The Breathing Sea I

Burning

E.P. Clark

Helia Press

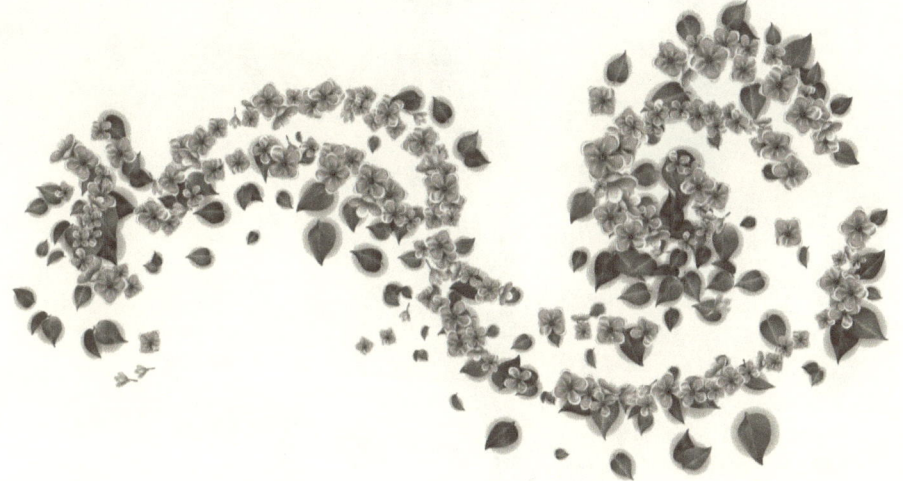

Newsletter Signup

Want to know how it all began? Keep up with the latest news and get freebies and insider information? Come say hi at epclarkauthor.net to sign up for my mailing list and get a FREE copy of the prequel collection *Winter of the Gods and Other Stories*. Or you can go to it directly by scanning the QR code below.

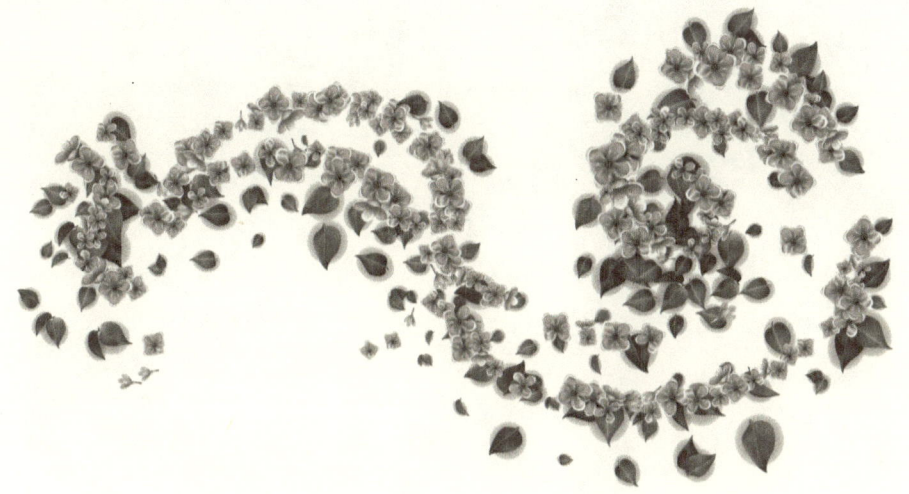

If You're Just Joining Us...

The main character of *The Breathing Sea*, Dasha, also known as Darya Krasnoslavovna or Darya Tsarinovna, is the daughter of the main character of *The Midnight Land*. In *TML*, Slava, our heroine, sets off on an expedition to the Far North, mainly to escape her unsympathetic and overbearing older sister, the Tsarina of Zem'.

While on her expedition, Slava conceives Dasha with Oleg Svetoslavovich, a lowborn hunter who has been granted prolonged life by the gods in exchange for serving them, primarily by fathering lots of daughters. Upon her return to Krasnograd, the capital city, Slava discovers that her sister has slid from unpleasant to insane, and, with the support of the community of gods and supernatural spirits, ends up taking her place as Tsarina. *The Breathing Sea* begins eighteen years later, and chronicles Dasha's own adventures as she struggles to deal with her legacy of magic, usurpation, and gods-given responsibilities.

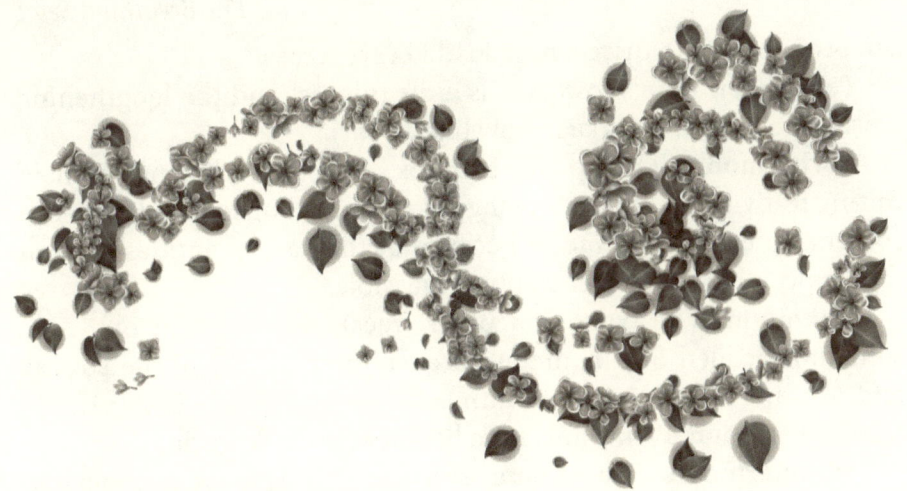

Zemnian Months

The Zemnian approach to calendar-keeping, like the Zemnian approach to timekeeping in general, is fairly relaxed and non-standardized. There are twelve more or less standard months, or moons, although some districts have thirteen, and several of the months have two or more possible names. The scholars and priestesses at sanctuaries are generally responsible for saying when a month or year begins or ends, but they do not necessarily coordinate their calendars with their sisters in other districts, so that it may be Wintermoon in the black earth district but Icemoon on the steppe.

The year is reckoned as beginning at Midwinter in Krasnograd, but some of the other districts, especially in the North, keep to the older method of reckoning the year as beginning on Midsummer, something that can still be seen throughout Zem' in the practice of counting a person's age by her number of summers, and declaring her a woman grown when she reaches her twentieth summer. Given the difficulty in keeping track of exact dates, many people do not celebrate their birthday on the day of their birth, but at the appropriate seasonal festival—Midwinter, Spring, Midsummer, or Autumn—along with all the other people of their village born in the same season.

Wintermoon. The winter solstice. Also sometimes called Darkmoon because it is the darkest month of the year. Midwinter festivities are held.

Icemoon. The coldest month of the year. Rivers and lakes are frozen over enough to drive a fully loaded cart across.

Pearlmoon. The snowcover is at its thickest and the lengthening days shine on it and make it glow like a pearl.

Springmoon. The spring equinox. The snow begins to melt. Spring festivities in which an effigy of winter is burned are held. Also sometimes called Mudmoon because of the vast quantities of mud that appear, making travel all but impossible.

Oakmoon. The oaks (and other trees) begin to bud out. Also sometimes called Sowingmoon because the majority of the sowing and planting is done in this month.

Flowermoon. Plants are at the height of their flowering.

Summermoon. The summer solstice. The days are at their longest, and Midsummer festivities are held. Midsummer of her twentieth year is when a woman achieves the age of majority.

Haymoon. The hottest month of the year, when much of the hay is harvested.

Harvestmoon. The days are already noticeably shorter, and the North and the Eastern mountains may experience frost at night. The majority of the harvesting is done in this month.

Autumnmoon. The autumn equinox. In some places, there may be an autumn festival in this month; other districts may hold a harvest celebration in Harvestmoon or a hunting celebration in Huntingmoon instead.

Leaffall. The leaves fall. Also known as Huntingmoon or Slaughtermoon in some places because it is considered the best time for hunting and slaughtering.

Frostmoon or Snowmoon. The leaves are gone and a hard frost sets in. Snow starts to accumulate on the ground, especially in the North and the Eastern mountains.

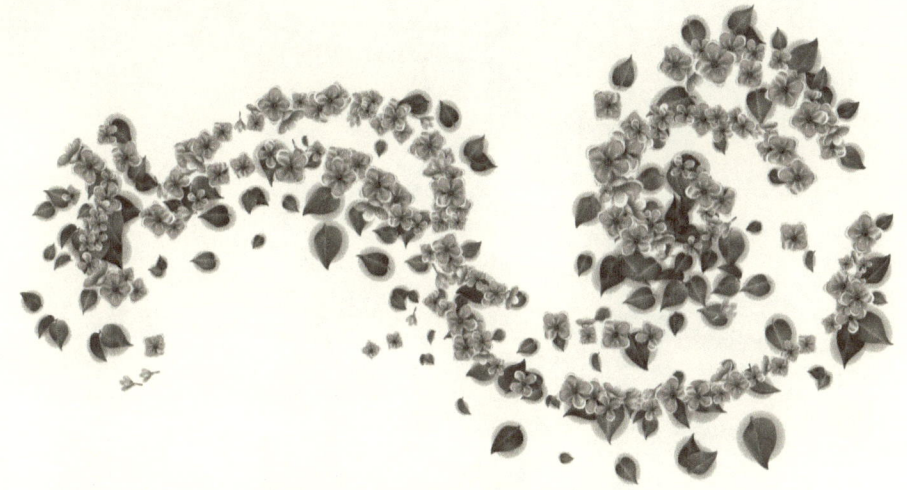

Epigraph

Some are made of stone, and some are made of clay—
But I silver and shine!
My business is betrayal, my name is Marina,
I am mortal sea foam.
Some are made of clay, and some are made of flesh—
For them the grave and the gravestone...
Baptized in the sea—and in my flight
Constantly broken!
Through every heart, through every net
Bursts my will.
Of me—do you see these wild curls?—
You will not make the salt of the earth.
Smashed on your stony knees,
With every wave—I am reborn!
Long live foam—merry foam—
Noble foam of the sea!
Marina Ivanovna Tsvetaeva

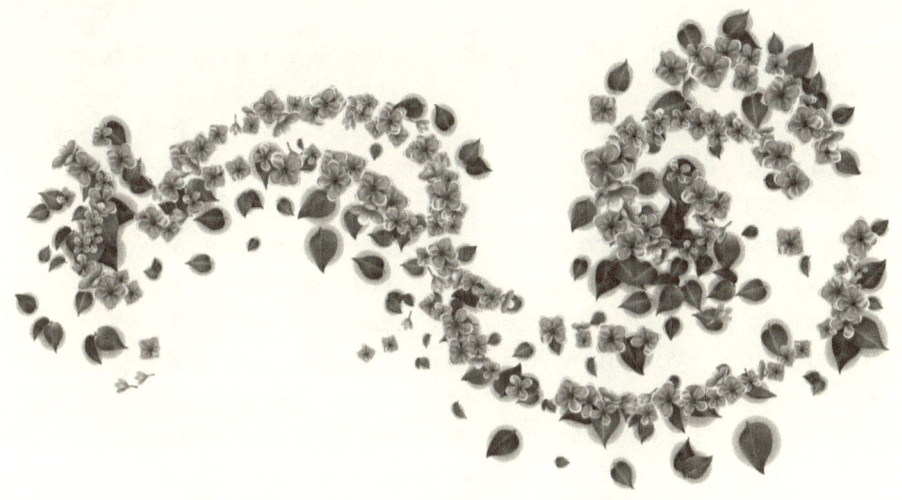

Chapter One

"Have some breakfast, dearest Tsarinovna," her maids urged her, but Dasha turned her face away.

"I'm sorry, I can't," she said. "Not the sausage. Maybe some porridge."

Kira and Olesya, her maids, fluttered anxiously about her, feeling her forehead and asking if she were ill.

"No," she answered them. "Or, no, no more than usual. I just don't want to eat sausage."

Kira and Olesya carried off the sausage and returned with a bowl of porridge.

"They promise down in the kitchen that they'll only send up bread and porridge from now on, Tsarinovna," Olesya told her, smiling with a sweetness that didn't mask her irritation with Dasha. "Since you're so finicky and all. Is it your moonblood hurting your tummy?"

"No," Dasha told her, trying, she hoped with more success, to mask her own irritation with Olesya for speaking to her as if she were still a little child. Dasha hadn't enjoyed it at seven, and she enjoyed it even less now that she was seventeen and stood head and shoulders over Olesya and most of the rest of her maids as well. "I just see where the sausage comes from. I can't eat something made from so much pain and horror. It's as if the blood still tastes raw, even when it's cooked, and I can hear the screams of the creature it came from as she was being slaughtered. It's like...biting down on metal soaked in sour wine, the way the cries of pain and terror grate on my ears and turn my stomach."

Olesya laughed nervously, while Kira looked down at the floor as if Dasha had said something particularly hurtful and indelicate. "Of course, Tsarinovna, of course," Olesya told her, her voice still so syrupy it made Dasha want to cough, as if she had bitten into an extra-sweet chunk of honeycomb. "Though you'll have to get over your squeamish ways before you take your mother's place, you know. It's good you think of others—you know you above all people have to be sure to be considerate and not to trample on others accidentally—but all of us in the kitchen, and who serve in your chambers, we deserve your consideration too, don't we? After all we've done for you? Of course, there isn't anything we wouldn't do for you, there isn't anything we wouldn't count ourselves lucky to do in your service, but it's a long way between here and the kitchen, and Anna Marusyevna made those sausages special for you, from a pig she hand-raised and slaughtered herself, and now she's sitting with her apron over her face wondering what she's done wrong, and all over a little girl's soft-minded foibles, and..."

"Thank you for your trouble, and please convey my thanks to Anna Marusyevna and the rest of the kitchen staff as well," Dasha said, before Olesya could say anything more. It was still a surprise to her, even after an (admittedly short) lifetime, to realize how completely oblivious those around her were to the things that touched her so deeply. To them, meat was meat, just as stones were stones and wood was wood, and they did not hear the echoes of the past and the possibilities for the future that surrounded each object. Which was lucky for them, to Dasha's mind, but not for her.

Sometimes—such as this morning—Dasha would find herself wondering if she really were of the world of women, as she appeared to be. Sometimes she didn't feel like a woman—well, a girl, in her case, but almost a woman—at all, especially when she looked at the other women around her. Sometimes she couldn't help but wonder if the blood that ran through her veins wasn't human at all, and if she didn't have more in common all the other creatures, the ones that ran on four paws or hooves, than she did with her two-legged sisters. And then she would look at her hands, and know that it was all nonsense, but it didn't make her feel any closer to other women, or more distant from other animals. Of course, some would argue that she wasn't of the world of women at all, was she, what with the circumstances behind her conception, but she was pretty sure she wasn't a god, either.

Gods got more respect.

Not that her maids and everyone else didn't give her respect of a certain sort. They, too, thought she was someone other than who she appeared to be, only in their case, they seemed to think she was someone much more dangerous than she seemed on the outside. As if all her seventeen years of smiling gently and speaking softly and never, ever giving offense to anyone had just been a sham concealing the monster beneath. Or perhaps she was just being fanciful. Quite possibly. It wasn't as if Dasha hadn't been told a thousand times that she was too fanciful for a future Empress. Consumed with her fancies, she slowly spooned the porridge into her mouth, looking out the window as she did so.

It was a wet, nasty day, the kind that only came in early spring, when the land was still worn down by winter and nothing was yet ready to bloom. It was the kind of day that made people doubt the possibility of true spring ever arriving, even though it was an essential precursor to that arrival, as everyone well knew. In short, it was a day guaranteed to dampen anyone's spirits, and Dasha, who had already awakened in a dark mood, felt her own spirits sink even further.

"Such a miserable morning," she exclaimed, and Kira, who had remained in her chamber after Olesya had bustled off on one of the innumerable errands that filled her day, hastened to agree that yes, it was a miserable morning, and likely to be a dreary day as well.

Dasha sighed and said no more until she had finished her breakfast and was left in peace by her ever-attentive, ever-adoring, kindly-hearted, well-meaning, and altogether admirable maids. No doubt every one of them would, just as they professed, consider their lives well spent if they spent them changing her linens and washing her dirty dishes, and that made it all the more terrible that she resented their (increasingly frequent) insinuations that they were slaving away for her out of the goodness of their hearts, and that she should be more grateful to them, more careful not to ask too much of them—except that when she tried not to trouble them, they grew resentful of that as well, and complained that she was shunning them or scorning them.

Unworthy as it was, especially given how much they did for her and how much they seemed to believe that they were sacrificing for her, Dasha dreamed more and more of getting rid of them. What she would do then, she didn't know, as she had never lived without them, but that was her dream, nonetheless. She turned her attention back to the window.

Drops of cold water struck it and ran down to the wall below. The sound of it chilled her tongue that had been warmed by the porridge, and in each one she could see the nearby river Krasna and the distant Sea of Ice that those drops had once called home, and one day would again. She wondered if they felt lonely and afraid, so far from their motherland and falling towards foreign earth.

The glass, too, had once been sand, sand from the ocean: perhaps it was lonely too? Or had it been transformed by the melting it had undergone and felt that its place was in the window where it now stood? Dasha could see the bellows and the panes of new glass, and then their journey packed in straw to the Krasnograd kremlin, and then... wind blew against the glass. A dark day. The bloody sausage rose up in Dasha's mind again, and she felt that it must herald some evil tidings. When there was a knock at the door she startled, expecting some bad news, but it was only her maids, returned from cleaning up after breakfast to escort her to her lessons.

Today there would be no riding, or swordplay, or anything out of doors, only lore of various sorts: history, healing herbs, distant lands... Dasha sat through all her lessons as best she could, but her fear of evil tidings grew rather than diminished as the morning wore on, and she answered her tutors' questions poorly. They all chided her for it, but somehow she did not hear them, even when they told her (gently and lovingly, but with that oh-so-stinging edge of sorrowful reproach that everyone's voice seemed to be armed with these days) that she was wasting their time and making their jobs more difficult than they should be, which was most unworthy of a Tsarinovna and future Tsarina, and especially one who had to guard against her more fiery impulses.

What these fiery impulses were, or where they had gotten the idea that Dasha possessed them, none of them said, and Dasha knew better than to demand an explanation. Finally Anastasiya Yevgeniyevna, her tutor in magic and spells, demanded to know if she were unwell, as that was the only excuse she could think of for Dasha's performance at her lesson, which was even poorer today than usual.

"Forgive me, Anastasiya Yevgeniyevna," said Dasha, and tried to mix the potion that Anastasiya Yevgeniyevna was describing, but knocked over her basin and her bundles of herbs instead.

"Child, what has overcome you!" cried Anastasiya Yevgeniyevna. "You *are* ill!"

"Perhaps," said Dasha, thinking that might be the easiest excuse. "Perhaps I have been struck by a chill."

Anastasiya Yevgeniyevna felt her forehead and looked into her eyes before shaking her head. "I see no chill," she said. "But you seem... cloudy, as one distracted. What is troubling you so much that you cannot pay attention to my lesson?"

"I don't know," said Dasha. "Today feels like a bad day, that's all."

"Young women are often prone to dark moods, especially on days such as this," said Anastasiya Yevgeniyevna, smiling with condescending indulgence. "It is your sympathy with nature, my dear Tsarinovna, telling you you must pass through all the muck of late winter before you reach your own spring."

"That's hardly comforting," said Dasha. "And what am I supposed to do until then: drip all over everything and force everyone indoors?"

Anastasiya Yevgeniyevna laughed, with an uncertainty that tasted of poorly cooked bread, and said she must not be in any real danger, whatever the cause of her black mood, and that she should run along and try to make the potion again at the next lesson. Dasha thanked her as courteously as she could in her present state of mind, and left to find her mother.

Her mother was busy when Dasha came upon her, listening to some very bedraggled-looking petitioners from the Western provinces, and before Dasha could catch her mother's attention, Princess Belova and Princess Zapadnokrasnova sent her away, telling her that they were speaking of things unfit for her ears. So Dasha set off to wander the kremlin, which seemed the only thing to do on a day like today.

Wandering the kremlin only made her more restless and uneasy, though. She kept feeling as if she could see something strange in the shadows out of the corner of her eye, although seeing something strange out of the corner of her eye was happening more and more these days, so she couldn't say it was unusual.

She tried to concentrate on what was really happening around her, instead of dwelling on her visions, but that just made her feel even worse. Everywhere she went she saw people with tasks and a clear purpose in life, reminding her that she had neither. She would have liked to stop to talk to them, or even better, help them, but she had never been trained to cook or clean or wash or stand guard or any of the other things that everyone else in the kremlin did, and her presence was only a bother and a distraction to the people who did know how to do those things. They were too polite to say so to her face—well, actually, some of them *did* say so to her face, but they did so kindly and politely—but it was clear in the way that they were rushing about that they were doing important things and had no time to spare for her, and that, much as they loved her, they would rather she were back up in her chambers, working on...what?

More and more it seemed to Dasha that she was completely useless and pointless, serving no purpose at all. Oh, there was the promise that she had been born for a special purpose, one chosen by the gods, but all she and the rest of Zem' had was her mother's word, because the gods had remained stubbornly silent on the subject since her conception (just thinking about that made Dasha grow hot all over with embarrassment and curiosity, so she quickly turned her thoughts away, but not quickly enough to prevent images she didn't want to see and yet was desperately keen to know more about from rising up before her inner eyes). Dasha may have been chosen by the gods, or so her mother said, but they had never actually made their thoughts on the matter clear to *her*. Of late she had been thinking more and more that perhaps it was all a lie, a trick of some sort, and that she really wasn't meant for anything at all, that she really was just as useless and pointless as she felt herself to be.

Of course that wasn't true, or so everyone would tell her if she were to speak to them of her worries. She could already see what would happen if she were to do so: whomever she had chosen as her confidante would smile, or maybe even laugh at her, their laughter like brine on a wound, and tell her she had nothing to worry about, she was just being silly, because even if the gods hadn't chosen her for some specific honor, one day she would rule Zem', like her mother and her grandmother before her, and until then she should devote herself to preparing for that heavy duty. Just picturing those smiles, which would want nothing but the best for her (or so their bearers would claim), and imagining those laughs, which would be provoked by nothing but the best of intentions, made her want to curl up and cry, and she knew that anything she did to ask for help would only make her feel even more miserable and alone, even as everyone around her claimed that their highest goal in life was to make her feel happy.

She knew that "they"—her tutors, maids, even her mother—were not completely wrong, and that she *should* be learning and studying in preparation for the day when she would take her mother's place on the Wooden Throne and rule, but lately, learning the uses of herbs and memorizing the names of places across the Middle Sea seemed a small and pointless thing, and anyway, there was little lore left to teach her. In everything other than magic, Dasha was a quick study ("frighteningly quick," said her tutors, their voices like peppermint), and she had already read everything in the kremlin library twice over. Which was why her mother had said she could go on a journey this year, her first real journey, in honor of her seventeenth summer.

Dasha had never left Krasnograd; in fact, she had hardly ever left the confines of the Krasnograd kremlin and the park with its prayer trees behind it. She knew from her books and from the words of others that beyond it there was a whole wide world, all of the Known World and even more world beyond that, full of interesting and exciting things that she could hardly even imagine, but she had never seen any of it. All her life she had been carefully protected, not just, she knew, from danger to her body, but from the danger of coming face-to-face with all the unpleasantnesses of life, all the evil that her mother claimed was out there but that Dasha had never seen.

Dasha knew that people suffered, grew ill, had accidents, even died, but she had never known anyone to whom those things had happened, no more than she knew anyone who had ever done the kinds of terrible things people were said to do, out beyond the kremlin walls. What those terrible things were, Dasha had only the haziest idea, and until recently she had never wanted to find out, but of late, with the restlessness growing stronger and stronger in her, she was growing ever more curious about the outer world, including all its bad sides. How bad could it be, really? Or so she would ask herself when she thought of it. And surely she would be strong enough to face it, whatever it was. After all, she *was* "frighteningly quick." Except at magic, of course. And many other things as well.

But in her private reveries she fantasized about encountering danger, evil, and all the ills of the world, whatever they were, and emerging unscathed and triumphant. In her daydreaming she never failed, and she certainly never had the sensation, which was overtaking her more and more, of being a complete and utter failure, not just at this one thing, but at everything she put her hand to. Some days she experienced real failure and imagined triumph a dozen times before noon, and she was becoming hard pressed to say which was the truth, which was reality: the one seemed as likely as the other, and any sort of sensible middle ground was becoming harder and harder to find. Which only made her sink into her daydreams even deeper.

But soon, so soon, she would get to test herself, experience every-thing she had dreamed of in person, when she finally left Krasnograd and went out to see the rest of Zem'. She could go with her father, her mother had promised, who would come down from the North es-pecially to be her escort, and she could travel out to her kin in the steppes and the Northern forests, and survey the land that she would one day rule.

"And there will probably be other journeys later," her mother had promised. "Journeys to foster and study with those who wish you well, and can teach you things you will not learn in Krasnograd."

"Like what?" Dasha had asked eagerly. "Like when?"

But her mother had only smiled and shaken her head and said that they would both find that out when the time came. This was a very unsatisfactory answer as far as Dasha was concerned, but it did giver her fodder for hours of speculation and daydreaming, as well as the hope of not one but *two* journeys in her future. But none of them would happen until the weather cleared. Dasha knew that this had to be so, but as winter waned the waiting grew harder and harder, and today she feared she might burst if she had to spend another day in this busy kremlin, watching rain run down the windowpanes.

By nightfall she had accomplished nothing except to fatigue her maids and guards with her incessant wandering, so that they be-gan to grow shorter and shorter with her, and their smiles took on a sharp, irritated edge. The sense of foreboding that had greeted her that morning only increased with the advent of darkness, so much so that she had to stifle a shriek when a servant came into the library where she was paging listlessly through a book on the great families of Zem' (there was nothing there of interest and never could be, as every description of every family always came back to "such-and-such a sister of the Zerkalitsa line," which Dasha already knew and which today threw her into despair at the thought that there was nowhere in Zem' where she could go to escape her family), and announced that it was time for her to make her way to supper, where the Empress was already waiting.

"Well, at least *she* might have some fresh news," said Dasha to her-self, and followed the serving woman to the kremlin's small private dining hall.

When she could, her mother preferred to take supper in her pri-vate chambers, with just Dasha for company, but this evening, as on many evenings, she had guests, and so she and Dasha must both dine with them. This evening they were princesses from Avkhazovskoye, the mountains in the far South of Zem'. They had long dark braids and flashing dark eyes, and they spoke with a strange accent, fragrant with roses and other heavy flowers and dark spices, when they rose and greeted "Darya Krasnoslavovna, beloved Tsarinovna." As they bowed all the gold that they wore on their ears, braids, necks, and wrists jangled like chainmail, and Dasha could taste the metal in her mouth and had a sudden vision of them as soldiers, come to defend their beloved Southern mountains from the rapaciousness of Northern Empresses.

Dasha wondered if this were the threat she had feared, but then the two princesses sat down at her mother's request, and they were just richly adorned noblewomen once again, and Dasha could see no threat in them, or at least not for the moment. They both peered closely at her, as new acquaintances tended to do, and Dasha had to bite her tongue to keep from telling them that no, there was nothing unusual about her appearance, nothing that would suggest she was anything other than a girl approaching her seventeenth summer and soon to become a woman grown.

If the gods had left any mark on her at her conception, it was not one that could be seen upon her face or body. Even her thick red hair, whose curls everyone so loved to admire, was something she shared with her wholly human Aunty Olga. And her father, of course. And presumably all those half-sisters whom she had never met (other than Aunty Olga) but who, according to her mother, were out there in the world, making their way as best they could and like as not with no knowledge that their very own sister (even if through the male line) was next in line for the Wooden Throne. A vision of a whole tribe of red-haired girls rose up around Dasha, girls who would finally make her feel as if she had found her kin, found others who were her kind...

"The Princesses Oridzhnikidze and Iridivadze honor us with their presence, my dear Dasha," said her mother, breaking off the vision before it could overwhelm her and make her do something strange and embarrassing. "I was just apologizing to them for my neglect of them, as I have been entirely taken up with the news from our Western borders today...but enough about that! I am glad to welcome them here this evening, and even more glad that you are able to meet them, for we see our Southern sisters far too rarely, although I hope it will be more frequently in the future, as Princess Iridivadze has graciously granted my request to foster her daughter here in Krasnograd. She is by all accounts a very worthy young woman, and just your age, my dearest Dasha, so it is our hope that you may become friends, and perhaps she might tutor you in Avkhaz. I greatly regret that the press of my duties has never given me the leisure to learn this noble tongue, but you are so quick to take in languages, my dear Dasha, that I am sure that with the benefit of Susanna Gulisovna's tutelage, you will be speaking it like a native before the year is out."

"I would be delighted," said Dasha, cheering up at this unexpectedly heartening news. While none of the wards her mother had taken on—and her mother did have a passion for taking on wards, as if to make up for only having one daughter—while none of the many wards her mother had taken on had become bosom companions for Dasha, not even Vladya from Severnolesnoye—she had been too old and too frightening for Dasha to ever truly become her friend, even if they were by some counts sisters—Princess Iridivadze's daughter did at least have the promise of novelty, and studying the language of the Southern mountains would be a useful task, and one that would while away the empty hours in the kremlin, when Dasha longed for action of some sort, but knew that her best action would be not to get in the way of the adults with serious duties. "When can I make her acquaintance?" she asked.

"Tomorrow, if it pleases you and your Imperial mother, noble Tsarinovna," said Princess Iridivadze, bowing low with every other word.

"If it pleases Susanna Gulisovna, let her come to me tomorrow morning," said Dasha, and there were a great many more bows and pleasantries, and it was settled that Susanna Gulisovna, heir to the great Avkhazovskoye province of Tflisi, Zem''s Southernmost territory and the only port that remained unfrozen year-round, would wait upon the Tsarinovna's pleasure immediately after breakfast the next day.

Extremely pleased with the promise of new adventures, even if they were only adventures of the mind, Dasha decided that perhaps she had been confused and that her forebodings had been forebodings of good rather than evil, but when the servants brought in a roast goose, it suddenly seemed to her that its long neck hung lifelessly from the platter and dripped blood from its slit throat onto the floor, even though the neck was gone and the blood had long been drained from its body, and the only thing in danger of spilling onto the floor was the grease in which it was swimming.

Dasha tried to convince herself that it was cooked, cooked because it was food and she should eat it because she was hungry and because it would make the others unhappy if she did not, but as soon as she lifted the first forkful to her mouth, her throat closed at the taste of blood and corruption. Luckily there was bread, and a dish of stewed apples and another of beets, and various other minor delicacies, so she was in no danger of starving, and the princesses did not seem to notice or care that she left the goose untouched, and her mother, after giving her a swift glance, also pushed her serving of goose aside and praised the bread and other dishes in a loud voice, and, even better, quelled the serving women with a stern glance when they tried to make Dasha eat the goose, and prevented them from complaining of the trouble she was making for them.

The dishes had just been cleared, and the princesses were just preparing to take their leave, when there was an urgent knocking at the door. Dasha's heart gave a great leap in her throat, and she knew that this was the moment, these were the ill tidings she had been dreading.

"Open the door," her mother commanded, and the guards jumped to do her bidding, interrupting the knocker, who was still banging unceasingly on the door with a strong fist, in mid-knock.

"Oleg!" her mother cried, and "Father!" Dasha cried after her.

Chapter Two

"What unexpected joy!" exclaimed her mother, but then stopped on seeing her father's face. "What is it?" she and Dasha both cried together. "Is it Olga?" her mother demanded, her voice rising anxiously with every word. "Or...Vladislava?"

Oleg shook his head. "It's Lisochka," he said.

"Oh!" cried her mother. "What happened to her? Is she?.."

"She walked out into the woods one day," said Oleg, as if the words hurt his mouth.

"Then she is...lost?"

"We found her body a few days later."

Her mother said nothing, but Dasha could see all the bones on her face stand out, as if her skin had suddenly gotten too tight. To her surprise, because she had never even met Lisochka, and what she knew of her made her feel nothing for her but dislike, Dasha felt her own eyes fill with tears. She tried to turn away from the others, but not before the princesses had noticed.

"It is no shame to weep for the dead," whispered Princess Iridivadze, and Princess Oridzhnikidze pressed a handkerchief into her hand and stroked her arm consolingly.

"Poor Olga!" her mother was saying. "Is she...is she much distraught over the...over it?" Through her own tears Dasha could see that her mother's hands were trembling, which only made her cry harder.

"She says no, but she is—very distraught. She and Lisochka...had words, as they often do—did, but this time Lisochka made good on her threat to run to her death. The whole family is...shaken. Even Vladislava is shaken, and has shed many tears over her sister's death. I came as soon as I could—I didn't want the news to come from strangers, I didn't want strangers to be the ones to tell Dasha that...that her sister...that she has lost a sister."

Much to her mortification, even though she knew that, just as Princess Iridivadze had said, there was no shame in weeping for the dead, Dasha began to sob loudly at that point, drawing the attention of her parents, who rushed to her side.

"The poor little dove mourns the loss of her sister," said Princess Oridzhnikidze, half-sympathetically, half-approvingly. "She has a noble and generous heart."

"She will make a good Empress one day," said Princess Iridivadze. "A good ruler cares for her kin, and feels their loss deeply."

"Yes," said Oleg, "even if they don't deserve it." But this only made Dasha cry harder, and he looked as if he wished he had kept his mouth shut.

"Let us retire to my chambers," said her mother, and she helped Dasha up with trembling hands, and, after many solemn declarations of sympathy from the Southern princesses, they walked slowly, surrounded by sad-faced guards who had not known Lisochka but were disturbed by news of the death of the Tsarinovna's sister, even such a distant sister as Lisochka, and made their way slowly to the Empress's private chambers.

By the time they had made it there, Dasha had managed to quell her sobbing, but she still, to her shame, clung to her mother's arm like a small child, an action that was particularly incongruous given that Dasha was more than a head taller than her mother and much sturdier in build, as large and strong as many of her mother's guards.

Once they had reached her mother's chambers, her mother gave way to tears, but only briefly, before taking command of herself and the situation once more.

"I am very sorry you have had to bear this grief, and the pain of bringing us such grievous tidings," she said to Oleg. "To...to lose a granddaughter must be very painful, especially under such circumstances."

Oleg shrugged, but he did so as if his shoulders were too tight to move properly, and Dasha could see that he was suffering, and much more than he had expected to. Lisochka would be glad to see how much everyone was sorrowing over her, Dasha thought, although most likely (she couldn't help but think) for spiteful, selfish reasons. In her mind she could see Lisochka running through the snow, racked with pain and yet still gloating over the pain she was causing others. Dasha was ashamed of her vision, but she knew it was a true one, and it would not leave her.

"She is at peace now," said Oleg. "Even the manner of her death was a peaceful one, and of her own choosing. Freezing is a pleasant way to die, or so they say, and perhaps now she can rest at last and find the peace in death she could never find in life—and stop troubling the rest of us as well. And if she had not died as she did, I don't know...I don't know what I would have done, what any of us would have done, for we would have had to take some black action, that we would have all regretted, and I'm glad to be spared that at least."

"What did she do?" demanded her mother. "Poor Lisochka!"

"She...we can speak of it later," said Oleg, with a sidelong glance at Dasha.

"Did she threaten Dasha?" asked her mother, her voice, normally light and clear as cool water, taking on the metallic edge it did when she was angry. "She was always full of envy for her, just as she was for Vladislava, and yet no amount of cajoling could convince her to be my ward, even though she begrudged her sister the honor greatly, and held it against her at every turn. Poor Lisochka! But I would not have held empty threats against Dasha as treason—I would have tried to help her."

"Yes," said Oleg. "And I would have done everything in my power to keep her away from Dasha. But her threats were not empty in the end, and I fear...I fear what she would have done. What she did was bad enough."

"What did she do, Oleg?" her mother asked, the blade of her voice sharpening with anxiety, while Dasha felt her breath catch, and knew that the night's ill tidings were not over and there was still something more terrible for her to hear.

"Dasha doesn't need to hear it," said Oleg. "Let her remember her sister as happily as she can."

Dasha thought her mother would send her away then, as she always had before, whenever there was dark news to be heard, and she didn't know whether to be glad or angry, but to her surprise her mother shook her head.

"Let her stay, if she has the strength to hear this sad tale," she said. "She's almost a woman grown, and one day she will rule Zem' and hear many sad tales then. Besides, if she does not hear the truth from you, no doubt she will hear garbled half-lies from some stranger, and that will be worse."

"I will stay," said Dasha, even though she knew she had no wish to hear what her father was about to say. He gave her an uncertain look, and carried on in a faltering voice that sounded strange coming from someone so strong and bold.

"She and Olga had harsh words, as they often do, and Lisochka fell into a rage, as she often does, and she took up the kettle that was heating on the stove, and she...she cast the boiling water onto...onto the dog that Dasha gave Olga as a gift."

Dasha and her mother both cried out involuntarily in horror, and for a moment Dasha thought she was going to be sick.

"Is she...badly burned?" she asked in a quavering voice, once she had regained control of herself. "Will she recover?"

Oleg shook his head tightly. "She was very badly scalded," he said. "She was suffering badly, and wasn't going to get better. She is at peace now. I made sure...I made sure it was a quick and painless end, and that she knew she was a good and brave dog and had done her duty by her mistress. I think Lisochka meant to cast the boiling water on Olga, but Dasha"—he glanced at Dasha, and said quickly—"I mean the other Dasha, the dog, stepped forward to defend Olga, and Lisochka screamed like a stuck pig and threw the water on her instead. Her injuries were so bad because she tried to save Olga, you know—she jumped forward instead of trying to flee.

"And Lisochka screamed that Dasha deserved it, she deserved to die, and I don't know which Dasha she meant—both, probably. And Olga struck her so hard across the face she fell down, and then she picked herself up and ran, still screaming hateful words at Dasha, and she ran all the way out of Lesnograd and into the woods. And if we had found her alive instead of dead, I don't know what I would have done—I wanted to kill her thrice over, once for hurting a good dog like that, once for destroying Dasha's gift, and once for threatening to kill Dasha—this Dasha. I think if Dasha herself had been there instead of her namesake dog, Lisochka would have thrown the boiling water on her with twice as much glee."

Oleg stopped, and then added, "She never should have been born. There's nothing in my life I regret more than letting Olga be forced into the ill-fated marriage that produced her. I'm not much given to fancy, but sometimes I think I can see evil sorceresses casting curses on their wedding day."

"Really?" asked Dasha with trembling lips. For a moment her horror over Dasha's fate was replaced with a vision of bent-backed sorceresses with long cruel fingernails, which they used to weave evil shadows on the wall, casting dark curses…

"No," said Oleg heavily. "No need to cast curses with magic on those two. They carried their own blood curses inside of them all along. As do…" Dasha could tell that he wanted to say *As do I*, but he stopped himself, and said instead, "It was an ill-fated day when that bargain was struck, when Olga and Andrey's mothers sealed their enmity with their children's flesh."

"Yes," said her mother, and Dasha could see through the fresh tears that this dreadful story had awakened that her mother also had tears in her eyes, and a much grimmer look on her face than usual. "That was truly an ill deed, but it cannot be undone. It does not always take magic to cast curses, and even non-magical curses are as hard to undo as gathering water back into an overturned bucket. The water always runs downhill, and I fear Lisochka was at the bottom of a very steep hill indeed. At least she is at peace now, and can do no more harm. And Dasha"—she turned to Dasha—"Dasha is at peace as well, now, and dreadful as this whole thing is, my love, she would have been glad to lay down her life to save her mistress. She was that kind of dog. She may have been happy at the very end."

"But she suffered!" Dasha burst out. "How could anyone make a dog suffer like that, and especially"—she choked—"my own sister. My own sister threw boiling water on an innocent creature! My own sister!"

Her mother's face gave a very queer twist, as if something more than grief were hurting her. "Yes," she said. "There is no evil greater than the hatred of sister for sister. There is no evil that one sister will not stoop to in order to hurt the other. It is terrible that little Dasha was caught between such hatred, but she is at peace now."

"I didn't hate Lisochka—until now!" cried Dasha. "There was no hatred between us—until now! It's good that she died as she did, for otherwise I would have gone to Lesnograd and poured boiling water on her myself!" She stopped, aghast.

"Luckily we are all spared such temptation," said her mother, after a moment. "For as you see, even being the victim of such hatred turns our thoughts to evil. This has been a dark day, but it is over! Both Lisochka and little Dasha are at peace. Perhaps the curse has run its course. In any case, don't let it carry on in you, Dasha! You gave little Dasha to Olga as a loving gift, and named her 'gift' after yourself to show your love for a loving aunt. The love will still remain, even if the gift is gone."

"That doesn't help Dasha!" cried Dasha. "She didn't deserve this!"

"No," said her mother. "But she no longer suffers, at least." And Dasha knew that there was no other answer to be had, and there was nothing she could do about the fact that Dasha had died an unjust, dreadful death at the hands of Dasha's own sister, even if a second-sister, and she would never come back to delight Dasha and Olga and everyone who had admired her loyal heart, not ever again, and no one could change that, and it was all because of a moment of malice on the part of someone who should have wanted nothing more than the happiness and well-being of the kinswomen she had hurt so terribly. Dasha could not have guessed that the ill tidings she had foreseen would be so very, very dark, for she had never experienced such sorrow firsthand, and she went to bed sadder than she could ever remember being, and what little sleep she got brought her slight comfort.

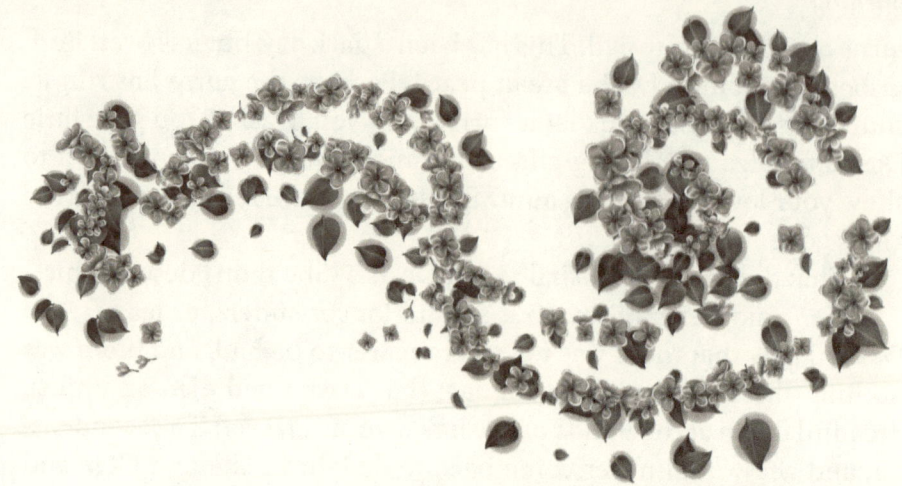

Chapter Three

She awoke the next morning feeling no more cheerful, but in a calmer frame of mind. As her mother had said, both Dasha and Lisochka were at peace now, and there was nothing she could do to help or hurt either of them.

"Do you wish to rise this morning, Tsarinovna?" asked Olesya, who was standing over her bed. "Or perhaps you would prefer to stay abed. Certainly it is one of the luxuries of your position."

"No," Dasha told her, sliding out into the dank chill air. The new-laid fire in the stove was crackling with a taste of dry sticks snapping in her mouth, setting off little sparks on her scalp, but the heat had not yet reached this side of her chamber. "I will rise. Staying in bed will do nothing for anyone." *If I could jump out of this bed and run all the way to Lesnograd and strangle Lisochka, I would,* she thought, but when she imagined how Olesya, who was some kind of fourth-sister to Lisochka anyway, would react to such a statement, she could see that biting her lip was her best course, so she did.

"We remembered, Tsarinovna," said Olesya, the self-regard in her voice making the area just behind Dasha's ears ache. "From yesterday. No sausages. Only porridge, with dried fruit and honey."

"You are too kind," said Dasha, and sat down to eat what they had brought her. Olesya sniffed in self-satisfaction at her own superiority, and Kira smiled in confusion at this latest freak of the Tsarinovna's. Dasha thought about trying to explain it to them again, but she knew it would do no good. Kira, even though she was not of noble blood, was no fool, and Olesya considered herself to be positively clever, but neither of them could hold two opposing thoughts in their heads any more than they could hold water in a sieve. If Dasha were to intimate that she thought they might, even if inadvertently, be doing something evil, she feared it would cause them to burst, or commit evil deeds of their own.

Perhaps, once the fuss over Lisochka's death died down, Dasha could ask her mother how to go about explaining such things to them. Unlike Dasha, Dasha's mother was very good at handling people. Not that Dasha often quarreled with people: quite the reverse. Everyone she knew thought they wanted nothing more than her happiness and her peace of mind, and since Dasha had always been a surprisingly well-behaved child (or so she had always been told), she had not done much to provoke those around her, and so her childhood had passed in as much cheerful tranquility as could possibly be expected for the heir of all of Zem'.

Which was why her outburst of the night before had shocked her so much. She could not remember another occasion when she had wanted to cause pain to another person like that. She could barely recall ever being angry, not really. She had vague memories of the tantrums common to a child of three or four, when her nursemaids would not allow her to have her way over something foolish and dangerous, but whenever they were unable to calm her, her mother would come to her and explain to her in clear simple words why she could not climb down from a high tower, or ride the swiftest steed in her mother's stables, or play with the weapons of the guards, and she would be appeased and forget her anger and allow herself to be diverted by blocks or dolls, and everything would go on as before, and she would feel safe and loved.

But now she knew she was in the grip of no childish tantrum, that her anger at Lisochka was justified, for she had caused an innocent creature to suffer and die needlessly, which to Dasha's way of thinking was the most evil of all acts, and she had done it out of hatred towards her own mother and Dasha herself. But Dasha also knew that that hatred was in its own way also justified, for Lisochka's mother had never loved her at all, even as she doted on Dasha, and so, through no fault of her own, Dasha was guilty of great wrong before Lisochka, one that she could now never repay, no more than she could avenge Lisochka's cruel murder of little Dasha, an act by which Lisochka had in one fell swoop earned all the misery she had already suffered, as if she had been determined to commit a crime that deserved the punishment she had been receiving her entire life. It was too dreadful to understand.

Dasha had no experience with such bitter quandaries, and she sat and stared out the window and wrestled with it until she was suddenly interrupted by the announcement that Susanna Gulisovna, heir to Princess Iridivadze, was outside awaiting the Tsarinovna's pleasure, if the Tsarinovna felt inclined to take visitors on this morning of mourning.

"Please, send her in," said Dasha, who felt no inclination to take visitors, but didn't want to be rude and send her away either, and had also already realized that sitting and staring out the window was no more useful than lying in bed all day and crying.

Susanna Gulisovna came sweeping in and made many bows that set all her golden trinkets jingling with a sound that was both metallic and warm, like a coin held in the mouth till it was at blood temperature.

"You do me inexpressible honor, Tsarinovna!" she cried, once she had straightened up from her bowing. Her Zemnian was flowery and fluent and only faintly accented. "And the sorrow I feel at the passing of your kinswoman is inexpressible too! Such a terrible loss for our great land!"

"Thank you," said Dasha. "There's no need to keep bowing all the time. Won't you sit?"

Susanna Gulisovna took a seat with a flourish and another jingle of jewelry. She was a tall slender girl, taller even than Dasha and much slenderer (Dasha couldn't help but regret, as she had many times before, her own sturdy build, which was very fine, no doubt, for hauling hay and carrying around sick sheep and feeding babies through long hungry winters and whatever else it was that her father's foremothers had had to do, but looked, she thought, lumpy and awkward next to Susanna's elegant litheness), with long black hair full of golden coins, strong black brows, and large fierce black eyes.

"My noble mother said that you were greatly stricken by the news of your sister's loss, great Tsarinovna, thus displaying the nobility and faithfulness of your own heart," said Susanna Gulisovna, once she had been seated, nodding her head with fierce emphasis. "Were you very close? Forgive me if I press your grief too hard: in the South, in Avkhazovskoye, we speak of these things freely, and count it no shame."

"Oh no, we weren't close at all," said Dasha. "In fact, I've never been close with any of my sisters. Prasha—Praskovya Vladislavovna, you know, my second-sister, the daughter of my, my aunt, the one who...my only aunt, that is—my mother offered once to foster Prasha here in the kremlin, once it became clear that my aunt's...condition would never improve, but she wouldn't hear of it, she wouldn't leave her mother's side, she said, and so I've never even met her, and she's much older than I am anyway, so even if we were to meet, we wouldn't be like sisters at all, and Lisochka, well...well..." Dasha gulped, and then, without quite meaning to, she poured out the whole sad story to Susanna Gulisovna's sympathetic ear: how Vesnushka, her own beloved dog from childhood, had had one last litter, and how she had chosen the sweetest and most loving of the puppies to be a special gift for her beloved Aunt Olga, kinswoman to her father, and how she had trained the chosen puppy herself, using only love and kindness, and then given her to Olga and named her Dasha because she was a gift and so that Olga would always have something of her close by, and how brave, faithful, noblehearted Dasha had met her terrible end by drawing the wrath of Olga's own daughter from Olga onto her, Dasha, and how Lisochka had run to her death screaming words of hatred towards Dasha the dog and Dasha the girl.

"What a miserable sister!" cried Susanna Gulisovna, jumping to her feet in her outrage. "What a pity she is dead! If she were my sister, I would ride to Lesnograd in all haste and throw boiling water on her with my own hands! Such should be the punishment for those who dishonor the gifts of their kin!"

Hearing Dasha's own desires come out of Susanna Gulisovna's mouth made Dasha uneasy. When Susanna Gulisovna spoke the words, she felt little of her white-hot anger against Lisochka, and could only see Lisochka's skin blistering under the boiling water. Besides, Dasha cared very little about the dishonor Lisochka had supposedly done her. If she had a choice between getting back her honor or Dasha, she would choose Dasha in a heartbeat, but she could not get either of them back.

"It does no good to dwell on it," she said instead, sounding unaccustomedly like her mother. "There is no one upon whom I could take vengeance, even if I wished to—and besides, my mother would never let me go racing off to Lesnograd on such an errand."

"Hmmm, yes," said Susanna Gulisovna. "That would be a problem. Of course, the usual counsel is that in matters of honor and love, a mother's command may be ignored, but when your mother is the Tsarina—what will you do, Tsarinovna, when you must ride off in search of a lover? Your situation has many complications!" And Susanna Gulisovna sat back down with a frown.

Much to her surprise, Dasha began to laugh at that thought, and after a moment of fear that she had said something untoward in her "Southern hastiness," Susanna joined her, and when they were done laughing, Dasha felt some of the horror that had gripped her since the night before lift, and she and Susanna talked of many interesting things the whole morning, and parted on the best of terms.

That afternoon the weather cleared enough for her to go out riding, and her father was granted permission to serve as her escort. Of course, he could go riding with her whenever he wished (when, that was, he was at the kremlin, which was not very often); the trouble was in getting rid of the guards. Boleslav Vlasiyevich, the captain of the Imperial Guard, did not care for Oleg one little bit, as he made abundantly clear every time Oleg came to Krasnograd to visit, and it was only after her mother had given direct orders that Oleg be allowed to take Dasha into the park behind the kremlin himself, that Boleslav Vlasiyevich— with many an untrusting glare—allowed that to happen.

At least that confrontation spared Dasha the complaints of her own guards about the trouble she was putting them to. Not that they would complain, exactly, but they would make it clear, just as her maids and her tutors did, that they were putting themselves out to do her a special favor, even if that special favor was just to do their jobs. But with Oleg accompanying her, Dasha was free of that for the afternoon.

Oleg and Dasha were both much grimmer than usual when they set off on their ride, and even Poloska, Dasha's horse, seemed out of spirits, but despite their somber moods, Dasha could not allow the opportunity to speak with her father alone pass unused, and as soon as they were away from the kremlin she demanded, "How long are you staying this time?"

"How long?" He raised an eyebrow at her. His voice was warm and red like it always was, like glowing coals, or his own hair. Or Dasha's hair. "Why, that depends on you and your mother, I suppose."

"We would have you stay for always," Dasha told him. "You know that." Indeed, although Dasha was not one to order others about, she did not understand why her mother had never put her foot down and insisted that her father stay in Krasnograd, with them, instead of wandering about the gods alone knew where. Well, and there was the problem, or at least part of it. Dasha knew that Oleg had been taken into service to the gods long ago, years before she had been born, and she also knew—although her mother had only hinted at it delicately, and the others around her hardly ever spoke of it at all, much to her relief—that his service had been to father her. Her *and* lots of other girls.

The very idea made Dasha want to squirm with revulsion, curiosity, and embarrassment. And sorrow. She knew—although again, it was rarely spoken of, at least in her presence—that this meant she had sisters, lots of sisters, none of whom she had ever met. Occasionally her mother would speak of this girl or that girl, and Dasha would realize she was speaking of one of Dasha's own half-sisters, but none of them had ever come to the Krasnograd kremlin, and since Dasha had never left it, she had never so much as laid eyes on any of them.

Sometimes—often—she wondered how much time her father spent with his other daughters, since he was gone so much, only coming back to his wife and *true* daughter (Dasha didn't like to think of herself that way, except when she was particularly angry with him, but she knew that others did) a few times a year, if that.

Well, his daughter and his daughter's mother. Dasha's mother had not even bound him to her with marriage, and although Dasha was not entirely sure why one would want to bind a man to oneself—that is, she understood why in theory, but whenever she actually thought about what it would be like to be married, many strange visions rose up in her mind, many of them less attractive to her than they seemed to be to other girls her age, and she also did not see why anyone would want to keep someone at her side against their will, which for some at least seemed to be half the thrill—she knew enough to know that that was the generally accepted practice.

She also knew that there were many who looked askance at the way her mother allowed Oleg to roam free and come back when he would, saying that she should either discard him as one did a peasant lover, or provide him with the honorable estate of marriage, as one did a nobleman, but not let him dangle in between, if nothing else because it gave other men the false idea that they, too, could roam free without the benefit of family, often to their own sorrow and that of their mothers. But Dasha said nothing of this to her father, both because she was embarrassed and because she guessed he already knew it, and so she only repeated, "We would have you stay for a long time."

Oleg sighed a sad sigh and said, "Maybe someday," in a tone that meant "Never." Dasha began to feel annoyed. Her father was one of the few people, in fact the only person, she knew who annoyed her on a regular basis. He was very kind to her just like everyone else, but the way he came and went as he pleased, with no explanation, always provoked Dasha's ever-hungry curiosity, and it was plain that he had many secrets, even beyond all the daughters he had supposedly fathered, which was even more provoking.

Most of all, he was alien in the world of Krasnograd and the kremlin, which was no flaw in and of itself, but sometimes it drove Dasha nearly to distraction to think that she knew so little and understood even less about her own father, whom she resembled so much in face and body, and so little in mind.

"How are your lessons?" asked Oleg abruptly, obviously intending to change the subject and show his fatherly concern in one fell swoop.

"Well enough," said Dasha. "Except for strategy. I'm *terrible* at strategy; my teachers all say so, and no matter how much I try, I make very little progress!"

"What's strategy?" asked Oleg, sounding genuinely curious.

"Oh, you know...battle strategy. Like how to order and command armies."

"Are you planning on fighting any wars any time soon?" said Oleg, now sounding amused, his voice rising like a flame as he tried not to laugh.

"No, of course not! But what if I suddenly had to? I'm simply *terrible* at it! Well, not so terrible at remembering the broad outlines of how old battles were fought, but when we play the games, I always get confused right away. My teachers say I have to envision all the possible moves and their outcomes before I do anything, but there's so many of them! By the time I'm two steps into the game, there are so many possible moves, all swarming all over the board in front of me, and I can't make them out, I can't make them out..."

"So, your strategy lessons involve playing board games?" Oleg clarified, still sounding amused.

"Yes, of course, it's an ancient training tactic—have you never played them?"

"My mother kept cows and my father was a woodsman," he told her. "Peasant boys don't play board games to train at battle strategy." His lips appeared to be twitching as he spoke.

"Oh," said Dasha, temporarily diverted from her woes by the appearance of this unexpected topic. Her father had never spoken about his family with her before; whenever he was there, they always talked about *her*, nothing but her, as if he had no past and no other life of his own. Which of course Dasha knew to be untrue, but that was always how it had seemed to her. "So...what did you do to pass the time on winter evenings, then?" she asked.

"My mother was always knitting or mending something," he said. "My father...well..." He frowned and looked away, as if the topic were unpleasant to him. "But my uncle taught me how to whittle and carve," he continued after a moment. "How to make those toys—do you remember the ones I gave you, the ones with the strings and such, the ones that move?"

"Of course," said Dasha. "I still have them. Well, my maids put them away somewhere, they said they were for little girls and were cluttering up my chamber, so they put them in some trunk somewhere, but I still have them, or at least I think so. So you would make things like that?"

"Yes, or fix things, or tell stories, or sometimes play games—but probably not the kinds of games you're talking about. You're talking about those games with a board and pieces that you move around, like checkers only fancier?"

Dasha nodded.

"No, not those kind. Are they hard then?"

"They are for *me*," said Dasha mournfully. "I told you: I get all confused! There are too many moves, and I can see them all at once, and I can't keep them straight! It's all too much!"

"What does your mother say?" asked Oleg. "Is *she* good at them?"

"She says no, she never was, but..."

"But what?"

"But *she's* managed to do all kinds of things, so it must not be true."

"Things like what?" asked Oleg.

"Well..." Dasha felt embarrassed about talking about it, because it was subject almost everyone almost always avoided, but then she blurted out in a rush, "Like how she came to power. She must have had to use all kinds of strategies to do that; it was practically like a war. It almost *was* a war, except that she avoided that—just barely."

"Ah, well..." said Oleg, no longer smiling. "Has she told you much about that?"

"A bit...there's probably more, though..."

"Probably," agreed Oleg. "But it might not be things she wants you to know."

"Like what?" asked Dasha before she could stop herself.

Her father grinned. "Like how she managed to conceive you with one man and use another to take down her sister. *That* might be something most mothers wouldn't want to share with their daughters."

"But..." Dasha found herself blushing, and wanting to argue with what Oleg was saying, and what he seemed to be implying, but she couldn't bring herself to talk about it, and so said instead, "No, that's not what I meant at all. But anyway...she must have been very clever to have done all that."

"Oh, she's clever all right, in her own way," he agreed.

"In her own way?! What does that mean!?"

"Nothing bad," said Oleg, looking amused again at her expression. "Just that she's clever, your mother, very clever, but no doubt she's right when she says she's not any good at those games you're talking about. Because if I understand them right, there's rules and so on that are fixed, and you can't just move the pieces around as you like?"

"Yes, of course," said Dasha.

"Well, there you have it, see. That's not the kind of clever your mother is, nor that you are either, I'll wager. She's more the kind of clever that looks at the game and says, 'Why are we doing it like *this*? It would be so much better if we did it like *that*,' and then she'd rearrange everything so that it was better. She isn't very good at following orders and following the rules, your mother, for all her seeming softness; she's much better at making the rules herself. Did she ever tell you about what it was like for her before, when she was still just Tsarinovna?"

"A bit," said Dasha.

"Well, there you see. Being the Tsarinovna was like playing one of those games you're talking about: all following rules that someone else had made up. And it didn't suit your mother at all, and she didn't do a very good job of it, or so it sounds. She was all overwhelmed by it, like you are with your games, and she thought she was going mad or something. But when she got free, when she left the game and started to live, where you make up the rules as you go and as you need, well then...she won. She won by doing what no one expected. Every time it seemed like she was trapped, she'd slip sideways and do something wild, something completely out of the rules, and then she'd march on and take whatever victory she needed while everyone was still scrambling to figure out what to do.

"That's how she won, by fighting to win instead of playing to play. And unless I'm all wrong about you, that's how you'll win if you ever have to. Besides," he added lightly, "you're *my* daughter just as much as you are hers, and I'm a hunter and a born good one. You say you're not clever about following the rules, but there's more to hunting and fighting than that. You have to be patient, and cunning, and when the moment comes, you have to be willing to kill. And that you have, my head for beheading."

"I...I don't think so," said Dasha tremulously. She didn't like hearing her father talk about hunting. This time it was worse than ever: a hundred dead animals seemed to be hanging before her eyes and littering the ground around Poloska's feet, and her father stood over every single one of them, his hands stained with blood.

"Well." Oleg eyed her with what appeared to be concern. "You might not see it yet, but it will come out when you need it, I'd bet my life on it."

This caused so many visions to appear that for a moment Dasha thought she might become so overwhelmed and confused that she would fall off of Poloska's back, and then she had visions of all the ways she could fall and be hurt and maybe cause Poloska to be hurt as well, and Oleg and his horse too, and...

"Dasha?" His voice cut through the confusion. "Dasha, what's the matter?"

"Nothing," she said.

"Is it..." Oleg sounded uncharacteristically uncertain, "...visions? Your mother told me," he added. "She said they've been...bothering you. Bothering you more and more."

"Yes," Dasha admitted in a very small voice.

"Aren't you training with sorceresses to learn to understand them?"

"It...it doesn't help very much," Dasha said. "And I'm not very good at it!"

"Not good at it?" her father repeated in surprise. "What do you mean, you're not good at it?"

"I'm not good at magic!"

He laughed. "I find that hard to believe."

"It's true! I can do a few things, if I work at it very hard, but the sorceresses say I hardly have any gift at all! It took me a month to make a flower bloom, and I can only do it half the time! And after years of study I still can't light a candle! Once I made a ripple in a basin of water, but like as not it just a stray breath of wind, not my magic, that did the moving. It takes me *ages* to learn even the simplest things, and I can only do it when everything goes right for me, and it would just be easier for me to do things without magic at all!"

"Have you told your mother? Maybe she can help. After all, she has the same gifts."

"Whenever I tell her about it, she just laughs and says she's *hopeless* at magic, which is true! She can't do a single thing, no matter how hard she tries, and she's never been able to! My teachers say...my teachers say that she has, has *negative* talent, that she's unusually *un*gifted, that an ordinary woman with no special gifts at all would be better at magic than she is!"

"Well, that may very well be, but it's no great loss," Oleg told her. "Magic doesn't mean much, here in Krasnograd. It only really works in the taiga or the steppe. Here you're better off lighting your candle from the stove like an ordinary person, even if you are gifted. And I don't think your mother is," he raised his brows, "'unusually *un*gifted.' Her gifts are just unusual, that's all. As they tend to be in your family."

"Yes, but," the thing that had been bothering Dasha the most came bursting out, "everyone's so *disappointed* in me! Everyone expected me to be *so* gifted, *so* talented, but I'm completely average! And I can see their disappointment and surprise every time I fail! They talk behind my back about how I'm gods-touched, about how I'm special, about all the expectations everyone has for me, and I always fail them!"

"And the visions?" her father asked. "Can the sorceresses help you with them?"

"They...the lessons, they...they just seem to make things worse," Dasha confessed, her voice going very quiet. "And now I'm...I'm...I'm scared." The last word came out as a whisper.

"All gifts weigh heavy," said Oleg, speaking unusually gently. "And you...well, it is no surprise that yours would weigh like a millstone. Is it...very bad?"

"It's...it's fine," said Dasha. She was already regretting having said anything. "It's nothing."

"Is it something someone can help you with? If not sorceresses, then maybe priestesses?"

"I...I don't know."

"Have you," he fixed her with a stern and piercing gaze with his blue eyes, that were so like and so unlike Dasha's own blue-green ones, "*asked* anyone?"

"Well...I don't want to be a bother...and anyway, who could help me? What could they do? It's just...it's just my gift, like you said," she said, more bravely than she felt. In fact, panic was welling up inside her, as it did now every time anyone discussed her gift. In truth she was terrified of it, so terrified that she had only recently begun to recognize the feeling for what it was. It had gone beyond the kinds of childhood terrors she had always associated with fear, and taken her with it into some realm where there were no ordinary thoughts and feelings any longer, just madness. Prickles ran over her scalp and up and down her spine at the thought of it, as they did more and more these days, making her shudder in order to release them.

"You'll never know if you don't ask, Dasha," he said. He was trying to speak lightly, but Dasha could taste the icy fear hiding behind his words, fear that he himself was only half aware of, and that frightened her even more.

"Mother says...she says she might know some people who can help," Dasha told him.

"Priestesses?" Oleg asked with interest, cheering up at the possibility of positive action.

"I...I don't know," Dasha admitted. "She didn't say. She just said that there are some people who have offered to train me, to help me, and that I should probably go to them, maybe soon."

"Well then," said Oleg, sounding very relieved. "There you go. No doubt they'll help you get it under con...help you learn to use your gift to your best ability. So, enough about that! How are..." he cast about for some safe topic of conversation, "how are the rest of your studies going?"

"Fine, I suppose," said Dasha. Then she became afraid she might have sounded sullen and ungrateful, so she said, "Everyone claims I make tremendous progress in everything except magic, and soon there will be no more to teach me, if only I wouldn't spend so much time daydreaming. Except that when I stop daydreaming and pay attention to them, we go through everything so quickly that they don't understand what's happened at all, and tell me that I haven't actually learned it. Which is probably true. But it's very confusing, because then they tell me again that I'm the quickest study they've ever seen."

"But you disagree?" asked Oleg, and the corners of his mouth turned up in a start of the smile he normally wore.

"The daydreaming thing—it's silly. That's what helps me learn the most, it seems to me, but everyone tells me I'm wrong. But as for being a quick study—I am often stupid and forgetful, and it seems impossible that the tiny store of wisdom that keeps falling out of my head could be all there is to know in the Known World."

"If I had twenty companies of men, each with forty soldiers, how many soldiers would I have?" asked Oleg.

"Eight hundred. What army has forty soldiers in a company?" asked Dasha. "You see! I thought I knew all the armies and how they were ordered, but I must have forgotten or never learned!"

"No army that I know of, I just made it up," said Oleg, now grinning broadly. "How many letters does the alphabet of Avkhaz have?"

"Forty-nine, because seven is sacred to them," answered Dasha promptly.

"And do you know all of them?"

"Of course; it's not difficult. I still read slowly, though, and I write and speak like a child of three, but Susanna has promised to help me, so perhaps, someday, I will be able to use it without shame," said Dasha, some her ordinary eagerness for her studies welling up in her, now that they were discussing something she felt at least a little bit competent in. "It's a very interesting language."

"I'm sure," said Oleg. "Well, perhaps you are not a complete half-wit, my dear Dasha. You sit a horse very—*very*—well for a city girl; can you wield a sword and bow as well?"

"A little, but very poorly," said Dasha.

"Oh? That's not what Boleslav Vlasiyevich says."

"Then he is flattering me, because he can hit a target with his bow from twice as far as I can, and whenever we spar, I only win if he lets me!"

"If the captain of the Imperial Guard could be outshot and out-fought by a softhanded girl of seventeen who spends too much time stargazing and daydreaming, then we would be in trouble," said Oleg with a laugh that quickly turned to a frown when he saw Dasha's face fall and her lips begin to quiver.

"Dasha my heart, I meant no harm," he said. "Your hands should be soft, and there's nothing wrong with stargazing and daydreaming, if that's what suits your fancy."

"Were your hands soft too when you were seventeen?" asked Dasha, her lips still trembling. "Did you spend all your time 'stargazing and daydreaming,' because you had nothing better to do?"

"Well, no," admitted Oleg. "When I was seventeen I'd already run away from home and put myself in the princess's service—Princess Severnolesnaya, that is. But I'm a bad example. You don't want to be like me. Let people with emptier heads do the sword-fighting, Dasha, that's my fatherly advice to you."

"But what if there is no one else?" said Dasha. "What if I have to do it, and I fail because I'm so poor at it? It's terrible! Susanna said she can shoot birds from the sky at a full gallop! Not that I want to shoot birds from the sky. I hate the idea of shooting anything. But what if I have no choice and I fail because of my slowness and stupidity?"

"By all the gods, you are just like your mother, only a thousand times worse," said Oleg, hitting his own forehead with his fist.

Dasha gave him an extremely aggrieved look, and her lips began to quiver again.

"By which I mean that if either of you has even a shadow of a chance to think ill of yourselves for not being as wise as scholars, godly as priestesses, kind as healers, and bold as steppe warriors, you both fall into a pit of despair that any other woman would sidestep with a proud toss of her head. Your mother means well, and she has done better by you than any other mother in the Known World, but she is right: it's time for you to leave her side and venture out into the world. Otherwise I fear you'll never be able to think well of yourself at all, my dearest Dasha. Well enough: I agree. I will stay in Krasnograd until the roads are clear for easy travel, and then I will escort you myself on your first great journey as a woman grown."

Chapter Four

To Dasha's delight and surprise, Oleg did not forget or deny his promise, and in fact the very next day he began making plans and arrangements for the journey. Even better, he began by taking Dasha into the library and going over maps with her, in order to choose the roads they would follow and show her where they would be going. Dasha had learned to read maps from her tutors, but when there had been no hope of a journey, poring over maps of places she thought she might never see had been more pain than pleasure.

Now, though, with her father's promise (and, more importantly, her mother's consent) that they would set off in the next moon and spend the entire summer traveling, or maybe longer, the library's dusty maps took on a new luster, and Dasha happily studied them and discussed with Oleg the best route to take, although as her actual knowledge of any of the places on the maps was minimal, it was less a discussion and more a conversation in which he said where he thought they should go, and she agreed.

This was a little annoying, but Dasha comforted herself with the thought that by next year, she would be an experienced traveler too, and she would be able to advise others on how best to arrange their journeys, instead of trusting others to arrange things for her. In the meantime, though, it was agreed that they would make their way North to Lesnograd, where Dasha would spend the summer with Vladislava, and then perhaps visit Naberezhnoye and her mother's friend

Dunya, and then come back down the Krasna to home.

"And perhaps next year you can visit the steppe," said her mother. "You should see the steppe too, my love: your own grandfather was a Prince Stepnoy, and you have close kin out there."

"Can I go visit them this year?" Dasha asked eagerly. "Can I go to the steppe first, and then Lesnograd?"

Her mother laughed. "That would be a very long journey, my love," she said. "You would be better served to make two journeys, one each summer, instead of trying to travel in winter."

"*You* traveled in winter," objected Dasha.

"True enough," said her mother, amused. "And never will I forget how unpleasant it was, getting up in the middle of the night to relieve myself in the snow. We all think we are above such things, until we discover that we aren't. Trust me, summer is better. And think of me, too: *I'll* want to see you again too, you know." Her mother smiled playfully. "I've gotten used to having you around, you see, and I don't know what I'll do without having you at my side all the time."

Her smile slipped away at those last words, and Dasha could see her mother sitting in her chambers, alone and lonely, worrying about Dasha and unable to do anything about it...and what if Dasha *died* while she was off on this journey, what would her mother feel then? How terrible that would be for her! Dasha could see the tears running down her mother's cheeks, a thousand times more tears than she had shed for Lisochka...

"Very well," she said. "The steppe next year. And you're right: I don't want to travel in winter."

"Well, winter travel has its charms," said her mother, kissing her cheek. "But you'll have plenty of time to discover that on your own. And being gone half the year is enough, at your age. Besides, you may have other things to occupy your time soon. You need to keep up with your studies."

"I don't see why," said Dasha. "They're not doing me any good."

"You never know when you might need to know something," her mother told her. "Just when you think you'll never have any use for that obscure bit of history your tutors forced upon you, up pops something to prove you wrong, and you see that you would have made a grave error if you hadn't known of it."

"I don't mean that," said Dasha. "I know I need to know my history and lore. But I'm *hopeless* at the other things, and it's not getting any better! Can't I stop? I'm just wasting my time and tormenting my tutors."

"Ah, well, as to that..." said her mother. "Perhaps you need better tutors."

"But who? I thought you said my tutors are the best in Krasnograd!"

"They are," said her mother. "But 'the best in Krasnograd' doesn't mean 'the best people to train you.' There are others who would like to train you, and who may be more adept, more fitting, than your current tutors."

"Like sorceresses in Lesnograd?" asked Dasha eagerly. "Aunty Olga says they're coming back to the city, after being gone so long after her mother sent them away."

"It wouldn't do you any harm to train with the sorceresses in Lesnograd," said her mother. "But there are others who could also train you. You know that there are others—spirits—who have claim to you as well."

"I suppose," said Dasha, trying and failing to suppress the tingles (of apprehension? Or was it something worse?) that began running up her spine at those words. "I suppose I should meet my father's companions. And perhaps they could help me."

"Yes, but not just them," said her mother. "Before you go, Dasha my heart, you should try once again to speak to the kremlin house spirit."

"I've tried dozens of times," said Dasha. "And so have you. And she's never once answered. I've never even *seen* her."

"That's not quite true," said her mother. "She was there for your birth, and she used to come visit you frequently, when you were a baby. So you see," she smiled, "you have seen her, you just don't remember it."

"It's all the same to *me*," said Dasha. "If I don't *remember* seeing her, then it's just the same to *me* as never having seen her at all. And I don't see why I should try yet *again* to speak to her, when she's made it clear she doesn't want to have anything to do with *me*."

"I know it seems like that to you, my heart," said her mother. "But she and all the domoviye have always taken a keen interest in you— took a keen interest in you even before you were born," she corrected herself, seeing Dasha's scowl, "and she and all of them would want to know if you were setting off on a journey, I'm sure of it. And they might be best suited of all to help you learn to use your gift as it is meant to be used."

"I don't see why," said Dasha. "Domoviye don't have visions."

"They must have something, as they have a great gift of foresight," said her mother, speaking tartly even as she smiled to take away some of the sting. "And they might be able to help you, when everyone else cannot."

"Why does everyone want to *help* me?" complained Dasha. It was unjust, she knew, but she couldn't seem to stop herself from letting all the complaints that were building up inside of her burst out, and this at least was a pretext for doing so.

"Because they love you, my soul."

"If they loved me, they would be here! They wouldn't disappear for years and years on end!"

"Perhaps they have their reasons," said her mother, and Dasha could *see*, to her tremendous irritation, that her mother was thinking of Oleg, and thought that Dasha was thinking of him too. Which wasn't true!

"I don't care about their reasons," said Dasha, looking down and kicking at the floor with the toe of her boot, making a sound so dry she thought she might choke on the dusty, rug-like taste of it. "I just want them to stop bothering me. Everyone always *wants* something from me. Everyone always wants me to do something, or be something, or change something. Everyone's always telling me what to do!"

She expected her mother to make some quick rejoinder, something about how it was Dasha's duty to help others, and that their demands were the price of who she was, or something else intolerable, but her mother said nothing. When Dasha stopped scuffing at the rug with her boot and looked up, her mother was standing there unmoving, staring at her with a very strange look on her face, as if she had never seen Dasha before, or she had just seen a vision or a spirit.

"What?" asked Dasha. "What is it?"

Her mother shook her head. "It's just...you...you looked so much like my sister, for a moment there. And sounded like her, too."

Of all the things her mother could have said, that was perhaps the thing that Dasha had expected least. It was, she was certain, not meant as a compliment, and when she thought that her mother might be *angry* with her, Dasha's throat closed over, and she had to blink back the tears that were always rising so irritatingly to her eyes these days.

"I'm nothing like her," she said.

"She is your aunt," said her mother. "Your close blood kin. I dare say you two are very alike. I had just never noticed it before. But no matter." She shook her shoulders. "After all, she and I are even closer. And if you do not wish to try to reach the domovaya here, I will do it myself, and hope that she answers. She can help, Dasha; all of them can help you, I am sure of it."

Well, I'm not, thought Dasha, but seeing how shaken her mother still looked, after the revelation that Dasha took after her sister, even in some very small way, she refrained from saying anything, and soon her mother turned the conversation to the upcoming journey, and all the interesting things she could expect to see and do while on it.

When she told Susanna that she would be leaving next month to visit her kin in the Northern forests, Susanna congratulated her heartily, but then urged her to come to the mountains as well as or instead of her planned journey, painting rapturous pictures of the beauty of the Southern mountains in spring and summer, the joy with which the local princesses would welcome her, and the figure she would cut amongst their sons, who, according to Susanna, were "a thousand times handsomer than these plain and pale-faced Northern milksops, and possessed of more passion than all the men in Krasnograd. Although...your Boleslav Vlasiyevich. *He* is a fine figure of a man, is he not? Not so big and tall as some, but still very handsome, and his hair is still almost as black as a Southerner's, even if his skin is pale and his eyes are gray. No wonder your mother has taken him as a lover."

"She hasn't!" Dasha blurted out without thinking.

"No? Then she is a fool and my mother is blind, and we both know neither of those things are true. Your father is gone half the year or maybe more, everyone says so, and every woman needs a lover at her side, everyone knows it. Have you taken a lover yet?"

"No," mumbled Dasha, looking at the floor and feeling herself blush so hotly that she thought her hair might catch fire.

"Well...if you must know," Susanna giggled, "I have not either. Not properly, you know. I am still waiting for a man whose blood is as hot as mine. But several young men have certainly caught my eye! You must come to our mountains, Dasha, you really must—the men are so handsome there, and they will all lose their heads for your red hair and curls. I'm sure they will even forgive your paleness and—what are those spots on your face?"

"Freckles," admitted Dasha, still looking down at the floor and blushing.

"Freckles!" Susanna repeated the Zemnian word carefully. "Freckles! I have heard of them, but I have never seen anyone with them before." She peered closely at Dasha's face. "I cannot say that I want any for myself. But on you they are not so bad," she conceded. "They make you look exotic. You will be so exotic when you came down to our mountains, Dasha. All the men will throw themselves at your feet. You will have to—how do you say? I do not remember the Zemnian phrase; something about sticks, I think. Anyway, you will have to fight them off with a sword in each hand."

Dasha blushed scarlet again and said she thought that sounded very pleasant, although in fact she thought no such thing. Perhaps for someone as bold as Susanna, the idea of having to fight off hordes of hot-blooded mountain men was attractive, but to Dasha it seemed rather terrifying. Although...she allowed herself to drift off in reverie for moment...maybe it *would* be fun. Other than her training with Boleslav Vlasiyevich, she had spent her whole life with other women. But on the road there would be men—a whole world of men for her to explore. People—such as Susanna—claimed that consorting with men was great fun, the best fun in the world. Perhaps there was something to that.

"And if you come to the mountains, dearest Tsarinovna, we will not be parted," continued Susanna, oblivious to Dasha's woolgathering. "My heart breaks at the thought of being separated from you for a whole summer, and just as we have become friends!"

"Yes," said Dasha, who, while less effusive about it than Susanna, was also dismayed at the thought of leaving behind her new friend. "If only you could come with me!"

"Oh, but Tsarinovna, I could!"

"Would your mother let you go off with a stranger for so long?" asked Dasha doubtfully.

"My mother does not control my coming and going, like that of a girl of three," said Susanna, tossing her head in a way Dasha wished she could emulate. "Besides, if the request came from *your* mother, she would not dare to say no," she added more practically.

"I suppose I could ask my mother," said Dasha, still rather doubtfully. It occurred to her as she said it that she had never asked her mother to use her influence as Empress on her behalf before, and she didn't like the idea. "I wouldn't wish your mother to agree against her will, or resent us for forcing her to agree," she said.

"She will agree happily," said Susanna, "or if she does not, she will be too proud to show that she does not like it. And I am almost a woman grown, and my own mistress, anyway. All you need to do is ask your mother."

Dasha agreed that it was a fine plan, but she decided to begin by approaching Oleg. She wasn't sure why she was so reluctant to ask her mother, other than it seemed too much like the action of a little girl who had to ask her mother's permission to go play, and she was no longer a little girl—but she was also not yet quite a woman who could command her own comings and goings, either. Dasha knew that this journey was meant to mark her becoming a woman, even though she would not officially come of age for three more summers, and that she must start to relate to her mother less as a child to a nursemaid, and more as one woman to another, but how to do that was mysterious to her, and so she put off the request until she could speak with her father.

Arranging to speak to him alone, however, turned out to be more difficult than she had anticipated, as when he was around he was always planning things—well, listening to other people planning things; Dasha soon realized that spending days and days planning things was not one of his favorite things to do, and that now that they had decided where to go, if it had been up to him they would have just set off one morning with nothing but the clothes on their backs and a pocketful of coin—and when he was free he disappeared.

Dasha wanted to ask him where he went to when he wasn't around, and if he would keep disappearing like that when they were traveling together, but she was too shy. According to the gossip of the maids and guards, though, he went off by himself into the park every day, and no one knew why. So it took two days before circumstances came together in such a way that Dasha felt that the time was right for her to attempt to ask him.

She waited until both her mother and father had gone off on business of their own, and then, guessing by the direction he had gone that her father had gone off into the park, she went out—*snuck* out, actually, by telling her guards she wanted to go to the stables, and then slipping off into the park on foot, as they were waiting for their horses to be saddled. Dasha had not tried to evade her guards for a good ten years, and had never done so successfully, and was astonished and a little terrified at how easy it was. She had simply thought *Don't see me!* and stepped out of the stable, and no one had seen her.

As she hurried to the park she had a hundred visions of the guards coming and catching her and shouting at her, of her mother becoming angry at her for her foolish and inconsiderate behavior, at the guards getting into trouble because of her (that was a painful thought), of harm befalling her because of what she had done—what if today was the day, for the first time in Dasha's life, when an assassin took it into her head to harm her, or she tripped and fell and broke something and no one was there to help her, or she got lost, or any of the other things that could happen to a girl walking around alone—of harm befalling her and her mother blaming the guards, of Oleg getting angry at her, of Boleslav Vlasiyevich getting angry at her and at her guards—the last was the most likely, and the most scary to think about. Boleslav Vlasiyevich took Dasha's safety very seriously, and he frightened her a little bit.

Not that he had ever given her cause to fear him; quite the opposite, from the point of view of sense. He had always been kind and attentive towards her, and trained her in fighting and shooting himself, as if she were his own daughter. But he had an intensity to him that Dasha had encountered in few other people, and she had the sense that there was little he would stop at, if he thought it necessary. Her father gave the same impression, and her mother, queerly enough, too, but whenever Dasha was around Boleslav Vlasiyevich, she could see things she would rather not see out of the corner of her eyes, things that, she was sure, he had actually done, even though she couldn't say what, exactly, those things were.

Dasha didn't think he would ever hurt her, but she had a strong feeling that he would hurt other people *for* her, which was almost worse. When she thought about it sensibly, she couldn't actually imagine her mother punishing the guards for Dasha's willful behavior, but she could easily see Boleslav Vlasiyevich doing so, no matter how unjust that might be, and if her mother forbade it, she guessed that Boleslav Vlasiyevich would find some way of doing it anyway, out of her mother's sight. At that thought, she almost turned around and ran back to the stables and begged her guards' pardon then and there, but instead she kept going through the trees, deeper and deeper into the woods.

The park was a strange thing, even to Dasha, who had been visiting it all her life. It was in the middle of the city, bounded by a fence, and a woman could walk around the outside of it in a small part of an afternoon. Dasha had done so once, and counted it as one of the greatest adventures of her young life. So it stood to reason that it would only take a short while to cross, as it must be less than a verst across at its longest point. But once inside it, the city seemed to disappear, so that nothing of its ordinary clamor could be heard, and you could ride around the park all day and not cover all of it. Or so it seemed to Dasha. Once when she had said as much to her mother, her mother had said that was because she was still young and untraveled, and thus was not used to calculating distances or keeping track of where she had been.

"I don't get lost!" Dasha had protested. "I can't! I always know which way West is!" It was her one gift that everyone agreed she possessed in abundance, although why and for what purpose, no one could say.

"No matter how well you know your compass points, even a very small park has many hidden corners," her mother had told her. "You can explore it all day, and not find all of them. But look, my dear: standing up on this tower you can see right across it to the brothers' sanctuary on the other side."

Dasha had had to admit that that was true, as they looked over the wall of the tallest tower of the kremlin, and surveyed the entire Northern side of the city. From here it looked as if she could just step over the park, which seemed small and ordinary and had clearly defined borders, and end up back on city streets.

But then her mother had admitted that sometimes distance and direction could play tricks on you, when leshiye and other creatures of the gods were involved, and that the park was very old and full of prayer trees, and who knew what that meant? It was true that people generally preferred to go around it when crossing the city, instead of through it, even though that made the walk twice as far, and no one went there after dark.

And whenever Dasha and her guards went riding in it, which they did almost every day, her guards kept her to the Southern edge of the park, which was crisscrossed with many paths, and stayed away from the Northern side. A few times Dasha had insisted that they take the one broad path that led so invitingly right through the center of the park all the way to the other side, where there was a large gate. They had done so, and nothing untoward had happened to them, but the guards were plainly made uneasy by it, and to be honest, so was Dasha. She had once suggested that they leave the path and go exploring in the groves to either side of it, but her guards had vehemently objected, saying that there were bogs there that would suck her right down into them, and for some reason that had frightened her so much she had never suggested it again.

Water frightened Dasha, especially deep, dark water, the kind where you couldn't see the bottom and that consequently gave rise to so many visions, visions as deep and dark as the water itself, and she didn't like the idea of sucking bogs right in the middle of Krasnograd at all. Which was silly. Bogs were just a place like any other, and lots of plants and little creatures made their homes in them. But Dasha had always kept strictly to the path after that, and stayed more and more on the Southern side of the park, where the ground was firm and dry.

Today, though, there was no part of the park that was firm and dry. Half-melted snow drifts stood by every path and under every tree, and the paths themselves, while mostly clear of snow, were less paths than pools and streams of melting snow, flowing over the still-frozen ground. Dasha tried to walk along the edge of the path and leap lightly over the puddles, but she soon slipped into the middle of the path and ended up in ankle-deep icy water, and as she struggled out of that she slipped again and fell onto her hands and knees into the snow drift that had forced her into the water in the first place.

Everyone would know she had gone into the park as soon as they saw her soaked and muddy clothing—the frozen ground had melted just enough to be covered with a thin layer of slick mud, making the footing twice as treacherous as it would have been had it been frozen through or wholly melted—she thought glumly, and she could already see the fuss her return would cause, wet and cold as she would be. No doubt on top of everything else she was in for a terrible scolding from her maids and tutors, who all lived in constant terror that Dasha would take a chill. Dasha had no desire to take a chill herself, but she had never suffered greatly from sickness, and any chill that had attacked her had always passed on by in a matter of days, leaving her none the worse for the experience, and so her maids' extreme fear of chills had always seemed excessive, even pointless, to her.

But they were unlikely to be swayed by her arguments—despite their claim to respect her above all other women, aside from her mother, and their promises to obey her in everything, they in fact considered themselves in their rights to run Dasha's life exactly as they saw fit, and ignore everything she told them, even though she was the one who knew herself and had lived her whole life, not them, not anyone else...but that had nothing to do with the task at hand. The task at hand was to find her father, wherever he might be hiding in this park, and ask him about bringing Susanna with them.

A task that, Dasha reflected as she slid along, would probably be best accomplished not by evading her guards and falling into the snow, thereby showing herself to be clumsy as well as foolish and inconsiderate, but that thought had come late, far too late, and since she was here already, she might as well go through with it...and perhaps her father would be impressed, or charmed, or amused, or put into some state that would make him well-disposed towards her.

Dasha tried to tell herself that she was doing just the sort of thing that he would do, and it would make him like her more, make him see her as *his* and not just some girl who took after her mother, but she rather doubted, as she slipped and fell into another snow drift, that she resembled her father at all right now, and even if she did, a little voice whispered to her that fathers didn't hold with their daughters doing the same things that they themselves would do. Not that she would know, would she, since her father had hardly ever been around her entire life, but he had said, he had said straight to her face that she shouldn't take him as a model...*And* she couldn't find him, either. She had been walking for ages, she must be halfway across the park by now, but she was still stuck in the Eastern side of it and she hadn't seen any sign of him.

She suddenly came to a fork in the path and recognized where she was once again. She knew from all her riding there that if she turned left she would end up back at the Southern gate, if she went straight, she would end up on the main path that led all the way to the Northern gate, and if she turned right, she would end up in a small grove of prayer trees. She also knew that this turning meant she had not gone very deep into the park at all, even though it felt to her as if she had been walking half the morning.

It's the mud and the ice, she told herself. *It's making it seem like I've been walking for much longer than I have, because it's such hard going. There's nothing strange about it at all.*

That thought made her feel a little better, but it didn't tell her which way she should go. She stood there for a moment in indecision. She knew that she should go back, but...she had gone this far, hadn't she? The path straight ahead would be the most sensible choice, as it would lead her deeper into the park, where she was more likely to find Oleg. The thought of going deeper into the park made her stomach twist queerly, as if with fear.

It's just the park, she told herself. *There's nothing here that will harm you.* But even so, her feet seemed to carry her of their own accord off to the right, to the prayer trees.

Despite how long it had seemed to take her to make it to the turning point, it seemed to take her, oddly enough, no time at all to come to the prayer trees, and she was about to step into the clear circle in the middle of the grove when the sound of voices made her freeze, half-concealed behind some bushes. For a moment she thought she had achieved her goal and stumbled upon Oleg, and that he really was talking to the trees, just as the maids and the guards said he did, but then she recognized the voice as belonging to Boleslav Vlasiyevich. And there was a second voice, too: a woman's. Her mother's.

Dasha knew that she should not eavesdrop on whatever her mother and Boleslav Vlasiyevich were discussing, but her curiosity—grown immensely after hearing the speculations of Susanna despite her denials of their truth—somehow held her there in the grove and out of their sight, and so, instead of slipping away or stepping forward and announcing herself, she remained half-hidden behind the bushes.

"You can't blame yourself for what Lisochka did," Boleslav Vlasiyevich was saying earnestly. "You can't, Slava, you can't! You did everything you could to save her from that path, but she'd already started down it a long time before you ever came along. You can't blame yourself for it!"

"I know." Dasha's mother stopped and softly fingered a swelling bud on a low-hanging tree branch.

"But you feel sorry for her, don't you?" said Boleslav Vlasiyevich, sounding more exasperated than Dasha could ever remember anyone ever sounding around her mother. She half-expected her mother to do something to put him in his place—for such a gentle person, her mother was surprisingly good at making other people feel small when she needed to—but she only shrugged and looked down, as if she herself were the one who felt small. This made Dasha want to jump out from behind the bushes and demand that Boleslav Vlasiyevich apologize right now, but she told herself to wait a bit and see what developed. Perhaps her mother already had something up her sleeve, and Dasha would only spoil it by appearing out of nowhere...

"Of course I do," said her mother tiredly. "Of course." She moved away from the branch with the newly-swelling buds, and Dasha could see, almost as if it had actually happened, a vision of her mother snapping and crushing their fragile new life in a fit of—what? Anger? Despair? Feelings that Dasha did not normally associate with her mother, anyway.

"If you're angry with her too, it wouldn't be strange," said Boleslav Vlasiyevich. "Many are, after someone they know takes their own life. And of course, after what she did to Dasha—I'm afraid Oleg Svetoslavovich was right. If she hadn't killed herself, we would have had to do it for her."

"Yes," said her mother tiredly. "Or rather, no, of course I wouldn't have allowed it, but I understand why you would think that way. What she did to Dasha...what she did to Dasha was...was unforgiveable."

Boleslav Vlasiyevich turned to look at her in surprise. "I never thought to hear you say that," he said, and it seemed to Dasha, strangely enough, that he was smiling, almost laughing, as he spoke.

"Of course I don't really mean it," said her mother, still sounding very tired. "But..." her voice rose in horror, "to throw scalding water on a dog! I cannot...I cannot..."

"I know," said Boleslav Vlasiyevich. "But I was talking about Dasha the girl, not Dasha the dog. To insult your daughter, the Tsarinovna, like that..."

"Oh, well." Her mother waved her hand dismissively. "Dasha will get over it." Her voice had taken on that metallic edge it got sometimes, and which made all her princesses and councilors quake in their boots. Dasha had never had it directed at her before, nor had she ever heard her mother say "Dasha will get over it" quite so directly. It was...strange, and a little unpalatable at first, but then Dasha realized that her mother was right, she *would* get over it, and she also felt a sense of pride that her mother thought so. She was no longer a little girl, not even in her mother's eyes, but practically a woman grown, and certainly a woman grown enough that she could get over an insult from someone of lower birth, who was dead besides.

Boleslav Vlasiyevich gave her mother a sideways look. "You're probably right, Slava," he said after a little while. "She will get over it, one way or another. She's a lot more like you than either of you realize."

"Of course she is," said her mother. "And," she smiled up at him, but her smile still looked tired, "I won't even ask what it is you mean by that."

"You got over a lot, Slava," he told her, looking into her eyes in a way that Dasha, although she had no experience at all in the ways of love, knew meant that they had to be lovers. "A lot. Too much, in fact. I don't want Dasha to have to get over so much."

"And neither do I, and the gods willing, she won't, but she'll still have to get over some things. She'll still have to be tough enough to rule, maybe sooner rather than later."

"Slava!" Boleslav Vlasiyevich grabbed both her hands. "Are you... unwell?"

"Not in the way you mean," said her mother. "It's just...the usual. What it's always been." She smiled a smile that had nothing of joy in it. "Just the curse," she said. "The one I've always had. Only it's bad right now. With what Lisochka did...and on top of all our troubles on our Western borders...it's just too much right now, it's too much."

"I see," said Boleslav Vlasiyevich, pulling her closer to him, so that he could cradle the back of her neck in his hands. "I see."

Her mother stepped in even closer and rested her head on his chest. Dasha *knew* that she shouldn't be watching this, that she should leave right now, but the fear of making a sound and the certainty that this was important, that she was about to learn something that she should know, held her in place.

"When I heard the news," said her mother, her voice muffled against Boleslav Vlasiyevich's chest but still audible. "When I heard the news, I was...I was...I thought, 'But that's supposed to be me!' And I was...envious. I was envious that she'd managed what I hadn't. And angry, because...because she'd stolen...she'd stolen what I'd always thought was *mine*."

"I see," repeated Boleslav Vlasiyevich, holding her tightly and kissing the top of her head. "I see." He looked around, making Dasha's heart stop for a moment from the fear of being found out, but his eyes slid past her hiding place without pausing. "And," he spoke cautiously, "do you have any...immediate plans?"

Her mother lifted up her head and laughed tearfully. "How can I?" she asked. "The season is past! The snow is almost gone. If I tried it now, I'd probably just spend a miserable night in the muck and have nothing but a terrible cold for my pains. Plus all the leshiye would no doubt drag me back to the kremlin kicking and screaming as soon as they got wind of what I was up to."

"And thank the gods for that," said Boleslav Vlasiyevich fervently. "Does that mean you have no plans to explore...alternative methods?"

Her mother shook her head. "I couldn't face anything else," she said, screwing up her own face in distaste. "Which no doubt means I'm not actually serious about it. It's just...I guess it's really just a fantasy I have."

"In that case it's a very peculiar one," said Boleslav Vlasiyevich, stepping back a bit in order to contemplate her but, Dasha was glad to note, still cradling her neck in his arms. Her mother smiled tremulously, and he grinned back at her. "Frankly, I'd like to think your fantasies were about something a bit...warmer."

Dasha blushed all over her entire body, but her mother only laughed a bit and shook her head. "And sometimes they are," she told him. "But...I need to have...I need to know that I *could* just run out into the snow and never come back. Sometimes that's the only thing that gives me any comfort. Sometimes the only thing that...that keeps me from ending it all right now is the knowledge that I could if I had to, and that someday maybe I will. And this...hunger will never leave me, you know. It is a sickness for life."

"I know," he said soberly. "I just hope you are willing to suffer it for a good deal longer, because I...I fear the cure."

"I'm afraid I probably will," said her mother, now beginning to sound brisk and business-like, as if they were discussing affairs of state. Which, Dasha realized, they were. "I cannot abandon my duties now. But...it made me think."

"Yes?" asked Boleslav Vlasiyevich, when she didn't continue. "Made you think what?"

"It made me think that I cannot do this forever," said her mother. "Or even for too terribly much longer. Once Dasha is ready, I will step aside, just as my own mother did, and retire somewhere peaceful."

Even through the bushes and in profile, Dasha could see the conflicting feelings run across Boleslav Vlasiyevich's face: relief at this non-fatal possible outcome, and—grief at the thought of losing her mother? The fear of being abandoned? She suddenly felt for him and his odd position, very strongly, and was glad when her mother stepped back into him to rest her head on his chest and say, "You could come with me, you know. Or not. It would be up to you."

"As if it would ever be up to me," said Boleslav Vlasiyevich into the top of her head. "As if I could ever stay away. You know I would never stop you from leaving, not even on that long last journey, if you really thought you had to, but I...I could never leave."

"If you wanted to..." her mother said, but he told her not to be silly, and then they broke apart and, with a coordination that spoke of long intimacy, both set off in the same direction at the same pace, Boleslav Vlasiyevich holding her mother gently by the arm.

Chapter Five

Dasha watched them go. She was ashamed to admit to herself that her first thought was of herself, of how hurt she was that her mother had never told her about—well, any of this, actually, and how foolish she felt that she hadn't figured it out on her own. She really was just a silly little girl, just as she feared...Boleslav Vlasiyevich and her mother were gone. She could come out from behind the bushes without any danger of being caught spying.

Only when she tried to step out onto the path, the slender branches of the bushes, with buds that were just beginning to swell with new life, caught at her clothes, and when she tried to pull free, they pulled back, surprisingly strong and flexible despite their apparent brittle thinness, so that the more she struggled, the more trapped she became. They had little briars, she discovered, that were sticking to her clothes and working themselves in deeper and deeper the more she moved.

It's just some twigs caught in my clothes, she told herself. *All I have to do is stop struggling and work them free, calmly and slowly. A girl of five could do it.* Only when she tried to reach her right hand over to where a twig had caught her left arm, another little branch caught it, and suddenly she couldn't move either arm. A nasty tingling ran up her spine and spread out behind her ears.

She twisted, trying to get free that way, but the only thing that accomplished was to make another twig slap her across the face, scratching her cheek with briars that had been so small she hadn't even noticed them at first, but now were large and sharp enough to draw blood. She tried to move her feet and back out of the bushes the way she had come, but her struggles had turned the half-melted muck into slick mud, and she slipped and nearly fell, stopped only by the embrace of the thorny branches. Her heart was racing as if she were running a race, and tingles of fear were slithering all over her body. Visions rose before her eyes of the branches engulfing her, strangling her, stabbing her, of the ground giving way beneath her and letting her sink into a bog, never to escape, drowning, drowning, never to escape, it was taking her down, taking her down...

"Dasha? Is that you?"

Oleg's surprised voice blew the visions away and allowed her to focus on him. "I'm here!" she cried in relief. "I'm stuck!"

"I can see that." He sounded more amused than concerned. "But how, by all the gods, did you get into this mess?" He came over and beginning to free her clothes from the branches that were now firmly stuck to her sleeves, her scarf, her hat, and her skirt. "And what are you doing here in the first place?" he added. "Your guards are frantic. They realized you were missing and went running off to confess to Boleslav Vlasiyevich, quaking in their boots, I might add, but when they couldn't find him, they came to me next, and I set off to look for you, and—here you are, stuck in a briar patch."

"I'm sorry," said Dasha. "I didn't mean...I didn't think about how they would get into trouble until after I'd snuck off, and then, well, I was already gone, so I thought...I thought I'd keep going. Only I got stuck instead."

"So I see," said her father mildly. He had freed the right side of her body and begun on the left, but when Dasha tried to help him, she only got trapped by the briars again, so she had to stand there and let him do all the work. "What made you want to run off?" he asked, still speaking mildly, as if he weren't angry at all. Dasha doubted even her mother would have been so calm. No doubt in his place her mother would have been displeased at the trouble she had gotten the guards into. No doubt her mother *would* be very displeased at the trouble Dasha had gotten the guards into, once she found out about it.

Not that she would do anything so very terrible about it, since she never did do anything so very terrible, at least not to Dasha, but Dasha could already hear her explaining, kindly and patiently, that Dasha's unkindness and impatience had caused trouble for others, and that

Dasha's actions affected more than just herself and that it was important to have consideration for all the others who depended on her... Dasha shook her head to clear it of those thoughts and looked at her father. He smiled back at her, for all the world as if he wasn't holding this mad adventure against her at all.

"I was looking for you," Dasha confessed to him.

"In a briar patch?" he asked with a laugh.

"No...I just got stuck...I was looking for you in the park. I...I wanted to, to ask you something, and I thought I might be able to find you in the park and talk to you, you know, in private, and, and so I...I asked my guards to take me out riding, and then I imagined that they couldn't see me, and then they *didn't* see me as I snuck off and came here, and I started looking for you, only I kept falling down in the mud and the snow, and I thought I was lost, but then I ended up here, only, only... well, I decided to hide behind these bushes, only then I got stuck, and, and...here you are."

"Here I am," he agreed cheerfully, freeing her left sleeve from the twigs stuck to it. He looked up and down the path. "Were you spying on your mother?" he asked.

"How did you *know*?" asked Dasha, astounded.

He laughed. "I hope I can read tracks well enough to know when someone has been walking up and down a path in deep mud," he said. "Your mother was just here with...some man." He raised a brow at her. "I hope you weren't trying to interrupt a tryst," he said, now sounding more severe, even though Dasha could tell he was still trying not to laugh. "Although it's a funny place for one," he added. "Most of us would choose a bed or at least a hayloft, this time of year."

"No!" Dasha protested. "I was looking for you, just like I told you! But instead of you, I found my mother. She was...taking council with, with, with Boleslav Vlasiyevich."

"Is that so," said her father. He spoke lightly, but Dasha didn't think he actually felt light about it at all. "A funny place to take council," he said, more to himself than to Dasha.

"She was upset about Lisochka," said Dasha, feeling the need to defend her mother, even though her mother had almost certainly been engaging in exactly the kind of thing that her father suspected, even if not on this particular day. "She was upset about Lisochka, and she...she came here to pray and to...to talk in private to someone who could help her. Like I came to talk to you."

"Probably not exactly like you came to talk to me," said Oleg, his mouth tight with sorrow and amusement. He shook his head, letting the amusement win out, and grinned at her. "So, Dasha, what is this thing you had to talk to me about so desperately that you abandoned your guards to Boleslav Vlasiyevich's tender mercies and your clothes to the mud and briars of the early spring woods?"

"Well…" Now that he was standing here before her, it seemed silly, or at least, going to so much trouble to try to find him alone did, especially given the outcome. "I wanted…" Dasha swallowed, "you see, Susanna wants to, to come with us, and I…I want her to come with us too, so I thought…she said my mother should ask hers, only I thought, if I asked you first, then…"

"Susanna? That Southern princess? You went to all this trouble to ask my permission for her to come along?" For a terrible moment Dasha thought Oleg was going to laugh at her, laugh out loud.

"Is that so bad?" she asked tremulously. "I guess…I didn't think it would be so much trouble…"

"It's no trouble at all," said Oleg, still looking as if he were restraining laughter only with extreme difficulty. "Well, I'm sure Susanna is trouble, but you bringing a companion is no trouble at all. In fact, people are insisting on it. It's just…" his shoulders appeared to be shaking with suppressed laughter, "why did you think you had to go sneaking off to beg my permission?"

"I don't know," said Dasha, staring at the muddy ground.

"Dasha, my dove," said her father, "did it never occur to you to *demand* that Susanna be allowed to come with you?"

"No," she said, in a tiny voice.

He sighed. "Your mother is right," he said. "You desperately need some toughening up."

Dasha thought tears might start to well up in her eyes at those words. She bit her lip to try to hold them back. The last thing she wanted to do was cry over being told she needed to toughen up.

"Oh don't look like that, my girl," said her father, pulling her free from the last of the briars. "There's nothing wrong with you. But you're Tsarinovna, and some day you'll be Tsarina. You should be able to order people around any way you please."

"My mother doesn't," argued Dasha, still staring at the ground.

"No, no she doesn't," agreed her father with a sigh. "She's much too terrifying for that. But you didn't have to go sneaking off to beg me this favor in private when all you had to do was say that you wanted Susanna to go with you and we all would have had to obey."

"People don't normally do what I tell them," Dasha mumbled at her feet.

"Surely your maids do," her father objected.

"Them least of all," said Dasha.

"Well..." he grinned, "having met some of the kremlin maids, I have to say you're probably right. But you need to learn how to *command*, Dasha. Surely you've been taught how to do that?"

"Everyone just fusses over me," said Dasha. "They fuss over me and say they want to help me and do anything I want, and then they boss me around and do whatever they want."

"Well..." he sighed again, "no doubt that's true, Dasha my dear. That's what comes of being Tsarinovna. So why don't we pretend you're not the Tsarinovna, when we're on the road?"

Dasha stared at him in astonishment. He grinned back in response.

"What, like...lie?" she asked.

"Not lie," he said, still grinning, obviously very taken with the idea. "We just won't tell anyone who doesn't need to know who you are. You'll just be...some traveling noblewoman. It will be...jolly."

"It doesn't sound very jolly," said Dasha, but she was already starting to smile at the idea.

"It'll be very jolly," said her father firmly. "Like a game! A real game, not like those strategy games you were telling me about." Now his eyes were sparkling like a boy's. "And you'll see and hear so much that you wouldn't if you were going under your own name. *And* you'll have to learn how to give commands, which every woman should if she's to be a proper woman and not a little girl. Really, I don't know how your mother could have neglected your training like this."

Dasha started to protest, but then she saw that he was still grinning and his eyes were still sparkling, and she realized that he was saying it as a joke and that she was supposed to find it funny too, and once she'd thought about it for a moment she *did* find it funny, so she smiled back at him in reply and said it sounded a clever idea and also like fun, and as long as her mother agreed, she would be happy to go along with it.

This made Oleg roll his eyes and say that most young ladies of her age were constantly looking for excuses to disobey their mothers, not seeking out their permission, but once Dasha had gotten over the hurt of that accusation and agreed that it was a fine plan, it was agreed that that was what they would do. Then Oleg said they should go back to the kremlin and find her guards and reassure them that she was still alive.

"And let's hope they haven't gone off to confess their crimes to Boleslav Vlasiyevich," said Oleg, not sounding particularly concerned about that possibility. "I told them to stay put and wait for me to come back, and not bother him about it, but you Krasnograd folk are so obedient, like as not they've already gone and volunteered for whatever punishment he's set for them."

"But it's not their fault!" cried Dasha in dismay. "I...I tricked them!"

"I very much doubt our Vlasiyich will see it that way," said Oleg, still not sounding overly concerned. "Our only hope for them is speed and silence. Come, let's go and rescue them from themselves, if we still can." He took her hand and led her out of the bushes and, moving at a half-jog, down the path. It ran straight and true for him, and in what seemed like a quarter the time it had taken Dasha to make the same distance, they were back at the gate and out of the woods and returning to the bustle and warmth of the kremlin.

They found the guards waiting unhappily by the stables. The sight of Dasha returning to them, safe and sound, caused them to brighten for a moment, but then Arkasha, who was in charge of Dasha's guard detail, began scolding her, most respectfully, but still scolding her, for her thoughtlessness. Dasha hung her head and apologized, which only made Arkasha scold her more, until Oleg burst in, more angrily than Dasha had ever heard him speak before, "Enough! Don't take out your own incompetence on the Tsarinovna!"

"But it really was my fault," argued Dasha, afraid of Oleg's anger and wanting to defend Arkasha from it, even though Arkasha's words had hurt her so much that a moment before she had thought she might start to cry. "I...I tricked them and slipped off on purpose."

"There, you see!" said Arkasha triumphantly. "The Tsarinovna admits her own willfulness! Really, Dasha," he added, turning to speak directly to her again, "I don't know what's come over you, I really don't. You used to be such a quiet, biddable little girl, but now you're..."

"A woman," interjected Oleg. "Soon to be a woman grown, and

heir to all of Zem'. Watch your tongue and your manners when you speak to her, Arkasha. She's no longer a little girl, and she never was, not for the likes of you."

Arkasha stiffened in offense. "I think I know a bit more about her girlhood than you do, Oleg Svetoslavovich," he said coldly. "After all, I was there for it."

The two men took a step towards each other, their hands clenched into fists. Dasha could feel her heart beating quick-quick-quick as visions rose up before her of them *fighting*, of them *hurting* each other. She had never seen anyone get into any kind of a fight, she had never even seen anyone get really angry before, not like this.

"I'm sorry!" she cried, taking Oleg by the sleeve. "Let's go, let's go. I'm sorry, I'm sorry, I'm sorry! I didn't mean to cause any trouble, I didn't...it's my fault, my fault! Don't fight, please don't fight!"

Arkasha looked pleased at her words and backed away slightly, relaxing his hands, but Oleg seemed, if anything, even angrier than before. He looked back and forth between her and Arkasha several times, before finally, to Dasha's extreme relief, stepping back too.

"Come, Dasha," he said. "I'll take you back to the kremlin. We need to speak to your mother, after all: that's what you came out looking for me for. No, you stay here," he said to Arkasha, who had moved as if to accompany them. "I'll guard my own daughter for the moment, thank you very much. You go back to the barracks."

"Boleslav Vlasiyevich..." objected Arkasha, while the other guards grimaced in a way that suggested they were also imagining what Boleslav Vlasiyevich would do to them when he found out what had happened, which he certainly would if they showed up back at the barracks in the middle of their shift.

"Whatever he does to you is no more than you deserve," said Oleg sharply.

"No, send him to me, send him to me!" cried Dasha. "Don't tell him, please don't tell him, Arkasha, and if he finds out, say it was my fault and send him to me!"

Oleg opened his mouth as if he very much wanted to object to that, but after glancing over—once it would have been down, but now he and Dasha were almost of a height—at her face, he did no more than shake his head in disgust before marching off towards the kremlin palace, with Dasha trotting anxiously behind him.

"What is the matter with you!" demanded Oleg as soon as they were out of earshot of Arkasha and the other guards.

"I said I'm sorry!" protested Dasha. "I'm sorry, I'm sorry, I'm sorry! I know I shouldn't have snuck off like that! It was thoughtless, just like Arkasha said."

"Not that!" said Oleg. "I'm beginning to think that sneaking off was the best thing you've done all day, maybe all year. Why did you keep apologizing like that? Why did you keep saying it was your fault?"

"Because it was! I felt so bad about causing trouble for others. And because he was so angry with me! You were both so angry! I was afraid you were going to fight! I saw…"

"What did you see?" asked Oleg, when Dasha didn't finish her sentence.

"Nothing," she said quickly, shaking her head. "It doesn't matter."

"It's your visions, isn't it?" said Oleg. "You saw…whatever it was you saw, and it scared you, didn't it? The visions are scaring you, aren't they?"

"No," said Dasha, but in such a way that both of them knew it was a lie.

Oleg sighed. "Let's go to your mother," he said. "She should know about this. All of this."

"I don't want to get anyone in trouble," said Dasha in a small voice. "They shouldn't have to get into trouble over my foolishness."

"But that's just the thing," said Oleg. "They should. Not about you running off to the park, but about everything else."

"What else?" asked Dasha, and then when Oleg's face darkened again at her words, wished she hadn't. It had never occurred to her to be afraid, really afraid of him before, but some of the visions he was making her see were of him…hurting her. It scared her even to think of it, but his anger had made her see out of the corner of her eye him shouting at her, slapping her, choking her, knocking her to the ground and kicking her…she had never actually witnessed anything of the sort, not by anyone, but she knew, from the whispers of her maids and guards, that many parents treated their children so, especially fathers. Part of her didn't think her father would ever actually do anything like that, not to her or to anyone else, but part of her, the part that was not only seeing but living the visions as they grew stronger and stronger, made her flinch away from him when he reached out to her, in order, she realized too late, to comfort her.

"Well, I suppose I deserved that," said Oleg after they both stood there for a shocked, awkward moment. "But I won't hurt you, my dove, I swear it."

"I know," said Dasha uncomfortably.

"Was it the visions again?" he asked.

She nodded miserably.

"What did they show you?" he asked.

But she was too ashamed to tell him, too ashamed to admit that the things she had seen were filling her head, when she shouldn't be able to think such awful things at all, so she only shook her head in refusal.

"Well," said Oleg. "Whatever it was, I suppose I deserved it. I...I won't hurt you, I promise. You're safe with me, Dasha, I promise. But if you saw bad things...bad things done to me, bad things done by me—you were right."

"It's nothing," said Dasha, and then, thinking he might take that to mean that she thought his suffering was nothing, added quickly, "I'm sorry! I didn't mean it like that."

"I know you didn't," he said. Dasha had the impression that she was, despite all her efforts to the contrary, trying his patience sorely, and that it was only with great effort that he was stopping himself from bursting out shouting. She tried to prevent herself from shrinking away from him again, but, judging by his face, she failed. She followed him in silence back inside the palace and up to the Imperial quarters and to her mother's chambers, where Oleg found a serving woman and demanded to speak with the Tsarina in a voice that made Dasha cringe back all over again, fortunately out of his sight.

Her mother appeared very shortly after that. "What is it?" she asked, looking back and forth between them in concern. "What is it?" she repeated, her voice growing sharper. "Oleg, has something happened?"

"How could you, Slava!" he burst out. Dasha shrank back towards the door, but her mother only looked at Oleg in surprise and asked, "Do what?"

"How could you let those...*people* raise our daughter!"

"I raised our daughter, Oleg," Dasha's mother said, so tartly her words were like unripe cranberries on Dasha's tongue.

"Not enough! How could you...how could you let those, those maids, and those tutors, and those guards...*do* that to her?!"

"Do what?" demanded her mother sharply.

"Make her...make the kind of girl who cringes and apologizes! To guards! She apologized to her own guards!"

Her mother sighed. "What did you..." She stopped herself before she could finish her accusation, and started again. Somehow that made it almost worse. "What happened, Dasha?" she asked.

"I'm sorry!" cried Dasha, for, it seemed, the hundredth time that day. "I wasn't thinking! I didn't...I didn't mean to get anyone into trouble!"

"I'm sure you didn't," said her mother. "But sometimes..."

"Oh stop it, Slava!" Oleg said before her mother could finish. "Don't lecture her on duty! Don't lecture her on consideration for others! There's been a great deal too much of that already, as far as I can see! You, you...you've failed her, that's what you've done! You're just like your own mother!"

Her mother's face went from calm to crumpled.

"That's not true!" Dasha cried, from where she was shrinking in the corner. She couldn't quite make out the visions that were hovering around her, trying to force their way into her sight, but she knew that Oleg had said the worst thing he could have possibly said to her mother, and she couldn't let him make her mother feel like that, not for a moment longer.

Her mother's face softened slightly and smoothed out, to her great relief. She swallowed and took a deep breath, and then said, with a calm that Dasha wished she could emulate, "What happened? What brought this on?"

"It was my fault!" Dasha said, before Oleg could say anything and make it worse than it already was. "I...I wanted to ask a favor, and I was...I was afraid to ask it in public, I wanted to ask it in private, and I thought the best place to do it would be the park, so I...so I tricked my guards and snuck off by myself."

Her mother stared at her and Oleg as if they all three had gone insane. "Is that all?" she asked after a moment, and Dasha realized that she was trying not to laugh out loud. "And here I thought you'd at least stolen Princess Stepnaya's prize broodmare or attempted to run off with her son. Not that she would begrudge you either of them, I'm sure, but...a quick trip to the park is hardly a cause for so much grief and consternation. How did you trick your guards, by the way?"

"I...I don't know," admitted Dasha. "I just...didn't want them to see me, and they didn't."

"Is that so," said her mother, looking thoughtful. "That is very interesting indeed. Have you ever been able to do anything like that before?"

"Slava!" interjected Oleg before Dasha and her mother could become distracted by this new piece of exciting information. "Now is hardly the time! We have more important problems!"

"I never thought you would be the one to worry over a little running-off and rule-breaking," said her mother, smiling at the thought.

"It's not that! It's Dasha! It's...she just kept apologizing and apologizing!"

"There's nothing wrong with saying you're sorry if you've inconvenienced someone," said her mother.

"There is if you're the Tsarina," said her father. "Besides, she did it a lot. And then that guard Arkasha was scolding her."

"I see," said her mother. She looked over at Dasha. "Dasha, my love," she said, "why did you do it?"

"I wanted to...to speak with him," Dasha confessed, nodding at Oleg. "In private."

"Yes, I understand that. But why did you sneak off?"

"Because...I don't know, exactly," said Dasha. "I just...felt like I had to. And...and I was scared to...to do the asking. I've never really...asked for anything before."

Both her mother and Oleg looked at her in surprise.

"Not like this," Dasha explained. "Not where I was asking for a favor that might...that other people might not like."

"All she wanted was to ask if that Susanna girl could come with us on our journey," said Oleg. "And still she went to all this trouble because she was so afraid to ask us for it."

"Afraid? Why afraid?" asked her mother, sounding even more surprised than before.

"I don't know," admitted Dasha, squirming and looking at the floor. "I just felt like it was...an imposition, somehow. I'm always an imposition, and I didn't want to make it worse. I'm sorry."

"You see!" exclaimed Oleg. "Apologizing again!"

"Ah, yes," said her mother. "Dasha, my heart, why do you think you're an imposition?"

Dasha squirmed even more. "I just do," she said, not wanting to get anyone into trouble.

"Have people been telling you that?" asked her mother.

"No," said Dasha quickly, but before she had even gotten the word out, she could tell that both her mother and Oleg knew that she was lying. She thought they were going to scold her for telling an untruth, but instead her father only rolled his eyes and said, "I've always been proud of all my daughters, as any man would be, but there is one terrible problem with trying to raise girls."

"Wha-what's that?" Dasha asked, her voice quavering.

"The trouble with girls," said Oleg, trying and failing to stifle a grin, "is that they're clever and easily taught."

"I don't see how that's so bad," said Dasha.

"It is when what people are teaching you is wrong."

"Oh, come now, Oleg," said her mother, her exasperated amusement like sandy sugar on Dasha's tongue. "You do Dasha a disservice if you think she's been entirely ruined by this…overzealousness on the part of a few. Perhaps there are those who said things that she…took too much to heart, but it wasn't *all* of them *all* of the time."

"It's that Arkasha, my head for beheading," said Oleg.

"He shouldn't get into trouble because of me!" protested Dasha.

"First of all, he'll be getting into trouble because of himself, not because of you, and second of all, that's no way for a Tsarinovna to talk," said her father sharply.

Dasha wanted to apologize again, but clearly her apologies made her father angry, so she said nothing, and only stared miserably at the floor some more.

"There's nothing wrong with a Tsarinovna—or even a Tsarina—not wanting to give trouble to others," said her mother.

"Yes there is," said Oleg. "How can she ever learn to rule if she's like this all the time?"

Dasha knew that he meant well with those words, but they gave rise to such terrifying visions of her failing, failing at the one thing she was meant to do in the world, that she was almost able to ignore the more simple hurt of his contempt. Her mother must have seen something, though, for she gave Oleg a swift sharp look and said, "Dasha will be ready to rule when she is ready to rule. *I* was hardly a model of courage and decisiveness when I was her age. I didn't come into my own till I was nearly twenty years older than she is now, as you know very well, and even now I'm sure there are those who would say I am too soft for a Tsarina, and we would do well to bring back my sister."

"I doubt that very much," said Oleg, a small smile now peering out of the corners of his mouth. "I doubt very much that there are any of your subjects who don't walk in fear and trembling of you."

"Not you, apparently," said her mother.

Oleg burst out laughing, blowing all the tension out of the room as he did so. "A fair point!" he said. "But you know what I mean, Slava. And you…" He turned to Dasha. "I didn't mean to hurt your feelings, my dove," he told her. "I just...worry about you. About what you need to be able to inherit all this." He waved his hand at the palace ceiling. "No one can doubt that you're clever and kindhearted and gifted, too, but that won't be enough when the time comes for you to take your mother's place. You'll have to be tough, you know, tough and proud and all those other things that don't seem like virtues except when they are, and it seems you haven't been learning them here in Krasnograd. Those maids and nannies and tutors of yours—they've been telling you you mustn't impose on anyone, haven't they?"

Dasha nodded in silent agreement, still unable to look anywhere other than at her feet.

"Telling you you have to apologize when you've caused someone trouble, haven't they?"

Dasha nodded again.

"I am not wholly without blame," her mother interjected. "And I had my reasons. We all had our reasons. There is nothing wrong with a noblewoman who knows how to be considerate of others."

"Oh, of course not, of course not," said her father. "But there *is* something wrong with a noblewoman who doesn't know how to stand up for herself, who thinks more about pleasing others than doing what is right. And how," he turned to her mother, "is she ever going to manage a husband if she doesn't learn to boss people around a bit?"

"The way I manage you, you mean?" her mother asked, with a pert smile.

"That's different," said Oleg, looking away.

"Oh indeed," said her mother. "For a start, most of the candidates have nowhere near your hardheadedness, Oleg. Although I *am* beginning to despair of ever finding a suitable set of them for us to consider. Dasha needs someone selfless and gentle, that's clear enough, but these young princes...my head for beheading, they're even surlier and more selfish than they were when I was a girl!"

"You only think that because you're no longer a girl, but they're still little boys," said Oleg. "There's still time. Plenty of time to make sure Dasha learns how to stop worrying so much about pleasing others at the expense of everything else."

"I don't!" exclaimed Dasha, now stung into self-defense. "I would never do something I knew not to be right, just in order to please someone!"

"Well, I'm glad to hear that," said her father. "But sometimes when you're caught up in pleasing others, it can be hard to tell the difference between right and wrong."

"I wouldn't..." repeated Dasha, and then stopped herself before she could say something that might offend Oleg, that might make it look like she was arguing with him, even though she was. Besides, how could she know he wasn't right? Probably he was. Probably she *was* so soft and quick to please that she *would* do something wrong, just because someone else wanted her to.

"Of course you wouldn't," said her father, with a glance that made it seem as if he had guessed her thoughts. "Because I'm going to teach you how not to. We'll take your Susanna, of course we will, and we'll go with our plan as well, the one we were talking about earlier."

"What plan?" asked her mother with interest.

"Of not telling people who she is," said her father. "She's been treated like a Tsarinovna her whole life, and look what that's brought her to."

"I don't think we can consider her to be wholly ruined," said her mother, with a fond smile.

"No, but she shouldn't be like this," said her father. "She should be...we all thought she would be..."

"She is exactly how she was meant to be," her mother put in sharply, before her father could finish. "There's nothing wrong with her at all. I'm sorry about what the maids and the guards have been doing, truly, my dove," she turned to Dasha, "I am. I didn't know. And they probably meant it for the best, but...but that is how many people are, even when they are acting for the best."

"That doesn't make it better," said her father, grumbling more to himself now. "And she *should* have been different. More...fiery. We were all expecting someone more...fiery. Like...like Olga."

"I'm sorry," said Dasha in a small voice, before she could help herself.

Her mother gave her a long cool look. Normally Dasha was not afraid of her mother's eyes, so gray and slanted, the way everyone else was, but this time she could sense how they were peering into her, seeing all kinds of things that she, Dasha, could hardly imagine about herself, and perhaps didn't want to admit to.

"I think she has more than enough fire," her mother said. "When the time comes...she will have all the fire she needs. You say she is not like Olga, and perhaps that is true, but she is herself, and that is more than enough. She has fire. And, since she is my daughter too, something else as well. You know what the domovaya told me when she told me I was carrying her: that I was made of water. And Dasha is too."

"I didn't father no watery daughters," said Oleg, with a smile that was supposed to be amused, but looked uncomfortable instead.

"Maybe not, but I gave birth to one," said her mother firmly. "You may have given her fire, true enough, but I gave her water, and she has both. So," she continued briskly, sounding more like her normal self, or at least her normal self when she talked to Dasha, "I have no doubt that she has more than enough of everything she needs for...whatever it is she needs to do. And I think your plan of not announcing her title is a good one. It's a good thing to be treated as someone other than who you are from time to time, especially if who you are is the Tsarinovna. People will say all kinds of things to you that they would never say if they knew who you were, and sometimes it's good to hear those things, even if it doesn't always seem so at the time. And if she and her mother are agreeable, I would be delighted to have Susanna join you. I will be sorry not to have her around the kremlin, but really, she'll be a better companion for you than for me. I've spoken with some of my sorceresses and herbwomen, and they all agree that the traveling season will start in a week's time, if not sooner, and that the signs are auspicious for a warm dry summer."

"Not too dry, I hope," said Oleg. "The last thing we need is to starve from a poor harvest."

"That is in the hands of the gods, as you know very well," said her mother. "But everything points to you being able to leave in a week, if you are ready."

"We'd be ready by tomorrow morning," said Oleg.

"You might be, but Dasha won't be, and Susanna most certainly isn't. They need traveling clothes, and weapons, and all sorts of things."

"Weapons!" exclaimed Dasha and Oleg together.

"Of course," said her mother with a smile. "We wouldn't send you off on a journey unarmed, would we? Not that I expect you to have to use your weapons," she added, "but you should have them nonetheless. In fact, why don't you go speak with Boleslav Vlasiyevich about it right now? Well, change into something dry first. But I'm sure he'd be glad to help you, and if there is any sort of...unpleasantness with the guards over your little trip to the park, you can smooth it out." She smiled again, in a way that said, very kindly, that they were dismissed, and turned and walked out of her chambers, with Dasha and Oleg following along behind.

She left them in the corridor, heading off to a meeting with her princesses or something of that nature. "Come," said Oleg, not looking particularly happy about it, "I'll take you to your chambers, and then to see Boleslav Vlasiyevich."

"I can go by myself," said Dasha.

He gave her a look.

"Well, I *could*. But I suppose you're right, and I shouldn't go anywhere unescorted, not even inside my own kremlin."

Oleg's lips twitched. "I'll escort you at least as far as the barracks," he said.

But they saw Boleslav Vlasiyevich walking across the square as soon as they stepped outside of the palace, and Oleg, who clearly wanted to avoid speaking with him, agreed when Dasha asked him that yes, he could leave her here, since Dasha was in sight of her mother's own captain of the Imperial Guard. He went off in the direction of the stables, and Dasha, feeling strangely alone and exposed without having a single guard or maid around her, went running across the square towards Boleslav Vlasiyevich, who was walking the other way and hadn't noticed her.

"Boleslav Vlasiyevich!" She caught him by the sleeve. "Boleslav Vlasiyevich, I have a request."

"Of course, Tsarinovna," he said, turning to face her with an expression of attentive politeness.

"I keep asking you to call me Dasha, like you did when I was little," she told him. "Everyone else does. And you have more right than most."

"Nonsense, Tsarinovna," he said, but he was smiling as he said it, his gray eyes light and soft as early morning pools of water.

"It's true," she told him. "After all, you're the closest thing to a father I've ever had." As soon as the words came tumbling out, she hated the sound of them, but Boleslav Vlasiyevich smiled as if they were the sweetest thing he'd ever heard.

"Well," he said. He stopped and swallowed. "I'm honored you think so, Tsarinovna. And this," he grew stern, "is one more reason I should come with you on this journey you're proposing."

"No!" she said quickly. "Someone needs to stay behind with my mother!"

"Well..." He shifted on his feet. "That's true enough, but..."

"But someone needs to watch over her," Dasha said, surprised at the firmness she heard in her voice. "I know that..." now she was floundering again, "her burdens oppress her greatly."

Boleslav Vlasiyevich sighed. "True enough," he agreed. "She's already lived enough lives for three women, she's already shed her old life and gained a new one many times over. Most of us remain the same mewling babe we were born as, clutching greedily at others' breasts and letting others clean and feed us. But she's left the mewling babe long behind, and become a woman instead. That wears on a person. She's always..." He was looking off in the distance. "She's always being called off on that last great journey."

"Then please, Boleslav Vlasiyevich, be at her side when she feels the call," said Dasha, not sure exactly what she was saying. "I couldn't stand the thought of you not being by my mother's side in my absence!" she added quickly. "Especially since there's something going on, I know there is, there's something going on on our Western borders, even though no one wants me to know exactly what, but it's something bad, I can tell!"

"It's not as if she's an inexperienced young girl who's never faced hardship and danger in her life before, about to leave the kremlin for the first time," said Boleslav Vlasiyevich, ignoring Dasha's words about their border troubles entirely. "She's a woman grown, a mother, and an Empress, who, by all the gods, led a magical army to overthrow her own sister. She could probably muddle along on her own for a few months."

Dasha tried to fix him with a stern glare, but found herself smiling instead. "Even so," she said. "I think part of the benefit of this journey will be for me to be on my own. Well, other than my blood father, my companions, and my guards, of course."

"Compared with the kremlin, you'll be so lonely you won't know what to do with yourself, Tsarinovna," said Boleslav Vlasiyevich. "And you're right. You should do this without either of us—your mother and me. It just pains me to let you go off like this. But I know it pains her more, and if she can do it, then I can too."

"Thank you, Boleslav Vlasiyevich," said Dasha. "I knew I could rely on you for—everything, really."

"Anytime, Tsarinovna. And speaking of your journey, have you been armed yet?"

"Well..." said Dasha, "my mother did send me out here to ask for weapons, but...I don't know...it seems so silly, me bearing arms..."

"Your mother's right. Anyone setting off on a journey should be properly armed. You said I've been like a father to you, but I've never even given you a proper piece of weaponry of your own, which is neglect of the worst sort. Come on, Tsarinovna, let's go to the armory and I'll fit you up with everything you could ever need." And, surprisingly lightheartedly after the conversation they had just had, they set off together towards the barracks and the armory in search of just the right sort of weapons.

Chapter Six

After giving Dasha a very fine shortsword, as well as a couple of daggers, which Dasha thought were actually much finer, and much more likely to be useful, than the sword, Boleslav Vlasiyevich walked her back to the palace.

"Where *are* your regular guards, anyway?" he asked.

"Oh, well..." said Dasha.

"Did Oleg Svetoslavovich send them away?" he said sternly.

"No..." said Dasha, even though he in fact had.

Boleslav Vlasiyevich half-smiled, but it wasn't a very nice smile. "Dasha, my love," he said, "don't try to lie to a man who asks others questions for a living. I may not be your mother, but I can separate out truth and falsehood pretty handily myself."

"Oh, well..." said Dasha again, not at all liking the pictures that those words engendered. She knew that one of Boleslav Vlasiyevich's duties was questioning criminals, at least the important ones, but surely that didn't mean anything *bad*, did it? Surely her mother wouldn't let him do anything *bad*, would she, especially since... "It was all my fault," Dasha said quickly, to stop that troubling line of thought as well as to attempt to forestall any of Boleslav Vlasiyevich's wrath.

"I doubt that very much," said Boleslav Vlasiyevich, with a smile that was fonder than it had been before, but still had an edge that his smiles so often did, much to Dasha's discomfort. Perhaps it was that doubtful, almost mocking smile that made Dasha insist hotly, "It was!

The others...it wasn't their fault! I tricked them!"

This, apparently, had not been what Boleslav Vlasiyevich had been expecting at all, for he stopped mid-stride to stare at her in amazement and amusement. "You *tricked* them?" he repeated. "Oleg Svetoslavovich, you mean? Or your guards?"

"Ah...the guards," confessed Dasha, growing uncertain again under his gaze.

"How?" demanded Boleslav Vlasiyevich, his voice and all the rest of him taking on that same hard edge that Dasha had seen in his smile. She didn't think it was aimed at her, but it made her shrink away from him nonetheless. He must have realized it, for he relaxed his stance—but Dasha could tell he was doing it deliberately, and that he wasn't actually relaxed or at ease at all.

For the third time that day, Dasha explained how she had wanted not to be seen, and her guards hadn't seen her.

"But please don't punish them," she begged. "It isn't their fault, it really isn't, not at all! It was me. I...I wanted to sneak off, even though I knew it was wrong, and I tricked them, I really did! And I think my mother thinks I used magic to do so, so it would be wrong to blame them for it, completely wrong, it was my fault, my fault..."

"I know, I know," Boleslav Vlasiyevich interrupted her before she could say anything more. "It's your fault, just like you think everything else is too."

"You think so too?" asked Dasha, astonished.

"Too?" asked Boleslav Vlasiyevich.

Glumly, Dasha described Oleg's reaction to her attempts to take the blame for her own misbehavior, and his...argument, for want of a better word, with her mother, and how they had decided she was too apologetic.

"I could have told them that," said Boleslav Vlasiyevich with a sharp snort, when she was done. "Anyone who's ever trained you could have told them that. You apologize every time you land a blow, and apologize every time you fail."

"I'm not very gifted with swords," said Dasha miserably, fiddling with her new shortsword, which, she was acutely aware, hung awkwardly from her hip, jouncing and banging against her leg, not at all like the way Boleslav Vlasiyevich's own sword seemed to move with him wherever or however he went, never getting in his way, acting like an extension of his body even when it was just hanging from his swordbelt.

She tried to straighten out her sword surreptitiously, and had a horrible vision of herself tripping and somehow falling onto the sword point and having it go in under her arm and right through her lungs, leaving her to cough blood and drown as everyone around her tried to stanch a flood that could not be stemmed.

"Your technique is perfectly serviceable," said Boleslav Vlasiyevich, distracting her from her foolish visions. "Better than that of most of my men, to be honest, since you always paid attention during training, and made an effort to improve. If you weren't the Tsarinovna but some prince looking to distinguish himself and make a good match, I'd tell you to keep training, because you'd have a good chance of getting really skilled. You're not as strong as you could be, but with your build you *could* be very strong indeed, as strong as your Aunt Olga Vasilisovna. You just don't..." he paused to think, "in order to be a good fighter," he continued, "you have to let the fight take you over, instead of trying to keep it under your control, and when the time comes, you have to be willing to go in for the kill. And you haven't learned how to do either of those things, at least not yet."

"I don't think I want to," said Dasha with a shudder, trying to ignore all the crowding images of her disarming someone, knocking them down, stabbing them again and again, until they would never rise again...but she only succeeded in replacing them with images of Boleslav Vlasiyevich doing the same thing, which was almost worse, because she suspected that those images had some basis in reality.

"I know you don't want to, Dasha my heart," he said. "But someday you may have to."

"Surely not," said Dasha, shaking her head in denial and smiling at the same time, trying to drive away such thoughts from both their heads.

"Sometimes," said Boleslav Vlasiyevich, speaking only half to her, "you find yourself doing things you really don't want to, things you never thought you would find yourself doing. And sometimes it's because those things need to be done, and there's no one else to do them. So promise me," and now all his attention was focused on her, "that if that time comes for you, you'll do *whatever* you need to do, to survive. Promise me you'll let the fight take you over, the...the hate, the rage, whatever you want to call it, take you over, so that you will live, even if means the other person will die."

"Surely that's not going to happen," said Dasha, trying to ignore the terrible visions floating before her.

"It happened to me," Boleslav Vlasiyevich told her. "That, and many more terrible things, too. You might think you're a good person, Dasha my heart, and you may even be right—in fact, in your case I'm sure of it—but that doesn't mean you won't one day find yourself doing terrible things, hurting people, destroying them in a way you would swear only the worst villains in the old stories would do, and you'll do it because you can't find any way around it, you can't find any better way of doing what needs to be done, what *must* be done. So promise me that if—when—you find yourself in the same situation I did, you'll do *whatever* you need to in order to survive, in order to live, in order to win, no matter how terrible those deeds are."

"I don't think you can be a good person if you do bad deeds," said Dasha, in order to avoid responding to his other words. For a moment Lisochka's face swam in front of her. Had Lisochka been a bad person? Probably. But she had had her reasons...and so, most likely, had Boleslav Vlasiyevich, and all the other people who had ever done bad things...so did that make them bad people? It did to their victims, Dasha thought. "I don't think you can be a good person if you hurt people," she said, trying to drown out her thoughts and her visions.

Boleslav Vlasiyevich smiled painfully. "Maybe not," he said. "Luckily, there's always forgiveness and redemption."

"Some things can't be forgiven," said Dasha.

"Maybe," he said. "But some of us are forgiven anyway. Don't... don't be afraid of not being forgiven, Dasha my love, not if it comes down to it. Survive first, and worry about the rest later. Because...well, no matter *what* you do, I'll forgive you, since it can't possibly be as bad as all the things I've done, and your mother will forgive you too."

"Will you even forgive me for sneaking away from my guards and running off into the park alone?" asked Dasha, speaking almost—she had never managed the trick of doing it properly, the way she saw the other princesses and even her maids doing it—saucily in her attempt to lighten his mood.

Boleslav Vlasiyevich grinned at her. "I suppose," he said. "Which means if I can forgive you that, Dasha my heart, I can forgive you *anything*, because there's nothing that would make me angrier than you endangering yourself. So...don't do *that* again, and you'll have nothing to worry about, you have my word. And..." he took her arm and started walking her towards the palace again, "don't let Oleg Svetoslavovich talk you into anything *rash*, will you?"

"I don't think he would do anything rash," said Dasha, causing

Boleslav Vlasiyevich to choke on his own laughter.

"I'm sure he cares for you as much as he is capable of caring for anyone other than himself," said Boleslav Vlasiyevich, which Dasha wanted to protest, but couldn't. "But he's not the type to watch over someone, not like I am," he continued. "I'm a guard, after all, while he's just a hunter, and we have very different views of the world. Which is why, since neither you nor your mother will allow me to go with you, I'll be assigning guards to accompany you."

"Not Arkasha," said Dasha quickly, before she could stop herself.

"Not Arkasha?" exclaimed Boleslav Vlasiyevich in surprise. "Well, I suppose he doesn't deserve it, not after letting you play that trick on him today—not that I'm blaming you, mind, but still…"

"I know he has a mother in Krasnograd, with no one else to care for her," said Dasha. It was true, although she hadn't been thinking of that at all (which made her feel even more guilty) when she had asked to have Arkasha left behind. But now that Oleg had pointed out how Arkasha and the rest of the guards that normally were in her detail had been treating her, she had to admit the justice of his complaint, and that she didn't actually like them very much at all.

"Considerate to the end, eh, Dasha?" said Boleslav Vlasiyevich, giving her an approving look that only made Dasha feel even more guilty. "Very well, then: not Arkasha. To be honest, he wouldn't be the best choice for a journey like this anyway. He's a city boy, and you'll need someone with a bit more woodscraft. Maybe Mitya…" They arrived at the palace doors, and Boleslav Vlasiyevich, still speculating over whom he should assign to her, handed Dasha over to her maids, telling them with a laugh to be sure not to let the Tsarinovna trick them with her magic and run away out from under their noses, and left.

Kira, who was the maid closest to Dasha in age and most friendly with her, told her excitedly as soon as they were inside that her mother was waiting for her in her chambers with several of her best seamstresses, ready to sew a set of travel clothing embroidered with protective spells.

"All my clothing already is embroidered with protective spells," pointed out Dasha.

"Oh, but these spells will be even better, Tsarinovna. Princess Zapadnokrasnova has brought in some of her best sorceress-seamstresses from her estate, and she's agreed to lend them to your mother for this task."

"I didn't know Zapadnokrasnovskoye or anywhere else in the black earth district was known for its sorceresses," said Dasha doubtfully.

"Oh, not normally, Tsarinovna, no, but they do have sorceresses, just like the rest of us—well, except for the mountains, of course—but anyway, they do have sorceresses, even if they're not as powerful as the ones up North or out on the steppe, and these two are very skilled, they say, very deft with a needle—you know that the black earth district *does* have the best seamstresses, no one denies that—you should see some of the designs they've made! They'd protect you from harm even without spells, my head for beheading, they're so beautiful no one would have the heart to attack a person wearing them.

"But they also have great magic, or so they say: they made all the clothes for Princess Zapadnokrasnova's son, and this winter he was thrown from his horse while out hunting, and everyone said he should have died from the fall, but he wasn't hurt at all, and then the wolves they were hunting should have turned on him and torn him to pieces before his guards could get to him—he always likes to race ahead of his guards, everyone knows that—but instead of turning on him and tearing him to pieces like everyone expected, they fled, and he got up and rode home without hardly a scratch on him.

"So now everyone's saying it's because of the clothes these seamstresses made for him, 'cause there's no other explanation—he should have been killed twice over, but he wasn't. So Princess Zapadnokrasnova wanted to make a gift of the seamstresses' work to the Tsarina, and the Tsarina—your mother that is—said she didn't need it so much for herself but she'd be mighty obliged if they'd make something for you, seeing as how you're about to set off on a journey, and they said they would, but they needed to see you in person before they could start. We told them they could take some of your old clothing to get their measurements, but they said they had to take them themselves, 'cause it wasn't just your body they were measuring." Kira gave a little shudder. "It sounds mighty queer, don't it?" she added.

"Don't talk like that, Kira," said Olesya. She was twice as old as Kira, which made her seem very old to Dasha, even though she was still much younger than Dasha's mother, who didn't seem so very old at all, and she was nobly born.

In fact, all of Dasha's maids other than Kira were nobly born. Some of them were wards her mother had taken in, and some of them were noblewomen in blood but not in money, in need of a warm kremlin and honorable service of some sort.

Kira, however, was one of a long line of kremlin maids who had never been anything other than maids. Perhaps that was why she was so much nicer to Dasha than most of the others, who were always trying to prove their nobility had not been stained by the servitude into which they had fallen, even as they tried to make their servitude as onerous as possible. Or at least so it seemed to Dasha. *And* they all picked on Kira, trying to show that they were nothing like her. As in what Olesya was doing right now, giving Kira a long lecture on how a maid of the Tsarinovna should speak, so that the Tsarinovna's own speech would not be polluted by the commonness of her companions.

"I don't think I'm in any danger," said Dasha hesitantly. She didn't want to argue with Olesya or make her feel bad, but she couldn't stand to listen to her criticism of Kira, and watch how Kira's face fell as she was being criticized, anymore. "I don't think my tutors would let me speak...in a way that wasn't correct, no matter how my companions spoke."

"Oh, but Tsarinovna..." Fortunately they arrived at Dasha's chambers just then, cutting off whatever Olesya was going to say.

Her mother was indeed waiting for her inside of them, standing by the pleasant little stove that was keeping off the spring chill as if it were her own chamber, which for a very long time it had been.

She was flanked by three women, two of whom Dasha had never seen before. The third was Princess Zapadnokrasnova, who had for the first time in years left her great estate on the West bank of the Krasna to come consult with the Tsarina on important business. She was a short woman, only about her mother's height, and like her mother was slight of figure, with a triangular-shaped face. But unlike her mother, Princess Zapadnokrasnova's slightness of figure made her look bony and withered, and her eyes were small and round, hooded with papery skin that stretched tight over her sharp cheekbones and pointed chin, making (Dasha thought) her look mean and sour, not wise and kind the way her mother did with her large slanted eyes and heart-shaped face that was somehow still smooth and soft, even though it was undoubtedly the face of a woman who was no longer young.

"Ah, Dasha," she said, smiling and stepping forward. "I see Boleslav Vlasiyevich has armed you, then. Do show us what he gave you."

Shyly, Dasha showed everyone the shortsword and the two little daggers, which were no larger than her hand.

"How charming," said her mother, turning the daggers over and examining them in the light. "Did Boleslav Vlasiyevich tell you how they were to be worn?"

"He said...however I felt most comfortable," said Dasha, feeling awkward about laying claim to the daggers and her preferred method of wearing them, which she hadn't yet decided on. "He said they could be carried at the belt...only I'll already have a sword...or in my boots... or up my sleeves...or, well...in my hair. Only he said I'd have to ask my maids to show me how to do that, since he didn't know how to fix hair. He said it was an art for noblewomen, not for..." She trailed off in embarrassment.

"Of course, of course," said her mother eagerly, holding up the daggers and looking at them even more closely. "I've never done it myself, but I know many women do." She looked hopefully over at Kira and Olesya. "I don't suppose either of you know how to put up your hair with daggers?"

Olesya said stiffly that she wasn't in the habit of going about armed, and Kira laughed and said no, her kind didn't hide blades in their hair, but that she imagined it was no different than doing it with sticks, which people did all the time.

"Oh, let's try," said her mother enthusiastically. "Come here, Dasha my love, and let's see if we can do up your hair with daggers."

But when pressed Kira said she would be afraid to do it, in case she accidentally nicked the Tsarinovna or did it poorly and caused the daggers to fall out and hurt her. Then her mother said boldly that she would try it herself, poor a hairdresser as she was, and unruly as Dasha's hair always was.

"Allow me, Tsarina, Tsarinovna," said one of the strange women then, stepping forward from where she had been standing by the stove. She was tall and slender, but, Dasha could tell, very strong, and she had sleek honey-colored hair and large gray eyes that were as slanted as her mother's. "I have the knack."

"Why thank you, Varvara Kristinovna," said her mother. "Her hair is very curly," she warned her, stepping back and handing her the daggers. "I'm afraid it's confounded all our efforts to tame it."

"That is good," said Varvara Kristinovna. "Every woman should have some part of her that can't be tamed." She ran her strong hands over the unruly braid that Dasha's hair had been braided into, and then deftly unbraided it, somehow smoothed it all out, and rebraided it into a much neater braid, that she then coiled into a knot and thrust the daggers into it.

"You will need sheaths for them," she said, stepping back. "Unless you want to be very careful never to turn your head too sharply."

"Can you make the sheaths?" asked her mother.

"I can make ones that will be serviceable, Tsarina," said Varvara Kristinovna with a bow. "I am not greatly skilled in the art, but they will do, and any blade you draw from them will strike true."

"Well, that sounds like just the sort of thing we need," said her mother cheerfully, while Dasha tried not to picture herself "striking true" at anything.

"It would be an honor, Tsarina," said Varvara Kristinovna. "As will outfitting the Tsarinovna with the garments she needs for her journey. If you will permit it, we would take her measurements now."

"Of course, of course," said her mother. "Dasha, my love, will you be all right if we leave you with Varvara Kristinovna and Sofiya Ariannovna for a bit? Princess Zapadnokrasnova and I have some matters we must discuss. We'll be back shortly, so that Varvara Kristinovna and Sofiya Ariannovna can tell us what they've envisioned for you."

"Of course," said Dasha. And in a moment she was left alone with Varvara Kristinovna and Sofiya Ariannovna, who looked enough like Varvara Kristinovna to be her sister. Dasha wanted to ask them if they were in fact second-sisters or third-sisters, but she was too shy, so she only stood there, holding out her arms, as they measured her with lengths of knotted string.

"You have a good figure, Tsarinovna," said Sofiya Ariannovna approvingly, when they had finished.

"No I don't," Dasha said, embarrassed, and then blurted out before she could stop herself, "Not like you do."

Sofiya Ariannovna laughed, a merry, musical laugh that caught in the back of Dasha's throat with its sweetness. Dasha was almost hurt by it, but then, for some reason, maybe because she could sense that Sofiya Ariannovna was not laughing at her, but at the idea that Dasha would not think her own figure was fine, she smiled in return. "Let me tell you a secret, Tsarinovna," Sofiya Ariannovna said, leaning close to Dasha and lowering her voice conspiratorially, "the best way to have a fine figure is to *think* that you have a fine figure."

"But it doesn't matter what you think about something like that," objected Dasha. "Either you have a fine figure, or you don't."

This made Sofiya Ariannovna laugh again. "Oh no, Tsarinovna," she said. "The main thing for having a fine figure is how you carry yourself, and if you believe you have a fine figure, you will carry yourself as if you do, and then you *will*. It's like magic." She laughed some more at that, and Varvara Kristinovna smiled a bit, too. "Hasn't anyone been teaching you things, Tsarinovna?" asked Sofiya Ariannovna.

"It's not important," said Dasha, shrugging uncomfortably.

"Not important!" said Sofiya Ariannovna. "Of course it's important, especially for the Tsarinovna! You must be able to make everyone fall in love with you, Tsarinovna, and there's nothing like a fine figure to accomplish that. But don't you worry, Tsarinovna: you have everything you need to make every eye fall on you, and every man fall in love with you, and what we'll sew up for you will make sure it happens. With a bosom like yours"—Dasha instinctively crossed her arms over her chest, and hunched her shoulders, making Sofiya Ariannovna frown.

"No, no, Tsarinovna, stand up straight," she said, gently uncrossing Dasha's arms and pulling her shoulders back, making her breasts stick out in a most mortifying way. "As if you took pride in your bosom, which, believe me, you should. Many a woman would trade her right hand for a bosom like that."

Dasha would have liked to object, but she was so surprised she had no words to argue with. Her bosom had suddenly appeared in her twelfth summer, and had swiftly made its presence known in no uncertain terms, requiring her maids to alter all her gowns drastically and causing a number of complaints on that score, along with sour remarks from some of the younger maids that the Tsarinovna would be expecting every woman to bow to her, and every man to fall at her feet, now that she was so well-endowed with a woman's most precious possession.

At first Dasha had not known what they were talking about, and then when she had figured it out, she had gone to her mother and asked if it were true, and a bosom was a woman's most precious possession, and the larger the better. To which her mother had responded with a blank stare, and, once she had realized that this was, inconceivable as it was to her, important to Dasha, the words that a woman's bosom was there to nurse children, should she have them, and as long as it gave milk, the size was unimportant.

When Dasha had pressed her to say what a woman's most precious possession was, then, her mother had given her another blank stare before finally saying, "Whatever she thinks it is, I suppose," and going back to the reports she had been reading. Which, Dasha now supposed, had been meant to be comforting and helpful, but it had not comforted Dasha's concerns in the least about her apparently outsized bosom and its powers—strange as it seemed to her—to draw a reaction from every person she encountered, and so Dasha had spent the last several years trying to hide her increasingly magnificent bosom in any way possible, with, it seemed, little effect.

It occurred to Dasha for the first time that her mother might not be very happy with her own appearance, which is why she never seemed to take much interest in Dasha's. Which was a funny thought. Dasha had never asked herself whether or not her mother were pretty. She was just...her mother, and looked like a mother should. Which was not at all like Dasha. Perhaps her mother was *embarrassed* by Dasha's figure! Perhaps she was envious! Perhaps she didn't know what to think or say about how Dasha looked, or what advice to give her, because it was a subject she knew so little about herself. Which was a very strange and uncomfortable thought, and one Dasha wanted to stop thinking right away.

"It's just a bosom," she said, hunching her shoulders and looking away.

"And your hair is just hair, Tsarinovna, and your eyes are just eyes, but every time you walk by, heads will turn, and people will think of love and fire and the sea, whether you like it or not. So you should use it, since it has been given to you. This is *your* figure, Tsarinovna, just as your hair is *your* hair and your eyes are *your* eyes, and you should take your rightful possession of them. Because if you do not, someone else will."

"I don't see how anyone else could take possession of my body," said Dasha.

"You would be surprised, Tsarinovna," said Sofiya Ariannovna, no longer smiling and merry. "But we will do what we can to help prevent that from ever taking place. Put on the clothes we will sew for you, and the stitches running through them will protect you from injury and accident, yes, and also help you take ownership of what is yours. It will not protect you entirely, no, but we will work spells into these garments that will make you understand that what is yours is *yours*, and that is a powerful thing."

"I don't know if I like the sound of that," said Dasha. "I don't know if I like the sound of spells working on my mind."

"Well, you're in need of something, Tsarinovna," said Sofiya Ariannovna, now smiling again. "Because you're not taking ownership of your body now, which is a thrice-cursed shame, seeing as how it's such a fine body to own. Besides," and now she winked, "how do you know I'm not doing the spell right now? Perhaps the spell is me just telling you these things I've been telling you, and nothing more."

"But that's just words," argued Dasha.

"As are all spells, Tsarinovna," said Sofiya Ariannovna. "Words, and the intent behind them. What do you think, sister," she turned to Varvara Kristinovna, "blue for her? It will go with her hair, and bring out her eyes."

"It will if it is the right shade," said Varvara Kristinovna seriously.

"And as it happens, I have just the right shade in my trunk!" Sofiya Ariannovna winked at Dasha again. "By this time next week, Tsarinovna, you'll be outfitted in clothes a Tsarina would beg to wear, won't she, sister?"

"That she will," agreed Varvara Kristinovna gravely. She looked Dasha up and down once more, and then said, "You will see the truth of Sofiya Ariannovna's words, Tsarinovna, trust me, you will. You have so much of you that is waiting to be revealed, and once you don our clothes, you will see that that is true."

"Does what I have to reveal include my bosom?" asked Dasha, half-jokingly, half-piteously.

Both the seamstresses smiled. "Not if you don't wish it, Tsarinovna," Sofiya Ariannovna assured her. "Which it seems you do not. Well, no matter. These clothes are for travel in any case, and travel in spring. You will want to be well covered."

"Yes please," said Dasha.

"As you wish, Tsarinovna," Sofiya Ariannovna told her. "But perhaps next year"—she winked again—"you'll ask us for something that will reveal more than your heart."

"I don't think so," said Dasha stiffly, but Sofiya Ariannovna only laughed some more, and said they would return for a fitting next week.

After the seamstresses had left, Dasha started sorting through the clothes she already had, in order to feel like she was accomplishing something to prepare for her journey. But as she had no idea what she should bring with her, it only made her feel more helpless, and when her mother returned, still with Princess Zapadnokrasnova in tow, she found Dasha sitting on her bed, her head drooping in despair.

"Are you not happy about your new clothes, my heart?" her mother asked.

"Of course," said Dasha, in a tone that really said, "Of course not."

"Well, you won't find better sorceress-seamstresses than Varvara and Sofiya," said Princess Zapadnokrasnova, in a tone that was probably supposed to be encouraging, but gave off an acrid odor of peevish scolding. Dasha had a vision of her scolding her son, and of him riding off in a rage and throwing himself down in front of the wolves in order to punish his mother by hurting himself. She couldn't tell whether the vision were a true one, or merely her own fantasies about what she would do if she were Princess Zapadnokrasnova's child. For a moment she felt a strange closeness with Prince Zapadnokrasnov, as if they were joined, even though they had never met.

"My daughters all *begged* me to let Varvara and Sofiya sew their clothes," Princess Zapadnokrasnova continued. "If I'd've let them, they'd've had them make *all* their clothes, and worn nothing else, but I wouldn't allow it, I wouldn't allow them to *hog*, yes to *hog*, my best seamstresses, the only ones capable of sewing spells—well, spells that work. No, not no matter how much they begged.

"'Your brother needs protection too,' I'd tell them, and it turned out to be true, for my girls do nothing but sit around all day whining, but my boy—he goes out and about, he goes out hunting like a proper man should. I tell you, if it'd been up to me, I'd've only had boys, I would—girls are such a trial! So uppity, always talking back to their mothers and aping you in a way that makes your skin crawl...you're too young to understand such things, Tsarinovna, you're still bothering your mother like a child, not helping her out like a woman should, not that daughters ever grow up to be proper women, they never stop being a burden...I'm sure *you* know what I'm talking about, Tsarina, I'm sure *you*..."

"I'm afraid I haven't the faintest idea," her mother interrupted Princess Zapadnokrasnova. Her voice was mild, but her eyes had the glint of steel to them that would have made a wise, or at least observant, woman change her course directly. Princess Zapadnokrasnova, however, continued complaining for some time about the trouble daughters caused, and how she would have a thousand times rather have had only sons, as she'd warrant most other mothers would, so that it took three more interruptions before she stopped, and then only because her mother said, the steel showing so clearly that Dasha was astonished Princess Zapadnokrasnova wasn't silenced completely, "There are many daughters in our land who do their mothers credit. Susanna Gulisovna, for example, has done us the honor of agreeing to accompany Dasha on her journey."

"Susanna Gulisovna?" said Princess Zapadnokrasnova, distracted from her lamentations on the curse of daughters. "Isn't she that Southern princess?"

"She is," her mother confirmed. "A very noble and high-spirited young woman. I was delighted that she and Dasha have become friends, and even more delighted that Dasha will have the honor of her company on her first journey away from Krasnograd. Princess Iridivadze has just given her consent, my love, as we knew she would," she added to Dasha. "She was more than happy to foster the ties between Avkhazovskoye and Krasnograd, and aside from Susanna's many charming qualities, it will do you good to spend time with an Avkhazovskoye princess and learn more about the region and the language."

"I suppose," said Princess Zapadnokrasnova doubtfully. "But you'd be better off with a girl from the black earth district, mark my words."

"If one of your own daughters would do us the honor, I am sure we would be overjoyed, and it would be a most beneficial opportunity for them," said her mother. "As Princess Iridivadze said, such a journey seems to come dear, but when you consider the good it will provide for years to come, all the connections, all the happy memories, what is a few hundred chervontsev?"

"A few hundred...to be sure, those Southern princesses can afford it, with their wine and their port fees...but I'm afraid my girls...well, you know how it is, they've both lost their heads over men, they're both dead set on getting married as soon as ever they can, with no thought to the trouble it causes the rest of us...and I don't see why they're in such a tearing hurry...it's not as if marriage ever made their mother very happy...and Sasha, my eldest that is, she's already with child, so what she needs a husband for I'll never know..."

"My best wishes for her health," her mother put in, before Princess Zapadnokrasnova could ramble on anymore. "We will be sorry not to have her join us, but under the happy circumstances, we can certainly understand. And I have no doubt that Susanna Gulisovna will prove to be more than adequate as Dasha's companion and confidante, in any case."

"Oh, well...at least she's not a steppewoman," said Princess Zapadnokrasnova. "A Southerner is one thing, but I would *never* let my daughter run off with a steppewoman."

Her mother laughed. "Whyever not?" she asked.

"Well..." Despite all her free words earlier about marriage and children, Princess Zapadnokrasnova suddenly seemed embarrassed. "*You* know." She gave Dasha a significant look. "I wouldn't want my daughter to be...corrupted. By, you know...the steppewomen, you know..."

"How could they corrupt me?" asked Dasha, puzzled. "I am partly from the Stepnaya family, anyway."

"All the more reason," said Princess Zapadnokrasnova meaningfully. "You don't want...I mean, perhaps the inclination is already there..."

"What inclination?" asked Dasha, even more puzzled. "For magic?" She began to grow excited. "Do you think I could be a steppe sorceress?" she said. "Is that what you're talking about?"

"Yes," said her mother dryly, just as Princess Zapadnokrasnova said, "No."

"Honestly," said her mother, speaking into the awkward silence, "I have not the slightest concern about anything that Dasha might have inherited from my father's family, and I have every intention of sending her out into the steppe someday. I'm sure she will find it very interesting and enlightening."

"As long as it's not *too* enlightening," said Princess Zapadnokrasnova, still speaking as if her words had some kind of special significance that was clear to her and to Dasha's mother, but not to Dasha herself. Dasha could feel herself beginning to grow irritated with her—even more irritated, that is, than she had been before—but her mother only laughed again and said she had no worries on that score, and that she and Dasha needed to continue their preparations for Dasha's departure.

"What steppe tendencies could she have been talking about?" Dasha asked as soon as Princess Zapadnokrasnova was gone and they were alone in her bedchamber, surrounded by clothes flung here and there and half-packed packs. "Was it magic? Did she think I might actually become a steppe sorceress?"

"My dear, everyone *knows* you will become some sort of sorceress," her mother replied. "You just have to find the right teacher."

"Well then, what?"

Now it was her mother's turn to look embarrassed, which was most unlike her. She even drummed her fingers on the top of Dasha's pack. "People can be...rather free in matters of love on the steppe," she said finally.

"Oh." Dasha could feel herself blushing painfully. "But..."

"But nothing," her mother said firmly, regaining her usual composure. "The black earth princesses don't like that kind of thing, they say it spoils the bloodline, or at least, makes it harder to keep track of—everyone knows it's good to freshen the bloodline from time to time, no matter how much some princesses might want to keep things in the family—and that it makes some people refuse to provide heirs at all, but plenty of mothers on the steppe still have daughters, so they must be doing something right. Don't let it bother you. People are going to make remarks about your bloodline, but pay them no mind. It's no different than anyone else's, and the strain that's from the steppe is hardly your biggest concern, especially the bit that she's worried about. Now, about your clothes…"

Chapter Seven

The next week went by for Dasha in alternating states of boredom and excitement, as the preparations for the journey continued. It had never occurred to her even for a moment that one rather short and safe journey could occasion so much trouble, but there were maps to be copied, clothes to be made, horses to be picked out, tack and weaponry to be repaired, money to be allotted, the guard detail to be assigned...on and on it went, requiring Dasha's presence and her ideas, which were frequently overruled by the other, older and more experienced, people.

The most exciting day, much to Dasha's surprise, was when Varvara Kristinovna and Sofiya Ariannovna returned, bearing Dasha's new-made clothes. There were three pairs of loose-fitting riding trousers that tucked into her tall boots, a knee-length blue kaftan made of wool with a high collar, tight-fitting sleeves, and elegant silver frog clasps down the front to keep it closed for the cold weather, and another, zipun-style kaftan with no collar, made of linen of a matching shade of blue.

A closer look showed that both kaftans were covered with embroidery, also done in the same shade of blue. Although Dasha's ability to cast spells was nonexistent, her lessons must have done her some good, for she could recognize the spells of protection and courage, stitched all over the kaftans, from collar to hem.

"They're like something a guard would wear," she said, inspecting them doubtfully. "Especially the zipun. I thought only peasants wore them."

"And why should you scorn a well-made peasant zipun, Tsarinovna?" said Sofiya Ariannovna. "Peasants wear them for a reason, you know: because they're comfortable and practical. And our own noblefolk wear them too: maybe not here in Krasnograd, but up and down the Krasna everyone wears them when they're doing anything outside. Come, try it on."

Feeling very self-conscious, Dasha put on one of the pairs of trousers and the woolen kaftan, only to discover that the seamstresses were right, and the outfit was both comfortable and—she looked fearfully in the mirror—more elegant in its lines than anything she had ever worn.

"I thought I would look like a man," she said.

Sofiya Ariannovna laughed. "Nothing you wore could ever make you look like a man, Tsarinovna," she said. "You could steal your father's clothes, or dress in nothing but an old horse blanket, and every eye would instantly know you for a woman. But in this case, we cut this outfit especially for you, and it will make you look even more like a woman than those gowns you are always wearing." She gave Dasha's sarafan, which was lying inoffensively on her bed, a disparaging look. "Did no one ever tell you to belt your clothes, Tsarinovna?" she asked.

Dasha shook her head.

Sofiya Ariannovna sighed. "I suppose it's a good thing our Tsarina is more concerned with affairs of state than how you both look, but as a seamstress it makes my heart ache to see a figure such as yours concealed by that...*sack*." She gave Dasha's sarafan and blouse another disparaging look.

"I always thought it was a very fine gown," Dasha objected, although not very loudly. In truth, it was one of her favorites. It was blue and red, with very pretty flowers embroidered across the neck and matching ones down the sleeves of the blouse, and was loose enough that it never hampered her movements or made her feel awkward.

"Oh, it's fine enough," said Sofiya Ariannovna. "If by 'fine' you mean made of rich materials. But with a cut like that, it might as well have been made of coarse undyed linen, for all the good it was doing you. No, Tsarinovna, you really must belt all your clothes—here, let me show you." And she fitted a sash around Dasha's waist, making her look even more elegant than before.

"I can't believe...I can't believe it's me," admitted Dasha.

"What did I tell you, Tsarinovna?" said Sofiya Ariannovna. "And you feel bolder now, too, I'll warrant."

"Ye-es," said Dasha. At first she was saying it only to please Sofiya Ariannovna, but then, as they continued to fit the rest of her new garments (along with the trousers and the kaftans, there were blouses, and underclothes, and a beautiful long dark green sarafan with a split skirt for riding, and a warm half-cloak, like what the guards wore thrown over one shoulder, and two very dashing-looking round hats, one that was tall and made of wool and one that was small, almost like a cap, and made of waxed linen, which Sofiya Ariannovna told her had been modelled off the hats that Southerners wore, in honor of Susanna's presence in the group), she realized it was true, and seeing herself in these clothes *did* make her feel bolder.

"It's funny," she said when they were finished. "I thought dressing like a man would make me feel worse, but instead it made me feel better."

Sofiya Ariannovna and Varvara Kristinovna shared a glance. "These are not men's clothes, Tsarinovna," said Varvara Kristinovna. "I know that here in Krasnograd most women wear only gowns, and men wear trousers and kaftans, but outside of Krasnograd things are different. Women wear trousers when it suits them, and some men— sanctuary brothers, for example, or scholars—wear robes that are like gowns. These clothes—any clothes—won't change who you are; they just show who you really are inside."

"But clothes are for covering up," argued Dasha.

"Clothes reveal at least as much as they conceal, Tsarinovna," said Varvara Kristinovna. She smiled. "And now I've revealed to you the greatest magic I know. All the rest of this"—she waved her hands at the pile of garments on Dasha's bed—"is just so much...I don't know what. Lesser magic, I suppose. But that...that is the true magic."

"It doesn't sound much like magic to me," objected Dasha.

"Most real magic doesn't," said Varvara Kristinovna. "Now, we'll take all this away for the final alterations, and have it ready for you by tomorrow, in plenty of time for your departure."

"How will you do it all so quickly?" asked Dasha.

"We measured true on our first try, Tsarinovna," said Sofiya Ariannovna. "There is very little to alter."

"Well then, how did you do it all so quickly the first time? How did you make all this between this week and last week? My own maids would have labored over something like this for a month."

"More magic," Sofiya Ariannovna told her with another wink, but Dasha saw that despite her merriness and her winks, her eyes were red-rimmed, and she had a vision of the two of them working long into the night, their hands growing cramped and their fingers sore from the pricking of their needles, to finish all this in time. That made her feel guilty, but then she had a vision of her mother giving them gold, so much gold that they wouldn't need to work again for the rest of the year if they chose not to, and even though she had no certainty that either vision was real, she felt better nonetheless.

After that she went down to the stables to take her horses out for a ride in the park with her new guard detail. True to his word, Boleslav Vlasiyevich had arranged for someone other than Arkasha to go with her. He and Oleg had had a short sharp disagreement over how many guards should accompany her, with Oleg wanting no more than two and Boleslav Vlasiyevich wanting at least five. They had compromised with three, which left neither of them happy, especially Boleslav Vlasiyevich, but he had been forced to admit that Oleg counted for at least two guards himself, and Susanna was also—he had tried her abilities several times, much to her delight—a fair swordswoman, and a dead shot with a bow, just as she had claimed.

"Not that it will ever come to that," he had said when he had proposed them, sounding as if he were mainly trying to convince himself. "It's not as if we have bandits roaming the roads, at least not the roads you'll be on. And Dasha can take care of herself if she has to, I'm sure of it"—he gave Dasha a meaningful look—"but better safe than sorry, better safe than sorry, and Mitya and the lads will keep you safe if anyone can."

Mitya was a young guard, no more than five-and-twenty summers, and Alik and Seva, the other two guards in the detail, were even younger, but Boleslav Vlasiyevich said they were three of his best fighters—"even better than Arkasha and his men, to be honest," he said, "just less steady and...less suited for standing guard over a young Tsarinovna day in and day out"—and skilled in riding and woodscraft as well, which made them ideal for the current duty.

"And, the gods help me, maybe Oleg Svetoslavovich will be a steadying influence for them," Boleslav Vlasiyevich had finished, shaking his head as if he couldn't believe those words were coming out of his mouth.

"You wrong me, Vlasiyich," Oleg had said coldly. "I would never do anything that would endanger the Tsarinovna."

"Not deliberately, no," Boleslav Vlasiyevich had muttered, so low that Dasha was almost sure she had been the only one to hear it.

Along with her new guards Dasha had been given a new horse to carry her packs. His name was Serovaty because he was a funny sort of dirty grayish color, but everyone called him Seryozha. He was at least as old as Dasha, which was not young for a horse, and he had a placid temperament that made Dasha doubt he would be willing or able to keep up with Poloska, but she had been assured that he could trot all day without slowing, and had a fair turn of speed when called upon, and most importantly of all, he was unlikely to spook at shadows or pick quarrels with the other horses and thus endanger Dasha.

"I know how to sit a horse!" Dasha had protested when these reasons for choosing him had been laid out.

"Of course you do, and very creditably, too, Tsarinovna," Alina Marislavovna, the kremlin mistress of horse, had told her soothingly. "But we mustn't inconvenience the others." Which Dasha had known had been an excuse, but she couldn't muster up any good arguments against it, especially since her objections to Seryozha were almost entirely based on vanity and a selfish wish to choose her own horse, instead of having her horse chosen for her. So she had merely nodded her acquiescence and resolved to develop the affection for Seryozha that he so manifestly deserved.

And now, two days before they were due to set off, they were all to go riding together in the park, for practice. Dasha knew that most groups managed to set off on their journeys without going for practice rides beforehand, but she also knew better than to argue against it, since Boleslav Vlasiyevich, her mother, and even Oleg were becoming more and more nervous about letting her go off. So she dutifully went down to the stables at the appointed time, surrounded by her new guards, and let them leg her up onto Poloska's back and put Seryozha's leadrope into her hand, and then everyone else mounted up, and they set off.

Once they were underway, Dasha's disgruntlement at being treated like a little child or an incompetent fool began to abate. It was a beautiful day, the first proper day of spring, with a warm sun shining down out of a deep blue sky, warming their skin, melting the last of the snowdrifts, and causing all the buds to swell so that Dasha was certain they would burst open at any moment.

They all trotted merrily down the main path through the park, all the way to the gate at the far end and back. With the bright sunlight and the bare tree branches, it was easy to see that park was just a park, a little fenced-in area in the middle of the city, and that there was nothing lurking anywhere in it, not even in the puddles of new-melted snow that filled the paths and the boggy hollows off to the sides, where black water was gathering in the low places between the trees...Dasha jerked her attention away from it and went back to chatting with Susanna, who was alternating between denigrating the landscape around them—the mountains were *so much* nicer in every respect, according to her—and speculating about the adventures awaiting them, and, when she thought they wouldn't be overheard, commenting on the looks of their guards.

"Mitya is handsome enough, I suppose," she whispered to Dasha, at a moment when Mitya had gone off to jump over a downed log out of sheer high spirits. "He is a bit pale and, how do you say it, pasty? But he has a good figure, even if he is heavier than we like our men in the mountains. But he looks like a proper man, at least. The others are just little boys."

"Well, perhaps to their eyes we're just little girls," Dasha whispered back. She thought her words were very sensible, but Susanna only tossed her head and laughed, with the air of a person who would rather die than be considered a little girl.

Just as they were going out the park gate to return to the stables, a girl suddenly jumped up from where she had been leaning against the park fence, and stood in front of them in the middle of the road, forcing them to rein in sharply to avoid running over her. She was tall, at least as tall as Dasha, and about the same age, and, what was even more odd, with the same curly red hair...Dasha felt something clench inside of her in a mixture of excitement and fear.

"Stand aside," Oleg told her sharply. "You're blocking the Tsarinovna's way."

The girl made to jump aside, and then—by force, Dasha could tell—made herself stand still and not give way.

"Stand aside," Oleg repeated, and the guards rode forward, fingering their knouts.

"I shouldn't have to stand aside for *her*," the girl muttered, her voice so low and muddy Dasha could hardly make it out. In spite of her bold words, she couldn't bring herself to look Dasha or anyone else in the face.

"Everyone stands aside for the Tsarinovna," Mitya told her. "Step aside, girl."

"No," the girl whispered, still not looking at them, her voice tasting of tiredness and cold and the remnants of a chill that she couldn't shake.

"You..!" began Mitya, raising his knout, as Oleg opened his mouth to say something harsh, and Alik and Seva looked to be about to do something violent as well.

"Which one are you?" Dasha interrupted, riding forward and pushing the guards aside. They were so surprised they let her get past, and when they tried to get in front of her again, she wheeled Poloska sideways and cut them off. "Which of my sisters are you?" she asked the red-haired girl, who looked...so much like Dasha she could have been looking in a mirror. No, she couldn't have, Dasha thought, after giving her another, more careful look: this girl's build was even sturdier than Dasha's, and her eyes were smaller and a pale blue, not the blue-green of Dasha's own eyes, and her face was squarer and had a cleft chin, instead of Dasha's own heart-shaped face and smooth chin, and overall there was none of that trace of the steppe, of the East, that Dasha wore in the slight slant of her eyes and the height of her cheekbones, but still, no one would ever mistake them for anything but close kin.

"You're quick on the guess," whispered the girl, her voice sour as unripe cranberries with dislike even as she couldn't bring herself to look Dasha in the eye.

"I think anyone could see it," said Dasha, as politely as she could. "And I have been waiting and hoping for this moment for a long time—my whole life, in fact. I've always longed to meet my sisters, and now here you are. Will you not accompany us back to the kremlin? Will you not tell us your name?"

For a breath the girl's face showed the same hunger for a sister that Dasha had always felt, but then she shook her head.

"Ask him," she said, pointing her chin at Oleg. "Ask him if he can recognize his own daughter."

"Of course I can recognize my own daughter," he said quietly. Then he smiled and said, "The gods know I have practice enough," which was, Dasha could tell as soon as the words left his mouth, the absolutely wrong thing to say. She flinched almost as much as the other girl—her sister, she reminded herself, even if only a half-sister through the male line—but instead of cringing, she found herself straightening her shoulders and saying, as warmly as she could, "You can't imagine how happy I am to meet you at last. Won't you ride with us back to the stables?"

"I don't have a horse," the girl said.

"You could ride with me," Dasha invited her.

"I don't need to be carried just to cross two streets," said the girl, now looking straight at Oleg. "I just want *him* to tell me my name. I just want *him* to show that he recognizes me."

"Svetochka's daughter," said Oleg. He sounded tired and sad.

"Is that all I am?" said the girl. "Just somebody's daughter?"

"At the end of the day, everyone is just somebody's daughter," said Oleg, still sounding tired and sad. "Or son. But you're Svetochka's daughter. I'd recognize that chin and those eyes anywhere."

"Just a chin," said the girl. "That's all I am to you. I ain't anyone to you at all, I ain't anyone special to you at all."

"All my daughters are special to me," said Oleg, even more tiredly and sadly than before. Dasha could tell that he meant it, that it was probably one of the sincerest utterances he had ever made, but also that it was exactly the wrong thing to say. And indeed, Svetochka's daughter, who had been growing bolder and bolder as they spoke, swelled up in indignation at the words.

"That's not true!" she exclaimed, jabbing her finger at Dasha. "*She's* the only one who matters to you at all!"

"That's not true," said Oleg, but he said it without any force.

"Then why are you riding next to *her*? Why do you know *her* name? Why? If that's not true, then tell me my name!"

Oleg sat and looked at her for a long time. "Svetochka," he finally said. He spoke flatly, with no trace of a question in his voice, but Dasha thought he was still guessing.

"You're just guessing," said the girl, echoing Dasha's thoughts.

"But I guessed true, didn't I?" said Oleg.

After a moment, the girl nodded in grudging agreement.

"Svetochka always said she'd name the child after herself, if it was a girl," said Oleg. "Do you have any other sisters or brothers?"

"Lots, apparently," said the girl, looking over at Dasha.

"No, I mean...through your mother. How is she? Has she had more children? Has she taken a husband?"

"She did." Svetochka's shoulders slumped. "But he didn't take her back, not in the long run. But you'd know that," her voice became waspish again, "if you'd stuck around."

"I'm sorry," said Oleg. "Do you at least have a little sister or two?"

"I..." Svetochka's shoulders slumped even more. "I don't know. My mother were expecting when I left, but you know how it is. She coulda lost the baby already, or died herself."

"Oh!" cried Dasha in dismay. Everyone turned to stare at her. "I mean...I'm sorry," she said. "So sorry." To her distress, she could feel tears begin to gather behind her eyes and clog up her throat, even though she had never met Svetochka's mother, and never met Svetochka until this very afternoon, and she knew Svetochka was saying those words to hurt her as much as anything. But visions of her losing her sister or her mother, visions that were cloudy but made up in sorrow what they lacked in detail, were filling her mind so that it almost felt as if she, Dasha, had lost a sister too.

"What do you care?" demanded Svetochka sullenly. "It ain't like they're *your* kin."

"Yes, but..." Dasha didn't know how to respond to that without sounding sullen and selfish herself, and so trailed off into silence instead.

"When was the child expected to arrive?" asked Oleg, with surprising gentleness.

"Now," said Svetochka, "and I ain't there to help with it!" She swallowed and looked away, so that Dasha knew that they were both feeling the same fullness behind their eyes, the same tightness in their throats, no matter what Svetochka might think. Surreptitiously, Dasha wiped at her eyes. Unfortunately, Susanna noticed and exclaimed loudly, "Now look what you have done! You have made the Tsarinovna cry!"

"It's no matter," said Dasha quickly, even as Svetochka said, "It's my sorrow, not hers!"

"I know," said Dasha, before anyone could say anything else and inflame Svetochka further. "And I am very sorry for your suffering. Please, will you not join us for some refreshment?"

"Re-fresh-ment?" asked Svetochka suspiciously, sounding out the word as if she had never heard it before.

"Food," explained Oleg.

Svetochka gave him a glare that would have smote a lesser man to ash, but, after a little back-and-forthing, succumbed to Dasha's urging and agreed to accompany them back to the kremlin and join them for some tea.

As they rode back to the stables, Dasha tried once again to convince Svetochka to join her, telling her that Seryozha was calm and sweet and would be happy to carry her, but once again Svetochka refused. She also refused to respond to any of Dasha's questions with anything other than a dismissive shake of her head, which Dasha found very strange. She was certain she was nothing like that, and neither was Oleg, so where had this ill temper come from? When they arrived back at the stables, she took advantage of the bustle that surrounded them as the stablehands came to take their horses, to sidle over to Oleg and ask him in a whisper, "Was Svetochka's mother very bad-tempered too?"

"No," Oleg whispered back, his mouth down at the corners in a way she had never seen it before, not even when he had come to tell them about Lisochka. "She was...she was just a...she was young and naïve, not...clever and wise like your mother, but she was a cheerful, good-hearted sort of girl. But..." He looked over at Svetochka, who was standing uncertainly by the stable doors, which were wide enough to admit half-a-dozen horses walking abreast, and tall enough to let a grown woman on a leggy racehorse ride through them without ducking her head. Not that Dasha would ever have come into the stable without dismounting first, as even if she had not been impressed with the dangers of riding inside the stable from her very first lesson, she could see all too well what would happen if a horse spooked and reared or threw her, smashing her head against the planks of the hayloft or the big beams, as wide as Dasha and twice as thick, that held up the roof...Dasha wrenched her thoughts away from accidents that were likely never to happen, and turned back to Svetochka.

She was now hugging her chest and fidgeting with her feet, looking overawed by the size and the richness and the busyness of it all, so that for a moment Dasha could see a vision of her own home, and how she had never seen a building this big or horses this fine or stablehands this smart and competent.

When she thought of it that way, it was easy for Dasha to see why Svetochka might act somewhat strange, but why did she have to be so... mean? And so hateful to Dasha? It was not as if Dasha had ever done anything to her...other than be given all sorts of things that Svetochka had probably wanted but never had, like Oleg's love and attention... not that Dasha had had overmuch of that, either, but Svetochka had no way of knowing that...it was like Lisochka all over again, Lisochka who had had so many wrongs done to her in her life that she had finally decided to do one great wrong to others, as if that would wipe the slate clean, instead of drowning it in muck so that it would never be clean again, and then kill herself, kill herself and with her any hope of any of them ever finding any forgiveness, her most of all...that would not be Svetochka's story, Dasha told herself.

With Svetochka, no matter what wrongs she had suffered, there was still hope, still a chance that she could be redeemed, forgiven, made whole again, so that she would not make others suffer whatever she had suffered herself. Maybe, Dasha thought to herself, this was her chance, her chance to make right everything that had gone so wrong with Lisochka, her chance to fix all the things that had been irremediably broken with Lisochka, her chance, her chance...

"I think we should take her with us," she said. Only when Oleg gave her a look of surprise and chagrin did she realize she had said it out loud.

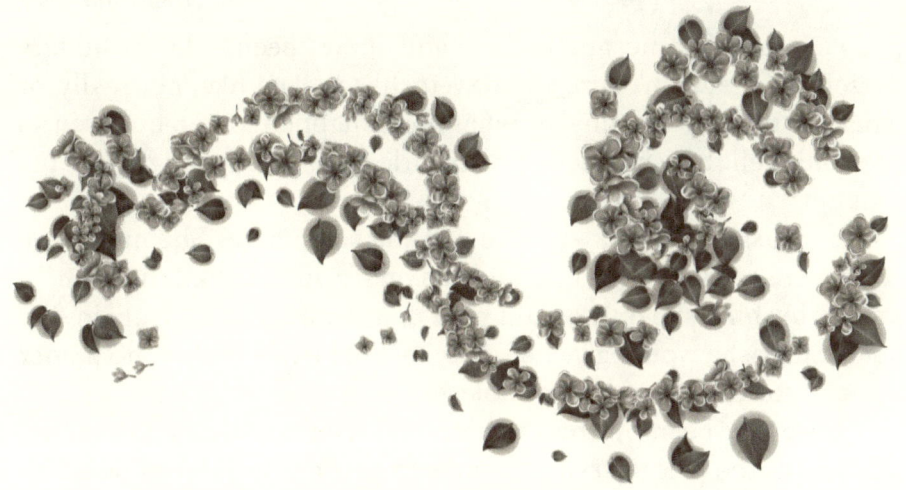

Chapter Eight

"I don't think..." said Oleg, and then closed his mouth on his objections. "I doubt she'll want to come with us," he said instead.

"She might," said Dasha. "She might need to, even if she doesn't want to. And we should...take her in, or something. Help her. We owe it to her."

Oleg gave her another look of surprise, and then said, his mouth quirked in a half-smile, "I dare say in a few years you'll have taken in as many ungrateful strays as your mother. You can't seem to help yourself any more than she can."

"Ungrateful?" said Dasha. "Who was ungrateful?"

"Lisochka, for a start," said Oleg. "Some might say I'm ungrateful as well. But..." He realized that the stablehands had taken away the guards' horses and the guards were coming back to them, and he swallowed whatever else he was planning to say. "We can speak of it more," he said. "Once we've found out what Svetochka's story is."

"She needs help," said Dasha.

"I'm sure she does. Whether she'll take it is another matter entirely. Come: let's at least see if we can get her inside and get her to take some food. She's not a skinny girl, but at the moment she looks like she hasn't eaten all day."

Svetochka did, Dasha thought as they drew up to her, look very wan and sickly underneath her natural ruddiness and good health, as if she...actually, Dasha had not seen very many sickly or hungry people in her lifetime, and had certainly never been sickly or hungry herself, so she wasn't sure what Svetochka looked like, not really, or what she might be feeling, or what might happen to her, but even so she could tell that she needed help, little as Svetochka might like the thought.

For, Dasha thought, why else had she come here? She must have come here seeking Oleg out, and judging by the dislike she seemed to bear for him, she only would have done so if she were truly in dire need. So Dasha would give her help, she told herself again, no matter what it took or how much she objected.

"Have you been on the road long?" Dasha asked her as they set off towards the palace, trying to smile in as friendly a way as possible. "Have you had a hard journey? Did you have to come far?"

"Why do you care?" said Svetochka, looking off to the side, maybe out of shyness, maybe out of sullenness.

"I...I..." Dasha was at a loss for words, but before she could come up with an appropriate response, Oleg said sharply, "Mind your tongue, girl! That's the Tsarinovna you're speaking to!"

"It is no matter," Dasha said quickly, knowing that once again that had been the worst thing Oleg could have possibly said. She had never thought of him as clumsy or awkward in this way before, because—she realized—he never had been. He was not so...elegant in his speech as her mother or her tutors, but he was...smooth-tongued, that was the word, he had always been smooth-tongued and quick-witted, ready with a laugh and a joke, able to anger others, yes, especially Dasha, but able to take away the sting of his words as well. But now he couldn't seem to stop hurting Svetochka, even though she was sure he had no wish to do so.

"Yes it is," he said. "Svetochka can't go around talking to you and about you like that. For her sake as much as yours."

"Why?" said Svetochka, still not looking at any of them.

"Because," said Oleg, "you need to win yourself friends here if you're going to get what you came for, my girl, and you're not going to win anything but hatred if you go around abusing the Tsarinovna. You're in Krasnograd now, not Khladniye Vody, so act like it."

Svetochka set her lips in a thin line, but thankfully said nothing, and they made their way in awkward silence to the palace and then up to Dasha's suite—she insisted on receiving Svetochka in her own chambers, even though Oleg spoke against it—where they left the guards outside (lucky guards, Dasha thought, and then suppressed that unworthy and probably untrue thought) and then waited in an even more awkward silence until Kira and Olesya brought in a samovar and trays of tea and sweet pies. Dasha sent them off and tried to pour Svetochka some tea herself, but Svetochka shook her head in angry refusal when Dasha tried to press it on her.

"Really, you must be thirsty," Dasha told her, after she had turned it down for the fourth time. Dasha had always found it irritating the way people would turn down tea—or anything else—three times before accepting it, in order not to seem greedy, not that she knew to name the scratchy feeling that always arose in her breast whenever it happened "irritation," but Svetochka's determination not to take the tea seemed more than mere politeness—the opposite of politeness, in fact. "You must be thirsty," she repeated. "If you don't care for tea, we have other things as well—compote, kefir, kumys, steppe tea—I'd be happy to send for any of it, or all of it, if there's something you'd prefer."

Svetochka looked at her for a long moment out from under her brows, which were drawn together to form sharp creases between her eyes and across her forehead. Dasha's maids and tutors and all her other caretakers had always warned her that frowning like that would make her look old before her time, and ugly once she did grow old. She had always been taught to keep her face in a smooth small smile, to look polite while also preserving her skin and keeping herself pretty. But Svetochka...

Dasha was willing to wager that no one had ever told her any of that, probably because no one had ever cared, or even if they had, it had seemed pointless, for what did Svetochka have to save herself for? Hard work and bearing babies didn't require a smooth face and a charming smile, not like ruling did. It was evident in every line of Svetochka's face and body that no one had ever taught her how to be gracious, or polite, or commanding, or to think about how others might perceive her and modify her behavior accordingly. At first glance no one would mistake Svetochka and Dasha as anything other than sisters, but a second glance would show that all they had in common was blood.

"Truly, it would set my mind at ease if you took some tea," Dasha told her, smiling as sweetly as she knew how, since she was at a loss for what else to do. Snapping at Svetochka the way Oleg had been doing was clearly not helpful, but she had a suspicion that part of the problem was her own good manners. Everything she did to try to put

Svetochka at ease only emphasized the gulf between them, the difference between her lot in life and Svetochka's. So when Svetochka only turned her head away from her, she decided to try another approach, and set the full cup down in front of Svetochka and poured tea for everyone else.

Then she put some of the pies, which today were little boat-shaped things of yeast dough, with apple jam in a hole in the middle and a glaze of sugar, on little wooden plates—at least the maids had brought in the painted wooden plates, which Dasha liked better anyway, with their cheerful patterns in red and black and gold, and not the porcelain plates, which she was sure would have frightened Svetochka so much she wouldn't have dared touch them—and handed them around, setting one down in front of Svetochka, who pointedly ignored it. Then Dasha turned her back on her and began discussing the state of the roads with Oleg and Susanna.

She kept at it, avoiding so much as glancing in Svetochka's direction, much as she would with a fearful dog, until they had all finished their first pastry and first cup of tea. When she went to refill everyone's cups and plates, she noticed, just as she had expected, that Svetochka's cup was also empty, and that there was nothing on her plate but crumbs. She poured her another cup of tea and placed another pie on her plate without saying a word to her, and went back to talking to Susanna, now about their travel clothes.

After everyone had had two pies and three cups of tea, and Svetochka was looking, if not exactly cheerful, then as if she were no longer in danger of biting everyone's head off, possibly because of the pie-induced somnolence that was making her eyelids droop, Dasha turned to her and said, as neutrally as she could manage, "Do you have any lodgings here in Krasnograd?"

For a moment Svetochka glared at her mutinously, but then gave a tiny shake of her head.

"We would be honored if you would stay with us," Dasha told her.

This jolted Svetochka out of her bad temper. "What, here in the kremlin?" she asked, incredulity making her look Dasha full in the face.

"Of course," said Dasha. "We are sisters, after all, and where else would my sister stay?"

"In the servants' quarters, I'll warrant," said Svetochka, regaining some of her earlier sullen shyness.

"Wherever you would feel most comfortable," Dasha told her gently.

"Where I would...where I would..." Svetochka shook her head, like a horse shaking off flies, and then asked, almost plaintively, "Why are you *doing* this?"

"I told you: because we are sisters. And because...because I think you need it, and there's no one else who can do this for you, not like I can."

Svetochka's face closed up again in resentment, but Dasha hurried on before she could say anything: "I would consider it a great favor, Svetlana, ah, Svetlanovna."

"I..." Svetochka opened and closed her mouth a few times, and then said, in a very different tone than she had used earlier, "No one's ever called me that. No one's ever called me by...by my proper name."

"Well, here you will certainly be called by your proper name," Dasha told her. "And I truly would consider it an honor if you would consent to stay with us."

Svetochka's face twisted, but this time it was not with resentment but with, Dasha thought, the need to hold back tears.

"Let us help you, girl," said Oleg, but this time he spoke gently. "You must've come to us for a reason, so let us help you. You said you wanted your due, so take it."

"I...I..." said Svetochka, and burst into tears.

After she had cried herself out and dried her eyes, she told her story to the rest of them. It was, to Dasha's shock and horror, even worse than Lisochka's, if such a thing were possible.

"After I were born," she began, "things seemed like they was going well for my mother. It were an easy birth, she said, an' I were a good baby, healthy an' so. Everyone said she'd be sure an' find a proper husband soon, pretty an' lively as she were, an' with a healthy baby already at her breast. Only...only..." She gulped.

"Svetochka was always very lively," said Oleg quietly. "And proud. Too lively and proud for most men, I'll warrant."

Svetochka nodded. "She said...she always said none of the village lads was good enough," she continued. "She didn't want none of 'em for a match, they was all too stupid, an' poor besides. An' then...an' then when I were still little, no more 'n three or four, she, she, she caught the eye of the, of the husband of, of, the village elder, next village over. The village elder, she weren't that old, not for an elder, but she'd taken a younger man as her second husband, once she lost her first to the cough, an' so...he weren't that young neither, forty if he were a day, but still twice the age of my mother. How she preened when he started chasing after her! I still remember, even though I could hardly say but a few words then, I were so little.

"So. He were chasing her, an' she were chasing him, an' her parents was telling her no good could come of it, no good could come of it, an' then...one night she, she, she went off, she went off for a tryst with him, an' when she came back she were crying an' crying, an' her lips was busted an' she had bruises on her neck—I still remember 'em, awful they was!—an' a cut, a cut right on her neck like from a knife or something, an' she made me swear not to tell anyone, she made me swear...her parents found out, though, 'course, but there weren't nothing they could do. It seemed this village elder, she liked...she knew what kind of a man she had, an' she'd...help him, you know, set it all up, seduce silly proud-headed young girls like my mother, talk 'em into a tryst, an' then...the wife'd come an' hold a knife to their throats while..."

Svetochka gulped again, and then said, "My mother weren't the first, we found out, nor were she the last, an' there weren't nothing we nor anyone else could do about it. Not until...Baba Anya, she heard what'd happened, not to my mother, but to another girl from our village—all the other girls was from Ozyorsk, the other village that is, which's why Baba Anya hadn't ever heard about all this before, not for sure, or so she said, but once she heard from this other girl, she said steps had to be taken an'...but she never did nothing about *him*, no one ever did nothing about *him*, but that fall when the wife, Anfisya her name were, the elder, she went into the woods to gather mushrooms, she...she never came home. An' no one's never heard nor seen sign of her since. An' he—Mark, his name was, Mark—he took over Ozyorsk, at least for a time."

"How *horrible*!" Dasha exclaimed. "And...and nothing has been done? Nothing has been done about him? Has anyone...you should go to Vladislava Vasilisovna, to the Severnolesniye that is, or to my own mother...they would do something about it for sure!"

"The rules ain't the same for us peasants as they are for you nobles, Tsarinovna," said Svetochka, some of her previous resentment returning. "They'd do something for you, I'd warrant, but not for the likes of me or my mother. We've got to take care of ourselves, 'cause no one else is gonna do it for us."

"They *would*," Dasha insisted. "My mother certainly would."

"You think so, Tsarinovna, but you don't know the truth of what it's like for us, for us simple folk," said Svetochka.

"The Tsarinovna is right," Oleg put in, before Dasha could make whatever retort she had been fumbling for. "The Tsarina certainly would do something, for no other reason than you are her daughter's sister, and she does whatever she can for all of the Tsarinovna's sisters." He sounded...ashamed, perhaps, about that, which Dasha thought was queer, but he said it anyway with enough conviction that Svetochka merely shrugged in grudging half-acquiescence before continuing her story.

"Anyways, after that things was calm for us for a while, an' my mother...she weren't never quite the same, you understand, but she... she got better, an' a few years ago, the predictions everyone'd been making, that she'd find someone as good as she were—though by then no one thought she were so good, anyway...but there were someone what caught her eye, a fellow who'd been serving as a guard away in Lesnogorod an' who'd just come back, come back home, an' he caught her eye, an' she caught his, an', well...he were a fine fellow, were our Tikhon, handsome, anyone could see it." She eyed Oleg critically, and added, "he looked a bit like you, to tell the truth, but then, most do up there. Handsome, as I said, an' always ready with a smile an' a joke, an' quick with his hands—he could make anything, or fix anything, afore you could tell him what you needed—an' he always sang as he worked, prettier 'n birds. An' afore we knew it, he an' my mother was wed.

"At first it were all sweetness an' singing, just like we'd been expecting, but then after half a year there were still no baby on the way, an' Tikhon were smiling an' singing less an' frowning more an' more, an' he kept asking my mother, 'When you gonna give me daughters? You got *this* one off some other man; when's my daughter gonna come? An' my mother'd say, 'A man who wants daughters needs to do his duty,' an' Tikhon'd scowl an' wave his hands an' walk away, an' half a year after that, when there was still no more daughters, he took to disappearing in the woods for longer an' longer, till he were hardly ever home, an' when he were, his brow were dark as thunder.

"This went on year after year, till everyone were after my mother to set him aside, saying, 'Svetochka, this man gives you no daughters, only scowls, you need to find another afore it's too late to give your daughter the sisters she deserves,' but my mother'd always say, 'No, I don't have the strength'—by then she weren't so pretty as she were when you knew her, she were all tired an' worn down—'to go chasing down another man after all the trouble the first two have put me through, an' one daughter's a far sight better 'n none, so I'll stop while I still can, I'll quit while I'm ahead.'

"An' then one day last fall Tikhon came home an' my mother told him his prayers had been answered an' there were a baby on the way. Only...he didn't take to the news so kindly, not like we'd been hoping he would. 'How do I know it's mine?' he shouted. 'After all these years, an' you expect me to believe it's mine? It's not mine! You've been running around with some other man an' now you want me to take his child as my own!'

"I don't think my mother were running around," Svetochka added. "I knew everything she did, we slept in the same room, in the same bed, when Tikhon weren't there, an' I'd've known if she'd've been running around with another man, an' she weren't. An' so I said to Tikhon, but he just shouted at me to shut my mouth, I didn't know what I were talking about, an' then he shouted an' shouted some more, about how we was tricking him but he wouldn't let us play him for a fool, an' then he stormed off into the woods again.

"He were gone for a month or more after," Svetochka continued. "An' when he came back, my mother were still with child, an' she were still telling him it were his, an' he were still saying it weren't, an' then... then my grandfather...it turned cold an' a chill took him off, an' Tikhon left us again, saying he weren't gonna stay around a sickly family, a mourning family, an' my grandmother, she didn't last too long after that, she sickened an' died soon after, an' it were just me an' my mother an' the baby on the way, an' no wood gathered for the winter—my mother'd been terrible sick at first, so she couldn't work at all—no wood gathered for the winter, no food set by, or not enough, anyways, 'cause every time she went to cook, my mother'd come over all sick from the smell an' have to go outside or go lie down—not enough hay for the cow an' no one to slaughter her—my mother never could bring herself to do it, my grandfather were the only one who'd do the slaughtering—an' we didn't know what we'd do.

"Others'd help us, 'course, but it'd been a lean year an' no one had overmuch in the way of supplies, an' we all knew some wasn't to make it through the winter, an', well, everyone thought it were our time, our fate. They wouldn't say it to our faces, but you could see 'em thinking it, even as they promised to help us. My mother couldn't keep her man at her side nor her parents alive, an' in hard winters them are the ones as dies.

"But then Tikhon came back, an' my mother, she were so glad, she cried when she saw him, an' called him our salvation, an' told him he'd keep us alive through the winter, but he...he said he couldn't. He couldn't be our support, he couldn't be the one to take care of us an' keep us alive when things was hard, he couldn't be the one to care for a woman with child an' a girl barely into womanhood through a long hard winter, he couldn't, he couldn't, he didn't have it in him, he weren't that kind of man.

"An' then my mother cried an' cried some more, an' told him it didn't matter what kind of man he were, 'cause we didn't have any other, an' she were already big with his child an' it wouldn't be safe for her to go out into the woods an' gather the wood we needed an' those sorts of things, an' he said, 'I don't know why not, you've been doing it all these years so far,' an' she said, 'But not when I were with child, an' I had my father to help me,' an' he said, 'And now you've got Svetochka to help you,' an' she said, 'No, *you've* got Svetochka to help you: I'll stay behind an' make the preserves an' stuff, get everything ready for winter, an' you an' Svetochka can go out an' gather firewood, there's still some left, I'm sure of it,' an' he said no, he weren't gonna go off, helping another man's child bring in firewood for another man's child, he weren't gonna let us trick him like that, use him like that, an' my mother swore up an' down again that the child she were carrying were his, an' then...an' then he left again."

Svetochka stopped to take a breath and swallow before continuing. "We thought we was done for then," she said. "I went out myself an' brought in what firewood I could, an' some of the other girls, they helped me when they could, but we was all so busy, an' they had families too, families that needed 'em just as much as I did. An' while I were out gathering firewood, my mother—she were feeling better by then, she said that's how it is, once your belly gets big you start to feeling better—she put aside what she could, she dried an' preserved everything that hadn't already spoiled, an' I..." Svetochka gulped and shivered guiltily, "I slaughtered the cow myself. It were much more awful 'n I thought it would be, an' I felt so bad about it, when she'd been feeding us all her life, but we didn't have no hay for her an' no one else would take her, she were already past her prime an' weren't giving so much milk as she used to, so...so I did it an' we salted the meat an' set it aside to freeze, only when we went to eat it the first time, our throats just closed up, an'...but then the weather got colder, an' we got hungrier.

"An' then one day...one day in midwinter he came back again, only he weren't alone. He were with...he were with Mark."

"What!" cried Dasha. "Why?!"

"He said...he said he couldn't take care of us, nor should he have to, not after what we'd done to him, but Mark could, he'd arranged it all an' we was to live with Mark. Mark'd even agree to marry my mother, so's he could continue running Ozyorsk. He'd been running it ever since his wife'd disappeared, but not everyone were happy with how he were doing it, an' there were talk that the village elder should be a woman, just like always, or that Mark should at least marry again, an' all the women was offering to take him, but he kept saying no, no, he didn't want none of 'em, but then somehow...there were a friendship between 'em, we figured out later, there were a friendship between Mark and Tikhon, they'd been hunting an'...the gods alone know what else they'd been doing, two fellows like that, but they'd been meeting out in the woods, all these years an' we didn't even know about it, an' when Tikhon'd told Mark all about our troubles, it seems Mark'd laughed an' said sure the child weren't Tikhon's, everyone knew what kind of woman my mother were, but he'd take her on anyway for old time's sake, an', an', an' it seems he'd had his eye on *me* for a while already, an' so he said he'd take us both in, an'...an' he an' Tikhon arranged everything between 'em, an' they came an' told us, an'...an'... my mother, she were so mad she cried, but, but, but the snow were already almost up the eaves, it took all I had just to clear out a path from our door to the privy an' the coldhouse, an' what mushrooms we had had spoiled, they was full of worms, an' our flour had gone moldy somehow, an', an', an'...an' so in the end we agreed. An' afore the week were out we was in Ozyorsk, with Mark.

"At first it weren't so bad, not like we feared. He had a big house, bigger 'n any house I'd ever seen afore, an' we had our own room an' he didn't bother us none, an' we could eat as much as we wanted, an' there was even other women, serving women, who did the food an' looked after the fires an' such. So at first we thought we'd struck it lucky, strange as it seemed. Only...only, that weren't so.

"The trouble started on the second week," Svetochka continued, after a brief pause to gather her strength. "There'd been a terrible storm, it'd been snowing for days, so's you couldn't see your hand in front of your face, soon as you stepped outside. And so everyone were growing bored an' restless, like you do, an' one day...one day my mother were in the kitchen, she liked it there, it were warm an' there were always company, so she were off in the kitchen, an' I were in our room, mending some footcloths, when...when Mark came in."

This time the pause lasted longer, until finally Oleg broke it by asking, "What happened to him?"

"How'd you know...?" said Svetochka, staring at him with the first sign of respect she had shown him since she had first appeared.

He smiled, though it was still a sad smile, as he'd worn ever since Svetochka had arrived. "I know Svetochka," he said. "And I know myself, and my daughters. What did you do to him?"

"I...at first I didn't understand, I didn't understand what he were doing, what he wanted—I'd never been one to fool around with the boys, so I didn't understand at first, but then I did—an' when I did, I tried to scream, to call for help, but he put his hand over my mouth, so I...I jabbed my needle into his hand, right into the back of his hand, so deep you could see the point trying to poke through on the other side. I thought that'd end it, but instead he got angry, crazy with anger, I'd never seen anything like it, it were like, it were like..." she shuddered and shook her head, "I don't know what it were like, I'd never seen its like afore an' I hope never to again, but he started screaming, not like a man, like, like...like some kind of maddened animal, an' he grabbed me, he grabbed me with his other hand, the one that didn't have the needle in it, an' even with one hand he was choking me, choking me, so I...I grabbed up the chamber pot an' smashed it against his head. Only...only that didn't stop him, not like you'd think it'd do, he were still crazy, crazy with it, an' when I tried to slip past him, he knocked me to the floor an' started kicking me, kicking me so's I thought I'd die, an' then...then my mother came bursting in, with the serving women behind her, an' they...they...they had knives."

"I see," said Oleg, when it became apparent that Svetochka wasn't going to say any more. "Did anyone cause you any trouble about it?"

"There were some trouble, with some of the older folk," Svetochka said slowly. "But everyone knew...what he'd done, what he'd been doing for years an' years, only no one had wanted to stop him, they'd all been looking the other way, an' they'd all hoped things'd get better, once his wife were gone, an' they did for a bit, but then...it's like he had a sickness or something, an' he couldn't stop himself, or so that's what everyone said, an' in the end...in the end it were us as had to stop him, so we did. An' we dragged his body off into the woods an' left it for the wolves, where it belonged. I never got that needle back, though, an' it were my best needle."

"Well, I'm glad justice was served in the end, at least, even if it cost you your best needle," said Oleg, trying to smile. "But I knew..."

"Knew what?" demanded Svetochka.

"I knew no daughter of mine would stand for that kind of thing," Oleg told her, now smiling at her fondly, the way a father should. For a moment Svetochka almost smiled back, but then she remembered herself, and looked away instead.

"What about Tikhon?" asked Dasha. "I can't believe he just...left you like that! What kind of a person would do a thing like that!"

"More than you'd think," said Oleg, no longer smiling.

"Tikhon, now...as I were making my way down here, I heard he'd gone off, he'd found another woman to take him in, over in Beryozovsk. He always were quick with a smile when he needed to be. An' I suppose...others told us that's a bad sign in a man, you can't trust a man who's smiling an' happy all the time, 'cause someday something'll happen that'll make it hard for him to smile at you, an' then he'll run off, he'll go running into the arms of someone who can make him smile, at least until that woman makes him stop smiling too.

"An' he...you could see he'd got it all worked out it in his mind, he'd explained everything to himself so's he didn't have any other choice, he'd convinced himself the baby weren't his an' we was tricking him, using him, an' he were doing us a favor by handing us over to Mark like that, just when we needed him most. We'd never needed him afore, not really, an' sometimes he'd complained about it, but when we did need him, when we really needed his help, well...he said we'd be better off without him," she said, smiling painfully. "He said we'd be grateful to him in the long run.

"An' maybe that's true. But...it'd have to be a very long run. He left us alone, in the middle of winter, with a baby on the way an' no one to turn to if we needed aid but Mark. So...I can't believe we was better off. I can't believe things wouldn't've been better for both of us if he'd stayed. I can't help but believe that, if only he hadn't been so craven and selfish, things might've been better. Although who knows. *I* survived, an' my mother did too, while Mark"—there was something wolfish in her smile now—"didn't. But still. He shoulda stayed. He shouldn't've run off an' left us like that, just when we needed him most." She gave Oleg a sharp look. "Just like you shoulda stayed," she told him. "If you'd've stayed with us like you shoulda, none of this woulda happened."

"I..." Oleg twitched his shoulders. "I...If I'd have known...I thought I was leaving you to, to, to something better than that. If I'd've known... but I *couldn't* stay, Svetochka, I couldn't."

"You managed to stay for *her*," said Svetochka waspishly, wrinkling her nose in Dasha's direction.

Oleg twisted his mouth into something that was sort of like a smile, but it was the saddest smile Dasha had ever seen. "No I didn't," he said softly. "I didn't stay, not even for her."

"You're here now," pointed out Svetochka.

"But only...only for a time. And...I was here much less than I wasn't."

"You was still here some," said Svetochka. "You was still here some, and you're here now. You was never *there*, you never came back for *us*, not once, only for her, only for her. It ain't fair. It ain't fair! It ain't fair!"

"Nothing ever is," said Oleg tiredly. "Some might say it wasn't fair that Mark ended up dead in the woods, food for wolves, after taking you in when no one else would."

"That's not...that's not...that's not right!" exclaimed both Dasha and Svetochka at the same time. They exchanged an awkward glance. "That's not...that's not how fairness works," said Dasha.

"For most people it is," said Oleg. "For most people 'fair' is just another word for 'other people giving me what I think I want, even if it hurts them.'"

"But...but..." objected Dasha. She gave another quick glance over at Svetochka, hoping she would be able to jump in and save Dasha from her confusion, explain to Oleg why he was wrong, why he shouldn't say things like that, but Svetochka looked too angry and too confused to be able to speak at all, so Dasha floundered on alone. "That's not... that's just not right," she said. "There's nothing that could excuse... what Mark did, what he wanted to do. There's nothing about that that could be 'fair,' that's not what 'fair' means, that's just not right, that's just not right..."

"No?" said Oleg. "Or rather, no, it's not 'right,' not in the way you mean, but it *would* be 'fair' for Mark to demand some kind of return for taking them in and feeding them over the winter, and it probably *wasn't* fair for him to end up dead."

"Well, no," agreed Dasha uncomfortably, "but...he was *bad*. He was a bad person who had hurt other people and was going to keep hurting them until he was stopped."

"I know," said Oleg. "And if I'd've been there, the outcome would've been the same, only quicker. But that doesn't mean what happened was *fair*. So don't go thinking the world owes you fairness, girl," he said, looking back over at Svetochka. "Nothing's been fair for you so far, that's true, and the way I've treated you, that's not fair either, but we could make the entire world 'fair' and it still wouldn't be right, or good, or anything else we'd want it to be. 'Fair' can be made to mean anything we want it to mean, and for most of us, 'fair' doesn't mean fair at all. It's just a word to try and take what you want when others won't give it to you. For those that've been given more than they've earned, more often than not 'fair' means that others keep giving and they keep taking, and those that've been treated unfairly, 'fair' is just another word for stealing and taking, only now it's them doing the stealing and taking. So put 'fair' out of your head, girl, and turn your thoughts towards better things."

"So what should we do, if we can't make things fair?" asked Dasha, at the same time as Svetochka burst out, "That's easy for you to say!"

"That's a question for your mother, not me," Oleg told Dasha. "She's the wise one for that sort of thing. And it doesn't matter if it's easy for me to say," he added to Svetochka. "What matters is what you're planning to do. Stop worrying so much about what you're owed, what should've happened but didn't and never will, and tell me what you're planning to do. Where's your mother?"

"She...when I left her she were still back in Ozyorsk," said Svetochka. "Someone there, the woman who were chosen as the next elder, she took my mother on as a helper, said she could stay there till after the baby were born, an' then start to work for her. But there weren't no room for me there. She said I had to make my own way, an' my mother...she said the same thing. An' she told me to go looking for you, that you'd help me, an' she...she'd heard you had some connection with the Severnolesniye, so she sent me to Lesnogorod, only when I got there, you wasn't there, but Olga Vasilisovna—she were the only one who'd so much as look at me—told me I might find you in Krasnogorod, she were the one who told me...about *her*," she pointed her nose at Dasha, "an' she were the one who told me to go looking for her, she were the one who said, who said, who said even if I, I didn't find you, I'd still get...get help from *her*."

"And she was right," said Dasha quickly. "Of *course* we'll help you. But you must have had a very fatiguing journey! And all by yourself, too. The roads...were the roads *very* bad? I've always heard you can't travel on them at all during the spring muds."

For a moment it looked as if Svetochka wasn't going to respond, but then she said, "You can if you walk. It's only those as has carriages an' sleighs as can't travel. If you can walk an' you ain't afraid of a little mud, you can travel just fine."

"Well...that's good, then, and we're very glad you made it here to us. But he's right: what is your plan? What do you want to do now?"

"I..." Svetochka opened and closed her mouth. "I want him to help me," she said finally. "I want him to help me like he shoulda all along."

"Help you how?" asked Oleg. "Help you with what?"

"With...with what you shoulda helped us with all along!"

He sighed. "I'm afraid that's not in my power," he told her. "Whatever you want me to do for you—I can't. If you want help, you'd best ask...ask your sister."

"She ain't the one as should be helping me!" Svetochka said indignantly. "She weren't the one who ran off an' left us! It were you, it were you, an' you're the one who's got to help me now! You can't...you can't just go running off whenever you want, I...all those weeks on the road, up to my knees in snow an' mud, freezing, not having enough to eat half the time, I...I thought an' thought, an' what I thought were this: Olga Vasilisovna, she told me a bit about you, she told me...she were the one as told me that you've got lots of daughters, not just me, that you've run off an' left all of 'em, not just me, an' I...I decided you're not going to do that any more, you're not going to do that any more, I'm gonna stop you, I am, I'm not gonna let you run off an' leave people like that!"

For a terrible moment Dasha thought Oleg was about to break out laughing at Svetochka's pronouncement. She could see him bite his lip and the inside of his cheek, and when he said, "And how're you going to stop me?" she could hear a hint of a smile bursting through his attempts at control.

"I'm..." There were two red spots high up on Svetochka's cheeks, and a red blotch creeping up her neck. Dasha could feel her own face and neck prickling in sympathy. "I'm gonna stop you, that's how!"

"But how?" Oleg repeated. "No one's ever managed to yet. Not even me. And no matter what you tried—I *can't*, Svetochka, I *can't*. I...my life belongs to the gods, not to you or me or anyone else. That's just... it's not 'fair,' as you'd say, but that's just how it is."

"That's just an excuse!" cried Svetochka.

Oleg sighed again. "You're not the first to say that, girl," he said. "But it doesn't matter if you like it or not, if you believe it or not. It's true either way."

"No it *ain't!*" insisted Svetochka, flushing more and more. "It's just... you're just saying it 'cause you're scared! You just want to run away 'cause you're scared, scared to stay an', an', an' face something you're not strong enough to fight! You're just scared that, that, that I *am* your daughter an' you'll have to take care of me like you should, an' you might not be strong enough but you shoulda done it anyway, only you run off! You're just scared to stay an' face, face, face the truth, that's what it is!"

Dasha expected Oleg to say something to refute that, to point out that, clearly, Svetochka was talking about Tikhon, not him, which even Dasha could see was the truth. But instead...instead he looked stricken, like she had stabbed him in the heart. Dasha couldn't ever remember seeing him look like that before, and, sorry as she felt for Svetochka, and true as she knew Svetochka's allegations to be, if not about Oleg then about Tikhon and all the other people in her life who should have acted like a father and taken care of her, but instead had tried to use her up and throw her away, she still wanted to defend him, to make some of that hurt go away.

"You may be right," he said quietly, just as she blurted out loudly, "That's not true!"

"Ain't it?" demanded Svetochka, rounding on her with an ugly expression on her face.

"It..." said Dasha.

"It may be," said Oleg, still speaking quietly, but cutting through their angry words. "But it doesn't matter. I couldn't have stayed with you then, and I can't stay with you now, no more than your grandmother and grandfather could have stayed with you when the gods called them away. Sometimes we just have to leave, even if things would be better if we stayed. It's just the way it is."

"It's not *fair!*" wailed Svetochka again.

"Do you want to stay in Krasnograd?" asked Dasha, hoping to break her thoughts away from the unfairness of it all, since, even though she wanted to cry out against the injustice of it all along with Svetochka, a part of her was forced to admit that Oleg was right, too. "If you wanted to stay in Krasnograd, I'm sure we could find you a position."

"As your serving girl?" said Svetochka sullenly.

"Well...no," said Dasha. It was on the tip of her tongue to say that Svetochka would never be fine enough to be Dasha's maid, but luckily her better sense overrode her honesty before she could blurt that out. "Something more suitable for you," she said instead. "Something like...I don't know. Do you like to cook? Or sew? Or care for horses? Or work in the garden? Or...I don't know. What do you like to do?"

"You think I ain't fit for nothing other 'n digging in the dirt," said Svetochka, by way of a reply.

"You're not leaving me much choice," Dasha snapped back at her, and then could have bitten her tongue for having raised her voice like that at someone who was both unhappy, and her sister. She found herself looking over at Oleg, expecting him to chastise her, but instead he appeared to be repressing a smile.

"If you would tell me what your skills are, where your interests lie, I'm sure we could find you a good situation," Dasha said, making an effort to speak more calmly. "If Krasnograd doesn't suit you, I'm sure there is work available out on someone's estate. Princess Zapadnokrasnova is here now, with two highly skilled seamstresses: perhaps we could arrange an apprenticeship with them, if you think such work would suit you."

"It ain't fair," Svetochka repeated, glaring up at Oleg self-consciously from under her brows as she said it. "It ain't fair that you'll get the spend your whole life in luxury, an' I'll have to slave away, working my fingers to the bone, even though we're sisters."

"My mother had to slave away her whole life, and so did yours," Oleg said. "The Tsarinovna is the Tsarinovna in spite of your sisterhood, not because of it. And if you had to become Tsarinovna, I doubt you'd like it as much as you think you would."

"No?" said Svetochka, and looked around Dasha's fine chamber expressively.

"No," said Oleg. "Your life has been hard, that's true, but sometimes being at the top can be as bad as being at the bottom, or maybe worse. It's best to be in the middle, but neither of you are ever going to know that. Well, *you* could, Svetochka my girl. The Tsarinovna's idea is a good one. Go apprentice with these seamstresses, or anyone else who takes your fancy, and with a little hard work you could have a better life than you would ever get back home in Khladniye Vody."

"It ain't fair I'll have to slave away in some apprenticeship," grumbled Svetochka. "Not when she had…silver spoons an' gold platters an' such just handed to her from birth."

"The Tsarinovna has already had to 'slave away in some apprenticeship' since she could walk, and will have to continue slaving away for years to come," Oleg said sharply. "And whatever you choose, girl, you'll have to work for it. There's not much that's certain in life, but work always is."

"*You* don't have to work," said Svetochka.

Even through his beard Dasha could see Oleg's jaw jumping, as he clenched it to keep from shouting at her. "Not like you're thinking of, maybe," he said after a moment. "But I still have to keep myself from freezing or starving to death, just like you and your mother do, and it's just as much work for me as it is for you."

Svetochka made a disbelieving face, and Dasha could tell that she didn't like the idea of other people struggling and suffering like she had, because that would make her less special and more like everyone else, and would mean that other people were real too, instead of just being props on her stage…Dasha told herself to stop being so fanciful. Perhaps her mother could see things like that, but she certainly couldn't. Just because she could feel that she was right, didn't mean that it was true.

"Well, where would you like to live, then?" Dasha asked, hoping to divert Svetochka from her resentment over her need to work. "Would you like to go back to Khladniye Vody? Stay here in Krasnograd? Or go somewhere else perhaps?"

"Where else would I go?" demanded Svetochka.

"Zapadnokrasnovskoye…"

"They'd never take the likes of me," Svetochka interrupted her.

At the moment Dasha heartily agreed, but she had the sense not to say so. "Krasnograd might be your best choice," she said instead. "There are many opportunities for a clever young woman here in Krasnograd."

For half a breath Svetochka looked tempted, but then she shook her head. "An' see you parading past me every day, looking down on me?" she said.

"I wouldn't parade past you!" protested Dasha. "And I certainly wouldn't look down on you!"

"You're looking down on me right now!"

It was very hard for Dasha not to say that was because Svetochka was making it impossible not to, but she held her tongue. "Many people enjoy living in Krasnograd," she said instead. "The advantages the capital has to offer..."

"Ain't of no interest to the likes of me," Svetochka put in sullenly before she could finish.

"Of course, if you would feel more comfortable back in Khladniye Vody..."

"I'm never going back!"

"Not even for your mother?" said Dasha, more sharply than she should have. For a moment Svetochka looked taken aback. Then she said, half-angrily, half-sadly, "She's better off without me around."

"You should go to Lesnograd," Oleg put in at this point.

Both girls turned to look at him.

"It's close enough to Khladniye Vody and Ozyorsk you could visit your mother when you wanted, but far enough away that no one from there would bother you. And the Severnolesniye would offer you a position, I'm sure of it."

"I don't want their charity," muttered Svetochka.

"If you're going to get anywhere, girl, others are going to help you on your way," said Oleg. "You're going to need a helping hand, at least at first. And isn't that what you wanted anyway? For your rich and well-connected family to give you a leg up? Isn't that what you keep saying you deserve? Well, if that's what you think you deserve, and it's being offered to you, then take it."

Svetochka looked abashed at that, but still managed to put up a resistance to Oleg's plan, saying, "Why would *they* help me out?" as skeptically as possible. "*They* ain't my family."

"Olga Vasilisovna is just as much family to you as she is," Oleg told her, nodding at Dasha. "And you say you don't want to be a seamstress or a maid or a stablehand, well, what about serving her? She's still out there, riding around, keeping order in Severnolesnoye and exploring beyond the borders, but she's always on the lookout for good companions, and she's not as young as she once was. And..." Oleg trailed off with a grimace of pain, and Dasha knew he had been thinking of Lisochka, and she guessed that he was hoping that Svetochka could be for Aunty Olga what Lisochka never had been, but he didn't say that. "And she might welcome a woman, and blood kin," he said instead.

"She'd never take me," muttered Svetochka, looking down at the floor in a way that Dasha knew meant that she liked the idea very much, and so was afraid to accept the offer.

"You've already proven yourself with your trek down from Ozyorsk, alone, in the worst season for traveling," Oleg countered. "That'd make her like you, even if you weren't blood kin, which you are. If you don't want to stay in Krasnograd, then come with us to Lesnograd, and let her take the measure of you. If it's what you want to do, she'll take you, my head for beheading."

"An' if she don't?" asked Svetochka.

"If she doesn't, then there are lots of other chances for a clever, hardworking girl like you in Lesnograd."

"How do you know I'm clever an' hardworking?" said Svetochka, the corners of her mouth turned up into something that was almost a sly smile. It was so like something Dasha might have said, or at least thought about saying, in the same situation, that Dasha had to fight the urge to laugh and clap her on the shoulder.

"You're mine, aren't?" said Oleg, and he was smiling too. "Or so you keep saying. And all my girls are clever and hardworking."

Now Svetochka really was smiling. "I...I suppose..." she began, but then frowned and said, "I ain't got no coin for the journey."

"We'll find it for you, I'm sure," put in Dasha quickly, at the same time as Oleg said, "But I do." He stopped and looked over at Dasha with a warm approval. "Don't worry, girl: we won't let you starve," he said, turning back to Svetochka. "We'll find you what you need, and a girl like you will always pull your weight and more than earn your keep on a journey like this, I'm sure."

Dasha was afraid that Svetochka was going to spoil it all by complaining that she shouldn't have to earn her keep, when Dasha and Susanna wouldn't have to, but instead she said slowly, "Well then... well then...I'll go with you, I guess."

"Good girl," said Oleg, as Dasha cried out, she wasn't even sure why (since it certainly was only very partially true), "I'm so pleased!"

Svetochka smiled a shy, uncertain smile at this. Maybe, Dasha thought, no one had ever been pleased to have her go along with them before. Out of the corner of her eye, she thought she saw Susanna roll her own eyes at all this, but she pretended not to notice, telling herself instead that it was all for the best and that soon, not only would she be going on a journey with her father, but she would have her new friend *and* her new sister at her side as well.

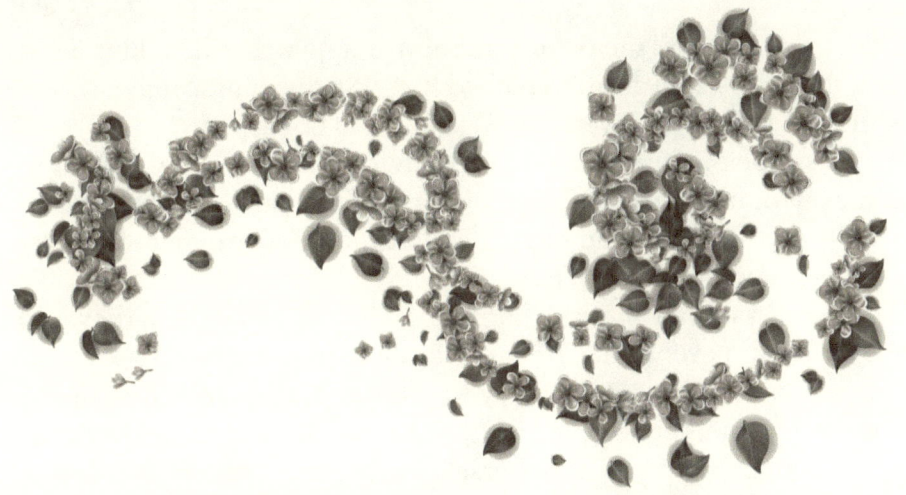

Chapter Nine

Dasha's mother was acquainted with both Svetochka and the plan to bring her with them to Lesnograd that very afternoon, and she offered, without any prompting from either Dasha or Oleg, to outfit her with any clothing or supplies she needed for the journey, and to loan her a horse.

Svetochka, who once she had gotten over her original shyness had been so bold in front of Dasha, appeared to be genuinely overthrown by being in the presence of the Tsarina. She didn't know how to get down on her knees and bow down to the ground properly, or Dasha was sure she would have, but as it was she hung her head and refused to look Dasha's mother in the eye or say anything to her other than "Yes, gracious Tsarina," even when Dasha's mother began reminiscing about Khladniye Vody and Svetochka's mother and how she had been carrying Svetochka when she, Dasha's mother, had stayed with her for the night.

"Anyone can see you and my Dasha are sisters," she finished, coming over and taking Svetochka by the chin in order to lift up her face so that she could examine it properly. "But you have your mother's look about you, too. She couldn't have been much older than you are now when I met her"—Dasha's mother flashed a half-mocking look over at Oleg, and he looked away, in shame, Dasha thought—"and she was so happy to be expecting you! It was all she could think off—well, almost all." And Dasha's mother flashed another look over at Oleg, one that

Dasha was sure was meant only for him, but he was still looking away, as if the whole conversation pained him. "Such a handsome girl, and so lively!" her mother went on. "I hope she is doing well?"

"Yes, gracious Tsarina," muttered Svetochka, which caused Oleg to come out of his stupor and provide Dasha's mother with a brief history of everything that had happened to Svetochka's mother since Dasha's mother had last seen her.

"I see," said her mother, her face falling. "I knew that...they told me that...but never mind. We must do something for her."

This caused Svetochka to try to protest, but in the end both she and Dasha's mother accepted Oleg's idea, which was to give Svetochka enough money to provide for herself and her mother over the coming winter, and send her to Aunty Olga.

"If Olga Vasilisovna takes you on, you won't need it and you can give it to your mother," Oleg told her. "And if she doesn't, you can over-winter where it suits you and not be a burden to her, at least."

Svetochka tried to argue against it, even though this was exactly what she'd said she'd come to Krasnograd looking for, but in the end agreed, and even agreed to Dasha's mother's suggestion that all three girls—Svetochka, Susanna, and Dasha—spend the remainder of their time in Krasnograd living together in Dasha's chambers, so that they could all get to know one another.

"If you can't live together in the kremlin, you won't be able to stand each other on the road," she said briskly. "So practice now, girls, and I'll come join you for supper. It will be a quiet affair, just the five of us."

Svetochka forgot herself for a moment and stared at her, horror-struck at the thought of an intimate dinner with the Tsarina, and became even more stricken when Oleg said he had things he would have to take care of, and wouldn't be joining them, but Dasha's mother ignored her discomfort, and said, with her most reassuring smile, "Even better, although we'll be sorry to miss you. But this way it will be just us girls. Dasha, my heart, please escort your sister to your—her—chambers, and see about getting her some more clothes for the journey. There's no time to make up a new wardrobe, but you're close enough in size that I'm sure you can find some of your things that will suit her."

Dasha agreed, and she and Susanna pulled the still-stupefied Svetochka away from where her mother was sitting on the Wooden Throne in the Hall of Council, hearing a bedraggled and desperate group of petitioners, and back to Dasha's chambers.

The dinner that night was just as awkward as Dasha had feared. Her mother and Susanna were in good spirits, and chatted the entire time about the weather, the upcoming journey, life in the Southern mountains—Dasha's mother expressed her regrets at not yet visiting them, and said that Dasha should, perhaps the following summer, and that some day, maybe when Dasha was ready to start ruling, she, the Tsarina, would make the journey herself.

"I don't know when I'm going to have time to rule if I go on all these journeys," Dasha blurted out, and then wished she hadn't. She sounded petulant and unhappy about the journeys, even though they were the thing she wanted to do above all else right now. It was because she was feeling petulant and unhappy about...what? She didn't even know what. It was just that things were moving so fast right now, which is what she had wanted, and yet it was still everyone else who was making the decisions about everything, not her. She felt as if, while attempting to go wading in the shallows, she had fallen into the depths of the Krasna and was being sucked along helplessly.

"I mean," she said, attempting to recover herself, "I'll be going North, up to Severnolesnoye, and then I need to visit the steppe, and the South, and, and...what about the Eastern mountains? I should visit them as well! It's just...when am I going to find the time for all of this?"

Her mother smiled, and then tried to hide it. "You will find the time, my heart, never fear," she said. "There are many things you must do, yes, and many journeys you must take, but you will find the time. And I thought you wanted to go to the South?"

"Oh yes!" added Susanna enthusiastically. "You *must* come to the South, Tsarinovna, you must! You will love it above all things!"

"I want to," said Dasha. "I just...it's just so many journeys, and I haven't even started off on my first one yet. *And* there's...there are so many other things I still need to learn. About ruling, and about...other things."

"True enough," agreed her mother. "Well, finish this journey, and then we can talk about planning the next one. And you are right in saying there are still many things you need to learn, but that is true for all of us, and sometimes there's no better way to learn them than on a journey. Don't fear, my dove: you'll fit in all the journeys and all the learning you need to fit in."

Her mother spoke sincerely, but Dasha knew that she was mainly trying to comfort her, and it was on the tip of her tongue to point out that there were many people who *didn't* fit in all the things they needed to fit into their lives, because their lives were cut short long before they could, for example, go on even one journey. But she remained silent, and her mother and Susanna went back to talking about life in the mountains.

After her mother left them, serving women came in and took away their trays and dishes, which, Dasha could see, both awed and disconcerted Svetochka, and then she, Susanna, and Svetochka had to arrange their things and get ready for bed. Kira came to help Dasha undress, and Makvala, Susanna's maid, came to help *her* undress, which left Svetochka with no one to help her. Dasha wanted to call for Olesya, but Svetochka, looking at them all very strangely, almost fearfully, said she thought she could undress herself, only, she admitted shamefacedly, speaking barely above a whisper, she didn't have anything clean or nice to put on for the night.

"Never you mind about that," Kira told her, smiling at her easily. Kira was being polite and friendly to her, but Dasha noticed that, as friendly and easy as she had always thought Kira's behavior towards her to be, she was twice as friendly and easy towards Svetochka. Dasha didn't know whether to be jealous, or to worry that Svetochka's feelings would be hurt by Kira's casual behavior, but after watching Svetochka's face as Kira spoke to her, she had to conclude that even so, Svetochka was overwhelmed by all the attention, and if Kira had bowed and called her "noblewoman," like as not she would have burst into tears.

"We'll find you something," Kira was assuring her. "No doubt one of my own nightgowns will do."

"Surely you can find one of mine that will suit her," Dasha objected. "After all, we're closer in size."

Kira gave her a surprised look, opened her mouth as if to argue, and then said, sounding, Dasha couldn't help but notice, much less cheerful than when she spoke to Svetochka, so that her voice jangled painfully, like an untuned balalaika, "As you wish, Tsarinovna. I'm sure it would be an honor for all of us," before leaving to go fetch another nightgown. Dasha was almost pleased by her obedience, but (as she had often observed before about herself), as she had no natural taste for demanding the obedience of others, when it did happen, it left a strange flavor in her mouth, and not one that she cared for. And furthermore, there was something about Kira's obedience, just as there was with everyone else's, that suggested that it was just another tool in her quest to gain control of Dasha, which all the maids and guards and servants seemed to want to do, even as they swore otherwise.

Kira returned, carrying Dasha's plainest nightgown, the one that had a frayed seam under the arm and—oh, the horror!—a stain from when her moonblood had come upon her unexpectedly in the night. She had tried to wash it out upon rising, but the blood had already set and when they had found out about it, her maids had told her it was pointless anyway, for such an old, wornout gown, and they had taken it away from her, saying they would wash and dry it and she could keep it especially for wearing when she had her moonblood, so that she wouldn't spoil her nicer sarafans.

And then later she had overheard them gossiping about it to each other and complaining about all the trouble she was causing them with extra washing. It was one of the more embarrassing memories of Dasha's life, even though part of her, the sensible part, knew there was nothing to be embarrassed about, but just looking at the gown made her cringe. It was folded so that the stain was hidden at the moment, but Dasha knew it was there, and she was sure that as soon as Kira unfolded it, it would loom out, even fresher and bloodier than when it had first been made.

"I know that is the most comfortable of my gowns, but perhaps my sister would prefer something...less worn," said Dasha, embarrassed not only at the memories the gown inspired, and the thought of Susanna and Svetochka seeing the stain, but also that Kira would think of loaning such a tatty sarafan to a guest, and hoping that Kira would take it away without ever unfolding it.

"It's a very fine gown," whispered Svetochka, hardly daring to look at it, as Kira—oh no!—shook it out and held it up for all to see. To Dasha, who was standing to the side of her and could see both the front and back of the gown, the stain seemed to leap out and burn her eyes, and she could feel her cheeks flushing the color of her hair. But when she dared look at the others, Susanna was busy letting Makvala unpin and brush out her hair, and Svetochka, who was standing directly in front of Kira and wouldn't have been able to see the back of the gown anyway, had only glanced at it before staring back at the floor.

"I think my blue nightgown would be more suitable," said Dasha loudly. "The one with the yellow trim."

Kira frowned. The blue nightgown was one of Dasha's finest.

"It's the loosest in the shoulders and...chest," Dasha continued, still speaking loudly. "This one is a bit tight there." Which was true, hence the frayed seams under the arms. "My sister will be much more comfortable in the blue gown."

Kira made a face as if she wanted to argue, but then, to Dasha's intense relief, she folded the worn gown back up, hiding the frayed seams and the shameful stain, and carried it back off to Dasha's wardrobe, returning a moment later with the blue gown in her arms. There was a short disagreement between her and Svetochka over whether or not she would help Svetochka into it, as Svetochka was adamantly opposed to the idea at first, but Kira insisted, saying that it had ties that needed a maid's help to do up properly without spoiling it, and when Dasha offered to help Svetochka herself, everyone was so embarrassed that Svetochka agreed to allow Kira's assistance, and then eventually, eventually, they were all ready for bed.

Dasha had expected that the presence of Svetochka would mean they would all spend the night in awkward silence, but Susanna, showing herself to be a true friend as well as an irrepressible spirit, started talking about men as soon as the maids left them, and soon even Svetochka was giggling over her stories, and confessing that no, she'd never had a man either, but was curious to try.

"But a nice one," she said. "Not horrid an' old, like..."

"Yes, of course," said Dasha and Susanna quickly. "Not like that at all. A young, handsome, well-behaved one." This soon devolved into a discussion of what kind of a man each of them wanted, and where they might find such a man, although it was apparent that none of them, not even Susanna, knew the answers to either of those questions, but that, Dasha could tell, was not the point of the discussion. The point of the discussion was for them to talk about it and laugh together in the dark, until eventually they started yawning, and one by one they slipped off into sleep.

The next morning Dasha's mother and Princess Iridivadze arrived with breakfast to tell them that a meeting of the Princess Council had been called, and that they should both attend.

"Your sister is welcome as well, of course," Dasha's mother said, nodding at Svetochka.

Svetochka looked like she wanted to object hotly to the idea, but only stared at Dasha's mother and gulped in fear.

"Of course you would be welcome to join me, but if you'd prefer to see Krasnograd, or..." Dasha couldn't think of what Svetochka might want to do, "see things," she repeated lamely, "there's no need for you to spend your morning locked up in the Hall of Council, listening to princesses argue." She went over to the window and peered out. "It looks like it will be a fine day," she said. "A proper spring day. If you'd like to spend it outside, I'm sure no one would object."

"A fine idea," her mother seconded. "Perhaps Oleg would want to show you around."

Svetochka looked little more enthused by that idea than by the thought of spending the morning at the Princess Council, but since she had to do *something*, it was soon arranged that Oleg would take her around to see the sights of Krasnograd while Dasha and Susanna accompanied their mothers to the Council.

"We called the session in haste last night," her mother told them as they walked down the kremlin's whitewashed corridors. The jingling of their guards' chainmail seemed to Dasha to be ominously loud. "A message came in yesterday with news from the West."

"From Seumi?" asked Dasha.

"No, from the South, from the Middle Sea—well, not exactly. You know, I'm sure, that the empire down there continues to grow. The word is that it is moving through Alemansko and Tansko, and is now threatening Rutsi. That's what I've been so busy with, these past few days—bands of Rutsi have been fleeing their own invaders right into our lands, where they've been attacking our people in turn. The tales they've been telling have been so dire that no one wanted you to hear them, but now I think you really must. You see, the Middle Sea empire has written to us, offering an alliance, and the Rutsi have asked for our help."

"An alliance!" exclaimed Dasha. "Our help! I thought they didn't like us at all!"

Her mother smiled faintly. "It's surprising how much fondness a large army can buy," she said. "And while we haven't used it in earnest since the last invasion by the Hordes, Zem' still has the most formidable army in all of the Known World. At least in theory." She frowned. "Truth be told, I have my doubts as to how it would fare against this Middle Sea army, especially as they recruit new soldiers as they go. Their territory must now rival our own, or it soon will, if they capture all of Alemansko, and Tansko and Rutsi as well." She looked over at Princess Iridivadze. "Not that that should be announced too loudly," she added.

"Understood," said Princess Iridivadze with a sharp nod. "But the South and Avkhazovskoye stand with Zem', I promise you!"

"I am glad to hear it," said her mother, not looking very glad about anything. "And the Avkhazovskoye warriors' reputation for prowess in battle is justly earned, as is that of our steppe army—but so is that of the Middle Sea army."

"Which they gained by fighting rag-tag, half-armed Western tribes!" said Princess Iridivadze. "Let them taste a little of our true steel, and see how they like it!"

"I hope it won't come to that," said her mother. "Those Western tribes might be rag-tag and half-armed, but there are a lot of them, and the Middle Sea army has been eating away at their territory since my grandmother's time, and recently has been cutting through them like a knife through butter. And our army—yes, we have true steel, and if the Hordes couldn't break our mounted warriors, I doubt anyone could, but our foot...other than the steppe, we do not have a standing army, as you well know, and most princesses have nothing more than a small garrison of guards. Not even here in Krasnograd do we have more, and proper soldiers take time to recruit and train, and money to feed and arm, and then what do you do with them? The men you send away to battle aren't the same ones who come back. It takes a generation or more to purge that evil out of them; many of them are ruined for life, never fit to be a husband or a father or even to live amongst civilized people."

She shook her head, like a horse shaking away a troublesome fly. "But there's no need to go borrowing trouble about what might happen in the next generation," she said. "Not when there's plenty to be had now. Even our steppe army—yes, it's strong, and I'd wager on it against any invader who made the mistake of trying to cross the steppe—but that's the steppe. Half its strength is from its sorceresses, and their strength comes from the steppe itself. They can still work their magic elsewhere, but not half so well. I fear if we sent it off to fight for foreigners in a foreign land, we'd lose. And even if we won, we'd look weak, much weaker than others take us to be now, and then we'd have to fight off our own invaders."

"We can stand against anyone!" exclaimed Princess Iridivadze boldly, and Susanna's eyes flashed in agreement.

"You may very well be right—I am inclined to agree with you, providing the battle takes place here, on Zemnian soil—but I'd rather not have to put it to the test. I'd rather not have any battle at all, since there's no such thing as a battle without cost." Her mother bit her lip. "And of course, there's the fact that the Rutsi and Tatchani can offer us little that we might want. The envoys from the Middle Sea, on the other hand, have much more to offer."

"But they're invaders, and slavers to boot!" Dasha burst out. Susanna nodded in emphatic agreement.

"So are the Rutsi and Tatchani," said her mother wearily. "They're just rather less good at it. But make no mistake: they will and often do sell their own mothers into slavery, and each tribe will steal another's land at every opportunity. So the question is not whether we should help our sisters and allies against raping, slaving war-mongers, but which set of raping, slaving war-mongers we should choose to ally ourselves with."

"Can't we just ignore them all?" asked Dasha.

"I'd like to think so," said her mother. "But that's also a form of aid, in its own way. Whatever we do, even if it's nothing, will affect what happens in the West. So we will see what my princesses think."

"Avkhazovskoye has no love for the Middle Sea and its empires, as you well know," said Princess Iridivadze. "It was their slaving that caused us to seek shelter with Zem'."

"Yes, I know," said her mother with a sigh. "And glad as we are to call you sister, that doesn't change just how hungry and rapacious this Middle Sea empire is, and how ready they would be to conquer and enslave us all, just as they're doing in the West."

"Would an alliance with them truly make them our allies?" asked Dasha, and then felt embarrassed when Princess Iridivadze gave her a look of surprised respect.

"The wisdom of the gods is speaking through her mouth!" she said approvingly. "They are making their presence known!"

Dasha wanted to argue that there was nothing particularly divine in the wisdom she had just shown, as anyone with a grain of sense would ask the same question, but she only looked away, her cheeks flaming, instead.

"I'd like to think so," said her mother. "But I'd like to think even more that there's nothing divine about the wisdom in her question. Anyone would want to know the answer to that."

"But in one so young!" exclaimed Princess Iridivadze.

"Dasha has had good tutors," said her mother, in the tone of one who did not care to continue the discussion of her daughter's divine wisdom, because she didn't believe in it at all.

"Maybe that is so," said Princess Iridivadze, looking unconvinced. "But whether the tutors or the gods speak through her mouth, the question remains the same: would an alliance with these stealing Southerners make them our allies?"

"No," said her mother with another sigh. "Conquerors and slavers have no allies, merely those whom they have not yet conquered or enslaved, or who have not yet conquered and enslaved them. And these men from the Middle Sea—they look at us and they see their mothers and their sisters, whom they keep in bondage and hold in contempt, and that's what they feel for us as well. As do the Rutsi, and the Tatchani, and most of the other Western tribes. If they were ever to unite and grow strong, if they were ever to believe that they could destroy us—well, they would, my head for beheading, they would invade us and burn Krasnograd to the ground if they could, sow the black earth district with salt, cut down the forests of the taiga, choke the steppe with fences, and enslave the mountains."

"They would die first!" exclaimed Princess Iridivadze.

"Yes, yes they would," her mother agreed. "But so would many of our own people, and I'd rather not risk it. So we must think of how we can best keep them weak and off-balance enough so that it never comes to that."

"Can't we...win them over?" Dasha asked, and then tried not to shrink away from the disbelief in Susanna and Princess Iridivadze's eyes.

"Perhaps," said her mother. "My sister, whose wisdom I always doubted, and with good reason, was trying to do that very thing before...before her collapse. Her methods were," her mother made a face, "not ones I would care to use myself, and were only somewhat effective, but they kept us out of war all throughout her reign, and mine as well. And not *all* Westerners are wholly steeped in evil. Some of them are people of sense, although precious few of them make their way to our lands as envoys.

"But I do believe that they could be won over. In the long term. In the long term, that is what I would wish very much to see, although I doubt I will see it in my lifetime. But in the short term, I fear a tenuous alliance is the best we can hope for. Although even a tenuous alliance is better than war, because almost anything is better than war. The question is simply with whom we will make our tenuous alliance. I hope my sister princesses will have words of wisdom on that score."

Both Dasha and Susanna repressed snorts, Dasha rather more effectively than Susanna. Princess Iridivadze gave her daughter a reproving look, but said, "Little hope of wisdom from that...pack of jackals."

"They could be worse," said her mother. "I also used to think that nothing could be worse than my Princess Council, but then I had to try to forge agreements and alliances with the men our neighbors send us, and I realized that our princesses are the soul of reason and agreeableness by comparison. Yes, they are quarrelsome, self-seeking, and foolish, but so is everyone. Many of them do try to do their best, and their best is better than what many others would do in their stead."

"That is terrible!" burst out Susanna, and Dasha couldn't help but agree. "They should be better than that! Things should be better than that! People should be better than that!"

"Oh, how I agree," said Dasha's mother, with the glint of a smile on her face. "Everything should be better than it is, but it isn't. So we will do what we can, and thank the gods that it is Zemnian princesses we have to deal with, and not war-mongering Western barbarians or smooth-oiled lying Southerners from the Middle Sea."

With that sobering thought, they entered the Hall of Council—going in through the main doors, instead of slipping in from the back entrance in the wall—and Dasha's mother took her place on the Wooden Throne, with Dasha sitting on a little bench by her side, and all the other princesses bowed and sat down on the benches placed in an oval in the middle of the hall, with the throne and Dasha's mother at the head.

"Thank you for coming, and my especial thanks to our sisters from the South, who have honored us with their presence," said her mother, nodding towards Princess Iridivadze and Princess Oridzhnikidze.

"With their courage, and all our combined wisdom, I am sure we can find a solution to this troublesome problem beyond our borders."

All the princesses sat up straight and looked proud and confident at these words. Dasha's mother had often told her that words were the truest magic she had, and once again Dasha could see the truth of that: with two simple sentences, her mother had turned these vain, quarrelsome, stupid (Dasha thought, and felt guilty for thinking it) princesses into women bent on working together to achieve a common cause.

It was a magic that Dasha herself seemed to lack utterly (she thought despondently); why couldn't she have inherited that instead of her stupid visions...discussion and dissent was already breaking out amongst the princesses, and Dasha tried to wrench her attention back to what was happening in front of her, but the disagreement made her feel ill, and all the noise made her feel like she was about to fall asleep, something that happened to her when things grew too loud or bright or violent or...too anything, really, as if her body were trying to protect her by putting her to sleep the way bears slept through the winter in their dens. Dasha tried to clear her head and concentrate on what was going on around her.

"Those Rutsi are *barbarians*," Princess Zapadnokrasnova was saying, her cheeks flushed with indignation. "I've complained on more than one occasion about their depredations—the *atrocities* they've committed on my lands, and what the Belovy have suffered is even worse!"

"Crops burned, livestock slaughtered, and what they've done to our people..." Princess Belova choked, but then swallowed and continued, her voice shaking with rage, "peasants murdered, or"—she glanced over at Dasha and Susanna—"violated and even taken away to be slaves, or so they say—they even take little boys! They tear little boys from their mothers' arms and take them away to be slaves! And grandmothers cut down in their own huts, their granddaughters smashed to pieces before their very eyes—I've seen it myself! I will never make peace with the Rutsi nor ally with them, never, never, never, and neither will my people! I hope these invaders from the Middle Sea destroy them root and branch, and I'd be glad to lend them all the swords and all the men I have to have it done!"

"And then what!" demanded both the Avkhazovskoye princesses together. "We'll have those Middle Sea...*monsters* at our borders! Is that what we want?" Princess Iridivadze drew herself up proudly, inhaling in preparation to speak until Dasha thought her bosom might burst out of her gown. "You Northerners may not know what you speak of when you call to join with the Middle Sea empire," she said, glaring at every other princess in the hall in turn, "but we in Avkhazovskoye have fought against them and their slaving, stealing ways for generations, and I tell you, they are worse than anything you Northerners can imagine. The very fact that we agreed to swear fealty to *you* should tell you all you need to know, if we chose to be conquered by *you* rather than them!"

This led to an outburst of indignant shouting, as some of the princesses of Zem' proper protested that Zem' was not, unlike her a neighbors, a slaving, conquering nation, and had never had any intent towards Avkhazovskoye other than the most sisterly and neighborly, while others cried that Avkhazovskoye had always been a weak nation, too weak to stand on its own, and there had been nothing of choice about its decision to submit to the might of the Zemnian army. Both arguments seemed to enrage the Avkhazovskoye princesses equally, and Dasha was beginning to fear that the meeting would devolve into fisticuffs, until her mother slapped her hand down hard on the arm of the throne and called out "Enough!" in a tone that made everyone else stop dead and look at her.

"I am glad you all have so much passion for the fate of our land," her mother said, once everyone had stopped quarreling with each other and was watching her instead. "You will need it, as will Zem' and Avkhazovskoye." There was some grumbling amongst the princesses farthest away from the throne about naming Avkhazovskoye separately from Zem', but those closer to her mother remained respectfully silent, and the two Avkhazovskoye princesses even smiled in gratitude at those words. "Certainly we none of us have any reason to love either Rutsi or the Middle Sea," her mother continued. "None of our neighbors have ever given us much reason to trust them. But they are still our neighbors, and unless we move the borders of Zem', they will continue to be our neighbors."

"Now there's an idea!" called out Yelizaveta Aryonovna, Princess Primorskaya's representative, and several of the other princesses nodded their agreement. "We've done it in the past," continued Yelizaveta Aryonovna. "Once all of Zem' was nothing more than a nest of warring queendoms, with every neighbor against her sister. It was your own gracious foremother, Tsarina, who changed all that, who united the queendoms and made Zem' what she is today."

Her mother's lips twitched, and Dasha knew it was amusement at the thought of Miroslava Praskovyevna, who had sacked every town the length of the Krasna, captured Krasnograd, and made the steppe bow down and kiss her boots, being called "gracious." But when she spoke, there was no trace of mockery in her words.

"Are you proposing that we seek to integrate our neighbors into our own lands, Yelizaveta Aryonovna?" she asked.

"Seumi has long been ripe for the picking, and like as not they'd be grateful for it," said Yelizaveta Aryonovna, warming to her theme. "And from there we'd have Rutsi on two sides, and weak as they are now, they'd fall into our hands like a late-autumn apple."

"And then we would be face-to-face with the might of the Middle Sea army," said her mother.

"Who have grown weary with long years of war far from home!" said Yelizaveta Aryonovna boldly.

"Or have grown worldly-wise and cunning," said her mother. "I would not care to face them in the field."

This led to loud outcries from many of the princesses that the Zemnian army could take all comers, including the Middle Sea army, and several hints that her mother was inexperienced in the ways of war, and by nature uninclined to wage it, which was making her unnecessarily timid in the face of this splendid opportunity.

"Very well," said her mother, after the princesses had said their piece. "Say that we *do* win, and we *do* conquer Rutsi, and make them swear fealty to us and become part of Zem'. What then?"

"No one will dare assault us again!" said Yelizaveta Aryonovna, with great enthusiasm.

"No one is assaulting us now," said her mother.

"The Rutsi are!" cried Princess Belova indignantly, and Princess Zapadnokrasnova nodded her emphatic agreement.

"Raids are not all-out war," said her mother.

"Tell that to my people!"

"I know they have suffered," said her mother, fixing Princess Belova with a firm gaze. "I know they have suffered greatly, and we must do something to protect them from further depredations. But raids are still not all-out war. And if we *do* take Rutsi, and maybe Tansko as well, then what? The Tatchani and the Rutsi, these raiders, these slavers, will now be inside our borders, will be living with our people. What shall we do with them? Shall we invite their village elders to sit on the Princess Council? Most of them do not even have princesses. Shall we bring their war-lords, stinking of blood and rape, and sit them down beside us, in this very hall?"

This led to some fallen faces and some discomposed muttering, which her mother interrupted before it could grow into actual speeches by continuing, "And that will still not take care of the problem of our borders. We will still have borders, just even longer and farther away and more difficult to guard, with barbarians now on either side of them."

"So what would you have us do?" demanded Princess Belova. "Stand back and do nothing while the Tatchani and Rutsi raid our lands? Become puppets and lapdogs of the Middle Sea empire?"

"We are still Zem'," said her mother, her voice ringing throughout the hall with the steel that was always just under the surface. "We are still the greatest, largest, richest, and most feared land in all of the Known World. I hope that there will be no occasion for anyone to become puppets or lapdogs, but if there is, then it will be them, not us. Princess Belova." Princess Belova looked up at her, startled. "Have you attempted to treat with the Tatchani and the Rutsi?"

"Treat with..." repeated Princess Belova, taken aback at the thought. "With barbarians? What do they know of treaties!"

"Very little, I am sure," said her mother. Her eyes were brightening in a way that Dasha knew meant she had just had a good idea. "But they must have some inkling, else they would not have begged for our aid. I am inclined to answer their request with a proposal of my own. Let them end the raiding on our lands, and we will help them in some way."

"With troops and arms?" asked Princess Belova, looking skeptical. "Like as not any arms we sent them would just end up being used against us."

"Like as not," agreed her mother. Her eyes were even brighter, and Dasha knew that her idea had formed in her mind, and was now ready to burst forth and astound everyone with its brilliance. Dasha wished *she* could have ideas that would burst forth and astound everyone with their brilliance. But instead all she had were these stupid visions, which did nothing for her except make other people think she was queer in the head. "Let us see if we can find something else that will sweeten them," her mother was saying. Dasha could feel the pressure of a vision building, one that would tell her what her mother's idea was, but...

"And what about the Middle Sea?" asked Princess Zapadnokrasnova, breaking off her vision before it could manifest itself. "What will we do about them? Risk open warfare?"

"Not by any means," said her mother firmly. "We will treat with them as well."

"How can we treat with them if we're also treating with the Rutsi and the Tatchani?" demanded Princess Zapadnokrasnova, while a number of the other princesses nodded at her words.

"Because we are Zem'," said her mother, with a faint smile. "We can treat with whomever we choose. I dislike this warring that is approaching our borders, threatening our people. I say we treat with both sides, and see if we cannot make them see sense, or at least take their quarrel farther from our lands."

"And if they refuse?" asked Yevgeniya Marislavovna, Princess Malogornaya's proxy in Krasnograd.

"A very good question, Zhenya," said her mother, favoring Yevgeniya Marislavovna with a fond smile. "Your mother still keeps half an army in her hall, does she not?"

"Ye-es, gracious Tsarina," said Yevgeniya Marislavovna hesitantly.

"Excellent. Would that all my princesses did the same." Her mother looked out over the hall and swept the princesses with her gaze, holding each one of them in turn. "Go and begin calling up your men," she told them. "It is time for them to earn their keep. I would have my black earth princesses ready what troops you can, in case we are called upon to use them. Call them up, and send them to me here in Krasnograd. Let us buy time with these Southerners and these Westerners while we arm and train our own soldiers. The gods willing, we will never have to use them, but I would rather have them than not."

There was a long, astounded silence.

"You want us to call up our armies again, Tsarina," Princess Zapadnokrasnova finally stated.

"I do," said her mother.

"There is a reason why your foremothers did not want other princesses to keep their own armies, gracious Tsarina."

"I know," said her mother. "But this time the armies will belong to Krasnograd, instead of being scattered all over Zem', warring more with each other than with our enemies. Let the black earth district have an army like the steppe does, at least for now." She rose from the Wooden Throne. "Do we have an agreement?"

There was some muttering and some glancing back and forth between the princesses, but after a surprisingly short time, every single one of them had given her agreement.

"Splendid," said her mother. "A fine day's work for all of us, then. I thank you again for your presence, and have every confidence that you will do everything in your power to bring about the successful defense of Zem'. I am particularly pleased that my daughter was here to see this noble decision. Come, Dasha: let us retire." And she swept out of the Hall of Council, Dasha and all their guards jogging after her.

They were still moving briskly down the corridor when Princess Belova came running up behind them. She was a stout woman of middle years, and that combined with her warm woolen gown and the brightly embroidered kaftan she had thrown over it was making sweat roll down her temples by the time she reached them.

"Tsarina!" she called, gasping for breath. "Gracious mother! And Tsarinovna!"

Dasha and her mother both stopped abruptly, causing a minor collision between some of the guards.

"Gracious Tsarina, little mother!" said Princess Belova, still panting. "I...I wanted to press upon you the urgency of our situation..."

"Believe me, I take it very seriously," said her mother. "Which is why I intended to ride out to our Western borders and survey the situation."

"You do?" said Princess Belova, looking as if such a possibility had never occurred to her.

"Indeed," said her mother. "And why not? As you said, the situation is urgent, and requires delicate handling. And besides," she smiled, almost girlishly, "it has been too long since I have left Krasnograd. My daughter's forthcoming journey has called up a similar longing for the road in my own soul. Perhaps," she turned her smile to Dasha, "we will even meet up somewhere upon your return."

"You are determined to go through with this, then?" asked Princess Belova, sounding displeased. "Sending your only heir on this...ill-advised journey?"

"Dasha is not my only heir," said her mother calmly.

"Well yes, but your niece—she's hardly fit to rule! We can't have her on the throne!"

"True enough," agreed her mother with a sigh. "But nonetheless, Dasha, dear as she is to me," she gave Dasha a small smile, "is not my only heir. None of us are the only ones capable of doing what needs to be done, whatever that is. There are many others who could take up that burden just as well, if only they would agree to it."

"Begging your pardon, Tsarina," said Princess Belova, looking a little frightened at her own temerity, but determined to say what was on her mind even so, "but there's *no one* who can replace the Tsarinovna. She's gods-touched, you've said so a dozen times, chosen by the gods themselves for her role, and there's *no one* who can step in and take her place, if something were to happen to her. She shouldn't be risked like this, on a whim. I know you may want to go on this journey, Tsarinovna," said Princess Belova, turning to Dasha and giving her a little bow, "and I don't blame you: I was the same when I was a girl, mad for traveling and adventure.

"But what your gracious mother just said about you—for me, that was true. I've two younger sisters, and half-a-dozen second- and third-sisters as well, and any of them would make just as good a princess as I ever would, maybe better. It's just that I was born first, but I didn't have to be, and I'm already thinking of when I can turn the rule of Belovskoye over to my daughter, and if something were to happen to her, the gods forbid"—Princess Belova spat over her shoulder, to ward off the evil of her words—"well, I have no shortage of nieces, all of them direct descendants through the female line. But *you*, Tsarinovna—there are other Zerkalitsy, that's true enough, but not so many as we can afford to waste them, and *you*—there's only one *you*, only one whom the gods chose to be born. If you were to be thrown from your horse, or bitten by a viper, or, or the gods know what..."

"Yes, of course, we understand." Her mother glanced over at Dasha and stopped Princess Belova before she could continue listing calamities that could befall Dasha on the road, but it was already too late. Dasha could see—no, Dasha could *feel* herself being thrown from her horse, being bitten by a viper, attacked by bears and bandits...it all felt so real she was surprised to glance down at herself and not see fang marks, and she had to restrain herself from clutching at her stomach from the real pain that her imaginary injuries were causing her.

"We understand," her mother repeated. "Life and health are such fragile things, even for those who have been...who have been favored more than others. But..." she glanced over at Dasha again, and then continued, speaking slowly, choosing her words, "I am not sanctioning this journey merely because Dasha asked it of me. In fact, although I knew it was what she wanted, *I* was the one who originally proposed it, not her.

"This journey is not just about Dasha—in fact, it's not really about Dasha at all, or not in the way you imagine. It's about the rest of Zem', and the fact that the heir to all of Zem' should have some idea of how her sisters live. I believe the small risk to Dasha that it entails is more than outweighed by the great benefit to Zem' that it promises. And as for the gods...I know my princesses love to think that my daughter is gods-touched, gods-chosen, and that is true—it was the bargain I made with them. But that was merely the bargain for her conception. Dasha herself is...just like any other girl. It is not as if the gods speak through her, or anything of that nature."

"And what about these rumors of visions we hear?" demanded Princess Belova.

"Are these rumors spreading all through my council, then?" responded her mother, looking displeased. "Do you have nothing better to think of?"

"Begging your pardon, gracious Tsarina"—Dasha could tell that her mother was already regretting her outburst, but that Princess Belova could not see that—"but no, we don't. Your daughter isn't just your daughter, as you said yourself, and there's nothing more important to us than—to *Zem'*—than how she develops, what gifts she has. Humbly begging your pardon, gracious Tsarina—I bow down before you, I bow down to the ground, but—it's all our business, more than anything else that happens in Krasnograd or anywhere else in Zem'."

Her mother bit her lip in chagrin, and then opened her mouth to reply, but before she could say anything, Dasha found herself blurting out, "It's true, I have been gifted with visions. They are strong, but I am only just learning to control them, so I fear they are not of much use—yet. But I have great hopes that on this journey I will find sorceresses who can help me in my training. As you know, the Krasnograd sorceresses are less able than their sisters in the North, but it is my—our—hope that while with my kin in Severnolesnoye, the sorceresses there will be able to teach me to harness my gift."

"Well!" said Princess Belova, and then added, smiling, "in that case, Tsarinovna, gracious Tsarina, I can see why the risk would be worth it. Visions, you say! Is it farsight, do you think, or foresight?"

"I am still uncertain," Dasha told her, more confidently than she felt. "But I suspect it is more...magical than that. I suspect they show me what, what *could* be, not what is. But this is why I wish to study with the most powerful and learned sorceresses and priestesses in Zem', and the North, Severnolesnoye, is the best place to do so."

"Of course, Tsarinovna, of course, but don't rule the steppe out either!" said Princess Belova, her face now shining with barely suppressed glee.

"Indeed, we have discussed the possibility that I will go to both," Dasha told her.

"Of course you have, Tsarinovna, of course you have!" said Princess Belova. "Well, I won't keep you then...the gods be with you, Tsarinovna, on your journey—we will all be praying for you—not that you could come to any harm, not with the gods watching over you—but we will be praying that you soon come into your full strength, and learn to use this marvelous gift—visions!" she exclaimed, and bowing several times and repeating the word "visions!", she took her leave.

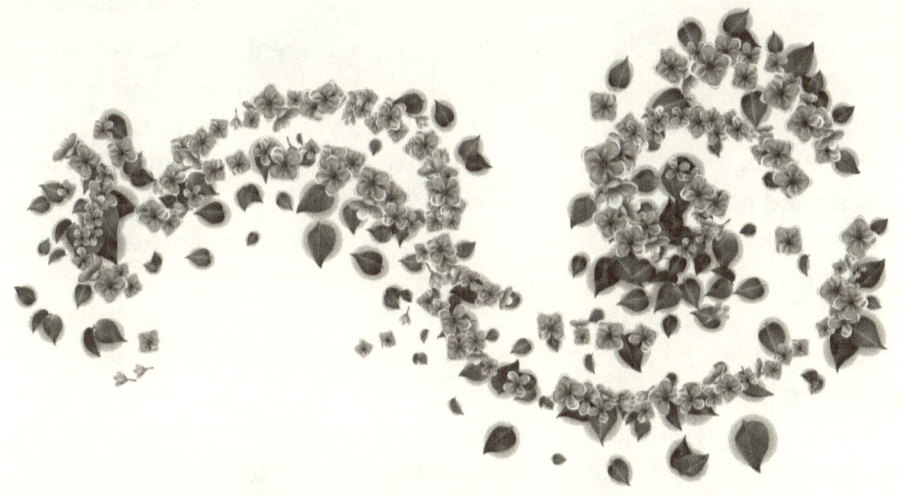

Chapter Ten

As they walked along the corridors, Dasha realized that her mother was observing her with a look of—what was it?—pride, it seemed. Pride, and approval, and something even stronger.

"That was very well done with Princess Belova," her mother told her as they approached Dasha's chambers. "Very well done indeed. I believe you have won her over completely, and with her, perhaps all the other Western princesses as well. You knew exactly the right thing to say to soothe her fears and dispose her towards you and your journey—and make her respect you as well. It was very well done. Worthy even"—her mother flashed her a grin—"of an empress."

"I didn't know I was going to do it," Dasha admitted. "And as I was doing it, I didn't know what I was doing. It just sort of...came out, like something was talking through me." A thought occurred to her. "Do you think it was the gods?" she asked, speaking hesitantly and not looking at her mother as she spoke, afraid to reveal just how much she hungered for it—even if she was afraid to admit it, even to herself, and even more afraid of what her mother's reaction might be if she learned of Dasha's desire for this sign of specialness, of exceptionality, of being something more than merely human. "Do you think they were speaking through me?"

Her mother pondered that thought for a moment, and then said, "No, my love, it seems very unlikely. I am not a priestess, and have not spent as much time in the company of priestesses as I should have, but my understanding is that when the gods speak to you, you hear them. That is certainly how it was for me. You hear them, and it is up to you to decide how to answer their call. They do not as a general rule speak through you. What you did must have been something else." She smiled again. "The magic of words, your father would say. He was the one who recognized it in me, you know, and charged me to bring it back with me to Krasnograd."

"Really?" said Dasha, temporarily diverted from her own worries by this unexpected piece of information about the circumstances surrounding her conception, of which her mother was normally so reticent. For understandable reasons, Dasha could see, and she cringed, inside at the thought of learning about the *actual* circumstances of her conception, curious as a part of her was about the act by which children were conceived, but the whole process by which her parents had become acquainted was also something shrouded in mystery, and she would have liked a little of that shroud to be pulled back.

"Really," her mother told her, smiling at Dasha with fondness and with the warmth of what Dasha could see was a happy memory. "He saw me do what you just did there, use my words to smooth things over with others, make others feel better, and he was the one who wanted to know if I would take my magic back to Krasnograd with me, and I realized then that I *would*, that I would use this simplest and deepest of magics to help all my sisters back in Krasnograd, who so desperately needed it. And I see you have it too. Of course I already knew that," she added, "but today you showed it in its full strength, just as I always suspected you would.

"And it was like that for me at first too," she told Dasha. "I wouldn't know I was going to say what I was going to say until I said it, and I wouldn't know what I was saying as I was saying it. It was like there were deep currents in my mind, that would suddenly show themselves when I came across the sandbars of strife and dissent, and propel me and my little craft over those obstacles safely." She smiled some more at the fancifulness of her image, and Dasha tried to smile with her, but in truth the thought of deep and hidden currents running through her mind was more frightening than welcome.

"And then?" Dasha asked, to take her mind off the visions her mother's words were trying to bring up. "What happened later? Is it different now?"

"Now," said her mother thoughtfully, "I have more control over it. Oh, it still acts on its own sometimes—more often than I would like, since like any gift it does not always act for good—but I can also think about how I would like to use it ahead of time, and make my plans accordingly. But that took years of practice, and no doubt it will for you as well."

"Oh," said Dasha, and tried to sound pleased and encouraged by this news. In truth, now that it was over, she couldn't stop herself from envisioning all the ways it could have gone wrong, all the ways she could have failed or made things worse instead of better, until by the time they entered her chambers, she was half-convinced that she had ruined everything with Princess Belova, or if not, that she had come only a hairsbreadth from doing so, and that next time she certainly would.

Her mother wanted to discuss the meeting more with her, and also make more plans for her departure, but before they had even sat down, a serving woman came with a message from Princess Zapad-nokrasnova, and her mother had to leave. Dasha was still in the grip of her visions of near-disaster, and was not entirely sorry to see her go, but once she was alone, she found herself worrying and worrying even more, and so it was a profound relief to have her solitude interrupted by Svetochka and Oleg's return from their tour of Krasnograd.

"Did you enjoy it?" she asked Svetochka. "What did you see?"

Svetochka looked over at Oleg as if for confirmation and support, realized what she'd done, frowned, and said, more loudly than she should have, "The beastmarket, the haymarket, some of the palaces, an' a tavern."

"A tavern?" said Dasha, surprised. "What did a tavern have that was so special?"

"Warmed ale and kvas," said Oleg. "The weather's filthy outside."

Dasha went and looked out the window. Sure enough, the fine morning had clouded over, and now there was a nasty rain mixed with wet snow, its chill palpable even through the wavy glass, pelting down onto the courtyard and filling it with slush.

"I hope it didn't spoil your tour of Krasnograd," she said. "You're not seeing it in its best light."

"The palaces was nice," said Svetochka. "Fancy. I don't see how people can live in 'em, though: they must have armies of servants to clean 'em!"

"They do," Oleg told her. "How do you think everyone else supports themselves, if not cooking and cleaning and running errands for princesses and their like?"

Svetochka frowned some more. "It don't seem right," she said. "It don't seem right as they should have so much, an' the rest of us should have to clean their boots an' empty their chamber pots. It ain't fair."

Oleg sighed heavily, but kept himself from saying anything more about his thoughts on fairness, which was good, Dasha thought, because it would have angered both of them. She had to agree with Svetochka: it wasn't fair. But she also had to agree with Oleg's unspoken thoughts: it might not be fair, but there might not be much they could do about it. After all, could Svetochka become a princess and rule others? No, Dasha had to admit to herself, she could not. Or at least she shouldn't.

"What did you think of the markets?" she asked, hoping to divert Svetochka's thoughts from the injustices of the world.

"The haymarket were good," said Svetochka, brightening. "So much hay! An' not just hay, but all sorts of other vegetables an' herbs, things I'd never seen nor heard of afore." She giggled. "Someone even offered to sell me herbs for a love potion!"

"Did you buy them?" Dasha asked, with genuine interest.

"I should say not!" said Oleg. "She doesn't need to be getting into that sort of mischief, and those sorts of potions don't work, anyhow. Not that she needs them." He surveyed Svetochka with something almost like fondness. Svetochka pretended not to notice, although Dasha could see by the hunch of her shoulders and the flush creeping up her neck that she *had* noticed, and was too embarrassed to acknowledge it, or respond with the fondness that Oleg seemed to want in return.

"What about the beastmarket?" asked Dasha, in order to break up the awkwardness that had fallen over them. "Did you see any interesting beasts?"

"Did I!" exclaimed Svetochka, brightening up again. "There was... there was dancing bears, an' wolves an' foxes in cages for skinning, an' horses from the steppe, an' birds of all sorts, even eagles an' such for hunting, an'...what was those creatures from the East called?" She giggled again. "Like horses but with two big humps on their backs, an' they smelled like a privy! What was they called again?"

"Camels," Oleg supplied. "A caravan had just come in from the East, from across the mountains," he explained to Dasha. "Some of their camels were foundering from the journey, and they'd brought them to the beastmarket to sell them for slaughter and skinning. Do you want to go see them?"

"Ah...no," said Dasha, trying very hard and failing to suppress the visions that were rising up before her from their words. She felt like a horrible coward—and she was!—for not wanting to see the camels, or the wolves, or the foxes, or any of the other animals that had been brought to the beastmarket for "slaughter and skinning."

As a child she had liked going to the beastmarket and admiring all the animals, laughing at the dancing bears, longing for a proper steppe horse instead of poky old Poloska—she was always ashamed of herself for thinking such thoughts, but whenever she saw the sleek steppe horses she couldn't help but want one, even though she suspected that her mother and her mistress of horse and everyone else was right when they told her that the steppe horses were much too hotblooded and difficult to handle for her to actually enjoy them, but even so the clean lines of the steppe horses always instilled in her a feeling that she thought must be lust, or something close—and oohing and ahing over the camels, whenever a caravan of them happened to come in, but she had never really thought about what it meant for the animals themselves.

And now that she had, she realized that for most of them, it meant capture, torture, and death, and there was nothing she could do to save them, for all that she was Tsarinovna. In fact, not only was she powerless to save them, but she herself was actually the cause of some of their suffering.

"The weather's still filthy, and I've seen camels before," she said, trying not to think about the fact that the sick and suffering camels were being forced to stand out in this filthy weather on this, their last day of life before they were to be killed, skinned, and chopped up into pieces. "I'm glad you got to see them, though," she told Svetochka.

"An' the people!" continued Svetochka, who did not appear to be affected by Dasha's gloomy thoughts at all. "Some of the people with the camels—they was so funny looking! Skin the color of honey or wheat, an' such funny eyes, like this!" She used her fingers to push up the corners of her eyes, laughing as she did so.

"Tribespeople from the Hordes," Dasha told her. "Sometimes they come here to trade." Although she had also always thought that they looked funny, and the gods knew that no one in Zem' had any cause to love the Hordes, even if their raiding was now mainly confined to the Eastern mountains and the steppe, and even that was more a nuisance than a real threat, Svetochka's laughter at them grated on her nerves. Had she ever looked and sounded like that when she spoke of them? What if she had! How awful! "They say that many Zemnians are half-Hordeswomen," she told Svetochka. "Our foremothers would take their warriors captured in battle as husbands sometimes, in order to freshen the bloodline."

"Or more commonly," put in Oleg, "we would give their women sanctuary, and take them into our families and give them our sons as husbands."

"Why?" asked Dasha and Svetochka together.

"The Hordes are a bad place for women," he told them.

"How?" asked Svetochka.

"You don't need to know," Oleg told her, his face closing. "And I'd best be on my way, now that I've brought you back to your sister. Try to stay out of trouble, girls, once you're on your own."

Dasha was about to tell him that she never got into trouble, but then she remembered how she had run away into the park without her guards, and had to hold her tongue on that score, promising him they would behave, instead.

"It ain't true, is it?" Svetochka asked, as soon as they were alone. "We ain't got Horde blood, do we?"

"Mostly in the steppe and the mountains," Dasha told her. "You probably don't, and I only have a little bit. You can't really see it in me, but you can see it in my mother. She has slanted eyes too, you know. Most people from the steppe do."

"Really?" Svetochka examined Dasha's own eyes closely. "I think yours are a bit slanted, too."

"Probably," Dasha said. "Just a bit." She grinned. "The Stepniye will be glad to see this sign of their blood in me. They're always moaning about how I'm not steppe-like enough."

"Hordeswoman!" cried Svetochka, grinning back and shaking her finger at Dasha. "Coming to steal our men!"

"Hordeswomen have to freshen the bloodline too!" Dasha said, and then they both collapsed into such a fit of laughter at the thought of freshening the bloodline by stealing a Zemnian man for a husband that they had to sit down on the bed to recover themselves.

"Maybe that's what my mother needs," said Svetochka, once they had calmed down enough to speak again. "Maybe she should steal herself a Hordesman!"

This led to more giggles, which ended when Dasha asked, "Do you think she wants another husband?"

"I...I dunno," said Svetochka, no longer mirthful at all. "She's had such trouble with 'em, you know? Running off an' leaving her just when she needs 'em." Her face fell further. "She musta had the baby by now," she said, after a moment of calculation. "And now I'll never know how it went! I'll never know if she's still alive, or if I have a sister or a brother."

"You could write to her," suggested Dasha.

Svetochka laughed, but this time it was not a very nice laugh, with nothing of merriment to it at all. "Write to her! Like either of us know any writing!"

"Well..." This was a complication Dasha had not expected. She knew that many people never learned to read or write, and that most of her guards, for example, could do no more than scratch out their names, but she had never met another girl or woman who was totally unlettered. "*I* could write her a letter, and she could find someone to read it to her and write out her reply," she said. "Surely the village elder of Ozyorsk knows her letters, even if your mother doesn't."

"As if she'd help out the likes of us with something like that!"

"She might, if you were nice to her," said Dasha, more sharply than she'd intended. And just as she'd feared, Svetochka bridled at her tone and snapped back, "*You* try being nice, after all the things as've happened to me!"

"Probably lots of things have happened to other people, too," said Dasha. "But many of them still manage to be nice." She had meant it to be conciliatory and helpful, but as soon as she said it she realized, both by Svetochka's expression and her own thoughts, that it had been pretty much the worst thing she could have said. "I know it's difficult," she went on hastily, hoping to smooth over what she had done. "I know you have good reasons for...how you are, but you can make things better for yourself if you can get other people to help you, and the best way to do that is to be nice to them."

"How would you know?" demanded Svetochka, her lip curled in a hurt that she was managing to cover up almost entirely with an unpleasant sneer. "*You* don't have to be nice to people to get 'em to do things for you."

For one awful moment, Dasha thought she was going to scream at Svetochka, slap her face, throw her down on the ground and smack her head against the floor until she forced her to admit how wrong she was and how much Svetochka was taking all her hurts and magnifying them into something much worse than they already were, in a vain attempt to turn herself into some kind of, some kind of, some kind of

Empress of suffering, that's what, as a way to make herself special and deny, not only the specialness, but the very existence of everyone else in the world, as if somehow erasing everyone else would erase her own pain, even though all it did was increase the pain of everyone around her while doing nothing to ease her own. No one had ever properly nourished Svetochka, nourished her in spirit the way a little girl and a young woman should be, Dasha could see it, see it with her true sight.

And so now Svetochka was desperately trying to feed herself, but the only way she could think to do it was by snatching sustenance from the mouths of others and stuffing it down the gaping maw of her own starving self-regard.

"What're you looking at me like that for?" demanded Svetochka. She edged away from Dasha. "You've come over all queer."

"My apologies," said Dasha. She clenched and unclenched her fists, and took a long deep breath in and out of her nose. "Sometimes I get these, these visions, and they...they make me come over all strange, as you said."

"Visions? Like what a sorceress'd get?"

"Sort of, I suppose," said Dasha.

"How'd you learn to do that?" asked Svetochka. She sounded genuinely curious, her enmity towards Dasha temporarily overcome by her interest in her abilities.

"I never really learned...our family has gifts, you know, and they manifest themselves in different ways in each person, so..."

"Not *our* family," said Svetochka, crossing her arms and going back to being angry at Dasha. "*Your* family, you mean. *Our* family don't have no gifts at all."

"Every family has some kind of gift," said Dasha automatically.

"But some are worth more 'n others. So where'd you learn to do these visions?"

"I didn't learn them anywhere. They just happen to me," explained Dasha.

"Can't you control 'em?"

"No. Not yet, at least. My mother says I should have some training, but none of the sorceresses here in Krasnograd are strong enough to teach me. She says I'll need to go elsewhere for my training, to others who are stronger in magic. The steppe, most likely, or maybe there will be sorceresses in Severnolesnoye who can help me."

"Hah," said Svetochka, trying and failing to conceal how impressed and how envious she was. "Seems like you shoulda started training ages ago. You mother shoulda sent you off years ago."

"The visions only became strong recently," said Dasha.

"You shoulda started training afore they became strong," said Svetochka, with an authority that puzzled Dasha. Svetochka had never mentioned any knowledge of magic before, nor had she ever shown any desire to be helpful to Dasha. So why was she giving her this advice now?

"Have you studied magic yourself?" asked Dasha. Perhaps Svetochka had been apprenticed to a sorceress, or something like that. After all, Dasha didn't actually know her that well. She could have lots of stories, lots of experiences, that Dasha knew nothing about.

"A sorceress?" said Svetochka contemptuously. "Me? Why'd I be 'prenticing to a sorceress? Where'd you get that idea from?"

"You spoke of magical training with such certainty..."

"It's just common sense, it is," said Svetochka loudly, overriding whatever else Dasha had wanted to say. "It's just common sense you should start training *afore* you start having problems, not after."

"What if you don't know that you need to start training until after you've started having the problems?" asked Dasha.

"What if...a fine sorceress you'd make, if you couldn't foresee something like that!"

"I don't think it's that easy," said Dasha doubtfully.

"'Course it is. Hain't you ever seen anyone do magic afore? It's easy as snapping your fingers."

"I think if it were that easy, everyone would be doing it," said Dasha.

"Hah! It's just 'cause the sorceresses don't want everyone knowing their secrets, that's why."

"I suppose that could be true," said Dasha. "Do you have any sorceresses back in Khladniye Vody, or Ozyorsk?"

"In Ozyorsk I don't know. I never saw any there, other 'n the traveling ones as'd come through two-three times a year an' sell their charms an' spells. In Khladniye Vody we had...well, we had Baba Anya. She weren't exactly a sorceress, but she weren't exactly not a sorceress."

"The one who...helped your mother with, with Mark's wife..."

"That's right. She were a good herbwoman, always could cure anything as ailed you. Lived off in the woods by herself, but she'd come quick enough if you needed her—half the time she seemed to know you was ailing as soon as you did yourself. Only last winter she didn't come. Everyone said she were gone."

"Do you think she...died?" asked Dasha.

"Some said so, an' some said death don't mean the same for the likes of her as it does for us. We never found no body, though, no nor sign the wolves'd come an' taken her. Some said she just went off into the woods, to be with...her kind."

"Her kind?"

"You know." Svetochka gave her a sideways look. "Like...like Oleg Svetoslavovich. Someone who serves the gods. Who's been taken by 'em, become a part of 'em, a little bit."

"You think Baba Anya was like that?"

Svetochka shrugged again. "Most likely. An' most likely she were called back to 'em. It happens, you know: they give you your life, more life 'n you'd've had without 'em, but then one day they call you back to 'em, an' they take it. You think that'll happen to Oleg Svetoslavovich? Well, it'll have to. You think it'll happen to him soon?"

"I don't know," said Dasha, to whom such an awful thought had never occurred before. "But I don't think so. I think he'll have to stay with us for a while, because of..."

"'Cause of you," Svetochka finished for her.

"And all of us," said Dasha quickly.

"Don't think they care so much about me." For a moment Svetochka no longer sounded angry, just sad. "I think once you came along, they stopped caring about the rest of us at all."

"You were born for a reason," Dasha told her. "Just like I was. You were born for a reason, and they must still care about you, too."

"You think so?" asked Svetochka, glancing up from where she was staring at her fingers before looking back down again.

"I'm sure of it," said Dasha. In the back of her mind she was uncomfortably aware that her certainty was the same kind of certainty that Svetochka had possessed when she had spoken about training in magic, but she still felt that those were the right words, and she had to say them. "Of *course* they still care about you, and you're still important to them. And to me too. So please, Svetochka, let me write a letter for you to your mother, so that you can find out how the birthing went, and how she is, and how the baby is, and everything else you want to know. And...and we can send them something, too. Money, that is, to help them, until you can go to them in person with the money you've been promised."

"I ain't got no money to send 'em."

"But I do. And I want to help them."

"Why're you doing this for me?" asked Svetochka again, but this time in a low, uncertain voice, and she looked away as she spoke. "For her? An' for the baby. Why're you doing this for 'em?"

"Because we're sisters. You and I are sisters, and that makes your new sister almost like a sister to me, too."

"She ain't your sister," said Svetochka, some of her earlier sullenness returning. "You an' me may be sisters, but you an' she ain't."

"But you and I *are*, Svetochka, we *are* sisters, and helping each other—that's what sisters do. So please let me help you in this way."

Svetochka bit her lip and looked down. Dasha could feel herself holding her breath, hoping that Svetochka would see reason, would agree.

"Very...very well," said Svetochka slowly, looking back up. "I'll...I'd be ever so grateful..." She choked on the last word, and stopped.

"Wonderful!" said Dasha. "Let's write the letter, then."

"What, right now?"

"When else?" asked Dasha. "We set off in the morning, so we need to have the letter finished and entrusted to a courier by this evening."

"A courier?"

"Someone who carries messages," explained Dasha.

"I don't think no courier would carry any of *my* messages," objected Svetochka.

"Well..." This complication had not occurred to Dasha. She corresponded regularly with her kin in Severnolesnoye and the steppe, and no one had ever begrudged her a courier to carrier her messages, but then, no one ever would begrudge a courier for a message from the Tsarinovna to a Severnolesnaya or a Stepnaya. But Svetochka...

"What's your family name?" Dasha asked her abruptly.

"It's only you nobles as have family names," Svetochka told her. "Not the likes of me."

"You *should* have a family name," Dasha told her. "Something like...like...what kind of name would you like?"

"I dunno." Svetochka was trying to appear indifferent, but Dasha could see that she was struggling not to smile at the thought of having her own family name, and at imagining what it could be.

"Khladnovodovskaya?" suggested Dasha, with a smile.

"The gods forbid!" cried Svetochka. "By the time someone got 'Svetlana Svetlanovna Khladnovodovskaya' out, I'd be long gone, or fallen asleep, or something."

"Hmmm...Ozyorovskaya?"

"I ain't no Ozyorsk woman," said Svetochka, her lips pursed in disdain.

"Severnaya!" suggested Dasha with a grin. "Snezhnaya! Ledyanaya!"

"Moroznaya!" said Svetochka, joining in the game with a matching grin. "Metel'naya! V'yuzhnaya! Zamorozhennaya!" By now she was laughing so much she could hardly get the words out.

"I wonder..." said Dasha.

"What?" asked Svetochka, still half-breathless with laughter at the thought of being a "Blizzard woman" or "Frozen woman."

"Do you know...does our father have a family name?"

Svetochka sobered up. "You'd know better'n me," she said. "I never heard nothing of it, but you'd be the one to know, not me. 'Course—weren't he wed, properly wed, to Princess Severnolesnaya as was?"

"Ye-es," said Dasha.

"Then he'd be a Severnolesny."

"I don't suppose you could take that as a family name," said Dasha with a sigh.

"Not likely," agreed Svetochka. Dasha had expected the thought to throw her into another fit of resentment and anger, but she only shrugged and said, apparently sincerely, "Not that I'd want it, either. But I suppose I could be..." she paused for thought, "Olegova? Olegovskaya?"

This provoked an extended fit of giggles in both girls at the thought of taking a man's name as a family name, which was only brought to an end by Dasha remembering the matter at hand, and saying, "Well, it doesn't matter at the moment. I'm sure we'll find someone to carry the letter to your mother, and she can't be that hard to find, no matter what name she does or doesn't have. Come: tell me what you want to say, and I'll copy it out for you."

Svetochka followed her, still giggling, over to her desk, but then, when Dasha sat down, took out paper and quill, and looked up at her expectantly, she froze.

"What d'you say in a letter, anyway?" she asked.

"Whatever you want," Dasha told her.

But this helped not at all, and Dasha quickly realized that the art of composing anything in writing was so foreign to Svetochka that she had no idea even how to bring her thoughts together enough to make a beginning, as she was overwhelmed by all the possibilities of what she could and should say, and made so many suggestions and then withdrew them, that Dasha had crossed out more than half a piece of paper before she was able to break in and say, "People often start off by wishing the other person well."

"What, like...like..."

"Like this," said Dasha, and wrote:

My Dearest Mother,

I hope you are doing well, and that you have safely been delivered of your burden, and I am able to welcome a new sister into the world. My thoughts and prayers have turned to you every day since our separation, and if the gods are good, they will have heeded them.

"That don't sound like me at all," objected Svetochka.

"Well, what would you like me to write?" asked Dasha, taking out another piece of paper.

"I...say...I dunno, say something like that, I s'pose, but...it's like, it's like those *are* the thoughts I were thinking, only, only the words ain't mine."

"It's how people write," Dasha told her.

"Well why don't they write like they talk?"

"It's also how people speak," Dasha said, with less patience than she would have liked.

"No it ain't!"

"It's how people who write speak," said Dasha, with, regrettably, even less patience than before. She expected Svetochka to explode at this statement, but, to her surprise, she nodded and said, "Yes, that's true enough. It's how *you* speak, ain't it?"

"More or less," said Dasha.

"Well then. I s'pose it'll have to do. And it *is* what I've been thinking. Now what?"

"You could tell her where you are, what you're doing."

"Do it," said Svetochka, with a decisive nod of her head. "Only... make it sound like writing, but like *I* wrote it."

Dasha puzzled for a moment over how to achieve this, and in the end gave up and wrote:

*I am pleased to inform you that, after a long journey, I am
safely arrived in Krasnograd, where I have been taken under
the care of my sister, the Tsarinovna Darya Krasnoslavovna.*

"That sounds grand," said Svetochka. "'Taken under the care of'!
Only it don't sound like something I'd write."

It was on the tip of Dasha's tongue to point out that nothing could
sound like something Svetochka would write, since she didn't write
at all, but she managed to stop herself before the words, which would
have caused nothing but hurt, got out. Instead, she dipped her quill
and continued silently:

*She has graciously invited me to accompany her on her jour-
ney to our kin in the North, and it was with great pleasure
that I accepted her kind offer.*

"That's not what happened," complained Svetochka.

"Yes, but it's how you would write about it," Dasha told her. "It's
how you will make your mother happy, when the letter is read to her."

"By lying to her?" Svetochka demanded suspiciously.

"It's not a lie," Dasha said. "It's just a way of explaining the truth
that will make her happy. And besides, it's how people write."

"You keep saying that. Don't people ever write the truth?"

"Generally what people write is the truth. Otherwise why would
they bother writing it down?"

"Hah. It sounds like lying to *me*."

"So what would you like me to write?"

"Tell her...tell her..." But once again the difficulties of composition
overcame Svetochka, and she waved her hand dismissively and said, "I
guess that's fine. Tell her I'm coming back to her."

Dasha dipped her quill in her inkwell again—only to see, as she
lifted her quill out of the ink and noticed how the plume bent and
waved as she moved it through the air, how the swan it had come
from—as the Tsarinovna, she had always been given *swan* feathers,
not goose feathers but *swan* feathers—had been raised in some pond
on the edge of Krasnograd.

And then one day the person who had fed him and kept him his
entire life lured him over with bits of bread, and then grabbed him

and—quickly, so quickly he had no time to fight back, but not quickly enough, no not quickly enough for him not to know that something was wrong, something terrible was happening, the worst thing in the world was about to happen and he couldn't escape—wrung his neck with an awful *crack*, and then plucked out the feathers, saving them for the Tsarinovna so that she could have her *swan* feather quill and her *swan* down bed, and cut up the body, ripping open and destroying the only thing the swan had ever had, the most precious thing in the world to him—no, not him, *her*, Dasha thought, it could have been a *her*, just like Dasha—ripping and chopping her all apart, so that the Tsarinovna and her mother and her guests could dine on swan flesh.

"Akh!"

"What's wrong?" Svetochka had grabbed her arm. Blotches of ink were spreading out all over the paper, ruining the half-written letter.

"It's spoilt!" Dasha cried. "You made me spoil it! Now I'll have to start all over again!"

"Me! You was the one twitching an' staring off at the wall like a half-wit! I were just bringing you back! What's wrong with you?!"

"It's...It's..." Dasha took a deep breath. "I apologize," she said.

"You say that all the time, but you don't mean it! What happened, Dasha?"

The sound of her name on her sister's lips, the first time she had dared use it, the first time she had treated her like a sister, calmed Dasha down, and gave her hope that perhaps Svetochka would listen to her with sympathy.

"I had a vision," she explained.

"Again! Can't you stop 'em?"

"Apparently not," said Dasha tartly. But instead of taking Svetochka aback, this only made her shake her head and say, "Well, you should try! You can't be having visions all the time like this, not if they're gonna be making you fall into fits like that."

"If I could stop them, I would!"

The two girls glared at each other. Dasha was the one to break first.

"My family's gifts are...not like ordinary magic," she said, looking away and speaking as much to the window as to Svetochka. "They're... they're often much more difficult to control, and they don't come when called, not like the magic of a sorceress. There's no one I can go to for help and training, not really."

"What about your mother!"

"Her magic isn't like mine."

"How ain't it like yours? You both have the magic of your family, don't you?"

"Yes, but...it manifests itself differently in each generation, in each person. My mother...well, she claims what she does isn't really magic at all. She just knows what other people are feeling. Not reading their minds, but feeling her way into their hearts. She says she gets visions sometimes, but they're just little visions, and they don't come very often. Whereas I...I have some of her skill, I think, I often feel what people are feeling, a bit, but not like she does, or at least not yet. While the visions...they come all the time now, faster and faster, stronger and stronger, and when they come they bring with them this strange awful feeling all over my body, that I can't get rid of except by having a fit, and...and trying to stand against them...it would be impossible, but even if I tried, it would...I think it would only make things worse."

There was a short, painful silence after this confession. Then Svetochka said, "Can't your mother help at *all*?" She sounded accusing as she said it, but Dasha still saw, or felt, in a flash of either one of her own visions, or her mother's power, that she was angry because in her heart she cared about Dasha, and was angry at the thought of her suffering, and no one being able to help her.

"No," said Dasha. "She says...she says that maybe there are those who can, that maybe...maybe I need to go off with, I don't know, leshiye or domoviye or something"—both girls shuddered involuntarily at the thought—"but she certainly can't, and neither can anyone else, not...not from the world of women, anyway."

"Oh." Svetochka looked like she wanted to argue against this, but instead she said, "What...what was your vision about?"

"Oh. It was...terrible."

"Like something bad'll happen to you?"

"No. Nothing like that. My visions—they're not visions of the future, not really."

"Of the past, then? Of far away?"

"No. Or yes. Or...it's more like...possibilities. Like I see how things are, or could be. Some of the things...I think some of the things I see are real, but a lot of the time it's of things that could possibly happen, or it's of...not exactly what really happened, not truly, but it's...the essence of what happened. Like what I see might not have all the exact details of what really happened or is going to happen, but I'll see... how things were. Inside. How everyone felt, and how...it's like, it's like someone telling you a story, you know? Like when someone tells you a story, and you see everything that they're telling you, and even though what you see isn't exactly what they see or what they saw, it's still 'real,' it's still 'true,' because it's what happened in the story, it's just how *you* see it, not anyone else."

"Oh." Svetochka looked as if she had only partially understood what Dasha had said, but had decided not to argue about it. "So...what did you 'see'?" she asked.

"I saw..." Dasha closed her eyes, and then reopened them. "I saw this quill...and then I saw where it had come from."

"Like...the village where it come from?"

"No. The swan."

Svetochka gave the quill another, startled look. "That's a swan?" she asked.

"A feather from one."

"That...do people usually use swan feathers to write with?"

"No. Usually they use goose feathers. I have swan quills because I'm," Dasha's voice became sharp, sharper than she had ever heard it before, "*special*. But it doesn't matter. Swan, goose—it's all death."

"Death?"

"They kill the birds to get the meat, and sometimes feathers too. That's what I saw," explained Dasha.

"Oh." Svetochka considered this. "But they'd kill 'em anyway, for eating, even if you didn't use the feathers, wouldn't they?" she asked.

"Yes, but...I'd never thought about it before, about how what I'm holding in my hand, what I use every day, it's...death. And not a natural death at the end of a long life, but some creature being killed just so that I can use its body. But then I saw it. It was...it was horrible."

"Oh." For a moment Svetochka looked like she wanted to argue with Dasha, probably to tell her she was too soft or something of that nature, but then she said, speaking low and fast and not looking at Dasha, "Like when...like when I killed our cow. That were horrible too."

"I'm sure," said Dasha sympathetically.

"I didn't think it would be," said Svetochka. "I...I never could stomach watching animals being slaughtered, I'd always hide inside with my eyes closed an' my hands over my ears on killing days—though it were fun afterwards, when we'd make balls out of their bladders an' fill 'em with air an' toss 'em back an' forth—I just couldn't stand the killing itself, but I didn't...didn't think it'd be as bad as it were. I...I told myself it were the only thing, the only thing as could be done, me an' mother'd agreed it were the only thing as could be done, an' she were so weak, I said I'd do it myself, an' she told me how to do it, an' gave me the knife, an' then...

"An' then I had to walk out to the barn myself, with that knife in my hand, knowing what I were about to do...it were the longest walk of my life, I never woulda believed how long it were, but that knife weighed so heavy in my hand, so heavy...I fancied as how I could see blood on it, old blood, but that were only me fancying things...an' then I were in the barn, I were walking up to her, an' she were looking at me as she always did, thinking I were gonna feed her..." Svetochka stopped and gulped. Dasha wanted to say something comforting, but no words came to her mind or her mouth.

"I...I hid the knife behind my back, thinking that way she wouldn't get scared, but she still knew something weren't right, as soon as I came up to her she sensed something weren't right an' she started snorting an' tossing her head, an' I...I had to drive her outside, an' she didn't want to go, she knew, she knew, an' I...I...I had to shout at her, to, to, beat her to make her go..." Now Svetochka was shaking. Almost without realizing it, Dasha reached over and took her hand. After a moment, she continued:

"An' the whole time I were thinking: 'How awful that she knows, if only she didn't know it wouldn't be so bad, but she knows, she knows, somehow she knows, an' that's the worst, that's the worst, what would it be like to be led to your death like that, knowing, knowing, knowing it's certain, it's certain, that in twenty paces, then ten, then one, you'll stop being *you* and just be...just be...just a pile of meat, not you at all, just a pile of meat for others to tear apart and swallow down an' shit out...An' I felt, I felt, right then I felt that it were the worst thing, what I were doing were the worst thing ever, a hundred times worse 'n hunting, 'cause with hunting they don't know it, they don't know they're being hunted, an' even if they know there's always the hope of escape, but with this...with this there ain't no hope, no hope, no hope..." Now Svetochka was crying, and Dasha could feel her own eyes filling up with tears as well.

"At least you were able to give her a quick death," she said. "Better than starving to death."

"That were what I were telling myself...but with starving there's still hope, still hope, but with this...it weren't her choice, an' she couldn't escape it, an' the more I thought that, the angrier I got with her, an' the more I shouted at her an' hit her, till I'd dragged her outside behind the barn, an' then...an' then it weren't such a quick death anyway, not like I'd thought it would be, she bellowed an' staggered around like crazy, blood going everywhere, an' she were scared an' hurt, scared an' hurt, an' if I coulda stopped it then I woulda, only I couldn't, she weren't dead yet but she were an' there weren't nothing I could do to stop it, nor nothing I could do to make her suffer any less, an'...an' the whole time I were thinking: 'What if she didn't have to die, what if it's all a mistake an' she didn't have to die, how much time we'd both have! How well I'd treat her, an' how much time we'd both have! 'Cause one day this could be me.

"An' then...an' then she were dead. She were dead an' neither of us had any time left at all. It were her lying there, only it weren't, 'cause she were gone, gone, gone, just like my grandmother an' my grandfather, an' then...then I looked up, I looked up beyond the barn an' I saw how the sun were shining, it were shining an' hitting the trees just so, the trees as was covered with ice an' hoarfrost, an' the sun were shining on 'em an' everything were shining an' sparkling like it were alive, an' I thought as how this were her now, she'd become this...this shining sun an' sparkling frost, only...even so, it still weren't her, no more'n the dead body lying at my feet were, nor the blood as had sprayed all over me an' ruined my clothes, an', an', an' I didn't understand none of it, an'...an'..." Svetochka was crying too much to continue, and Dasha had joined her.

"That's what I saw too, in my vision," she said, once she had brought herself back under control. "Only it was a swan instead of a cow."

"Well..." Svetochka shook her head and wiped her eyes, and then said, "It's how things are, though. There ain't nothing as we can do about it."

"There has to be," said Dasha.

Svetochka gave her a strange look. "No there don't," she said. "Why should there be? It's the way things are, is all."

"I...I think...I think..."

"You having another vision?" demanded Svetochka, when Dasha paused and stared off at the wall.

"Perhaps. Perhaps I'm having a vision telling me that there is a reason why we both had these same visions," said Dasha slowly.

"I didn't have no vision! You're the one with visions!"

"But I saw...I had a vision very similar to your actual experience, and you...you had a vision too, while you were...while it was happening."

It took a little while for Svetochka to puzzle through all this and work out what Dasha was saying, but once she had, she shook her head stubbornly, her former distress at the memory of killing her cow already forgotten, or perhaps firmly squashed down, and said, "You're the one as has visions. I don't."

"We're sisters," Dasha argued. "It stands to reason that we would both have visions."

"No it don't! 'Cause your visions come from your mother!"

"Well...yes. But...the gods wanted us born, you know. They wanted *both* of us born. So maybe you can have visions too."

"That don't make no sense!"

"Well," Dasha gave her as encouraging a smile as she could manage, "you must have *something* special about you. After all, they wanted us for *some* reason."

"They wanted *you*." Svetochka's resentment was twisting up her face and growing in her voice. As if looking at her from somewhere far away—was this another vision?—Dasha could see that by nature she was a warmhearted girl, if a trifle hot-tempered, but that half the time, her natural warmth was distorted into something...malevolent. Or potentially malevolent. For a moment Dasha could see her balanced on the edge of a precipice, wavering, about to fall...

"Why're you shaking your head?" Svetochka demanded.

"I beg your pardon," Dasha told her. "I was thinking of something else. But it's true, you know: they *wanted* you. How many of us are that lucky? How many of us are born because we're wanted?"

"*You* was," said Svetochka sourly. "Not me."

"You were too," Dasha argued. "The gods wanted you, and your mother must have wanted you too, otherwise, why did she carry you?"

"No one wanted me," Svetochka insisted. "I'm not like *you*, I'm not *special* like you, I'm not wanted like *you*, I'm not like you, I'm not like you, I'm not like you..."

"You are," Dasha interrupted her.

"So why..."

"Why did I grow up in a kremlin and you grew up in a village?" Dasha said. Svetochka's jaws clenched and her cheeks flushed.

"Stop reading my thoughts!" she snapped.

"Well don't be so obvious with them!" Dasha snapped back, and then wished she hadn't, but it was too late to take back her words, which triggered such a flood of complaints (many, Dasha had to admit, justified) and invective (not justified at all, to Dasha's mind) on Svetochka's part that Dasha was entirely unable to stem the flow, and could do nothing but listen to her until her ranting had run its course, and then ask her if she wanted any tea. Which enraged Svetochka so much that she ran out of Dasha's chambers, slamming the door behind her.

Chapter Eleven

The door had not even stopped shaking from the force of Svetochka's anger when it swung open again, letting in her mother.

"Was that Svetochka?" she asked. "Have you girls quarreled?"

"I'm sorry!" cried Dasha. "I didn't mean to!"

"Quarrels are like that," said her mother, her mouth quirking. "The worst ones happen when you're not expecting them, and then— babakh!—they hit you in the face out of nowhere."

"*You* never quarrel," Dasha said.

Her mother's mouth quirked up at the corners even more. "No? It seems to me I quarrel with people every day."

"I mean, not like this. Not like we did. Not over..." Dasha swallowed, and then forced herself to say, "stupid things that you shouldn't have said or done."

"Ah," said her mother. "That kind of quarreling. Well, I'd like to say I've outgrown it, but in truth, it's surprisingly difficult to outgrow. Like spots on your face: you think once you reach your twentieth summer and become a woman grown that you'll have left them behind forever, but for most of us that's not true at all. They keep coming back; for years and years they keep coming back, long after you think you've left all your girlishness behind."

"You've never had any spots on your face," said Dasha in surprise.

Her mother laughed, but without any malice. "Oh, how I wish! I was plagued with them when I was your age, and it wasn't until you were born that they went away completely." She gave Dasha a fond smile. "You cured me of them. They say that happens sometimes: you bear a child, and all the little problems—spots, and itching, and strange headaches—that plagued you when you were a girl go away, once you become a mother. To be replaced by other problems, of course, but there's nothing like novelty, especially in ill health.

"But as for quarreling and saying the wrong thing without meaning to, well, all I can say is that practice helps. If it's something you want to learn how to avoid, how to manage so that you say the right thing instead of the wrong thing, then practice helps. Just like when you said the right thing this morning with Princess Belova. You *knew*, a part of you *knew* what to say, you just had to get the rest of yourself out of the way. Not quarreling with people is sort of the same. Part of you knows how to say the right thing instead of the wrong thing, and you just have to give that part of you control, and not let the other part, the part that wants to say the wrong thing, take over and blurt out all kinds of awful things that you can't take back."

"I don't think what I said was so *very* bad," said Dasha, and then thought back on what she had said, and started to worry that she had said something terrible, something unforgivable that she couldn't take back.

"I very much doubt that it was, my heart," said her mother.

"I just...she made me so *mad*, I was trying to make her feel better and tell her that we were sisters, that we were alike, and she got so angry with me, well, not with me exactly; she's angry because she grew up in a village and I grew up here, and she's angry with Oleg for coming here instead of going to her, and, and, and she's so mad about everything, and the things she's mad about, well, she's right to be angry about them, I would be angry about them too; in fact, I *am* angry about them too, on her behalf, but she doesn't believe me, she doesn't *want* to believe me, she doesn't want me to help her, even though that's why she came here, for our help, but when we offer it to her, she wants to knock it to the ground so that it dashes into a thousand pieces, and, and, and," the thing that had been bothering Dasha most about Svetochka finally came bursting out, "she doesn't want to believe that anyone else has any troubles, she acts like because she has suffered, no one else has, that no one else could possibly ever have the troubles that she's had, or that other people's troubles couldn't possibly be as bad as hers, but that's just not true! It's selfish and mean, and it's just not true! I know that I haven't had the troubles that she's had, but she...when I tried to explain to her about the visions, she wanted to act like they were all my fault, and no trouble besides, and...well, all she thinks about is herself and her own troubles!"

"Yes," said her mother dryly. "It's funny how the troubles we aren't having always seem so much better than the troubles we are having, especially when they're happening to other people. And as for her turning away your help, well, I'm afraid that's only to be expected. People who've been hurt, you see, they expect to be hurt again. They see the outstretched hand and they think it's reaching out to hit them and push them down, not lift them up. Because that's the way it's always been before. And, maybe even worse, they want to hit others and push them down just like has been done to them, but they're too afraid to do it to the ones who need it, the ones who did it to them. They want to rebel, but they're too afraid, so instead of rebelling against the ones who are holding them down, they rebel against the ones who are lifting them up. After all, those people won't hit them back."

"That's just stupid!"

"By some measures, yes," said her mother. "But not by others. And that is how it happens. It takes a very strong woman indeed to break that pattern. And maybe one day Svetochka will be that strong of a woman, but right now she's a frightened girl who's had to leave behind her mother and the only home she's ever known, and so that's how she's acting."

"I know I should feel sorry for her," Dasha continued unhappily, "and at first I did, I felt sorrier for her than I had ever felt for anyone in my entire life, but now, even though her suffering hasn't gotten any less, I feel less and less sorry for her! The more she tries to make me feel bad for her and bad about myself, the angrier I am with her, and the less bad I feel for her, and the worse I feel for myself! And I hate it! I hate that she's making me into a, a *bad person* by trying to force me to be a good person! She's making me selfish against my will!"

For one awful moment, Dasha thought her mother was going to laugh at her, but then she sighed instead. "Yes," she said. "Such is the way of many people, I'm afraid, especially those who've suffered. You know, they say that suffering ennobles. And maybe it does. Or rather, sometimes it does. Certainly you can never be a truly good person without undergoing at least a little of it. But it depends on the suffering, and even more on the person doing it. Some people—many people—can only handle a little bit of suffering before it breaks them down, and with enough suffering, anyone can be broken."

"That's awful!" cried Dasha. "It's...it's not fair that Svetochka should have been given more suffering than she was able to bear!"

"Yes." Her mother sighed again. "It *is* awful, and unfair, and that's also the way the world works, sometimes. There's no," she gestured up at the ceiling, "power watching over us and balancing everything out so that everyone receives exactly what they need and deserve. There's just life, which only cares about going on living, and not about any of the things that we women believe are so important and hold so dear."

"But the gods..." protested Dasha.

"The gods most of all," her mother said firmly. "The gods are in the business of life, and nothing else. Whatever justice, or mercy, or fairness, or goodness we're going to find in the world of women, we'll have to make for ourselves."

"So what can I do?" Dasha had meant that to come out as a demand, but it sounded more like a whine to her ears, and she would have taken it back if she could.

"About life? Not much," her mother said. "About Svetochka? Well, I know she can be...annoying, and difficult, and all those other things, but that doesn't change the fact that she's your sister and that her suffering was real."

"Sometimes I doubt it," said Dasha, more waspishly than she would have liked.

"I know," said her mother, giving her, to her surprise, a sympathetic smile instead of chastising her as she would have expected. "And maybe you're right and her suffering was not as great as she believes it to be. Certainly others have suffered as much, or much much more. But that doesn't mean that she isn't unhappy, or that she doesn't need your kindness and compassion, no matter how much she might try not to deserve it."

"And if she refuses it? Because she seems determined to refuse it!"

"She must walk her own path," her mother told her. "As must we all. But that doesn't mean you shouldn't keep offering her a shoulder to lean on, whenever you see her falter."

"It'll only make her mad," Dasha predicted gloomily.

"That," said her mother with a smile, "is her problem."

"Not if she takes it out on me!"

"Well," said her mother, with another smile, "in that case, don't let her." She patted Dasha on the shoulder. "I know it's a trying situation," she told her, "and there isn't a good way to fix it, not right away, but she *is* your sister and she *does* need your help. And you're going to be going on a long journey with her, so you'll all have to spend lots of time together and help each other out, whether you want to or not. So just... keep being patient and kind. It's remarkable how that tends to wear down even the most obstreperous opponent."

"But it's so hard!"

"There would be no merit in it if it were easy," her mother told her. Which shouldn't have been comforting, but it was. And then Susanna came back, laden with packs from where she had been packing her things in her mother's chambers, and Dasha's mother invited all the Southerners to join them for a farewell supper in her chambers, and when the time came they all crowded in there together and consumed large amounts of food—although Dasha passed on the roast boar, she hoped unobtrusively—and drank a number of toasts of vodka and mead on honor of the girls' adventure.

Dasha's mother sent serving women off in search of Oleg and Svetochka, to invite them as well, but they all came back with the report that Oleg Svetoslavovich had taken his daughter off to a tavern to hear the performance of a famous singer, one who had gotten her start singing with Lyudmila Krasnoslavovna, Svetochka's (and Dasha's, of course, although Dasha had never met her) half-sister, and who had promised to give Oleg Svetoslavovich and his daughter a full report on Milochka's doings, and so he thanked the Tsarina for the generosity of her invitation and promised to return Svetochka in one piece by the end of the evening, but he couldn't return to the kremlin until he had spoken with the singer.

Dasha felt bad for feeling glad that Svetochka wouldn't be joining them, but without her anger and self-pity, the group was much lighter and merrier, and they passed a very cheerful evening (probably helped by the large quantities of vodka and mead they consumed), which included several rounds of Southern songs sung very loudly and poorly, before Dasha's mother and the princesses kissed Dasha and Susanna several times on both cheeks and told them to get as much sleep as possible before their big journey. Which words ensured, of course, that they would be up half the night with the excitement of it all, along with the need to run (staggering slightly) to the privy over and over again to relieve themselves of all the vodka and mead they had drunk. No one had ever warned Dasha of this queer effect, but Susanna said it was normal. In that case, Dasha resolved to be more circumspect in her imbibing in the future, and in the present had to settle for lying on top of the bedclothes and fanning her flushed cheeks and hoping the drink would pass through her sooner rather than later.

Sometime in the middle of the night Svetochka came stumbling into their chambers, giggling and tripping over the furniture.

"You're drunk too!" Susanna and Dasha both hissed at her, sitting up.

"Too?" she asked, and giggled some more.

"Our mothers had a seeing-off party," Dasha explained, still slurring her words slightly. "There was vodka and mead. And toasts. Lots of toasts. We had to. It was a seeing-off party."

"You had to!" Svetochka started to laugh, all-out earnest laughter. "I...I..." she was choking on her own laughter, "I had to too!" Now all the girls were snorting and choking on their own laughter, until they all collapsed onto the bed together.

"Where did Oleg take you?" Dasha whispered.

"Why're you whispering?" Svetochka said, very loudly, by way of reply.

"The maids might hear us," Dasha replied, still whispering.

"So what!" said Svetochka, still much too loudly, sitting up and trying to get off the bed, while Susanna buried her face in her pillow to stifle her uncontrollable laughter.

"So...so..." Dasha couldn't think of why that mattered. "So we don't wake them up," she finished lamely.

"Aha." Svetochka nodded with owlish solemnity. "Aha. Aha. Aha. So's we doesn't wake 'em up. Aha. Aha. Aha..." Her "ahas" turned into more laughter, which turned into sobbing, which turned into hysterical shrieking, so that Dasha and Susanna had to jump up and wrestle her back down onto the bed and cover her mouth with their hands, until her shrieking turned to tears, and her tears to silence.

"I don't think I like being drunk," she said, once they had decided she was ready to be released, and took their hands from her mouth.

"Me neither," agreed Dasha, wiping sweat from her face and wishing she could open the windows. She knew it was really too cold outside to do so, and she would never hear the end of it from her maids, and maybe even her mother, if she did so, but between the drink and the wrestling she was sweating all over, as if she had just come from the bathhouse.

"Oleg Svetoslavovich," said Svetochka, speaking very slowly and deliberately, "took me to a tavern," there was a brief outbreak of giggling, quickly suppressed, "where he told me a lot of stuff, an' then introduced me to some singer he said knows...knows our, our sister Milochka."

"And did she have anything interesting to say about Milochka?" asked Dasha, pricking her ears at this information. She had always been curious about Milochka, about whom she had heard so much from her mother. She had discovered last year that Milochka came frequently to Krasnograd, but that she had never been taken to meet her, which she considered strange.

When she had pressed her mother on it, her mother had looked, most unusually for her, uncomfortable, and then confessed that there were members of the Princess Council who objected to Dasha's peasant blood, or rather, objected to the idea of her spending time with her low-born sisters and becoming friends with them, and so, in order to keep the peace, her mother had acquiesced to their demands that Dasha be kept apart from her sisters, even Milochka, who had won fame for herself the country over with her singing, and who, under other circumstances, would have been invited to the kremlin on every opportunity to entertain them.

"It isn't fair," her mother had told her. "Not to you and not to Milochka. But some of my princesses were...extremely adamant about it, and some things, like a lot of strife, are worse than a little injustice. Someday you will have the opportunity to know your sisters, I promise you."

"Which princesses?" Dasha had demanded, but her mother had told her it was better for her not to know, and much as it pained her to admit it, Dasha had to agree. Her mother's princesses were her mother's princesses, closer and more important, it could be argued, than any half-sister through the male line who didn't even live in Krasnograd, and peace with them and between them was worth almost any price.

"She's in the North," Svetochka told them, her tongue struggling to pronounce the "r" in "North." "She spent the winter in Pristanogorod. An' she had a child. Another child. Fourth or fifth. Something like that."

"So I suppose," said Dasha, weighing this strange idea in her head as she spoke, "that makes us aunts."

"I ain't no aunt!" Svetochka protested automatically.

"If our sister has children..." began Dasha.

"She ain't our sister!" Svetochka interrupted her. "She ain't no sister to me! She ain't never done nothing for me!"

"Mmm," said Dasha. Part of her wanted to say that Milochka was their sister whether they wanted it or not, whether they ever met her or not, but she could sense that that would only enrage Svetochka further, so she held her tongue.

"Maybe you will meet her in Pristanograd!" said Susanna, who was clearly not restrained by such considerations.

"I ain't going to Pristanogorod!" cried Svetochka.

"Mmm..." said Dasha again. "But if we stop there..."

"But you're stopping there *after* Lesnogorod, ain't you? An' you'll be leaving me behind in Lesnogorod, won't you? You'll be leaving me behind, won't you? Leaving me behind!"

Dasha wanted to tell Svetochka, and rather sharply too, that she had things all wrong, but she didn't know how without making things even worse. Susanna, however, said, with a cheerfulness that was guaranteed to be even more irritating than anger, "Do not be silly, Svetochka! Of course we will not be leaving you behind!"

"You *will*! You'll be dumping me off with Olga Vasilisovna, an' leaving me behind!"

"Dumping?" repeated Susanna, looking at Dasha in her bewilderment.

"Like throwing away," Dasha explained to her.

"Ha!" Her linguistic confusion resolved, Susanna laughed with easy contempt at the notion. "Do not be silly, Svetochka: of course we will not throw you away—'dump' you. If you want to stay with Olga Vasilisovna, stay; if you do not want to, do not."

"That's easy for you to say! I hain't got nowhere else to go!"

"Of course you do!" Susanna told her, still speaking with that breezy contempt-tinged good cheer that Svetochka was—and, Dasha had to admit, rightfully so—finding so maddening. "You have lots of places you could go! After all, you went all the way to Krasnograd, did you not?"

"Yes, but I don't want to go through that again, an' I spent all my money besides."

"So get more!"

"How?"

"Work for it. Or ask your sister."

This didn't smooth things over at all, and it took a while to soothe Svetochka's hurt feelings and convince her that she wasn't going to be thrown away, dumped, or anything else terrible, while they were on the journey, and that if she didn't want to stay with Olga Vasilisovna, they would arrange something else for her, although she kept saying she didn't know what else she could do, and all the suggestions they gave her were met with scorn and distaste. It wasn't until they were able to distract her by getting her to talk about the dishes she had tried in the tavern—fresh camel meat had been on the menu; Dasha almost cried out at the vision this news evoked, but managed to pass it off as indisposition caused by drink—that they were able to calm her down enough to convince her to get into bed and get some sleep.

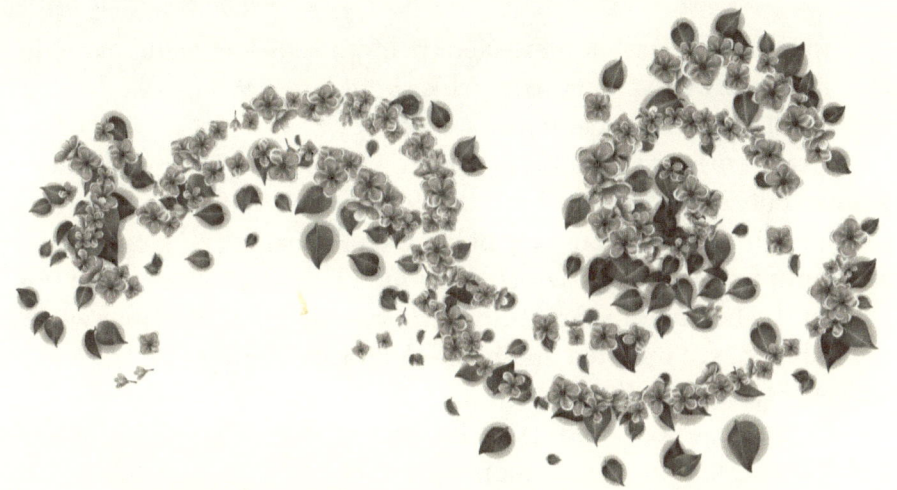

Chapter Twelve

Kira came bustling in much too early, or so Dasha thought, the next morning, although when she had woken them all up and Dasha dragged herself over to the window, she discovered that the sun was already breaking over the kremlin walls, and that it was high time for them to be up and about and preparing for their big journey, little sleep as they had gotten the night before.

"I think I have a...what do you call it? A *hangover*," said Susanna, pushing herself upright against the headboard of the bed. She considered that for a moment. "I must be a proper woman now!" she said, a tiny bit more cheerfully. "A woman grown, to have a hangover!"

"Why?" asked Svetochka sullenly. "Did that mead come with a man last night?"

"Alas, no," said Susanna. "I wish it had!"

"Once you've known men like I have, you'd say different," Svetochka told her, with even more ill humor than before.

"Why?" asked Susanna. "How many men have you known?" Dasha couldn't tell whether she was genuinely curious or trying to take Svetochka down a peg: probably both.

"Enough," said Svetochka, looking away as she said it in a way that let them both know that, just as she had already told them, she hadn't known any men at all, not in the way Susanna had meant.

"I do not think that one horrid old man who tried to grab you is the same as real experience," Susanna said. "It only counts if it is fun!"

"Your letter!" Dasha interjected, before Svetochka could explode with resentful accusations. "Svetochka, your letter! We should finish it and give it to a courier before we set off!"

This led to more grumbling, which, Dasha thought privately, was at least half caused by what looked to be a vicious hangover; while Susanna felt fresh enough to brag of her own ill health, and glory in this marker of womanhood, Svetochka sat for a long time slumped on the edge of the bed before she could summon the will to rise, and when she did, her eyes were red and bruised, and she moved as if her head were a precious egg about to crack.

"I'll go see to our breakfast," Dasha said, and slipped out of her bedchamber into the maid's room next door.

"Kira!" she hissed, interrupting her from where she was setting out things for the girls to wear. "Oh, good morning, Makvala! Kira, what do you recommend for hangovers?"

"Too much mead last night, Tsarinovna?" asked Kira, with a smile that was meant to be solicitous but had a little too much amusement in it for her to carry it off entirely.

"No, it's not for me. Actually, I don't think I'm hungover at all," said Dasha. "Which is strange: I must have drunk just as much as the other girls."

"It's the blood of the gods," said Kira, nodding significantly.

"I never heard of the gods protecting anyone from a hangover."

"The gods work as they will, Tsarinovna," said Kira, her conviction in Dasha's divine protection strong in her voice.

"Well, be that as it may, it's not me who has need of a cure, it's Svetochka. Is there something you can bring her?"

"Her!" said Kira. "Not that you'd expect any better from her!"

"It wasn't like she was out being...dissolute," said Dasha. "My father...our father...took her out to a tavern last night to hear word of our...our sister Lyudmila Krasnoslavovna, and, well, she must not have much of a head for drink."

Kira snorted in contempt at this news of Svetochka's weak head for drink, although a moment ago she had been prepared to believe that Svetochka was an inveterate drunkard.

"And Susanna Gulisovna as well," Dasha said, turning to Makvala. "Not so bad, but she is suffering too. If you happen to know of some potion, some concoction from the South, perhaps..."

"My mistress suffers?" exclaimed Makvala. "I go now! To kitchens! I know! I know what needs...what is needed! I bring herbs from mountains, good herbs, helping herbs. I go now, I make everyone tea."

"Thank you, Makvala," said Dasha.

"Just don't you go drinking any of that 'tea' yourself, Tsarinovna," Kira told her, once Makvala had left the room. "The gods alone know what she'll put in it. She gave me something yesterday, some strange thing she said was a sweet, but it weren't sweet at all, not like a proper sweet, and so full of herbs I couldn't hardly choke down a bite, and I swear my tummy kept turning all the rest of the day from it. Let them others drink the tea if they want it, but don't you go drinking it yourself. The gods know we've enough trouble today without calling in a healer for you as well."

"I'm sure Makvala wouldn't do anything to harm her mistress," Dasha told her. "She seems very respectful of her, and cares for her greatly." Then she was worried that Kira would catch the meaning in her words and take offense, but if Kira did, she gave no sign of it, shooing Dasha back into her bedchamber and telling her they needed to be dressed before Makvala brought up breakfast, if they wanted to set off before the sun reached midday.

And by the time Makvala and Olesya brought in the trays with their breakfast, all three girls were dressed in their traveling clothes, with their packs lined up against the bed. The sight made something go fluttering in Dasha's chest and stomach in a way that was almost pleasurable, and almost painful as well.

Dasha had worked up quite an appetite by this time, but both Susanna and Svetochka were still sitting listlessly at the breakfast table and waved the food away with a squeamishness that Dasha suspected was real in Svetochka's case, and feigned in Susanna's. The tea that Makvala had promised looked rather like any other tea to Dasha's eyes, with a pleasant, slightly sweetish, very spicy smell. Susanna downed several cups in quick succession, and managed to persuade Svetochka to try some too.

"It ain't bad," said Svetochka, perking up a bit after a few swallows. "I thought it'd be foul, but it ain't bad at all. What's it got in it?"

"Ah, what do you call it...cinnamon?"

"What's cinnamon?" asked Svetochka warily.

"A spice from the East," Susanna told her. "From very far away. Very dear, but so tasty, and so good for health! And ginger. Also a spice from the East," she added, guessing Svetochka's next question. "And mint and...chamomile, I think you call it? Take some, Tsarinovna: it is very good for health!"

"Well, there's certainly nothing there to be afraid of," Dasha said, and, checking that Kira was off in the other room, tried a cupful. It was spicy, just as she had guessed it would be, but not unpleasant, and far from sickening her, made her feel clearer-headed and revived.

"Come," she said, rising from the breakfast table and going over to the desk where she kept her writing things. "Let's finish your letter, Svetochka, before we set off."

Svetochka made a face that showed just how little she liked having Dasha suggest things to her, even if they were things for her benefit that would only be completed if Dasha took charge of the process. A vision of the air-filled bladders of slaughtered animals Svetochka had told her about yesterday filled Dasha's eyes, telling her...telling her that Svetochka was just like one of those bladders, always bouncing but only moving because she was hit, and only going in the direction that others sent her, as if she had never learned how to direct her own behavior towards anything at all, only away. But that was much too cruel a thought for Dasha's comfort, and made her wonder if the same couldn't also be said about herself, so she quickly suppressed it and took out the letter they had begun the day before.

"Would you like to tell her that you will come visit her?" Dasha asked. "Or tell her where to direct her letters to you? Perhaps to Lesnograd?"

"When'm I ever gonna be able to see her!" Svetochka demanded petulantly.

"I'll tell her to direct her letters to you to Lesnograd, then," Dasha said.

"She won't write to me! Even if she wanted to, she wouldn't know how!"

"You never know," said Dasha. "Perhaps she'll be able to find a scribe. There must be some lettered women there, even up in Ozyorsk." Although she had to admit to herself the truth of Svetochka's words, she had become oddly determined to have her own way in this matter, and ensure that Svetochka sent a letter to her mother, even if Svetochka was determined to thwart her. Accordingly, she moved her breakfast dishes aside, set down the letter and writing instruments, and, dipping her quill in the black pool of ink—which, she thought, should be the red of blood, to signify the bloody source of her writing tools— and wrote:

> *It is my hope to take up service with Olga Vasilisovna Sever-*
> *nolesnaya; if I am successful, I may have the opportunity*
> *to call upon you during my travels. In the meantime, if you*
> *happen to have the occasion to reply to this missive, even*
> *with just a few lines to assure me of your health and happi-*
> *ness, I would be most grateful. Until you hear from me oth-*
> *erwise, you may direct your letters to me to the Lesnograd*
> *kremlin.*
>
> *I bow before you and offer you my heartfelt duty, embraces,*
> *and prayers for your continued health and prosperity.*
>
> *Your loving daughter,*
> *Svetlana Svetlanovna*

"What're you saying?" Svetochka demanded, craning her head over Dasha's shoulder and squinting at the letters forming in shining black ink.

"We should teach you to read while we're on the road," Dasha told her.

This, predictably, provoked a minor tantrum on Svetochka's part, but once Dasha and Susanna between them had calmed her down and convinced her that the offer was real, not mockery, and that learning her letters would be both possible—Svetochka insisted several times that she didn't have the mind for it, and nearly cried with outrage and indignation when Dasha and Susanna both insisted that she did—and beneficial, she listened quietly enough to Dasha's recitation of the letter's contents. Once Dasha finished, though, there was another round of protests, denials, and complaints, which was only cut short when Dasha's mother, Princess Iridivadze, and a whole host of guards and serving women came in and told them it was time to depart. Dasha used the moment of distraction to slip the letter, unchanged, into Kira's hand and ask her to send it to Ozyorsk by the next courier North. A part of her told her she should be ashamed of her deception, but another, new and brash, part of her told her that the only way to help Svetochka, paradoxically enough, was to go behind her back until she was healed enough from whatever had made her this way to act with sense.

"Is everyone ready?" Dasha's mother asked. "You are? Marvelous!

It's a beautiful day to begin a journey—I quite wish I were going with you, but," she smiled almost girlishly in her excitement at the thought, "I may be joining you on the road soon enough. Oleg and the guards are already waiting for you down on the yard, with the horses. Some of the princesses wanted a grand sending-off in the Hall of Council, but I said no—it's late enough as it is, almost mid-morning, so I told them that if they wanted to send you off, they could come down to the square like the rest of us. Is everyone ready? Are all your things packed up?" She cast her eyes around the chamber, and, finding nothing that should have been packed away, said with almost feverish cheerfulness, "Grab your packs, then, and let's set off!"

She led them at a brisk pace out of Dasha's chambers and down the corridors and stairways that led to the yard, chattering with that feverish brightness the whole time, probably, Dasha realized, to distract all of them from Princess Iridivadze's tearful words of farewell to Susanna, and Susanna's concomitant embarrassment. Or maybe her mother wanted to cry just like Princess Iridivadze was doing, and was trying to stop the flow of tears with a flow of words?

This was a startling thought to Dasha. She knew that parents always complained of the sorrow of parting with their children, but that had always struck her as strange, given how inevitable such a parting was, and how much most parents complained of the burdens their children laid upon them as long as they were still living under their roofs, and it struck her as particularly strange that her mother, who had organized the whole expedition, would be struggling not to break down now that the moment was finally here.

Only...it was too awful...even though this was the most anticipated moment of Dasha's entire life, now that she was actually walking down to the yard, her shortsword buckled onto her belt and her packs slung over her shoulder, she wanted to turn around and run back to her chambers and hide, and when she thought of not seeing her mother for months on end, a lump rose in her throat and threatened to choke her. And it could be longer than months, too, it could be forever: Princess Belova was right when she said traveling was dangerous. A dozen ways that she could be crippled or killed appeared in Dasha's mind, threatening to choke her even more than her unshed tears. For an instant she thought she might be sick, or scream.

"You see!" said her mother, as they came out of the palace and onto the yard. "Such a perfect day to set off on a journey!" And it was true that the spring sunshine was so bright it was almost blinding, so that for a moment Dasha had to cover her eyes and couldn't see anything, not even where her horse or her father or her guards were.

"What's everyone doing here?" hissed Svetochka. "Why're there so many people?"

Dasha unshielded her eyes. It seemed as if half the princesses of Zem' had come out onto the square, along with their households, and they were all clapping and cheering. At them, Dasha realized. For them. They were clapping and cheering for Dasha, because she was about to set off on a, a ride. A long ride, true, but a ride, just a very long version of the picnics she would take in the park. She wanted to shout at the princesses that they were being silly, coming out to cheer her for going off on a ride, which she had done almost every day since she had grown large enough to sit on a pony unassisted.

"Wave at them!" her mother told her, lifting her own hand and giving a stately wave to the princesses and servants and everyone else who had come out to see Dasha off.

Dasha wanted to argue that it was silly, it was all silly, the whole thing was silly, ridiculous even, and she didn't want to encourage it by waving at all her wellwishers...that word snapped her out of her sulk, and made her realize how, well, *silly* she was being herself, like a little child, so instead of saying all the things she was now embarrassed for having thought, she lifted her hand and gave a little wave too. The onlookers cheered even more enthusiastically than before, making Dasha want to cringe away or shout at them that she hadn't done anything special and they were wasting their time by cheering her.

She turned to say something to Susanna about it, but Susanna was waving and smiling at everyone, and so was her mother, their earlier tears and embarrassment forgotten. Which was—could it be true?—maybe this was the point of the whole exercise? For everyone, nobles and commoners alike, to see the Tsarinovna walk out onto the square side-by-side with the heir of the most powerful princess in Avkhazovskoye, and her own common-born half-sister.

Dasha glanced over at her mother, hoping to catch some kind of confirmation of her suspicion in her eyes, but her mother was looking around and smiling and waving just as she always did, in a way that made others feel good about themselves, without losing any of her own authority. Which may have been confirmation in itself. This whole thing could have been carefully staged, Dasha realized, to demonstrate the Tsarinovna's close relations with the newest, most troublesome, least loved, proudest and angriest province in Zem', as well as her blood relationship with the common people. Which was… Dasha didn't know how she felt about that.

She wanted to be outraged, both at being used that way and at the calculating nature of it all, but…her mother's smiles seemed genuine, as did the enthusiasm of all the people who had come to see them off. It was all genuine and real, Dasha thought, even if it had been staged to be so, and it was truly making things better for everyone there, even if they were also being manipulated. And it wasn't entirely artificial, either, since they did have to set off from somewhere, and that somewhere needed to be the square or the stableyard, and the square was the most convenient, so it was as if everything had been made to fall together in a way that was completely natural and yet also staged for everyone's convenience. Which was altogether a very confusing thought, one that Dasha was glad to stop thinking.

"Is that Seryozha? Is that whom they gave you?" her mother asked, pointing to where Oleg and the guards were waiting for them with the horses.

"Ah, yes," said Dasha, eyeing Seryozha's fleabitten, dirty-gray coat with disfavor. While the other horses were all looking around with interest and even sidling back and forth in their excitement, Seryozha was just standing there, his head hanging and one hindfoot cocked, looking even more unprepossessing than she remembered.

"Such a good horse!" said her mother encouragingly. "I remember when he was born. He's half-brother to my Rozochka, you know. They both have the same sweet nature."

"Yes," said Dasha. Her mother was passionately fond of Rozochka, and still visited her regularly, even though she had been retired out to pasture the year before. Rozochka, though, was a beautiful rose-gray, and even in her old age still arched her neck proudly and pranced like a filly of two. Whereas Seryozha just looked as if he hadn't been groomed properly, was unattractively slab-sided, ewe-necked, and angular (Dasha thought uncharitably), and appeared to be about to fall asleep. Dasha looked over at the huge black stallion that was Susanna's horse, who was currently snorting his delicate nostrils and dancing back and forth in his impatience to be off, his muscles rippling under his coat that had preserved its shine even though he was shedding, and felt nothing but embarrassment at her own horses. True, Poloska was fine enough, neatly built and with a brilliant chestnut coat that dappled in the summer, but she was at least a hand shorter than Susanna's horse, with none of his brilliance, and Seryozha…Seryozha looked like he wasn't good enough to be a packhorse for the guards, let alone her horse. Dasha was ashamed of her thoughts, but that didn't stop her from thinking them.

"And I thought we were going to have to wait here all morning!" her father said by way of greeting as they came up to him, much to Dasha's annoyance. She made a painful and half-hearted attempt to smile at him as the stablehands took their packs and buckled them onto the saddles and legged them up and handed Dasha Seryozha's leadrein, and then her mother and Princess Iridivadze were squeezing their hands and reminding them to take care and to write every chance they got, and Dasha thought her mother was choking back tears, and then Oleg was saying it was time to set off if they wanted to get anywhere at all that day, and they were setting off at a sedate walk—although Susanna's horse was crowhopping and sidestepping out of impatience at their slow pace, and Svetochka was proving herself already to be no horsewoman at all, clutching fearfully at the pommel of her saddle with one hand as she yanked confusingly on her reins with the other, and looking even angrier and more frightened than before when Oleg and the stablehands tried to correct her, while her horses, Dasha had to admit, were behaving themselves perfectly—and everyone was cheering and crying out well-wishes, and her mother was definitely crying now, and then they were past the barracks and the stables and had turned onto the street that led past the park, and very soon they were past the park and out into Krasnograd proper.

They kept their slow pace as they made their way down Brother Street, named for the brothers' sanctuary set against the Northern end of the park, to the haymarket, where between the two of them Svetochka and Susanna's horses nearly knocked over a wagon carrying a load of last year's precious hay, and then down Northgate Street to the North Gate. Mitya, who was in charge of their guard detail, wanted to pick up a trot then, as otherwise they'd spend half the day just getting through Krasnograd, and Seva and Alik seconded him, but Oleg said no, Svetochka hadn't learned how to trot yet and he didn't want to risk it until they were out of the city, and Susanna's Chernets was likely to explode if they let him go any faster than his current crabwise jigging, besides.

"He just needs to be given his head!" Susanna said, at the same time as Svetochka declared indignantly, "I do too know how to trot! I've ridden before, plenty of times! Just not with a saddle."

"Let me guess," said Oleg. "Riding the plowhorses home after a day in the fields?"

"There's nothing wrong with that!"

"No," said Oleg. "But it's not really the same as real riding, either. Poor Sverchok," he added, nodding at Svetochka's horse, who was plodding along with his head down, at least as placidly as Seryozha. "Teaching a new rider's never any fun. Well, he'll teach you soon enough, if you're able to learn."

"I can ride!" insisted Svetochka, her cheeks stained with an angry flush. "I can even trot!"

"Hmmm," said Oleg. "Which would you prefer: for me to teach you, or for your sister to do you the honor? To be honest, she'd probably be the better choice, if she'd deign to do it, seeing as how she's been trained to it since before she could walk, and has the sweeter temper besides, but it's up to you."

"I'd be happy to teach you," said Dasha, but when Svetochka only glared at her, dropped the subject.

"There is hardly anyone out on the street right now," Susanna put in. "We should trot, like Mitya said."

"Not till we pass the gates," Oleg told them. "And why the hurry? This is your chance to see Krasnograd, girls! The Northgate road isn't as pretty as the South Gate and the Southgate Road, it's true, where the finest of the sanctuaries are located, as well as the palaces of the steppe and mountain families, or Black Earth Street, where all the black earth princesses keep their palaces, but there's plenty to see nonetheless—merchants' houses, and traders from the North, and all such things."

"I would rather see traders from the East," said Susanna.

"They'll be coming down the Eastgate Road," Oleg told her.

"I wish we had gone out the East Gate, then!"

"No you don't," Oleg said. "The East Gate isn't a very nice place. That's where all the poor folk live, and where they pen the beasts before bringing them to the beastmarket, and where they're building an abattoir."

"What's an abattoir?" Susanna and Svetochka both asked at once.

"A place to slaughter animals," Oleg explained. "Lots and lots of animals, to feed all of Krasnograd."

"Well, that is good," said Susanna.

Dasha found herself catching Svetochka's eye, even though neither of them relished the contact, and she knew they were both thinking of the same thing, of Svetochka's story about killing her cow. Suddenly a fierce rage rose up in Dasha, one that made her feel as if something were catching fire inside of her, threatening to lift her up right out of her saddle and carry her away to where the people building that abattoir were working, so that she could strike them down and burn them to ash. She had to cling to that image, the one of her killing everyone working there and of smashing and burning the abattoir itself, to keep the other images, the one of the animals being killed, from overwhelming her and making her scream out in pain. She was so focused on her inner vision that she hardly saw anything of Krasnograd itself until they crossed through the North Gate and were riding through Outer Krasnograd.

"This is dreadful," said Susanna, looking around at the hovels and the muddy streets with distaste.

"You should see it by the East Gate," Oleg told her. "Then you wouldn't think this was bad at all."

"No thank you," said Susanna, wrinkling her nose. Dasha found herself wrinkling her nose as well, from the smell more than the sights: there was a rich smell of mud from the churned-up streets, and an even richer, although that was probably the wrong word, smell of every kind of manure, including human.

Dasha knew that her mother had set scholars to studying the methods of the Middle Sea, of the empire they were currently so concerned about, for ensuring clean water and waste removal, in hopes of cleaning up Krasnograd, particularly Outer Krasnograd, and reducing the fluxes and poxes and other nasty illnesses that raged through the city every year, especially in the poorer districts where there was no clean water at all. But many people, including the very people who would benefit from it the most, that is, the people living in Outer Krasnograd, were suspicious of the idea and thus far had resisted all her attempts to introduce a system of collecting clean water and running it through pipes and troughs to the neighborhoods in need.

Many scholars and sorceresses held that boiling water before drinking it would also prevent many of the fluxes that ravaged the city, especially in the spring, and Dasha's mother had insisted that the water served in the kremlin be boiled before drinking, but that cost more time and fuel than the people who needed it most had to spare.

Dasha tried not to imagine diseases emanating from every person they passed, or rising up from the street and caking their horses' legs with the mud they were slogging through, but once the thought came to her, it became firmly fixed in her mind and she couldn't shake it.

She told herself that she had never been seriously sick, not even with the measles or scarlet fever that every child underwent, so that her nurses had said she was protected by the gods, and when she had cut herself, none of her little wounds had ever turned putrid, but looking at—and smelling—all the dirt around her, she couldn't help but think that even the gods wouldn't be able to protect her from infection here.

These unpleasant thoughts were dissipated when they left Outer Krasnograd behind and began riding through the fields that stretched for versts and versts in every direction away from Krasnograd. The snow was almost completely gone, with only a few drifts left here and there in the shadows under groves of trees, which were budding out in a haze of sticky green buds. Some of the fields were already greening with their crops of winter wheat and rye, the plants pushing up through the soil after lying under the snow all winter. Groups of peasants were already out plowing and sowing other fields, preparing them for the barley crop, and their own horses neighed in greeting at the horses in the fields, who pricked up their ears and whinnied back.

"Let us *go*," Susanna urged. "The ground is good, and we cannot walk all day! Let us *go*!"

"Very well," said Oleg. "Let's trot a bit. Dasha, you can instruct your sister in the art of rising to the trot."

"I know how to trot!" Svetochka insisted once again, but as soon as they began trotting, it became manifestly obvious that that was not true. She jounced in every direction and at every moment except the one when she should have been rising from the saddle, when she always managed to smack down on it hard enough to make Dasha wince, and all the men look away. But when Dasha told her she need- ed to feel for when her horse's feet were moving, and know which foot was moving forward and move her body with it, Svetochka glared at her as if she were insane, and responded by yanking cruelly on Sver- chok's mouth instead.

"Sverchok's never done anything to deserve that!" Dasha said, or rather, shouted, at her. "And you never punish your horse in the mouth anyway! Imagine what that would feel like if someone did it to you!"

But this only made Svetochka even angrier and less able to listen to Dasha's instructions, which made her bounce around even more painfully, so that Sverchok, probably the placidest horse in the krem- lin stables, began to lose patience and trot more and more quickly, until Dasha had to reach over and grab his reins and bring him back to a walk, and Oleg quickly called a halt for a rest.

"I'm never getting back on that horrid beast!" Svetochka exclaimed tearfully, once she had slid gracelessly, almost tearing her kaftan, from the saddle.

"It'll be a long walk home, then," said Oleg. Out of the corner of her eye, Dasha could see that the guards were snickering at Svetochka's distress, and not even bothering to try and hide it. And she had thought they would be better than the ones they had left behind! But guards would be guards, it seemed. She slid off of Poloska and went over to Svetochka, stepping carefully to avoid the worms that had come wriggling out of the warming soil by the side of the road, driven by the rising tide of life that was lifting everything out of the ground and up towards the sky.

"Riding really isn't that difficult," Dasha told Svetochka, hoping to distract her from her pain and from the guards, whose laughter she hadn't yet heard but would soon, if Dasha couldn't drown it out. "I can teach you, you just have to listen."

"Riding really *is* that difficult, if you haven't learned it from childhood," Oleg put in, to Dasha's irritation. Didn't he understand what she was trying to do? Apparently not, as he continued, "It's the most difficult thing I've ever learned to do. But it's easier and safer for women than it is for men, so if I can learn to do it, so can you." His voice was stern as he spoke, but he gave Svetochka an encouraging smile when he finished, and, to Dasha's relief, instead of bursting out into tears or a tantrum, she almost smiled back in response. "And your sister really can teach you," he went on. "She knows more about this than any of the rest of us and has by far the best seat and hands, so listen when she tells you something. No, don't sulk about it. How many other girls will get to say they've had the honor of being trained in the arts of the saddle by the Tsarinovna herself?"

"I don't think I have the best seat..." Dasha began to protest, uncomfortable with the praise and not wanting to make this conversation any more about her, when it was supposed to be about helping Svetochka, but Oleg cut her off.

"You have *by far* the best seat of any of us here, and the best hands too. Why have your horses behaved so well, when the rest of them have been nothing but trouble?"

"They're just calm," Dasha argued.

"Alik," Oleg called. Alik looked up from where he and Seva and Mitya, having stopped snickering at Svetochka, had been dividing up some pies. "Weren't you telling me about the time you tried to ride

Poloska once?"

"Oh, that." Alik wrinkled his nose. "Never again, I swear by all the gods, never again. I thought she was going to jump halfway across Krasnograd at every gust of wind—and I'm from the steppe, and know about riding."

"You just have to be calm, is all," Dasha said.

"Yes," said Oleg, with a small smile. "Be calm, and have a seat and hands a steppe warrior would envy. The Stepniye will be proud to claim you. So listen to your sister, Svetochka, and she'll see you right. And stop fighting with your horse: your sister's right, he's done nothing to deserve the treatment you're giving him."

Dasha held her breath, afraid Svetochka was going to explode again (why couldn't she be calm with her the way she was with Poloska; after all, Alik was right: Poloska *could* be a bit jumpy if you weren't calm around her, but you just had to not fight her about it—could Svetochka be handled the same way? Of course, Poloska was just high-spirited, not vicious the way Svetochka was, but it might still be worth a try, Dasha thought, tucking that idea away for future contemplation and experimentation), but Svetochka merely grimaced and, letting Dasha check and adjust the tack for her, since it turned out she didn't know how to do it herself, heaved herself up onto Sverchok's back like a sack of turnips.

To his credit, Sverchok stood there without making any fuss, when another horse, Poloska for example, would have tossed Svetochka onto her backside for that, and deservedly so. Dasha knew that they would have to have lessons on proper mounting and dismounting, but seeing how impatient all the others were, and how embarrassed Svetochka was by her own inability to manage even that simple task gracefully—not that she seemed to have much notion of grace; it would be more accurate to say that she was embarrassed by what she thought of as her own weakness, even though strength had little to do with it—she decided to wait until later, preferably somewhere out of sight of the guards, who had gone back to snickering at Svetochka's struggles.

The others all wanted to trot again, and Oleg said that if they didn't, they wouldn't reach the first waystation by nightfall, and would have to spend the night in the fields or beg for shelter in some village and risk bedbugs and worse. So Dasha said that she and Svetochka would stay to the rear of the group and go slowly, so that Svetochka could practice trotting, without slowing the others down too much.

Only that plan brought all sorts of problems with it. Dasha wanted to hand Seryozha over to Susanna so that she wouldn't have to concentrate on ponying him while she taught Svetochka, but when they tried to make the handoff, Chernets lunged at Seryozha, knocking him into Poloska and nearly causing them both to go down and take Dasha with them. This made Oleg shout at Susanna for endangering Dasha, to Dasha's acute embarrassment, but Susanna only tossed her head and said that's what happened when a horse like Chernets was forced to crawl along like a snail, and anyway, it was probably Poloska's fault, as she was most likely about to go into heat, now that spring had come. Oleg looked like he wanted to shout a number of responses to that, but clamped his jaw shut on his recriminations and took Seryozha himself instead. Susanna and Chernets immediately sprang away and set off down the road at a pace that the guards, whom Oleg ordered to follow them, had to canter to keep up with.

"By all the gods," said Oleg, watching them race down the road, "if she weren't a princess and your chosen companion, Dasha, I'd..." He checked himself from saying whatever it was he was thinking and ended with, "Southern blood, eh?" instead, but his tone and his face were far from jovial. "Well, if she gets herself into trouble, I won't be held accountable for it. If she gets the guards into trouble, or if we get into trouble because they had to go after her, well..." He ground his teeth so that Dasha could see the muscles in his jaw jumping.

"I'm sure she's just bored," she said. "She doesn't mean to cause any trouble."

"No doubt," said Oleg, not looking placated in the slightest by that thought. "Well, luckily enough for all of us there's not likely to be any trouble on this stretch of the road, except maybe a fall or a bowed tendon. Come, Dasha: show us how a proper princess rides and guides her companions."

It was on the tip of Dasha's tongue to say that she wasn't a princess at all, but the Tsarinovna, which was entirely different, but fortunately the words remained stuck behind her teeth, and when she next opened her mouth it was to explain to Svetochka once again the basics of the art of rising to the trot.

And for the next several versts the journey was...everything that Dasha could have hoped such a journey would be. The fluffy clouds above them did little to block out the warm sun that shone out of the bright blue sky down on their backs and slowly dried out the muddy dark road, smelling so pungently and yet not unpleasantly of warming earth, and the greening fields alternated with little copses of birch and oak, fuzzy in their first green growth. Poloska, Sverchok, Seryozha, and Oleg's horse Belka, so named because of her luxuriant chestnut tail and the fluffy feathers that covered her fetlocks, all jogged along peacefully, and Svetochka listened attentively to Dasha's instructions and honestly tried to follow them, and then broke into a warm grin when Oleg praised her for her progress. It was like they were a real family out for an afternoon ride on a warm spring day.

Things soured a bit when they caught up with the others, who had stopped in a copse of fir trees to rest and wait for them. Seva had decided to while away the time by kicking the rotten snowdrifts hiding in the shadows under the fir boughs, and had gotten his boots, which it turned out were old and in poor repair, thoroughly soaked. Once again Dasha could see the muscles in her father's jaw jump as he struggled not to shout at him, and struggle even harder once they had mounted up and set off again, and Seva started complaining of how his wet boots were rubbing holes in his calves and toes. Then Chernets tried to attack Seryozha again, and Susanna, instead of apologizing, insisted that it wasn't her fault, but Seryozha's, for coming too close to Chernets, and complained some more about the slow pace they were keeping.

"We need to stick together," Oleg told her. "We're approaching a village, and we need to stick together."

"We can take care of ourselves!" said Susanna, with a toss of her head that set all the gold coins braided into her hair to jingling. Only one of the gold coins came loose, and when she let go of the reins to catch it, Chernets lunged at Poloska, making her squeal and jump back and almost crash into Sverchok, which made Svetochka scream and drop her reins.

"I can see," said Oleg, blank-faced, once everyone had gathered up their reins and gotten their horses pointing in the right direction. "But let's stick together even so. And let's keep Chernets away from the other horses."

Susanna sighed at that, as did the guards, but they did as they were bid, and walked through the village, although Chernets almost kicked a little boy, no more than two, and wearing nothing other than a dirty shift and so much mud on his legs he looked to be wearing hose, who ran out into the road and shouted at them in his excitement at seeing strangers. This caused his mother to grab him and slap him hard on the face, and then glare with resentment at Chernets and the rest of the group. Dasha was surprised at the sharp spike of anger that drove through her chest at that: the boy shouldn't have been allowed to run out into the road and endanger himself and everyone else (what if he had caused one of them to be thrown, or one of the horses to stumble and bow a tendon?), and the mother shouldn't have hit him like that, or glared so hatefully at these strangers who had never done anything to her other than ride through her village.

This line of thought caused a series of visions to cascade before Dasha's eyes, starting with one of her being thrown because of someone else's foolishness and being crippled or killed, which led to one of how her parents would react, which led to one that she wished she could erase, but that, she feared, would haunt her forever. In it she was a mother herself, with a little child like that little boy, and a moment of inattention on the part of either her mother or her father (the vision kept cycling through her head again and again, in different but dreadful versions every time) would lead to a crippling or fatal accident, so that her parents were, through no malice of their own, responsible for the death of her child, which—the vision grew more and more awful as they left the village behind—led to rage, recriminations, unending guilt, and suicide all around.

"Are you all right?" Oleg asked, startling her.

"I'm fine," she told him.

He gave her a look full of doubt. "Was it a vision?" he asked.

"Yes," she admitted. "A terrible vision."

"What was it about, then?" He smiled. "Tell me, and I'll carry it for you."

But Dasha could only shake her head in refusal. Giving words to the vision felt like it would make it more real, more likely to come true, and she couldn't bear to burden him with it, and she was afraid that if he knew the kinds of visions she was having about him, he would get angry with her, so angry that he would disown her, maybe abandon her here on this empty road in the middle of this empty field...

"Come now," he said, still smiling. "It can't be that bad, can it? What kind of vision could a girl like you have that could possibly be so bad that you can't tell me about it? Unless," he smiled even more broadly, "it's about a boy." He winked at her. "Is it about a boy, then? Is that why it's a secret?"

"No." Dasha shook her head, her throat and neck so tight that even forming that simple word, and making that simple movement, was difficult. "It wasn't about a boy."

Oleg gave her a look that was much too sharp for her liking. "Well then," he said more gently, "when we get to Lesnograd, we'll see what the sorceresses say. They'll know the answers to your problem; they'll know how to teach you to control your visions. Or maybe...the priestesses at the sanctuary where you were..." He cleared his throat. "Well, anyway. There's a sanctuary no more than a day's ride from Lesnograd; some of the sisters there are very wise, and very close to the gods. They might know something. We should go talk to them, ask them for their guidance."

"Is this the sanctuary where Lyubov' the Kind lived?" Dasha asked, brightening up a little at the thought of one of her favorite foremothers. "My mother told me all about her, and about her own time at that sanctuary!"

"All about it?" repeated Oleg, giving her a funny look, half-amused, half...she wanted to say apprehensive. "What did she tell you?"

"Oh, just that they were very kind and helpful to her there, and gave her scrolls about Lyubov' the Kind, and that the gods, or at least the spirits of the forest, gave her guidance."

"Well, that is true," Oleg agreed, nodding and smiling a smile that seemed to be more for him than for her.

"Could we really go there? If we went, do you think we might meet...I don't know...my mother said that animal spirits showed themselves to her. I'd love to see an animal spirit! I know that some of them stayed with her for a while after she returned to Krasnograd, and I have these memories of the fox—she stayed till I was at least four—but the snow hare returned to the forest when I was still a baby, I've only ever heard my mother's stories about him, and the fox left us soon after that, so that I barely remember her. Just that she was so fluffy!

"My mother said that the city wasn't the right place for them, and they stayed only long enough to be sure I was safe and well, and then they had to go back to their homes, for all that they were imbued with the power of the gods. And I haven't seen any since then. But I'd like to. I'd even like to meet Gray Wolf—do you think he's still alive? My mother said he would live much longer than an ordinary wolf, but still...she said he was enormous, the size of a pony or larger. I used to have nightmares about him, but now I think I'd like to meet him, even if I would be scared. Do you think he's still alive? Do you think he might show himself to us, if we went out there to the prayer wood around that sanctuary and prayed?"

"Oh, he's still alive," Oleg told her. "And I'm sure he'd show himself to you, if you needed him to, or if you just asked nicely. But it's best to wait till we're well away from towns and such. A prayer wood is what he and those like him like best, but any wood will do. No doubt we'll see them before this journey is over. He has a special interest in you, after all."

"Really?" exclaimed Dasha, the horror of her visions pushed away by this exciting thought. "That would be wonderful! I'd be sure to be very polite and respectful towards him."

Oleg laughed. "And I'm sure he'd find that very amusing," he told her. "But I think he'd like you more if you showed him a little of your fire. Wolves respect strength, you know."

"I don't think I have enough strength to make someone like *him* respect me," said Dasha doubtfully.

"Well, we'll see about that," Oleg said. "We'll see about that. And maybe sooner rather than later."

Chapter Thirteen

The sun was just disappearing behind a copse of birches, causing their long shadows to reach out across the fields all the way to the road where they were riding, when they came to a long low ramshackle building that Oleg said was their stopping place for the night.

"It's not the finest place in the world," he said, "but it's big and comfortable and safe, which is all you need when you're traveling." He looked it over with a critical eye. "It's gone downhill since I last stayed here," he went on. "It was never fancy, but now it's positively shabby. But it's better than sleeping in the woods."

"It will be an adventure!" said Susanna. "We will be sleeping with the common folk!"

Alik, Mitya, and Seva all snorted with laughter, and Oleg looked as if he wanted to join them, but instead he turned to Svetochka and asked, "Did you stay here on your way down to Krasnograd? Do you know what it's like now? I, well," his voice faltered, "I was in a hurry on my way down from Severnolesnoye, and I raced right past it."

She shook her head. "I didn't much stay in waystations. No money. I stayed with people who'd take me in, or crept into haylofts an' stayed the night there."

"Well." Oleg gave her a smile. "You'll be sleeping a little more comfortably this time around, at least. It may be shabby, but you girls will have your own chamber."

"What if there's no room for us?" asked Dasha.

"There will be room for the Tsarinovna and her companions," Oleg told her, now sounding as if he were explaining the most basic things to a girl of three.

"But I thought we were going to pretend I wasn't the Tsarinovna," objected Dasha.

Oleg slapped his forehead. "Of course!" He grinned. "How could I have forgotten our little game? Listen, everyone: there's no need to tell everyone who our Dasha is here. She'll be safer and happier if no one knows she's the Tsarinovna. She can just be...a noblewoman traveling to her kin in the North. And there's no need for anyone to know who Susanna Gulisovna is, either. They'll both be safer if they're just a pair of traveling noblewomen. Not that anyone will think that Susanna Gulisovna's anything other than a Southerner, but you'll be safer," he addressed Susanna directly, "if they think you're just some minor noblewoman, not heir to the greater part of Avkhazovskoye. And I wouldn't talk too much about Avkhazovskoye, if I were you, or talk too much in general—people might not feel too friendly to Avkhazovskoye, and you don't want to rub it in their faces."

"*I* am the one who should be offended, not them!" said Susanna, with another one of her head tosses that endangered everyone around her with her wildly waving coins. "Avkhazovskoye was taken by Zem', not, not," she struggled for the right words, "not the opposite!"

"Yes," said Oleg, after giving her a long, level look. "But the common folk of Zem' are unlikely to see it that way, and if you make them so angry they attack you, the only thing you're likely to get for your trouble is a split lip."

"I can take care of myself!"

"Against one, perhaps, but against an entire waystation of people?" Susanna looked as if she wanted to argue with that, but he forestalled her, saying, his voice sharp, "Just don't do anything brash and foolish. Just don't do anything to put the Tsarinovna in danger. You are her companion now, and your prime responsibility is to ensure her safety. It's a matter of honor."

This argument seemed to sway Susanna, and she nodded in a way that was almost compliant, and asked, "Should she have a new name?"

"A new name?" asked Oleg.

"If we are pretending she is not who she is, should she have a new name?"

"Ah...no," decided Oleg. "There are lots of Dashas about; one more or less either way won't catch people's attention. Remembering to call her something else will be too much to keep in mind on the road. Just don't call her 'Tsarinovna.' Call her by her name instead."

"And where should we say she is from?" pressed Susanna. "What is her story?"

"Her story? Ah, her story..."

"I'll be your companion," Dasha put in. She could see that, strangely enough, Oleg, who was so quick with his words when on the spot, was having a hard time thinking up a story for her ahead of time, maybe because making up stories in the abstract was not something he was good at. Which was a strange thing to find difficult, since it was so ridiculously easy, but that was what it seemed like to Dasha. "I'll be your companion," she told Susanna. "A minor noblewoman from the North, who was raised in Krasnograd and is returning to her kin. You took a fancy to seeing the North as well, and hired me to attend you on your journey."

"And her?" asked Susanna, nodding at Svetochka.

"Ah...." It was on the tip of Dasha's tongue to say that Svetochka was their servant, which was by far the most believable explanation, but one look at Svetochka's face showed that would start another tantrum, so instead she said, "We'll tell the truth. We'll say that she's my sister—maybe my second-sister? Ah, from the poor part of the family"—Svetochka's face turned dark as thunderclouds, but Dasha plunged on, determined not to stop just because Svetochka was being difficult—"and now we're going back to, to find my other sisters and escort them back to Krasnograd, where I've found a good situation, ah, attending your family..."

"I ain't no serving girl!" Svetochka burst out, unable to stay silent before this outrage a moment longer, just as Susanna said, "Will that not make others guess? To say that you are sisters?"

"No one knows," Dasha told her. "Not outside of Krasnograd. At least I don't think so." She turned to Oleg. "Do they?" she asked.

"Svetochka knows," he said. "Milochka knows. And a few others. But I think we'll be safe. Don't make it too complicated when you're making up a story. And you're a serving girl," he added to Svetochka. "Or near enough. So stop whining and be helpful."

This made Svetochka's face go even more thunderous than before, but she said nothing as they rode up to the sagging porch that stretched the entire width of the building, and were hailed by a boy of ten or so with shaggy blond hair and smears of dirt on his face.

"Looking for lodgings?" he called to them, jumping off the porch and running over, a broad grin on his grimy face. His eyes were large and blue and shining with good nature and self-importance with the task he had been given. "You can't do better than us! We've got space! Space for..." he counted them, "seven! Perfect! We've got seven empty stalls in the stables!"

"I'm glad to hear it," Oleg said. "We'll need stalls for the horses, a place in the loft for our three guards, and rooms for the rest of us."

It hadn't occurred to Dasha that the guards would have to sleep in the hayloft, and she wanted to protest, but she didn't know how, and before she could figure that out, the boy who had greeted them and a second boy, clearly his older brother, had taken the guards and all their horses and led them all off towards the stables to the side of the inn itself, and Oleg was sending the girls into the inn.

"I'm going to go check on the horses," he told them. "Go in and order dinner, and I'll join you in a bit."

The thought of going into a strange building and ordering dinner from strangers filled Dasha with an unexpected shyness, and she realized—strange thought!—that she had never gone into a strange building before in her life, and she certainly hadn't ever ordered strange food from strange people, and, simple a deed as it was, right now it seemed almost overwhelmingly frightening.

"I should lead the way," said Susanna, sounding not at all displeased by the idea. "Since you are serving me."

"Yes, of course," agreed Dasha, relieved not to have to take charge, even as she castigated herself for her cowardice. But Susanna *was* right, and happy enough to take command, it seemed. She walked boldly up onto the porch and into the inn, where she said to the harried-looking man who greeted them at the door that they would be spending the night, and that they wanted dinner.

"'Course, noblewoman," he said, bobbing up and down in a jerky half-bow. "For your serving women as well?" He glanced at Svetochka and then did a double-take upon seeing Dasha. "My 'pologies, noblewoman," he said, jerking his head in a cringing movement that was probably supposed to be an apology and a bow all in one. "I din't know..."

"It is all right," Susanna interrupted him. "Understandable. They are both waiting upon me, but they will join me for dinner and in my bedchamber. They are also of noble birth, as you see, and you will treat them as such."

"Ah...'course, noblewoman, 'course. I'll...dinner tonight's just cabbage soup and black bread, but we've a bit of sausage set aside, or I could...I s'pose I could send my boy to kill a hen, we've got some old ones as need killing soon anyway..."

"No need," Dasha found herself saying, before Susanna could respond. "What you have offered us is more than sufficient for our needs, and we thank you for your generosity."

There was an awkward pause while the innkeeper tried to make sense (Dasha realized with embarrassment) of her temerity before her mistress, but then, when Susanna nodded and said, "Dasha is correct. Your regular fare will be fine," he jerked his head again and led them through a large dark room full of tables and benches, up a set of broad but sagging stairs, and into a chamber that was almost entirely filled with a huge, sagging bed.

"It's the best room as we got, noblewoman," the man said, looking anxiously at Susanna.

"It will do," Susanna told him, after a brief but imperious survey. "It will do for the three of us. We will need another chamber for...for our male companion. The stables are not good enough for him."

"We got a...another room, noblewoman," said the innkeeper, looking terrified at the thought of something not being good enough for them. "But he might have to share it. It's empty now, but if someone was to come in..."

"It will do," Susanna interrupted him. "He is not too, not too refined. It will do."

"Good, noblewoman, good," said the innkeeper, bobbing his head. Then he told them, with evident embarrassment, how to call for water and where the privy and the chamber pot were, before rushing off to what must have been the kitchen, with the promise that his boy would serve them their dinner whenever they deigned to join everyone down in the main room.

The boy who brought them their dinner once they had dropped off their packs and gone back downstairs (was he the same boy who would have been called upon to kill one of the old hens if they had requested it, Dasha wondered, and who in that case would end up killing all of them anyway), who by his looks must have been the older brother of the two who had taken away their horses, was only a year or two older than them, and, all three girls agreed once he had brought them a loaf of black bread and gone off to the kitchen for their soup, very handsome, with his broad shoulders, slanted gray eyes, and thick hair the color of ripe wheat. And the perpetual smile he wore on his face didn't hurt either. He revealed to them when he came back with steaming bowls of a watery half-cooked cabbage soup that his mother had died the year before and it was now just him, his father, and his two younger brothers running the inn.

"My aunt said it weren't no business of ours to be running the inn, that one man an' a bunch of boys would run it into the ground afore the year were out, but we're doing all right," he told them proudly. The shabby appearance of the inn belied his words, but his face was so handsome that the girls were quite willing to overlook all the other deficiencies of their surroundings, and agreed that the inn looked to be doing quite well, and didn't complain of the burnt bread and watery, half-cooked cabbage soup at all.

"After all," said Susanna, when he had gone back into the kitchen, "with a face and form like that, he will have a wife before the year is out, and she will put everything in order. Or her mother will." She nudged Svetochka. "*You* appear quite taken with him," she said. "Are you considering making an offer yourself?"

"No!" said Svetochka, but then added, "But when I do, it'll be to someone like that."

"Well, what are you waiting for?" demanded Susanna. "Take him before someone else does! Not only is he handsome, but he has an inn! You could do much worse."

"His father has an inn," Svetochka corrected her, although she looked not displeased by the thought. "An' his aunt wants to take it away, an' maybe will. We don't know who it really belongs to—maybe his wife's family could take it whenever they wanted to."

"Not if his eldest son had a good wife, and they took her into the family as official heir," said Susanna. "Then the inn would be hers."

"That would depend on the will," put in Dasha, intrigued by the idea in spite of herself. She felt guilty about disposing of someone else's life so casually, even in fantasy, but it *was* only fantasy, she told herself, and it was no more than what was going to happen to him anyway in real life. At least they were acting out of good will, rather than greed.

"Nonsense," said Susanna, waving aside all considerations of the will with an airy hand gesture. "Peasants like this, they would not have proper wills, would they? So everything would go to the heir, who would be the eldest daughter. Is that not how things work in Zem'? And if there is no heir, the family can adopt one by marriage?"

"Yes," confirmed Dasha. "That's how things work here in Zem', most of the time. Families do all sorts of things, though, depending on what they want and need. Sometimes sons even inherit outright, if it suits the family's purposes, or if the mother is very tenderhearted."

"Well then. Either way, the girl who marries him will get the inn— *and* a handsome husband for her bed."

This led to a lengthy bout of giggling, which was only interrupted when Oleg returned from the stables, looking tired and as if...Dasha struggled to find the right thought...as if he were done for the day and wanted nothing more than to retire somewhere and be done with them all. Which was a strange thought to have of her father; that he could be tired and harried from just spending the day riding in their company. Still, he managed to raise a smile for their giggling. "I'm afraid to ask," he said.

"We are planning to marry the serving boy," Susanna explained, her black eyes sparkling and her gold-and-black braids jingling with her merriment.

"What, all three of you?" asked Oleg.

This caused even more giggling, and a proposal from Susanna that they do exactly that. "He is certainly handsome enough," she said. "And he looks strong, too. What do you think, girls: would he be enough for all three of us?"

"And more, I'll warrant," said Svetochka. "What d'you say, Dasha? Would you share him with us? Or keep him all to yourself?"

"Ah..." said Dasha, not knowing how to respond to that, and blushing furiously at either possibility.

"Leave the poor boy alone," Oleg put in, before she could say anything more. With his tiredness wearing away his usual good cheer he looked almost angry, or even...he was disgusted, Dasha saw. Disgusted with all of them, even with her, at the thought of them taking the boy as a lover. Disgusted even though he had been joking with them about getting married and taking lovers in a way that seemed he had been encouraging them to do so.

But now that the real possibility of them doing so was facing him, or maybe now that they were talking about it themselves instead of reacting with embarrassment to his insinuations, he was afraid. And not because he was worried for them, but because he was afraid for the boy, afraid of them, afraid that they would hurt him. The thought of any of them hurting the boy seemed ludicrous to Dasha, both because they were only joking about something that wouldn't hurt him even if it did become reality, which it wouldn't, and because it wasn't normally boys who had to worry about being hurt by girls, now was it, it wasn't boys (or men) who had to worry about taking someone violent and selfish into their hearts and into their beds, but nonetheless, Oleg was, Dasha could see with hurtful clarity, horrified on the boy's behalf that they might take him as a lover, more worried about the boy and his wellbeing than what might happen to any of them.

Because, Dasha saw (she wasn't sure how she was seeing this, since there weren't any actual visions; it must be more like the heart-reading that her mother did), when he looked at the boy, he saw himself, but when he looked at them, he saw something repulsively terrifying and alien, even though he had only caught a single glimpse of the boy, and Dasha and Svetochka were his own flesh and blood. Perhaps this was why her mother had never put her foot down and forced him to stay. For a moment Dasha could feel herself swelling up to shout at him, but she stopped herself. If he saw her as terrifying and alien, then shouting at him wouldn't win him over.

"It was only a bit of fun," she said instead.

"To you maybe, but not to him," said Oleg, still speaking angrily, and still looking at them as if they were loathsome monsters, not three girls (two of them his own daughters) indulging in a playful bout of high spirits.

Susanna opened her mouth, probably to say that the boy would find it a bit of fun too, but Dasha forestalled her by saying, "We're sorry. We didn't mean anything by it. We didn't mean to hurt your feelings." Which, as she had guessed it would, made Oleg frown even more. *Now*, she thought with more triumph and spite than she was able to admit to, even to herself, *he can think about how he's made me act in the way he doesn't want me to act, and maybe he'll stop blaming me and blame himself a bit instead.* "How are the horses?" she asked, telling herself that she wasn't being manipulative, or rather, that she was manipulating him for good reasons. It would do none of them any good to get into an unwinnable argument over a silly subject, so they were better off talking about the horses.

"Well enough," he told them, giving her a look as if he had half-guessed what she was up to, but couldn't quite believe it. "The stables are in even shabbier shape than this room, but we made them comfortable enough, and the guards will take turns sleeping in the hayloft, when they're not standing guard."

"Do we really need them to stand guard over us while we're in an inn?" Dasha asked. "And sleep in the hayloft?"

"Yes," Oleg said. "And the hayloft is where guards normally sleep. They're used to it, and they won't mind."

"But *I'll* mind," said Dasha. Where was this boldness coming from? Was it because Oleg was tired and out of sorts and had annoyed her? Was she really so weak and mean? Was it wrong if weakness and meanness propelled her into the courage to stand up for others? "Wouldn't they rather have a chamber?" she found herself saying, even as she worried about all these things. "That way they won't have to climb out of the hayloft and come over here when it's their turn to go on guard. Surely we can afford it."

Oleg gave her a long look. "Is this just another plan to get more men near your bedchamber?" he asked. Susanna laughed, but Dasha could tell he wasn't really joking, and that in his current state of tiredness and low spirits, he really did think they would do something like that, and was disgusted and outraged with them because of it.

"If you're going to be like that," Dasha told him, not believing her own ears as she heard her words, "I'm not going to speak to you anymore. Do as you will; I'm retiring for the night." And she rose from the table and strode out of the main hall and off to her bedchamber before anyone could stop her.

Once she had thrown herself onto the sagging, musty bed, she was overcome with shame. How could she have spoken to Oleg like that? She should run right back downstairs and apologize to him and beg for his forgiveness! Only...what if that made him even angrier with her? She couldn't do anything without displeasing him! Why was she such a terrible daughter? Why was she such a terrible person who couldn't do even the simplest thing without hurting everyone around her?

She never should have gone on this journey! She should have stayed home in Krasnograd and readied herself to rule. Only if she couldn't even manage to get along with her own father, she probably shouldn't be ruling either! She shouldn't do *anything*! She...she...she started to panic at the thought of not being able to do anything at all. If she couldn't do anything, what *would* she do? Maybe she should run away and join a sanctuary? Surely they would take her in, even useless as she was?

Although the last thing she should be doing was inflicting her worthless presence on the sisters of a sanctuary. And if she didn't ready herself to rule Zem' one day, who would? Her mother couldn't do it forever, and if she, Dasha, didn't take over for her when she was ready to step down, who would? There was no one else. Or rather, there were other candidates, but they were all even worse than Dasha, terrible thought as that was. Which meant that she would have to do it, but she was sure to fail, sure to fail...

There was a knock at the door. Thinking it was Susanna, Dasha pulled herself off the sagging bed and took the one step to the door, which she had to open carefully in order to avoid crushing herself between it and the bedframe. When she had completed that tricky operation, she found Oleg standing at the threshold.

"Oh!" she said, stupidly.

"Can I come in?" he asked. There were dark circles under his eyes, Dasha noticed, and his whole face seemed to want to sag towards the earth. She stepped back to let him in.

"I'm sorry," he said once he was inside the chamber. "I shouldn't have teased you like that. I'm sorry. I..." He sighed and sat, or rather flopped, down onto the bed, which creaked in protest. "I'm not used to...to being a father," he told her.

"That's funny, because you have lots of daughters," said Dasha, and then could have slapped herself. She hadn't meant for it to be cruel at all, but as soon as the words came out, she knew that it was pretty much the worst thing she could have said. If her mother were here, she would have taken back everything she had said about Dasha's abilities with words, she was sure. Yet another sign of her absolute and utter failure...

"I deserved that," said Oleg, with a pained smile that wasn't really a smile at all.

"No you didn't," Dasha said. She had meant to sound comforting, but her voice came out hard and sharp instead.

Oleg smiled another pained smile. "Yes I did, but it's kind of you to argue with me."

"I wasn't arguing with you," said Dasha. What was wrong with her voice? Why couldn't she sound as kind and comforting as she needed to right now? Instead she sounded as if she were ordering him around or winning an argument against him, which was the last thing she needed to do. "I was just telling the truth," she continued, still speaking with an edge that she couldn't seem to get rid of. "I lost my temper."

She really, really should be speaking more conciliatorily, instead of laying everything out with the firm precision of the Councilor of Justice laying out a case against a criminal, but she couldn't seem to find the right words or tone or anything else. Just like with Princess Belova, something had taken over her and was speaking through her, but instead of saying all the right things in the right way, she was saying all the wrong things in the wrong way. "I lost my temper and I wanted to hurt you and show you that I wasn't weak and sniveling like you think I am." Was she being possessed by the gods? Was that what was happening? Perhaps the Black God had taken over her tongue and was using it for his own evil ends? It was the only rational explanation. She should clap her hands over her mouth and hold them there until the fit passed or Oleg left.

"Weak and sniveling?" Oleg looked like…oh by all the gods…he looked like he might *cry* at those words…this was even worse than Dasha had feared… "I don't think you're weak and sniveling."

Dasha tried to open her mouth to tell him that she knew that and she hadn't meant to say that, but her jaw seemed to be locked shut.

"I don't think you're weak and sniveling, Dasha," he repeated. "I think…I think you're like your mother. Soft like water."

Dasha didn't know what to say to that, so she said nothing. His face was changing, warming up, as if…as if she hadn't said the wrong things after all! Maybe her mother was right and she *did* know how to say the right thing, even when she didn't realize it herself!

"Soft like water," he repeated. "Life-giving. Like water." He smiled just a little less tiredly. "Dangerous. Like water. You've got to…see the thing is…water might not seem like much, Dasha, it might seem soft and ordinary, but it'll…it'll make the crops grow, it'll carve out mighty riverbeds. And it'll wash away cities if it floods in the wrong place. So you've got to make sure it floods in the right place. You've got to make sure it quenches your thirst, and doesn't drown you. So…I'm just afraid…I'm afraid that you're being turned into…that your force is being allowed to spill out uselessly onto barren ground, or dammed up till it floods where it shouldn't and washes everything away, and I just…I want to make sure that doesn't happen. Only I don't know how."

"Oh," said Dasha.

"And I don't think I really can," he added. "No one can. You've got to...you've got to carve out your own riverbed, Dasha, and if the rest of us, if we try to change your course too much, well...you know, you can bridge rivers, if you do it in the right place, and you can sail on them, if you do it carefully, and you can even make little dams and channels to help with, with watering your crops and such, but if you try to change their course, dam them completely closed, well, they'll just rise up and flood everything, and you'll have ruined them and you too.

"So...I want to help you, Dasha, I want to help you make sure that you hold the course you need to hold, that you carve out the banks you need for yourself to keep from flooding out and destroying everything and losing yourself in the process, but I...I don't really know how. I don't think anyone does. I think we can just kind of give you nudges in what we think is the right direction, but only...I don't even know if the river knows its own direction, not really. Maybe it just has to follow its course, and its direction is revealed to it as it flows. So..." he sighed again, "I want to help you, I really do, and I worry that others are damming you up and cutting you off and I want to stop that, but I...I can only do so much. Most of it wrong, like as not."

"Well then," said Dasha, once he had fallen silent. "That's not so bad, though. Because in the end, a river always goes where it needs to go. All that other stuff—all the dams and bridges and everything else—they might get in its way for a little while, but in the end, the water will always run to where it needs to run."

"I guess that's one way of looking at it," said Oleg.

"And I'll...I'll try not to lose my temper in the future," added Dasha.

"No?" Oleg grinned, now looking a lot less tired. "Good luck with that. I had a *terrible* temper when I was your age."

"Really?" asked Dasha.

He laughed. "You say it like you're surprised. Which only shows how little you know me. Really, a terrible temper. Just awful; you can't even imagine. Everyone when they're your age, they have a temper—it's just part of growing up. All the fire you need to push you up and out and into your life—it builds and builds until you just have to burst. So you do. And I...I burst all over the place. All the time. Till I ran away from home. And even then I kept exploding, lashing out..." His voice sobered. "You don't want to be like that, Dasha, truly you don't. But," he smiled again, "I doubt you have to worry about that. You won't be like me, Dasha, not in that way."

"But what if I *am*? I...I'm afraid of my temper sometimes," she admitted.

"You'll get over it," he told her. "Trust me. You'll learn how to bank your fires, and you'll get over it. After all, *I* did."

"How can you be so sure?" she demanded.

"Because I'm older than you. A lot older, in fact. More than old enough to be your grandfather, and then some. Which isn't always a good thing. But in this...I've seen a lot, Dasha, a lot of other people, a lot of myself, and so I can tell you: you'll learn. Maybe not today, or even this year, but one day, you'll learn."

"I want to learn now!" said Dasha. "I don't want...this is all so *unpleasant*. I'm unhappy all the time, and I keep hurting people without meaning to, which makes me even more unhappy, and I don't know what I should do or even what I want to do, and, and...I don't know what to do, and I can't stand it!"

Oleg laughed. "That's what it's like to be a girl of seventeen," he said. "Or a boy, for that matter: I was the same. And if...if I could give you everything I've learned in all the years between then and now, so that you could know what I know now, well then...I still wouldn't. Because it wouldn't do you any good. The only way you'll learn any of that is by doing it yourself, and no one else can do it for you."

"But what if I make mistakes?" demanded Dasha.

"Mistakes are how you learn," said Oleg. "You'll never learn anything by doing everything right the first time. You have to do it wrong a few times before you can even know what right is."

"But what if it's a *bad* mistake?" said Dasha. "What if it's such a bad mistake that I don't get the chance to make any more mistakes?"

"Is that what you're worried about?" Oleg gave her an intent look, with eyes that were so like her own, only a little more blue and a little less gray and green. "That you'll...get hurt? Have you"—his voice grew tight, even though she could see he was struggling to keep it calm—"seen something?"

"I see things all the time! That's the problem! I see things all the time! Every time I so much as walk down the stairs, I see myself tripping and falling, and every time I get on a horse I see my head smashed in, or my body impaled on a jagged branch, or, or...every day! I see it every day, no, every hour of every day, I see myself torn, pierced, smashed to pieces, and, and *I can't tell which of the visions are real!*"

"I see." Oleg made a move as if he wanted to put his arms around her, but then pulled back and asked, "Have any of the visions come to pass?"

Dasha shook her head.

"So they're not true visions, then."

The pain that stabbed Dasha's left eye, and the burning tide rising up her neck, and the funny taste in her mouth, were all so strange and intense that at first she didn't recognize them for what they were, which was rage. For a moment she thought she might actually throw herself at Oleg and bite his face with her teeth, which were actually itching with the desire to sink themselves into something and rip till the blood flowed. How could he...he couldn't possibly have said anything worse, that was the worst thing he could have possibly said, because, because, because, because it showed that he, that he, that he...

"You don't understand it at all!" she cried. "You don't understand, that's not how it works, how could you say that, how could you say that..."

"I was just trying to understand..."

"But you did it by calling me a liar and a fraud! You did it by saying that I'm not real!"

"That's not what I said," protested Oleg.

"Yes it is." Suddenly Dasha felt herself growing calm again, now that she had grasped just why what he had done was so terrible. "You said that you are more real than I am, and that you are able to decide what is real and what isn't, and you are real and I'm not. Because that's how the visions work, you see: they show me all the realities beyond the surface. And that's what they've shown me here. They've shown me that you don't think I'm real."

"I..." Dasha could see Oleg starting to cry, and she could see him getting up and striking her, knocking her down in his rage, and she could see him storming out of the room and abandoning her, and she couldn't tell what he was actually doing or was going to do. "I..." he said, shaking his head and clearing his throat. "That's not what I meant to say. What I meant to say was that you haven't been...hurt like that, so it's not...it's not real in that way. It's just inside your head."

"The inside of my head is real too, as you'll see if I dash my brains out tomorrow on a rock," snapped Dasha.

"Yes, but...that's not going to happen."

"How can you know that?"

His shoulders slumped. "I can't," he admitted. "But it's not very likely. And your visions...they don't sound like foreseeing, not like what some of your foremothers could do. They would see someone falling from her horse in the morning, and by the evening she would be lying in a healer's bed. This sounds...different."

"It is! But that doesn't mean it's not real!"

"No. But...this sounds like a matter for sorceresses. Or priestesses. Or both. Probably both." He stood up from the bed and then bent over and kissed the top of her head. She couldn't remember him ever kissing her before. "I know it's scary," he told her. "I was scared when I was your age, too. Still am, actually, but it's not as bad as it was when I was your age. Scared, and angry, and all sorts of other bad things, too. And you're right: I don't know what tomorrow will bring, but I have faith. I have faith that the gods wouldn't have brought you into the world just to sacrifice you to a cruel accident."

"Not everyone can have that faith," she objected. "Lots of people are sacrificed to cruel accidents."

"Yes but...you can't go through your life afraid that that's going to happen to you. And it's less likely to happen to you than to anyone else in the world, so...I'm sure the visions are bad, but we'll find help for you, we'll find those who can train you so they don't take you over like this anymore, so in the meantime, have faith."

"In what?" Dasha asked, her voice, to her shame, shaking.

"In the fact that you're real and no one can change that, no matter what they try to do about it," Oleg told her, and, with another kiss on the top of her head, left.

Susanna and Svetochka came up shortly after that, still giggling over the boy who had served them their dinner, or boys in general, or...it soon became clear that the real reason for their giggles was the beer they had been given after Dasha had left.

"It weren't like our beer back home," Svetochka said. "It were all dark an'...thick somehow. Sort of like kvas, but stronger." She laughed for no reason and half-sat, half-fell down onto the sagging bed, which made an ominous creaking sound. "I liked it!"

"That is why you need to marry that boy!" said Susanna, also half-falling onto the bed. "Then the beer will always be yours, and you can have as much as you want!" Both girls laughed themselves breathless.

"I need to pee," announced Svetochka, once she had gotten her breath back.

"Then go to the privy," Susanna told her sternly.

"What if something's already in there?" objected Svetochka.

"Like what?" asked Susanna, wrinkling her face in confusion.

"Like...a domovaya."

"Oh. You Zemnians, you believe in these spirits of the house?"

"They're real!" insisted Svetochka. "Don't you have 'em in the South?"

"We have spirits. But they are different. Have you seen one? A 'domovaya'?"

Svetochka shook her head.

"Then how do you know they are real?"

"Everyone knows! An' I think I might've seen one on the stairs!"

"Here?" asked Susanna. Her face wrinkled up again, and then she burst out laughing. Svetochka joined her.

"No, I think I saw one," she insisted, once she'd stopped laughing. "There was shadows on the stairs, an' I saw...something in 'em. An' now I don't want to go to the privy. What if it jumps out an' gets me?"

"Domoviye wouldn't do that," Dasha found herself saying.

"Have you met any, then?" Susanna asked. "Do you know them?"

"I've...I've never met any myself. Well, once when I was a little girl...I think when I was a little girl, really little, the one in the kremlin used to come to me, but she stopped, I guess. I don't really remember it: it was when I was really little. But they wouldn't do anything to hurt you. They're...beneficent."

"Beneficent?" Susanna and Svetochka asked together.

"They're good," Dasha explained. "They have good intentions. They don't want to hurt us. They're not wild, like leshiye or animal spirits, who might help you or might hurt you. You don't have to be afraid of them."

"I don't want 'em peering at me when I'm in the privy!" said Svetochka with a shudder.

"I don't think they would do that," said Dasha.

"Or catching me when I'm on my way! Jumping out of the shadows an' grabbing me!"

"Let's all go together, then," said Dasha.

Which was how they found themselves stumbling down the darkening corridor from their room to the privy, laughing and trying not to trip in the shadows that were rapidly filling up the hallway.

"Domovaya!" shrieked Svetochka as they entered the darkness at the end of the corridor where the privy was.

"Domovaya!" Susanna shrieked back, pinching her and making both of them shriek even more.

"Will you girls be quiet!" shouted someone from inside a near-by chamber. "Some of us have to sleep, you know, instead of fooling around all night!"

Susanna and Svetochka both looked with apprehension at Dasha, and she realized that she was supposed to be offended, and that if she wanted to, she could go complain to her father and her guards and the innkeeper, and they could come and take the woman shouting from behind that door and...do what? Something bad, probably. At least make it so that she wouldn't be able to sleep all night.

"Our apologies," Dasha called back. "We beg your forgiveness, and we won't make any more noise, we promise."

"You can start by shutting up now!" the voice shouted. "Instead of pretending to be as fancy as noblewomen."

The three girls looked back and forth, and then exploded into another round of giggles that didn't end until they had all gone to the privy and returned to their chamber. It must have been the laughing, Dasha told herself, that made her think that she had seen something in the shadows in the corner of the corridor. Her eyes had been crinkled up and her head had been shaking and she had been looking at Susanna and that was why it had seemed that she had seen a little figure crouched in the darkness, watching her with shiny black eyes like a dog's. It had just been a trick of her eyes, nothing more.

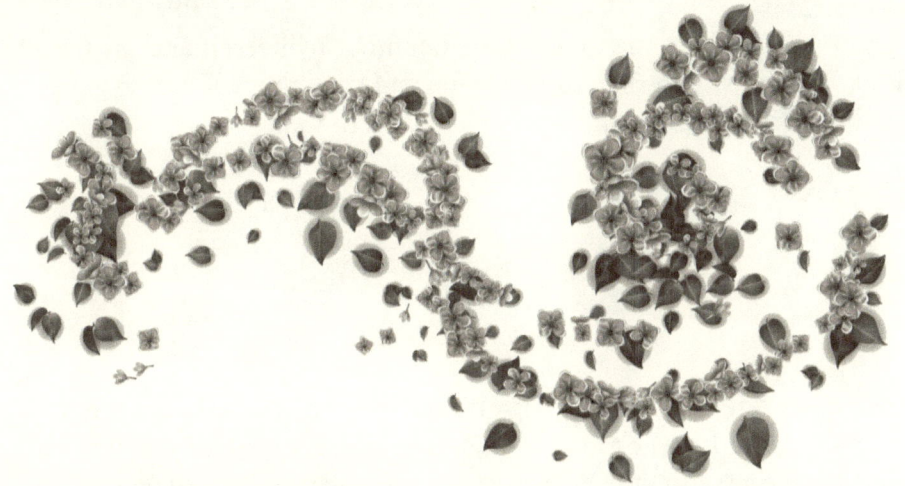

Chapter Fourteen

The lumpy, musty-smelling bed was not conducive to sleep, nor was the strange room. Dasha realized, lying there, that she had never slept in a bed that was not her own. Or a bedchamber. The wooden building (she had also never stayed in a wooden building) creaked and made funny noises, and people kept walking up and down the stairs and past them down the corridor all night.

Also, she kept thinking about little creatures lurking in the shadows. Telling herself that, firstly, they weren't there, and secondly, if they were, they were domoviye, who were *beneficent*, as she'd so grandly told Svetochka, was surprisingly little help, which was very annoying. It was as if her own mind were beyond the reach of reason. And she wanted to toss and turn, but she knew that would disturb Susanna and Svetochka, so she had to lie there until she had to get up and go to the privy again, which meant that now she was one of the people tromping up and down the corridor keeping everyone else awake.

And Mitya was standing guard at the end of the corridor, and wanted to escort her to the privy, and had to be dissuaded firmly from doing so. Although she then regretted her insistence on going alone, because as she tried to tiptoe back and forth as quietly as possible, the shadows seemed to lap at her feet like the waves of a rising river...*Stop it stop it stop it!* she shouted at herself in her head.

Her rising had woken up Svetochka and Susanna, or maybe they hadn't been sleeping either, and they both had to go to the privy too, which left Dasha to lie there in the chamber by herself and try not to look into the shadows in the corners, and then they all had to get settled back into the uncomfortable bed, and then...

The dawn greeted Dasha entirely unexpectedly. She had been sure that she would never fall asleep, and that she hadn't slept a wink all night, but one moment she had been lying there trying not to look into the shadows, and the next thing she knew, the shadows were drying up and melting away like the snows of winter under the sun of spring, and she realized she had in fact slept through most of the night, with no memory of anything other than a peculiar tune running through her head, one that must have come to her as she was dreaming.

She sat up cautiously, not wanting to disturb the other girls and not sure what she should do. No maid was going to come to dress her and bring her breakfast, she realized, which was fine, except that she had no structure to her morning. What was she supposed to do? Should she get up and get dressed and go down to breakfast? Or maybe to the stables to see to their horses? Should she go look for Oleg and the other men? Should she wake up Susanna and Svetochka, or leave them? When were they supposed to set off?

"Did you wake up?" Susanna murmured, sitting up as well.

"Ah...yes," Dasha said, resisting the temptation to make some kind of smart remark about how *obviously* she had woken up. Susanna must have meant to ask if she was awake, but had gotten it mixed up in her half-awake state.

"Good!" said Susanna, and threw back the covers and jumped out of the bed. "Time to go to breakfast!"

"We won't be disturbing anyone?" Dasha asked.

Susanna went and looked out the little window that peeked out just below the eaves. "If we disturb them, they will deserve it," she said. "They should have made breakfast already. It is after dawn." She went back over to the bed and shook Svetochka by the shoulder, none too gently. "Wake up!" she commanded. "Time for breakfast!"

Svetochka grumbled and complained and spent a while sitting

on the edge of the bed moping while Susanna and Dasha dressed, but by the time the sun was well and truly up and Oleg had come and knocked at their door and told them it was time to come down to breakfast, she had managed to get dressed and follow them, stumbling and still complaining, out the chamber and down to the main room, where Oleg and the guards were already waiting for them.

"Sleep well?" asked Oleg. The shadows under his eyes and the tiredness in his face of last night were gone, and he looked hale and hearty and ready to take on the world, or at least another long day of riding. The guards looked slightly less ready for the day, but they still thanked Dasha for insisting that they be given a chamber instead of the hayloft, and by the time they had finished their breakfast (tea, something that was probably supposed to be kvas but that Dasha couldn't bring herself to drink, and half-burned boat-shaped pies with a little dot of jam in the center), they were bouncing with energy and half-ran out of the inn to the stables, punching and slapping each other in their exuberance.

"I'll go make sure the horses are saddled and ready," Oleg said, watching the guards and their play-fighting with amusement. "The gods alone know what those three will do without me. Go gather your things and meet me out on the porch, and we'll pay and go."

The girls went back to their chamber and gathered their things, which took Dasha no time at all, as she had already put her things back into her pack when she had dressed, but was a laborious process for Susanna and Svetochka, who had both managed to empty out their entire packs while undressing the night before, and toss the contents all over the chamber. Just looking at them poke around the room, miss things that were in plain sight, and argue over whose things were whose started to give Dasha a headache—she had never been able to tolerate too much disorder in her chambers, it made her uneasy and confused—so she grabbed her own packs and went back downstairs.

"Girl!" called someone, as she was walking through the main room, and then, more loudly and insistently, "Girl!" A hand fell on her arm. Dasha instinctively shook it off and whirled around, preparing to strike down whoever had accosted her, just as Boleslav Vlasiyevich had taught her. But there was no need, as it was just the innkeeper, cringing back from her bearing and the look in her eyes.

"Don't you answer when people call you?" he asked, but he wouldn't meet her gaze as he said it.

"I apologize," Dasha said, trying not to be annoyed with him.

There was something about his groveling temerity that was calling up an urge she had never experienced before, at least not so clearly: an urge to give him a good slap, or maybe a kick, just because he seemed to be asking for it. Which was dreadful. What an awful thing to think, let alone to want to do! "I didn't realize you were speaking to me," she said, as gently as she could.

"I don't see no other girls here," the innkeeper said, still not daring to look her, but unable to stop himself from whining even so.

"Ah...true," agreed Dasha. "I just...people rarely call me 'girl.' I wasn't expecting it. I apologize again."

"What, don't your mistress ever call out for you? Or what's she say when she's scolding you?"

"Ah...my name," said Dasha. "Can I help you with something?"

"Oh. Right. The bill," said the innkeeper. "You wasn't thinking of slipping off without paying it, was you?"

"No," said Dasha. She was too surprised by the accusation to take offense at it, although once again there was a faint tingle in her hands, as if they were just begging to reach out and give him a little slap. "I fear I carry only a little money, but if you figure the total for me and it's more than I have, I'll be happy to tell my...our escort the sum, and have him pay you, as soon as he comes back from the stables."

"Right," said the innkeeper. He hesitated. "Right," he said again. "Let's just go over there then, where I does my accounts."

"Please," said Dasha, and followed him over to the bar at the back of the main room, where he found a slate and a piece of chalk.

"Now let's see," said the innkeeper, looking at her with a fearful, self-conscious resentment. He held the slate and chalk as if they were foreign objects. "That's seven beds at thirty grosh apiece, seven dinners at twenty grosh each, seven breakfasts at ten grosh each, and one night's board for seven horses at thirty grosh a head..." He made some marks on the slate, looked at them in confusion, cleared them off with his hand, which was now sweating, made some more marks (the chalk was no longer writing well, now that the slate was damp with sweat) and wiped them off again, and, growing more and more agitated, kept trying to figure their bill, every time coming up with a different sum.

"It's three chervontsa and thirty grosh," Dasha told him finally, as kindly as she could. It seemed like such a paltry sum of money for everything they had received during their stay, compared with what little she knew of Krasnograd prices, but on the other hand, they hadn't received Krasnograd service, had they? "Here," she said, reaching for her coin purse. "I have enough: I can pay you right now."

He glared at her out from under the hair falling in his eyes. "Now don't confuse me, little girl, don't confuse me," he said, and went back to figuring, arriving at sums that were each more incorrect than the one before.

"It's three chervontsa and thirty grosh," Dasha repeated after a while, when she could stand it no more. "Here." She took the necessary coins out of her coin purse and tried to hand them to him, but he only shook his head in refusal.

"You can't know that," he said. "You're just guessing! Now don't confuse me!"

"I'm not just guessing," Dasha insisted, as politely and patiently as she could. "That's ninety grosh for each of us, and there are seven of us. Nine times seven is..."

"Ninety grosh!" the innkeeper interrupted her before she could finish. "None of that's ninety grosh!"

"It was thirty grosh per bed, thirty grosh for food, and thirty grosh for each horse," Dasha said. "Which means that..."

"Thirty for food!" the innkeeper interrupted her. "Dinner were only twenty!"

"And breakfast was ten," explained Dasha. "So together they make..."

But the innkeeper only interrupted her again, begging her not to confuse him, and growing more and more muddled as he tried to work his sums, and angrier and angrier when Dasha tried to convince him that the total for each person, counting their horses, was ninety grosh, which meant that the total for the seven of them was six hundred and thirty grosh, which worked out to three chervontsa and thirty grosh. The matter was only resolved when Oleg came back to announce that the horses were ready, and, seeing the problem, threw some coins down on the table in front of the innkeeper and announced that they were leaving immediately.

"How do you I know you're not cheating me!" demanded the innkeeper.

"That's three chervontsa and fifty grosh," said Dasha, counting quickly. "So we should take this twenty-grosh piece back..." But the innkeeper snatched up all the coins before she could take back the change that he owed them, and Oleg hustled her out of the door, followed by the innkeeper, who continued to complain that they must be cheating him.

"He *cheated* us!" cried Dasha indignantly, as soon as they were mounted up and on their way. "He *cheated* us, and you let him!"

"With the money your mother gave us for this journey, I'd rather lose a few grosh than another moment arguing with the likes of him," said Oleg. "Besides, he'd never be able to figure the bill anyway, so it was the only way out of there." He looked over and saw her face. "If it makes you feel any better, I don't think he was trying to cheat us," he told her. "And he probably gets cheated all the time by his other customers, poor as his figuring is."

"He wouldn't let me help him," said Dasha, half in wonder, half in annoyance. "I knew the right answer, and I told it to him, but it only made him angry and untrusting, and the more I tried to explain how I had gotten the right answer, the more upset and scared he was! And he wouldn't let me help him at all, even though I knew how to do what needed to be done, and he didn't."

"Welcome to the wide world, my love," said Oleg, with a dry half-smile. "Those that are least capable are the ones that insist most strongly on having their way in matters they don't understand."

"But..." said Dasha, but since she had just witnessed it herself first-hand, she could find no objection to his words, other than her own dislike of that truth, so she made no more attempt to argue it, and allowed herself to be distracted by Susanna and Svetochka's good-natured—well, good-natured on Susanna's part—ribbing of each other over the boy who had served them dinner, and merry plans—at least on Susanna's part—to conquer a new heart at every inn they stopped at.

It was another sunny day, even warmer than the one before, so that by midmorning Dasha found herself unfastening her kaftan, and when they stopped for their midday meal she took off her hat and put it in her pack. Oleg tried to argue against it, on the grounds that she might catch a chill if the sky clouded over or a wind came up, but his resistance was half-hearted at best, merely to salve his conscience, and when she mounted up after their meal with her hat still in her pack, he said nothing about it, not even when a breeze really did come up and lift her hair so that it streamed behind her like, as Susanna said fancifully, a flame.

The road and the earth being turned over in the fields they trotted past was black and moist and smelled of the beginnings of life: a pungent, not entirely pleasant smell, but rich and heady, even as it whispered of death as well as birth. Whenever the wind would pick up, pollen would float down from the trees and get in their nostrils, causing everyone to sneeze violently. Which Dasha didn't mind at all, but when Sverchok went into such a fierce paroxysm that he had to stop dead and rub his nose against his knees, Svetochka slid out of the saddle and right down his neck onto the ground.

"Bad!" she shrieked, yanking on the reins and kicking him in the face. Sverchok, who had never been treated so in his entire blameless life, didn't even think to defend himself from her assault, and merely stood there, stupefied and terrified by this unexpected attack.

"No, Svetochka!" Dasha shouted, jumping down from Poloska and grabbing the reins from her. "I told you! *Never* punish your horse in the mouth! Or in the face! What is wrong with you?!?! You scared him! You could have hurt him! You could have made him hurt someone else! How would you feel if someone did that to you?!?"

"I been hit in the face plenty of times," was Svetochka's sullen reply. "It never did me no harm."

"That's not true!" Dasha blurted out before she could stop herself. "If it's made you act like this, then it's done you plenty of harm! Don't treat my horse like this!"

"He ain't your horse," said Svetochka, even more sullenly than before. Telling her that being hit in the face had done her harm had been the wrong thing to do, Dasha could see, even though it was true. She should speak gently with Svetochka, try to help her rather than antagonize her further.

"He's more mine than yours!" was what came out of her mouth, though. "And I won't let you abuse him like this! If this is how you're going to act, then I don't want to be with you at all!"

"Fine!" Svetochka actually stamped her foot on the spongy earth beneath her. Tears were starting in her eyes, and her whole front was covered with dirt and grass stains. Behind her, Dasha could hear the guards snickering. "I don't want to be with you—any of you—either! I'm going home!"

"Don't be ridiculous! Where would you go? How would you get

there?"

Svetochka gave Dasha a look that was almost as betrayed as the look Sverchok had given Svetochka, and began to cry in earnest.

"You don't want me!" she got out between sobs. "You don't want me! And it hurts so much! I can't stand another moment in that cursed saddle, the Black God take it! I never hurt so bad in my entire life."

"I didn't mean it," Dasha found herself saying, softening at the sight of Svetochka's tears.

"Yes you did!"

"Well..." Dasha slid all three sets of reins onto her arms, and reached out and took Svetochka's hands in her own. Luckily none of the horses were in a mood to fight, not like Chernets, who was picking a quarrel with Seva's horse even as they spoke. "I was upset," she said, ignoring the disagreements that were going on behind her. "I can't stand to see anyone hurt a good horse, not even if she's my sister. But I don't like to see you in pain, either. I know it hurts a lot—more than anything in the world—when you first start riding, going on real rides, and I know your first fall is very frightening. The first time I fell off, I cried too."

"Really?" asked Svetochka, wiping her eyes and looking up, almost catching Dasha's eye.

"Really," Dasha told her. She thought it best not to mention that she had been a child of four—or was it three?—at the time. "I cried and cried when they picked me up off the ground, and cried even more when they put me back on."

"Back on!" repeated Svetochka.

"Of course. You have to get right back on after a fall, everyone knows it. That way you won't be scared. So come on: let's apologize to Sverchok and get you back on."

"Apologize to a horse!"

"Better than to a human," said Dasha, leaning forward with a conspiratorial smile. "After all, he might actually listen. And forgive you."

This elicited a watery smile from Svetochka, which turned into more moans when Dasha actually legged her back up into the saddle. Dasha had to suppress a wince at that: the pain in the sitting bones riding could cause when you weren't used to it was enough to make the bravest woman want to cry, as it felt the flesh between your legs had been stripped away entirely, leaving nothing but nerves and bare bones in contact with the saddle. Dasha herself was feeling more than a little sore after all this time on the road, and she knew Svetochka must be in agony, and her muscles must be sore too, unaccustomed as they were to holding her in the saddle for verst after verst. But, as she whispered to Svetochka once she had gotten her as settled as she was going to be, at least she wasn't a man. However painful the experience was for her, it could be worse, much worse. Svetochka almost giggled at that, and soon they were on their way once again.

They rode along quite merrily after that for a while, or at least, Dasha rode along merrily, and Svetochka only moaned a little bit from the pain. After another verst or so they came to a fork in the road, and took the right-hand path.

"This is the road that'll lead us to Lesnograd," Oleg told them. "If we'd gone left, we'd have carried on to Pristanograd and Vostochnoye Selo."

"Is that the way my mother went on her journey?" Dasha asked.

"I suppose," Oleg said. "I wasn't with them. But there aren't very many roads leading North. She probably took the left-hand path on her way up, and the right-hand path—the one we're on—on the way back down."

It felt very significant to Dasha that she was taking a different path from her mother, even if it was just the same one in the opposite direction. "Is this the way you came down?" she asked Svetochka.

"For a bit," Svetochka told her, trying to smile but only grimacing in pain. "I were on this bit of road for sure. But most of the way I were on smaller roads, where I knew I could find folks as'd help me."

"Well then, you'll get to see something new too," Dasha said, with an encouraging smile, which Svetochka attempted to return. This, Dasha thought, must be what having a sister, a proper sister, was like.

But, unfortunately, the rapprochement between Dasha and Svetochka had, it soon turned out, been bought at a high price. The snickering Dasha had heard behind them when she had been shouting at, and then helping, Svetochka, had not been her imagination, but had been the expression of the guards' genuine amusement and joy at the sight of Svetochka falling off her horse and being chastised by her sister. Even though Dasha had not meant to say anything so very terrible, and had, she thought, made things right between her and Svetochka afterwards, her words had somehow told the guards that Svetochka was now fair game for anyone who wanted to amuse himself at someone else's expense.

At first Dasha didn't understand what was going on, since the guards were respectful enough towards her and Susanna, and appeared to be somewhat afraid of Oleg, calling him "Oleg Svetosla-vovich" and bowing their heads whenever he spoke, even as they made faces at him behind his back—Dasha wasn't supposed to see that, she was sure, but after he had reprimanded them—gently, but still a rep-rimand—for laughing amongst themselves over Svetochka's fall, she saw them wrinkling up their noses and sticking out their tongues in his direction.

Which made her wonder: how often did her guards do the same thing to her? Were they all secretly sticking out their tongues at her when she wasn't looking? She would have liked to think that they weren't, but she had to guess that at least some of them were. Which certainly explained some things about the behavior of people like Ar-kasha, but she would have liked to think that Mitya, Alik, and Seva were different: after all, that's why they had been chosen. But appar-ently not.

As the afternoon wore on, Dasha noticed that whenever Oleg wasn't paying attention to them, they teased Svetochka about all kinds of things that Dasha didn't think were funny at all: her red hair, her cleft chin, her full figure, the mistakes she made when she spoke (even though they made many of the same mistakes themselves), the fact that she was wearing borrowed clothes—none of that seemed like a source of mirth to Dasha at all, but for the guards, it was an endless font of amusement, especially when they didn't have anything better to think about.

And what was worse, if Svetochka got angry and lashed out at them, which she did several times, they only teased her even more often and more mercilessly, but when Dasha tried to intercede and ex-plain to them that what they were doing wasn't very kind, they argued angrily that they were just having a bit of fun and it wasn't very kind of *her* to stop them from having their bit of fun, in a way that made Dasha feel terribly guilty and also a little bit afraid of what would happen if she were to try to argue with them again, and the next time, when Susanna reprimanded them for their behavior, they sank into a sullen sulk that was even more frightening, and went right back to teasing Svetochka before they were even another verst down the road.

When Oleg found out what was going on, he also tried to put a stop to it, using rather more forceful and threatening language than either Dasha or Susanna had, but met with little more success. It was as if the guards, for all their appearance of being good-hearted lads—and maybe they were, as good-hearted as lads could be—had realized that there was one person in the group who was beneath them, and they were determined to pour out all of their malice onto her, and trying to make them stop only made them more malicious.

By the end of the day, Svetochka had stopped arguing with them, or even paying attention to them, which Dasha had thought might make things better, but no—the more she ignored them, the more they teased her. All three girls were in near tears over it when they stopped for the night.

"We have to do something," Dasha decided, as they stowed their packs under the bed of the little chamber they had been given at the waystation where they were staying. It was less rundown than the previous one, but smaller, and so far they hadn't seen anyone as handsome as the boy who had served them dinner the night before, which was a disappointment. On the other hand, the sheets in their bed smelled better.

"It ain't worth it," said Svetochka. Her shoulders were slumped, and her voice and her face were dull with resignation.

"Yes it is!" Dasha said. "We just have to figure out how to stop them."

"We could ask Oleg Svetoslavovich to step in again," suggested Susanna, the doubt she felt over the efficacy of such a step clear in her voice.

"No," said Dasha. "It didn't work the first time, and besides, these are *my* guards. I'm the one who needs to take them in hand. I just don't know what's gotten into them!"

"Young men can be like that," said Susanna sagely, while Svetochka nodded in listless agreement. "Once they are out from under their mothers' control, they feel the need to prove themselves as men."

"By harassing and hurting people?!" said Dasha. "That doesn't sound very manly to *me*." To herself she had to admit that she only had the vaguest notion of what it was to be "manly," but she was certain it didn't involve making the most vulnerable member of their own party miserable.

"Their mothers, if they have done their duty, will have told them that it is wrong," said Susanna. "So they think they are rebelling, as grown men should. I have seen it dozens of times."

This seemed to Dasha to be one of the silliest things she had ever heard, so silly that she had a hard time giving it any credence at all, but Susanna looked so sincere, and it did explain so much about the behavior of the guards, that Dasha decided to take it on faith for the moment.

"Very well," she said. "Then we have to...think of some way to make them act right, without making them feel like they're under the thumbs of their mothers. Although if this is how even the best of lads behave if they think they can get away with it, perhaps they need to stay under their mothers' thumbs for life!"

This made Susanna giggle, and Svetochka smile wanly, in agreement. With this encouragement, they went down to dinner, ready for confrontation.

The confrontation that Dasha was steeling herself for had to wait, however, as the guards were not in the main room when they came down, only Oleg.

"Where are the others?" Dasha asked, as she, Susanna, and Svetochka all sat down on the same bench, opposite Oleg.

"In the stable," Oleg told them. "Having their dinner with the stablehands." He leaned forward. "There was talk in the stables of thefts of tack and even horses, so they're spending the night there tonight. I've arranged for my chamber to be next to yours tonight, and you should each stand watch tonight, just in case."

"Are people being attacked in their chambers, then?" Dasha asked, trying not to show how alarmed she was at the thought. Alarmed, but also excited at the idea of standing watch herself.

"Not yet, but it's a small step from stealing horses to stealing people out of their bedchambers, and you need a watch over you every night in any case. So the guards will stand guard over the horses, and we'll stand guard over each other. I'll stay up all night in my chamber, and you can take turns in yours."

"You shouldn't have to stay up all night!" said Dasha. "We'll all stand guard over each other! We'll stand guard over you as well. Besides," she added, "that way we can each stand shorter shifts."

Oleg smiled a small, and, Dasha thought, proud smile. "We'll have to sit out in the corridor, then," he said. "So that we can keep an eye on both doors."

"I don't mind," insisted Dasha, and Susanna nodded in agreement. Dasha could tell that she was just as excited as she, Dasha, was over the idea of standing her own guard, and the idea of doing it out in the corridor, where others could see them, made it seem even more exciting.

"Very well," Oleg agreed with another little smile, as if he could guess their thoughts—which perhaps he could. Perhaps, Dasha thought, he had had exactly the same sorts of thoughts when he was their age. "I'll go first, so everyone who passes by can see me standing there and know the chambers are under guard, and then you can take your turns once everyone's gone to bed. But," now he was grinning, "are you ready for it? Are you ready to stand guard in the depths of the night, your nerves quivering with every gust of wind, every creak of the floorboards, imagining all the things that could be lurking in the shadows…"

"Stop it!" Dasha cried. "You're just trying to scare us!"

"And it's working too, I can tell," he told them, still grinning. "And good. I don't want you falling asleep on your duties, and a little fear's the best way to keep the sleepy guard awake, in my experience. Especially the unlucky person who draws the middle shift, when the night is at its darkest…"

"*I'll* take the middle shift, then," said Dasha, stopping him before he could continue. Susanna opened her mouth, probably to object, but Dasha forestalled her, saying, "Svetochka isn't a morning lark like the rest of us, so she should take the shift right after Oleg, so that she doesn't have to get up any earlier than she has to, and you should take the last shift, since you know best how things work in waystations and you can go make sure that breakfast is ready and the horses are fed and saddled and ready for us after your shift is over, since you'll already be up and dressed."

"It is good that no one is watching us," said Susanna. "Because they would guess right away that I am not your mistress." But she agreed readily enough to Dasha's plan, and so, once they had finished their dinner, they went straight up to their chambers at Oleg's advice, to get as much rest as they could before their interrupted night.

Chapter Fifteen

That night Dasha made yet another new discovery about life on the road, namely, that the knowledge that you will have to get up early makes it much more difficult to fall asleep, especially if you have decided to go to bed early in the hopes of not losing too much sleep. She lay awake listening to people pass by in the corridor outside their door, many of them stopping to talk to Oleg and make jokes about the mistress they assumed he was serving, even though they could be heard clearly through the thin walls. She was still awake when Oleg came in and got Svetochka, and she assumed she would still be awake when Svetochka came for her, but in fact she had just sunk into a deep sleep when Svetochka shook her roughly on the shoulder, and she was still groggy when she stumbled out into the hallway after her, trying and failing to buckle on her swordbelt.

"There's someone else standing guard as well," Svetochka whispered to her. "There down at the end." And indeed, Dasha could dimly see a figure leaning against the corridor wall, down by the stair. "You see how the moonlight's coming in through the window?" Svetochka continued. "When you can't see the moon no more, it'll be time for you to get Susanna. Understand?"

Dasha nodded, wondering how that could possibly be misunderstood, but not wanting to get into a pointless discussion about it in her half-awake state. "Understand?" repeated Svetochka, apparently thinking that Dasha was confused or being difficult.

"I understand," Dasha whispered. "When the moon disappears from the window, I'll come get Susanna." Svetochka's hurt glance, clearly visible in the moonlight flooding in through the window, suggested that she hadn't managed to keep her contempt for the question as veiled as she should have, but Svetochka forbore to argue about it, and with a sharp nod of her head, went back into their chamber, leaving Dasha to finally buckle on her swordbelt properly (feeling ridiculous as she did so—who was going to attack them in the middle of the night in a waystation?—but also a little frightened—what if someone attacked them and she had to defend the others?) and arrange herself as comfortably as possible.

That proved to be more difficult than she would have guessed. There was nowhere to sit except the floor, which seemed like a bad idea, both because of the dirt and the discomfort, as well as because if Dasha *did* have to spring into action, it would be very difficult to do so from a sitting position.

After a furtive glance at the other person standing guard in the corridor, she copied him by leaning against the wall, but it was hard and a cold draft was blowing in through a crack between the window frame and the glass. And then, once she had finally gotten herself settled into a position that was slightly less uncomfortable and inconvenient than all the other positions she had tried, she realized that she was still sleepy and terribly bored, and the moon was nowhere near setting.

She had never experienced before how tedious and unpleasant guard duty must be, and for a moment the realization of the immense quantity of suffering that had been taking place around her every day of her life, right in front of her but without her awareness, loomed so large before her that she wasn't sure how she was going to stand it, and she had to bite down on her lips to keep from crying out.

Stop it! she told herself sharply. *It can't be **that** bad!* But she knew that was nothing more than the feeble excuse of someone who doesn't want to admit how much suffering she is causing others—or was it? It certainly *could* be, but was it in this case? After all, lots of things that she considered to be terrible didn't seem to bother other people at all. So which was it here? Was standing guard really as terrible for everyone else as it seemed to her, or did her guards not actually mind so much? Perhaps they even enjoyed it? Or were glad not to be doing something worse—working on the road crews or the mines, for example.

Not that any of them would have had to choose between the road crews and guard duty, because there were no criminals in the Imperial Guard, unlike the guard companies that some of the other noblewomen kept, who were made up almost entirely of criminals and other desperate men trying to escape their pasts...like her father...if he'd come running to them, to her family, for help, they most likely wouldn't have taken him in; it was Princess Severnolesnaya's lax morals and low standards that had saved him: saved him and indirectly brought her, Dasha, into being, because if the old Princess Severnolesnaya hadn't taken him in and then taken him as her husband, then he never would have been chosen to father her, Dasha...or *would* he? Perhaps that had been fated long before he ever ended up with the old Princess Severnolesnaya, and if he hadn't been taken in by her, he would have ended up with Dasha's mother some other way...perhaps Princess Severnolesnaya had actually delayed things rather than speeding them along, and Dasha's parents should have met long before they actually did, and Dasha should have been ten years older than she really was, and not the Tsarinovna at all, but merely the daughter of the Tsarinovna, third in line for the throne...only the gods had their plans for her, didn't they? Either way, they still would have wanted her to end up on the throne, wouldn't they?

But perhaps if she had been born earlier, their plans and their desires for what, exactly, she was supposed to do for them would have already been revealed, and she wouldn't still be worrying about it, because it would already be over, which would be good, because she didn't like to think about what the gods were planning for her; it scared her almost as much as her uncontrollable visions: no, more, it made her sick to her stomach just to think of all the wants and needs and possibilities and expectations hovering around her, lurking, looming...

"AKH!" Dasha shrieked, hitting her head against the wall as she jumped. The other person standing guard had come over and was trying to get her attention.

"Sorry," she whispered, hoping she hadn't woken anyone up, particularly her father, with her shriek. She waited, barely breathing, for a moment, but all remained quiet in Oleg's chamber. She must not have shouted as loudly as it had seemed to her.

"You're a jumpy little thing, ain't you?" the man whispered back, his grin visible in the moonlight that was still flooding in through the window, although, Dasha noted with relief, already at a different angle than when she had started her shift. Soon the moon would set and she could go in.

"I'm as big as you are," Dasha whispered, saying the first thing that came into her mind. And it was true: the man was probably twice her age, she guessed, but no taller than her, and she probably outweighed him. But it must have been the wrong thing to say, for he wrinkled his nose in offense.

"Bold, too," he said, still whispering, but more loudly than before. He was leaning awfully close. "What's so special about your mistress, anyway, that she needs guarding? Is she that high an' mighty? You'd think she'd've taught you some manners in that case."

That seemed like a very strange question to Dasha: of course her mistress was high and mighty, if she had a guard standing outside her door, even if as it happened the mistress was Dasha herself. It was as if his questions weren't about what they were supposed to be about at all. "She'll be angry if we wake her," Dasha whispered, instead of replying. "And shouldn't you be at your post yourself?"

"Feisty!" said the man. "You remind me of my daughter, you know: she's just about your age. And she has hair like yours."

"Oh?" said Dasha politely, and then she was even more puzzled when the man reached out and squeezed her buttocks. It didn't hurt, but it seemed like a very strange thing to do, so she tried to sidle away, but then he grabbed her breast with his other hand, which also didn't hurt but seemed like an even stranger thing to do: what could he possibly be thinking? He'd said she reminded him of his daughter, who was just her age!

A sick feeling was growing in the pit of her stomach, and she wanted to shrink away from him, but there wasn't anywhere for her to go, and he wasn't hurting her, was he? Oh, but now he was leaning in as if for a kiss—what should she do? So far he hadn't hurt her, not really, but she certainly didn't want any of his kisses, and now his hand on her breast really was starting to hurt her, and it was starting to occur to her, as she felt sicker and sicker, that something terrible might be about to happen if she didn't stop it, but she didn't want to *hurt* him, especially since he would probably scream, and that would wake up everyone in the surrounding chambers, and then they would be angry with Dasha for disturbing them...

"AAKH!" shrieked the man, jerking away from her and stumbling, almost falling. "AAAKH, AAAKH, AAAKH!" He was jumping and kicking as if a wasp had gone down his boots and started stinging him.

"WHAT BY ALL THE MOTHER-RAPING GODS IS GOING ON OUT HERE!" Oleg had come bursting out of his chamber wearing nothing but his trousers. He grabbed the man by his throat and threw him up against the wall, holding him pinned there as he still kept kicking and fighting his own boots. Doors were opening up and down the corridor. "What did you do?" Oleg hissed. He gave the man a shake. "Look at me and answer! What did you do?"

"AAKH!" cried the man by way of response, flailing his boots against the wall and then, suddenly, slumping into submission.

"Did he hurt you?" Oleg demanded, looking over at Dasha. "Dasha!" he said, when she failed to respond. "Did he hurt you?"

"I'm sorry?" Dasha said, dragging her eyes away from where they had been transfixed on the man's boots. She could have sworn that wisps of shadows had come crawling out of them and disappeared into their sisters in the corners of the corridor. "No..." she said. "He didn't...hurt me...exactly...he just..."

But she didn't know how to describe the man's strange behavior in a way that both explained how truly peculiar (to her mind) it had been, and how he had not, in fact, actually hurt her. "He...I don't know what he was doing..." she went on, and then fell silent.

Now that it came to it, she discovered that, for some reason she couldn't explain even to herself, she was ashamed to tell Oleg what had happened, even though she hadn't done anything wrong...or had she? Perhaps she had done something terrible without even meaning to. Suddenly, clearly, she could see that, even though she still couldn't find the words to tell Oleg what had happened, she was already feeling a squirming sickness in her stomach when she thought about it.

Even though she truly hadn't done anything wrong, even though it was the man who had done something wrong, whatever that was. But—this was the truly sickening part—she *could* do something wrong, something terrible, without meaning to. If Oleg or anyone else were to find out that this man had been thinking of doing—the word *rape* couldn't even make it into Dasha's consciousness—to the Tsarinovna, his life would be over, only there would be a fair amount of suffering before it actually ended. Dasha opened her mouth to try to explain things in a way that save him from a little bit of that pain.

"It were her!" the man blurted out before she could speak. "She drew me over, an'...it were her!"

"It was not!" Dasha cried, irate at the unfair accusation, her intentions to shield him from his own misdeeds forgotten. "He came over on his own, and then...but he didn't have time to hurt me, because...because they got him!"

Oleg frowned briefly at that, confused by the "they," but then forgot about that in favor of slamming the man against the wall again, so hard that the boards shook and Dasha cried out in shock.

"He's been punished enough!" she said. "They got him, they rescued me from him, and he's already been punished! Don't hurt him!" She reached out and put a hand on Oleg's arm. "Please," she said, "don't hurt him. I don't want to see you hurt him. He's not worth it."

Oleg looked over at her. His jaw clenched, and then he nodded curtly. "Who does this...piece of shit," he suddenly stepped back and let go of the man, causing him to collapse onto the ground in surprise at the unexpected release, "belong to?"

"What you done that for?" demanded a woman, coming up to stand beside Dasha and giving her a look that would have etched, or possibly melted, glass. "What you talking about him like that for? He ain't done nothing! It were her!"

"It was *not*!" protested Dasha, growing angrier and angrier at the assumption that she must have done something when she most certainly hadn't. "I was just standing here, standing guard, when *he* came up to *me*! And then he..." She trailed off in confusion and embarrassment. Why couldn't he have kept his hands off of her? Or why couldn't he have accepted the punishment he had been given and slunk off in silence? Why did he have to involve the entire inn in his foolishness?

"What, you ain't got the nerve to lie about it to our faces?" jeered the woman. She was small and slight, no bigger than Dasha's mother, with short spiky hair that was sticking up in every direction, and she smelled as if she hadn't bathed or cleaned her teeth in days. Dasha couldn't help but have a little vision about what it must be like to work for her, watch over her...share her bed? That was what the vision was saying. Tfoo! Dasha shook her head to try to clear it.

"I am not lying," she said. The woman stiffened, and Dasha could hear in her voice the tone, as clear as crystal and sharp as shards of glass, of her mother when she was displeased about something. There was no anger in it, which it made it even more frightening, because it said that anger was for the weak, but the possessor of this voice had no need of it to make her will be done.

"I am not lying," she repeated, and tried not to take pleasure at the way the woman flinched from the lash of her voice. "*He* came up to *me*, and *he* was the one who attempted to force himself upon *me*, to his regret. Because I am under the protection of this roof and the spirits who dwell beneath it, and those who would seek to harm me or my companions will suffer for it. There is no need to punish him further," she added, speaking now to Oleg. "They have already given him his due measure of punishment for his trespasses against me. Let him go, and let us retire back to our chambers."

"Who you think you are!" cried the woman, but her voice shook as she spoke, and she had involuntarily taken a halfstep back from Dasha.

"Someone in the favor of the gods," Dasha told her. "Come, father: let us leave them and retire."

"We can't just let him go," Oleg objected. "Else he'll just do to others what he wanted to do to you."

Dasha glanced over to the corners of the corridor. She thought she caught sight of movement in the shadows that shouldn't have been there. "I leave him to the justice of those who watch over this roof, and dwell under it," she said. "They will instruct him in the error of his ways more thoroughly than we ever could. Come." She stepped away from the woman and Oleg, and went back into her chamber. After a moment, there was a thud and a yelp behind her, as if Oleg had given the man one final kick, and then Oleg followed her into her chamber, where Susanna and Svetochka came running over and were hovering around her.

"Are you hurt?" demanded Susanna. "No, I can see that you are not! But by his screams, he was!" She grinned wolfishly at that. "You gave him what he deserved!"

"I don't know about that..." began Dasha. She still didn't know how to explain to the others that the man hadn't really hurt her, but he had done something that was now seeming almost worse than hurting her, as she remembered the sick feeling that had bloomed in the pit of her stomach at his touch, the sense that something terrible was about to happen, that he wanted to do something terrible to her, even if it didn't seem that way to anyone else, including him. "He...it wasn't me," she said. "It wasn't me that drove him off. I think it was the domoviye."

"The domoviye!" exclaimed everyone at once. "Domoviye don't do that kind of thing," Svetochka said, dismissively. "They don't stand up for you, not even if you need it. That ain't what they do. They never stood up for me or anyone I knew, not once. You gotta stand up for yourself, not go looking for spirits an' stuff to do it for you."

"I didn't know what to do...I was afraid of making a scene and making everyone angry with me for disturbing them...and he kept talking about how I reminded him of his daughter..." Dasha faltered and fell silent at the look on Oleg's face, which grew so thunderously angry at those words she instinctively shrank away from him, thinking that she had somehow proven that she really was at fault for what had happened. But rather than shouting at her, or striking her, as Dasha had feared, he simply strode out of the chamber, still looking like thunder.

"Anyway," she continued nervously, "then he started screaming, and then I thought...I thought I saw"—she was interrupted by the sound of a slamming door, shouting, and what sounded like fighting.

"We should go stop them," she said uncertainly.

"Nonsense!" said Susanna. "Only if you want to hit him yourself!"

"Certainly not! But I don't want..."

"Dasha," Susanna stopped her before she could continue. "I know you do not...spend much time with your father. He was not with you so often when you were a child. And perhaps things are different here in Zem', but not so much, I think. You see, a father does not like it when something like this happens to his daughter. A proper father, that is. There are many bad fathers, of course, like that man there. Many. But a proper father's duty is to protect his daughter and every other father's daughter from men like that. Your father knows that in his heart, even if he does not know it as an Avkhazovskoye father would. He must punish that man, and he must make it so that he does not hurt his own daughter or anyone else's daughter in the future, because he will. He will unless he is stopped, and your father needs to do it."

"Oh," said Dasha. The sounds of fighting had died down in the other chamber. "But I don't want him to do anything really bad for my sake, especially since I wasn't actually hurt," she said.

"Let him be the judge of that," Susanna told her. "My father...if something like that were to happen to me, or something even worse, the gods forbid...my father is a good man, he knows his place, but if something like that were to happen to me or my sisters and brothers, then no one could stop him from taking his vengeance and stopping the man who did it from doing it again. You have to let him do this, Dasha."

"Do what?" asked Oleg, stepping back into their chamber. The knuckles on both his fists were bloody, Dasha noticed.

"Taking your vengeance," Susanna told him.

"Too right," said Oleg. "That man...the gods alone know what he's done to his daughter—his own daughter! And that woman he's with—

not his wife!—she's been taking him into her bed, she tried to defend him when I went in there! He has to be stopped, Dasha my love, no matter how much it upsets you, he needs to be stopped."

"But how?" asked Dasha. "We can't just send him off to the mines for one little thing...and we have our journey, we can't go dispensing justice..."

Oleg grinned, even more wolfishly than Susanna had. "Some justice has already been dispensed," he told her. "He won't be going anywhere anytime soon, and that should keep the world safe from him for a bit. And then...I think you're right, my dove. The domoviye *are* watching over you, and I think they'll be taking an interest in him, as well. I caught sight of one creeping into the room as I left, and she looked none too happy. And now everyone here knows what kind of man he is, or will soon. So justice will be served, one way or another."

"The domoviye!" cried Svetochka. "Why...why are they protecting *her*?! Why are they standing up for *her*!? It ain't fair!"

"No," said Oleg. "It's just life. And now I think we should leave. It's practically light out already, and the sooner we're away from here, the better. Pack up, girls, and let's get out of here."

They packed up as best they could, although between the shaking that had suddenly overcome her whole body, and her annoyance at Svetochka's moaning about how unfair everything was, Dasha could barely get her things into her pack, and was convinced that she had forgotten something, but couldn't figure out what that might be, and by the time the sun was up, they were simultaneously bolting down breakfast and mounting up, and soon they were on their way in the early-morning chill.

There was frost on the budding leaves and the grass that was just starting to come out by the side of the road. Dasha hoped it would burn off soon enough, once the sun began to warm them, but the sun, after peeking out briefly at dawn, hid itself behind thicker and thicker clouds, and instead of growing warmer, the air grew colder and colder, until little flakes of snow were drifting down around them, whirling this way and that in the eddies caused by the gusts of wind that was picking up. After a couple of versts of this, when it became apparent that it was not going to stop snowing and the day was not going to get any warmer, they all stopped to pull out their warmest clothing from their packs and wrap it around them.

"I thought it was supposed to be spring!" Susanna complained. "It does not snow in spring!"

"Maybe not down in the South," said Oleg. "But up here in Zem' it can snow well into Flowermoon, and it's still early in the month. We could be riding through many more of these little snow showers, all the way to Lesnograd and maybe beyond."

"But it was so warm yesterday!"

"That's spring for you," Oleg told her. "One day it's one thing, and the next it's different. So pull your kerchief tight around your face, and let's get on with it. Mitya!"

Mitya looked up from where he was fussing with his stirrup and whispering with the other guards. Dasha had a sinking feeling that she knew what they were whispering about. They hadn't given the guards any details of why they had had to rush off before breakfast, but they must have guessed at least the broad outlines of what had happened.

"I want to make sure we're not being followed," Oleg told him. "It's come to my mind that our friends must have plenty of acquaintances in these parts, and I want to make sure none of them are looking for us to," he looked over at Susanna, "take their own vengeance."

"They have no right!" Susanna said hotly. "The fault is all theirs! Anyone can see it!"

"I don't know how it is in the South, but here in Zem' people can be surprisingly blind to their own faults," Oleg told her dryly. "Better safe than sorry, that's what I say. Those two are from these parts: who knows what friends they might have, who might take it into their heads to come after us and deal with us as they see fit."

"They would not dare!" cried Susanna. "And if they did, we would fend them off!"

"Better safe than sorry," repeated Oleg, the corners of his mouth quirking in a hint of a smile, whether out of sympathy with Susanna, or amusement at her confidence, Dasha couldn't say. "So Mitya, you ride on ahead, and Alik and Seva, you ride behind us, and keep a watch for anyone coming or going our way."

"I want to ride ahead too!" said Susanna.

"Then by all means, ride on with Mitya," Oleg told her. "It'll be good for Chernets to stretch his legs."

Chernets, who was in a particularly foul mood from the cold air, which his thin Southern skin and coat didn't appreciate at all, pinned back his ears and snapped in Oleg's direction in reply, but neither he nor Belka responded, and soon everyone had their warm clothing wrapped around them, their saddles and stirrups adjusted—Mitya's was giving him trouble, rubbing against his leg, but Dasha was able to help him angle it just right once he was mounted up so that it wouldn't bother him so much—and they were trotting down the road again, accompanied by the snorting of the horses in the chill air, and Svetochka's moans at the pain she was enduring.

Which, Dasha had to admit, was probably intense, even though her moaning was annoying. Dasha tried to coach her as best she could, but the only real way to learn to ride was by riding. Of course, it helped to have a little grace and self-awareness, too, gifts Svetochka seemed to be singularly lacking in, or possibly intent on spurning with every grain of strength she possessed, but even someone as determined not to learn as Svetochka couldn't fail to make at least a little progress over the next few hundred versts. And the guards were too far away to engage in their mockery of yesterday, which was a mercy.

As the morning whiled on, Svetochka, worn down by the pain and the cold and the interrupted night's sleep until she could no longer fight Sverchok's movements and Dasha's suggestions, even seemed to improve slightly, moving in concert with her horse instead of trying to make him match her own graceless bouncing. When Dasha—foolishly, she realized in retrospect—praised her for it, and pointed out that her success was due to the fact that she was no longer fighting against everyone, including her own horse, Svetochka went into a sulk, but she didn't try to quarrel with Dasha, and she didn't, as Dasha feared for a moment she might, deliberately ride worse out of spite. So all in all, despite the cold wind numbing her fingers and slipping in under her kerchief and her kaftan, Dasha was pleased with the morning and the journey, and considered it a success.

They came to a tiny village, hardly worthy of the name, around midday. Dasha expected them to ride straight through and stop for their midday rest once they were out of sight, but instead Oleg rode up to the first of the half-dozen huts crowding around the road, and called over the fence into the yard, "Is Agafya there?"

An older, lined-faced woman, with a worn kerchief pulled tightly around her head and an elaborately embroidered and horned headdress placed on top of it, popped her face over the top of the fence and called back, "Who's asking?"

"It's about her father," Oleg answered.

The woman made a sour face. "He ain't welcome here, even if he is my son," she said. "They say sons is the most important in a mother's life, but granddaughters come higher, to my mind. Let him stay with that woman, her as ruined him an' took him away."

"Is Agafya well, then?" asked Oleg.

"She is now that he's away," the old woman told him. "And she will be long as he stays that way."

"He will, if he knows what's good for him," Oleg told her. "Anyways, he's promised."

"He's promised a lot of things," said the woman.

"Be that as it may, this promise may have a little more force to it," Oleg said. "And he won't be in any fit state to come bothering you for some time, if I'm any guess."

That made the old woman's sour face split into a grin. "Like that, is it?" she asked. "Finally met someone who'd stop him, did he? What'd he do? Go after your daughter?"

Oleg gave a curt nod, making the woman grin even wider for a moment, before her sourness came back. "So he had to go after some noblewoman's daughter afore any justice could be done," she said. "His own daughter weren't enough, as well as all that thieving an' the other stuff he did. But he goes after a noblewoman's daughter..."

"He is your son," Oleg interrupted her, before her complaint could pick up any more force. "He lived in your village." He looked around. "I don't see anyone other than his own people who could be responsible for him and his actions."

For a moment the old woman had the grace to look ashamed. "He always were a willful one," she said. "Came out backwards, he did, near tore me to pieces, an' he were just as willful an' difficult ever since. But his father...he were the apple of his father's eye, an' his father were the apple of our headwoman's, so..."

"I understand," said Oleg. Most of his face was hidden under his hat and scarf, but Dasha could see the muscles jumping in his jaws even so. "But he's crossed the wrong family now, do you understand? I don't think he'll be coming back, but if he does...if he does, and he offers any harm to Agafya or anyone else, you take what justice you need to, or if that won't work, you come to Krasnograd, to the kremlin, and you ask for Oleg Svetoslavovich, you understand? Or," his jaw muscles jumped again, and Dasha could see how hard it was for him to say the words, but he said them anyway, "or if you can't find me, you ask for Boleslav Vlasiyevich, and you tell him who you are and who he is and that I've sent you, and you tell him that this man raised his hand against our Dasha. Against our Dasha, do you understand?"

"Against our Dasha," the woman repeated doubtfully. "And this

Boleslav will do something about it?"

"You tell him that, and he will, I swear it, my head for beheading," Oleg told her. "But I doubt you'll need it. Not if he has any sense."

"He never did," said the woman. "But old age makes sages of us all, eh?" She grinned again, exposing a mouthful of missing teeth. "Even my no-good son. Children are a burden, by all the gods, children are a terrible burden, leastwise, mine was. But he got me my Gafenka, so I can't complain too much, can I?"

"Wise words," agreed Oleg. "Remember what I said, and my best wishes for Agafya's health and happiness."

"I'd call her out to hear those wishes from you direct," said the old woman, "but I don't want her to hear all of this with strangers present, 'specially nobles. Let her hear it from me, when it's quiet. She's had enough trouble in her life already, what with her mother dying an' her father...being what he is; she don't need this too. Let her hear it when it's quiet. Gone for good, you said?"

"Those who are stronger than I am have taken an interest in him," Oleg told her. "Taken an interest in stopping him from harming anyone else."

"Stronger than you..." the woman repeated slowly. "You don't mean...spirits an' such, do you?"

"Something like that," Oleg told her.

"What'd he do to fall afoul of such as them?" asked the woman.

Oleg said nothing, but nodded expressively in Dasha's direction, much to Dasha's embarrassment.

"The spirits have an interest in her?" asked the old woman doubtfully. "What'd she do to catch their eye?"

"She was born," Oleg told her. "Sometimes that's enough. But anyone who crosses her...do you understand?"

"Must be nice," said the old woman, with a grim little smile. "To have spirits an' such standing up for you."

"Nice for you too," Oleg told her. "Since they'll be keeping your Agafya safe as well, when you wouldn't. But if he comes back...don't be afraid to call on them. Call on the domoviye, or the leshiye, or any of the other spirits of the forest, tell them that this is the man who hurt our Dasha, and they'll come for him. Understand?"

"I understand," said the old woman. "An'..." she swallowed, and then said grudgingly, "thank you. For stopping him, an' for coming to tell me of it. Our minds'll be much easier, knowing he won't be coming back for us."

"Good," said Oleg. "Be well, then. Come on, girls, we've more road to ride before sunset." He and Belka wheeled away from the fence and back onto the road, and everyone trotted after him.

"Did the domoviye really put a stop to him, then?" asked Dasha, once they were clear of the village. It wasn't what she really wanted to ask, which was what Agafya's father had done that was so terrible, but part of her could guess, and another part of her told her that it would be better not to speak of such things openly, for fear of what it would do to her, and even more for fear of what it would do to Oleg.

She could still see the muscles in his jaw jumping. She knew, sort of, that sometimes parents did terrible things to their children, especially fathers, but she'd never encountered anyone who had suffered such things, or committed them, before. She saw the scene between her and the man in the inn again in her head, and her stomach clenched and her skin crawled. At the time it had seemed more...silly, she would have to say, or puzzling, than anything else, but as she understood it better and better, it seemed more and more sinister, and made her feel sicker and sicker to remember it. Not just because something really terrible could have happened, but because, she was realizing, something terrible *had* happened.

That man had been a terrible person who had done terrible things to his own daughter, and had been intent on doing terrible things to her, and even the brief brush with him had...she wasn't quite sure what it had done...tainted her? Not exactly, but...but it had exposed her to something ugly, brought something cruel and disgusting into her life, and even though it had only been a tiny drop, and even though she had been completely innocent of any wrongdoing herself, it was still poison, and poison was deadly even if drunk accidentally.

"You were right," Oleg told her, by way of answer. "The domoviye did come to save you. They came to us in the room, they came out of the shadows in the corners as I stood over that man, hearing his confession"—Oleg's mouth twisted, and he spat onto the road before continuing—"and wondering if I should kill him then and there, or at least cut off his...administer swift justice, I mean, make sure he never harmed another—"

"You wouldn't have killed him!" cried Dasha in horror. "Or done anything else to harm him!"

"It would have been no more than he deserved, Dasha, and it would have kept others safe from him. The old woman was right: not everyone has protectors as you do. You wouldn't have him go on to hurt others, just because they can't defend themselves as you can, would you?"

"No, but..." Dasha knew there was some flaw in Oleg's reasoning, some reason why he was wrong, but she couldn't find it. "We don't give people what they deserve," she found herself saying, just as she had heard her mother say so many times before. It had always annoyed her: of *course* you should give people what they deserved, what else? How else could there be justice in the world, other than by giving people what they deserved? After all, they *deserved* it. But now for the first time it made sense. "We give people what they need," she finished.

Oleg sighed. "True enough," he agreed. "Well, to my mind he *needed* to be stopped, and by whatever means necessary. Only just as I was standing there and he was sniveling at my feet and that shriveled-faced hobgoblin he'd joined up with was screeching at me and trying to scratch my eyes out, the domoviye came slipping out of the shadows, first no more than wisps, then fully formed. They're small, you know, no bigger than a child—or a dog—but even Gray Wolf wouldn't want to stand against them when they're riled. And they were riled then, though you might not have guessed it right away, not unless you know them like I do. And they came and crowded around that man, and pushed me away, and told me not to worry, they would deal with this, make it so that that man never threatened you nor anyone else ever again, and then they all leaned over him and laid their hands on his head, and...and he fell silent."

"Dead?!" cried Dasha.

"No, not dead, just...tamed. Or something. I don't know. They told me to leave then, and I did. But they tamed him, or broke him, or something like that, and I don't think he'll be a threat, ever again. And good riddance, too!" Oleg gave his shoulders a shake, and then said, in a much more cheerful voice, "And now we know that they're watching out for you, Dasha my love, so all in all, there's been more good than harm from this little adventure. Life on the road, eh?"

"Yes," agreed Dasha, trying to smile back at him. "Life on the road."

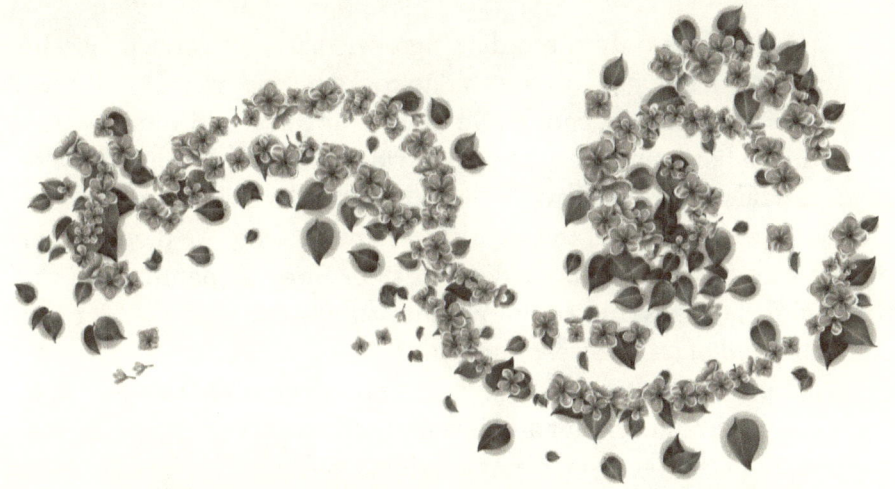

Chapter Sixteen

he snow showers continued for the rest of the day, so that by the time they arrived at their waystation for the night, the horses' hooves were leaving scuffed prints in the snow that was building up on the road, and there was a thin layer on everyone's hats and shoulders. Svetochka was moaning again about the pain she was in, which to be fair, must have been considerable, and Dasha herself wasn't sure if she would ever get any feeling back in her fingers. Until they went into the waystation and began thawing out, and then she got far too much feeling in them, and was hard pressed not to moan about it herself.

"How much farther to Lesnograd?" she asked, once the throbbing pain in her hands had reduced to a dull ache, allowing her to concentrate more fully on how incredibly hungry she was. A serving girl brought them bowls of borshch and a loaf of black bread.

"Are there sausages?" Susanna asked.

"For an extra ten grosh," the girl told them. "They're good: from pork. It were a good fat pig we slaughtered last fall."

"Bring us all sausages, then," Susanna told her.

"None for me," Dasha found herself saying.

Susanna gave her an incredulous look, and started to argue, but Dasha repeated, turning to Oleg, "How much farther to Lesnograd?"

"About two weeks," he told her. "Or more."

"It was two weeks or more when we set off from Krasnograd!"

"And that was only three days ago," he said. He looked like he wanted to grin, but was still too cold to make his face move.

"A whole three days ago! We've ridden for versts and versts!"

"And we have many more versts to ride before we get there. We've covered a fair stretch of road, yes, but there's still a lot more road to go, and we don't know what the weather will be, or what we'll encounter on the way. So it's still about two weeks or more, depending on the roads and the skies and so many other things that aren't under our control. Tired of travel already, are you?"

"No," protested Dasha. She took a spoonful of soup. It was surprisingly good, with sauerkraut and bits of dried mushroom in it. "I'm just curious. But it will get warmer as we ride, won't it?"

"As to that." Oleg started tearing the loaf of bread into chunks. It must have been baked that morning, for it was already starting to go stale, and he had to fight to break it. "As to that, I can't say."

"But it's spring! It's supposed to get warmer!"

"Yes, but," he handed around the chunks of bread, "it's still early yet, and we're riding North. It could be warm and sunny all the way, or we could spend the entire road from here to Lesnograd riding through the snow. You just don't know."

"I hope it doesn't keep snowing," Dasha said, shuddering at the thought. "Winter is past."

"It *cannot* keep snowing," said Susanna, with the voice of someone who expects her wishes to be obeyed, even by the weather. "One day of spring snow was enough! I can tell my friends of it back home, of how is the Zemnian spring, but I do not need any more. The sun must come out!"

Oleg smiled to himself, but said nothing in reply, and Susanna forgot the threat of snow when the sausages appeared. The serving girl had brought some for Dasha, even though she had asked her not to, and this led to a minor quarrel when Susanna tried to force her to take them, and Dasha tried to convince her to take them for herself instead, which only made Susanna more determined to force Dasha to join her in partaking of them. She seemed to take it as a personal affront that Dasha didn't want them, and refused to listen to any of Dasha's excuses and explanations, until Oleg put an end to the whole thing by spearing the offending sausages with his knife and eating them himself.

Dasha was grateful to him for resolving the quarrel that way, but as they left the main room and made their way up to their chambers, she was still irritated with Susanna. What business of hers was it what Dasha ate? Why was it so important to her to assert her will over Dasha in this matter? Dasha could feel the answers to those questions hovering just out of sight, but she could also feel that she wouldn't like them when she finally saw them, so she tried not to look at them.

Which only caused her to look at herself, and tell herself that refusing the sausages had been stupid and petty, since the pig was *already* dead and there was nothing she could do to bring her back to life, and Oleg had eaten the extra sausages anyway, so...so it was a problem that couldn't be solved, at least not tonight, and probably (something whispered to Dasha) not by that type of thinking. Trying to add things up as if they were sums was likely only to cause her to come up with the wrong answer. So instead she burrowed in the bedclothes, selfishly grateful that she had the side of the bed closest to the tiled stove that filled up at least a third of their chamber, and tried to warm herself enough to fall asleep.

"Is it still snowing?" asked Susanna, when they woke up the next morning.

Dasha got reluctantly out from under the warm covers, shivering in the dank chill of the air, and cracked open the shutters—there was no glass in the window—to look out on the stableyard. "No," she said. "It's raining."

Susanna and Svetochka both groaned.

"We should stay here," Susanna said. "Travel in rain is bad for health."

There was a loud knock on their door. "Girls!" Oleg called from the corridor. "Time for breakfast! We have a long day ahead of us!"

"We should stay!" Susanna called back to him, not getting out from under the covers. "It is raining!"

"It's spring," Oleg called back to her. "It rains in spring. If we only rode on dry fine days, we wouldn't reach Lesnograd till Midsummer. Put on your warmest clothes and come down! The boys are already saddling the horses."

Dasha dashed off to the privy, dashed back to their chamber, and hastily began to wash and dress herself. By the time she was done, and had packed away her nightgown and her little kit with her things for her teeth and hair, Susanna and Svetochka had gotten out from under the covers and were moaning and complaining about the cold air and the rain that was still falling steadily outside. The chamber, as usual, looked as if they had opened their packs and shaken every single thing inside them out onto every available surface.

"I can't find my kerchief," Svetochka was complaining, even as Susanna was lamenting the fact that not only her kerchiefs, but her best kaftan, had disappeared entirely. Dasha backed out of the chamber and went down to the main room, leaving them to their searches.

The men were all sitting at a big table that had once been splintery but was now greasy and worn. Plates of steaming buckwheat were set out in front of them, and there was a pitcher of what turned out to be, when Oleg poured her some, kefir. She tried to push it back over to him when he handed it to her.

"Don't you want it?" he asked.

She wrinkled her nose and shook her head. "I don't like it," she told him. "Or anything made from milk in general, to be honest."

This led to protests and denials from the guards, as if they knew what she liked and disliked better than she did. Which was so annoying that it made Dasha fight off her first impulse, which was to take the kefir and drink it simply to keep the peace and avoid hurting their feelings, and instead repeat that she didn't like milk or anything made from it, and that they should have her kefir, since they were the ones that liked it, not her. She thought that was rather clever, and that they would be sure to agree to her scheme and stop harassing her about it, but it only seemed to make them even more scornful of her, and more determined to force her to drink the kefir than they had been before.

"How can you not like milk, Tsarinovna?" Mitya demanded, while Alik pushed the cup he'd poured for her insistently into her hand.

"Tsss! Keep your voice down!" Oleg told him sharply.

"Forgive me, Oleg Svetoslavovich. But you can't not like milk, ah, Darya, ah Krasnoslavovna, you just can't. The gods themselves must drool for it!"

"I wouldn't know," Dasha told him. "But I think it tastes like…" she tried to find a polite explanation, "other products of the body," she said.

This led to a lot of guffawing from the guards, who found this vastly more funny than she would have expected. She couldn't help but suspect that they thought she had meant something other than what she had, although what that was, she didn't want to say. She pulled her plate of buckwheat over to herself and began eating as quickly as she could. Only that drew more attention to her as well, as once the men had stopped trying to force her to drink the kefir, which she had always thought was like drinking sour snot, they started commenting on her appetite for buckwheat, and how she would soon be twice her current size if she kept eating like that.

Part of Dasha knew that they meant no harm, that they were trying to atone in some way for their rudeness over the kefir, but since people had been commenting on how big she was ever since the moment she had been born—although she didn't remember her birth herself, of course, she couldn't count the number of times people had told her what a fine, big, plump baby she had been, and how surprised everyone had been to see such a big thing as her come out of such a tiny little woman as her mother, and how lucky they had been that it had been a quick, clean birth, given her size—she instinctively tried to shrink herself or hide whenever people remarked on her stature and figure.

But the men, even Oleg, all chattered on about it obliviously, until she gobbled down the last of her buckwheat (she had considered storming off in a huff rather than eating it, but she really was very hungry, and it was going to be a long cold day on the road, so she ate every last grain instead) and hurried off to her chamber, where she found Susanna and Svetochka had just finished dressing and packing up their things.

"You'd better hurry," Dasha told them. "Everyone else is almost done with breakfast."

"Then let them wait for us," Susanna said grandly, and searched around the corners of the chamber once more—she had found her kaftan and put it on, but one of her kerchiefs was still missing, and despite the fact that there was nowhere for it to be but in her pack, she was still convinced that she must have taken it out and lost it somehow during the night—before making her way slowly out the chamber and down the stairs, Svetochka trailing hesitantly behind her. Dasha considered following them and joining them at the table, but the thought of having more kefir pressed upon her, or hearing more complaints about the weather, made her clench her teeth, so she went out to the stable and waited with Poloska and Seryozha instead.

The rain had slacked off to a drizzle by the time they were ready to set off, but chill gusts from the North kept blowing it in their faces and under their hats and collars, lifting every hem and making a mockery of their felt and oilcloth. Dasha kept telling herself that it would get better as the day wore on, but by midmorning the drizzle changed back to a heavy rain, and by midday they were all soaked through, and the horses were stumbling and sliding through the muck, their heads down and their ears pinned back against the wind. Even Chernets was too miserable to pick fights with the other horses, but trotted grimly on, his head down and his tail clamped firmly against his body.

"We should stop!" called Mitya, when they rode into a little copse of fir trees. "It's not much, but it's better than nothing! We can't keep going, not while it's raining like this!"

"There's a waystation a verst or two ahead," Oleg told him. "Let's make for it, and stop there till the weather clears."

"Till tomorrow, then," muttered Mitya.

"I'd rather not stay the night there if we don't have to," Oleg told him.

"I'd say we'll have to!" said Mitya, gesturing at the cold water pouring down between the fir boughs around them. "'Less we want to die of cold, or catch a chill!"

"We'll see. Maybe the weather will break," said Oleg. "But in the meantime we might be able to shelter there for a bit."

It was hard to leave even the minimal shelter of the fir grove, but the thought of a waystation just a verst down the road spurred them on (much to the horses' disgust—they were of the opinion that they should all huddle together there with their tails to the wind for the rest of the day), and sure enough, they had barely left the copse out of sight when another copse appeared, this one mostly of pines and large enough that it was practically a small woods, and when they rode into it, they discovered a clearing in the center, with a half-rotten palisade fence surrounding what turned out to be, when they rode through the broken gate, a falling-down waystation.

"Are you sure there are people here?" Susanna asked, looking around with suspicion, and more than a little disgust.

A horse whinnied from the stable, and then several more joined in.

"Yes," said Oleg. "But we'd best not stay long. I'll go ask if we can shelter in the stable till the rain passes."

Alik and Seva groaned at that, and Mitya said, "Oleg Svetoslavovich, surely we can at least take a bite to eat while we're here? This rain isn't passing any time soon; we might as well have some hot food."

"I wouldn't recommend the food here..." Oleg began, but the guards all overrode him before he could finish, insisting that no food held the same terror as starvation, and that if they didn't get something hot to eat forthwith, they would be forced to eat their own horses.

"What do you know of starvation..." said Oleg, shaking his head, but just then a boy of about twelve came running out onto the porch and asked them if they wanted any dinner, and Mitya and Susanna both said "Yes" before Oleg could say no, and so, with a look of disgust, he acquiesced.

"On your own heads be it if anything happens," he hissed to them as they all dismounted and handed their horses' reins over to three more boys, all also of ten or twelve summers, who had come running out from the stable. "We won't be stopping for the night," Oleg told the boys. "Don't unsaddle them, just loosen their girths and slip their bits and give them a bite of oats and a bit of hay; we'll be leaving as soon as the rain slackens."

"The rain ain't slackening anytime soon, uncle, if I'm any judge," the oldest of the boys said, but he promised that the horses would be ready to leave whenever they were, nonetheless.

"Mitya," called Oleg sharply, as soon as the boys were taking their horses away. "Mitya, wait up!" Mitya stopped his dash towards the porch and the inn and looked back, waiting reluctantly. "Listen to me, all of you," Oleg continued. "Keep your heads down, and don't cause any trouble, no matter what happens, you hear me?"

"What might happen?" asked Susanna, just as Mitya and Alik said together, "Nothing's going to happen! It's just an inn, same as any other we've stopped at!"

"Listen," Oleg repeated, more insistently than before. "This inn... it's...unsavory. You're not going to like it nearly as much as you think you will. But keep your mouth shut and your head down, whatever happens, and we'll leave soon as we can."

"As long as there's hot food, I'll love it!" declared Mitya, and, with a toss of his head, continued his dash over to the shelter of the porch and the welcoming warmth of the door.

Oleg chewed his lip, what Dasha could see of his face wrinkled up in distaste, but then he sighed and said, "Come on, girls. You'll be safe enough, I hope: otherwise I'd never've agreed. It's the boys I'm worried about, but...maybe it'll be a lesson for them." He grinned a not very nice grin and led the girls onto the porch and into the inn.

Dasha's first impression was one of pleasant surprise. After the ramshackle appearance of the outside, she had expected the interior to be just as unkempt, but the main room was large and clean, with well-made tables and benches, most already holding occupants, a sturdy bar along one end of the room, and a raised dais at the other end.

"Who holds audiences here?" she asked Oleg. "Is this the seat of some noblewoman?" She tried to remember who would be the noblewomen in these parts, but since she wasn't entirely sure where she was, and she knew only the great noble families, not the minor noblewomen of each village, she couldn't even begin to say.

"Ah...no," he told her. "Definitely not. It's for...performances."

"Ah," said Dasha, nodding in understanding and feeling a little trill of warmth run through her at the thought. She'd always enjoyed watching all manners of performances. "What kind of performances?" she asked, excited. "Do they have tumbling and dancing? Or is it plays and scenes? Do you think they'll hold a performance while we're here?" She looked around. There was a good-sized crowd in the room, although there was something a bit strange about it. "There are certainly enough people here already." She looked around again, realizing what it was about the crowd that had struck her as strange. "Only...where are all the women?" she asked.

"Ah...women don't normally come here," Oleg told her. "And I certainly hope they won't be holding any performances while we're here."

Dasha frowned, disappointed at missing the chance to see a spectacle but also bothered by the complete absence of women. She realized that she had never before been anywhere without any women, and it felt strange to her now, strange and alarming somehow. She tried to look at the men all sitting on the benches again, and had to look away when she caught their eyes. Some of them looked shocked or embarrassed, but others had the same look of horrified revulsion she had caught on Oleg's face when she and the other girls had been joking about marrying the boy at the inn they had stopped at their first night on the road. It was as if she were a viper who had suddenly fallen into their midst, and they didn't know whether to crush her to death, or flee in terror. She tried to tell herself that she was being overly fanciful, but instead, the images of hatred and violence rising off the men like steam only grew stronger, till she had to look away and pretend that they weren't there at all.

A man about Oleg's age—well, the age Oleg appeared to be—came over to them, bowing several times as he approached them. He was small and slender, with fine features that were cleanly shaven, light intelligent eyes, and dark hair that had been as carefully cut and arranged as a nobleman's. He reminded Dasha strongly of Boleslav Vlasiyevich, except that whereas Boleslav Vlasiyevich always radiated a strength that was threatening and reassuring at the same time, like a well-made blade, this man radiated a fidgety, nervous energy, like a high-blooded horse who had been badly treated.

"Welcome, welcome," he said, "you are very welcome. Nasty weather, eh? Well, we'll warm you up quick enough! There's a free table over there, and we'll bring you something warm to eat soon as we can. Anya! Anya, over here!"

Dasha looked around hopefully, expecting to see a serving girl, but instead it was a boy of about her own age who came over to them.

"This is Andrey," the man told them, "but we all call him Anya, don't we, Nyusya?" He slapped Andrey on his rump. "Bring the visitors some beer, Anya, and some hot food. And we'll be having a performance soon, so that'll be something to look forward to!"

"What kind of performance?" asked Dasha excitedly, as Oleg gave a groan.

The man gave them both a surprised look. "You're a *very* pretty one," he said. "So...girly! It's almost real!" He looked over at Susanna and Svetochka. "All three of you...are you interested in a spot with our players? Especially you, you black-eyed beauty," he told Susanna. "The men would be all over you! But all three of you...we could do all kinds of things with all three of you..."

"This is my daughter," Oleg said, putting his arm around Dasha's shoulders. She couldn't ever remember him doing such a thing before. "My two daughters and their nobly-born companion. There will be no performances while we're under your roof."

"Your daughters! Some of our customers do like their little jests, but I assure you, there's no need of pretense here."

"Open your eyes, man! These are my," Oleg gave Dasha a little shake, and nodded in Svetochka's direction, "*daughters.*"

The man reached over as if to touch Dasha's cheek, but Oleg jerked her away.

"Possessive, are we?" The man laughed. "Don't like to share, do we?" He laughed some more, but nervously, as if trying to hide from himself the truth that was staring him in the face.

"You have no idea," Oleg told him. "If it were up to me, none of us would be here, but the rain had other ideas. So let us shelter here and bring us something warm, and we'll pay you handsomely, but no one is to touch these *girls*, no one is so much as to look at them, and *no performances!*"

"Or what?" asked the man, with another brittle little laugh. "You'll report us to the Tsarina? Because she knows, or at least her councilors do." Now his laugh was decidedly bitter. "They had better, after all we've paid them."

"I know she knows," said Oleg, as Dasha blurted out, "The Tsarina's councilors have been *taking bribes*?"

"She's a clever little thing, isn't she?" said the man, giving Dasha a look in which all trace of his former goodwill had vanished.

"You have no idea," repeated Oleg.

"Which councilors?" pressed Dasha. "Which councilors have been taking bribes?"

"Why?" asked the man. "What business is it of yours, little girl? What are you going to do, clean us out, send us out to starve by the wayside, and then go back to Krasnograd and clean all the bribetakers out of the kremlin while you're at it? And then admire your handiwork while we all die of hunger?"

"No, of course not!" said Dasha indignantly. "I don't want anyone to starve! But I don't want any of my mother's councilors..." She trailed off into silence as she realized what she was saying, but not before the man had realized what she was saying as well.

"So," he said, giving her a look in which fear and outrage were equally intermingled. "Come here to shut us down, have you?"

"Have the sense the gods gave you, man," Oleg told him sharply. "If Krasnograd had come to shut you down, would they have sent three girls to do it? No. They'd have sent guards."

"I see guards," replied the man, looking over at Mitya, Alik, and Seva, who, oblivious to the confrontation going on between Oleg and the innkeeper, were chatting with gusto with some men at a nearby table.

"Only three! Think, man, think: if we'd come to shut you down, would we have brought only three guards? No! All we want is a dry place to stop until the rain passes. We won't cause any trouble if you don't cause us any trouble. So keep your mouth shut and bring us something to eat, and we'll be on our way before you know it."

The innkeeper looked at Oleg, and then at Dasha, and then back at Oleg, and then sighed and said, "Very well. It's not as if I have a choice, now do I? I just hope none of my other patrons grow restless, waiting for the performance that *you* have made me cancel."

"You can still hold it once we're on our way," Oleg told him dryly. "Waiting makes some things better, you know."

The man almost smiled at that, but instead sniffed and led them over to their table. Andrey had already brought out steaming-hot pies, and a platter of sausages.

"That man looks very much like Boleslav Vlasiyevich, doesn't he?" Dasha whispered, once the innkeeper had retreated out of earshot.

"I think they're third-brothers, or something of that sort, but I wouldn't go talking about it to Boleslav Vlasiyevich, if I were you," Oleg told her.

"They are? He's never mentioned anything about him. I wonder why not."

"He has his reasons," Oleg said shortly. "Now eat up, and let's be out of here as quick as we can."

The guards fell ravenously upon the sausages, and then had to spit them back out.

"Hot! Hot!" cried Alik, waving his hands in front of his mouth to cool it off.

Dasha broke cautiously into a pie. It appeared to be stuffed with sauerkraut and bits of dried mushroom, and proved to be excellent, once she had allowed it to cool down to an edible temperature. The guards made another attempt at the sausages, this time successful.

"By all the gods, a man could go a long way in search of a sausage this good," declared Mitya, closing his eyes in ecstasy as he swallowed his down. "It's not every inn that serves sausages like this, I'll tell you that now. Are there more?"

Out of the corner of her eye, Dasha thought she saw the men at the table next to theirs snickering. By the silver and gold thread embroidered into their kaftans, she guessed them to be the sons of merchants or noblewomen, and wondered where their mothers or wives were. The sons of wealthy women were not generally allowed to travel about unsupervised—the gods alone knew what kind of trouble they could get into. But here were four young men, clearly from families of means, staying on their own in an inn full of other men, and with no women other than herself, Susanna, and Svetochka in sight. A prickling of unease spread out from her belly and up her chest, and her visions tried to tell her something, but what that was, they didn't know.

"Hey," said one of the men at the neighboring table. He was the youngest, but wore the most richly decorated kaftan, with silver frog clasps holding closed the collar, and lace with a metallic, golden sheen at the throat and cuffs. He leaned over so that his thick hair, the color of old gold and smelling faintly of rosewater, almost brushed Dasha's shoulder, and slapped Mitya on the shoulder. "Hey," he said again, and now Dasha could smell the vodka on him, overpowering the scent of rosewater. He laughed, even though nothing that was happening struck Dasha as particularly funny. "Is this your first time trying the sausages here?" he asked.

"Yes, but it won't be my last!" declared Mitya, sounding as if he had partaken in some of the same vodka that was affecting their neighbor, even though Dasha knew that he hadn't. The golden-haired man laughed some more, and a spasm of pain crossed Oleg's face.

"Once you've had some of Yaroslav's sausages, you'll never want anything else!" the golden-haired man said, with a drunken wink that seemed to be trying to say something that Dasha couldn't make out. She tried to edge away from him and his reek of vodka, but only succeeded in turning his attention onto herself.

"And who's this?" the man asked, bringing his face too close to hers. He must be only a year or two older than she was, Dasha realized, still more a boy than a man. "He's a *very* pretty one," the boy said. "Do you share him? Surely you'll share him with me!" He tried to stroke Dasha's cheek. Startled, she jerked back, but that only made him grab her by the chin.

"Hands OFF!" Oleg's own hand flashed past Dasha's face and dealt the boy a ringing slap, even as Susanna reached over and pinched his ear.

"OW!" cried the boy reproachfully, letting go of Dasha, who was sitting there in stunned immobility. "Very well, no sharing, no sharing, I understand! But you can't blame me for trying, can you? Anyone would have done the same!"

"What's happening, what's happening!" The innkeeper came rushing over to them, his head turning this way and that as he tried to look at all of them at once. Even in her state of shock at the young man's behavior and, increasingly, shame at her own inaction, Dasha couldn't help but notice how much he looked and even moved like Boleslav Vlasiyevich, only different somehow, as if this man had the same energy but it was the energy of high-strung nervousness instead of the force of barely contained outrage. But both of them, Dasha thought, edging as far away from the young man as possible, gave off the air of someone who didn't quite fit in with everyone around them, which marked them as kindred even more than their dark hair and light eyes.

"Svyatopolk," sighed the innkeeper, once he had come up to them. "Are you bothering the other guests again? We talked about this! We talked about this! One of these days it's going to get you into trouble!"

"It already has," Oleg told him. His face was almost as thunderous as it had been when he had come out into the corridor and found out about the man who had tried to grab Dasha. "And it will only be worse for him when *your brother* finds out about this."

"My brother?" The innkeeper gave Oleg a puzzled look. "What does Yaromir have to do with anything?"

"Not that brother. *Boleslav.*"

"Oh." The innkeeper swallowed. "Of..." he gave Dasha a look of extreme squeamishness and distaste, "of course. I should have guessed." He tried to square his slender shoulders—like Boleslav Vlasiyevich would have done, Dasha thought, only he didn't have enough shoulder to square—and swallowed again. "So that's it?" he asked, his voice high and cracking. "One foolish move by one customer who didn't know what he was doing, and you're just going to come and...shut me down, send my brother to stand over me and laugh as you shut me down and turn me out of house and home, leave us all with no place to go?"

"No!" exclaimed Dasha, before Oleg could answer. She turned to Oleg. "It was just a foolish mistake, just as he said. He shouldn't have to suffer for what someone else did in a moment of drunkenness, and I wasn't hurt anyway."

Oleg's jaws clenched, and he gave her a look that seemed almost angry—why? Why was he angry with her? *She* hadn't done anything, other than plead for mercy—before turning to the innkeeper and saying, "It seems you're in luck, Yaroslav. For today, at least. But I *will* be telling your brother about this, you can be sure of that, and what he'll do then, well, I can't answer for his actions."

"He won't do anything!" insisted Dasha. "I'll ask him not to!"

She thought Oleg had to fight not to roll his eyes at that, but he nodded and said, "And like as not he'll listen, seeing how it's you doing the asking." He gave Yaroslav something that was sort of like a smile. "How's it feel, needing the help of a woman?"

Yaroslav made a sour face and turned away to berate the men at the neighboring table, until they gathered up Svyatopolk, who was so drunk he was having a hard time standing, and dragged him out of the inn.

Oleg wanted to leave then, but everyone was still eating and it was still raining heavily, so he agreed, with very poor grace, that they could stay for a little while longer. Dasha also wanted to leave, since she thought that now everyone would be staring at them and speculating as to the cause of the altercation between them and their neighbors, but once Svyatopolk and his men were gone, everyone else appeared to forget about the matter entirely, including her own guards.

She herself was having a harder time forgetting the feel of Svyatopolk's hand on her face. As with the man at the inn two nights ago, he hadn't hurt her, but it was almost as if he had done something worse. Dasha was aware that she had never really been hurt, that no one had ever really hit her, but she had received her share of bruises learning to ride and training to fight with Boleslav Vlasiyevich, and none of them had ever bothered her the way these seemingly innocent touches had. Even when her pony had bitten her and left a scar, she hadn't minded so much—that was what ponies did when they were in a bad mood, and it had been her fault for not getting out of her way in time.

But this—both Svyatopolk and the other man had wanted to...do what? Dasha shied away from the thought of rape, but then forced herself to face it. That was what they had wanted, wasn't it? She had only the haziest notion of what rape would entail, or why it was so bad, but when she remembered their fingers on her face...tfoo! She had to struggle to keep herself from spitting at the very thought. Because...because, because, because when they had touched her, they had meant her ill, they had meant her ill in some particularly horrid way that Dasha couldn't consciously fathom, but that she instinctively felt made everything that they had done a hundred times more awful than that time she had fallen off of Poloska and wrenched her shoulder and had to wear a sling for a week, or the time Boleslav Vlasiyevich had tripped her full length onto the hard paving stones and swatted her with his wooden sword so hard she'd had a bruise for a month.

That had hurt, but Poloska had just been shying at a squirrel, and Boleslav Vlasiyevich had been trying to help her learn what she needed to learn in order to protect herself from...from...people like the ones who'd been grabbing at her lately. Only he must not have hit her hard enough, because she hadn't been doing a very good job of protecting herself, had she? Both times she'd been frozen stockstill while others came and rescued her. This thought, combined with the memories of the men's nasty hands creeping over her, made her want to squirm with shame and embarrassment, and beg forgiveness from her companions...

"Still raining out?" Mitya's question interrupted her thoughts before they could get any more foolish, and made her look in the direction in which he was speaking. Six men had come in and sat down at the table next to them. They were dripping wet, and were shaking their heads and running their fingers through their hair to try to dry it.

"It's pissing down like an old soldier on his sixth mug of beer," said the man closest to them, his voice as warm and golden as...it was like beer, Dasha told herself. Like beer, not...the other thing. Oleg must have felt the same way, though, for he made a face and twitched as if he were about to jump up and tell the man not to talk like that in front of the girls, but then sat still, although, Dasha could tell, at the cost of considerable strain.

Mitya, however, shared none of Oleg's distaste for their new neighbors, and laughed expansively and winked back, much to the obvious delight of the newcomer, who reached over and gave him a slap on the shoulder. Why Dasha thought that was odd, she couldn't say, since it was the kind of thing men did all the time, but this time it seemed to her that Mitya shouldn't actually enjoy the wink and the slap as much as he did.

She looked over at Susanna to see if she felt the same way, but instead of catching her eye in return, Susanna was gazing at their new friend with even more admiration than Mitya. Even Svetochka appeared to be warming to him. Well, Dasha had to admit to herself, he did draw the eye: he was big, almost as tall as Oleg and even broader through the shoulders, with thick dark-blond hair that flowed down to his collar, and the big round blue eyes so common here in the black earth district. But even better than that, he seemed to make the air around him...warmer, or something like that. Like beer or...the other thing. Like there was something special about him, and he knew it, and instead of being repulsive, this drew others in. Dasha could feel it acting on her, too, even as the unpleasant pressure began building up in the back of her head like water behind a dam after a rainstorm, signaling that something was soon to happen.

"What's the food like today?" asked the man, leaning over and looking at the remains of their meal. "Pies?" He wrinkled his strong, straight nose, which somehow made him even more handsome. Why was she noticing handsome men everywhere these days? Every place they'd stopped at had been full of handsome men. Was it them, or her? It must be her. "Pies are for children!" he exclaimed. "'Specially if they've made with"—he reached over and picked up half a pie that was lying on the platter in the middle of their table—"sauerkraut. Tfoo! What kind of food is sauerkraut, I ask you?"

"The kind of food you eat at the end of winter, before the spring's crops come in," said Oleg evenly, while Mitya, Alik, and Seva all laughed and nodded in agreement.

"Trust an old man to take all the fun out of eating!" cried the newcomer, which made the others all laugh and nod even more fervently. "Well, old man, lucky for the rest of us that you're not the one serving us! We have more agreeable servants, don't we, lads?!" Everyone other than Oleg and Dasha laughed even more at this, and the newcomers all winked at each other in a way that suggested that those words had some special meaning, although what that was...the pit of Dasha's stomach twisted. She looked over anxiously at Oleg, expecting him to lash out or make a scene, but he just sat there, stonefaced, which made her even more anxious.

"But it looks as though it hasn't been *just* sauerkraut," the man went on, digging through the rest of their food. "Is this sausage I see?" He held up half a sausage. "Now, that's just wrong," he said. "Refusing one of Yaroslav's sausages. Why, there's many a man who's gone begging for them, but all in vain. What little fool's been turning down Yaroslav's sausages?"

"It were her," said Seva, pointing at Dasha. "She don't like sausage."

The newcomer turned to Dasha, his blue eyes brightening even more, like candles that had been set into sconces. He was, Dasha thought, the handsomest man she had ever seen, with both good looks and something that was even better: a kind of magic that sucked you to them, like water rushing into a waterfall. Dasha could feel it pulling on her, even as a painful prickling crept up the back of her head, setting her teeth on edge and making her want to curl up and moan, or reach back and tear apart her scalp till the pain drowned out the crawling sensation of the building explosion.

"You *are* a pretty one," the man said, flashing his white, even teeth at her. "Almost like..." He stopped, then laughed again. "You're a *girl*," he exclaimed. "An actual girl."

"Of course I am," said Dasha. "What else would I be?" She knew she was being rude, but the crawling in the back of her head was spreading down her spine, making it harder and harder to speak civilly, or at all.

"I don't know, I don't know," said the man, grinning some more. "You get all sorts in here. So you don't like sausage, do you?"

"You take it, if you want it," Dasha told him.

"Oh, I will, I will," said the man, now grinning hugely. The tingling and crawling was spreading across Dasha's shoulders and over to her breasts. "But I can't believe you don't like it like you say you do. Maybe you just haven't had the right one."

"I've had sausage before," Dasha told him. "Lots and lots of times. My maids used to bring it to me every day. But..." She stopped in confusion. The men at the other table were doubled over with silent laughter, their shoulders shaking and their faces contorted. The tingling and crawling had reached the base of Dasha's spine and then stagnated, locking her whole upper body in misery, refusing to pour through her and out and dissipate. She wriggled her shoulders, hoping to find some relief, but all it did was make the others laugh more.

"Well," said the man, once he had regained control of himself. "I think we need to remind her of what she used to enjoy about sausages so much, don't we, lads?" He leaned in close to Dasha, bringing the cold half-sausage up to her face. Out of the corner of her eye, she could see how avidly everyone else was watching and hoping for her to have the sausage stuffed into her mouth against her will. Even Oleg wasn't doing anything to help her. She could smell the herbs that had been used in it, and an underlying unpleasant scent of...what?

Death and corruption! screamed the vision in her head, splashing her inner eye with blood, and her shoulders and head jerked so hard she was thrown against Oleg, who had to grab her to keep her from falling off the bench.

"That's *enough*," he growled, as the others laughed some more.

"What, is she gods-touched or something?" asked the man. "Better than any performance!"

"Yes," said Oleg. "She is. And only the gods are to touch her, is that clear?"

"If you say so," said the man, with another big grin. "Although she might be hankering for something a little more substantial, if you get my drift." He faltered in the face of Oleg's glare. "Fine," he said, forcing out another smile, but edging away from them. "Fine. Fine. We'll leave her be. There should be a performance starting soon, anyway. A proper performance, like what we've come here to see."

"A performance?" asked Dasha. She pulled herself away from Oleg. The crawling pressure was gone, and everything seemed clear and happy. "What kind of performance?"

"Not one you'd enjoy," the man told her, with a sly little smile.

"Oh no," said Dasha eagerly. "I *love* performances. I've never seen one I didn't like, even when the actresses were...not so good."

"Well then," said the man, with another sly little smile. "Maybe you'll enjoy this one too, then, though it'll be full of things you just said you don't care for. But maybe you were lying about that, like girls do."

"That's it," said Oleg, standing. "Rain or no rain, we're leaving." Dasha obediently rose as well, but everyone else in their group remained mutinously sitting. Oleg ordered the guards to get up and go get their horses, but Mitya began a strenuous objection, seconded by Susanna, and when Oleg wouldn't come up with any concrete reasons that they should leave directly, Svetochka and the other guards began to argue for staying longer too, and while they were going back and forth over that, everyone else in the room began clapping and stamping their feet and calling for the expected performance, until finally Yaroslav came out, looking very harried, and said that the performance would happen, whatever Oleg thought, and anyone who didn't want to see it would just have to leave.

"We're going, Dasha," Oleg announced, throwing down a handful of coin onto the table, grabbing Dasha by the arm, and dragging her in the direction of the door.

"But..." she said, trying to pull out of his grasp and failing. "The others..."

"They made their beds; let them lie in them," he said grimly, and marched her outside.

"But if they're in danger..." she objected, once they were on the porch. "We can't just leave them! What if something were to happen to Susanna or Svetochka!"

"I doubt they're in any danger," he told her. "Especially Susanna and Svetochka. Except maybe from having their eyeballs burned out. That was a joke," he added, at Dasha's gasp of horror. "I just meant they're likely to see things they'll wish they hadn't seen."

"Like what?" she demanded. "What could be so bad about the performance that you don't want me to watch it? It's just a performance! I've seen dozens!"

"Not like this, you haven't."

"Like what? What is it? Father, what is it?"

His face softened for a moment at the word "father." "You're a good girl, Dasha," he told her. "But that means there are lots of things you haven't seen, and don't need to."

"Like what?" she demanded again. "What could *possibly* be so bad about this place?"

"Dasha!" he exclaimed in exasperation. "Open your eyes! This is a, a place for men!"

"Ah..." said Dasha, confused. "Like...a barracks, or something?"

"Well...there's nothing here that doesn't happen in most barracks, too, that's true, but no. It's a place of...entertainment. For men. For a certain kind of men."

"What kind?"

He shrugged his shoulders in discomfort. "The kind that...that prefers the company of other men," he said in a low voice.

"Most men seem to prefer the company of other men," said Dasha, puzzled.

Oleg gave a short laugh. "You may not be wrong there," he told her. "But these men...they prefer the company of other men...as lovers."

"Oh." Dasha frowned. "How...how does that work?" she asked, curious in spite of the blush rising in her cheeks at the thought. "Never mind," she added hastily, seeing how Oleg cringed at the question. "It's not important. So was that why there were no women there, and everyone thought we were boys?"

"Yes," said Oleg.

"But why would they think we were boys, when we're dressed as girls? Or did they just not recognize our clothing?"

"No, they recognized it," said Oleg, his voice full of resignation for the conversation that was happening despite his fervent wishes that it were not. Dasha wanted to tell him that they didn't need to talk about it anymore, but the curious part of her couldn't let her stop him. "Some of them..." he was speaking as if the words were cutting his tongue on the way out, "some of them like to dress as women, or take...lovers who dress as women."

"Oh." Dasha considered that. "That doesn't sound so bad. I mean, they're not hurting anyone, are they?"

Oleg made a face. "No," he admitted. "Not in the way you mean, or not always. Anytime—why am I the one who has to tell you this? Why isn't your mother here to tell you this?—anytime there are men, Dasha, there tends to be," he swallowed, "rape and cruelty. And the more men you have, the more it tends to be that way. So that's one thing, although...I *have* known men," he said very reluctantly, "who treated their lovers with tenderness. But this...*performance*"—he said the word as if it hurt his lips—"will be, if it's like all the others I've seen of its ilk, of men dressed up as women in order to show how much they hate women. And then they'll be raped at the end of it, because that's what everyone has come to see."

"We should stop it!" cried Dasha. "And rescue the performers!"

But Oleg shook his head. "They won't thank us for it," he told her. "They agreed to this of their own free will, Dasha my love, and this is how they earn their coin, and how everyone here gets their pleasure. You'd think you were doing a good thing, but you wouldn't be, at least not for them, and they might...show their displeasure in violent ways."

"But...the performers...and there are young boys working here!"

"Would it be better if it happened to girls?" he asked.

"Well...no, of course not, but..."

"Better these boys than someone else," he told her. "Better that all this ugliness stays between men, and doesn't touch women."

"But..."

"You can't fix it," he told her sharply. "And if you try, you'll only make things worse. For yourself, and for the ones you want to help, too. So just go the stables, get Poloska and Seryozha, and leave without looking back. You can't save these men, Dasha, and most of them don't want or need saving. At least this way they're not hurting anyone who doesn't want to be hurt."

Dasha wanted to argue against that very strenuously, but just then the door swung open and Susanna, Svetochka, and Mitya came stumbling out, their faces frozen in deep grimaces of shock.

"The performance..." gasped Mitya.

"Not what you were expecting?" asked Oleg.

Mitya shook his head, looking slightly green, but then turned back towards the door. "The others..." he said. "They're still in there! We have to go get them!"

"I'll go," said Oleg. "It's nothing I haven't seen before, after all." Ignoring the appalled expressions that provoked from the others, he gave himself a little shake, like someone about to jump into cold water, and then flung open the door.

Although Dasha knew she shouldn't try to look in, somehow she found herself in just the right position to look through the door and catch sight of the dais where she guessed the performance would be taking place. Two men—boys, really—were dressed up in tasteless women's finery. There was something about the choice of every item of their wardrobe that set Dasha's teeth on edge, as if it had all been chosen not to make them look like women, but to make them look like every woman's nightmare of how others might see her in her deepest fears. As if there were nothing more to a woman than her clothes, and these men were trying to...before Dasha could figure out what these men were trying to do, other men, in ordinary men's clothing, grabbed them (there had been arguing going on between them, in which the "women" had been speaking with ridiculous voices that seemed deliberately done in order to hurt the ears), and, despite their protests, which were obviously meant to have no force, began to rip off their fake finery and push them down onto the ground...Oleg came out the door, with Alik and Seva under each arm.

"Dasha! Susanna! Svetochka!" he snapped. "What are you standing there for! This is no place for you! Go get the horses!"

Dasha shook herself out of her state of petrified horror, and ran through the cold rain towards the stable. By the time she got there, she realized that the others had remained on the porch, arguing about the wisdom of going out into the rain, which was still coming down hard, but since she was already at the barn door, she opened it and went in, leaving the others to follow or not.

It was dark in the stable, with no sun to come in through the chinks and the small windows under the eaves, but Dasha could tell by the smell that despite its outward shabby appearance, it was clean and well-kept inside, with fresh straw in the stalls and good hay in the mangers.

For some reason this surprised her, but when she thought back to men she had seen in the inn, many of them had worn nice clothes and obviously been from good families. And the food had been good, and the tables and benches well-made. And the whole thing was run by Boleslav Vlasiyevich's third-brother, and showed the same neatness and attention to detail that had always marked Boleslav Vlasiyevich, which was a strange thought...of course, Boleslav Vlasiyevich had never married, and spent most of his time in the company of men...could the relationship between him and her mother be nothing but rumors? Was he really..? Dasha imagined herself asking him, but the only answer her visions gave her was a picture of the extreme embarrassment she would feel.

And she surely hadn't imagined the scene between him and her mother in the park...or had she totally misread it? Or...more visions closed around her, but she couldn't make out what they were trying to tell her, other than that love was a much more complicated business than she had always been told. The stories and songs made it sound as if you just saw your beloved and instantly knew that he was the man for you, and then he either fell into your hands like a ripe apple, or first you had to outsmart his cruel mother or unworthy suitors, and then he fell into your hands like a ripe apple. In either case, you and everyone else knew what was supposed to happen. The possibility that he might not want to be with you, or that he might prefer another woman, or other men, or that he might hate you and want to mock and hurt you, rarely seemed to come up.

But surely none of that would happen to her, Dasha told herself: just because some men were difficult didn't mean that *her* man, whoever he was and however he was brought to her, was going to be like that. Surely not! Because...because he was probably going to be chosen for her by her mother and the Princess Council. Funny how she had never really thought about that before, or about how unpleasant that would be. For him too. If she were a noblewoman's son whose only duty in life was to be married off to a bride of his mother's choosing and provide her with children, she might run off to some place like this too...there were funny sounds coming from the big box stall to her right. Like someone was being hurt. Maybe one of the stableboys had been kicked or fallen from the loft?

"Hello?" called Dasha uncertainly. "Are you hurt? Should I call for a healer?"

Cursing erupted from the stall. Dasha ran up to it, just in time to make out in the gloom what looked like a half-naked man jerk away from a boy—Andrey?—who was kneeling in the straw, and deliver a sharp slap to his face.

"Stop!" cried Dasha. "What's wrong with you!" She wrenched the stall door open, and then stumbled as the man rushed out, shouting something about interruptions and lashing out with his foot as he went past her. This time, instead of freezing in surprise, Dasha blocked his foot with her own, just as she had been taught. The man cursed again, and, clutching his trousers and limping from the force of Dasha's counter-kick, half-ran, half-hopped off. For a heartbeat Dasha thought about going after him, but she had no confidence in her ability to wrestle him to the ground and subdue him, and she didn't want to leave Andrey. So she went into the stall instead.

"Andrey? Are you hurt?" she asked, glad to see that he was pulling himself to his feet, at least, even if he was rubbing his face and wiping his mouth.

"What is wrong with you!" he shouted at her. He stopped to spit in the straw, and then shouted, "Couldn't you wait even a moment! Couldn't you wait till he were done! That's fifty grosh you cost me!"

"Fifty grosh?" Dasha repeated stupidly. "For him to hurt you? Why would..." There were so many questions she wanted to ask, but she settled for, "Why would you do that?"

"'Cause I need the money, you stupid rape-child! Not everyone got a rich mama to feed you sweets an' dress you in, in stupid mother-raping spell-embroidered silk kaftans!"

"My kaftan is made of wool," Dasha said, aware even as the words came out of her mouth that it was probably the stupidest thing she could have said.

"I ain't got money for wool neither!" Andrey shouted at her, furiously dashing away the tears that were rolling down his cheeks. "Not less I do this! 'Sides," he added more calmly, "it don't hurt so much. Fifty grosh for the mouth—you gotta learn how not to choke, but once you got that, it ain't hard an' don't take long. A hundred grosh for the ass—that hurts more at first, but after a while it ain't so bad neither, an' it's over quick too an' you've got a hundred grosh in your fist."

"I see," said Dasha, although she didn't see at all. Or rather, she could make vague guesses, but they were so horrifying that she told herself she must be wrong. "If you need money, why don't you enlist as a guard?" she asked. "You're still a bit young, but we're always looking for boys to join the guard in Krasnograd. And a lot of the princesses will be hiring now too. I'm sure you could find a place in a guard somewhere."

Andrey gave her a look that said she had taken leave of her senses. "If I joined a guard, it'd just be the same, only I wouldn't get paid for it, an' I'd have to fight as well," he told her, speaking as if explaining the most basic facts to a small child.

"Oh. Well...you should let me help you."

"What're you going to do?" he asked, curling his lip. "Petition the Tsarina?"

"Well...yes..."

"Like that'd do any good. Even if she listened, which she wouldn't, she'd just shut us down an' put us in the guard, an' things'd be even worse."

Dasha tried to argue against this, but Andrey adamantly refused to agree with her or accept any of her offers of help, so in the end she settled for slipping him a hundred grosh when he helped saddle up their horses. The coins, at least, he took with alacrity, and almost smiled when they clinked in his hand.

It was still raining when they mounted up and rode away, and everyone else was complaining and lamenting, but Dasha ignored them and rode up to Oleg.

"Why didn't I know about this?" she demanded.

"Know about what?" he asked warily.

"About...all of this. Why didn't I know that, that," she blushed, but kept going, "that men take each other as lovers, and that places like this exist, and that," her voice rose in indignation, "boys like Andrey have to sell...their favors, I suppose? To make enough coin to live."

Oleg sighed and bit his lip. "It's not a pretty thing," he told her.

"Which part of it?"

"All of it. It's all an ugly thing. Any time you have too many men together, like I told you—it's not a pretty thing. Men, the way they treat each other—it's..." he made a face, "ugly. You don't need to know about it."

"I do! These are my people as well. I need to know about their suffering. And *you're* a man, and *you* don't do things like that!"

"Yes, but," he sighed again, "lots of bad things have...happened to me, Dasha my heart, and I've done lots of bad things myself. Things you don't need to know about."

"But I could stop it! If I knew about it, I could stop it!"

"Could you? How?"

"I don't know! But I would!"

"Even if you could, which you couldn't, they wouldn't thank you for it."

Dasha wanted to argue against that, but she had to admit that Andrey certainly hadn't wanted her help, other than her money. Even when she had given him perfectly good advice, he'd done nothing but argue with her, and told her straight out that it would only make things worse for him, because...because wherever he went, he'd be a man—well, a boy for the moment, but soon a man—who'd have to live amongst men, and that meant things would be just as bad, no matter where he went. Dasha refused to believe that that was true, and told herself that *surely* men couldn't be that bad, but, looking at the expression on Oleg's face, she forbore to say what she was thinking. Instead she asked, blushing and stumbling, as she did so, "And...women?"

"What about women?" he asked cautiously.

"Do they also...the same...like that..."

"Well, not like that, of course, since they're women. And here in the black earth district it's frowned upon, since it doesn't lead to children, but plenty of women take lovers in secret anyway. And on the steppe it's done openly. As long as you get a child, no one cares about your other lovers. Many women keep other women openly for years, and treat them as their husbands."

"Oh," said Dasha. "That explains it, then."

"Explains what?" Oleg asked.

"Princess Belova was saying something about..." Dasha squirmed in the saddle, "how I might be too...steppe-like, when she found out that I was taking Susanna and Svetochka with me. I didn't know what she meant, but now I guess I do."

Oleg laughed out loud at that. "Well, in that case, I expect it'll be all over the kremlin by the time we get back."

"I don't think I'll like that very much," said Dasha, squirming even more at the thought of everyone gossiping about her that way. "Not very much at all."

"Oh, don't worry about it," he told her. "With all your steppe blood, it's no more than what everyone'll expect, but no one'll care too much either. As long as you get a child as well. Preferably two or three. But after that—you can do as you wish."

"Oh," said Dasha. His words were less comforting than he had intended them to be. Finding and taking a lover! Or letting her mother and her princesses find one for her to take. Which would mean plunging herself full-length into the world of men, which she had thought would be fun and exciting, but instead, now that she had dabbled her toes in it, was turning out to be frightening and disgusting.

She wasn't sure if she *could* take a lover, even if she wanted to, which right now she didn't. Especially if she wouldn't be given much choice in the matter. And everyone would be gossiping about it, and asking her impertinent questions, and know everything about it, and waiting and praying for a child! And what if she couldn't conceive? She would be a failure, and everyone in all of Zem' would know and talk about it. What if, what if...

"I wouldn't worry about it," Oleg interrupted her.

"How did you know what I was thinking about?"

"I didn't. But I could guess. And I wouldn't worry about it. What'll be, will be, and you'll do what you need to do when the time comes, and until it does, don't worry about it. Worry about the ten versts we need to ride to the next waystation instead."

"I'll try," she promised. Fortunately, the weather was so filthy that the misery from the rain lashing in her face and pouring down the collar of her kaftan soon took her mind off everything else.

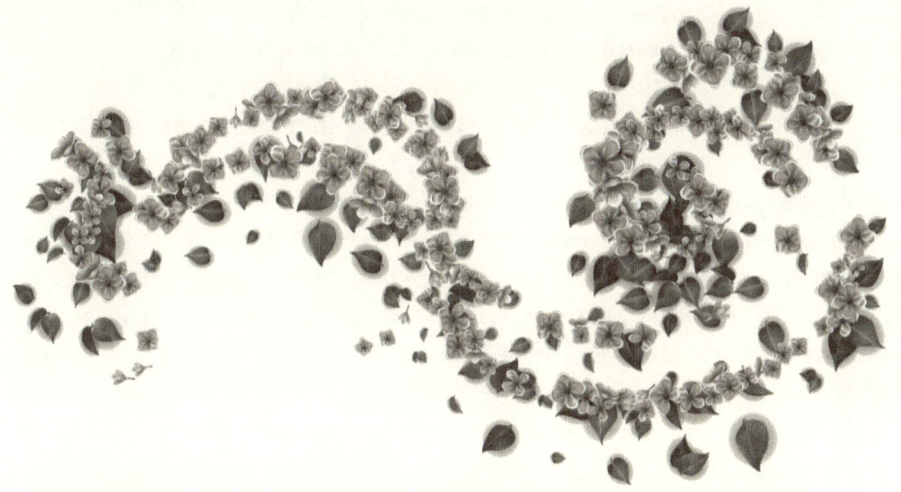

Chapter Seventeen

At first the relief of getting away from the waystation and everything about it was great enough that the cold rain lashing down didn't seem so bad, but after a verst or so, that all changed. They were riding through a thick fir wood, which should have given them some shelter, but the wind was blowing straight down the road and into their faces, driving cold rivulets of water under their collars and cuffs, no matter how tightly they pulled their clothes shut and wrapped themselves with kerchiefs and scarves. And then they rode out of the firs and into open fields, and the wind started gusting at them in all directions, lifting up the hems of their kaftans and blowing cold rain up their backs, despite all their attempts to belt their kaftans closed.

"The rain's all soaked through the waistband of my trousers, an' now it's running down the seams like wax down a candlewick," Svetochka complained.

"Mine too," Dasha told her, her teeth chattering as she spoke. "It's really awful."

"It happens," Oleg said brusquely. "Keep riding, and it'll be over soon!"

But it certainly didn't seem soon at the time. That afternoon ride through the rain, brief as it was compared with so many other rides Dasha had been on and would go on again afterwards, seemed both at the time and in retrospect to be one of the longest, most miserable experiences of her entire life. Every half a verst she would tell herself that she couldn't ride a step more, and that she was going to collapse and fall off of Poloska from the strange sleepiness that was overtaking her, or just from sheer shivering, at any moment.

And then she would keep riding, and another half a verst would go past, and she would have the same thought again, and keep riding, and on and on, until she thought she was trapped in this misery forever. She couldn't even say why it was so bad, really—it was only rain, with a little sleet mixed in. The road was level and smooth, and no one was attacking them, or hunting them, and they all knew perfectly well that they would soon reach warmth and shelter. But even so it was absolutely awful, much worse than Dasha could have imagined something so insignificant as a little rain could be. Which made her feel even worse, since if a little ride through the rain could reduce her to such a state, what would happen when she actually had to face something that was truly unpleasant? What would she do if things got worse?

Then the wet seam of her left trouser leg began to catch on her stirrup leather, and she found out. Mainly what she found out was that it was not courage, but shame that kept her from moaning and whining and crying out from the pain. Every time she thought a complaint would burst forth from her lips, she could see in her head how the others would react, and her lips sealed shut again, even as the rest of her begged her to say something, do something, at least let everyone know how miserable she was and thus spread the misery around.

But instead she kept silent, and tried dropping her stirrup. Which relieved some of the rubbing on the inside of her calf, but made it worse on the inside of her knee, and caused the stirrup to bang painfully against the inside of her ankle. Which made her even more angry at herself, because *of course* she knew how to keep her stirrups from banging around when she dropped them, but she was so stiff and shivery that making sense of what was happening was peculiarly difficult and no part of her body was working properly, and so she was hunched over and jouncing around on the saddle like, like, like Svetochka, which must be horribly uncomfortable for poor Poloska, which was horribly unfair to her, to have to suffer the cold and the rain *and* Dasha's inept riding, and if she had to trot one more step she was going to cry, she was going to scream...

"Waystation," called Oleg. "Up there." Everyone tried to cheer, but their jaws were all locked up with chattering too much for them to get much sound out.

No one came out to greet them when they rode into the waystation's front yard, but they dismounted anyway—Dasha staggered and nearly fell when her numb feet hit the ground, and her numb knees refused to bend to take the impact, and her numb hands failed to grab onto Poloska's mane—and led their horses into the blessedly, blessedly warm and dry stable, where they found a collection of young stablehands playing cards in the hayloft. They came swarming down to take their horses right away, though, with promises to rub them down thoroughly, and the information that their mistress had already gotten the bathhouse heated for any traveler who came through on this filthy day, and that they should go straight over and steam before they did anything else.

Stepping out of the stable back into the rain was hard, but Dasha, saying they couldn't possibly get any wetter than they already were, grabbed Svetochka and Susanna by the hands as they stood at the door, wavering and complaining, and ran in the direction the stablegirls were pointing, dragging the others behind her as they stumbled and slid on legs that weren't working as well as they should, until they burst into the women's bathhouse and slammed the door behind them. They peeked in from the antechamber and saw that the stove was already red-hot, but that no one else was in there steaming.

"Oh good," said Dasha. "I wouldn't want to steam with strangers."

"Quick, quick, quick," Susanna was muttering to herself in Avkhaz, already trying to tear off her sodden clothing, but with little success. Dasha tried to help her, but her own fingers were also stiff and unresponsive, and figuring out how to work the buttons and laces, and in what order to undo everything, was strangely difficult and confusing. Now that she was no longer in the cold and the rain, she was becoming aware of how slowly her mind had been working, and how much she wanted to lie down and never get up...she and Susanna had somehow between them managed to remove Susanna's kaftan, but the laces of the sarafan she was wearing over her shirt and trousers were completely beyond them, and they were, she realized, standing there helplessly, not even attempting to undress.

"Let's just take off our boots and go warm up with our clothes on," Dasha said. "We can undress the rest of the way once we've thawed out."

Pulling off their soaked-through boots was harder than it should have been, but between the three of them they managed to remove each other's boots, after which they staggered into the main chamber. As soon as the hot air from the stove hit them, they started shivering so hard they could barely stand, and threw themselves onto the benches and lay there without speaking.

After a while Dasha felt her jaw and her stomach unclench, and she was able to get up, strip off the rest of her clothes, and hang them up around the stove, where they promptly began emitting steam. Which was very satisfying to see. She stumbled back to her bench and lay back down. Her eyes kept wanting to close, but she forced them to stay open. Falling asleep in the bathhouse was dangerous. You could overheat, or become fume-struck.

So she examined the sores on the inside of her left leg instead. They were surprisingly small for something that had caused her so much pain. There was one on her calf, no bigger than her thumbnail, and the one on her knee was no bigger than her pinkie nail, and neither of them were particularly bleeding. How embarrassing! It had felt as if her entire inner leg were being flayed, but in fact it had been nothing more than a few layers of skin, not even worth calling a healer for. And that tiny rub-raw had driven her almost to distraction with the pain! How would she ever be able to handle any *real* pain, if she couldn't even tolerate something like this? So far on this journey, which, she knew, had been as easy as a journey could be, she'd had to be rescued from people who weren't even that dangerous, and been almost completely undone by an afternoon of rain and something that wasn't even a real injury. How pathetic! Surely the chosen of the gods should be tougher than this!

"Why is it so dark in here?" Susanna mumbled from the bench she was lying on, still fully clothed.

Dasha stopped castigating herself for her weakness and looked around. Or rather, tried to look around, since it *had* become rather dark in there, so dark that she could barely make out the other girls on their benches, and the far corners were completely hidden in shadow.

"It must be getting dark outside," Dasha reasoned. "And"—she looked over at the lamp by the door—"our lamp is burning down."

"We must fix it," Susanna mumbled, but made no move to get up and do anything about it. Svetochka appeared to be sound asleep. Dasha told herself she should get up and check on Svetochka and adjust the candle in the lamp, which was probably drowning in wax, but she was so tired. They would both be fine for a little while longer, she told herself. She was finally almost warm through. As soon as she was well and truly warmed up, she would feel better, and then she would get up, pour out the extra melted wax in the lantern, wake up Svetochka, and make them all get dressed—back in their wet clothes, tfoo!—and go to the main building, where there would probably be supper waiting for them.

Her stomach told her that she was ravenously hungry, but the message seemed to be coming from very far away, as if her stomach belonged to someone else's body. As did everything else that should have been hers. She was acutely aware of her arm resting against the bench, but she could barely feel her feet, and her head felt as if it had wandered over to another bench, or was floating somewhere up in the rafters above them.

Open your eyes, she told herself. *Open your eyes and get up. It's so dark because your eyes are closed. Open your eyes and get up. Open your eyes and get up.*

It won't do any good, you know, the little voice next to her said.

I can't see unless I open my eyes, she objected.

True. But you have to open them right.

There's only one way to open your eyes.

True, but you still have to look at the right thing once they're open. Look over there, in the corner.

Dasha turned her head in the direction the little voice was indicating. Only she was mired down in sleep, and when she tried to turn her head, it caused her to jerk and twitch so hard she nearly fell off the bench.

"Akh!" she cried, hitting her head on the hard wood and causing Susanna and Svetochka to jerk awake as well.

"What is it?" demanded Svetochka, still half-asleep but looking around wildly.

"No-nothing," Dasha told her, also looking around wildly but failing to see anything other than the stove and the bathhouse walls. "I started to fall asleep, but then I jerked awake, you know how you do sometimes. We should go in. We've been here long enough. It isn't good to over-steam, and supper is probably waiting for us." She dragged herself upright and forced herself to start wriggling back into her still-damp clothes.

"You fixed the lamp," Susanna said, going over and taking it off its nail by the door. "It is not dark anymore."

"No," Dasha said. "I didn't do anything." But it was true that the lamp was now burning bright and clear, with no sign of drowning in wax and guttering out.

I must have dreamed it, she told herself. *I must have dreamed the dark-ness. You dream all kinds of strange things, when you're just falling asleep.*

They dragged their wet boots back on with considerable difficulty, and then ran the two steps from the bathhouse to the back door of the main building. Dasha had expected night to have already fallen, but the sky, while still dark and full of rain, was gray, not black. And then they were inside, and serving girls found them in the corridor and showed them to their chamber for the night, and waited while they changed out of their wet things and into dry—well, dry-ish—clothing, and then took away all their wet clothes.

"We'll hang it up to dry overnight, noblewomen, don't you worry," the two girls waiting on them promised.

"Burn it," Susanna told them. "I never want to see it again."

"Don't," Dasha told the girls, who looked confused. "She jests. Please just hang it up tonight, and bring it to us in the morning, once it's dried. Is there supper?"

"That there is, noblewoman! Cabbage soup or buckwheat; what do you want?"

Susanna made a face at the choice, but Dasha ordered cabbage soup for all of them, and, when they came downstairs and joined the men, was delighted to discover that it was steaming hot and quite good. Although anything would have seemed good by then. Even Susanna, despite complaining about barbaric Zemnian fare, gulped down all of hers as quickly as the rest of them.

"I do not think I like traveling anymore," she complained, once the first pangs of hunger were satisfied. "Not up here in the North, anyway."

Oleg laughed. "This is hardly the North," he told her. "Up in the North proper, that would have been snow we'd've been riding through today, not rain."

"Snow would have been better!"

"You're right there," he agreed with her. "But rain in spring hap-pens. Tomorrow will be better."

"Do you promise?" Susanna asked, sounding as if she expected him to make the promise and keep it.

"Absolutely," he told her solemnly. "I swear by all the gods that tomorrow will be better than today. The skies can only hold so much rain, after all."

"True enough," agreed Susanna, and then yawned hugely. "I am so tired! Even after that nap in the bathhouse!"

"You shouldn't nap in the bathhouse," Oleg told her.

"I know! But we did it anyway!"

"Well, I suppose no harm came of it," he said. "To bed with you! We have another long day tomorrow!"

Everyone groaned at that, but let him chivvy them off to their chamber, where they threw themselves onto the lumpy bed—the bed was considerably less comfortable than everything else about this waystation—and soon fell fast asleep.

Dasha woke up twice that night, shivering and convinced that the chamber was strangely dark, but why she thought that, she couldn't say. Until she got up the next morning, and realized that her throat was scratchy and sore, her head hurt, and she felt hot and cold at the same time.

No! she cried to herself. *I can't be sick! I'm on a journey!*

As if you can't get sick on the road, was the answer. *The road is the best place to get sick!*

I'll hide it from the others, she decided. *We've been going slowly enough, and I don't want to stay here.*

Are you sure that's a good idea? came the reply. *You risk turning a little chill into a cough, and a cough is nothing to mess about with. Coughs kill.*

I've never been sickly, she answered. *I've never even been seriously sick. I'll be fine.*

No you won't, she was told. *But it will be for the best.*

Why? she asked, but the voice in her head made no reply. Another voice in her head told her that she should be concerned about hearing voices in her head. Not that she didn't often have many thoughts and opinions come floating through there—in fact, she could hardly get them to shut up—but they rarely spoke in fully formed sentences like this, or argued with her. Maybe it was a result of the sickness, she thought. That must be it! She was vaguely aware that that hardly made it any better, but everything seemed hazy and far away, and so she dressed herself with hands that seemed to move around her like weeds in water, and floated downstairs like a leaf on the flood.

She expected, inasmuch as she was capable of expecting anything in her current state, the others to notice her indisposition instantly and raise a great hue and cry and insist that she return to bed for the rest of the day. Certainly that was what her maids would have done. But the only person who said anything at all was Oleg, who merely remarked that she looked a little tired, but that she'd wake up as soon as they started riding.

"I'm sure you're right," Dasha agreed, and followed him out of the inn and over to the stable, where the horses were saddled and waiting for them, even though it seemed as if she had arisen only a moment ago, and that not nearly enough time had passed for them to be dressed and breakfasted and ready to set off.

But set off they did. The clouds had all been blown away by the keen wind that cut through their clothes like...well, like a keen wind in early spring, and the brilliantly blue sky spread over them like...like the sky. It seemed to fly impossibly far above them, and also to press down on Dasha's head like a blanket smothering her, and she kept fancying that she could see bits of it moving and wriggling around the edges of her vision, where things seemed to sparkle like in midwinter, when it grew so cold that water froze out of the air and fell like crushed diamonds out of the clear blue sky. Only it was spring, not winter, and the blue of the sky was the wrong color for cold-snow and hoarfrost, and, and, and...Dasha forgot what she had been trying to think.

"A fine day to get more freckles," Mitya was saying. "I reckon we'll be covered by 'em by the time the day is out, lads, what do you say?"

"I reckon some of us'll have so many freckles, they'll all just turn into one big freckle and make us dark as Hordeswomen," said Seva. "What do you reckon: will they just cover our faces—those of us as has 'em—or the rest of our bodies as well?"

"I don't know," answered Mitya, with mock doubt, as Alik muttered, not looking at the rest of them, "There's nothing wrong with Hordeswomen."

"Those of us as has freckles has a lot of body to cover," Mitya continued, paying Alik no mind.

"Stop it!" shouted Svetochka, her voice shrill and petulant. Dasha looked over and realized—somehow it had never really struck her before, although of course she'd seen it—that Svetochka's face was covered with freckles, even more than her own was. And it *did* seem as if they were increasing by the day. Well, of course they were: freckles

grew with the sun, and they hadn't had any sun all winter until now.
"It's not funny!" Svetochka insisted.

"Sure it's funny!" said Mitya, and he and Seva both laughed at
length in proof of that, until Svetochka's lip started to tremble, and her
face turned so red the freckles were all but drowned in blood.

"It's not funny!" Dasha interjected. "I don't see why you keep teasing her like this! It's not nice, and it's not even funny!"

"If it's not funny, why are we laughing?" demanded Mitya with a
grin, while Seva nodded his head in agreement. Alik rode off abruptly
to join Susanna at the front of the group.

"Because you laugh at things that aren't funny!" Dasha told him.

"If you're laughing, it's funny," reasoned Mitya. "And we don't
mean no harm!"

"You're hurting her!"

"How are we hurting her? I don't see any cuts and bruises, do you,
Seva?"

"Not a one," said Seva, shaking his head. "Nor a drop of blood,
neither."

"So we can't be hurting her, then," Mitya said.

"But you *are*! You're being mean!"

"We ain't being mean!" Mitya was starting to get angry. "What's
mean about telling the truth? She's got freckles, don't she? We're just
telling the truth! You're supposed to tell the truth! What do you want
us to do, lie?"

"You're hurting her because you want to! You're hurting her because you want your words to be mean, so they are! The truth isn't the
only truth! If there's a lie behind it, or meanness, then it's hurtful and
untrue! It's what's behind your words that's most important!"

"What's this?" demanded Oleg, coming up to them from where he
had been riding in the back of the group. "Are you quarreling like little
children?"

Mitya gave Dasha a very sullen look and muttered something
about "Little girls who don't know what funny is," before riding ahead
to join Alik and Susanna.

"I shouldn't have said that," Dasha lamented, just as Svetochka
said, "Why was you so mean to him! There weren't no need for you to
go off on him like that!"

"He was teasing you! He was making you miserable!"

"I can handle myself!" insisted Svetochka, despite all evidence to
the contrary. Dasha opened her mouth to point out exactly that, but a

wave of nausea overcame her, and she had to snap her mouth shut and swallow hard to keep the contents of her stomach where they were supposed to be.

"I can't be having this," Oleg said, to no one in particular. He looked back and forth between Dasha and Svetochka, and focused on Svetochka. "I can't be having this," he repeated. "I can't be having them tease you and make fun of you, and you sulking and whining like a little child. Nothing tears a traveling party apart so fast as that, when you're on the road and you don't have anyone other than each other to rely on. So either you make them stop, or you let those who can do it for you."

"*She* certainly can't," Svetochka muttered sullenly, with a sideways glance at Dasha.

"No, but at least she's trying, and she's made them feel ashamed of themselves. Whether it'll make it better or worse, I don't know. But what you're doing—you're making yourself a victim for them. Everything you do makes them want to attack you more."

"It ain't my fault!"

"Maybe not. But it's still your problem, and not just yours. You're endangering the rest of us as well. I can speak to them, and that might help, but you'll have to do your part too." He looked back over at Dasha. "You both will."

"It's just so hard," complained Dasha. "What they do is so bad not because of what it is, but because they want to be mean, like I told them. But there's nothing to hang onto, nothing to tell them that they can't do, because it's not what they're doing, it's how they're doing it. And if you say that, they'll just twist your words and make you look bad."

"Yes." Oleg exhaled sharply through his nose. "This is how bullies behave, and most people are bullies, under the right circumstances. I'll speak to them, but you'll have to do your part too, and that means not giving them a target, not being a victim, and making them like you."

"I don't know if they're capable of liking us," said Dasha.

"Sure they are. Oh, you're right, there are those who can't feel anything for others, who can't ever like other people, but these lads aren't like that. They're just doing a bit of bullying because that's what they know how to do. They just need to be retrained a little, and you're the ones who'll have to do it."

"It's not fair," objected Dasha. "We shouldn't have to protect ourselves from them, and we shouldn't be the ones who have to retrain them."

"No, it's not," agreed Oleg. "But it's still up to you to do it, because no one else can, and you'll be the ones who suffer the most if you fail, so I'd think hard if I were you about how you're going to go about it. At the very least, you two should figure out how you're going to work together on this. After all, you're sisters, and this is the kind of thing that sisters do for each other. And—you'll be Tsarina some day. It's time for you to learn how to show everyone who's always seen you as the little girl who has to do what they say because their duty is to protect her that you're not that little girl anymore. It's time for you to learn how to make them do what *you* say, instead of you doing what they say. I'll speak to them this time, but this is something you'll have to learn how to do on your own."

He rode forward, presumably to go speak with the guards about their behavior, leaving Dasha and Svetochka to look at each other in shame-faced silence. Dasha made one attempt to bring the matter up, but Svetochka was still sulking and resolutely refused to discuss it, so Dasha had to content herself with strategizing in the quiet of her own head. Which proved to be barren of any good ideas. She was forced to hope that what she had already done would prove to be sufficient, or that she would be struck with a brilliant idea later. But mostly she was taken up with the soreness in her throat, and the uneasiness in the pit of her stomach, which occupied more and more of her thoughts as the day wore on.

She was briefly distracted from her discomfort by the sight of clouds billowing out of the ground, off to the right. As they came closer, she saw that there was a path leading off from the main road in the direction of the clouds, and as they rode by the turnoff she saw that the clouds came from a deep ravine, in which—she stood up in her stirrups, and just managed to catch a glimpse of it—a village was standing. The ravine was large enough that even the village roofs were concealed, and the only sign of it were the clouds, which turned out to be smoke and steam. Oleg told her that the ravine was full of clay, and the villagers made bricks there and sold them all over Zem'.

"Is that what the steam is coming from?" she asked, temporarily forgetting her rising illness in her interest in this novelty. She was quite taken with the idea of living hidden away down in a ravine like that, although when she had actually looked down in it, for the two strides she had been able to see anything, a cold chill had run up her spine. Probably fever, she told herself.

"Maybe, although like as not it's laundry day," he told her.

"Can't we stop there?" Dasha asked, even as another cold chill ran up her spine. The steam had taken on a very ominous look, somehow.

"There's no waystation there," he told her. "And it's only midafternoon. We'll ride another ten versts or so before stopping."

"Oh," said Dasha, relieved that they wouldn't have to descend down into the threatening—why was it threatening?—steam, but trying not to let her dismay at the thought of riding another ten versts show. A nasty pain was now gripping her head, and the bright sun was hurting her eyes. It was finally growing warm, but even so, she found herself shivering.

I should tell him I'm sick, and say that we should stop for the day, she thought, but when she thought of stopping for the night down in that ravine, another cold chill gripped her spine and made her shudder all over. She held her tongue, and soon the ravine and the village were behind them, and they had to keep riding forward, whether she wanted to or not.

What if I'm really sick, she found herself thinking. *After all, I hardly ever fall ill. This must be something special and bad. What if I'm really sick. What if I'm putting myself and everyone else in danger by not saying anything.* A series of visions of herself becoming ill, really really ill, and then dying, and of her mother's grief—no, first her father would have to inform her mother, and how terrible would that be?—her parents' agony, the disarray her death would throw Zem' into—what if her sister Prasha ended up becoming Tsarina? *That* would be a catastrophe. She should say something.

But—what would her father do if she told him right now? They would have to keep riding on to the next waystation in any case, and it would only make him anxious and guilty. Dasha tried to imagine her father anxious and guilty. It was not something she'd ever witnessed before. But her visions told her that if she were to fall really ill while on this journey with him, he would feel guilty and afraid, and the fact that that would be so out of character for him made her even more determined to protect him. So she said nothing, and told herself that she was *not* really sick, and that a night of rest would heal her completely.

The waystation, when it finally appeared, was small but neat and comfortable, and its mistress was a large, motherly woman, whose good nature was as expansive as her bosom. She took one look at Dasha and said, "Caught a chill, have you, my heart?"

Dasha opened her mouth to deny it, but was overcome by a sneezing fit before she could get the words out. The waystation mistress, who introduced herself as Baba Alina, even though she was closer to Dasha's mother's age than her grandmother's, immediately put her hand to Dasha's forehead, and proclaimed her ill. "Though luckily it's nothing but a little chill," she pronounced briskly. "Come, my dear, let's get you to the bathhouse."

"How long have you been ill?" Oleg demanded. "Why didn't you tell me?"

"I didn't want to delay us," Dasha told him. "And what could you have done, anyway?"

"You should have told me. You can't go risking yourself like this. You..."

"Now, now," Baba Alina interrupted him. "I know it's vexing when your child's taken ill, but it ain't her fault. A body can't decide when to take ill and when not to."

"Her mother..." began Oleg, his face knitting together in that thunderous expression that Dasha found so intimidating, especially now that it seemed to be aimed at her.

"I know, I know," Baba Alina said, before he could continue. "Her mother's entrusted her precious darling to you for the first time, and she's gone and gotten sick on you, hasn't she? I've seen it before, my dear, I've seen it before. There ain't much I hain't seen, here on the road. I've been at this inn more'n fifty years, an' I've seen it all, I've seen it all. But don't you worry: we'll have your girl right as rain in a day or two. You!" she called to Svetochka. "You're her sister, ain't you? Come over here an' help her with her things!"

"I ain't her sister," Svetochka muttered, but sidled over in Dasha's direction.

"Like that, is it?" said Baba Alina, with a sharp-eyed glance at Oleg. "Different mothers, is it?"

"How do you *know*?" asked Dasha. "Do you have a gift? Are you farsighted or foresighted?"

Baba Alina laughed. "Oh, by all the gods, no, my sunshine, not in the slightest! You do an old woman an honor she ain't never earned. No, I've just seen it all, my love, seen it all, an' a blind woman could see you two are sisters, an' daughters of that handsome fellow," she nodded towards Oleg, who looked to be trying to ignore her, while still keeping an eye on Dasha, "over there. It happens, you know, that a man'll have daughters by two different mothers, it happens more'n you'd think. What'd he do," she took Dasha by the shoulder and began leading her in the direction of the bathhouse, "run off an' leave your mother? Or was it the other way 'round, an' she stole him? For I see you're noble, as noble as they come—now, don't try to deny it!—an' your sister is as common as can be, an' your father too, by the looks of it. So who stole whom?"

"Ah," said Dasha, writhing a little in embarrassment. "Well, ah, nobody *stole* him. He's, ah, he's kind of his own man."

"Well!" exclaimed Baba Alina. "So that's how it is, is it? An' handsome as he is, who can blame your mother—or hers! An' it's kind of your mother to let you go off with him—many a mother wouldn't so much as think of it. Is he taking you to meet your kin?"

"Ah," said Dasha. "Yes."

"An' I'm sure they'll be more'n pleased to meet you, such a fine high-born girl as you are!" Baba Alina stopped at the door to the bathhouse and looked Dasha up and down. "My, but you're a noble one, anyone with half an eye can see! You must be from one of the very noblest families!"

"My grandfather was a Stepnoy," Dasha told her.

"A Stepnoy! You don't say! A Stepnoy! My, but your grandmother must've been glad to catch him! Did he train you like they say they train you, out on the steppe?"

"He died before I was born," Dasha told her. "You know. Fighting the Hordes. But I ride pretty well."

"'Course you do, 'course you do, noblewoman!" said Baba Alina. "Well, a granddaughter to a steppe warrior ain't going to be brought down by a little chill, are you? Have a nice steam, an' you'll be feeling right as rain in no time. Go on in, an' you'll find towels an' such in the front chamber. The stove's all hot, an' there's plenty of water, so steam as long as you like. I'll come get you when it's time for supper."

Dasha thanked her, and went into the bathhouse, which was small, but clean and tidy, like everything else at the waystation. She hung up her clothes in the antechamber and, feeling peculiarly as if someone were watching her, went into the hot room, where she threw so much water on the rocks that soon the entire chamber was filled with steam, and if anyone was watching her, they wouldn't be able to make out her figure. Or so she told herself. She laid out her towel and lay down on the bench, wondering if the others would come join her. Steaming alone was dangerous, everyone knew that...

The moist heat soon cleared out her nose and eased her aching muscles. *I should go in now,* she thought to herself. *No one's coming to join me, and it won't be good for me to over-steam. I should go in now. I wonder if I'll still be sick tomorrow? No, surely the steam will sweat out all the sickness. The steam's already dissipating: I should throw more water on the rocks if I'm going to stay here. But the bench is so comfortable.* This was not strictly true, as the hard wooden slats pressed through the thin towel she was lying on, and dug into her shoulderblades. She flipped over onto her stomach and pillowed her head on her arms, but that only made the slats dig into her breasts, and her neck soon grew sore from being turned to the side, so she flipped back over onto her back. The steam was almost gone, revealing the dark shadows in the corners.

I should get up, Dasha thought drowsily. *I certainly mustn't fall asleep in here by myself. If I already have a fever, then too much steaming would be particularly bad for me. It can make the fever settle in the brain. Roll over and get up!* But her body ignored her command, and she continued to lie there, her only motion to fling one arm over her eyes, as if that would hide the shadows in the corners from her, and her from them.

In the silence as she continued to lie there her ears seemed especially sharp, perhaps from her fever, and she could hear and taste the coals snapping and cracking as they burned and cooled in the stove, and the sound of footsteps approaching...*It must be Baba Alina, coming for me,* thought Dasha, and tried to sit up, but once again her body refused to obey her thoughts.

At last.

At last what? thought Dasha.

At last you come to us, as was promised!

What promise? asked Dasha.

The promise your mother gave us, that you would come to us to be trained. Some of us were beginning to despair, some of us were beginning to fear that she had gone back on her promise, or that you would never leave Krasnograd, but here you are! We have been following you since you left the kremlin, and now...

"Noblewoman?" called Baba Alina.

Dasha jerked awake. For a moment she saw the darkness in the corners reaching out, reaching for her, almost touching her...

"Noblewoman?" repeated Baba Alina, her footsteps loud on the wooden floor as she came into the bathhouse. "Little noblewoman? Are you done with your steam?" She opened the door into the hot room and poked her head in. "You've gone an' fallen asleep an' gotten overheated, hain't you, my heart," she said, sounding worried. "I should've come to check on you sooner, but I wanted to make sure you had a good steam, an' there was so much to do..."

"No, no, everything's fine," Dasha assured her, pushing herself upright, but then swaying as she attempted to wrap her towel around her.

"You have, you've gone an' overheated, you poor thing," said Baba Alina, running over in order to help Dasha over to the antechamber.

"Maybe a bit," Dasha admitted, allowing Baba Alina to give her her arm. "But I don't think any harm was done, and with luck I'll have sweated out the sickness."

"With any luck, little noblewoman, with any luck! Come, let's get you back in your clothes an' back inside. I'm going to put you to bed an' bring you a warm broth for your supper. My mother always swore by it, an' she passed the recipe on to me, an' I nursed both my daughters to health with it whenever they got their childhood illnesses, an' now they're nursing their own little daughters to health with it, whenever they catch a chill or a flux. Depend upon it, in a day or two you'll be right as rain."

Baba Alina fussed around Dasha and hustled her into her clothes and out of the bathhouse so peremptorily that she was never able to look back into the corners and see if the shadows were still stretching out towards her. And she had to acknowledge to herself that she didn't look very hard. She was fairly certain that it had been the domoviye, although whether it had really been them, or she had just dreamed it, was an open question. In any case it had been unsettling, more unsettling than it should have been. Perhaps it was the fever disturbing her brain. Perhaps it would all seem different tomorrow.

Dasha allowed Baba Alina to lead her to the chamber she had set aside for her and Susanna and Svetochka and, as promised, put her to bed like a little child and bring her a tureen of steaming broth and stand over her until she finished it. Either the broth had sleeping herbs in it, or Dasha was even more exhausted by the events of the day than she knew, for she fell asleep soon after finishing it, too tired even to clean her teeth.

She was walking down the road, no more than seven or eight, holding her father's hand in a way she never had in real life, because he had hardly ever been around, and when he had he hadn't taken her for walks down dusty roads out in the provinces like this. They walked over the top of a rise, Dasha hanging back and Oleg dragging her forward.

"I don't think we should go down there," she said, as he pulled her over the rise.

"Nonsense," he told her harshly. "We have to. We have to get down there."

As they crested the rise, she saw there was a village down there, down in what was almost a ravine at the bottom of the hill, so that the only thing she could see of it from the road was the smoke rising from its chimneys—or was it steam rising from vats of laundry? She could feel it scalding her skin even from here. She whimpered and tried to pull back harder, but her father only dragged her forward with redoubled strength. Dasha twisted around to try to run the other way, but as she did, she caught sight of...something coming down the road after them.

"Look!" she tried to scream, but it came out as a whisper. "There's something behind us!"

"Oh," said her father, unconcerned. "That's just Gray Wolf."

Dasha looked back. "No it's not," she screamed/whispered. "It's a bear, and he's...he's running! He's running after us! He's running after us!"

"Let's cross here," said her father, and pulled her across a narrow bridge made only of two birch poles, spanning a deep cleft in the earth.

"Now we're safe," said her father, as the bear leapt across the cleft and continued after them. Or was it a bear? It looked more like a domovaya...no, a bear...no, a wolf...it was very fast.

"He's still coming!" Dasha screamed/whispered, as she tried to drag him down the road faster. "He's still coming!"

"Look," he said, pointing at a horse and cart she hadn't noticed before. "We can ride on that cart."

"No," she said, now trying to pull him in the other direction. "No, no...that horse can't pull us, she can't pull us..." But her father was oblivious to her protests, and dragged her down the road until they drew level with the horse and cart.

"No..." said Dasha, but no one paid any heed to her, none of the people suddenly gathering around her from out of nowhere paid any heed to her, least of all her father, who threw her roughly into the cart and shouted at the horse, "Go!"

The skinny horse, covered in sores from her harness, tried to move forward, but Dasha's weight was too much for her, and she fell to her knees instead. Dasha jumped out of the cart and ran to her head. Flies were buzzing all around her face, tormenting her and making sweat and water run from her eyes as if she were crying. It was Poloska.

"No!" shouted Dasha. "Poloska! It's Poloska! Father—father, help her! Help her!" She tried to undo the harness straps, but her small childish fingers only fumbled helplessly over the knots and buckles. The onlookers were all laughing now, laughing at Poloska's misery and her distress.

Her father stepped up behind her, filling her with relief. He would help her, he would save Poloska. He moved—and kicked Poloska in the ribs, kicked her so hard she groaned and tried to get up, but she staggered and fell back to the ground instead. "Mine!" he shouted. "Mine, mine, mine!"

"NO!" screamed Dasha, but her father kept kicking Poloska, and then the others were all surrounding them, pushing Dasha out of the way despite her struggles, and they were kicking and beating Poloska, kicking and beating her and laughing and laughing and screaming "Mine, mine, mine!" as she tried to get away from them, but couldn't, pinned down as she was by the harness and her own weakness.

Dasha ran around to her head and grabbed her reins. "Come *on*, Poloska, come on!" she screamed, tugging at the reins, knowing that the only way she could save Poloska was to get her to her feet and away from these people who were laughing, killing her and laughing as they did so. And Poloska tried, she even made it to her feet, but then someone landed a savage kick to her near fore fetlock, and she collapsed again, looking so mournfully, so reproachfully, at Dasha. Dasha could see herself reflected back in Poloska's eyes, and somehow she knew that Poloska could see herself reflected in Dasha's.

"Come *on!*" she screamed again. "Come *on,* come *on,* come ON!" She pulled at the reins again, screamed, tried and failed to push the others away, screamed and pulled some more, and then she was hitting Poloska too, screaming and hitting her just like the others, with just the same rage, as she tried and failed to save her.

"She's *mine!*" she screamed at the others. "Stop it, she's mi—" She was cut off mid-word by a tremendous shove from behind that knocked her to the ground. When she twisted around, she saw the bear—no, wolf—no, domovaya—looming over her, claws and teeth extended towards her face.

"Mine!" cried the domovaya triumphantly.

Dasha's eyes snapped open. She was in her bed in the inn, lying in the dark next to Svetochka and Susanna. Her heart was pounding, and she felt sweaty and sick. She pushed herself convulsively upright, thinking to get out of this awful bed, to go out, to have some water and try to calm herself. She slid out of the warm blankets into the cool air... and froze, one foot on the floor. There was something in the corner, something watching her out of the corner of the room.

"Svetochka!" Dasha hissed, shaking Svetochka on the shoulder. "Susanna! Svetochka!"

Svetochka groaned in protest and rolled away from her. Susanna half-sat up and looked around groggily.

"What is it?" she asked.

"There's something in the corner!" whispered Dasha.

"Where?"

Dasha pointed. Susanna squinted into the darkness.

"There is nothing there," she said.

"Nonsense..." Dasha looked again. A ray of moonlight came in through the window, illuminating the corner and showing that there was absolutely nothing there.

"It is the fever," Susanna told her groggily. "It is the fever making you see things. You must go back to sleep."

"I'll just...I have to..." Dasha got the rest of the way out of bed and, staggering slightly, made her cautious way out the chamber and along the corridor to the privy. She kept thinking that something was moving just on the edges of her vision, but whenever she turned her head, nothing was there. She staggered back—her head still ached and spun fiercely—to the chamber, crawled into the bed, and shut her eyes firmly, determined not to look out again until the sun rose.

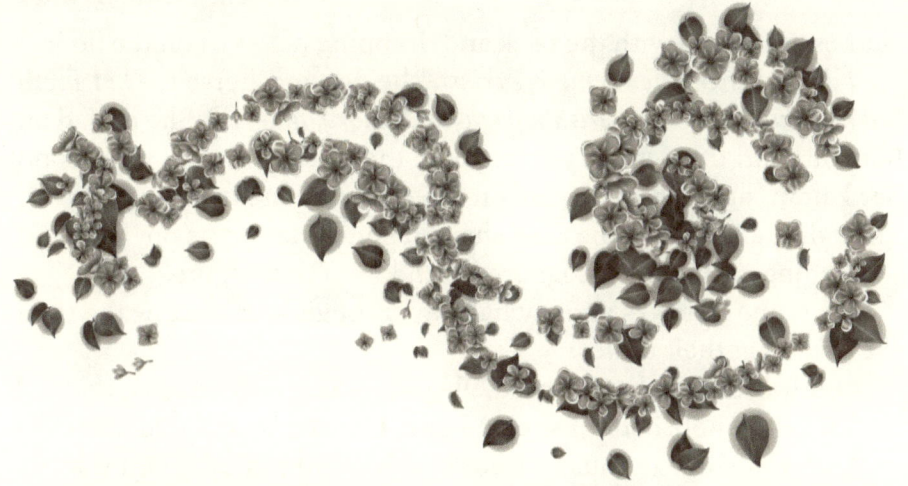

Chapter Eighteen

Despite her intention to go directly back to sleep, the horrid dream haunted Dasha, holding her trapped in a fitful doze until the kitchen started to stir below, at which point she fell deeply asleep and was only awakened when Svetochka shook her awake and asked her if she wanted any breakfast.

"Breakfast?" She sat up. "Yes, I'll be down directly. I'm sorry I overslept."

"You well enough to get up?" asked Svetochka doubtfully.

Dasha slid cautiously out of the bed. "I feel better," she said. "I'll be down directly."

"I'll tell 'em, then," said Svetochka, and left. Dasha went over to her pack, got out her little packet of linen and dried mint, and began cleaning her teeth. She *did* feel better, she told herself: she definitely wasn't as feverish as she had been the night before. She glanced over into the corners and saw nothing other than some dust and cobwebs.

Or was that something creeping up on her...she looked away quickly and felt her forehead. A little warm, but not bad, she told herself, although she wasn't really sure what a feverish forehead should feel like. Probably hotter than hers was right now. She really was better. Still a little weak, but definitely better than yesterday. Her throat certainly didn't hurt as much, and neither did her eyes. Which meant she must be improving, and wasn't in any danger anymore. She struggled to put away her things for cleaning her teeth and to take out her clothes, fumbling with the pack and dropping her shirt on the floor.

I'll feel better after some breakfast, she assured herself. *That broth last night wasn't very nourishing. I'm just hungry, that's all.* She pulled on her shirt and trousers, struggling with the laces, and then slipped on her kaftan, her fingers clumsy on the clasps as she tried to put them through the loops. By the time she had gotten her boots on, her head was aching again, but she ignored it and went downstairs.

Everyone else was already halfway through breakfast by the time she arrived at their table.

"Feeling better, then?" asked Oleg, sounding relieved.

"Yes, definitely better," she told him. *It's not a lie*, she told herself.

"Are you sure? Because we could stay another day, if you wanted to recover more."

"No. Let's keep going."

"Good," said Oleg, sounding even more relieved. "No point in hanging around here any longer than we have to. We're already going slower than I'd hoped."

"Up on your feet already, my sunshine?" asked Baba Alina, coming over to their table and peering intently at Dasha's face. "Your fever's broke," she announced, feeling Dasha's forehead. "But you still look very pale."

"I just need some breakfast," Dasha told her.

"If you say so, my heart," said Baba Alina, sounding much less convinced than the others had been. "If I were your mother I'd keep you here another day, or better yet, a week, but I know how you young people like to be on the road."

"We'll have a short day," Oleg assured her. "Maybe just a half-day."

"There ain't another waystation closer 'n fifty versts down the road, which if you're healthy ain't so bad, but if you're sick, it's fifty versts farther 'n you'll want to go," Baba Alina told him. "But there's a cabin, oh, about fifteen or twenty versts from here, an' Baba Sofroniya's the best healer an' herbwoman we've got in these parts. I'd've sent for her anyway, if you weren't better this morning."

"That's a long way to send for a healer," Dasha remarked.

"Ah well, Baba Sofroniya's light on her feet. She gets around quicker 'n most, an' she's the one you want by your side if you're poorly. If you're set on getting out of here, I'd tell you to go to that cabin, an' send for her. She don't live but half a verst from the cabin—you'll find her hut if you go looking for it, an' she wants you to find her."

"Then that's what we'll do," declared Oleg. "We'll ride to the cabin, and send for Baba Sofroniya. Unless Dasha wants to keep going, and then we'll carry on to the next waystation." By his voice, Dasha knew that he was hoping that she would want to keep going. She told herself that she could ride the fifty versts, it would be no trouble at all, but when she imagined actually doing it, her heart sank, and she knew it would be profoundly unpleasant.

No it won't, she told herself. *It won't be so bad. You can do this!* And she set to eating as much breakfast as she could stomach, ignoring the voice in her head that was telling her that she was lying.

When she stepped outside onto the porch to join the others, who had all finished before her, her mouth kept filling with saliva, the harbinger of the vomit that wanted to burst free. The day was sunny, but there were dark clouds on the horizon, and a cold wind from the North hit her as soon as she left the shelter of the waystation walls, and caused her to start shivering.

"Are you ready?" Oleg, who was already mounted up on Belka, called to her. "Svetochka already brought your things down and put them on Seryozha."

"All ready," Dasha called back, and, swallowing down her breakfast and forcing herself to stop shivering, she went over and, after a little surreptitious wavering and fumbling, swung herself up onto Poloska's back.

See, she told herself as they set off down the road. *It's not so bad. You're definitely better than yesterday, and this isn't so bad.* And in truth, after a verst or so her stomach began to settle down, and the strength from breakfast began to spread throughout her limbs, displacing the shivering. *By the afternoon maybe I'll be completely recovered!*

They rode through a stand of freshly budded birch trees, and between fields whose rich black earth was already being covered with a green haze of new growth, and then up and down over swelling hills too steep for crops, and which were instead being left to grow grass for hay, until they came to a little river winding its way lazily through the greening hills. The cold wind from the North had died down, and in the sun it was almost warm. For an instant Dasha thought she caught a glimpse of a rainbow off in the distance, where the dark clouds were shedding their load of rain. From this distance it looked like steam rising up from the ground. Dasha tried not to shudder at the thought, which reminded her of her horrid dream.

"We'll cross the river and stop for a rest on the other side," Oleg announced.

"How?" asked Susanna, looking down at the little river with doubt. "There is no bridge."

"There's a ford," Oleg told her. "See, over there. The road leads to a shallows, and there's a ford there."

"A ford?" repeated Susanna, her forehead creasing in confusion.

"A shallow place where you can cross," explained Oleg.

This caused some snickering amongst the guards, who, despite their general admiration of Susanna, appeared more than willing to abandon their mockery of Svetochka for a time in order to take advantage of this opportunity to laugh at Susanna's ignorance of the Zemnian language. Dasha knew that she should do something, say something, but she couldn't think of anything to say, and her lips felt sealed shut.

"Tell us the Avkhaz word for ford, or shut up," Oleg said sharply. All three guards immediately fell silent. Why hadn't she thought of that? Simple, elegant, and just. Why couldn't she ever think of things like that? Dasha was aware that her thinking was both muddled and whiny right now, but she couldn't seem to stop it, couldn't seem to stop it, couldn't seem to stop it from going in circles...

"There is a lot of water in this 'ford,'" said Susanna, still looking very doubtful about the whole enterprise.

"Only to be expected in spring," Oleg told her briskly. "But the ice has passed, so if we're careful, it should be safe enough. Boys! Stop your sulking and go ride ahead. You can be the first to cross, to test the waters."

The guards looked less than thrilled at that prospect, even though it most certainly fell within the scope of their duties, but they rode ahead nevertheless. The rest of them started down the hill leading to the ford more slowly. As they drew closer, Dasha had to agree with Susanna: the water was running awfully high and fast. It would be all too easy for the horses to lose their footing and fall, or even be swept away...she could see, so clearly she could almost feel it, Poloska's near forefoot coming down on a loose rock, causing her to lose her footing and be carried off in the current, spilling Dasha headfirst into the cold, muddy waters...

No, no, no, she told herself. *It's just a vision. It's not real. Stop thinking about it and keep up with the others.*

Once they reached the bank, Oleg sent Alik and Mitya across first, leading Strelka and Nyusenka, the other packhorses. The water came up above their horses' knees in the middle of the ford, almost high enough to reach their stirrups, and the current was strong enough that both horses struggled and slid, but they made the crossing and were soon on the far bank.

"Good," said Oleg, once they'd made it. "The water's not as high as I feared." He sounded more relieved than he should have, considering how confidently he'd spoken before. "Susanna, you, Svetochka, and Seva cross now. Try to stay together, but not so close that if one of you stumbles, it'll bring down the others."

"I don't want to cross," said Svetochka, while Susanna made a face and muttered something about "'fords.'"

"Well, you can cross now, or spend the night by yourself on the ground and cross tomorrow," Oleg told her.

"We can cross together," Dasha offered. "I'll ride right by your side, and even hold your reins, if you want. That way you can hold onto the mane with both hands."

"I don't need you to lead me!" Svetochka cried out in indignation, while Oleg said, "No, Dasha, you cross with me."

"But Svetochka needs me," objected Dasha. "She needs my help."

"I do *not*!"

"Enough!" shouted Oleg. "No more quarreling! Svetochka, you go with Susanna and Seva, and Dasha, you go with me. Now go!"

Susanna, despite her earlier reluctance, started down the bank and into the water without any hesitation. Chernets pawed at the water as if thinking about lying down and rolling in it, but she legged him forward. Svetochka and Seva followed, with Svetochka holding her head up proudly as if to prove to Dasha that she didn't need any help. That lasted until the moment Sverchok first stepped into the water.

"He's being carried away by the current!" Svetochka cried.

"No he's not!" Oleg shouted back in impatience. "Susanna, wait!"

But Chernets had already crossed the ford in a few leaping bounds, snorting and shaking his head, and it was clear to everyone that if Susanna tried to make him stop in the water, he would do something unwise, like lie down and roll. Svetochka would have to make her own away across. And she had made it to the midpoint of the river, when Sverchok slipped and almost went down in the current and Svetochka shrieked, and when he regained his footing and tried to carry on, she jerked on his reins and screamed, "Stop!"

"Keep going!" shouted Oleg, waving his arms. "Don't stand there, keep going! You need to keep going!"

"I can't! I can't! He'll fall!"

"He won't, but only if you keep going!"

But Svetochka responded by shaking her head and yanking on Sverchok's mouth again, even though he had done nothing more than shift his weight as he tried to keep his balance in the current.

"Is the water running higher?" asked Dasha. It was washing over the bottom of Svetochka's stirrups.

"You're taking a perfectly ordinary river crossing and turning it into something dangerous!" shouted Oleg in disgust at Svetochka, ignoring Dasha's question. "Get going!"

Instead of moving forward, Svetochka clutched at Sverchok's mane and began to cry. Seva, who had gotten ahead of Svetochka and was almost to the far bank, tried to turn around in order to come back and get her, but Ryzhechka, his horse, stumbled and went to her knees when she tried to turn in the current. Seva, who had been paying attention to Svetochka rather than his own horse, slid forward out of the saddle and onto her neck.

"Get back in the saddle!" Oleg, Mitya, and Alik all shouted at once. "She can't get up when you're on her neck like that!"

Seva tried to scramble backwards into the saddle, but Ryzhechka's own scrambling as she tried and failed to get back to her feet made him slide around to the side of her neck instead, so that he was hanging from her by his arms.

"Jump off!" shouted Oleg.

"I can't!" Seva called back. "My foot's caught in the stirrup, and if I jump off, I'll end up upside down in the water!"

Sverchok, upset by the water and by Ryzhechka's distress, started moving forward in little half-hops that were the closest he could get to a trot in the high water. Svetochka shrieked and, in her desperation to clutch at his mane, dropped her reins, which he promptly put his near foreleg through.

"I'm falling off!" Svetochka cried, as Seva slid further and further under Ryzhechka's neck, and his foot became more and more twisted in his stirrup. In a few breaths, Dasha could see even without her visions, his wet hands were going to lose their grip, or Ryzhechka was going to shy or maybe even go down completely, and he would end up head-down in the water, which definitely was rising, no question about it now, or possibly even trapped underneath Ryzhechka. Meanwhile, Sverchok was tossing his head, trying to free himself from the reins that were caught around his leg, but only succeeding in causing Svetochka to begin her imagined slide out of the saddle in truth.

"You have to go get them!" Dasha told Oleg.

"I can't leave you here by yourself! I can't leave you to cross on your own!"

"I'm the best rider. You said it yourself," she told him. "You go get them, and Poloska and Seryozha and I will cross once the ford is clear."

"By all the mother-raping gods!" Oleg swore, as Svetochka came out of the saddle and landed with a splash in the swiftly-running current, which promptly tumbled her over and rolled her under Sverchok's prancing legs. "Svetochka, get OUT of there! I'm coming to get you, just get out of there! Mitya, go get Seva. Susanna, Alik, wait and be ready!" He gave Dasha a sharp glance, which clearly meant, "Don't do anything foolish," and plunged into the water.

"I'm drowning! I'm drowning!" Svetochka was screaming as she splashed around in the water, making Sverchok jump in fear and almost kick her in the head. He missed, but lost his footing and was swept several yards downstream, towards a spot where the shallows of the ford ended and the water tumbled and swirled as it poured into a deep pool. Dasha shrieked in horror without meaning to and almost dropped all her reins.

It won't do anyone any good if I drop my reins and Poloska or Seryozha get hurt, she reminded herself, and forced herself to sit still and do nothing, as Sverchok went down onto his knees and struggled back to his feet, his hindquarters sliding perilously close to the deep pool.

"I will get him!" shouted Susanna, and before anyone could stop her, she legged Chernets forward. They leapt back into the water and across the ford in a few plunging strides, Chernets's long legs seeming to half-dance across the surface of the water instead of getting caught up in the current as the smaller, weaker horses had been, until they reached Sverchok's side. To Dasha's mingled terror and amazement, Susanna guided Chernets over to Sverchok's far side so that she was between him and the edge of the ford, putting herself and Chernets within a hoof-width of the churning waters tumbling into the deep pool. The current pushed Sverchok up against Chernets, who pushed back and nipped Sverchok on the neck for good measure. With a squeal and an angry toss of his head, Sverchok thrust himself away from Chernets, using him as a wall to brace against, and jumped back into calmer waters.

"Come here boy!" Alik called, and rode forward to catch him and lead him to the far shore. "That was clever!" he shouted at Susanna, who grinned in reply and legged Chernets forward and away from the tumbling whirlpool and back up onto the far bank.

Meanwhile, Oleg had pulled Svetochka to her feet and was guiding her, as she clutched to his stirrup and staggered through the thigh-deep water, falling and half-floating, to the others on the far shore. Somehow—Dasha had missed it in the excitement—Mitya had extricated Seva from his predicament and was now leading Ryzhechka to the bank while Seva held onto her saddle and half-walked, half-swam beside her.

"You all made it!" cried Seva, once they were all on solid ground. "Everyone made it across..." They all looked at Dasha, standing there alone holding her horses.

"I'll come across!" she shouted at them. "Wait there and I'll come meet you!" *There used to be a rock in the middle of the current*, she thought. *But you can't see it anymore. No, there it is—you can see the water tumbling over it. If I go upstream of it, the crossing will still be shallow enough.* She began riding forward.

"Wait!" Oleg shouted back. "Wait for me to come get you!"

"The water's rising!" she objected. "It's raining upstream, and the water's rising! I need to cross right now, or not at all!"

"Well then...start now!" Oleg told her. "And I'll meet you in the middle!"

When they reached the edge of the water, Poloska snorted in distaste and stopped. Dasha had to agree that the water didn't look very inviting at all.

"We have to cross now," she told her, stroking her neck clumsily, Seryozha's reins clutched in her hand, which despite the chill in the air had grown slippery with sweat. "We have to cross now," she repeated more boldly. "See? All your friends are on the other side. We just have to go meet them."

This argument was sufficiently persuasive to convince Poloska to step into the muddy, swirling waters, and after a little balking, Seryozha followed her. Oleg and Belka were already in the water and coming towards them, although the water was now up to Belka's belly.

The water's shallow there—over there, Dasha told herself, and carefully guided Poloska upstream. "See, this isn't so bad," she said aloud, as much for herself as for Poloska.

And when the water was only up to the horses' knees, it wasn't. Poloska took slow, careful steps, feeling her way across the bottom, and Seryozha followed willingly enough. Oleg and Belka were moving towards them, and in just a few steps, Dasha thought, they would reach

each other and they would all make their way to the shore together.

"Watch..!" cried Oleg, but before he could say "out" a large branch came tumbling down through the waters and crashed into Seryozha's legs. He squealed and tried to jump forward, and Poloska followed suit, just as a large wave washed over all of them, lifting the horses' feet right off the bottom of the river and forcing them to swim desperately to keep from being bowled over.

"Drop his reins!" Oleg shouted at Dasha. "He'll make his own way to the shore!" Dasha obediently flung Seryozha's reins over his neck, hoping to keep him from getting tangled up in them that way, and tried to guide Poloska in the direction of the far bank.

Poloska managed to get herself facing the right way and struggle over to a shallow spot, where she regained her footing. Looking around, Dasha realized they were near the big rock in the middle of the ford, on the downstream side of it. To make it to the far shore, they would have to cross the deep spot formed by the water tumbling over the rock.

"Turn around!" shouted Oleg. "Turn around and come towards me!" He was standing in the shallowest place in the ford, upstream of the big rock, but the water was now rushing over his boots, and Belka was staggering and struggling against every wave and ripple.

"I can't!" Dasha called back. "I can't ride upstream! I'm going to swim across! Come on, Poloska!" And before Oleg could object, she urged Poloska forward, into the deep water.

She guided her towards the downstream side of the small pool, as far as possible from the waters tumbling and swirling off the rock. Seryozha, she saw, had already made it to the others and the safety of dry ground. She felt Poloska's hooves lift off the bottom of the river, and her body stretch out as she started to swim. They were being carried downstream in the current, but, just as Dasha had hoped, they only went a few lengths before they came against the edge of the deep pool, and Poloska was able to pull herself up it and into shallower waters.

"Good girl!" shouted Oleg. "Just a few more lengths, and..." Dasha felt Poloska's near forefoot slip on a loose rock, and Poloska go down underneath her, the current lifting her off her feet and spinning her around, making Dasha slide sideways. She only had time to think *Just like in my vision* before the current caught her too, spilling her head-first into the churning waters.

The shock of the cold was the first thing that hit her, followed immediately by the shock of the water slamming into her. She was lifted up and then down, down till her face dragged against the rocks and mud of the river bottom.

Not caught in the stirrups, she thought. *That's good. Got to get my feet under me.* She tried to flip herself around, get her head pointing up and her feet pointing down, but the water swept her over the shallow bottom of the ford and dumped her into the deeper pool beyond it before she could even make sense of which way was up and which was down. The heavy wool of her long kaftan was soaking up the water and tangling around her limbs, immobilizing her arms, and her boots were filling with water. She tried opening her eyes, but all she got for that was stinging pain and a glimpse of opaque muddy water.

Got to get out of boots, she thought. The current tossed her up to the surface for a moment, and she half-gasped, half-choked on the mixture of air and water that she sucked into her lungs. She caught sight of the others and the far shore—how had they gotten so far away?—before she was whirled around and saw the uprooted tree caught on the sandbar ahead of her.

*I'm going to slam...*she thought, and then the current sucked her back down towards the bottom, grinding her against a rock and then tossing her back up, right into the roots of the downed tree.

Ground, she thought. *There's solid ground, and the tree. I just have to get out from under these roots, and I can pull myself onto the sandbar.* She bobbed up to the surface for a moment and sucked in another choking breath of air and water. She was caught between the roots of the tree, which was lying on top of her, and the edge of the sandbar. The water pulled her back down and then tossed her up again. She could catch little breaths like this, but she was trapped under the tree. A wave washed over her, pushing her head back down under the water. She tried to pull herself back above the surface and struggle free of her boots, which were dragging her down, but something was holding her back. Something was caught on her right boot, something that felt like little hands, gripping it.

It's a branch, she told herself, and kicked as hard as she could. The boot came free and she shot up above the surface of the water, gasping for breath and grasping at the tree with all her strength. She got one arm wrapped around a branch and used it to pull herself higher, so that she was half-sitting on the edge of the sandbar, with the tree above her. She tried to squirm higher, to free herself from the tree entirely, but the space was too narrow for her hips to fit through.

"Dasha!" It was Oleg, standing on the shore nearest to her. He'd stripped off his boots and shirt. "Dasha, hold on, I'm going to come get you!"

"You can't swim through the current!" she shouted back.

"Just wait there!" He jumped into the water, but another wave washed over Dasha, blinding and choking her, before she could see what had happened to him.

I have to get out from under this tree, she thought. *I have to swim under the tree and then pull myself up over the other side of it. The water's still rising: if I stay here any longer, I'll be trapped and drowned.* She pulled herself as high as she could and tried to peer through the tree branches and find Oleg, but all she got for her pains was another faceful of water.

Do it! she told herself. *Do it now!* She tried to kick off the other boot, and once again had the sensation that little hands were grasping it and pulling it off of her.

It's just branches, she told herself, and pushed herself down and away from the tree as hard as she could.

The current caught her and slammed her against the sandbar. She kicked against it with all her strength, launching herself forward and, she hoped, under the tree. Something caught at her back.

No! she thought. *Not a branch!* But instead of holding her down, the thing caught at her back tugged her forward. She had a confused impression of scraping through branches and roots, and then she was being dragged away from the tree, out into the channel. She struggled, trying to free herself from whatever was holding her, but it only gripped her more tightly, its fingers moving against her clothing like a living thing.

"Dasha! Dasha, over here!" It was Oleg, clinging to a log that was resting precariously on another little sandbar halfway across the channel. Dasha kicked and swam in his direction, the little hands on her back and now around her waist pushing her along.

"Dasha, grab my hand!" She was already almost within reach of Oleg, and he was stretching out a hand towards her.

Dasha. The little hands suddenly pulled her down under the water. She had a quick glimpse of Oleg's horrified face, his mouth forming the word "No!" and then the muddy waters closed over her head.

Dasha. This is your element. Remember this. Remember this. And then the little hands shoved her upwards, so hard that half her body flew out of the water, and Oleg grabbed her by the hair and dragged her into an embrace.

"Come on!" he shouted into her ear. "We can wade to shore from here!" Still clutching her hair with one hand, he put the other hand under her arms and, wading, swimming, and crawling, pulled her to shore, where they both lay there gasping.

"Dasha!" It was Susanna, looming over them on Chernets. "You are alive! I thought you would die!"

"Help her," said Oleg, getting to his feet and pulling Dasha up after him. "Take her back over to the road and the others." He tried to lift her up onto Chernets's back, but Chernets sidled away unhappily. For a moment Dasha was afraid that Oleg was going to shout, or hit him.

"I'll walk," she said quickly. "I need to warm up and dry off anyway." And then she coughed so hard she thought she might throw up.

"Here, hold onto me," said Oleg. "That's it, take it slow. Nice and easy. No need to strain yourself any more than you already have." His arm around her waist tightened. "That was quick thinking," he went on, his voice thick. "Using that branch to help you swim over to me."

"Branch?" repeated Dasha, and coughed some more.

"You grabbed a floating branch," Oleg told her, helping her straighten up from her doubled-over posture once the coughing fit had passed. "You went down under the tree—I thought I'd lost you"—his voice shook—"and then you popped back up, holding a branch, and used it to swim over to me."

"There was no branch," Dasha said.

"You might not have known what you were doing. But you grabbed a branch, and used it to keep afloat while you swam. Quick thinking!" He grinned down at her, for a moment almost like his usual self. "I always knew my blood would come out one day!"

"Ye-es," said Dasha doubtfully. "There...there wasn't any branch. It was...something grabbed me."

"Something?" asked Oleg.

"Do you think..." (she coughed so hard she started to retch) "might it have been...a water-spirit?"

"Vodyaniye aren't much for consorting with humans," said Oleg. "They're even shyer than leshiye."

"But it *could* have been. *Something* grabbed me. *Something* spoke to me."

"Spoke to you?"

"It told me that this was my element."

"Drowning?" asked Oleg.

"Water."

"Well, if that's the case, then you'd best grow gills," he told her, as another coughing fit overtook her and held her in its grip as the others came running up to meet them, embracing her and slapping her on the back (which helped expel a little more water) and telling her how clever she was, to grab a branch like that and use it to swim to shore.

"There was no branch," she told them all.

"Oh, but we saw..."

"Something helped me." But another coughing fit, followed by a spell of shivering when a gust of cold wind hit her, stopped her from saying more.

"Quick, dry clothes," ordered Oleg, who was also coughing and shivering. "Don't hang about! Dry clothes! For Svetochka too," he added, looking over at Svetochka, who was huddled up next to Sverchok, shivering and coughing, in her own sopping clothes. "Everyone into dry clothes!"

"There's no place for the Tsarinovna to change," objected Mitya.

"So turn your back. Quick! Where are those dry clothes!"

Struggling out of her wet clothes and into slightly dryer, but still rather damp, clothes in the middle of the road was even more awkward than Dasha would have thought, even with all the men looking the other way as they changed their own clothes, and by the time she was done she was shaking and coughing so much she could hardly stand, and covered in road dirt besides.

"And I lost my boots," she said, through chattering teeth. "They were brand new, and I lost them!"

"Better them than your life," said Oleg. "Here." He took a kerchief and wrapped it around her head and shoulders, his movements brusque and jerky. He must be freezing as well, Dasha thought, and on another person she would have said his expression meant he was about to cry. Or shout at someone, which seemed more likely. "And here are some footcloths," he told her, pulling some rags out of his pack. "We'll strap them on as best we can, and they'll get you far enough. You can put on your old pair when you've dried out a bit."

"How far do you reckon we still have to go?" asked Mitya.

"No more than ten versts," said Oleg.

Ten versts! "Do you think we might come upon someplace to stop sooner?" Dasha found herself asking, her voice shaking so that everyone, judging by the looks they gave her, could hear it.

"If we do, then we'll stop," said Oleg, turning away from her. "But I don't know where that would be, and we need a healer."

"Oh." Dasha wanted to protest that she would never be able to make another ten versts, but what choice did she have? Lie down in the dirt and die? "It's still early," she found herself saying, her voice almost encouraging. "And the sun's out. We should make it well before dark."

"Yes," said Oleg, looking off at the horizon, towards the rainclouds, rather than at her. "The sooner we set off, the sooner we'll arrive. Let's go."

Riding warmed her at first, especially as they rode up out of the river valley and through the greening fields on the other side of it. For the first verst or two, the wind lay still, and the sun beat down on their heads in almost summery fashion. Oleg had wrapped the footcloths around her feet and legs so cleverly that riding without boots was less difficult than she would have thought, and as they went along she began to feel flushed and cheerful, as if she had taken a sip of vodka. But then the wind picked up, bringing with it the scent of rain from the North.

"We're going to get hit by that rain," Mitya warned them.

Oleg frowned at the horizon. "Then we'll just have to dry off," he said. "Since there's no way around it."

I've already gotten as wet as a person can get, Dasha told herself. *A little rain isn't going to make things any worse. And we've already done at least two versts. And it's probably just a short little band of rain, and we'll be through it and back in the sunshine in no time. And then we'll find shelter and a healer and everything will be fine!*

"There's been enough of this," Oleg was saying behind her. Why could she hear him? He was speaking low, so low she shouldn't have been able to hear him, but all of a sudden her ears seemed to have grown twice as sharp as usual. She turned to see whom he was speaking to, but blue crackled across her vision, distracting her.

"It was one thing when it was just you," Oleg was saying, still speaking in that low, angry tone. "It was one thing when you were just making a fool of yourself. We all make fools of ourselves, especially when we're your age. But when you start endangering your sister, it has to stop."

Svetochka, thought Dasha.

"It weren't my fault!"

Definitely Svetochka.

"Not all of it, no. Not the rising water, nor the fact that we all should have listened to Dasha and walked you across the river like she suggested. But you didn't have to make such a mother-raping fool out of yourself!" Oleg's voice rose at those last words, making everyone turn to look at him and Svetochka, who was hunched over Sverchok's neck, sniveling.

"Don't talk to her like that!" The words left Dasha's mouth just as pain slammed into her temple so hard she reached up to feel for the rock she was sure had hit her. Only there was nothing there, and now the pain was jumping around to the other temple.

"She put you in danger!" Oleg said. "If it hadn't been for her foolishness..."

"It wasn't her fault. It wasn't her fault. It was ours. And it had to happen."

"It did not have to happen! It never should have happened! You—you could have died back there in the river! Don't you see that you could have died! And it would have been..."

"It had to happen," Dasha interrupted him. "It had to happen so that they could speak to me."

"So that who could speak to you?"

"Them," said Dasha, flinching as another sharp pain stabbed through her head, this time above her left eye. She wriggled her shoulders, trying to shake off the sensation of power building up in her spine, spreading its tingling way across the nape of her neck and the back of her head. If she could just twitch and scream, everything would feel better, but the thought of making any sudden movements made her head throb. Blue crackled across her vision again. "They had to...Ah!"

"What is it!" Oleg cried.

"I just thought I saw something out of the corner of my eye. I was wrong. They just had to"—she turned in the saddle to face him—"speak to—AKH!"

Chapter Nineteen

"I can ride by myself. I don't need you to help me."

"Yes you do! You had a fit and you almost fell off! And you're sick!"

There was nothing Dasha could say to argue with that, since both points were absolutely true, so she bit her lip and wrapped her arms around Oleg's waist. When she had had her near-fit and almost (but not actually!) fallen off Poloska, he had made her get down so he could check her over. He had proclaimed her feverish (which she had to admit was true) and insisted that she ride behind him on Belka.

"That will just slow us down," she'd argued. "We can go faster if I'm on Poloska, and the faster we go, the sooner we'll reach Baba Sofroniya."

"Unless you have another fit and fall and break your neck or your head," Oleg had said, his brows drawn together in a way that told her it would be very difficult to change his mind. And she *did* feel terrible, she had to admit. So she'd allowed Mitya to leg her up onto Belka. She'd tried to argue when they'd taken away Poloska's and Seryozha's reins, but Oleg had told her that she wouldn't do them any good if she had another fit and dropped their reins and they ran away.

"They wouldn't," she'd protested.

"They would if you had a bad enough fit," he'd told her. "They'd know something uncanny was going on, and like as not they'd bolt. Horses don't like to be anywhere near anything strange."

Burning

This, too, was unarguable, so Dasha had, with (she had to admit to herself, feeling more shame than she would have liked) rather poor grace, handed over the reins to Seva and Alik, and was now putting her arms around Oleg's waist as they set off. Not that she needed to hold onto him, since he was keeping their pace at a sedate walk.

"We'll never make it to Baba Sofroniya's if we keep poking along like this," she complained. It had taken them simply ages to pass through the fields by the riverbank, which would have been a good place to trot or even canter (which would have been easier for Dasha to stay on, and they could have covered ground quickly and then rested the horses by walking again, but Oleg didn't want to hear about it), and now they were descending into a wooded valley and the road was steep enough that Dasha supposed it was sensible for them to be walking, but they could have gone faster, they could have...

"I don't want to jostle you," Oleg told her, his voice tight and angry, not comforting the way a good father's (Dasha thought) should have been. "You might've gotten a knock on the head when you were in the water."

"I *didn't*! I would have remembered. And it's not my fault, anyway! You don't have to be angry with me! It's not my fault!"

"I'm not angry with you."

"You are!"

Oleg released a sharp sigh and guided Belka around a branch that had fallen onto the road. They were down in the bottom of the valley, and the trees seemed to crowd around and over them, blocking out the sky and making it hard to believe that just half a verst away there were hilltops and open fields. "I'm not angry with you," he repeated, his voice flat. "I just don't want you to get hurt any worse than you already have been."

"So stop being mean to me! That hurts me more than anything!" Dasha was aware that she was being whiny and difficult, but she couldn't seem to stop herself. Part of her knew that Oleg must have gotten a terrible fright when she had gone under the water, and another one when she had had her almost-fit, but she couldn't find it in herself to be patient with him even so.

Now that it was all over, the near-drowning and the fit were scaring her too, and the words of the presumed vodyaniye were scaring her even more. She wanted someone to tell her that she had been very brave and everything was going to be fine, but instead her father, who *should* have been the one to help her, was being short-tempered and

289

unpleasant, as if he needed to take his anger at what had happened out on someone, and since she was closest, he was going to take it out on her, even though that wasn't fair *at all*.

"Stop whining," Oleg said, still in that same flat, awful voice. To her horror, Dasha could feel tears welling up in her eyes in response.

"And by all the gods, stop crying. There's nothing actually wrong with you: you'll be fine just as long as you don't do anything stupid."

"Why do you always do the worst thing possible! You couldn't have said anything worse if you'd tried! *And* you're lying! You're scared for me, I can tell! So stop lying and bullying me about it!"

Oleg opened his mouth to make a retort, and then shook his head. "We're wasting time," he said, and kicked Belka forward into a canter.

"You didn't have to kick her like that! Why are you so mean to everyone!"

A muscle jumped on Oleg's jaw, but he said nothing. Dasha could feel the strain in his back and shoulders. Was it because he was angry with her? Most likely. Was it because he wanted to *hurt* her? What if he wanted to hurt her? What if she'd made him so angry he was going to hurt her? Fathers did terrible things to their daughters all the time! If he attacked her, would the others step in and stop him? Susanna probably would, but maybe not the others. Would she and Susanna be enough to stop him? What if the others took his side! What if, what if, what if...

"Hold on to me!" he told her, still not looking at her.

"No."

"You'll fall off if you don't hold onto me."

"No I won't. And I'd rather fall off than touch you when you're being so mean to me!"

"Stop being silly."

He *did* hate her! Dasha slid back as far as she could away from him without getting her legs tangled in Belka's hindlegs.

"What foolishness are you doing now! Hold onto me!"

"Leshiye!" shrieked Dasha, making Belka jump and causing her, just as Oleg had predicted, to fall off.

After that things were very confusing. Not because Dasha had lost consciousness or had another fit, because she *hadn't*, she kept insisting, but no one would believe her. She did feel strange, as if her head were floating half a yard away from the rest of her body, but she hadn't *fainted* and she wasn't delirious, no matter what they said.

"There were leshiye!" she told them for the fourth or fifth time. "There were! I saw them! Peering out from between the trees!"

"Nothing was peering out from between the trees," Oleg told her, still speaking in that awful flat voice. "I would have seen it."

"Why? Why couldn't I be the only one to see it? *I'm* the gods-touched one, aren't I? Maybe they showed themselves just to me!"

"You're feverish," Oleg told her, feeling her forehead for about the dozenth time, but still not looking at her. "You can't trust your eyes."

"I can!" Dasha decided not to say anything about the shimmering on the edge of her vision, and the blue crackling that went across it like lightning every time she turned her head, or how everything seemed too quiet and too loud at the same time, or how time kept dragging and jumping, so that she had lain on the ground for what seemed like half an eternity after falling off, and now they were climbing out of the valley and had covered half a verst or more and she couldn't have said when or how.

"How much longer?" she found herself asking, despite her earlier intention not to speak to Oleg again for at *least* a day. But she was feeling all hot and cold at the same time, and she just wanted to lay her head down on Belka's mane and slide right off onto the ground and go to sleep even though she was also strangely jittery and funny tingling sensations were running up and down her arms and...

"I don't know," said Oleg, sounding even grimmer than before. "But it won't go any faster for asking."

Dasha couldn't tell whether it was anger or sickness that caused the sudden throb of pain that went through her head at those words. She really was very hot, even though she was shivering and her hands were cold, but they were slippery with sweat too and...they must have covered at least another half a verst, they would be there in no time, but how would she make it until then, she hurt all over...her head really hurt, like something was pressing on it...the blue crackling in her eyes was getting worse and worse, that was quite a flash...

"Lightning!" cried Mitya. "There's a storm up ahead!"

"And we're riding right into it!" added Alik.

"Nothing we can do about it," said Oleg. "Keep riding. It's just a spring storm. It won't be so bad."

Things were floating around on the edge of Dasha's vision, trying to catch her attention and distracting her from what was really happening, but even so she saw Alik start to argue and then look in her direction and fall silent. She wanted to tell him he had no reason to worry or spare her feelings, but all she could make herself do was rub her forehead, where the pressure was building and building. There was a funny feeling in her ears too, and it was getting harder and harder to stay in the saddle. What if she fell off and couldn't get back on? What if she couldn't stay in the saddle even while being led at a walk? What if, what if, what if...

There was another brilliant flash of lightning, followed by a crack of thunder that made all the horses toss their heads and prance sideways. A huge cold raindrop landed on Dasha's nose and slid off. More followed, splashing down on her hands and running down her neck and leaving big fat marks on the road.

"It'll be a short shower," Oleg said, sounding as if the main person he was trying to convince was himself. "It'll be a short shower, and we'll be through it soon." He glanced over at Dasha and then looked away quickly, his jaw set.

"I feel better," Dasha told him.

He looked back up at her, surprised.

"I feel better," she repeated, as the rain ran down her face in rivulets. "The rain's making me feel better. It's taking away my fever." And it was true. After the first cold shock, the shivering and sweating had stopped, and the pressure was gone from her head. "Maybe it was just the weather making me ill," she told him. "Just the oncoming storm."

"Maybe," he said, sounding unconvinced. "We'll be there soon enough."

It wasn't actually that soon, but to Dasha's confused time-sense it seemed like no time at all before they came to a little path leading off from the main road, and when they followed it they came to a travelers' cabin, with another little path leading off deeper into the woods. The rain had stopped and the sun had come out, making everything seem so bright and sparkly it was difficult for her to look at any of it. Or maybe that was still the fever, weakening her eyes.

"That must be the way to Baba Sofroniya's cabin," Oleg said, looking down the path leading away from the cabin. "Dasha and Mitya and I will go. The rest of you, stay here in the cabin till we come for you. And," he gave the others a very sour look, "try to stay out of trouble."

"Nothing to worry about," said Alik, forestalling Susanna and Svetochka's indignant replies that they were (all evidence to the contrary) completely capable of taking care of themselves. "We'll be safe as can be here. And quiet as mice. Take the Tsarinovna to the healer, and don't worry about us for an eyeblink."

"I'll send Mitya back when we find her," Oleg told them. "Like as not, Dasha and I'll spend the night there with her."

"Spend the night there?" blurted out Dasha. "Can't we come back here?"

Now it was her turn to receive a sour look from Oleg. "You'll do as Baba Sofroniya says," he told her. "And like as not, she'll tell you to spend the night there with her, where she can watch over you, and I'll do the same."

Dasha wanted to protest that she didn't need to spend the night at some strange old woman's hut (which sounded very unpleasant, not at all like spending the night at an inn, which she had thought would be jolly but had turned out to be less jolly than she had expected—but spending the night in some hut out in the middle of the woods with some strange old woman was sure to be even less jolly, and in fact sounded terrible, even worse than being sick), and also that he shouldn't talk to her like that, like she was a naughty little child, but she sensed that it wouldn't do any good, so she said nothing, and seethed with outrage on the inside instead, all the way down the narrow winding path until they came to a little hut in the middle of a tiny clearing.

The hut was no bigger than a single chamber, and instead of standing on the ground, it was raised up on stumps, whose roots spread out over the worn bare ground like chicken claws. It was surrounded by a palisade fence that was topped here and there by the skulls of various animals and even... "Is that a human skull, there on the gate?" Dasha asked, leaning down to whisper her question in Oleg's ear, forgetting about her recent pique against him.

"Yes," he told her quietly. "Don't worry about it."

"Don't worry about it! It's a human skull!" Out of the corner of her eye, Dasha could see Mitya nod in agreement, as he edged a little farther away from the skull, and then, looking ashamed of himself, edged back around so that he was between her and it.

"Healers often have things like that around."

"But why?!"

"Because they do," he told her curtly. "Now be quiet, and don't let

293

her know what you think of...all this. You don't want to offend her."

"What about her offending me?!"

"It's up to you not to be offended by her," Oleg told her, speaking as if this were the most obvious thing in the world, and she was a silly little child not to have guessed it already, and that having to explain it to her was almost more than he could bear. Which was so annoying! And unjust! Why didn't anyone care about how she thought or felt? Why was her own father being so short with her? *Obviously* he didn't love her at all! She should just slip off Belka and run away, back to her mother, who would comfort her and help her understand what was happening and how she should deal with all this...they were past the skull and through the palisade gate (Mitya giving a little shudder as they passed through it) before she could put her plan into action, which in retrospect was a good thing, because what would she do once she had started to run away? She certainly couldn't make it back to Krasnograd on her own. And she was a woman grown, or soon would be, and shouldn't have to be running to her mother over every trifle and slight. She should know how to deal with it on her own. Only she didn't, and no one seemed to be interested in teaching her how...

"Well come." The woman who had appeared on the steps of the hut was less strange and deformed than Dasha had been expecting. She was a tiny thing, even smaller than Dasha's mother, and much older, with pure white hair, but she stood tall and straight, with no sign of weakness. She held a broom in one hand, and Dasha could see in her mind's eye how she swept the area around the hut every day, and that was why it was so bare and clean. "You are in need of healing," the woman said, looking at Dasha.

"How did you *know*?" asked Dasha, torn between discomfort and delight at the woman's knowledge.

The woman gave her a small smile. "I am a healer, child. I know the sight of a girl in need of healing when I see it."

"Oh. So...nobody told you, then?"

The woman gave her another small smile. "Only my own senses, child. I'm afraid my companion there," she nodded to the skull by the gate, "is much more silent than people seem to think."

"Oh." Dasha's cheeks hurt from the blush that leaped up in them. "How did you know about...that too?" she asked.

"A lucky guess," said the woman, smiling a little more. "Everyone thinks my companions are more than what they are, which is scarecrows to keep the birds off my garden."

"Oh. How did you know we were here?"

"By smell," said the woman, and then laughed at Dasha's expression. "In truth, I can smell your company and your horse a bit, but it was your footsteps that told me, and the fence rattled as you walked past it."

"Oh. Isn't it strange, having a skull where you can see it all the time?" Dasha asked before she could stop herself.

"Not once you get used to it," the woman told her, now smiling at her in an almost kindly fashion. "Now come here, child, and let me examine you. That's it, Oleg Svetoslavovich, lead her over to me, and I'll help her down from the saddle. You can send your companion back now," she added. "He can tell the others that you are safe and in good hands, and will be spending the night with me."

"How did you know that too?" asked Dasha eagerly. Now that she had met her, she almost liked Baba Sofroniya. Another person who seemed to know things that others didn't! Maybe she could help her! "And how did you know who my father was?"

The woman laughed. "Everyone knows Oleg Svetoslavovich, my child," she said. "Everyone who knows things, that is." She gave Dasha what appeared to be a meaningful look. "Just as everyone knows that I am Baba Sofroniya—because that's who you came to see, isn't it? Now off with you," she said to Mitya, not waiting for their answer. "Go tell the others that your mistress is here and being cared for, and will return to you in the morning."

Mitya gave Oleg a questioning look, and, receiving a nod in reply, turned and set off down the path back towards the cabin at a walk that was so brisk it was almost a jog.

"I'm glad to see that I can still affect those who need it," said Baba Sofroniya, watching him go. "Now come here, child. That's it, right into my arms. I've got you, you won't fall. You can take your horse to the stable around the back," she told Oleg. "I hope she doesn't mind sharing a stall with a goat. There's some hay if she'll take it, and plenty of water from the well."

Oleg led Belka, with several backward glances, off to the back of the hut, where there was another, even more ramshackle structure, although this time on the ground rather than raised up on stumps.

"Why is your house like this?" Dasha asked, too curious to be polite. "Why is it raised up like this? It looks like it's on chicken legs."

"It does, doesn't it, my child? It keeps it out of the snow, so that I don't have to dig out my front door."

"Why aren't more houses built like this, then?" asked Dasha.

"Well, it is a little difficult to make very *large* houses like this, my love," said Baba Sofroniya, leading her up the steps and through the door, which was so low they both had to duck down to go through it. "In fact," she went on, as they stopped in the middle of the small single chamber, "such houses are normally for just one person. Have you never seen one like this before, my child?"

Dasha shook her head.

"Such a young thing," said Baba Sofroniya. She sounded almost sad. "Such a young thing, with so much sorrow still ahead of her."

"Have you seen something, then? Have you had a vision of my future?"

"A vision? I have no need of visions to know that you will learn the meaning of such houses someday, my child, and that it will be a day of sorrow for you."

"Why?" asked Dasha, starting to walk around the little room. She knew that she should be more polite towards Baba Sofroniya, and that Mitya and even Oleg seemed to find her uncanny, but she felt as if she were talking to someone she had known forever, as if Baba Sofroniya were her grandmother, the grandmother she had always wanted but had never had. Oh, she had her own grandmother, of course, her mother's mother, but she had only come to Krasnograd once, when Dasha was ten (her mother said that her grandmother had also come for Dasha's birth, but Dasha didn't remember that, so as far as she was concerned, it didn't count), and she and Dasha hadn't gotten along nearly as well as Dasha had hoped.

Dasha had thought that her grandmother would be both kind and wise, and would love Dasha more than anything in the world, but instead she had asked her mother over and over again whether Dasha's gods-touched nature and fate had manifested itself yet, and talked constantly of Prasha, Dasha's disgraced sister, who lived in the same sanctuary as their grandmother.

Dasha supposed that she couldn't fault her grandmother for loving the granddaughter whom she saw every day more than the one she saw only once every ten years, but it had still been disappointing, especially since she had seen nothing in her grandmother that looked to her like wisdom. It had been hard to believe that the elderly woman sitting before her and criticizing her had once been a beloved Tsarina. Dasha supposed that she also had another grandmother, on her father's side, but she had never heard anyone say a single word about her, and she guessed she must have died years and years ago. But Baba Sofroniya made her feel as if all her wishes for a proper grandmother, someone who would help her and council her, had just come true.

"How did you get the stove in here?" Dasha asked, without waiting for Baba Sofroniya's answer to her previous question. "How did it fit through the door? And how does the floor hold it up?" One whole corner of the little hut was taken up with a stove, the kind that had a cooking area and a sleeping shelf. Nobles rarely had them in their houses, but Dasha had heard about them from her maids and had always wanted to sleep on one.

"We brought it in and then put in the front wall," Baba Sofroniya told her. "Houses such as these rarely have front walls, you know."

"No, I don't," Dasha said, going over to examine what turned out to be a giant mortar, so big she could have gotten inside it herself, standing on the floor, with a huge pestle, almost as tall as she was, beside it. "What do you use this for?" she asked.

"Making medicine," Baba Sofroniya told her. She had come up behind Dasha without her noticing and was now standing right at her shoulder, so close they were almost touching. "Tell me, my child, what direction does my front wall face?"

"West," Dasha answered promptly.

"And how do you know that, my child?"

"I always know which way West is. I don't know why, I just do. Not that it's a very useful skill. What's the use of knowing which way West is, when you don't know where anything else is?"

"Someday you may find out, child." Baba Sofroniya no longer sounded cheerful, but tired, almost sad. "What direction is West? What is it the direction of?"

"It's the direction of...of the setting sun," Dasha told her, her voice faltering.

"The setting sun, yes," said Baba Sofroniya, her hand coming down to grip Dasha's shoulder, her voice tasting of stone. "And what is that the direction of?"

"Of..." Dasha's voice sounded thin and frightened in her ears. "Of death."

"Very good." Baba Sofroniya's hard hand on her shoulder spun her around to face her. "And what kind of a house do you think this is, then?"

"A house of...of death?" asked Dasha, sounding incredulous to her own ears.

"A house of death, child, a house of death. Or a house of the dead, at least. It is in houses such as these that we lay out our foremothers, and let their spirits go free from their bodies. And they are always raised up off the earth, and they always face West."

"Why do you live in such a house?" Now Dasha could taste the outrage in her voice, sharp and metallic as blood. "Who would want to live in such a house?"

"Someone who wanted power, my love," Baba Sofroniya told her. "Someone who always knows which way is West."

"What kind of power is that!"

"The kind that lies in life—and in death, which is just the other side of life. *Your* kind of power, my love."

"No!"

"Yes." Baba Sofroniya's hand closed even more inexorably on Dasha's shoulder, pressing her down so that she was sitting on the edge of the heavy stone mortar (how had Baba Sofroniya gotten that into the hut? It was surely much too heavy for a single woman to lift), feeling as if she were about to fall backwards into its depths. "Yes. Your kind of power, your kind of magic. Which is the same as every other kind of magic and every other kind of power."

"But...I'm no good at magic," Dasha admitted. "I've been training with sorceresses for years, and I can barely do even the simplest spell. I'm practically hopeless. And my mother's worse, even though everyone says she has great power. But neither of us do! Neither of us are any good at magic, even though everyone thinks we are, and everyone's expecting so much of me! Everyone's expecting so much of me, expecting me to be so good at magic, and I'm completely hopeless! Everyone thinks I have this great power, all this magic, and I *don't*! All I have are visions that don't make any sense and don't do any good!"

"Do you know how magic works?" asked Baba Sofroniya.

"Why? What does that have to do with anything?"

"If you understood how magic works, then perhaps you would understand all the rest," Baba Sofroniya told her, smiling, but still holding her down on the edge of the mortar implacably. A shiver suddenly racked Dasha, but Baba Sofroniya never loosened her grip, nor looked away.

"There is power in the world, which we can reach out and use, if we have the ability," Dasha answered, feeling as she said it that her answer was feeble and imprecise. By Baba Sofroniya's smile, she felt the same.

"So many of our sisters would teach you," she told her. "But that's not quite right. Magic is...everything. Magic is us. We are all full of magic, because we are a part of the wide world, and the wide world is a part of us. We are not separate, little islands—or maybe we are, but islands are not truly separate from everything else, either—but one with the world.

"And if we see that, and accept it, we can reach out and affect the world around us, just as it affects us. Sorceresses are just those who understand this, with their hearts if not always with their minds, and let themselves be taken by magic—by *life*, which is all that magic is, the ability to make something that taken together is greater than all of its parts, taken separately—they let themselves be taken by magic, so that they can take of it in return. But it works best where you are truly one with the world, where you and everyone around you can allow the world to take you, instead of you taking from it without giving back.

"In the steppe—the sorceresses there are so powerful because the steppe is their place, the blood and the bones of their foremothers have fertilized it for generations, and they have become one with their magic and their land. The same in the North, in the taiga. In Krasnograd and the black earth district—there is some magic left. We are still tied to the land enough that the land is still tied to us, but the ties are tenuous. We are cut off from it more and more here, as we think of it as something to take from without giving anything of ourselves to it in return. And in the mountains—they fear magic there, they fear giving themselves to the land there, and the land fears them. And so they mine for metal, and take and take without giving back, and now there is almost no magic left there at all."

"Oh," said Dasha. "So, ah, how does that help me learn to control my own gift?"

"You have to stop being afraid of it," Baba Sofroniya told her. "You have to accept it for what it is, and stop trying to run away from it, or twist it into something it isn't. You have to learn how to give yourself to your visions so that they can give themself back to you, just as your mother gives herself to the people around her. And once you do that, as she has, there's not a lot left of yourself to give to what most people would call magic."

"I'm afraid."

"Of course you are. And rightly so. If there were nothing to fear, it wouldn't be worth doing. The trick is doing something dangerous without succumbing to the danger."

"How do I do that? How do I protect myself from it?"

"By learning how to give of yourself without losing yourself. By learning how to be great enough, strong enough, that what you give, you gain back tenfold."

"That doesn't make any sense," objected Dasha. "You can't just turn nothing into something, or something small into something big. That's not how things work."

"It's how *life* works. And thus, how magic works, for magic is just life, directed for our own ends."

"That doesn't make any sense," Dasha repeated. In fact, it did, but she didn't want it to, so she was arguing against it. She wanted it to be logical, because that was how her tutors had taught her to understand things, and even though it hadn't come naturally to her, now that she had grasped it, she didn't want to give it up, and she wanted to force everything around her to comply with its rules. And if she did give up logic, which sometimes—often—seemed like the only thing standing between her and the madness of her visions, how would she keep herself from plunging into a sea of possibilities and fears, until she didn't know what was real and what was not? "That doesn't make any sense," she said for a third time, as if she were finishing a spell, a spell to protect herself from what she could already sense was the truth.

"It doesn't matter whether or not it makes sense to you, my dear," Baba Sofroniya told her, suddenly pulling her back to her feet. "What matters is whether or not it works. And right now what you're doing isn't working, is it?"

"No," Dasha admitted.

"Well then. Let's worry less about sense and more about results. But in the meantime, let's start by curing you of this chill you've taken."

"Will you train me?" Dasha asked.

"Me, child?"

"Yes. Will you train me?"

"It would be"—Baba Sofroniya cleared her throat—"it would be an honor, child. But I fear it will not be mine. You have better teachers waiting for you."

"I can't imagine anyone better than you! I want it to be you!"

"Oh child." Baba Sofroniya hugged her, her head only coming up to Dasha's chin. "Rarely have I heard something that has touched me so much. But you still have better teachers waiting for you. Now come and drink this tea. It will help with the fever."

"What is it?" asked Dasha.

"Willowbark."

"Oh. They use willowbark back in Krasnograd too."

"So they do, child, so they do. But it isn't *my* willowbark." And Baba Sofroniya winked at Dasha before dropping some willowbark into a cup and pouring hot water from a kettle she'd had sitting on the stove into it. "Let it sit till the steam stops, and then drink up. I'll add a little honey for sweetness. And you'll spend the night on *my* stove, and in the morning you'll be right as rain again."

"I like the sound of that," said Oleg, stepping into the hut and coming over to stand beside Dasha. "So it's nothing serious, then?"

"Serious? Nothing but a little chill!" Baba Sofroniya reached over and felt Dasha's forehead. "And it's already passing. She'd heal herself on her own, if you'd let her be. But it's good that you came to me anyway. There are other kinds of healing, healing that she needs more than from this chill. That's it, drink up, child—I know it's bitter, but this honey will make it sweeter—drink up, and then go lie down on the stove. That's it, on the blankets. Don't worry, there's nothing there that will harm you. Lie down and have a rest, and when you wake up, we'll have some cabbage soup. And in the meantime your father can pay for your healing with his help. I've stones in my poppy seeds, and I'll need you to sift them out."

"You must be joking," said Oleg flatly.

"Joking? Stones in your poppy seeds are no joke! I almost lost a tooth to one last week. I bit down on a roll and—crrck! I still can't chew on that side of my mouth."

"That must have been unpleasant," said Oleg. "But you can't think that I would do a good job sifting through your seeds. I'm hardly fitted for the task."

"You came to me, did you not? I don't see anyone else who can do it. You came to me to heal your daughter, and this is the payment I require, and I don't see anyone else who can pay it. So you had best become fitted for the task."

"But..."

"Sit down," Baba Sofroniya told Oleg. Dasha, who had climbed up onto the stove's sleeping shelf, watched drowsily—had the tea had more than willowbark in it?—as Baba Sofroniya sat Oleg down at the table and placed a large bowl of poppy seeds in front of him.

"Go through them one by one," she told him. "Put the clean ones in this dish here, and toss out any stones and dirt you find."

"But..."

"You think it will be tedious, do you not?"

"Very," admitted Oleg.

"You think you'd rather do anything other than this, do you not?"

"I'd be more than happy to muck out your stable, move your privy—anything. And I'd do a better job, too. This kind of tedious, fiddly stuff—I'm no good at it."

"Too bad. Because this is what needs to be done. *I'll* go see to the stable, and when I come back, I expect you to be finished."

Oleg protested a bit more, but Baba Sofroniya ignored his arguments and, taking up her broom, went outside, closing the little door firmly behind her and filling the entire hut with darkness that was lit only by the candle flickering next to Oleg on the table. He began picking through the poppy seeds one by one, cursing softly under his breath. Dasha told herself she should get down off the stove and go help him, but her limbs felt so heavy, and her eyes kept closing. When she did try to stir herself, her head spun and she found herself lying back down and slipping into blackness.

She rose up from sleep with the same difficulty with which she had pulled herself out of the river, and with just as many plunges back into the current. When she finally did manage to open her eyes and keep them that way, she saw that Oleg was standing by the stove, looking down at her.

"You're awake," he said. "How do you feel?" His voice was low and rough, without that horrible flatness that had filled it earlier.

"Tired," she told him. "Thirsty."

"Baba Sofroniya said you would be, when you woke up. She's made some cabbage soup for us, which we can have as soon as she's back from the woods. She went looking for more herbs. And in the meantime, she said for you to drink this." He offered her a mug of some kind of tea. Dasha sniffed it suspiciously, but all she could sense was chamomile.

"I'm sure it's safe," he told her.

"I think there was something in the last one," she said. "Something that made me sleep."

"Probably. But it didn't do you any harm, did it?"

"I suppose not." Dasha sipped at the tea. It tasted like chamomile, and seemed to have no effect other than to quench her thirst. "Did you finish your task?" she asked.

"Yes, the gods help me," he told her, rolling his eyes. "And I may never be able to stand straight again, but it's done."

"That's good. She won't be angry with you, then."

"No," said Oleg, and reached out and smoothed her forehead. "Your skin feels better," he said. "Less feverish. The sleep did you good."

"I still feel like I can't wake up, though."

"Well, you'll have plenty of time to wake up. We'll be spending the night here, and not leaving till tomorrow morning at the earliest."

"Oh. Hopefully I'll feel better by then."

"I'm sure you will." He stroked her head again. "I haven't done a very good job of taking care of you, have I?" he burst out suddenly, his mouth twisting into a sad half-smile. "We've barely been on the road a week and already you've been insulted, assaulted, and taken ill. What your mother will say when she finds out I'm afraid to guess."

Dasha wanted to agree, to point out to him what a terrible job he'd been doing as a father, just as he had for her entire life; she wanted to generally sulk and complain and let him know just how she felt about the way he'd always left her to fend for herself (not that that was a very just accusation, since her life in the Krasnograd kremlin could hardly be called "fending for herself," but that was still how she *felt*, and the accusation was most definitely true for all her other sisters, starting with Aunty Olga and ending with Svetochka and—were there more sisters after her? Svetochka was the youngest that Dasha knew about, other than herself, but perhaps there were more that he'd kept a secret from her and her mother), but instead she found herself saying, "I don't think she'll be happy about it, exactly, but I think this is why she let me go off with you."

"So that I could put you in danger?" he asked, still smiling that painful little half-smile, that in the shadows and half-darkness made him look more like a little boy than a father.

"Sort of. I don't think my mother can bear to see me suffering, or in danger. But she believes it's something I need in order to become a good Tsarina, so she let me go off with you."

"Glad to be of service," he said, with a mocking half-bow that made him look even sadder than he had before.

"I'm sorry!" she said.

He grimaced in displeasure, but she went on regardless. "I didn't mean it like that. What I meant was that you can give me more freedom than she can, you can show me things that she can't. Not that they're always good things, but I shouldn't only see the good things in life. I should see—and know—danger and suffering and illness and all those sorts of things, because everyone experiences them, and I need to know about what my people experience, how they live."

"You've almost persuaded me," he told her. "But," he grinned one of his old grins, "I'm still going to keep a much sharper eye on you from here on out. No more going anywhere by yourself, no more going out in the rain or doing anything at all if you so much as sneeze, do you hear me?"

Privately, Dasha thought that was a doomed enterprise, partly because it would be impossible in general and partly because she had no intention of obeying him, but since telling him that would only make him feel worse, she smiled up at him and said, "Of course. No more danger or illness or anything else for the rest of the journey."

He narrowed his eyes and gave her a sideways look. "I think you're mocking me."

"I can't imagine where I learned to do that," she told him.

"The gods help me!" he groaned. "No father should have to look at his daughter and see his own cocky little self! What have I done to deserve this!"

"It's good for you," she told him.

He tried to groan and grumble about it a bit more, but with a smile that said he was really relieved and proud. "And I'm sorry if I was short with you earlier," he said.

"I know. But…"

"But?" he prompted.

"You have to stop being so angry all the time," she said, all in a rush. "If you're angry I'll know, and I'll think you're angry with me. Because you *are* angry with me, even if it's something that's not my fault, but only because I've ended up in danger."

"One day you'll have a daughter, and you'll see that's easier said than done," he told her.

"I don't care. That doesn't matter to *me* at all, when you're angry with me. When you're angry with me, all I care about is what you might...what you might do to me," she finished in a low voice.

"Dasha...Dasha...I would *never* hurt you."

"Yes, but...you might without meaning to. And when you're angry, it hurts me, even if you don't mean to."

"Oh." He was silent for a long time. "This is some kind of lesson for me, isn't it?" he said eventually. "About patience or something."

"I think so, yes. I think I'm supposed to learn to be braver and tougher, and you're supposed to learn to be more patient."

"I wish it could have been in some easier fashion than sorting through all those gods-forsaken seeds. I don't think I'll ever be able to straighten my neck out again, at least not without a good hanging."

Dasha looked at him, and he looked back at her, and then they both started giggling, and didn't stop until Baba Sofroniya came in and demanded to know what was so amusing, and then shook her head at them when they couldn't explain to her why they were laughing and told them to stop playing the fool and come sit at the table and eat some cabbage soup.

"And now back to bed for you," she told Dasha when they were done. "You and I will sleep on the stove, and your father can take the table."

"I'd rather have the floor, if it's all the same to you," he said.

"Squeamish, are you? *Still* afraid? Well, you'll be laid out on a table one of these days, afraid or not."

"I'm not squeamish, I'm tall," said Oleg, his mouth twisting to show that he was, in fact, squeamish about being laid out on the table. "I'd spend the whole night falling off onto the floor anyway, so I might as well start there."

"Well, have it your way. Come child, let's retire for the night, and let your father do the cleaning."

Oleg started to object, but Baba Sofroniya told him it was part of his payment for Dasha's healing, and so he began the washing up without any further complaint, while Baba Sofroniya made Dasha drink another tea. It must have had more sleeping herbs in it, for as soon as she had returned from the privy and climbed up onto the stove, Dasha found her eyes closing, and she was sucked down into sleep.

Chapter Twenty

"Wake up, child, wake up. Wake up, child, you're having a nightmare."

"What?" Dasha mumbled, although it came out more as "agh?" Her eyes were still sealed shut, and she felt like she was falling through the hard surface beneath her, falling, falling...

"Wake up, child. Wake up." Something was shaking her. Somehow Dasha managed to crack open one eye, and then the other. Everything was still dark. She tried to sit up, and hit her head on something hard.

"Careful, child, careful. You're tall, and the ceiling is low."

"Sorry," said Dasha, rubbing her head. At least the pain was waking her up, allowing her to remember that she was on the stove in Baba Sofroniya's strange hut. Her shoulders and back ached from the hardness of the sleeping shelf. The nest of blankets she had been lying in had compressed while she slept, and now offered little protection between her and the hard clay beneath her.

"What are you sorry for?" asked Baba Sofroniya.

"I don't know."

"Well then, don't apologize for it. Come. You were having a nightmare. Come. You need some fresh air."

Dasha crawled stiffly down from the stove, almost tripping over her father, who was lying on the floor at the foot of the stove. She stepped unsteadily over him in the dark, and followed Baba Sofroniya, wavering as she walked, to the front of the hut and then down the steps to the yard outside.

"I don't feel good," she said. Even now out under the moonlight she was having a hard time walking, wavering back and forth as if the ground kept shifting underfoot, and she felt too hot and too cold all at once. And everything seemed darker than it should.

"Come," said Baba Sofroniya, ignoring her complaint. "Come, follow me."

Dasha thought they were going to go blundering off into the woods, but instead they only went into the stable, which was full of Belka and a large collection of goats.

"How do you fit all them in here?" she asked, squinting and trying to count.

"Normally I don't have a horse in here," Baba Sofroniya told her. "Normally there are fewer of them, but Rybochka has just kidded. Twins, a boy and a girl. So now I have six to feed."

Dasha staggered over to Rybochka, who was placidly chewing her cud, and admired the two kids lying next to her. "They're so sweet," she said. "I wish I could take them home."

"And what would you do with two goat kids, my child, back in Krasnograd?" asked Baba Sofroniya.

"I don't know. Play with them. Train them."

"Thus speaks someone who knows little of goats," said Baba Sofroniya, and Dasha didn't have to see her face to know that she was smiling.

"So teach me," said Dasha. "I don't know anything about goats because no one's ever taught me anything about them. They've only taught me things I'm no good at. Maybe goats are what I'm good it."

"I doubt it," said Baba Sofroniya, and Dasha could still hear that smile in her voice. "So tell me, my child," she continued, "what was your dream about?"

"I don't remember," Dasha told her.

"I don't believe you."

"I don't! It's true. I'm all asleep and I can't seem to wake up, and I don't remember what the dream was about. I don't even remember dreaming. Whenever I think about dreaming, all I can think about is..."

"Yes?"

"It doesn't matter."

"Tell me, my child. Did you have a dream that troubled you, troubled you particularly?"

"Ye-es," admitted Dasha. "The other day. But it's nothing."

"Tell me anyway."

"I was a little girl, with my father, even though he didn't ever hold my hand like that when I really was a little girl, and we were being chased by a wolf or a bear or something like that, and we tried to go down into the village in the ravine, the one full of steam, and we...we killed Poloska," Dasha finished in a horrified whisper.

"We?"

"Other people were hitting her, and I tried to save her, only I...I think I was the one who killed her. I was trying to save her, but I became just the same as them. And then the domoviye came for me."

"I see," said Baba Sofroniya.

"Do you think...do you think it meant anything?" Dasha asked.

"All dreams have meaning, my child."

"That wasn't the answer I was hoping for."

"I know, my child, I know, but it is an answer that is true. But what kind of meaning—that I cannot say. Except for the obvious."

"Yes?" asked Dasha.

"Why, that you are being pursued by something you fear, my child. But that should be obvious to anyone. And that failure stalks you, haunts you, but that should be obvious as well. And that it is well to be cautious when helping others, as it is just as easy to do them harm as it is to do them good."

"Oh. Well, that's not very helpful," said Dasha, disappointed.

"Did you not just hear what I said to you? It is harder than you think to help others, even when they need it. You want my help, or think you do, and I want to help you, or think I do, but it would still be difficult for me to give you the help you truly need, and for you to receive it. Helping others requires a light hand, lest you break them in your quest to save them. A hard lesson to learn, no matter which side of the story you find yourself on. I would take you in, train you, help you, save you from whatever it is you fear, truly I would, Dasha my child, but it might not be the help you were looking for, and it might not even be help that you need."

"Oh. But you're wise! Surely you could help me!"

"Well." Baba Sofroniya snorted in a half-laugh, half-sniff. "What would you say, my child, if I told you I thought you should be stronger, braver, tougher? Less shrinking, more the daughter of your foremothers, who were formed of fire and steel?"

"I'd say...I'd say you're probably right."

"You would, wouldn't you? And so would many others. And what if I told you that I could cure you of your softness? Would you agree to that?"

"I—I suppose."

"You suppose. See how you shrink and hesitate, even over such a small supposition. I also suppose. And I suppose that I could make you tougher, cleanse you of this shrinking, make you a woman ready to be Empress, rather than a shy little girl. And I would indeed start by teaching you about goats."

"Really?" asked Dasha, startled. "Why?"

"Because, my child, because raising animals is a cruel business. They sicken and die so easily. And even when they don't, why, what do you think we raise them for? What if I fancy some kid stew? Why then, I would give you a knife, and tell you to slit the throat of that little boy there"—Baba Sofroniya pointed to the kid lying closest to Dasha—"and bring me his body, so that I—*we*—could feast on it."

"I wouldn't!"

"So you say now, child. But if you truly wanted to learn the lesson I had to teach you..."

"I *wouldn't*! I wouldn't, and that's final! And I don't think that's the right lesson for me to learn, anyway."

"Is that so, my child?" Baba Sofroniya gave another low laugh. "And what is the lesson you need to learn instead, my child?"

"Not to do what other people tell you to, just because they think it's a good idea!"

Baba Sofroniya laughed again. "And you may be right, my child. You may be right. But you see the problem. I offered you my lesson in all honesty, fully believing it was the right lesson for you to learn. And I still do. But you threw it back in my face and chose to learn a different lesson instead, and perhaps you are right and I am wrong."

"You're not really going to kill him, are you?" Dasha asked.

"It is his fate, child. It is his purpose in life."

"No it isn't! That's just what you think! But maybe you're wrong about this as well!"

Baba Sofroniya leaned forward and peered closely into Dasha's face. Despite the darkness, Dasha thought she caught a flash of gold, bouncing off her cheeks like candlelight. "Maybe so," said Baba Sofroniya. "Very well. I will spare him, if I can. But that only means that some other goat will die in his place."

"No it doesn't! You're thinking about it all wrong!"

"Is that so, child? And how should I be thinking about it?"

"I...I don't know," Dasha admitted. "Not yet. But I *will*. And I know I'm right."

Baba Sofroniya was quiet for so long that Dasha began to be afraid that she had offended her beyond apology, and that she really was about to do something terrible, just like it had seemed she might when they first arrived. "Maybe you are, child," she told Dasha, after the silence had gone on unbearably long. "Maybe you are. And when you can explain to me why, I will listen. But I think we have proven one thing here tonight. That *I* am right, and I should not be your teacher. You will find better, fitter teachers farther down the road."

"I'm sorry about...everything," Dasha said. "I wish you *could* be my teacher."

"And perhaps I already have been," Baba Sofroniya told her, now speaking briskly. "Teachers come in all sorts. Now come, child. Time to go back to bed."

When Dasha next woke, bright morning sun was streaming in through all the chinks and cracks.

"Isn't it cold here in the winter?" she asked, sitting up and looking down at Baba Sofroniya, who was cooking porridge on the stove's cooking shelf below her. "How do you keep the cold air out?"

"Magic," Baba Sofroniya told her with a wink.

"More like straw," said Oleg, coming into the hut. "Stuffed into the cracks."

"That still doesn't sound like it would keep the cold out," said Dasha, climbing down from the sleeping shelf.

"I keep the stove stoked," Baba Sofroniya told her. "And sometimes I bring the goats in for warmth."

"How do they fit?" asked Dasha, looking around. The hut seemed cramped with just the three of them in there; it was hard to see where goats would fit as well. "And don't they make a mess?"

"Huddling together keeps us warm," Baba Sofroniya explained, taking the porridge off the stove and ladling it out into wooden bowls.

"And I train them not to make a mess."

"You told me you couldn't train goats," Dasha said.

"That's where the magic comes in," Baba Sofroniya told her, with another wink.

"Oh. Well...why don't you go live somewhere else? Somewhere with people?"

"There are lots of people here," Baba Sofroniya said, putting a dollop of honey on each portion of porridge. "Goats, bears, elk, wolves, squirrels..."

"I meant humans," said Dasha, digging through her things and finding her little packet of herbs for cleaning her teeth. Her mouth felt less nasty than she would have expected—had the herbs Baba Sofroniya given her also cleaned her teeth?—but she couldn't stand to start the day with a dirty mouth, and always cleaned her teeth as soon as she got up, and after breakfast as well.

"Well, why didn't you say so, child? As if there were only kind of person. What is it you have there? Linen and herbs. Good. Strong teeth are the foundation for strong health. Here, give me your packet, and I'll add something to it."

"What?" asked Dasha, watching with some trepidation as Baba Sofroniya sniffed at the packet of herbs and salt, and then began going through her wooden jars of supplies.

"I have to find just the right thing to mix with what you already have...here you go. Fennel."

"I think it already has fennel in it," objected Dasha.

"But not *my* fennel, my child. Bring me that mortar and pestle. We'll grind it up while we wait for the porridge to cool." Seeing Dasha's expression, she laughed and said, "Go out first, child. It'll still be here when you come back. Go, go!"

When Dasha came back from the privy, Baba Sofroniya declared the oat porridge cool enough to eat. It was well enough, Dasha thought, but very plain, with almost no salt and only a tiny dollop of honey. If she hadn't been so hungry after her illness (which seemed to be almost gone), she wouldn't have liked it at all.

"Why don't you go live in a village or something?" she asked again. "I'm sure people—*humans*—would pay you for your services."

"They do, child, they do. Where do you think I got these oats from? Do you see any oat fields around here?"

"No, but...you could have a much nicer house, I'm sure, and have neighbors, and..."

"Have you not been listening, child? I *do* have neighbors."

"Yes, but..."

"Yes, but you think I should go live in Krasnograd or Lesnograd or some place like that so I could have a big house and wear fine gowns and not have to bring goats in with me in the winter for warmth."

"Well...yes."

"Look at me, child. Do I seem like someone who would look well in fine gowns?"

"Actually, yes," said Dasha. "I think you'd look just like a princess if you had a fine house and wore fine gowns."

Baba Sofroniya laughed. "And you may be right, my child. What is a princess if not an ordinary woman who has a fine house and fine gowns?"

"I don't think that's how it's supposed to be," said Dasha, but doubtfully. Many of the princesses she'd known had mainly been notable because of their houses and gowns, it was true.

"Perhaps not, but that's how it is, my child. But the price for those grand houses and silk gowns and all that gold and jewelry is high. More than I am willing to pay."

"But if you lived in a city, you would have the money!"

"I wasn't talking about money, my child," said Baba Sofroniya. Her voice had taken a steely edge. "I wasn't talking about money. I was talking about freedom."

"You don't seem very free *here*," objected Dasha. "You seem...just as trapped here as you would be in a town. You still have to stay with your house and your goats, and you don't have any money!"

Baba Sofroniya laughed some more. "An apt observation," she said. "None of us are ever truly free, after all. But here I have the kind of freedom I desire, or perhaps it would be better to say that I am trapped in a way I can bear. I have known your town life, Dasha, and I have no more need of it."

"Were you a princess once?" Dasha asked.

"Well spotted!" cried Baba Sofroniya. "Well spotted, my child. How did you guess?"

"You talk like a princess," Dasha told her.

"And so I do, my child, so I do. And you are right: I was a princess, or near enough, once, long ago, when I was your age. But that was not a life I wanted to live. That was not a trap that I could bear. And it was not where my gifts lay, anyway. My gifts always lay in magic, no matter how faint it was, or how little my family wanted me to work it, and so—"

"Are you from the mountains?" Dasha interrupted her.

"Well spotted again!" cried Baba Sofroniya. "I can see you're a true Zerkalitsa, my child. Yes, I was from the mountains, where there is little magic, and less trust in it, but my gift was strong nonetheless. And so I traveled West, following the setting sun—the direction of death, but for me it was the direction of life—until I ended up here. And here I intend to remain. Here, where my magic is strongest. Because if I did settle in some town, I would soon find my magic drying up, and then where would I be? I need to be here, where the land and I are one. Which is a kind of non-freedom, you are right, but it is the non-freedom that pays for all the freedoms that matter to me."

"Oh," said Dasha. "Will I also be trapped like that, if I come into my gifts?"

"I don't know, child." Baba Sofroniya reached out and placed a hand on Dasha's forehead. It felt cool and dry, but soothing. Pain and tiredness that she hadn't even known she'd had melted away under that touch. "You will be trapped, unfree, because we all are, especially those of us with the most obvious gifts, but what form the bondage will take, I cannot say. That is more your business than mine. I heal; you are the seer."

"I don't see anything worth seeing," Dasha complained. "Even when I saw what was going to happen at the ford, it didn't do any good."

"And why should it? Did you think the understanding of your gift would come to you quickly and easily, with no effort of your own? Learning to use a gift takes sacrifice and suffering, and many, many mistakes. Now come," she said, standing up briskly and pulling Dasha up with her. "Let's clear away the dishes, and let your father do the washing up while you and I pack some things for your journey."

"I already have all my things," Dasha said.

"But do you have *my* things? I think not. You will need herbs and supplies, and that I can give you, even if I cannot give you the training you are seeking."

"What do you want in return?" Dasha asked.

"Your father has already given me your payment. But if I think of something more, I will tell you."

"I don't think I should agree to make some unspecified payment for some unspecified service at some unspecified date," said Dasha.

"And thus begins the path to wisdom," said Baba Sofroniya. "In that case, just promise me that you won't try to drag me off to Krasno-grad because you think I would be better served by living there."

"But what if you're sick and that's the only way to save you?" objected Dasha. "What if you can't live out here on your own anymore?"

"If I can't live out here on my own anymore, then I will be ready to die, my child," said Baba Sofroniya.

"But…"

"And such is the second step on the path to wisdom," Baba Sofroniya told her, before she could voice her objections. "Sometimes it is best to let go, even when what you're holding onto is life."

"But…"

"No more buts!" said Baba Sofroniya briskly. "It's a hard lesson, but one we all learn eventually. Some things can't be fixed and some wounds can't be healed. Now come. I have herbs for you."

Dasha had thought that preparing the herbs and mixtures that Baba Sofroniya wanted her to have would be tedious work, at least as tedious as Oleg's task of washing up the breakfast dishes, but in fact it was interesting, even enjoyable. Baba Sofroniya told her the properties of each herb, and where she had gathered or bartered for it, and how best to administer it. It was how Dasha had always imagined being with her grandmother would be. Why hadn't her own grandmother done this with her? She kept the herb garden at her sanctuary, or so Dasha had been told. Why hadn't she spent her time with Dasha teaching her about herbs, or ruling, or *anything*, instead of criticizing her and worrying over her? Why hadn't she tried to help her, the way Baba Sofroniya was helping her? Dasha voiced her complaint to Baba Sofroniya as they finished preparing a mixture of willowbark and valerian that Baba Sofroniya told her would help with the pain of moon-blood.

"Maybe she thought she was helping you, my child," Baba Sofroniya said.

"But she wasn't!"

"Maybe she thought she was," Baba Sofroniya repeated. "It can be hard to tell. I can give you this mixture and think I'll be helping you, but the taste will be bitter, and if you take too much, you might get sick or collapse. Helping people is not as easy as you think it should be, as I already told you. Healers learn this early on, if they're any good, and everybody else learns it eventually, if they ever gain any wisdom at all.

"Maybe she thought you didn't need to learn about herbs, or you would be bored by it. Maybe she thought she didn't have anything to teach you about ruling—and maybe she was right. Maybe she thought that pointing out your flaws to you was helping you—and maybe she was right. When you set a bone it doesn't feel like healing, but it is. The true test of healing is not how it feels at the time, but how it feels down the road. And your grandmother may not have done right by you, but she did the best she could. Whatever love and help she had for you, she gave to you. A woman with only one coin in her purse cannot give you two, even if you are starving. That is the true tragedy of poverty, and it is just as true for love as for any other kind of coin."

"But..."

"But nothing," Baba Sofroniya interrupted her. "She did the best she could, even if it wasn't good enough. And perhaps no grandmother, nor mother either, could do right by you, child. Any mother is doomed to failure, and with a gods-touched child like you, she is doomed twice over. So it's up to you to finish the job, and do all the raising that no one else can do for you. Now let's wrap this up, and you'll be on your way. Be sure to keep it dry, and to take it as I told you to."

"Can I come see you again?" asked Dasha.

Baba Sofroniya smiled. "Of course you can, child, of course you can. My home will always be open to you. But I think it will be a while before you come this way again."

"Why? Have you seen something?"

"It doesn't take a seer to see that you have a long road ahead of you, child. A long road. Now let's go gather up your father and your horse, and send you on your way. And try not to catch any more chills."

Impulsively, Dasha reached over and hugged Baba Sofroniya. She was surprisingly thin and frail under Dasha's arms, and Dasha felt her heart squeeze at the thought that she most likely did not have many years left before she disappeared entirely.

"It's not so bad as you're thinking, child," Baba Sofroniya said into her ear.

"What isn't?"

"Dying. It's not so bad as you're thinking. I was always full of magic, and one of these days, magic will be full of me. Which is how it should be. Now off with you!" She pushed Dasha away, almost roughly. "It's already midmorning and you're still here. You'll never get to Lesnograd if you keep on like this."

"I'm not sure I want to get to Lesnograd," Dasha admitted. "I want to see Aunty Olga, but I've heard that Lesnograd isn't a very nice place."

"And so it isn't, my child, but you should go anyway. We can't always just do things that are pleasant, and you'll cheer up your aunt at the very least."

"I will come back," Dasha promised.

"If you do, you'll be welcome. Now come! Your father's brought your horse 'round, and it's time for you to be off."

As they rode away down the path, Dasha turned her head to watch Baba Sofroniya receding and disappearing amongst the trees. As the forest swallowed her up, Dasha thought she might have caught a flash of gold, like sunlight on water, even though there was no water to make it.

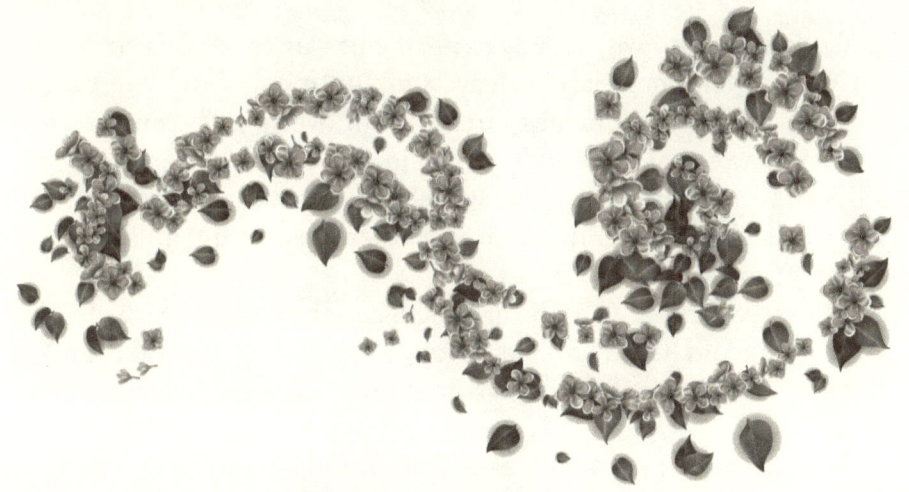

Chapter Twenty-One

"Where *were* you?" Svetochka demanded, as soon as they rode up to the cabin where the others were staying, and where they were currently all gathered at the gate, come to greet Oleg and Dasha. "We thought you'd gone off an' left us!"

"Some of us did," put in Mitya, with a sour look at Svetochka. "Others of us were sure you wouldn't run off without good reason."

"You were gone for so long!" complained Svetochka.

"It's only midmorning of the next day," observed Oleg, as he and Dasha dismounted from Belka. "We could have been gone for days, if Dasha had taken a turn for the worse. I noticed that none of you came to check on us. We were only half a verst away. You could have run over before breakfast, if you were really that worried. Or if you'd wanted to find out how the Tsarinovna was doing. Out of sisterly concern, you know, or the loyalty of someone in her service."

Svetochka glared at him, and Mitya looked abashed. "We didn't want to disturb you," he mumbled, looking down at his feet.

"You didn't want to see Baba Sofroniya again, more like," said Oleg. "By all the gods, man! She's just a healer."

"Healers are uncanny," said Mitya, still mumbling at his feet.

"Well...true. She's an uncanny woman, I won't deny. But she healed the Tsarinovna, and we're ready to be on our way as soon as you are."

Getting everyone ready to leave took up most of the rest of the morning, so that the sun was already high overhead when they set off. They rode out of the woods, which just yesterday had seemed still half-dead from winter, but today were lushly green, and back onto the main road, which serpentined up and down over rolling hills planted with new growth.

"What crop is that?" Dasha asked Oleg as they rode past the fields.

"Rye," he told her. "For black bread. They plant it in the fall, and it overwinters under the snow and comes up in the spring. Some wheat is the same."

"It must be heavy work," said Dasha, remembering the people they had ridden past the previous week who had been working the fields. "Plowing and sowing."

"Pretty heavy, yes," Oleg told her.

"Have you ever done it?" she asked, suddenly emboldened to ask about his past life. What did she know about him? So little. She didn't even know if he'd ever worked a field, even though he was her father.

"Some," he told her. "When I was your age or younger. My family had a field, and I had to help work it, starting as soon as I was old enough to walk.

"That sounds like fun," said Dasha. "I'd like to work a field some day."

He laughed. "You say that now, but you'd change your tune quick enough if you ever actually had to do it. Nobles often get a hankering to come out and work the land, become one with it, become a true Zemnian and a daughter of the earth, so on and so forth, but after a morning of slogging through the mud behind a plow or wielding a scythe or sickle, they find out it's not so much fun as they think it's going to be. It's either too cold or too hot, the ground is either too muddy or too hard, and scythes and sickles give you blisters, especially if you have soft hands that aren't used to hard work. So they throw down their tools and go home."

"I wouldn't," said Dasha.

"Maybe not. But we're all still lucky that we don't depend on you to bring in the harvest."

"I'm not *completely* useless," said Dasha, stung.

"I didn't say you were useless. I said you probably wouldn't be much good working a field." He looked over at her and sighed. "I didn't mean to hurt you, Dasha. I didn't mean to act like I was angry with you. I just meant...this isn't what you're meant for, so don't get distracted."

"Maybe I need to go work a field in order to figure out what I am meant for," said Dasha. "Maybe it would reveal something important to me, even if I'm not any good at it."

"Maybe," said Oleg, sounding not at all convinced. "But I think we all already know what you're meant for."

Dasha thought that he probably meant to be comforting, but his words sent a cold shiver up her spine, and she fell silent and looked around her instead, at the rye, which had been reborn from under the snow and was now sprouting vigorously after the rain and waving in the warm breeze.

When they stopped for a rest and a meal, Dasha went to examine the young heads up close—and jumped when a brown and yellow snake popped up out of the rye and hissed at her, smiling. Dasha leapt away, her head snapping back hard enough to make her shriek.

"It's a viper," said Oleg, pulling her back. "A female expecting young. Let's move on, and leave her be."

"Is she dangerous?" asked Dasha, shaking tingles out of her shoulders.

"Vipers won't normally chase you down, but they'll strike if you bother them, and females with young are always dangerous. Come." They backed away and led their horses a few yards farther down the road, and the viper disappeared back into the waving rye. Dasha knew that she should be afraid of her, that she should be repulsed by her, but mainly what she felt was a curious sense of...kinship. As if she and the viper were sisters, which couldn't be right, but was.

"Do you think it was a warning?" she asked Oleg, as they walked away.

"A warning not to bother her," he said.

"No, I mean...a sign or something."

He gave her a sharp look. "Did it *feel* like a sign to you?" he asked.

"I don't know. Yes. It was like she wanted to say something to me."

"Like what?"

"I don't know. Like she wanted me to be like her, or something like that."

"I don't think you're very much like a viper," said Oleg, smiling at the thought.

"I know. But it was like we were sisters, like we had some kind of connection."

"Well, maybe you need to become more like a viper," said Oleg. He grinned. "In fact, I'm sure of it. Especially your fangs. You need to grow better fangs."

She reached out and slapped his arm, hard enough startle the horses and make her palm sting.

"I see the transformation is already beginning," he said, grinning some more.

"I'm being serious!"

"So am I. If it was a sign, Dasha my love, if you felt a connection with her, it was most likely because you *do* need to become a little more viperish."

"I think I'm more of a mouse," she said. "I like mice. They're so sweet. I'd rather be a mouse than a viper. I'd rather be a mouse than a *girl*."

"Maybe you should be both," he told her. "A mouse *and* a viper, and a girl as well. Here, this looks like a good spot. Entirely viper-free."

They finished their meal undisturbed by any more vipers or other visitors, and set off again down the road, which was steaming slightly under the warm sun. For the first time in days, Dasha felt light and strong, without any of the creeping threat of an impending fit crawling up the back of her neck, and without any visions hovering at the edges of her eyes. Perhaps, she thought fancifully, the viper had taken all that. Perhaps she was cured! Probably not. Probably it was best not to think on it anymore, and concentrate on her riding instead.

They rode through more fields, and crossed another little river (this time there was a bridge), and entered a stand of birch trees just as the sun was growing low in the sky.

"There's a waystation on the other side of these woods," Oleg told them. "We'll stop there for the night. It's not as far as I'd've liked to make, but we don't want to tire the Tsarinovna out, and we've made good enough time overall."

"How much farther until Lesnograd?" Dasha asked.

"A bit more than a week, if our luck and the weather holds. Ten days maybe?"

"Luck!" exclaimed Susanna and Svetochka together, and then looked at each other awkwardly. Their week on the road together had not, as far as Dasha could tell, drawn them any closer, even though they had ridden together every day, and shared a bed every night.

"If that was luck, I'd hate to see misfortune," muttered Mitya.

"We're all still alive, aren't we?" said Oleg, who had overheard him. "We still have all our arms and legs, don't we? We can all still walk, can't we? We still have all our money and clothes and things, don't we? I call that pretty lucky. There's many who're much worse off."

"Yes, well..." Mitya looked abashed by Oleg's reprimand. "No thanks to *them*," he said, nodding towards Susanna and Svetochka. "They're trouble, the pair of them. Especially that one." He pointed at Svetochka. "The sooner she learns to ride, the better!"

"Svetochka can ride!" cried Dasha. "She's learning!"

"Not fast enough. Maybe if she stopped whining so much, she'd learn a little faster and stop putting the rest of us in danger. Thank the gods she'll be leaving us in Lesnograd; maybe we can make it back home a little safer than we've been so far."

This led to a spirited denial from both Svetochka and Dasha—although Svetochka made it clear that she found Dasha's support irritating rather than helpful—that Svetochka was a burden, which only made Mitya shake his head in disagreement, joined by the other guards, which soured everyone's mood, even once they had all fallen silent behind tightly closed lips. Dasha had hoped that the guards would have stopped their bullying of Svetochka by now, but, it had to be said, Svetochka had certainly done her best to provoke another round of it with her behavior at the ford.

Which wasn't entirely her fault, but, but, but...Dasha had to admit to herself that she was secretly looking forward to Svetochka leaving their company too, as much as she disliked this fact about herself. She and Svetochka *should* have been such good friends, but instead Svetochka always seemed to be annoying them and dragging them down...Dasha was so deeply sunk in such thoughts, her earlier good mood forgotten, that she didn't notice the deer until it stepped out onto the road in front of them, causing the horses to spook.

"What a beauty!" she breathed, as the deer—it was a young doe—stood there looking at them, showing no fear.

"She'd be even prettier at the end of my arrow, or better yet, on a spit," said Mitya, who was also still in a bad mood, and, it seemed, hungry as well. Dasha expected the doe to flee at the sound of his voice, but she remained standing there.

"Do you think she's trying to tell us something?" Dasha whispered.

"She's a deer," said Mitya. "What could she be telling us? Kill me now?"

Dasha urged Poloska forward, and after a moment's hesitation, Poloska responded, stepping cautiously towards the doe until they were practically nose to nose. The doe sniffed Poloska, and then, to Dasha's immense wonder and delight, reached her long neck over and sniffed Dasha's knee. Dasha wanted to reach down and stroke that soft neck, but stayed her hand: surely that would make the doe bolt, even if nothing else had yet. The doe carefully sniffed her knee and up and down the rest of her leg, before emitting a loud snort and bounding off, making Poloska jump once again.

"Did you see that!" Dasha exclaimed, once the doe had disappeared. "She sniffed me! She came up and sniffed me!"

"So she did," said Oleg, smiling.

"It *must* mean something! First the viper and now the doe! It must mean something!"

"Maybe it does," said Oleg.

"Like what?" demanded Mitya.

"I don't know," admitted Dasha. "But it feels like a sign."

"Then it's not a very good sign, is it, if you don't know what it means?"

"Well...maybe I'll figure it out later," said Dasha. Mitya didn't look very impressed by that answer, and went back to muttering to himself, but Dasha rode ahead so that she couldn't hear him, and they all more or less kept the peace between themselves as they rode out of the birch woods. They reached a big waystation that was bustling with other guests just as the sun was setting redly in the West. That, too, seemed like a sign, but Dasha tried not to see it as such, for it couldn't possibly be a good one.

Despite all the other guests already there, the waystation mistress welcomed them with a bustling gusto that had more of gloating than

of joy to it, finding them empty rooms and sending them out to the bathhouses (there were two, one for women and one for men) before supper. Mindful of what had happened last time, Dasha spent only the minimum amount of time in the bathhouse, and left as soon as she could convince Svetochka and Susanna to go. Which meant they were some of the first to enter the main room in search of supper.

"Had your steam, my dears?" asked the waystation mistress as she seated them. She was a large woman, as tall as Dasha and much broader, wearing a plain gray sarafan covered in food stains and with her hair tucked up under a simple headdress that had small horns curving up on the sides. She gave them a warm smile, but, Dasha thought, there was something cold and angry underneath it. "That didn't take long, did it?"

"We weren't very dirty," Dasha told her. She didn't think there was anything particularly funny about that, but the waystation mistress laughed heartily nonetheless. Tingles ran up and down Dasha's spine at the sound. She wriggled her shoulders to rid herself of them. She hoped she wasn't about to have a fit, here in the front room, in front of the waystation mistress. She tried not to think about how they had been getting worse of late.

"You're a bold one, aren't you?" said the waystation mistress, with another warm, motherly smile that wasn't very warm or very motherly at all. "With your daggers and all!"

"My daggers...oh." Dasha reached up and touched the daggers she had shoved back in her hair when she had put it up after steaming. She didn't know what to say to the waystation mistress about them, so she settled for a weak smile.

"Fancy yourself quite the adventuress, don't you?" said the waystation mistress, with a smile that was supposed to be sympathetic, but was resentful instead.

"No," said Dasha, which she thought would smooth things over, but instead only made the waystation mistress give a disbelieving sniff, before plastering on another broad smile and changing the subject to if they wanted to eat.

"Yes," said Dasha, resisting the urge to point out that they wouldn't have come down to the main room if they hadn't wanted to eat.

"Well, it looks as if your menfolk are still steaming, the lazy fellows, so you'll just have to get the best of the food before they get here," the waystation mistress told them, winking broadly, as if inviting them to complain about the laziness of men. When no one accepted her invitation, she continued, sounding more and more irritated, even as she tried to sound cheerful and friendly, "Borshch all right, my dears? It ain't much, I fear, but I've the first of the dill to put on it, and even a smidge of sour cream. Our cow dropped a calf this month, and the first sour cream is just ready today."

"Borshch sounds nice," said Dasha. She was less thrilled at the thought of sour cream, which brought with it visions of the calf— what would happen to her? Or even worse, him?—but she held her tongue, not wanting to set off the waystation mistress, whom she was liking less and less, or to hear the others' criticisms and complaints if she were to say what she was thinking.

"Do you have any sausage?" asked Susanna. "We have been riding all day! And last night we were in a cabin and had only buckwheat to eat!"

The waystation mistress laughed. "My, you're an even bolder one, ain't you, my dear!" she said. "This other one's been doing all the talking, but you must be the leader of this group, and no mistaking." Her eyes watched them brightly—like the viper's, Dasha couldn't help but think—as she waited for an answer.

"Well..." said Susanna, looking over at Dasha.

"She certainly is!" said Dasha firmly. "She's a princess from the South, and we're both her serving women, escorting her on her tour of Zem'."

"From the South!" exclaimed the waystation mistress, her eyes going round in what struck Dasha as contrived surprise. Her voice continued to grate on Dasha's spine as she continued, "Now that's a fine thing, and no mistake! It must be mighty cold here, compared with what you're used to, though, my dear," as if she were pressing them, hoping to push them into a mistake, trying to make them reveal themselves as something other than what they were. Which was justified, Dasha thought uncomfortably. No one had ever questioned their story before of Dasha as Susanna's serving girl, but this woman seemed to suspect something.

"Very cold," agreed Susanna. "So could we have some sausages?"

"Of course, my dear, of course! And you two take care of your mistress," she added to Dasha and Svetochka, wagging her finger at them. "Don't let her get too cold! We wouldn't want our Southern guest to catch a chill before she goes home, would we?" She bustled off before they could reply. Dasha involuntarily caught Susanna's eye, and then Svetochka's as well, and for a moment they almost laughed together at the very awkwardness and ridiculousness of it all, but then the moment passed, and they went back to sitting in uncomfortable silence.

They waystation mistress brought out steaming bowls of borshch, which, Dasha noted with resignation, already had sour cream floating in them, and then a pile of still-sizzling sausages, followed by a loaf of black bread. Everything smelled delicious, and everything went well when they started off on their soup (which was delightful—or maybe that was just the effect of the ride and Dasha's return to health—with just the right amount of beets, and dried mushrooms and beans as well as cabbage and carrots), but then Susanna started handing around the sausages, and Dasha refused hers.

"You are not *still* not eating sausages?!" Susanna exclaimed. "When will you stop this!"

"I don't know," Dasha told her. "What business is it of yours, anyway?"

"You heard her," Susanna said, nodding towards the waystation mistress, who was at the other end of the main room, serving the only other people currently in it. "Take care of your mistress! We wouldn't want her to catch a chill!" Her imitation of the waystation mistress was so perfect, even with her Avkhazovskoye accent, that Dasha and Svetochka both burst out giggling, and had to stifle their laughter with their hands, casting furtive glances in the direction of the waystation mistress, who, fortunately, had her back to them as she chatted with the other guests.

"I think she was talking to me, not you," Dasha said, still stifling her giggles. "My disguise is working! She thinks I'm a simple serving girl. Which is lots of fun. I didn't think it would be this much fun to trick everyone like this, but it is. I've always wanted to be someone else, haven't you?"

"No," said Susanna, "that is for little girls. And why would you want to be a serving woman?"

"I don't know, it's just fun to pretend to be someone else. I've always liked to do it. I used to dress up and pretend to be a guard, or a warrior from the Hordes, or...all sorts of things. And I also wanted to be a horse, of course, and a swan, and, well, I wanted to be a firebird, but they're not real, are they?"

"Why does it matter?" asked Susanna. "You cannot be any of those other things, anyway."

"Well...no. But I can be a serving girl! Maybe I should have had the seamstresses make coarser clothing for me."

"No," said Susanna, shaking her head and starting to smile. "My serving girls always wear nice clothing. I do not think you are dressed finely enough. You should have some proper clothing, Southern clothing. I will have some made for you, when we return to Krasnograd. Then you can wear it when you come with me to Avkhazovskoye. And you *can* be a proper princess, a Southern princess, like me."

"That sounds like fun," said Dasha. "Would I get to change my name?"

"Of course! We should give you a proper Avkhazovskoye name. Hmmm...Ketevan! Or Tamar."

"Those don't sound like proper names," said Svetochka. She had been watching them with a confused expression on her face, but now she was starting to smile too. "They sound like men's names."

"Don't you have any names that sound like real names?" Dasha asked. "Girls' names?"

"Hmmm...Natela?"

"I like Natela," said Dasha.

"It's almost like Natalya," agreed Svetochka.

"It is agreed, then," said Susanna solemnly. "When we return to Krasnograd, we will sew you some real clothing, Southern clothing, and name you Natela, and you will come with me back to Avkhazovskoye and become a proper princess and marry a handsome man, a real man, from the mountains, and he will give you many children and you will rule his lands."

This provoked another round of giggling, even from Svetochka. Dasha had to admit that it also provoked some very jolly visions, of her holding court in a beautiful stone kremlin high up in the mountains, with gold coins jingling in her hair and a beautiful dark-haired daughter on her lap...*NO*, the visions said, and fell into a thousand pieces, and blew away, as a shudder shook her body.

The sudden dispersal of her happy fantasies disconcerted Dasha a little, but she hoped that the whole thing had at least distracted Susanna from her determination to force her to eat her share of the sausage. However, as soon as they started eating again, Susanna went back to harping on about the sausage, and refused to heed Dasha's refusal.

"I don't want it!" Dasha half-shouted at her, after they had been over the same ground at least half a dozen times. But Susanna placed some on her plate anyway.

"There," said Susanna, with a smug smile. "Now you *have* to eat it."

"No I don't!" Dasha looked around the room, seeking salvation, and caught sight of a nose peering out from behind the bar, still empty, in the corner of the room.

"Here girl!" she called, holding out the sausage. The nose cautiously poked out farther, revealing the gray-brown head of a very disreputable-looking dog.

"Here girl!" she repeated, waving the sausage in what she hoped was an enticing manner. Still moving cautiously, as if expecting a beating at any moment, the dog slunk out from behind the bar and crept over, stopping just out of reach of Dasha. She was tall, with a long shaggy coat, and Dasha thought there must be wolfhound in her ancestry, but mostly she looked thin and hungry and frightened, and she walked with a limp.

It took several more tries to get her to accept the sausage, and when she did she snapped it out of Dasha's hand and then retreated to the corner, where she crouched over it, looking around fearfully and growling slightly as she ate it.

"Hey you, stop that!" cried the waystation mistress, catching sight of her. "What're you doing, you plague! I'm sorry she took your sausages," she told Dasha, bustling over in her direction. "I'll send some more out direct. Get out, you!" She aimed a kick at the dog in passing.

"I gave her the sausage," Dasha said, her fear at confessing to something she could see the waystation mistress wouldn't approve of overcome by the sight of the dog cowering back from the attempted kick.

"You shouldn't've done that, girl, you shouldn't've done that," said the waystation mistress, trying to sound jocular, but with her anger showing through. "She showed up last week, begging, and I've been trying to drive her away ever since, but she won't go, and my youngest won't stop feeding her scraps, no matter how much I try to beat it out of her."

"She's hungry," Dasha said. "And injured." She could hardly recognize her own voice. It had the metallic edge that her mother's took on when a princess had done something particularly bad.

"This ain't a sanctuary," said the waystation mistress. "And you should learn to hold your tongue, girl."

Susanna and Svetochka both looked nervously at Dasha. She sat there for a moment in silence, trying to make sense of the strange heat rising up in her breast, threatening to choke her and explode out of her. Then she picked up the rest of the sausages and carried them over to the dog.

"You're just encouraging her," said the waystation mistress angrily. "You're just spoiling her. Ain't you going to stop her?!" she demanded of Susanna, when Dasha continued to feed the dog, ignoring her.

"No," said Susanna.

"You should teach your serving girl better manners!"

"No," repeated Susanna. She stood up. Tall as the waystation mistress was, Susanna was taller. "If she wishes to feed the dog, she will feed the dog," she declared. "And she is right. The dog is thin and injured, and you should take care of her."

"I can't be taking in every stray that comes my way!"

"I did not say 'every stray,'" said Susanna. "I said this one. As did the Ts...as did Dasha. And you must have plenty of food. If you were hungry and without food, you would be thinner."

The waystation mistress gave an audible gasp. "Don't they teach you to respect your elders in the South?" she cried.

"They teach us to defend our honor in the South," said Susanna. Her hand, Dasha noticed, was on the hilt of her sword, which she had worn into the inn. Dasha had also worn her sword into the inn, she realized, but the idea of using it was so alien that it hadn't even occurred to her.

"This is how you foreigners are?" cried the waystation mistress. "Threatening respectable women?"

"We do not threaten *respectable* women," said Susanna.

The waystation mistress sucked in another shocked breath. "Susanna," Dasha called. "Susanna. Leave her be. She is no threat to us. We'll take the dog with us."

"If you are sure," said Susanna, still standing there with her hand on her hilt.

"I'm sure. It will be jolly. She can spend the night with us tonight"—"I won't allow no dirty dog in my rooms!" protested the waystation mistress—"and we'll take her with us when we leave in the morning."

"She might not be able to keep pace with us," said Susanna.

"Then we'll carry her. She can ride on Seryozha. Or we'll find someone to take her in at the next village."

"I won't be having no mess in my rooms!" put in the waystation mistress, clearly feeling left out of the discussion and wanting to exert her authority.

"If there's a mess, we'll clean it up," said Dasha.

"Or pay for it," said Susanna.

The waystation mistress perked up at this. "There'll be an extra charge, of course," she said.

"An extra charge for what?" asked Oleg, who had just come in, still flushed from the bathhouse.

"This dog!" said the waystation mistress, pointing dramatically at the dog. "They want to keep her in their room!"

"Dasha, you can't steal this woman's dog," said Oleg.

"I'm not stealing her," said Dasha. There was some small part of her that was hurt by Oleg's accusation, but the warmth in her breast, that she was beginning to realize was rage, was so strong she hardly felt it. Her voice was strangely flat, like Oleg's had been the other day when he had been angry, and still had that metallic edge of her mother's to it. "She's a stray. She's been trying to drive her away and not feed her, and she just tried to kick her."

"I see," said Oleg. She thought he would be angry with the waystation mistress, but instead he was looking at her with something that looked like tenderness, even pity. "Of course you can keep her. We'll be keeping her," he told the waystation mistress.

"I don't see why," she replied, folding her arms and sniffing. "A mangy old dog like that. She won't do you any good. She's no good for anything other than eating food best kept for other people. You'll just waste time and food on her, and like as not she'll die anyway."

"As much could be said for the rest of us," said Oleg. "Dasha, if you're done with your supper, take her out and then take her to your chamber. You'll probably need to take her out again later. With all she's eaten on her shrunken stomach, she's likely to feel sick later."

"You see!" cried the waystation mistress triumphantly. "She'll make a mess!"

"I said I would clean it up if she did," said Dasha, still in that flat, metallic voice that felt funny in her mouth. Funny but good, as if this was how she had always been meant to speak.

"Flighty young girls can't be trusted to do anything!" insisted the waystation mistress, her face now almost as red as Oleg's.

"Be that as it may," said Dasha, and stood up. "I will do as I say. Unless you keep annoying me, that is. Come girl: let's go upstairs." She gently encouraged the dog to follow her out the main room and up the stairs to her chamber, leaving the waystation mistress and her cries and complaints behind.

The dog was nervous about entering the chamber, and hid in the corner for most of the evening. Dasha managed to coax her to drink some water, and then to go outside, before settling into bed herself for the night. The dog watched her fearfully from the corner, before eventually slinking over and settling herself on the floor by Dasha's side. She jumped back when Susanna and Svetochka came into the chamber, but once they were all in bed, she crept back over again and lay down, close enough that Dasha could reach down and stroke her back. She could feel every rib, and each bone of her spine.

"You'll be plump enough soon," she whispered to her.

Dasha thought that she should have pleasant dreams that night, but as soon as she closed her eyes, she thought she could sense something lying in wait for her in the corners of the chamber. She opened her eyes and looked around, but could see nothing. The dog shifted uneasily, but then settled back into sleep. Dasha forced herself to close her eyes again.

Something was coming out of the darkness, coming for her. Was it a bear? It looked like a bear. Or a wolf. Dasha was running, running over a bridge of two birch poles spanning a ravine, just as she had before, but the creature came thundering across the bridge after her. Dasha threw herself forward as fast she could, tree branches catching her clothing and tearing at it, so that soon she was running in nothing but tatters, the moonlight shining down on her bare flesh. Suddenly the trees ended and she plunged headlong into a river.

I'm in the river, she thought. *Let the river carry me. I'll drown soon.* And then she screamed as something touched her foot, making her mouth fill with water.

Climb onto my back and I'll carry you to shore, the thing touching her foot said, and she tried to climb onto its back, but it was slippery and sinuous, slithering back and forth across the moonlit surface of the water, its scales glinting brown and yellow under the golden light.

It's the viper, she thought, as it moved muscularly beneath her. It dumped her onto the shore, amongst waving grass higher than her head, and she began to run again, struggling against the grass, the sound of pursuit close behind her. The dog was bounding by her side.

I won't let them get you, she promised, and then screamed again as something swiped at the dog, catching her flank and making her stumble and cry out. Without stopping to think, without even any conscious thought, Dasha lashed out at the attacker, and heard a whimper of pain and smelled the sharp scent of burning hair. She began running again without stopping to look back and see what it was that she had hit, or what was happening to it.

Come to me, Dasha! something cried, and she raised her head, finding herself in a forest glade, with the deer standing in front of her, and the dog still at her side.

Come to me, Dasha! repeated the deer, and Dasha tried to move towards her, but a heavy hand fell on her shoulder. The dog leapt up, teeth bared, but the hand—or was it a paw?—knocked her to the ground, causing her to yelp with pain and then lie there unmoving. Dasha tried to dive down to her, but the hand gripped her shoulder once more.

Mine! said the domovaya.

Dasha jerked awake. The dog was sleeping soundly, lying in a patch of moonlight. Dasha's eyes hurt, and she felt sweaty and shivery. Perhaps that was why it seemed to her that shadows were creeping around the edge of the moonlight, reaching out towards the dog.

"Shoo!" she hissed at the shadows. "Shoo, get off her!" But instead they glided over the dog and straight at Dasha, grabbing her arms.

"Mine!" they declared.

Chapter Twenty-Two

Dasha couldn't decide when she woke up the next morning whether what she thought had happened had been real, or just another part of the dream. She had shifted, trying to shake the shadows off her, and then they hadn't been there and she seemed to have gone back to sleep, or maybe just stayed asleep, and then woken up later. There were no marks anywhere on her arms, and the dog seemed unaffected as well. Dasha took her outside as soon as she got up, and then had her breakfast upstairs in her chamber, feeding half of it to the dog, who responded by rubbing her head affectionately against Dasha's leg.

"You're very thin," Dasha told her. "We'll have to fatten you up. And what happened to your leg?" Now that the dog trusted her more, she decided to try examining her. There was a half-healed cut across her upper leg, like someone had bitten or slashed at her. Dasha also found numerous other old cuts and scars all up and down her body.

"What happened to you?" she asked her, mixing some of the herbs Baba Sofroniya had given her with a little water and applying the paste to the wound. The dog sat there stiffly but made no move to snap at her.

"Dasha, are you ready?" Oleg called through the door. "The rest of us are done with breakfast, and we're about to go get the horses. How's the dog?"

"She's well enough," Dasha called back. "Although I think we'll have to carry her. And she's covered with old wounds."

"What kind of wounds?" asked Oleg, coming into the chamber.

"Like this," Dasha said, showing him some of the worst scars. "Like she's been bitten all over."

"Like as not she has," said Oleg, examining the scars. "Either she was savaged by wolves, or she was a bait dog. Probably the latter."

"A bait dog? You mean people used her as bait for wolves?"

"Or for other dogs," Oleg told her. "To get their bloodlust up before a fight."

The vision that rose up in Dasha's head was so strong and so horrifying that for a moment she could see nothing else, nor feel anything other than the sweat of rage that prickled across the back of her neck.

"They should be killed," she said, not even realizing the words were going to come out of her mouth until they did. "People who do things like that should be killed."

"You'd have to kill a lot of people, then," said Oleg.

"Well, maybe they need to die!"

"You'd have to kill an awful lot of people," he repeated, his voice all flat again. "Come on, let's go. She can ride with you, if she'll tolerate it. She might not want to sit on a horse. And Poloska might not let her."

"Poloska and I have ridden with dogs before," Dasha said, hardly hearing the words from the anger, no, the *rage*, that was still coursing through her. "I'm sure it will be fine. Come on, girl, let's go. Let's get you out of here."

The dog followed her out of the chamber and down the stairs, pressing closely against her legs and giving Oleg half-nervous, half-defensive sideways glances. She pressed even closer to Dasha when they came out onto the yard and found everyone else in their party milling around, preparing to mount, and a number of the other guests doing the same.

"Come, girl, meet Poloska," Dasha told the dog, going over to where a stablehand was waiting with Poloska and Seryozha. They both sniffed the dog with interest, and, after a brief hesitation, the dog sniffed them back. "See," said Dasha. "Everything will be fine."

"I'm glad to see that," said Oleg. "I'll leg you up, and then hand her up to you. Let me know if you have any trouble."

"There won't be any trouble," Dasha insisted. Oleg only shrugged and legged her up onto Poloska's back. The dog whined with anxiety at the separation, and backed away from Oleg when he tried to grab her.

"You're frightening her!" Dasha told him. "You shouldn't loom over her like that!"

Oleg gave her an impatient look, but squatted down and tried to lure the dog over to him. Instead of coming over to him, though, she hid between Poloska's legs. Dasha had to dismount and catch her and put her in Oleg's arms herself, before remounting Poloska and letting Oleg hand her the dog. The dog got very nervous when they tried to situate her on Poloska's withers, and squirmed and shifted so much she almost fell off again. Dasha supposed that sitting like that wasn't actually very comfortable for her.

"We'll have to get something for her to sit on more comfortably," Dasha said.

"No time for that now," said Oleg, sounding more and more impatient. "If we find something later, we can do it then. Or leave her somewhere. Come on, let's go." He turned and went over to Belka, his shoulders tense with irritation. Dasha wanted to apologize for annoying him, to cringe away from him, but a sudden surge of anger at him stopped her. She was the one trying to help, and he was just upset because it inconvenienced him and made him feel bad for some reason! He had no right to be annoyed with her, and he was a bad person for getting annoyed over something like this!

"Never mind," she told the dog, scratching behind her ears. "We'll figure something out for you. And maybe you can run alongside us for a while, too."

"You!" The waystation mistress came striding over from behind the stables, a hatchet in one hand and a beheaded, still-squirming chicken in the other. "You! I knew you'd try to sneak off! What kind of mess have you left in my rooms!"

"There's no mess," Dasha told her.

"So says you! Trying to sneak off like this!"

"Here." Dasha put Seryozha's leadrein under her knee and dug around in her kaftan awkwardly, trying not to drop either the dog or the reins, and pulled out her coin purse. She fished out twenty grosh and tossed them towards the waystation mistress, who didn't even attempt to catch the coin, instead glaring at Dasha as if she wanted to use her axe on her as well as on the chicken.

"What're you doing?" she demanded. "Are you making fun of me?"

"No," said Dasha. "I'm paying you. There's no mess, but I'm giving you money for your trouble anyway."

"You insolent little brat! I should teach you some manners, since your mistress won't!" The waystation mistress came striding over in Dasha's direction, her hatchet raised high, her other hand heedlessly squeezing the dying chicken so that blood came out of his severed neck and ran over her hand and onto her sarafan.

"No, NO!" cried Susanna, who was on the far side of the yard, keeping Chernets away from all the other horses. She tried to ride over towards Dasha, but other guests and their horses were between them, and didn't want to give way. Svetochka was closer, but facing the other direction, and couldn't get Sverchok to turn around. Oleg and the guards, who were discussing something amongst themselves, heard Susanna's cry and started over too, but they had also been facing the wrong direction and there were other horses in the way.

"No!" repeated Susanna, as the waystation mistress came up to Dasha, still flourishing her hatchet. Dasha sat there in numb petrification. She knew she should do something, move, back up, do *anything*, but a thousand visions of what might happen, each worse than the one before, were assaulting her, filling all her senses, chaining her limbs. Tingles began to build up her spine, and she knew she was about to have a fit, but she couldn't stop it, any more than she seemed to be able to stop anything else that was about to happen.

"You get down right now!" screamed the waystation mistress, dropping the now-dead chicken on the ground and reaching for Dasha with her bloody hand. "You get down right now and let me teach you some manners!"

"NO!" Dasha burst out, as all the visions condensed into one and she *knew* what was about to happen, but couldn't stop it, she should have stopped it, she could have stopped it but her hands were too slow and feeble, too slow and feeble...she tried to hold onto the dog even though she knew it would do no good, but the dog slipped easily out of her grasp and launched herself at the waystation mistress as the woman started to shake Dasha, trying to pull her out of the saddle. There was a deep growl, like something a wolf would make, not a beaten starving dog, and the dog landed on the waystation mistress's chest, knocking her back and grabbing the hand that had been grasping Dasha with her jaws. Before Dasha could scream again, even though she *knew* what was going to happen, the waystation mistress brought up her other hand and slammed the hatchet into the back of the dog's skull.

Now Dasha could scream, and she did, almost but not quite drowning out the horrible, stomach-turning whimper that came out of the dog. Without even knowing what she was doing, Dasha found that she kicked her feet out of the stirrups and launched herself at the waystation mistress too, knocking her back as she started to rise from the ground. Moving independently of her thoughts, her right hand drew back and then struck out, hitting the woman's cheekbone with a closed fist backhand strike, just as Boleslav Vlasiyevich had taught her to, the very first punch he had ever taught her. The woman shrieked and sat back down heavily. Blisters popped up across her cheekbone in the shape of Dasha's knuckles, and smoke began to rise from her hair and headdress. Dasha drew back her fist for another strike—and found it caught before she could land the blow. Strong arms closed around her, and she was dragged backwards, away from the woman, away from everything.

"I have to go to her! I have to go to her!" Dasha screamed, and she didn't know whether she meant the woman or the dog. Probably both. Rage like she had never know before was still coursing through her, giving her the strength to pull out of Oleg's grip...only to stop when she saw that his coat was on fire. Without thinking, she slapped the flames, quenching them instantly. He tried to grab her hands, but she jerked away from him before he could catch her, and ran over to the dog.

Before she even touched her, Dasha knew by the angle of her neck and the bloody mess that was the back of her head and the way she was lying still, so still, that there was nothing that could be done, but she dropped to her knees even so and laid both hands on the dog's body, trying to remember everything she could about healing, everything she knew...some had the power to lay their hands on the sick and heal them, especially out on the steppe, but she had never noticed any such power in herself. But maybe, maybe...the dog's body felt so limp and cold under her hands, already so limp and cold...

"Dasha." Oleg placed his hand on her shoulder. "There's nothing you can do. It's too late. It was always too late. There wasn't anything you could have done. Come, we have to go. Come on, we have to go."

Dasha found herself rising up on stiff, awkward knees that couldn't bend properly and yet threatened to buckle at any moment. Power was building in her, running up and down her spine, and her skin crawled so that she wanted to tear it off, tear it off and show the hatred inside to the world. She turned to the waystation mistress, who had been pinned to the ground by Mitya, Seva, and Alik. Dasha raised her hand.

"NO!" shouted Oleg, grabbing her wrist and pulling her into his arms again. "NO, Dasha! You *can't* set her on fire, no matter what she's done!"

"Wha...?" Dasha wriggled out of his grasp and looked at her hand. Smoke was still rising from it, and her cuff was singed. She looked over at Oleg, and saw that his hand was blistered and red, just like the waystation mistress's face. "What did I do?" she asked, looking back at her hand.

"You burned her, Dasha, you used your magic to burn her! And me," Oleg added. "You were trying to set her on fire!"

"It's no more than she deserves!" cried Dasha.

"Even so," said Oleg. "You won't make things better by setting her on fire. You won't bring her"—he nodded towards the dead dog—"back, any more than Lisochka's death brought little Dasha back, and you might make things worse. Come, we should go. We should go right now."

Ignoring him, Dasha walked over to stand in front of the waystation mistress. "You killed her," she said. "She was only trying to protect me, and you killed her, just like you killed that chicken. How many others have you killed? You must kill every day. But one day that will all come back to you. I'm not going to set you on fire now, like I want to, because one day that will all come back to you. One day," the words were warm in her mouth, like fire, and also cool and quenching, like water after a long thirst, and tingled like vinegar, or the power that ran up and down her spine before a fit, "one day, everything that you've done will all come back on you."

"Dasha." Oleg took her by the shoulder once again. "Dasha, what did you do?"

"I told her the truth," said Dasha.

"No, it was more than that, I could feel it. Dasha, you cursed her."

There was a sound of everyone on the yard sucking in their breath at once. The people who had been gathering around to try to help the guards, to try to help the waystation mistress, to try to stop Dasha, to try to stop Susanna from reaching her—all of them froze, and then edged away.

"I don't care," said Dasha. "She deserved it. Whatever terrible things happen to her, she deserved them. She brought them on herself. It's only just." She shook her head, and realized that the tingling and the crawling and all the signs that heralded an oncoming fit had disappeared. The people on the yard were starting to mutter amongst themselves, and edge closer to her, an ugly look in their eyes. Susanna made another attempt to ride over to her, and was forced to stop when half a dozen people grabbed at Chernets, heedless of his pinned ears and snapping teeth.

"Don't you see!" hissed Oleg. "This isn't a matter of justice! This is a matter of life and death, and what kind of a Tsarina you are going to be. Are you going to be the kind of Tsarina who rules by fire and fear, or the kind who rules by mercy? Because you have to decide right now, before someone dies. Before someone else dies," he added, glancing at the dead dog.

Dasha held up her right hand again. Flames danced between her fingers. People were muttering, just on the edge of her hearing, saying something that sounded like, "Look at her eyes!" Why they were looking at her eyes instead of her hand she didn't know. It didn't matter. "Mitya, Seva, Alik, let her up," she commanded. "Let her up!" she repeated, when they failed to obey. "She has already been judged, and given her punishment," she said, loud enough for everyone on the yard to hear. "I am inclined to issue a similar punishment to everyone else here. No doubt you all deserve it. But I won't. I could, but I won't. I will be merciful. I will let you all go free and unpunished, so that you may spread the word of how Krasnograd deals with those who harm others."

"Krasnograd!" cried the waystation mistress, grimacing as she pushed herself to sitting, the guards letting her go only with reluctance. "And what has Krasnograd to do with us!"

"Are you a fool, old woman?" demanded Mitya. "Who do you think this is?"

"Some insolent little serving girl," said the waystation mistress, but with less confidence than before. "Someone who, who, who…"

"Who travels with members of the Imperial Guard," Mitya finished for her. "Think, old woman, think! Who do you think that might be?!"

"She ain't the Tsarina," insisted the waystation mistress. "She ain't! She's too young. She's young enough to be…" Her face drew taught. "Her daughter," she finished. She looked like she wanted to throw up, or leap up and smash in Dasha's head with her hatchet as she had the dog's, or all of those at once. Seeing her, Dasha had a vision of what might have been, if she hadn't tried to trick her, hadn't pretended to be someone else, someone the woman could safely attack. If the woman had known Dasha was the Tsarinovna, she never would have argued with her, never would have tried to teach her manners, never would have attacked her dog...the dog would still be alive, and none of this would be happening, if only Dasha hadn't tried to pretend to be someone she was not. Or so said the visions.

"By rights we should be dragging you back to Krasnograd in chains, to face her mother for justice," Mitya told the waystation mistress. "And I will, if she gives me the nod." He looked over at Dasha.

"No," said Dasha, after a pause. "I meant what I said. She has been punished enough. If the curse takes effect..." She stopped. By the look on her face, whatever the waystation mistress was imagining was a hundred times worse than anything Dasha could think up. Which, from what little she knew of curses, meant that was how it was likely to happen. Her rage jumped gleefully in her breast at that thought.

"Come," she said. She closed her right hand into a fist, extinguishing the flames that had been dancing there. She wondered how she had done that. She had never seen anything like that demonstrated by any of the sorceresses she knew. "We should bury her," she said, going over to the dog. "She should have a proper burial."

"No time for that," said Oleg.

"No, she has to have a proper burial!"

"Very well," he said, looking down at her face. "Very well. Seva, you and Alik take care of it and meet us on the road."

"I should do it myself," Dasha protested.

"No, you need to leave," he told her firmly. "Come on. And let her through!" he shouted at the people holding back Susanna. "She's the Tsarinovna's companion, and a great princess in her own right. Let her through!"

The people around Chernets stepped back reluctantly. Dasha was pleased to see that he nipped and kicked at them as he passed, and that Susanna did nothing to stop it. Her hand was on the hilt of her sword, and she glared at each person she saw. Most of them glared back. Now that the rage-fueled magic was no longer coursing quite so hard through her veins, Dasha could feel the dangerous mood of everyone around them. They had been frightened when she had burned and then cursed the waystation mistress, and even more frightened when Mitya had said she was the Tsarinovna, but the fear was now only adding fuel to the anger and resentment they felt.

Towards her. For trying to defend the dog. For attacking one of them for what she had done to someone they considered well within her rights to attack. Dasha wanted to scream at them that what she had done was justice—mercy, actually, compared with what could have been done to the waystation mistress in times past, in the reigns of her foremothers—and that it was they who deserved a hatchet to the back of the head, for the things they no doubt had done to others, and probably continued to do every day.

The power was already starting to build up in the back of her neck again, and she was already starting to get little flashes of visions about all the people around her, telling her that some of them were rapists, many of them beat their children, and all of them killed animals, sometimes for food, sometimes for sport. All of them would suffer horribly if she were cast the same curse on them as she had the waystation mistress.

And they knew this as well, and wanted to strike out at her because of that, wanted her gone before she could do anything else to them, before she could bring to them the justice they only wanted for others. For an instant flames danced through Dasha's fingers again, and when she heard muttered complaints about how the dog's body should just be dumped in a midden, it was wrong to bury her as if she were a person, she almost lashed out and let the fire spread till it burned down the entire waystation and every person in it.

The vision of how satisfying, how *right* that would be was so compelling that she almost gave into it and made it reality, but then she had a second vision, one of all the horses that would be trapped in the stable, or who would starve because their riders were no longer there to feed them, and she closed her fist down around the flames instead, and let Oleg lift her up onto Poloska's back.

There was more sullen muttering as they rode by, more angry, resentful faces, and Dasha almost lashed out again at that, but she held herself back, even as she thought of all the things she was leaving undone, all the cruelties and injustices that she was leaving behind unsolved and unrevenged. She wanted to turn back, she even opened her mouth to tell Oleg that they must turn back, they couldn't leave things like that, when there was still so much more that needed to be done, but he cried out, "Let's go!" and urged Belka into a canter as soon as they were clear of the yard, and the other horses all leapt forward to follow before Dasha could object.

They cantered—galloped, really, or as close as Seryozha and Sverchok could manage—for a good two versts before Oleg reined Belka down to a walk.

"We'll give the horses a breather and go slow till Alik and Seva catch up with us," he announced.

"*If* they catch up with us," muttered Susanna. "I did not like that crowd! We should have stayed with them."

"Yes, we should have," Dasha chimed in, nodding in agreement. "Who knows what those people will do to them?"

"Well, you shouldn't have insisted on burying the dog, then!" Oleg burst out.

"We couldn't just leave her like that! They were going to throw her in the midden, or, or, do the gods alone know what to her!"

"She wouldn't have cared," Oleg said tightly, the strain of not shouting at her plain on his face. "It wouldn't have mattered to her, and it was dangerous for the rest of us."

"It mattered," said Dasha stubbornly. "Even if it didn't matter to her—and we can't know that!—it still mattered. It mattered that we didn't leave her there like garbage. If we'd have left her there like garbage, we'd have been just the same as *them*. And we shouldn't have run off from them like that either. There were still so many other things we should have done, so many other cruelties we could have stopped."

"Could we?" Oleg demanded. "Could we? You see how trying to stop the mistreatment of that dog turned out! Like as not anything else you tried would have ended just the same, or worse."

Now it was him that Dasha wanted to set on fire. She had a vision of him wreathed in flames, and it was much more tempting than it should have been. Even the thought of his screams of pain did little to quell her rage. She opened her mouth to say—what? She didn't even know. Something hateful. Something that would hurt him just as much as he had hurt her. Something, something, something...tears were filling up her throat, choking off her words and threatening to spill out from behind her eyelids.

"You can't go rushing into things like that," Oleg was saying. "You can't go endangering others just because you think you're doing the right thing! Think of all the lives you endangered today! And if something had happened to *you*—by all the gods, why are *you* crying! What do *you* have to cry about!" He was staring at her with the same revulsion he had shown when she and the other girls had been joking about marrying the boy at the waystation: as if she were a loathsome monster, completely alien to him, certainly not his own flesh and blood. As if just looking at her made him want to vomit, as if he would strike her down like a viper, smash her like a bug, if he thought he could get away with it.

Set him on fire! Dasha thought. *No, don't, don't set him on fire—yes, burn him, burn him, burn him! Let him know what it is to burn! Set him on fire—no, don't, don't, don't—yes, do it, do it, no don't, don't do it, don't do it—*"Akh!" she screamed, as the power that had built up in her spine sought release, and denied the flames, took the only way out it could, and sent her into a fit.

"Stop it!" shouted Oleg. "Stop it, stop it, stop it! You almost *killed* people, you almost *died*—"

"Shut up!"

Everyone looked at Svetochka in surprise. She flushed and looked down, but mumbled, barely loud enough to be heard, "She were only trying to help the dog. I wanted to help her too. It weren't her fault the others was so crazy. It were them, not her."

"That doesn't change things! Just because others are likely to do the wrong thing doesn't mean you aren't responsible for not provoking them! You don't tease a beaten dog!"

"I'm sorry!" Dasha shouted. "Is that what you want to hear? I'm sorry! I'm sorry, I'm sorry, I'm sorry! Should I ride back and say that to them as well? Maybe I should apologize to everyone! Maybe I should only say 'I'm sorry' for the rest of my life. Is that what you want? Is that what you're trying to teach me? Because that's what I'm learning!"

Oleg's face twisted, showing her that she had found the words to hurt him the way he needed to be hurt. "No, that's not what I..." he began.

"I don't care! You can't go around hurting people just because you think you're doing the right thing! You have to think before you act!" Dasha took a moment to savor Oleg's expression, like someone who had been struck in the back by a loved one, before kicking Poloska forward and riding off down the road, leaving them behind, she hoped very much, to suffer the pangs of remorse without her.

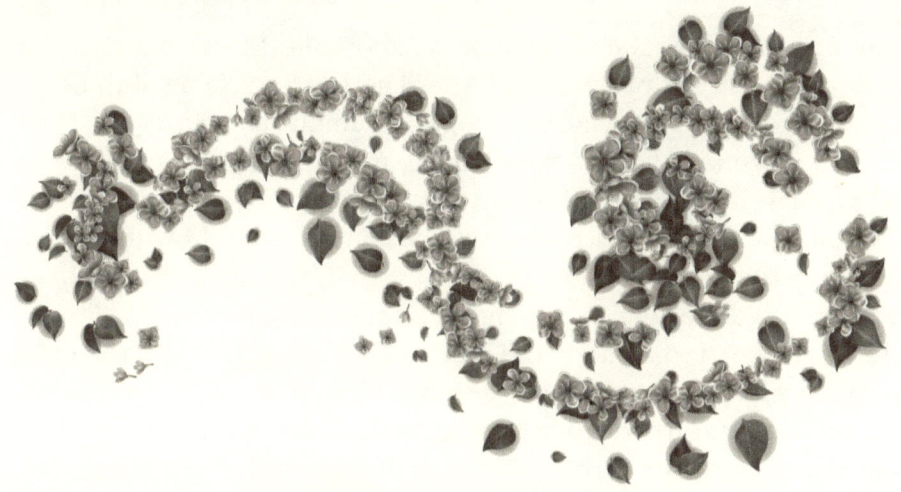

Chapter Twenty-Three

Dasha thought, with mingled trepidation and joyful vengeful-ness, that the others would never want to speak to her again after her outburst, and that she was now on her own and would have to make her own way either back to Krasnograd, or on to Lesnograd. A whole series of visions rose up before her, mostly of her getting lost or attacked by other travelers or by wolves or starving to death or any of the other things that could befall a traveler by herself.

Those thoughts were horrible, but even worse was the thought that it was all her fault, and she could have saved the dog if only she had told the truth about who she was, or if she had done something different, said something different, acted faster, grabbed the dog be-fore she had jumped, struck down the waystation mistress with her sword before she had threatened Dasha. Her visions were now telling her that there were dozens of things she could have done, if only she had thought to do them, if only she hadn't been so blind and stupid and selfish. Tears rose in her eyes, and wouldn't be stopped or brushed away.

She tried to distract herself by looking up at the sky, but that only told her that it was full of dark gray clouds, threatening a drenching rain later in the day. Prickling tingles ran up and down her spine and over her scalp. Was she about to have another fit? Most likely. *And* she had no food in her packs. Or did she? Did she have some of the supplies in Seryozha's packs? She thought she might, but the fact that she didn't know made her angry at herself and her own lack of preparation.

And even if she did have food, what would she do with it? She had only the haziest notion of how to turn barley or buckwheat into something edible. Like as not she would ruin half of it learning how. If she hadn't been so angry with Oleg, and also so afraid that he would turn away from her and tell her he never wished to speak to her again, she would have turned around and gone back to her group. The desire was already strong, almost as strong as the self-disgust she felt for her own weakness and cowardice.

But before she had gone even a quarter of a verst, Susanna came riding up beside her. For a moment Dasha was pathetically grateful, and then for a moment all she could see was a vision of her reaching out and setting Susanna on fire like she almost had the waystation mistress. She could see herself burning Susanna, burning the horses, burning everyone, everyone...

"Dasha," Susanna began, and then stopped when Dasha turned to look at her.

"What?" demanded Dasha. "Why are you staring at me like that?"

Susanna shook her head. "I do not know...I thought...it does not matter...but your eyes...they were a strange color. Like flame, or gold. Only now they are not."

"You were probably imagining things," Dasha told her, and then hunched her shoulders against the tingling that was threatening another fit, and turned away, not wanting to talk to Susanna or anyone else. Now that she wasn't alone anymore, the thought of making her way by herself to wherever it was she needed to go was much less terrifying and much more attractive than it had been when she had actually been by herself.

"It was too bad about the dog," Susanna said, after an awkward moment of silence. "She was a good dog. That woman should not have done that."

"Yes." To her shame, Dasha realized she was crying—again! She dashed the tears away, but more came pouring out in their place.

"And you did right," continued Susanna. "You did right to strike her down, and to curse her. It was right. You should take your vengeance, and you did."

344

"Yes," said Dasha, but with less certainty. When she thought of her actions as justice, or as stopping bad people from doing more harm, they seemed right. But when she thought of them as vengeance—vengeance was not what she had wanted.

Yes it is, the flames whispered within her. *Vengeance is what you want, and vengeance is what you shall have!*

"And your people should learn to fear you," Susanna went on. "What we have been doing—when you pretend to be my serving woman—it is interesting. It is good to know what your people are thinking. It is good to pretend to be one of them, sometimes, in order to discover how they live and what they think. But it is not good to do it too much. You are not one of them, and neither of you should forget that. They must still remember to fear you, if you are to rule them. I do not think you have ever learnt how to make people fear you, have you?"

"No," Dasha admitted. "But I don't want them to!" she added, the words tumbling out with passionate intensity. "I don't want anyone to fear me, any more than I want my horses or my dogs to fear me! I want them to love me! And they're not my people! They're not my people! Anyone who could do something like that—we have *nothing* in common! Those people at the waystation—they're not my people. They're *not*. I don't know who my people are, but they're not them! I don't think I have a 'people'! They're not like me, and I don't want to be—I *can't* be—like them! I don't even want to be human! I want to run away and never have anything to do with anyone else ever again! I don't want to be human, I don't have a people, and I don't want to be human!"

"Well, what would you be, then?" asked Susanna, brows knit in puzzlement.

"I don't know! A dog, maybe, or a horse. Anything other than what I am!"

"If you were a horse or a dog, you would still have to be around humans," Susanna pointed out.

"Then a wild animal! A wolf or a bear."

"You cannot even force yourself to eat a sausage," said Susanna. "How would you hunt?"

"I don't know! I don't know! Why are you hurting me like this? Why aren't you helping me?!"

"I am trying to help you," Susanna told her, still looking puzzled. "I just do not know how. I know about being a princess, but not about becoming something you are not, or avoiding things that cannot be avoided. I do not like this dark sky"—she raised her eyes up to the heavy clouds above them—"or this cold wind, but they will pour rain down on my head whether I want it or not, and I cannot stop it. I could run away, but even if I ran a thousand versts to the South, to my home, rain and snow would still find me. I do not think you could become a dog or a wolf even if you wanted to, any more than I can live in a land without winter, and if you did become a dog or a wolf or a bear or a wild animal, you would not like it.

"I think you are a girl, and the only thing you can become is a woman. You are also the Tsarinovna, and that means you must become the Tsarina. So I think you should learn how. I think that is the only thing I can help you do. And I think that what you did today was a good thing. I think that was a good step on the path to becoming the Tsarina. To make people fear you—that is good."

"I told you—I don't want them to fear me!" *But maybe they should,* she found herself thinking. *If you are a person to be feared, then others should know to fear you. Otherwise they could put themselves in danger, through no fault of their own other than ignorance and foolishness.* "I want them to love me," she said uncertainly.

"Of course." Susanna nodded in understanding, seeming relieved that they were no longer talking about turning into a bear. "Princesses often think that way. I think that way too, sometimes. We all want love. But—do you love them?"

"Not the ones who are cruel and stupid, and, and, and attack their children and kill innocent animals! I told you—they're not my people, and I don't want to have anything to do with them!"

"Of course." Susanna nodded her head again. "Of course not. But why should they love you?"

"Because...because I'd help them stop!"

"But what if they do not want to stop?" pressed Susanna. "Or what if they do not want you to help them stop?"

"Why wouldn't they? Why would they want to go on doing those sorts of things, leading the miserable lives that they're living!?"

"My mother often says that people are stupid," said Susanna. "And also that they like to do things their way because it is their way and not anyone else's, even if someone else's way would be better. And I think she is right. And she also says that sometimes you have to decide for them and make them do what you want, even if they do not want to, because that is better than not doing anything at all."

"But that's...that's...isn't that dangerous? Couldn't you do more harm than good? Isn't that what..." Dasha's voice dropped, "everyone thinks I did?"

"My mother says sometimes you have to do it anyway," said Susanna. "And I think she is right. Sometimes you have to do something, even if you do not know how it is going to turn out. You did not know that woman would do what she did. You did not know. You only knew the dog needed help. She would have died if you had done nothing, you know. She surely would have died. And she lived a bad life, but she died a good death. She died in battle, defending her mistress. It was a good death, better than any other death she could have had."

"But she shouldn't have died at all!"

"It was her time," said Susanna. "Everyone dies, and it was her time. You merely made it possible for her to die bravely in battle. I know what kind of dog she was. I do not remember the name in Zemnian, but the dog that other dogs attack before they fight. I have seen it myself. Most of them die terrible deaths, the death of a coward. But she died a hero's death, and all because of you."

"But...what about the curse? I—I *cursed* that woman, Susanna! I know I did! I...felt it. I felt the power build up in me, and then it was just gone, and I *knew*! I'm sure I cursed her!"

Susanna shrugged. "She deserved it."

"I know she did!" For a moment Dasha's self-righteous certainty returned to her. The woman certainly deserved to be cursed, and some would say there was no one living who did not deserve Dasha's curse. It was, after all, the most perfect form of justice, to have what you had done to others be done to you. But, but, but...all those thoughts sounded so right in Dasha's head, but hearing them come from Susanna's lips made them sound so harsh and cruel.

"What is done is done," said Susanna. "You cannot take it back, can you?"

"I don't think so," said Dasha. "Curses are difficult to take back, and can't really be undone. I suppose I could try to fix it somehow..."

"No," said Susanna firmly. "Let her live with her curse. Let her know her justice, and be a warning to others who would not fear the Tsarinovna. Let everyone remember that you are to be feared. She was not a good woman, Dasha, but she could become a good lesson to others, and that is more than many people will do in their lives."

"Well..." Once again, everything Susanna was saying sounded so right, so sensible, and if Dasha had had those thoughts on her own, she most likely would have considered them to be right and proper, but hearing them spoken aloud made them sound...evil. As if this were another facet of the same evil that had driven the waystation mistress to do what she had done. Dasha looked over at Susanna. She rode tall and straight, her face serene. Dasha could sense no evil in her. Her visions were quiet. And she was the one who had come riding over to be with Dasha, when no one else would, and she was the one who had tried to save Dasha twice before, once in the river and once there on the yard. But, but, but...

"Look," said Susanna, raising her hand to point to a small copse of woods at the top of a rise ahead of them. "A deer."

"With a fawn," said Dasha. A doe and fawn had just stepped out from the copse and were standing in plain sight, and, it seemed to her, watching them. Dasha and Susanna slowed their horses to a walk, not wanting to frighten the deer any sooner than they had to.

"She is not afraid," said Susanna, as they rode closer. "Most deer would run away by now."

"I know," breathed Dasha, not wanting even to speak too loudly, in case that would startle the deer. The doe stood there at the top of the rise, her head raised, looking down at them. The fawn, who must have been no more than a few days old, was standing and watching too, instead of kneeling down and hiding the way fawns were supposed to do.

"I wish I were a deer," Dasha said in a low voice. "I wish I were a doe instead of a girl. *That's* what I want to be."

Susanna took her eyes off the deer for a moment to give her a startled look. "Why?" she demanded.

"I don't know. I've always liked deer. Whenever I see them, which hardly ever happens because we don't have that many in Krasnograd, just a couple in the park, I feel like, like we're sisters. And looking at her now, I feel it even more. After all, who would want to be human?"

This thought appeared to startle Susanna even more than the previous one, but before she could argue against it, the deer gave a snort, and, instead of bounding off as Dasha had expected, began to walk closer.

"I think she's coming over to the road!" cried Dasha, forgetting to keep her voice low in her excitement. Then she clapped her hand over her mouth, sure that she'd frightened off the deer with her exclamation, but instead the doe kept making her stately way towards the road, the fawn wobbling along behind her. She stopped right by the road's edge and stood there, her head high, as Dasha and Susanna drew close. She drew in a great breath, her nostrils flaring, as Dasha stopped in front of her.

"Do you want to tell me something?" Dasha asked, speaking softly, but still loud enough for the deer to hear her, as if she expected her to answer.

The deer stood there silently. Dasha knew she should ride on, but she was loath to do so. Surely this was a sign, although of what Dasha couldn't guess. The prickling tingles, which had abated as she had been talking with Susanna, suddenly came back, making her jerk and shudder as a little half-fit struck her. The deer drew in another breath, so sharply her nostrils quivered and Dasha could hear the sniffing sound she made. Dasha bit down on her lip, hoping to stop the fit she knew must be coming—and then realized that the tingling was gone.

"Thank you," she told the deer. The doe nodded to her, and then suddenly whirled and bounded off, the fawn trotting unsteadily behind. In a moment they had disappeared back into the copse, and were gone.

"That was strange," said Susanna.

"I think she came to help me," Dasha said. "I think she came to take some of my magic."

Susanna frowned. "How could she do that? And how could that help?"

"I don't know how she could do it. But my magic—it's not really under control. And I think it's getting worse. I think it's getting stronger and stronger, and more and more out of my control."

"Stronger, yes," said Susanna. "The flames this morning—that was wonderful. Few sorceresses could do that. You should have let that woman burn!"

The flames leapt within Dasha again, telling her that Susanna was right, and in a way, Dasha knew, she was. "No," she said. "I wanted to, and I still do, but...no. Especially not since I have so little control over what I'm doing."

"You had much control over what you did this morning! That was magnificent. Zem' is lucky to have such a powerful sorceress as her Tsarinovna."

"Well," said Dasha. "I didn't know what I was doing this morning. I didn't know how to do what I did before I did it, and I wouldn't know how to do it again now. But I think that's what's causing me to have these fits. The magic is growing inside of me, and I don't know what to do about it, and neither does anyone else. But the deer—I could feel the magic growing inside of me, trying to set off another fit, but then it was gone, and I think she took it away."

"That still does not sound like a good thing," said Susanna, frowning some more.

"Better than a fit," Dasha told her.

"Do you think she took it all away?" asked Susanna.

"No. I can feel it building up again. I think she just stopped me from having a fit. And I think she came to let me know she could do it, and she wanted to help me. Maybe I'm right! Maybe I really *am* a deer!"

"I do not think so," said Susanna. "I think you are being silly. Oh look, Seva and Alik have arrived, and so have the others."

Dasha turned around and saw that the others, including Seva and Alik, were riding up to them. Oleg appeared intent on ignoring her, but Seva and Alik filled any silence that might have been uncomfortable by talking loudly about how they had buried the dog by the side of the road, despite the opposition of some of the people from the waystation, who, according to Alik, "had been in a rare mood," and put a marker over the grave.

"If we'd've had time and someone who could write, we'd've done something fancier," Alik told her. "A stone carved with a description of her deed, and how she'd died defending the Tsarinovna. But we marked the spot good, with a cairn of stones and some branches and ribbons and such, and left some vodka as an offering, so the gods'll watch over her, and you can send someone to put in a proper marker, or bury her in a proper graveyard, later if you like."

"Thank you," Dasha told them. "I was afraid something might happen to you, that the others might attack you. I shouldn't have left you to do that task."

"Nonsense, Tsarinovna," said Alik with a grin. "What're we here for, other'n stuff like that? And she was a good dog, and died a hero's death. She deserved no less. We sure couldn't leave her for them to throw her in the midden like they wanted to."

"Ah now, you've made the Tsarinovna cry," said Seva. "Don't cry, Tsarinovna: I know you wanted to save her, but you did the next best thing for her: you turned her from a mangy old stray into a hero. And that spell you did!" He kissed his fingertips. "I'd never seen such a thing! You know, people talk about how you're the chosen of the gods, but I hadn't never seen any sign of it, begging your pardon, until this morning. But that fire! And cursing the woman—we all felt the curse, didn't we, boys?"

Mitya and Alik both nodded, and, Dasha noticed out of the corner of her eye, so did Svetochka.

"That was a proper curse, a curse of a Tsarina," Seva went on. "A person can respect someone who can cast a curse like that." And even as he smiled at her like an older brother, in a way he had never smiled at her before, he was also looking at her with a respect bordering on fear neither he nor anyone else had ever demonstrated towards Dasha. She wanted to say that she didn't like it, but she had to admit that she did.

"Let's go," said Oleg brusquely, not looking at Dasha. "We want to get as far as we can before those clouds break."

Dasha looked up at the ominous sky, feeling the prickles crawl across her scalp as she did so. When she looked back down, she saw that the others were all looking at her, waiting for her to second Oleg's order before they obeyed.

"Let's go," she said, trying to ignore the flare of hatred his refusal to acknowledge her sparked.

"Was that lightning?" asked Mitya. "I thought I saw something flash, like lightning."

"I didn't see anything," she said. "Let's go."

They made good time that morning, spurred on by the threat of rain. Everyone remembered the last time they had gotten caught in the rain, and no one wanted to relive that experience. The guards were in good spirits, better spirits, in fact, than Dasha had seen them in since they had set off from Krasnograd.

Which was puzzling and annoying. Had they been hoping and waiting all along for her to almost kill someone? Not that she had done anything wrong, oh no, not that that woman hadn't deserved what had been done to her, oh no, certainly not, certainly not, but still, but still...Dasha had to admit that, in her heart of hearts, *she* didn't like or respect herself more for what she had done that morning. If she had been able to save the dog, now that would have been another story...those thoughts led to more tears, although if the others noticed, they said nothing. And perhaps they hadn't noticed at all: the guards were busy talking amongst themselves, Susanna was riding ahead to keep Chernets from quarreling with the other horses, and Svetochka and Oleg were riding in the back and not speaking with anyone. So even though she was surrounded by the others, Dasha was essentially alone.

As usual, she thought. *These are not my people, any more than those people at the waystation this morning were.* Then she felt bad about that thought, but not enough to unthink it, or deny its truth.

They stopped at a cabin to eat their midday meal and wait out the rain that had started to fall. There was some talk of stopping there for the night, but by early afternoon the rain had ceased and they de-cided—once again with Dasha having to give the final consent to the plan—to carry on for the rest of the day. Much to Dasha's relief, as Oleg was still being grim and silent, and hadn't spoken a single word to her for the entirety of their stop. The thought of being trapped in the cabin with him for the rest of the day and night was almost un-bearable.

But the sun obligingly came out shortly after they had finished their meal, and he declared, looking out the cabin door, his back turned to the rest of the group, that they should carry on. When Da-sha said into the awkward silence that followed, "Yes, let's," the guards jumped to their feet and went to bring the horses around, and soon they were able to escape the confines of the cabin and the tension that had filled it.

Pools of water stood in the road as they set off, and the sun spar-kled on raindrops that hung from every branch and leaf.

"We'll have a job cleaning up the horses after this," said Mitya, as they splashed through the mud. "Will we be stopping at a cabin to-night, do you think, or a waystation?"

"There's a cabin about twenty versts down the road," Oleg said. "We'll stop there. I don't want..." He shook his head and didn't finish the sentence, and Dasha knew that he had meant that he didn't want to stop at a waystation, not after what had happened. Which made her angry all over again, even though she knew it was only sensible.

They made good time despite the mud, and reached the cabin by late afternoon. Dasha would have liked to press on, in order to spend less time sitting around in the cabin with Oleg, but she said nothing when he gave the order to stop, not wanting to argue the point, not wanting to start any more fights with him, and also not wanting to lose the argument, which she was fairly certain was what would happen. Which made her angry yet *again*. Prickles were crawling all over her body, and no deer came forward to rescue her from them. Which meant that she had another little fit as she was leading her horses to the stable.

Oleg was the one who reached out to catch her as she gave a jerk and screamed, but as soon as she was stable, he only shook his head at her and said, "Be more careful!" before stalking off into the stable. This set off a whole series of visions of Dasha setting him on fire, of her burning down the cabin and the stable, of her setting the whole forest on fire...she tried to block them out, wash them from her mind, tell herself they weren't real, but she couldn't block out the voice telling her that they *could* be, that all those things she was seeing *could* happen, and maybe some of them should or would.

Supper that night was a strained affair. Oleg normally cooked for them, but he spent so long out in the stable that Mitya eventually took over the cooking duties. The stew he made of barley and dried mushrooms was surprisingly passable, or maybe they were all just very, very hungry after having to wait so long for it.

Oleg came stalking in as the rest of them were finishing, and ate without saying a word to any of them. Dasha found the atmosphere so oppressive that, after setting up the bedclothes in the chamber she and Susanna and Svetochka were to share, she slipped out of the cabin when no one seemed to be paying any attention to her, and went to sit in the stable.

The horses were all peacefully eating their hay, even Chernets. Dasha leaned against Poloska's stall door, and, lifting the lantern she had brought with her to illuminate the semi-darkness, looked her over and saw that she had been thoroughly groomed. Dasha had cleaned off the worst of the mud that had caked her legs and belly when she had unsaddled her, but they had both been so hungry that she hadn't wanted to spend too long on it, and then afterwards she hadn't wanted to come back to the stable and be alone with Oleg. But it looked as if he had spent his time in here grooming her horse. Dasha went on to the next stall and looked in at Seryozha. He, too, was as clean as if one of the stablehands at the kremlin stable had just prepared him for a parade.

"You're a good boy," Dasha told him. "I didn't want to take you with me at first, but I was wrong. I couldn't have a better packhorse."

Hearing her voice, Seryozha turned around with difficulty in the cramped stall, which he seemed to be tolerating patiently, even though it was half the size of the stalls he was used to, and came over to sniff and lip at her hands.

"I'm sorry," she told him. "I don't have any apples or carrots. All I have is this lantern." She lifted up the lantern to show him, causing him to step back. His motion triggered a vision, one of Dasha dropping the lantern and setting the stable on fire. She clutched it more tightly, but that only made it feel even more slippery and fragile in her hands.

The prickling tingles started at the top of her scalp and spread across her head and onto her face. She could drop the lantern, set the stable on fire, and then the cabin would catch fire too and then so would the whole forest! One tiny slip of her fingers could kill all her companions and destroy an entire district! Or perhaps they would only be horribly maimed by the fire, and she would have to decide whom to kill out of mercy, and whom to try to save! Or everyone would hate her for what would start out as a tiny, trivial accident. If they hated her this much after what had happened this morning, how much more would they hate her if she actually burnt something down? She could destroy her life and the lives of her friends and companions, and countless more lives as well, all by a moment of clumsiness.

The prickles continued to spread, moving down her neck and across her shoulders, and she knew she was about to have another fit. Holding onto the lantern as hard as she could, Dasha whirled around and tried to race out of the stable, hoping to avoid dropping the lantern until she was away from the wood and hay and out on bare ground. The latch of the door resisted her, refusing to open to her clumsy, one-handed fumbling. Another vision came, this time of her being trapped in the stable as it burnt around her. She rattled the door desperately, hearing the horses moving restlessly in their stalls in response to her own panic—and then almost tumbled headfirst through the door and out onto the ground when someone pulled the door open from the outside.

"Be *careful!*" Oleg cried, catching her as she came stumbling over the doorframe and half-fell into his arms. He snatched the lantern out of her hands as she went into another fit. "Be careful!" he shouted again when she was finished. "These fits—you have to stop having them!"

"I can't!"

"Try harder! Be more careful—you almost set the stable on fire there!"

"I know!" she shouted back. "I know, I know, I know! And I *can't* be more careful! Don't you understand? This is as careful as I can be! I don't have control over what's happening to me, and it's getting worse! I can't stop it, and it's getting worse! And no matter how much you try to lie to yourself and run away from that fact, I can't escape it! I didn't mean to almost set you and that woman on fire this morning, but I did! I didn't mean to curse her, but I did!

"And I've been having fits and visions of setting things on fire all day, and I can't stop it! I just...I came out here because I thought I would be safer, everyone would be safer, and as soon as I came out here, I started having visions of setting everything on fire, and then a fit started coming on and I knew I *could* set everything on fire, the visions might come true, so I tried to leave, but the fit was already coming on and there was nothing I could do. I can't stop it and I can't control it and it's getting worse and there's nothing anyone can do! My mother can't do anything about it, the sorceresses in Krasnograd can't do anything about it, Baba Sofroniya turned me away and said she couldn't help me, no one can help me and it's getting worse and worse!

"And you're making it worse too! You're doing everything you can to make it as bad as possible! You hate me, I know you do, you look at me like I'm a monster or something, something you need to drive away or kill, like a viper or a rabid wolf, but it's not my fault and there's nothing I can do to stop it! Why are you staring at me!" she demanded.

"Your eyes. They're...they're flashing. Like with flame, or sunlight on water."

Dasha brought her hands to her eyes. "They don't feel any different," she said.

"It's gone now," he told her, his voice flat.

"You see!" she cried, returning to her earlier grievances. "Things are happening to me, things I don't understand and can't control, and you—you speak to me like you're mad at me, like you hate me!"

Even in the moonlight, Dasha could see how the muscles in Oleg's jaw jumped at her words. For a moment she thought he might hit her.

"I don't hate you," he said in a low voice.

"Then why do you act like it?!"

"I..." He ran his free hand, the one not holding the lantern, through his hair in frustration. "I don't hate you, Dasha. I don't. It's just that... you almost died this morning, you could have been killed over a stupid misunderstanding, one I should have stopped. You almost *died*, Dasha, and then what would we have done? If you die...most of us, we're not that valuable, not in the grand scheme of things. Most people, if they die, it doesn't matter that much. Harsh but true. But if *you* die—that would bring all of Zem' to its knees, open us up to those armies to the West and South that see our riches and think they should belong to them. What," he added, seeing the surprise on her face, "don't you think I can understand such things too? Your mother told me all about what's going on on the Western border, and I've heard about it from others, as well. I may not be on the Princess Council, but I know *some* things."

"I didn't know you cared," said Dasha.

"I care, Dasha, I care. And...not just about that." His voice dropped. "I also...when I think of something happening to you, Dasha, I—I can't stand it. You know," he was looking off at the night sky now, not able to bring himself to look at her as he told her this, "I've lost daughters before. Not all of them have had the good fortune to be born, and not all of those that have been born have had the good fortune to grow up. That's how it is. That's just how it is. And it hurt, but the hurt passed quick enough for me.

"But if something were to happen to you...I couldn't stand it, Dasha, I couldn't stand it! And I can see that you're suffering, that you're getting worse and no one can seem to do anything about it, and I can't help but wonder...I don't have the gifts you do, I don't get visions, but when it comes to you sometimes I do, or maybe there's nothing magical about it, it's just the ordinary visions of a father for his daughter, and I also...I also see bad things," he finished, almost in a whisper.

"So help me!" Dasha told him.

"I wish I could. I've been praying, asking for help, trying to think of what I could do, who could help you, but so far all that's happened is you've gotten worse, and almost died, and...and I can't bear to watch it!"

"If I can bear to live it, you can bear to watch it," Dasha told him impatiently.

"I know. Or rather, I know that's how it should be. But I think you might be stronger than me, Dasha, braver than me. Or maybe just younger." He half-smiled, but the smile was laced with pain. "When I look at you, I see myself at your age. And when I remember what I was like then, all the pain I caused myself and others by my foolhardiness," he gave a rueful smile, "I'd spare you that if I could. I'd give anything to be able to spare you that. Only I don't think I can, any more than I can spare you the pain of your gifts, or the heavy burden of rule that is going to land on your shoulders, or any of the other sorrows that are sure to come to you, because they come to everyone.

"Your mother and I—we'd spare you that, keep you safe from all that, and for the most part we have so far, but we can't forever, and, and, and when I think of all that awaits you, all that I'd save you from but can't, all that could happen to you, it makes me so angry and help-less I feel sick, I want to run away and never come back, and, and...and that's why I've seemed angry with you today. I'm not angry with you, not really, I'm angry at how things are, and how I can't change them."

"That doesn't help me very much," said Dasha, but more gently than she had spoken before. "It still hurts me when you're angry. It still makes things even worse for me than they already are."

"I—I know, and I'm sorry. I'd spare you that too, if I could."

"So spare me," said Dasha, her voice sharpening. "*That* is some-thing you have control over, even if you can't control any of the rest."

"Oh Dasha!" He tried to smile, but it came out as more of a painful grimace. "I'm afraid it's not under my control as much as I'd like it to be, any more than your fits are."

"Well, try," said Dasha sternly. "You say you want to spare me suf-fering: try harder, then."

He laughed, although it was a jagged laugh, with the taste of tears behind it. "That sounds *exactly* like something I would have said when I was your age," he told her. "And your mother as well, like as not. Well, I will try harder. And soon enough, I think, we'll find someone who can help you. Maybe in Lesnograd. Or the sanctuary. You're right: you should go there, to the sanctuary your mother visited when she was in the North. You'll be able to find help there even if you can't any-where else. The gods wouldn't have made you this way and not had a plan to help you with your gift."

"Maybe the gods don't have very much control over this either," said Dasha. "I'd think they would have organized things better, if they did."

This time Oleg's laugh sounded much more like a real laugh. "You may be right," he told her. "It's true they don't have nearly as much control over every little moment in our lives, the way we think they do. Most of the time they don't even care. But in this case I don't think they will want to waste you."

"That should sound more hopeful than it does," said Dasha.

"Well, it's the hope we have," he told her. "So let's hold onto it. Come on. Let's go back to the cabin and go to bed. We've another long day tomorrow."

Dasha followed him back towards the cabin. The moon, while waning, was still bright enough when it broke through the clouds that they cast shadows as they moved through its light. Some of the shadows, it seemed to Dasha, moved and reached out towards her. Prickles ran up and down her spine, but she shook her head and wriggled her shoulders to dispel them, and they made it into the cabin unmolested.

Chapter Twenty-Four

There was another storm during the night, and the next morning dawned bright and hot, the clouds temporarily rained away but the air still full of the moisture they had left behind. They all put on their lightest shirts and left their kaftans in their packs, and were still sweating, as were the horses, by midmorning. Despite the sun that was shining down on them, hurting their eyes and turning everyone's necks red, the sky seemed to hang oppressively over them as if it were about to storm, without a breath of wind to provide any relief. And the mosquitoes had all chosen this particular morning, it seemed, to awake from their winter slumber and feed.

By midday they were all covered with itchy blotches and streaks of blood from where they had slapped mosquitoes who had already managed to gorge their fill. The horses were at least as unhappy as the humans, and Chernets kept snapping at the others and almost threw Susanna when a whole swarm of biting insects attacked his belly. Their stop for their midday meal was cut short by mutual agreement: the only thing worse than riding through the clouds of mosquitoes was standing still and trying to eat while they swarmed around everyone's face and ears, getting into their food and biting every bare surface of skin they could find.

"We should smear ourselves with mud," Oleg said. "That'll keep them off." Svetochka and the guards promptly went over to a patch of mud in a hollow near where they had stopped, but the attack by the mosquitoes that rose out of the mud was so fierce that Susanna and Dasha decided to abstain, not counting the gain in future bites prevented worth the cost of more bites now, plus the unpleasantness of wearing mud. Dasha had never been allowed to get muddy if her nannies and maids could prevent it, and the last times she had gotten dirty, during her fall into the river and her ill-fated venture into the park in search of Oleg, had been so unpleasant and so disturbing that she had no desire to repeat the experience, or have anything to do with dirt and water.

"You'll wish you had soon enough," Oleg told them, but in fact they had barely ridden another two versts when a great gust of wind suddenly hit them, blowing away all the mosquitoes and bringing with it more wind and dark clouds, which filled the sky more and more menacingly as the day progressed, and by late afternoon began to scatter droplets of rain onto them as they rode. They were passing through open fields and meadows, with no sign of any woods that might shelter them if the clouds were to open and pour down on them.

"There's a cabin up ahead in another verst or so," Oleg told them. "We'd best stop there for the night, and not try to go any farther, or we'll be soaked for sure."

Everyone agreed to this plan, and they pressed forward eagerly as the rain splatted down harder and harder on them, and the air changed from oppressively hot to threateningly cool.

As they came around a bend in the road and drew within sight of the cabin, which was tucked against a swell of ground, which gave it a little shelter from the elements, they caught sight of a lone horse and rider up ahead, clearly making for the same cabin as themselves.

"Mitya, go see who that is and what they want," Oleg told him. "I doubt they're a threat to us, whoever they are, but go check on them anyway, and reassure them we're no threat to them either, providing they do us no harm." He squinted. "It looks like some young boy—or is that a girl?—traveling alone; like as not he's more afraid of us than we are of him."

Mitya rode up to the solitary figure, who appeared to try to flee from Mitya's approach, but Mitya soon caught up with her—as they drew closer Dasha could see that she was wearing a sarafan, and a very gaudy, ill-made one—and spoke to her. The girl appeared to be rejecting whatever Mitya was saying to her, but then the clouds broke in truth and they all had to race to the cabin, the girl allowing Mitya to coax her along with him.

Once they arrived at the cabin, there was a confused rush to get out of the rain and put the horses away, which allowed Dasha little time to speak to the girl, or even look at her. Every time she did, though, her visions told her that there was something...off about her. Not— she sidled over closer to the girl as they dried off their dripping saddles, hoping to get a better read on her—threatening, just...off. Seeing Dasha so close to her, the girl jumped back and then stumbled as she almost fell over her own saddle, sitting on its rack.

Which was odd, because she was large, at least as tall as Dasha and just as solid in her body, and Dasha would have expected her not to be so skittish. But then, Dasha could be pretty skittish herself. Dasha gave her what she intended to be a warm and sympathetic smile. The girl responded with a look that was peculiarly reminiscent of the revulsion with which Oleg sometimes regarded her, and, ducking her head, hurried off without speaking. Which was all very odd, and made Dasha's skin prickle in answering distaste, even though the girl hadn't done anything to deserve it.

It was the same once they had finished with the horses and gone into the cabin. Dasha couldn't tell what was wrong with the girl, only that there was something about her that grated at her nerves. Her face, her figure...she had never seen anyone wear a gown so poorly, even though the girl, when she wasn't being frightened by the others, seemed to think she looked very fine in it, even as she hunched her shoulders and fussed with the fabric awkwardly.

She knew it was rude to stare, but she had to fight the impulse every time her eyes strayed the girl's way. Dasha felt as if she could only get a proper look at her, only figure out what it was that she wasn't seeing, all the pieces would fall into place. Even looking at her out of the corner of her eyes, which was all she allowed herself, caused all sorts of visions to cascade before her, but none of them took enough form for her to make any sense of them, instead only increasing her sense that there was something odd, something wrong, about the girl.

Susanna had no such compunction about looking, and stared at the girl as if trying to burn holes in her face, all the while asking question after question about where she was from. But the girl hunched her broad, awkward shoulders and refused to name her family or her home village, only saying that her father had sent her away in disgrace, and she didn't have a family or a home or anything other than her clothes and her horse.

"That's more than most of us got," said Oleg, who obviously disliked the girl even more than Susanna, if such a thing were possible. "Count yourself lucky you still have the skin on your back. And you have to have a name. Make one up if you want, but we need something to call you."

"F-F-Fedya," said the girl, her voice trembling as if she were about to break into weeping. There was something wrong with her voice, too, but Dasha couldn't say what. Pity and irritation battled inside of her, and pity won.

"You are welcome to travel with us, Fedya," she told the girl, giving her the most welcoming smile she could muster up. Out of the corner of her eye she could see that Susanna and Svetochka didn't look so welcoming, and the guards looked positively sickened at the thought of Fedya joining them, but she, emboldened by their recent fear of her more violent abilities, ignored their displeasure, and continued as cheerfully as she could, "You will be safe with us, and perhaps we can help you find a suitable situation. Do you have any skills? Cooking, weaving, needlework, reading and writing?"

Fedya had shaken her head miserably as Dasha had listed possible skills until she came to reading and writing, when she brightened and said, "Oh yes, I read and write better than any girl!"

"Oh," said Dasha, not sure how to respond to this statement, while Oleg gave a bark of laughter and shook his head in amused scorn. Fedya shrank fearfully away from him.

"I like to read too," Dasha told her, going over to sit between her and Oleg, hoping to distract them from each other. "Especially tales of magic, but also histories and stories of foreign lands. What do you like to read?"

"I...I...we only had...the priestesses let me read a couple of histories, but they wouldn't...they wouldn't take me in."

"Wouldn't take you in?" asked Dasha, puzzled. "Wouldn't take you in to their sanctuary? But...but priestesses...I've never heard of anyone being turned away from a sanctuary before."

"It's a lie! They turn people away all the time!"

"People like you, yes," said Oleg, giving Fedya a look of even deeper dislike than before.

"It's not fair!" cried Fedya hotly.

"That may be, but it is what it is," said Oleg. "And you're a bigger fool than you look if you thought they would just let you in for the asking."

"They're supposed to let everyone in! It's a *sanctuary!* But instead they just...they just *laughed* at me! And said...and they said...and they said it would never happen!" Now Fedya really was crying, all hunched up on her chair, the most graceless figure Dasha had ever seen.

"Then we'll find you another sanctuary," said Dasha, overcoming her instinctive revulsion at the idea of touching Fedya, and patting her arm. It felt wrong somehow under Dasha's hand, not at all the way an arm should feel, but she didn't know why. "A better one. One that will let you in. I'm sure there must be plenty of sanctuaries that would be happy to take you in."

"Oh, there are," said Oleg, casting Fedya another scornful look, his mouth twisted in distaste. "Plenty of them. I'd be happy to take you to one tomorrow, Fedya."

"There, you see?" said Dasha encouragingly. "My father will escort you to one himself. And if he asks, they'll *have* to let you in."

"Oh, I'm sure they'll let Fedya in," said Oleg. "But it sounds like Fedya won't accept their offer."

"But she said she wanted to enter a sanctuary..." objected Dasha, even more confused than before.

"Oh, I don't think it's the godly life Fedya is after," said Oleg. "I don't think Fedya knows what she wants at all, do you, Fedya?"

Fedya had been hunched over her chair, crying like a little child, but now she straightened up and said, shooting Oleg a look so poisonous a weaker man would have reeled back, "I *do!* Everyone says I don't know what I want, but I *do!* I know! I know! I know!"

"Well, maybe you do, then," said Oleg. "But that doesn't mean you're going to get it, nor that you should."

Fedya's face crumpled up again. "*Stop* it!" cried Dasha. "Can't you see you're hurting her feelings? Leave her alone!"

Oleg smiled sourly. "As you wish," he said. "I'll just go set up the beds. But where we'll put you," he said to Fedya, "I have no idea. In the stable with the horses, maybe."

"*Stop* it!" cried Dasha again, but Oleg only bowed at her and strode off, leaving Dasha to sit at Fedya's side. No one else seemed interested in sitting with them. Dasha was hurt by this, but she could also understand it. Even as she pitied Fedya more and more, and became ever more determined to protect her, she still found her grating on her nerves, although why, she couldn't say.

Oleg soon had supper ready, and they all sat down to eat it readily enough. He seemed to have forgotten his threat to put Fedya in
the stable for the night, and while they ate their stew and cleaned up
afterwards, everything went well, and Dasha began to hope that whatever it was that was making him so unpleasant, it had passed. Men had
queer moods sometimes, or so she had heard. Perhaps that was all it
was.

But when it came time for them to retire for the night, things began to unravel again. Dasha said that she, Susanna, Svetochka, and
Fedya should all be in the same chamber, and began to carry their
things to the room she had selected.

"You, Susanna, and Svetochka, maybe, but not Fedya," said Oleg,
reaching out and grabbing Fedya by the arm and stopping her from
following the other girls into the chamber.

"Where else is she going to sleep, then?" asked Dasha. "Not the stable! She shouldn't be sleeping in the hay, especially after the soaking
we all got!"

"Oh very well," said Oleg, sounding exasperated almost beyond
bearing. "Fedya can sleep here, in the front room."

"She should sleep with us!" insisted Dasha. "It will be warmer, and
jollier, too." She looked over at Susanna and Svetochka for support,
but both of them looked like they would sooner take a viper into their
bedchamber. Fedya cringed away from all of them. *If only she wouldn't
cringe so much*, thought Dasha. *It makes her look ridiculous, and makes me
want to slap her face, too.*

"Over my dead body," said Oleg. "Fedya will *never* share a bed or a
bedchamber with any of you."

"But *why*?" demanded Dasha. "She hasn't done anything! She
hasn't done anything but ask for our help!"

"Should you tell them?" asked Oleg, looking at Fedya. "Or shall I?"

"There's nothing to tell!" insisted Fedya, but her voice and her
stance and everything about her proclaimed her words a lie.

"Tell them," said Oleg, and his voice frightened even Dasha. "Or I
will."

"No," said Fedya in a small voice, shaking her head. The guards,
Dasha noticed, were watching her with a cruel gleam in their eyes,
obviously expecting something terrible to happen to her, something
nasty that they could relish. "No, no, no, no..." She kept shaking her
head and saying "no, no" even as Oleg reached over and grabbed the
hem of her skirt, but made no move to oppose him, didn't even try

to pull away or claw at his hand as he began to lift up the skirt of her sarafan...

"What are you *doing*?!" shrieked Dasha, launching herself forward and doing what Fedya would not, grabbing Oleg's arm and trying to twist it to break his grip as Boleslav Vlasiyevich had shown her. It was hard, much harder than she had thought it would be, and all she did was stop him for a moment, even though he wasn't even fighting her very hard, but it was long enough for her to push Fedya away from him, put herself between him and Fedya...and then freeze in shock as their bodies came into contact.

"You..." She whirled around so that she was facing Fedya. "You...you...you..."

"Figured it out, have you?" asked Oleg dryly.

"But *why*? Was it...was it to disguise yourself?" Dasha could understand that. Perhaps he had run away from his cruel parents and disguised himself as a girl for his own safety. But Fedya only shook his head silently in answer to her question.

"Then *why*?"

Fedya huddled up inside himself and looked miserably at the floor, then resentfully at everyone else in the room, then miserably back at the floor.

"Come," Dasha found herself saying. "Let us go visit our horses. And perhaps we can talk of it there, just the two of us."

"You're not going anywhere alone with him," declared Oleg, while Susanna nodded her head in support.

"I don't think he means me any harm," said Dasha. Now that she knew Fedya was not a girl at all, but a boy, probably about Dasha's age, both her sight and her visions were making more sense to her. She could see sorrow and cruelty in Fedya's past, which made her wary, but she saw no threat to herself in Fedya's present. "Come," she said, taking Fedya by an arm whose awkward boniness now felt less strange under her hand, and led him out of the cabin and into the stable.

"You shouldn't've done that," said Fedya sullenly, once they were alone.

"Done what?" asked Dasha, puzzled.

"You shouldn't've told 'em all. Now they'll...they'll..." He seemed to be struggling not to cry again. Dasha had never met anyone so prone to crying. Other than maybe herself.

"I think I was the only one who didn't know," she said. "Even the ones who hadn't already guessed knew there was *something* wrong with your disguise. But now that we know, we can help you make a better disguise. Maybe you can be a guard or something." She had meant for that to be comforting, but it only made Fedya more upset.

It took several more rounds of questions, each of which seemed to hurt Fedya's feelings in one way or another, even though Dasha was trying to be as kind and understanding as possible, before the true story came pouring out, but when it did, it was even stranger and sadder than Dasha had been expecting. Fedya was the only child of a minor merchant from a small town in the black earth district. He had always been clever, more clever than any of the other children in the town, but different. He had taught himself to read by the time he had reached the age of four, to his parents' prodigious pride.

But their pride turned to concern as he grew, since instead of playing with the other little children, he preferred to read or play indoors with his mother's cloths and spices, inventing long and complicated stories for them, dressing up as the characters in them, and screaming hysterically whenever his parents tried to stop his games.

Even worse, he had developed a number of queer obsessions. He had taken to reading about the lives of the most pious and gods-touched sanctuary sisters and brothers, and had become determined to emulate them and be touched by the gods himself. To that end, he had taken to fasting, wearing chains and other uncomfortable things under his clothes, and whipping and cutting himself.

At first his parents thought he would grow out of it, but instead, he had become more and more convinced that not only was he meant to be touched by the gods, but that he had been born in the wrong body, and that he should have been given a woman's body, not a man's, a conviction that only grew as his body did, betraying him with its bulk, its hairiness, its terrifying and uncontrollable stirrings of lust. If only he had been born a woman, he was sure, none of this would be plaguing him, making his days a living torment of awkwardness and fear.

"You only say that because you've never had your moonblood," Dasha observed at this point.

"Moonblood! Why do girls always bring up their moonblood!" Fedya cried out indignantly. "As if there's something special about bleeding uncontrollably every month! As if *that's* what makes you a woman!" Before Dasha could think of how to respond to that peculiar outburst, Fedya was already spilling out more of his story, heedless to anything Dasha might say or think.

He had taken to dressing in his mother's clothes, and when she had forbidden that, he started stealing away rags and old gowns and making his own clothes, which, Dasha thought but had the kindness not to say, explained a lot about the sarafan he was currently wearing. When this had been discovered, his father had beaten him for it so hard he had thought every bone in his body was broken, and then paraded him naked through their town so that everyone could see that his words were a lie.

"How horrible!" Dasha cried. "What parent would do a thing like that?!"

"He thought the shame would cure me," Fedya said, shuddering and gulping. "Lots of people think that in our town. Everyone gets shamed one day or another. Only it didn't change my mind! It didn't!"

"I'm sure it didn't," Dasha said sympathetically. Tingles of rage and magic were running up and down her spine at the images of cruelty that Fedya's story was creating in her mind. At that moment she felt almost as sorry for Fedya as she had for the dog.

"Your eyes!" said Fedya, momentarily distracted from his own woes. "There's something funny about them. I thought...it must have been the lantern light..."

"No doubt," said Dasha quickly. To her relief, Fedya forgot about this mystery and plunged back into the recitation of his own troubles.

After the ineffective public shaming, he had then told his parents he wanted to join a sanctuary. His mother had begged him with tears in her eyes to reconsider, telling him she considered him as good as a daughter and that she had always raised him to succeed her in the business when the time came, and his father had said that maybe the brothers at one of the stricter sanctuaries would be able to knock some sense into him, and at any rate a few months there wouldn't hurt him, but he had said no, he didn't want to become a merchant and he didn't want to go to a men's sanctuary, he wanted to go join a women's sanctuary and become a priestess.

When both his parents had told him that that was impossible, and his father had threatened to send him off to be a guard—"It's not *fair* that men have to be guards!" he cried passionately at this point, and glared at Dasha with redoubled spite when she told him it wasn't fair that women had to bear children, no more than it was fair that the peasants had to work their fingers to the bone, and the nobles had to rule—he had put on his women's garb, gathered up all the coin he could find, stolen one of their horses, and ridden off in the middle of the night, till he came to a sanctuary and asked the sisters to take him in.

Despite all his arguing, cursing, and pleading, though, they had refused to take him in as a sister, and so when they tried to send him to their brothers nearby, he had ridden off again, and had been riding around ever since, not sure where to go and growing steadily lower on coin and more frightened and angry at the unkind treatment he had received from everyone he encountered. Dasha was the first person he had come across who had been at all nice to him, and now even she had ruined that.

"Well, where *do* you want to go?" asked Dasha, when he had finished the recitation of his sad tale and was wiping away a few more tears.

"I told you! I'm meant for a sanctuary! I'm meant to hear the voices of the gods! Only...only first I have to get rid of *this*!" He gestured contemptuously at his body.

"But you can't," said Dasha. "You can't get rid of your body. It's just not possible. And you can't be a girl, either. You just...can't."

"Why not?" demanded Fedya sulkily. "*You're* a girl, and you're not even very good at it."

Once again Dasha didn't know what to say to that. It had never occurred to her to wonder whether or not she was any good at being a girl. She had just...always been a girl, and that was that. Oh, for a time she had thought it would be splendid to be a man and wear jingling chainmail and carry a shiny sword—she had been very taken with the kremlin guards, and when she was smaller she had liked to dress up and pretend to be one. But already she was beginning to see the childishness of that. All the suits of "chainmail" her nurses had knitted her, and all the toy swords they had given her, would no more make her a man than the finest gown in the world would make Fedya a woman, no more than telling people she was Susanna's serving woman would make it so. Just as Sofiya Ariannovna and Varvara Kristinovna had told her, wearing "men's" clothing didn't make her a man, or even make her look like a man: it made her look more like a woman, and by wearing them on her woman's body, she had turned her trousers and her guards-style kaftan into women's clothes.

No more than pretending to not to be human would ever make you anything other than human, anything other than exactly the same as those people you hate, a little voice said in her head, but she quelled it, even though now that she was looking at Fedya, she could see that the same thing had happened with him: the sarafan he was wearing was only making him look taller and bigger, showing that he had the wide shoulders, narrow hips, and flat chest of someone who would never bear or nurse children.

Which she supposed might be very sad for some. Perhaps—she had never thought about this before, but as soon as she did, her visions told her it was true—some men, even many men, desperately wished for the ability to bear and nurse their own children. Which was sad. And even discounting that, she could see why someone might want to become a woman, if being a man meant not inheriting his mother's lands and title, or being forced to go serve as a guard, but that did not seem to be the case for Fedya, or at least, not his main trouble. He just...didn't want to be who he was, and was convinced that being someone else would be better.

Like you, her visions whispered to her again.

Not like me! she shouted back at herself. And then her visions showed him to her, dressed as a woman, simpering in that awful way those men at that horrid waystation—not the one where the dog was killed, the other one—had done when they thought they were imitating women, and growing more and more sour and more and more ugly with every passing year.

Was that what was in store for him? Was that what was in store for *her*, if she didn't gain control of her magic soon? Would she be reduced to crawling around and whining, complaining that she wasn't who she was meant to be, she wasn't who she was, and making a spectacle of herself in the process. She caught a glimpse of herself hunting down deer and dressing herself in their hides, killing the animals she thought she loved in order to become one with them. Tfoo! The very thought made her ill, but her visions were telling her it was possible, even probable, if she didn't stop herself from going down that path. She shook her head to clear it.

"I think if you're meant to serve the gods, it doesn't matter what kind of a body you have," she said, instead of saying all that. "I think it's more about what's in your heart. I think the priestess at home used to say something like that: something about how the line between truth and lies is as thin as a sword edge, and often depends more on what's inside of you than what's on the outside. I think you might have fallen off that sword edge onto the wrong side. But you could fix that if you concentrate more on what's in your heart than all the other things."

Dasha thought that sounded very wise and comforting, but Fedya only responded by crying out, "What good can I have in my heart when

I'm forced to wear *this*!" in such a plaintive voice that she thought tears might come to her eyes, except that it also made her so annoyed with him she wanted to shout something angry in return.

"You're not wearing your body," she argued, speaking more sharply than she should have. "You *are* your body. You can't be something you're not." Somehow the words sounded much truer and more sensible when she was saying them to someone else, than when someone else was saying them to her.

"That's easy enough for you to say!" cried Fedya, as if reading her mind. And then he spoiled it by continuing, "When you were born with the body and the heart you were meant to have!"

Dasha desperately wanted to tell him how wrong he was, and how if it had been up to her, she would have been born something else entirely, such as a deer. But did she really want to become a deer? She thought she did *now,* but did she *really,* and would she always? *I don't want to be like them,* she thought, by "them" meaning all the people who had disgusted her since she had left Krasnograd, and, if she were honest, before she had left Krasnograd, as well, but would turning into something else save her from that? She thought about telling Fedya all this, pouring out her heart to him and showing him that they really weren't that different, the two of them, but when she envisioned telling him how she felt about humans, how she felt she wasn't really human, she could sense that that wouldn't help her win her argument.

"Come," she said instead. "Morning is wiser than evening. Perhaps we will find a solution to all this tomorrow. And we must consult with my father. He...he is very knowledgeable about the gods."

"Him!" cried Fedya in contempt. "Not him! He's...he's *awful*!"

Although Dasha was angry with Oleg for how he had treated Fedya, it made her equally angry to hear Fedya speak that way about Oleg. But instead of quarreling about it, she bit her lip and insisted that they return to the cabin.

Once there, though, they encountered more problems. Fedya wanted to sleep in the girls' chamber, and Dasha had to agree that he couldn't be allowed to share a chamber with the other men. The incidents at the waystations had made her very wary of men and their intentions. She would have liked to think that no one in their party would rape someone just because he was weak and miserable, but she wouldn't put it past them to commit some more minor cruelty, not even her father. So Fedya couldn't stay with the other men.

But Susanna and Svetochka were unyielding in their objection to him sharing a bed with any of them, and Dasha had to admit that she was unwilling to share a bed with him either. For starters, because he was big, even bigger than Dasha, and wouldn't fit. So in the end he ended up making up a bed on the floor of their bedchamber. He complained bitterly that this was unfair, but when Dasha said she would take the floor then, Oleg said no, absolutely not, Dasha was not sleeping on the floor and Fedya, having made his bed, so to speak, would have to lie in it.

"What are you?" Fedya demanded resentfully. "Some kind of princess?"

"Yes," said Oleg tersely. "And don't you forget it. And also don't forget I'll be standing guard at the door all night."

"That's not necessary!" objected Dasha, embarrassed at what he was implying and at the thought of him staying up all night for her sake.

Oleg got a stubborn look on his face, and Dasha's heart sank, knowing that she wouldn't be able to convince him that Fedya posed her no threat and she was going to have to suffer the embarrassment, but Susanna rescued her, saying, "It certainly is not necessary. I sleep with a dagger at my side, and I know how to use it!"

Oleg gave her a measuring look. "That you do," he said grudgingly.

"I don't *need* a dagger to fight off such a mewling coward," said Svetochka contemptuously.

"That you don't," agreed Oleg, softening slightly. "I'll wager even Dasha could take him on single-handed."

Dasha wanted to shout at them that she was not so helpless as that, and that they shouldn't talk that way about Fedya right in front of him, as if he weren't even there, but she could see that that would get them nowhere, so instead she bit her lip again and let them all take their places, ignoring the grumbling as best she could.

She had hoped that once they had retired to their tiny bedchamber, things would go more smoothly, but the awkwardness and hurt feelings continued. No one wanted to change into their nightgowns in front of Fedya, or watch him change into his nightclothes, which meant shuffling in and out of the chamber repeatedly. And then Susanna said that her moontime had come upon her suddenly and she was in pain. Dasha offered her some of the mixture that Baba Sofroniya had given her, but Susanna said she didn't trust any of that Northern medicine, and adamantly refused it despite Dasha's assurances that it was perfectly safe, that Baba Sofroniya wouldn't have given her anything that might hurt her.

So in the end Dasha and Svetochka could do nothing but gather around her, rubbing her back and stomach and soothing her until the pains ceased (temporarily, they all knew) and she could fall asleep, while Fedya looked on with mingled envy and revulsion, obviously wanting to be part of their group but not knowing what to say and, Dasha could see, disgusted at the thought of touching or even being near a girl who was bleeding.

No one slept very much that night, but not in the happy way of girls staying up to giggle over stories; it was the painful silence of people who didn't know what to say to each other and wished they were not in the same room with each other. The only comfort Dasha could take was that nothing appeared to be watching her from the shadows, but given all the other awkwardness that was currently filling their chamber, she couldn't say that she wouldn't have preferred dealing with her nighttime stalkers.

Chapter
Twenty-Five

The next morning Dasha arose full of determination to do something about Fedya, find him a proper place in the world, whatever that might be. Perhaps helping him would make up in some slight way for all her failures to help all the others who had needed her help and not gotten it...Dasha bit back a sob at the thought of the dog, and, forcing herself to smile, went over to Fedya.

The sight of him hunched in a corner over a basin, shamefacedly shaving off the beginnings of a beard that had grown in during the night, obviously hating himself and his body for its betrayal, gave her pause, even as it made her pity him more. The look on his face...it was the look she had often wanted to wear whenever her moonblood came, the despair at being trapped by her own body, helpless before its insistence at its own primacy, its determination to obey its own laws instead of her will, the clear, unequivocal, unavoidable sign that her flesh was not just her flesh, but part of something greater, something that would trample her, use her, make her just one link in a long chain of mothers and daughters, whether she willed it or no...Fedya cursed as he nicked himself under the chin, and, wiping the drop of blood off with his sleeve, looked as if he were about to cry again.

"You're lucky," he said sullenly, catching her watching him. "*You'll* never have to shave."

Suddenly Dasha's pity evaporated. It was not the first time she had heard men complain of the burden of shaving—Seva moaned about it constantly—which had always seemed ridiculous to her. If they didn't like doing it, why didn't they just stop? More than half the men she knew had beards of various lengths, and they seemed perfectly happy with them. Shaving was an entirely voluntary activity, so why complain about it when you had chosen to do it of your own free will?

"You don't have to," she told him. "You don't have to shave if you don't want to. My father doesn't shave when he's on the road. He just trims his beard when it starts to annoy him. You could do the same thing."

But Fedya only gave her a look as if she had proposed that he murder his first-born daughter, which made her feel even less pity and more annoyance than before. He thought shaving was inconvenient? He felt burdened by *shaving*? she thought to herself angrily. He had no one to blame but himself!

She looked over at Susanna, who was curled up in a ball on the bed, her hands kneading at her middle, trying to make the pain stop. Let him try getting his moonblood, Dasha thought angrily, when the spasms were so bad he would want to throw up or scream, and the blood came pouring out, threatening to stain anything he wore, and he still had to go about his business, pretending that nothing was wrong and that other people's concerns mattered as much or more than his own. That, her mother had always told her, was part of the test, the test the gods had set to see who was worthy of becoming a woman, becoming a mother, and who was not.

"Just as a seamstress trains with her needle, and a soldier with his sword, a mother trains with her moonblood," her mother had told her, the first time she had found Dasha doubled over in pain, unable to believe that something so terrible was happening to her, and unable to accept that it would go on happening, month after month, year after year, until she was as old as her grandmother, off in the sanctuary. She had begged her mother then to tell her it would get better, but her mother, normally so gentle and comforting, had for once given her only comfortless words, telling her that sometimes the gods were *not* good, especially when it came to women and motherhood, and that it was the lot of every woman to undergo this cruel training, whether she wished it or no. "And only those who can take the training can pass the test," her mother had told her.

"What test!" Dasha had cried out. "Whatever it is, it's a test I don't want to pass!"

"Someday you will," her mother had told her. "When it comes time for you to have a child, you will want to face and pass that test as well, and you will be glad for all the training you have undergone."

Dasha had disbelieved her words at the time, and she still, when the pain was severe, had a hard time crediting them, and even, in her worst moments of weakness, wished she had been born a man instead, not for the shiny trappings, but for freedom from this terrible gift. Any little inconveniences that resulted from manhood seemed inconsequential in comparison with running from the privy to her bed and back again, biting her lip to stifle the moans of pain that threatened to break loose, hour after hour, every month, sure as fate, and with the equally sure knowledge that it would only be worse, not better, when she actually bore a child, and that the only salvation from this torment lay in old age and death.

In those moments Dasha would have given up a good deal to be free of this gift, which to her mind was more of a curse, and the test that went with it, and looking at Fedya now, she could feel nothing but rage at the thought that he was sulking over not being forced to face this test, a test that Dasha lived in fear of. A test he would never be able to pass, or even undergo, because only those who had been chosen by the gods were given this test, and he had not been chosen. Which was terribly unfair, since he obviously thought he wished that he *had* been chosen. Dasha sighed.

"We've got to do something for you," she said, going over to him and patting him on the shoulder. An acrid scent, one that only men gave off when they hadn't bathed recently, rose up from him. The next time they came to an inn or a village, Dasha thought, they would have to steam, and what would they do then? They couldn't let Fedya steam with the other men for his own safety, even if he would agree to it, which no doubt he wouldn't, but she also doubted very much that Oleg would allow him to steam with her and the other girls, even if they would consent to it, which—Dasha suppressed another sigh—no doubt they wouldn't. *She* certainly had no desire to steam with him.

If only—Dasha suppressed yet another sigh—men weren't such rapists. If it weren't for that, Fedya could be safe from the other men, and no one would have cause to be afraid of Fedya. But as it was, Fedya had good reason to fear the other men, and the others had good reason to fear Fedya, even if he himself didn't want to see that. If she were a man, Dasha thought, she would probably want to be a woman too, just to be rid of such a burden, which—since she was currently free of its pain—at the moment seemed even worse than moonblood. "Don't worry," she said aloud, much more boldly than she felt. "I'll help you. We'll find something for you, some place where you'll be safe and happy."

Fedya made no response, still sulking over his cut chin, but Dasha thought his shoulders unhunched a tiny amount. Encouraged by this sign of acceptance, Dasha left the chamber on her quest to find some way of helping him.

She first went to her father and asked what he thought they should do.

"A sanctuary," said Oleg. "That's the only place for him. But he'll have to give up this nonsense about joining a women's sanctuary. If he'll accept a place at a men's sanctuary, it'll...it'll give him as much peace as he's ever likely to find."

The day before Dasha would have argued that Fedya should be allowed to join whatever sanctuary he liked, but after spending the night with him, she heartily sympathized with the priestesses who had sent him away, and agreed that they should offer to take him to the brothers at a men's sanctuary that Oleg said was only a day's ride away, and in the right direction for them. But when they broached the suggestion to Fedya when he came out of their chamber and joined them for breakfast, he refused.

"Well, what *are* you going to do?" asked Dasha. Once again she saw visions of him all around her, but this time they were of him going hungry, getting lost, being attacked and robbed, maybe worse...no, no, no, they could not permit that. "We can't just leave you," she told him.

"Why not?" he demanded. "Since you're not going to help me!"

"We're *trying* to help you," Dasha told him, with patience that was already wearing very thin. To her horror, her voice sounded worrisomely like Oleg's when he was annoyed about something and looked and sounded like he was angry with her. She tried to soften her tone, but the words that came out next were, "But be reasonable. Where are you going to go? What are you going to do? You can't just disappear into thin air. You have to go *somewhere* and do *something*."

Fedya repeated his intention to become a priestess, and his overwhelming horror of being labeled a man and being forced to join a men's sanctuary, or, just as bad if not worse, of going home.

"We should just send you to the castrates and be done with it," exclaimed Oleg in disgust, after they had gone several rounds over this, and seemed no closer to resolving it.

"The castrates?" asked Dasha, as she, Susanna, and Svetochka all wrinkled their noses in instinctive distaste at the notion. "Who are they?"

"Madmen," said Oleg, with even more distaste than the girls. "But maybe they'll do for the likes of him, or he'll do for them, or both."

Further prodding caused Oleg to reveal, his lip curling in disgust as he spoke, that there was a sanctuary, with a compound in Severnolesnoye and another in Pristanograd, where the brothers (it was mainly brothers) and the occasional sister who joined them held that the creation of children and all the acts and organs involved in it were the cause of all death and corruption, and that by foreswearing the act of love and cleansing themselves of the offending body parts, they could become as gods, immortal and all-powerful.

"Not that the gods are immortal and all-powerful," said Oleg. "But they're a far sight stronger and longer-lived than we are. Still, these castrates, these madmen, they've got it all wrong. They die just the same as anyone else, only often faster, because so many of them don't survive the cutting, the 'seal' as they call it. The men cut off their manhoods"—all the men in the room made a protective gesture towards their groins, and Dasha thought she might be sick at the thought—"and the women cut off their breasts"—Dasha, Susanna, and Svetochka clutched at their own breasts—"and, they say, sew themselves up sometimes, too."

"Sew themselves up?" said Susanna, with the voice of someone who was desperately hoping she has misunderstood what she had just heard. Her hands made a convulsive movement towards her lower belly, and her face twisted in a grimace of pain, which led to her biting down on her lip to keep from crying out. Dasha could tell, as surely as if it happened to her, that those unhappy words had brought the moonblood pain back, this time worse than ever.

"Sew up the entrance to their wombs, and sometimes they cut off… everything that can be cut off down there, as well."

For a moment no one could say anything, so horrified were they by what they had heard, but then Dasha found voice to say, "I don't think we can send Fedya *there*."

"Why not!" he demanded. "Why do you think you get to decide where I go?"

"But surely you don't want to go *there*," she told him.

"Why not?" he repeated.

"You heard what Oleg said! They...they would...they would cut off...the pain, Fedya, the pain would be...and you could *die* from it..."

"I'd rather be dead than live like this!" shrieked Fedya.

"I *can't* let you do this!" insisted Dasha. "If something were to happen to you, Fedya, I couldn't live with myself."

"It isn't for you to decide," said Fedya sulkily, stabbing the last sausage on his plate as if it had personally offended him. He looked over at the pan in the middle of the table, which had a single sausage left in it, the one that had been cooked for Dasha but that she hadn't taken. "Are you going to eat that?" he asked Dasha.

"No," she said, trying to ignore the smiles of the others, who were, she just *knew*, thinking that a girl wouldn't have still been hungry after all the food that Fedya had put away that morning. "You have it," she said, pushing it towards him, hoping to distract him from the faces and the too-obvious thoughts of the others. "I..."—why was this so difficult to tell people, especially people like Fedya, who, she thought, should be sure to understand? "I don't eat sausage," she said quickly.

"Why not? Don't you like it?"

"I..." *He'll understand, he'll understand, he'll understand, he's not like the others, he knows what it's like to be different, he'll understand*, Dasha told herself. "When I look at it, I have visions of the suffering of those who made it," she said.

"What, like, the butchers?"

"No," she said. "The pigs. Or cows, or...whoever else."

To Dasha's astonishment and dismay, instead of nodding sympathetically, or perhaps even offering to join her in her abstention from slaughter, Fedya gave her a look of such withering superiority she could feel her spine trying to curl up into a ball and slither under the table as she sat.

"You...you care more about pigs than you do about me!" he cried, his voice full of self-righteous accusation that in no way prevented him from spearing the sausage and cutting lustily into it. Out of the corner of her eye, Dasha saw the others wincing, and once again just *knew* that they were thinking of the castrates, and wishing that they weren't.

She had to admit she was wishing that she weren't, too, but luckily, Fedya continued (eating the entire time) on his tirade about Dasha's petty selfishness and the fact that she was a horrible, selfish person for caring more about pigs than about him and for making everyone around her feel bad instead of being just like everyone else in order to spare their feelings. Not that he put it in exactly those words, but it was clear enough that that was what he was thinking, along with a certain amount of pleasure at finding someone else to needle for being different, just as everyone else had always needled him.

The guards, Dasha noticed with disappointment if not surprise, nodded along in agreement, temporarily on Fedya's side, now that he was voicing all the angry, hateful things that they had wanted to say but couldn't, now that they were afraid of Dasha's newfound abilities to set people on fire.

"I thought you said you wanted to be a girl," Dasha burst out, no longer able to contain herself. "But instead you keep acting like a man. If you really wanted to be my sister, you would have stood by me then, not tried to hurt me to impress the other men!"

Fedya flushed bright red and clutched his knife as if he wanted to leap up and stab her in the face. Dasha instinctively looked over to Oleg. He caught Dasha's eye and winked, which let her know that he, at least, was on her side, unexpected as that might be, and made her feel a little better.

"Well you must want to be a pig, the way you keep going on about them!" cried Fedya, once he had gotten himself under control enough to speak.

"No *pig* has ever annoyed me," Dasha snapped. She regretted saying something so hurtful, and regretted it even more when Svetochka jumped into the argument to say that pigs could be pretty annoying sometimes, so that you couldn't help but want to stick them till they squealed and bled their lives away, which was not at all the argument that Dasha had wanted to make. It was on the tip of Dasha's tongue to remind Svetochka of her story of slaughtering the cow, and how terrible she had felt about it, but she didn't need any special visions to know that that would just cause more arguments and bad blood between them, no matter how true it was, and so she bit down on those words, and said, as peaceably as possible, "So which direction do you intend to travel today, Fedya?"

In the end it was agreed that Fedya would accompany them on their journey, since he didn't have anywhere else to go and he was just as likely to find whatever it was he was looking for with them as anywhere else. So they packed up their things and groomed and saddled their horses and set off, although everyone was in a very irritable mood.

Susanna and Svetochka clearly considered Fedya to be ridiculous, and Susanna's spasms were worse than ever, so that she had (after finally acquiescing when Dasha had pressed her very hard) eaten nothing but Baba Sofroniya's willow bark mixture that morning and was riding with one arm pressed over her middle, her face drawn. Dasha's own middle hurt in sympathy, especially since she knew very well that that could be her in a few days, but other than offering Susanna willow bark and telling her that the pain would pass soon, and with no ill effects, she didn't know what to do for her, and so tried to cheer the others up instead.

A tiny part of her couldn't help but think that Susanna wasn't being very brave about it: Dasha well knew how painful the spasms could be, and how hard it was not to groan and cry out from them, but she had never yet succumbed to the temptation to show her pain in front of others the way Susanna was. It seemed so out of character for the boldness that Susanna had always claimed for herself...but maybe the pain really was very bad, Dasha told herself, and so who was she to judge? She stopped such thoughts as best she could, and went back to trying to cheer up Susanna, and when that failed, Fedya.

But there she met with equally little success. Their guards wouldn't have anything to do with Fedya, other than to laugh at him, and Dasha knew that she could only be grateful that they weren't doing any worse to him, and that they were tolerating him as well as they were only for her sake, but that she was making herself look foolish in their eyes by her protection of him, losing much of the respect she had gained by cursing the waystation mistress.

Oleg also obviously considered Fedya to be the worst sort of fool, although Dasha could see that he had, grudgingly, decided to try to help him for her sake. He spent the first part of the morning riding next to Fedya and trying to find out more about him and to give him some guidance in serving the gods, but Fedya stubbornly refused to listen to any of his suggestions and advice, saying that Oleg couldn't possibly understand anything about him, Fedya, and was only trying to force him to do things he didn't want to do, until Oleg threw up his hands in exasperation and declared, half-laughing, half-angrily, "By all the gods, boy, you've been sent to me as a trial and a judgment. Now I know what my father, and my uncles, and all the other men in my village, and all the other men I served with when I ran away, must have gone through with me. I swear, my head for beheading, you're as pig-headed stubborn as I ever was, maybe worse."

"I'm not a *boy*!" cried Fedya indignantly. "And I'm nothing like you!"

Oleg laughed, his lip curled in amused contempt, and rode ahead, leaving Dasha to ride next to Fedya so that he wouldn't be alone.

The next two days continued in this pattern. No one else wanted to have anything to do with Fedya, and, Dasha had to admit, he did his best to push away any outstretched hands of friendship, and drive away the person who offered it. Which left the entire burden of being his companion on Dasha. It was a burden she would have liked to lay down, only she knew that as soon as she did so, the others would drive him away even more viciously than he was trying to drive them away, and then what would become of him? As irritating as he was, Dasha couldn't stand the idea of him going off, cold and hungry and alone, or worse, falling prey to all the predators, four-footed and two-footed, that roamed the woods and roads.

Dasha had hoped, naively, that once he realized that they, or at least she, wanted to help him and make him happy, he would be easier to deal with, but instead the reverse was true. Now that he had joined them, everything seemed to be about Fedya all the time. He seemed to want them to rearrange everything, from their sleeping arrangements to their travel plans, to suit him, no matter how great the inconvenience to the rest of them, to which he was generally oblivious, although if it was pointed out to him, he would say, sullenly, that he had suffered enough, and deserved a little consideration.

He also wanted Dasha to give him lessons on how to be a girl, which she did, but even as he kept asking her for advice, he kept telling her that she herself was being a girl all wrong, although when he tried to show her how she *should* be acting and moving and dressing, Dasha couldn't see what any of it had to do with being a girl. It smacked of... it smacked of...suddenly, after one of the most ridiculous sessions, in the travelers' cabin where they had stopped for the night, when Fedya kept trying to make her parade back and forth across the floor of their bedchamber (after a couple of nights of nothing terrible happening, Oleg had stopped muttering dark imprecations about their sleeping arrangements, and it was an understood thing that Fedya would share a chamber with the girls, even though they still made him sleep on a separate bed or, when one wasn't available, on the floor), Dasha realized what it smacked of: it was as if, just as Sofiya Ariannovna had warned her might happen, he were trying to take over her body, possess her body for his own.

Once she had thought about it, and particularly after seeing what had happened to the boys at *that* inn, Dasha had assumed that Sofiya Ariannovna had meant rape, and maybe she had, but what Fedya was trying to do—Dasha tried to squelch the thought as soon as it arose, but it thrust through her barriers insistently, forcing her to recognize its truth—was in its own way another form of rape, or something like it. He was trying to use her and her body for his purposes, at any rate, and seemed to think that was why she existed, and he certainly had no qualms about trying to force her to do things with her body that she didn't want to do. He was unhappy with who he was, and wanted to become someone else, but he didn't know how to go about it, and so was trying to steal from others, force himself on others, just as he obviously felt had been done to him.

Was that what I was like, when I was pretending to be a serving girl? Dasha couldn't help but wonder. *Was I forcing myself on others under false pretenses with no thought of anything but myself? Is that what I would be like if I tried to run away from being Tsarinovna and became a, a, peasant girl, or a sister at a sanctuary, or a creature of the forest?*

These thoughts were very unpleasant, but they kept bubbling up, whenever Fedya tried to grasp whatever it was he thought it meant to be a girl. Most of what he seemed to think was essential for their mutual (because he kept telling Dasha she wasn't a proper woman yet, not with the way she acted) transformation into womanhood seemed to Dasha to be either silly, or overtly insulting, involving wearing silly clothes and speaking in a funny voice and prancing around like a ninny, and the more she went along with it, the more she began to suspect that part of pleasure in it for him was in making her feel bad and look foolish.

It got so bad that finally, after their third day on the road together, she burst out and told him, "I don't think you really want to be a woman. I think you want to hurt women because you're not one of them."

"How can you say that!" cried Fedya, his lips quivering. "I...I...I *am* a woman! I'm *nothing* like those...those brutes who, who, who..."

"Then why are you trying to hurt my feelings and make both of us look silly like this?" she asked.

"I'm...I'm...how can you *say* that?" he demanded, his voice rising to a shrill pitch that, Dasha had to admit, was rather feminine. It was sometimes said that one of the reasons men were unsuited to rule was because they couldn't raise their voices to a high enough pitch to force others to hear them when they didn't want to, but Fedya seemed to have acquired that skill, at least.

"Because it's the truth," she snapped, and then felt terrible as his face crumpled, and he turned away from her and stared off at the wall, refusing to talk to anyone. Only the longer this went on, the less guilty and more annoyed she felt, until she stormed out of the chamber herself and, running out of the cabin, cornered Oleg in the stable, out of hearing of the others, and asked, her voice quivering with a tremulous tang, whether he thought that Fedya was deliberately trying to hurt her feelings, or whether this was what men really thought girls were like.

"Losing patience with our little dove, are you?" asked Oleg with a laugh. "I knew even your temper wouldn't be able to stand him for long."

"It's not that!" insisted Dasha, although it was. "But...is it *really* what men see when they...when they look at me? Do I really look that...*silly* to you? That...*awful*? Do you—do men—really," her voice quavered again, to her embarrassment, but the question that had been haunting her ever since they had encountered the men and the boys at the waystation after the rainstorm and had seen how they had pretended to be women, "do they really...hate me that much? And if Fedya hates me—us—so much, why does he want to be a girl?"

Oleg gave her a long look. "As for Fedya, I can't say what's going through that little head of his," he said eventually. "I wouldn't worry about it, if I were you."

"But...but...it's as if...as if he despises me, despises girls, even though he says he wants to be one! And he tells me I shouldn't tell him what to do or how to be, but he's constantly trying to tell me how *I* should be! It's...it's...it's...it's *not fair*, that's what it is, even though he's the one constantly complaining about how things aren't fair! I know what you said about fairness, but he's the one who keeps talking about it, who keeps talking about how things aren't fair towards him, and maybe that's true, but...but he's making it worse! He's making things more unfair, not less! *And* I'm the only one who's being nice to him, but he treats me worse than any of the rest of you! He's polite, or as polite as he can be, to you and Susanna, but he's always criticizing me and trying to boss me around, even though *I'm* the one trying to help him, *I'm*...well, I think I'm the only friend he has in the whole world, really, or as close to a friend as he can have, and he treats me worse than anyone! It's like the more I help him, the more he wants to control me and hurt me!"

"I'll send him away tomorrow," said Oleg, his face darkening.

"No! No, don't send him away. We can't send him away. Where would he go?"

"Somewhere where he wouldn't be hurting you."

"He's not really hurting me," said Dasha quickly.

"Yes he is," said Oleg. "And he's likely to hurt you more before this is through. The beaten dog bites the hand that feeds it, and the trapped wolf bites the hand that frees it."

"You mean...you mean there's nothing I can do to help him?"

Oleg gave her another long look. Then he sighed. "Sometimes I wonder if you're really my daughter," he said.

"Wh...what...you mean..." Dasha's lips were trembling uncontrollably now, and she could feel tears welling up behind her eyes, threatening to spill out and shame her, show the world how little control she had over herself and everything around her. How could Oleg not be her father? Had her mother *lied* about that? Why? Why would she do such a thing? Or did Oleg not want her? Maybe...maybe...so many images, so many possibilities whirled through her head, faster than she could catch sight of them, each one more heartbreaking than the one before it...

"Oh stop it," said Oleg, exasperated, as if he could guess what she was thinking, which he probably could. "Don't be silly. Of *course* you're my daughter. Aside from the fact that I was there at your carefully planned conception, and the fact that your mother would never lie about something like that, not to you, me, or the gods, a blind person could see that I'm your father." He grinned at her. "I'm afraid you're stuck with me, my dove, whether you like it or not." When Dasha failed to grin back at him, he continued, trying and failing to sound patient, "What I *meant* was that I see this Fedya and all I want to do is knock some sense into him, but *you*, my dove, can only think of helping him, little as he deserves it, and difficult as he is determined to make it for you."

"Knocking some sense in him is also a kind of helping," said Dasha tremulously.

Oleg laughed. "And so it is. Well, it must be true, then: you're my daughter, and you'll just have to make the best of it." He turned serious again. "But with Fedya...you can try to help him, and it will be a noble effort, but...it may be that you won't be able to do anything for him, any more than you could for those boys at the waystation, or the dog. You can only help people who will take your help. Otherwise they *will* bite you when you reach out your hand to them, even if your hand is the only thing holding them back from being swept away in the flood that is threatening to claim them.

"And as for whether he hates you, whether he really thinks what he's showing is what girls really are like, or should be...some of it is only confusion. Not everyone has clear sight like your mother, you know, not everyone has visions like you do."

"My visions only confuse me and cloud my sight," said Dasha glumly.

"Maybe, in some ways, but no matter how much they trouble you now, *I* can see that in other ways they show you true. Because Fedya and everyone like him—they *do* hate you, in their heart of hearts, or at least fear you, and desperately want to be you, to be women. Fedya is just a little more honest about it than most boys, even if he is silly and going about it all wrong. But make no mistake: there are many other boys, and men too, who resent what you have, what you are, and will try to control you and hurt you even more than Fedya, to usurp what you are without taking up the burden that that involves.

"You see, they want the power of, of," Oleg stumbled over his words for a moment, and Dasha realized to her surprise that he was embarrassed, something she had never thought to see him be, "the power of the womb, but not the burden, not all the blood and pain that comes with it. But you cannot have the one without the other. Power is always a burden, power always comes with blood and pain at its side, its ever-present twin.

"You can pretend to have it, as Fedya is trying to do, but that is like pretending your wooden sword is made of steel. Or you can steal it for a time, as, they say, so many outside our borders have done, where they say that they keep their women as their slaves, but in the end there will only be more blood and pain, for those who tried to sidestep it, steal what they wanted without paying the price, and for all those who cross their path, as well. So be sure that you do not pay the price for crossing Fedya's path, and I will do likewise."

"It seems so unfair," said Dasha, before she could stop herself from saying something she knew Oleg would think was silly. "It's so unfair that he should be so unhappy, and want something so much that he can't have."

"Life, as I keep trying to teach you, is unfair," said Oleg. "It's unfair that the only price I paid for your birth was some scratches on my shoulders," he seemed to regret saying that, and hurried on before Dasha could puzzle out his meaning, although it seemed by his face to be something that Dasha shouldn't know about, "while your mother had a lifetime of preparation by blood and pain to bear you, and months of sickness and exhaustion to carry you, and brought you forth in pain and danger, and lost her sister and her freedom over it besides. But there you have it. You are learning the same hard lesson she had to, which is that power breeds enemies, even if you don't even know that you have the power. So just remember, Dasha: when he tries to hurt you, it's because he's weak and scared and full of envy, and can't think of anything better to do."

"So what should I do?" said, or rather, wailed, Dasha. "I can't just... send him away, but...I can't just let him hurt me either. Not just because I don't want him to hurt me, but because he might do the same, or worse, to everyone else he comes across."

"Well, if you're determined to keep him, then keep him, at least until we find a place for him. The castrates, most likely. For some people, a place like that is the only place they can be happy, no matter what it might seem like to us. But maybe once he's there, he'll find...whatever it is he's looking for. Better than he will anywhere else, at least. And in the meantime, if he insults you, or hurts your feelings, *tell* him. Don't let him get away with it."

"I don't know how to do that," Dasha admitted.

"Just *tell* him," said Oleg, exasperated. "Just *tell* him that, and if he tries to make you do something you don't want to, just tell him to stop."

"That sounds too easy," said Dasha doubtfully. "I don't see how it could be that simple."

Her father laughed. "It depends on how you say it," he told her.

"What...what do you mean?" she asked.

He stood up from where he had been leaning against the wall, and took a step towards her, leaning in so that he almost seemed to loom over her, holding his hands in a way that...Dasha took a step back, her heart beating fast.

"You see?" said her father. "I frightened you, didn't I?"

Dasha nodded nervously.

"But why? Did I hurt you? Did I say I was going to hurt you? Have I ever hurt you?"

Dasha shook her head.

"And yet all I had to do was take one little step, and you, who have never known a day's hurt in your life, were shrinking back against the wall, trying to get away from me. If I had told you to stop doing something, would you have?"

Dasha considered that. "Maybe," she said. "It would depend on what you wanted me to stop doing. Maybe I need to keep doing it, even if you don't want me to."

Her father laughed again. "The right answer!" he said. "But let's say it's something you shouldn't be doing in the first place, and you and I both know it. Would you have stopped?"

"Probably," Dasha admitted. "But I don't want to have to *scare* people like that," she added. "And even if I did, I don't think I could."

"As for wanting to...I know you don't want to, my heart, and often it's best not to, often it's best to use smooth words to get what you want, but sometimes a bit of a threat works better than all the smooth words in the world, and sometimes there are things that you have to do, that you have to make other people do, even if the only way to go about it is to scare them. Or so I've found. But oftentimes you don't have to scare them the way I scared you: a hint of a threat is all you need, such a faint hint that it's nothing more than the thought in the back of your mind that if you had to, you could smash them."

"I don't think I could smash anyone," objected Dasha. "And even if I could, I don't think I should be thinking things like that."

"Come here, girl," said her father. "No, don't be scared, come here, come stand right beside me. That's a good girl. Now tell me: am I bigger than you?"

"Yes," said Dasha. This close, he seemed to loom without even trying. A tiny part of Dasha wondered how he and her mother, who was so slight in comparison, had ever managed to conceive her...she flushed and looked at the floor, ashamed of her thoughts and afraid that Oleg would guess them.

"No, don't be scared, don't be shy," her father said, apparently not guessing her thoughts, or not caring, if he had. "You say I'm bigger than you, and it's true, but look at me, look me in the eyes. Can you do so?"

"Yes," said Dasha faintly.

"You see? You're not so much smaller than me after all. I just stand taller than you, I just make sure people know that I'm bigger and stronger than they are, and everyone believes it, even if it's not always true." He grinned at her. "And those shoulders..." He gave her a light punch in the arm. "Those are my shoulders, sure enough. You'd overmatch nine women out of ten who came at you, my head for beheading, and half the men, too. You're big and strong, Dasha, you were born to be big and strong, like me! No doubt your mother never thought to teach you about this, tiny little thing as she is, but the thing is, Dasha my girl, for people like us, all we have to do is stand up tall and speak up loud, and people will obey us.

"Your mother...your mother can make people obey her when she has to, and better than either of us, but...for us it's *easy*, Dasha, it's easy! I wonder..." He paused and looked at her speculatively. "I wonder if that's why the gods...wanted me for your father. I wonder if...now that I think on...being big and tall and handsome is a gift, Dasha, the only gift I was ever really given, and the only gift I can be sure to pass on to you and all my other daughters, so," now he was smiling again, "don't throw it away! The gods wanted you to have all the advantages they could give you, for...whatever it is they have planned for you, and so they gave you your mother's gifts and her cleverness and her heart and, of course, her bloodline and her money and power, but they also gave you what she doesn't have: they gave you my body. They made you big and tall and handsome like me."

"You don't think my mother's handsome?" asked Dasha, hurt.

"She's better than handsome," said Oleg. "She's been touched by the gods, and you can see it soon as you lay eyes on her. But you and I...we've also been given this more ordinary magic of our bodies and our faces. And it *is* magic, and it *is* a gift, so don't be afraid to use it. Maybe...maybe," he said thoughtfully, "that's what I should be teaching you. No," now he was speaking decisively, "that's *definitely* what I should be teaching you. And the lessons start right now, this very evening. Come. Stand up straight and look me in the eye. That's it. You know how to fight, don't you, how to spar hand-to-hand?"

"Yes, but I certainly don't want to fight with Fedya—or anyone else!"

"I know," said her father. "And I don't want you to, either. But when you go to talk to him, like I said, you need to have that thought in the back of your mind that you *could* take him if you had to. Carry that thought, whisper it to yourself when you need it, and nine times out of ten, others will stumble all over themselves to do what you tell them."

"And the tenth time?" asked Dasha.

"The tenth time they'll try and fight back," he told her. "Like that waystation mistress—although maybe she wouldn't have tried, if you'd've stood up to her, frightened her, sooner." The guilt that flared in Dasha's heart at those words must have shown on her face, because Oleg went on quickly, "Not that there was much you could have done with what you had at the time. Some things can't be changed, and there's no point in worrying about the past. But the knowledge that you can take on anyone who comes at you can change a lot of things in the future. Which is why you need to make sure that that thought is true, which is why we're going to start by sparring here a little. Turn and face me. Yes, like that. Now, I'm going to try and hit you."

Oleg made a lazy punch at her face, which she swatted aside easily. "Good," he said, grinning. "I see Boleslav Vlasiyevich hasn't failed you completely. Now I'm going to try again."

"I don't think anyone actually attacking me would warn me ahead of time," said Dasha.

Quick as a cat, Oleg's right hand flashed out at her left cheek, but she slapped it aside. Oleg's grin widened. He tried a punch with his left hand, but she blocked that one too.

"Now what?" he asked.

"What do you mean?"

"Now what are you going to do? I've attacked you and you've stopped me. Now what are you going to do?"

"Ah...run away?" she suggested, smiling to show it was a joke, but also really meaning it. What else *would* she do? Boleslav Vlasiyevich had trained her to defend herself, but he had made it very clear, as had her mother and everyone else, that she was most definitely not to start fights herself, and if anyone ever attacked her, she was to evade them as best she could and then run away as fast as possible.

"What if you can't?" asked Oleg. "Or you don't want to?"

"If I couldn't run, I don't think I could fight very well either," Dasha objected. "And why would I want to fight when I didn't have to?"

Oleg tried to keep his face still, but she could see he was biting his lip, as if he wanted to laugh at her, or shout at her, or both. "You're trying to think this through like...like it's one of those games you told me about," he told her. "The ones with pieces that you move around on a board, pretending it's a battle. Only now we're not pretending. Well, we are, but we're not pretending in that way, and if it ever comes to it, if it ever really happens that you have to fight someone for real, that won't be pretend either. You're thinking about it like it's...like it's something you can work through the way you work through sums, where there are rules and, and..."

He paused, struggling to come up with some explanation to do with sums, which, Dasha realized, were not something he was comfortable with. She saw, flashing before her eyes, that unlike her he had never spent his days playing with columns and tables of numbers, trying over and over again to break the rules and discovering that it was impossible, that numbers obeyed their own rules no matter what you wanted them to do. She knew that he could calculate how much someone owed him in a heartbeat, but other than that, she realized, numbers held little significance in his life, and never had, and that the idea that there were rules that couldn't be broken and things that always added up was alien to him.

"You...you're saying I shouldn't use logic to, to solve this problem," she said.

"Yes," he told her, nodding in appreciation of her words, and she suddenly thought that, smooth-tongued as he was, using words to say that one thing was like another thing that on the surface bore it no resemblance was also alien to him, and that, unlike her and her mother, he lived in his body, not his imagination. It was a strange thought to have about someone who was the second-closest person in the world to her, to realize that on some fundamental level they were completely foreign to one another.

"My tutors always told me logic was the best way, the *only* way, to solve problems," she said, instead of sharing what she was really thinking.

Oleg snorted. "Problems on paper, maybe," he said. "Problems for scribes and book-keepers. But for most problems, logic just makes things worse."

"Well, how *do* you solve them, then?" asked Dasha. Her father's words sounded kind of like reckless nonsense to her, but they also... made sense in a way that none of her tutors' words ever had, they chimed with the part of her, perhaps the biggest part, that had always whispered rebelliously that the most important thing was what really was, not the rules you tried to stuff it into. The part of her that her tutors had so assiduously tried to teach her to repress, for, she could see, good reason, but still, perhaps they shouldn't have, or perhaps she shouldn't have let them, because her father spoke true, he spoke true...

"What would your mother say?" he said, interrupting her thoughts before she could follow them off into some land where he couldn't follow.

"She would..." Dasha thought about it for a moment. "She would...I think she would say problems should be solved with...I don't know, wisdom, maybe. And compassion. And she would tell me...I think she would tell me to look for what was really there, and to feel how I was a part of it, how I was connected to it."

"That does sound like her," said Oleg. One corner of his mouth was quirked in amusement, but his voice was fond. "And for her kinds of problems, I'm sure it's true. But that's not what we're dealing with here. We're not dealing with numbers, that can be solved with logic, or your mother's princesses, who can be handled with wisdom. We're dealing with a fight. And for a fight what you need is the will to win. For a fight what you need is the understanding that sometimes you can't run away even if you want to, and that you'll have to win even if you're hurt and scared and the other person's bigger and stronger than you and all your logic says he's going to win and all your wisdom and compassion say you shouldn't be fighting with him at all. But you are fighting with him, and there's no way around it and you can't back down or beg for mercy, because he's not going to give you any. So once again: *what are you going to do*?"

He leaned in towards her as he spoke. She leaned back.

"What are you going to do, Dasha?" he repeated, leaning in more, so that their faces were almost touching. "How are you going to get out of this?"

She tried to slip to her right, but he grabbed her arm.

"Good," he said. "I'm right-handed, and you've made me grab you with my left hand. Good. But can you get away from me now?"

She tried to wriggle out of his grip, but instead all he did was grab her other arm. "You should have taken me out while you had the chance," he told her. "While I was still holding you with only one hand. You should have taken me down then. But you can still do it now, it'll just be harder. So what are you going to do about it now?"

Boleslav Vlasiyevich had taught her that in this situation, she should try to kick a woman in the knee, and knee a man in the—she blushed just thinking about it—groin, but she didn't want to do that now, for fear of hurting Oleg. Only he was gripping her arms really hard, he was hurting her, he was going to leave bruises...she dropped to the ground. Not prepared for the sudden weight, he let go of her, and before he could grab her again, she rolled away and jumped back to her feet.

"Good," he said, sounding...pleased with her, pleased in a way she didn't think he ever had been with her before. "Very good. Only you should have knocked me down while you had the chance. I know you've been taught to run away, and that's good, but sometimes the only thing you can do is fight back."

"I can't fight you back," she objected. "You're bigger and stronger than me, and a better fighter as well."

"When that's how you're thinking, that's true. But have you ever tried to hold onto a cat that doesn't want to be held?"

"Ye-es," said Dasha, not sure where this was going.

"And?"

"And I got all scratched up, and she got away."

"Was she bigger than you?"

"No."

"Stronger?"

"No."

"A better fighter?"

"Obviously, since she got away," said Dasha.

That made Oleg laugh. "But had she ever trained to fight, like you have?"

"Well, no, not that I know of."

"And yet she still injured you and got away. Why? All your logic would say that you should have been the winner, not her."

"Why...she just kept wriggling and clawing, until I let her go."

"Exactly," said Oleg. "She wanted to win more than you did, and she wasn't afraid to hurt you, so she won, she escaped. I'm sure your tutors would have some kind of a lesson there for you."

"They did," said Dasha. "They said the lesson was not to try and grab cats that didn't want to be grabbed."

"A very important lesson," said Oleg, grinning and nodding gravely at the same time. "One we should all learn. But the other lesson is that you have to be like that cat. You have to fight to win, even if that means wriggling and biting and clawing until the other person gives up and lets you go. So what should you have done there?"

"But I got away," pointed out Dasha.

"To where? We're still inside this stall. I could still catch you easily enough. You need to make it harder for me to catch you."

"Ah...but how?"

"Think, girl, think!"

"Ah, well...I suppose if I knocked you down..."

Oleg nodded encouragingly. "Yes. Knocking me down would be good. Kick my feet out from under me as you go down."

"But what if I hurt you?"

"You *want* to hurt me, remember?"

"But I mean, what if I hurt you while we're practicing?"

"I'll take my chances," said Oleg dryly. "Now, let's try again."

They tried the same thing again, and then again and again, until Dasha had swept Oleg's feet out from under him and made him go down three times in a row. After the third time he rose slowly and, limping over to the stall door, said, "I think that's enough for tonight, but...well done, well done."

"I've hurt you!"

"This?" He grinned at her. "Nothing but a few bruises. You have to learn to take a few bruises in life. And these I'll boast of for sure!" He grinned at her even more widely, and said, with a warmth in his voice she had never heard directed at her before, "Only my own daughter could give me bruises like this. Only my own daughter could knock me around like that. You just have to see what's really there. You can't let your fear show you terrors that don't exist, but you can't let it make you shut your eyes to the real terrors, either. You have to see what's really there, what's really happening in each breath as you fight, and deal with it as best you can, not waste your time wishing things were different, or running away from what you can't change and only making things worse for yourself."

Dasha thought it funny that their practicing together had made him think that she was more like him, when it had made her see how far apart they really were. At least in some ways. In other ways, perhaps he was right. In some ways perhaps she really did have a lot of him in her. It was a strange thought, and she decided not to share it with him. It was, it seemed to her, the kind of thought she could share with her mother, but not with him. Which only strengthened her belief that in some ways they were nothing alike at all...but not in all ways. It was all very confusing.

"Come on," said Oleg, still looking cheerful from the sparring, and proud from her performance in it. "Let's go have some kvas." Apparently for him it wasn't confusing at all. "Let's go have some kvas, and we should really practice like this every evening."

"What about the others?" asked Dasha.

"You mean the guards?"

"No, I mean Susanna and Svetochka...and Fedya too, I suppose."

Oleg sighed. "And Fedya too, I suppose. Well, he won't be with us long, and it wouldn't hurt him to know how to fight a little too." He grinned at her. "If nothing else, it'll give me pleasure to watch you knocking him down!"

Dasha didn't find that nearly as amusing as he did, but, not wanting to threaten the good will and the connection that was finally growing between them, she managed a wan smile and a promise to knock all the others down like so many dead trees in return, which elicited her a clap on the shoulder and the words, "Good girl! You'll be a fighter in no time!"

This conversation with her father, while it didn't make Fedya any better, made Dasha feel a little better about dealing with him, and she was able to tell him, when he found out she'd been sparring with her father and tried to criticize her for her lack of girlishness, that she couldn't possibly do it wrong, since she *was* a girl, and therefore everything she did was girlish. This made him sulk, and criticize her all the more, but she ignored it as best she could, and—oh, the wonder!— soon he fell silent, and ignored her too.

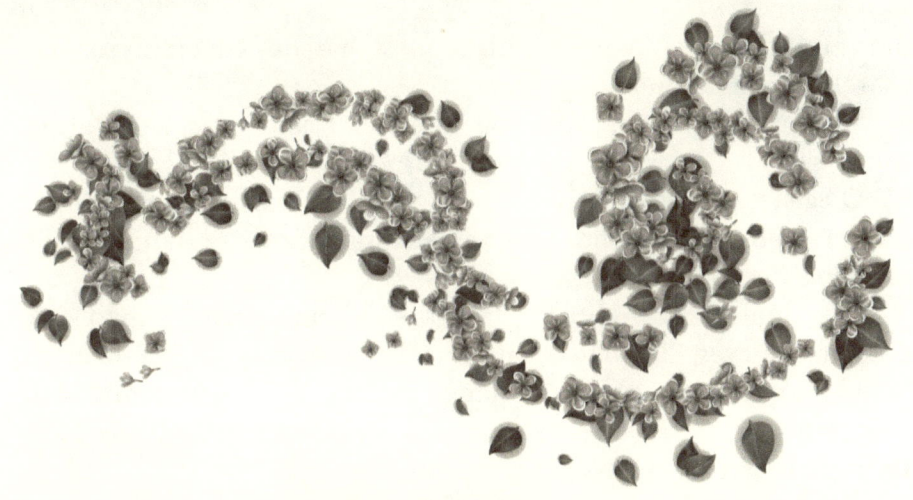

Chapter Twenty-Six

Oleg insisted that the rest of them join Dasha in her sparring lessons the next evening. Susanna agreed with delight, Svetochka said she didn't think she'd be any good at it and would only hold the others back, and Fedya sulked and complained that they were just trying to bully him into doing something he didn't want to, just like back home.

"And what do you think living at a sanctuary will be like?" Oleg asked him. "Do you think they'll let you only do what you feel like doing on any given day? Discipline is strict, especially amongst the castrates. You'd best get used to it, laddie."

"I haven't said yet that that's where I'm going to go!" protested Fedya.

"Well, where else are you going to go?" demanded Oleg.

"Do you want to come with us to Lesnograd?" asked Dasha. "Perhaps we could find a place for you with my Aunty Olga."

"Doing what? Counting coins? I'm not going back to another miserly old merchant like my mother!"

"Aunty Olga isn't a merchant," said Dasha. But he paid no mind to her words, carrying on with his complaints until Oleg shouted at him that he had half a mind to drop him off with the castrates even if he didn't want to go to them, with the request that they cut off his tongue as well as his manhood.

"You just say that because you hate me!" cried Fedya, and started to snivel.

Oleg stopped what he was doing, which was showing Svetochka how to avoid an opponent's punches, and walked over to stand in front of Fedya. Everyone froze.

"Son," said Oleg, taking Fedya by the chin and forcing him to look Oleg in the eyes, "if I hated you, I would have dragged you back to your parents, or left you by the side of the road the day we found you. Certainly that's what you deserve, annoying as you are. But instead I'm trying to help you, as best I can."

"Well, you're doing a terrible job!"

"That may be. Helping others isn't easy. But you're never going to get what you think you want. Things are never going to be perfect for you, or even easy. Young as you are, you've already seen to that, and maybe that's the only way it can be. Not everyone is destined for a happy life, or an easy one, and I don't need the gift of foresight"—he nodded at Dasha—"to see that you're never going to be happy. And that's fine. It isn't happy people who do great deeds. Great deeds are done by the desperate.

"So it's up to you to decide what great deed your desperation will drive you to. And you can start by deciding where it is you want to go next. Lesnograd, with us? We'll find you a place there, if that's what you want. You have useful skills that others would be willing to pay for, if you'd be willing to work for them. The men's sanctuary outside of Lesnograd? They're a good sanctuary, dedicated to the forest. They take in orphan and runaway boys, and treat them well. You'd have a good life there, and you'd be able to help others, others even less fortunate than you. Or the castrates? Maybe that's what you're really looking for."

"No!" cried Dasha in horror. "Go to the men's sanctuary, Fedya, go to the sanctuary! You heard my father: they'd treat you well, and you could do good for others in return. Go to the sanctuary!"

"You can't know that that's the right thing for me," said Fedya, and for once he sounded, not whiny and weak, but calm and certain. "Only I can know that. And I think...I *know* that the right choice...the right choice is the castrates."

"No!" protested Dasha, and tried to argue some more against joining the castrates, and for joining the other sanctuary, but Fedya's opposition to the idea was adamant and unyielding, probably the only adamant and unyielding thing about him. So in the end, after many disagreements, horrified exclamations (on Dasha's side) and tears and sulks (on Fedya's side), it was agreed that they would make a detour and take him to the sanctuary of the castrates, which Oleg said was also more or less in the same direction as Lesnograd, although a few days' journey out of their way.

"It will mean losing as much as a week on the road," he warned them. But Fedya, having gotten his way, showed no signs of understanding why that would be a problem, or any compunction about inconveniencing them in that way, and Dasha said they should do it, and so, when they came to a fork in the road the next afternoon and Oleg told them that the left-hand road would take them straight to Lesnograd, but the right-hand path would take them to the castrates' sanctuary, they turned right.

This new road was much narrower than the main roads they had been riding on since Krasnograd. Even at its widest points it would barely admit two horses abreast, and in many places they had to ride single file. The fields had become smaller, and the woods larger and darker, as they rode North, and now, Oleg said, they had left the black earth district behind and entered the taiga.

"There are still fields up here, as there are everywhere people live," he told them. "But it's mostly forest. We can expect not to see a lot of sky between here and Lesnograd."

They rode all afternoon through a thick fir wood, the only sound their horses' footfalls, the wind in the trees, and the occasional bird call. Despite the shade, the air was warm and close, and Dasha found herself more than once growing drowsy in the saddle, jerking awake just at the last moment to prevent herself from falling right off Poloska and onto the ground. Every time that happened, she had the sensation that her visions were trying to tell her something, but what that was, she couldn't say—the visions always dispersed along with her drowsiness, only to return the next time her eyes grew heavy.

There were no proper waystations or travelers' cabins on this secondary road, but they came across a little settlement at a crossroads, and arranged to spend the night there, in a large barn that the inhabitants used for storing hay and also rented out to the few travelers who passed through.

"Normally it's just hunters, and the occasional traveler to the...the castrates," said the headwoman, whose name was Fyokla, showing them the barn. "Which are you?" she asked, staring at all of them, and especially Fedya, with naked curiosity.

"The latter," Oleg told her curtly.

"Well," she said, when it became apparent that Oleg was going to say nothing more on the subject, in spite of her obvious desire to learn more about their business. "If you want to light a cookfire, don't do it in the barn. There's a pit out in the yard. I ain't got much, but if you want some fresh bread, I just baked some this morning. An' if you've got any silks or any such thing, I'd be glad to trade for it," she added, looking at Fedya again with interest.

"If we find something worth offering, we'll come to you," Oleg told her. She waited a moment, and then shuffled off when she realized he wasn't going to say anything more.

"You should trade her that sarafan of yours for trousers or a robe or something, and get her to throw in some fresh bread," Oleg told Fedya as soon as she was out of earshot.

"I'm not wearing trousers!" cried Fedya, clutching his sarafan to himself as if Oleg had just threatened to rip it off him by force.

"Then a robe," said Oleg. "They're not going to let you keep it once we get to the sanctuary anyway, so we might as well get some use out of it."

Fedya huffed and stomped off to the far corner of the barn, but when Oleg had started a cookfire in the pit in the yard, and, having set Mitya to watching their stew, called the others over to practice sparring while they waited, he came slowly over and said, looking down and hunching his shoulders, "I'll do it. I'll trade my gown for a robe, if she's got one, and bread or any other food she can spare. If you don't make me spar."

Oleg laughed, his face lighting up the way it did when Dasha had done something that particularly pleased him. Fedya looked up at the sound of his laughter, ready to cringe or take offense, but then started to smile in response.

"That's my boy," said Oleg, clapping him on the shoulder, making him stagger under the force of the blow. "I knew we'd make a sanctuary brother of you yet."

"Some of the ribbons are made of cloth-of-gold, and I embroidered some of the designs in silver thread," Fedya told him, still mumbling but smiling a bit as well. "We should get a good price for it. A robe *and* bread *and*..." he tried to come up with another item they should demand, "something else," he finished.

"I doubt she'll have much else, but I'll ask," said Oleg. "You stay here and...well, I won't make you spar with the girls, but...watch the cookfire so that Mitya can spar with them. I'll be back in the blink of an eye." And Oleg strode off, looking happier than he had in days.

Fyokla accepted Fedya's clothes with obvious delight, although she shook her head over them for a long time, saying that she'd have to take them apart and redo them completely in order to make them fit to wear. Luckily Fedya wasn't around to hear her saying that, as he was off in the barn putting on the robe she had brought him in trade.

"It were from a sanctuary brother," she said. "They don't always stay, you know, not that they have anywhere they can go, after...well, you know."

"I know," said Oleg. "And thank you."

"Can't you talk him out of it?" asked Fyokla, running her hand over the fine cloth of the sarafan again. "Can't you put your foot down for his sake and stop him?"

"Maybe," said Oleg. "But he'd probably just do something even more foolhardy if I did."

Fyokla shook her head over this, but brought them several loaves of bread, as well as some dried mushrooms and a few spring onions for their stew.

"If I had more, I'd give it to you," she said. "This gown's worth more, but this's all I've got."

"It's more than enough," Oleg assured her. "The gown won't do him any good where he's going anyway."

This also made Fyokla shake her head and sigh, before she scurried off, clutching the sarafan and shirt to her chest like the precious objects they were for her. The rest of them went back to sparring, but Dasha's movements were distracted and halfhearted, weighed down by the thought of what Fedya was getting himself into and her inability to talk him out of it. Why couldn't he see that what he was doing was a *terrible* idea? He should...he should...Dasha didn't know what he should do, since he seemed determined to be unhappy no matter what he did, just as her father had said. Whenever she looked at him, her visions whispered "sanctuary," but she didn't want him to go to *this* sanctuary. But short of chaining him up and dragging him off with her, she couldn't stop him, and if she did that, he'd probably just run off as soon as he could, just as he had before from his parents. Why were people so stupid?!

"It's a good thing you're the Tsarinovna and I'm the guard," said Alik, pretending to hit her in the face, and almost succeeding because she utterly failed to block him, distracted as she was with her thoughts. "'Cause you can't fight at all!" He grinned, probably thinking he was softening the words, but Dasha could see he was telling the truth. Which made her angry, but it was a sad, diffuse kind of anger that only made it more difficult for her to concentrate. When Fedya came out of the barn dressed in his new robes, she left the sparring and hurried over to him, glad at this chance to escape.

"You look nice," she told him. And it was true. Now that he was wearing a robe rather than that horrible sarafan, he looked...more like himself, somehow.

"It's too short," he complained, pulling at the cuffs that were indeed at least two inches too short. "And it's dirty and scratchy." But he smiled a tiny smile nonetheless, as if he could also sense what she could, that the robe was what he was meant to wear.

To Dasha's great relief, Oleg announced that supper was ready and they should stop sparring. They all sat on logs around the firepit in the yard as they ate, which was a novel experience for Dasha and would have been great fun if the wind hadn't died down and allowed the mosquitoes to descend on them with a vengeance. Fyokla, who had joined them with her own supper—"It's always nice to have a bit of a chat with travelers whenever they come through, and hear about what's going on out in the wide world"—retreated to her house, and they soon were forced to retreat to the barn, where they set up shields against the mosquitoes as best they could using blankets and spare clothing.

"You always think traveling in winter is the worst, and then you try traveling in summer," Oleg observed, slapping away half a dozen mosquitoes before crawling into his makeshift shelter. "Pray for wind, everyone."

Dasha did in fact try to pray for wind, but she kept being distracted by the pain in her belly. Supper was not sitting very well with her, and she didn't know why. Nothing had seemed bad about it. Unless...

Oh no, she thought. *Not yet!* She curled up in her own shelter, and, pulling her knees up towards her chest, prayed most fervently for the indisposition to pass.

Her eyes flew open and she lurched out of the shelter and stumbled through the barn across the yard to the privy, barely making it there in time for her bowels to empty themselves out so thoroughly she didn't think she could ever have to use the privy again.

Why now!? she cried to herself, recognizing the pain in her belly and the sticky dampness in her underclothes. *Because it's time,* she told herself, looking up at the moon, so thin it was almost gone entirely, as she dragged herself back to the barn, struggling not to whine and cry. It wouldn't do any good.

"What is the matter?" asked Susanna, sitting up and watching sleepily as Dasha fumbled through her pack.

"My...my moontime," Dasha told her, embarrassed by the admission, even though she knew Susanna wouldn't be bothered by it at all.

"Oh." Susanna made a face. "Do you need anything?"

"No," said Dasha, finding the cloths and the packet of herbs she was looking for. "Only...I don't want to go all the way back to the privy to change...".

"Do it right here," Susanna told her, turning her back to her. "No one can see us in this tent. Do it here, so that you do not have to go back."

Dasha felt ridiculously awkward about it, but she really didn't want to have to go all the way back to the privy, which was dirty and strange and full of mosquitoes as well, so she stuffed the cloths into her underclothes as best she could (along with a few very scratchy pieces of hay, she later discovered), and swallowed down the willow-bark and valerian mixture Baba Sofroniya had given her, choking on its dry bitterness and wishing she had tea and honey to go with it, not just a swig of tepid water. Then she curled up again into as small a ball as she could, and, assuring Susanna (with more confidence than she felt) that she was going to be fine, tried to go back to sleep.

She did sleep eventually, and when she awoke in the morning the pain was not so bad, which she tried to take as an encouraging sign for the rest of the day. Some months the pain was not too terrible: perhaps this would be one of those months. She managed to breakfast with the others more or less normally, and remembered to fill her pockets with the necessary cloths (how was she going to wash them? Of course it had to happen *now*, while they were in the woods, far away from civilization and also, strangely enough, privacy), and herbs to combat the pain.

It was another hot, oppressive day, with the trees keeping out the breeze just as much as they provided shade from the sun. Mosquitoes and flies whined around them as they rode, driving them all, especially the horses, almost to distraction. Dasha couldn't help but think, even though she kept telling herself it was a silly fancy, that they targeted her in particular, as if drawn by the scent of blood. Surely not. Although...could the others smell the blood on her? She had had no chance to wash, and it sounded as if she wouldn't tonight either, and perhaps not for several more days. Her skin felt sticky and itchy at the very thought, and she became convinced that the reek of blood hung over her, even though the others were treating her no differently.

It became even worse (in her mind, at least) when they stopped for their midday meal and she crept off to change the cloths she was wearing, earning several mosquito bites in sensitive places as she did so. She tried to rinse the used cloths, which were soaked with clotted blood, with water from her waterskin, but she didn't have nearly enough water, and there was no stream around for her to get more.

She ended up stuffing the damp, still-bloody cloths into her pocket, wrapping them in the bit of oilcloth she had been using to keep her herbs dry. She swallowed down another dose of willowbark and valerian, and told herself, beginning to creep back to rejoin the others, that it would keep the pain at bay, and that the others wouldn't know why she had been gone so long.

I'll just tell them I got lost, she thought, and then tripped over a fallen branch in her distraction and fell onto her hands and knees. When she rose, she realized that she *was* lost, or at least disoriented enough from her fall not to be able to remember which way she had been heading. She had gone over a slight rise and into a hollow thickly wooded with fir trees, the better for privacy.

Now she was climbing out of the hollow, but she had twisted as she fell, and she couldn't tell whether she should go straight or turn left once she got back to her feet. The others were by the side of the road, which should be only a few yards on the other side of the rise, but the rise ran in a long ridge, and she wasn't sure where she had crossed it. She should be able to find the road, but her visions were showing her coming out either ahead or behind of the others, not knowing which way to go, and heading the wrong direction down the road.

Don't be ridiculous, she told herself. *You'll recognize the road if it's a section you've already ridden before.* But her heart was beating so hard in her chest her head was actually swimming, something she had heard of but had never experienced before.

Look for your tracks, you silly girl! she told herself. She tried to force herself to focus past the sparkling spots floating in front her—was it from terror? Or was she about to have a fit?—and see the ground clearly, but everything seemed too bright and too dark at once, and all the fir needles littering the forest floor looked exactly the same to her, with no sign of footprints or scuff marks.

Listen for them! she shouted at herself. They should only be a few dozen paces away: if they were talking she should be able to hear them, or perhaps one of the horses would whinny or snort. But when she strained her ears, even closing her eyes in her effort to catch the faintest sound indicating the location of her companions, all she heard was the whining of mosquitoes in the still air. And suddenly that went silent.

This can't be good, she thought. Her eyes wanted to remain shut, not wanting to see whatever it was that had silenced the mosquitoes. She forced them open, ignoring as best she could visions of wolves, bears, hostile wood-spirits, and all the other dangers of the forest, as well as the prickling tingles of power that were building uselessly in the back of her neck.

Nothing was there. Nothing was...was that a footstep? What was that *smell*? Like dog, but...the wolf appeared. Between one heartbeat and the next she appeared in the space between two fir trees, and then stopped, seemingly as startled to see Dasha as Dasha was to see her.

She was tall, almost as tall as a wolfhound, but broader, with a shorter, thicker grayish-brown coat, and eyes that were amber and slightly slanted rather than brown and round. Those eyes regarded Dasha with an intelligence that was both nakedly assessing and entirely non-human. The fear that filled Dasha from her predatory gaze was so great that she couldn't even whimper in terror. The blood-scent that clung to her seemed to become the strongest smell in the world, overwhelming her senses so that she thought she might gag, or faint.

The wolf sniffed and took a cautious step towards her, still contemplating her but already, Dasha could tell, dropping down in preparation to crouch and spring.

Sword! Dasha screamed at herself, from a very long way away. *Sword, sword, sword!* And when she couldn't get her hand to move in the right direction, the same voice screamed, *Daggers! Grab your daggers!* And then another voice chose this moment to ask, *Is this how the waystation mistress felt, when the dog jumped at her?*

The wolf crouched lower, her body tensing to jump. Dasha's mind was screaming at her to shout, to wave her arms, to do anything to ward the wolf off and drive her away, but her body was frozen, until—"Akh!" she shrieked, and jerked all over as a fit took her.

The wolf rose from her crouch and regarded her with patient curiosity, cocking her head this way and that and sniffing.

"Be on your way," Dasha told her shakily, still quivering from fear and the aftermath of the fit. "I mean you no harm. Be on your way."

"Serenkaya? Are you there?" A girl's voice called out from between the trees, followed shortly by the girl herself, who slipped out from between the firs to come stand beside the wolf, whose back she stroked as affectionately as Dasha might stroke one of her dogs.

She was about Dasha's age, with slanted gray eyes and light-brown hair braided in a crown, a style that in the black earth district had not been worn, Dasha thought, since the youth of her grandmother. She was dressed in a shabby sarafan that was short enough to reveal even shabbier boots. Such short sarafans had not been in style in the black earth district for years and years, either. Girls Dasha's age in Krasnograd wore gowns that swept the toes of their boots. Perhaps this girl was wearing her grandmother's hand-me-downs. Or was she in a sanctuary robe? Dasha blinked and rubbed her eyes, bringing forth sparkling spots that wouldn't go away.

"Hello," the girl said. "I'm Vika. What are you doing in my woods?"

Dasha rubbed her eyes again with a trembling hand, but the sparkling spots in her vision remained. Vika herself appeared to shimmer, like sunlight on water or the ground on a hot summer's day. "I'm..." Dasha cleared her throat. "I'm traveling. I stepped off the road to, well..."

"Were you looking for water?" asked Vika, coming over to stand beside her. Even at only an arm's length away, she still appeared to Dasha's eyes to shimmer. A breeze picked up, ruffling Dasha's hair and bringing with it the scent and coolness of bogs and brooks.

"I didn't think there was any water nearby," Dasha said.

"There's my stream," Vika told her. "Come: I'll show you."

"I need to get back to my companions," Dasha said. "They must be missing me by now."

"Don't you need water?" asked Vika. "It's a hot day and your water-skin is empty. You must need water. Then you can show your companions where you found it, and they can have some, too."

"I should go to them first and tell them where I'm going," Dasha said. She *knew* that was the right thing to do, but when Vika told her, "My stream's on the way to them!" she began to follow Vika, even though they headed, not towards the road, but deeper into the woods.

"How far is it to your stream?" Dasha asked, as they pushed through fir boughs. The cool breeze was blowing briskly now, driving away the mosquitoes. Even so, beads of sweat were running down out of the braided crown around Vika's head, and down the back of her neck.

"Not far!" Vika assured her, turning back to smile at her. Her face was dripping with sweat too, soaking the collar of her shirt, and the chest of her sarafan was so wet Dasha could have wrung it out like laundry. But there was no scent of the sweat of an unwashed human: instead, all Dasha could smell was water.

"Does your family live here too?" Dasha asked. She was surprised at how normal the words sounded. She felt as if her mind were floating far above the rest of her, separated from her mouth by a thousand versts or more. The air was filled with shimmers, and there was a rushing sound in her ears, like falling water.

"Just me and Serenkaya," Vika told her cheerfully. Serenkaya, who was walking in front, stopped and looked back at the sound of her name. Dasha thought her gaze looked mournful. And also pleading, as if she were begging Dasha for help. But with what? It was probably all in Dasha's mind.

"Where do you live?" Dasha asked, stumbling along behind them. Vika's pace had quickened to a half-jog, and Dasha was struggling to keep up, but she was desperate—why was she so desperate?—not to be left behind.

"By my stream, of course," Vika told her with a smile. "There." She came to an abrupt stop. Dasha almost plowed into her, and had to grab a tree branch to keep from falling off the streambank on which she found herself, and into the waters below.

"Where's your house?" Dasha asked, staring down into the shimmering, flowing water that swirled beneath her. The stream was narrow here, no more than a couple of paces across, but deep, with overhanging banks as tall as she was, and water that was deep enough she couldn't see the bottom.

It would be easy to drown here, she thought. *One stumble, and—splash! You couldn't climb out.* She turned to face Vika, who was standing very close to her, so close they were almost touching. "Where's your house?" Dasha repeated.

"Here, of course," Vika told her. "Right here." She was no longer smiling. Dasha thought that tears might be mingling with the sweat on her face.

"Vika," said Dasha. "How long have you been here?" She reached out and took the other girl's hand, and was unsurprised when her hand passed right through Vika's, with no trace of their contact other than a faint tingling dampness.

"A long time," Vika said. "Alone. Always alone."

"You have Serenkaya," Dasha pointed out.

Serenkaya whined, sounding so much like a dog that Dasha wanted to run over and comfort her. But she remained where she was, facing Vika, who was now shimmering so much Dasha could hardly bear to look at her.

"That's true," said Vika. "But that's not who I wanted."

"Who was he?" Dasha asked.

"Just some boy," said Vika.

Dasha waited, saying nothing. The woods were completely silent, other than the sounds of wind and water.

"We were at the sanctuary," Vika said suddenly. "We were both supposed to take the seal. We both…it was what we wanted, more than anything. What we thought we wanted. Only we met each other."

Serenkaya whined again. Dasha nodded but said nothing, waiting for Vika to continue.

"We started sneaking out at night to…to tryst," said Vika. "And then I realized I was with child."

Serenkaya whined and came over to stand beside Vika. But not to touch her, Dasha noticed. It seemed she could no more touch Vika than Dasha could.

"Did you try to run away?" Dasha asked.

"We...we..." Vika was sobbing now and twisting her hands. "We got this far and..."

The tingling prickles of power were building up again in Dasha's spine, spreading out across her shoulders and head and demanding release. As was the rage that was filling her chest, trying to choke her. And then it was as if they met, and Dasha's mind, which had been floating along so high above her, slammed back down into her body, and instead of having a fit, or a dozen useless visions, she had one single vision, that told her what she must do.

"Come here," she said, holding out her arms.

"What? No!" Vika jerked back from her like a burned child from a hot stove.

"Yes," said Dasha. "It's what must be done. You know it. Come here."

"But...but..." Vika was shaking her head and trying to back away, but her body, now solid, stumbled over Serenkaya, who was blocking her path. Dasha took the opportunity to leap forward and wrap her arms around Vika's wet, shimmering body.

Dark, moonless night. Stumbling through the forest, already feeling the sickness of early pregnancy. "Come on, come on, not much farther now," her lover calling to her. "Once we cross the stream we'll be beyond their borders, and they won't come for us. Come on." Stopping here in the darkness, begging for a pause to catch her breath, and then strong hands pushing her from behind, sending her right over the edge and down into the water, a terrifying slippery slide and a cold wet splash, water filling her nose and mouth, trying to climb back out, trying, trying, trying and sliding, sliding, sliding, until the hand she thought was extending a branch in order to pull her out drew back instead. Exploding pain in her head, darkness, darkness and cold. Waking up in the shallows a few paces downstream, still so cold. Her body **beside** *her, and a wolf worrying at it, tearing at the fragile flesh, and she felt nothing other than cold, cold, cold, and the need for vengeance. Vengeance against her lover, against the sanctuary and all who sought it out. Pulling herself up and standing* **beside** *her body, commanding the wolf to stop tearing at it, to drag it back into the water and let it float away, but* **she** *was still there, still standing, still taking vengeance...*

"I'm sorry," said Dasha, and opened her eyes. The only person standing there was Serenkaya.

"I'm sorry," Dasha repeated. "You were just hungry, the same as anyone else. But you ended up feeding her, didn't you? She kept herself alive, well, half-alive, through you, didn't she, and kept you both here, half-alive, for—how many generations? Three? Five? Far too long."

Serenkaya regarded her with her amber, slanted eyes, and then blinked.

"But she's free now," Dasha told her. "And so are you."

Serenkaya blinked at her again.

"I've...taken her, I think. Let her return to where she needed to go, and taken what she shouldn't have. So I suppose I've taken a bit of you, as well. But I don't think I've harmed you. You'll live out the rest of your life the way you were meant to."

Serenkaya came over and licked at Dasha's hand, her breath hot and her large teeth touching Dasha's flesh without scratching it. Then she turned and ran off. A heartbeat later Dasha was alone.

"Wait!" Dasha called after her. "How do I get back to the road? How do I..." She staggered, the sparkling spots that had filled her vision suddenly turning to black as a spasm gripped her belly so hard she retched and fell against a nearby tree.

After a moment the pain loosened its grip, and she tried to start walking in the direction she thought the road lay in, but after only a few paces another spasm of pain took her, so hard that she barely managed to pull her trousers down in time before emptying her bowels.

That brought some relief, but she knew, as she stood up shakily, that the next spasm would come upon her very shortly, and the next and the next. She clung to a tree branch, trying to get her addled wits to decide whether she should attempt to find the road, or stay where she was. She hated the thought of the others seeing her like this, and knowing the cause of her suffering, but she also wanted to escape this oppressive forest and this place of death and return to the safety of her companions. And they must be searching for her already, and they wouldn't rest until they found her. Although if she were to wander around, especially in her current state, she could be carrying herself farther and farther from the road, farther and farther from the others, without even knowing it, and end up lost forever amongst these firs.

Another spasm gripped her, causing her to claw at the tree and whimper. She had heard others describe the pain of moonblood as being like claws or hooks tearing them from the inside out, or like being crushed in a giant fist, but for her it was just its own pain, unique and awful and greater than any other pain she had ever known. And this time was much worse than it had ever been before. Along with the pain in her belly, the entrance to her womb ached as if she had crashed down onto the hard pommel of a saddle with all her weight, and she could feel clots of blood slipping out of her, which was not painful in and of itself, but was still unpleasant and made her wonder if she was staining her clothes.

The pain released her, making her feel giddy with joy. Just then she thought that everything her mother had said was true, that she could handle the pain and that it was making her stronger, that it was a gift. And that she could certainly find her own way back to the road. She took a few more steps in the direction she thought it to be in, before the next spasm made her stop and whimper again.

"Why is it so bad?" she asked the air. "Why is it so bad this time? Why this time? This is the worst time for it to be so bad! *And* I took the herbs!"

The air responded with a repressive silence. Dasha told herself that the herbs took time to take effect, but that by the time she was back with the others, they would have taken away the pain, and forced herself to take a few more steps. She had come this way, hadn't she? Following Vika? At the thought of Vika, another spasm took her, pulling an involuntary whimper out of her mouth. But should she be retracing her steps? After all, she had already been a little bit lost when Vika had come upon her. She should try to return to the road, which should be South of her. If she could find the sun, she would know which way was South.

Dasha looked up at the sky, but all she saw were more fir boughs. The sun was somewhere up above her, pouring down its relentless heat, but where it lay in the sky, Dasha couldn't tell.

She suppressed another whimper. What if she *was* doomed to wander these woods until she became a water-maiden like Vika? Although—could she become a water-maiden without being murdered? The stories all said they were the ghosts of young women who had been murdered by faithless lovers, or who had drowned themselves over a broken heart. And Vika's story, which Dasha could still feel twisting coldly inside of her, supported that. So surely she couldn't become a water-maiden.

Unless by doing...whatever it was she had done to Vika, she had become one herself? Dasha found herself pinching her arms and cheeks, trying to see if she was still warm flesh and blood. It seemed that she was, but how was she to know how water-maidens felt to themselves? Perhaps it was only others who felt them to be nothing but shimmer and water.

The air *was* very shimmery around her: was this a sign that she was transforming, or had already transformed? She would have to ask the others as soon as she found them...if she found them...why weren't her visions helping her, why weren't they helping her...they had helped her, they had shown her what to do about Vika—if that had been the right thing to do—but now all they were showing her was herself wandering around the woods, or coming out onto the wrong part of the road and failing to find her companions and stumbling around until she starved to death...if only she knew which way was South...

You utter FOOL! a voice screamed in her head, and Dasha found herself stumbling to a halt, whimpering and kneading at her belly to try to drive away the pain, but also laughing as a vision revealed itself to her, and laughing even more as the pain released her and she could straighten up and see and hear the vision, which was perfectly clear now, showing her telling Baba Sofroniya that she always knew which way was West. Dasha looked to the West and laughed again, before straightening up and turning so that West was to her right, and began walking briskly to the South.

She had to stop twice more as the pain took her, but already she could feel the herbs taking effect and easing the spasms, or perhaps it was the walking, or the relief from knowing which way she was headed. The second time she stopped, she caught sight of movement out of the corner of her eye.

"Is that you, Serenkaya?" she called.

A single amber eye peered at her from behind a fir bough, and then Serenkaya came out and trotted briskly past Dasha and over a little rise. Dasha scrambled after her. By the time she reached the top of the rise, Serenkaya had disappeared—but the road was right below her.

"Thank you!" Dasha called, and raced down the bank onto the road. "Thank you, thank you, thank you!" The pain was gone, leaving her shaky and lightheaded in its wake, but she still found herself laughing in joy, and then crying, and then laughing some more as she realized that she recognized this little rise and this stretch of road, and knew that they had all stopped not a hundred paces down the road, just out of sight around the bend.

Dasha half-ran, half-staggered in the direction of the others. When she rounded the bend and came to where they had stopped, she expected them all to turn to greet her, but only Svetochka and Fedya were there, with all the horses.

"Dasha!" cried Svetochka. "Where *were* you!?"

"I was lost!" Dasha started to say, but her words were drowned out when Fedya put his fingers in his mouth and emitted a piercing whistle.

"Everyone went in search of you!" Svetochka told her. "They left us here with the horses, and told us to whistle if you showed up. And you did! Why're you so wet? What'd you do, fall into the water? Why'd you wander off like that? Don't you know any better than that?! You should be more careful!"

Dasha opened her mouth to defend herself, but before she could get any words out, there was a crashing noise in the trees, and then Oleg came running of the woods. Dasha thought she caught a flash of gray-brown fur between the boughs, and an amber eye blinking at her, and then Oleg caught her in an embrace that was half joy, half anger.

"Where *were* you?" he demanded, squeezing her and shaking her at the same time. "We thought you'd fallen and broken your leg, or gotten lost, or, or...why are you so wet? Did you fall into a bog?"

"I...I...a girl came up to me," Dasha said.

Oleg stiffened.

"I thought I was lost, and she came up to me and told me she'd lead me back to you, only she led me off in the wrong direction, and I couldn't turn around even though I knew I was going the wrong way, and she took me to a stream, and then, and then..." Dasha was shivering now, shaking and laughing at the same time, and she had to clutch at Oleg's arms to keep her knees from buckling under her. "And then I *took* her," Dasha concluded, wiping her face and nose on her shirt.

"Took her?" Oleg repeated, his voice careful.

"I...I thought I was going to have a fit, and she was telling me what had happened to her, and I got so angry, and then...I just *knew* what to do, my visions told me what to do, and I reached out and...took her. I think she's inside me now. And then I was sick and I didn't know how to get back to the road, but then my visions told me that I *did* know, and...here I am." She sniffled and wiped her nose again. Oleg pulled a kerchief out of his shirt pocket, and handed it to her wordlessly. Dasha thought she might have rendered him speechless with her revelation. She could sense his pulse racing as if he were running.

"Did Serenkaya come for you?" she asked. "Was that her I saw with you?"

"What? Oh. Yes. I suppose. I was following your trail when a wolf stepped out in front of me and told me to follow her back to you, so I did."

"Told you?" asked Dasha. "She could speak? She never spoke to me."

Oleg shook his shoulders in discomfort. "I spend a lot of time with wolves," he told her. "They don't need words to tell me things. Although some of them do 'speak' to us when they need to. But that's not important." He held her out at arm's length to examine her, and then held a hand to her forehead. "You're chilled," he told her. "And feverish too. And soaking wet. Let's sit you down. And get you some water."

"Not from the stream!" Dasha cried, seeing once again the deep pool where Vika had drowned.

"Not from the stream," Oleg assured her. "I never even got that far before the wolf came for me, anyway. This is the water we took from Fyokla's well and boiled this morning. Here. You sit here. Svetochka, sit with her. Fedya, get out the pot. We're going to make some tea. Dasha, do you still have the herbs Baba Sofroniya gave you?"

Dasha clutched at the packet of herbs in her pocket, and flushed as she found the lump of dirty cloths as well. Then she realized those weren't the herbs he was talking about.

"In Seryozha's righthand pack," she told him. "In the pocket at the top. In oilcloth. Yes, that one. That's it. But I don't know which ones to take."

"Dasha!" Susanna came running out of the woods, followed shortly by the guards. "Dasha, you are here!" Susanna dropped down beside her and flung her arms around her, while the guards all gathered around, grinning and clasping each other's hands in relief.

"Give her some air," Oleg ordered, bringing the packet of herbs over to Dasha and pushing Susanna and Svetochka back. He opened the packet. "Is there something with rue in it?" he asked Dasha.

"Yes." She reached a shaky hand and pointed to one of the little pouches of linen inside the packet. "That one has rue and betony in it. It's supposed to be used as a ward..."

"Good enough," said Oleg, and dumped the entire contents of the pouch into the water that was heating over the fire. "Come here," he told her. "The rest of you, give her some air. Come here and put your head over the pot. Breathe in the steam."

Dasha complied, feeling silly as everyone watched her with wide, solemn eyes as she crawled over to the fire and began breathing in the steam coming from the pot. When the water began to boil, Oleg took the pot off the fire and set it on the ground, telling her to keep breathing in the steam until it stopped rising from the water.

Dasha knelt there, breathing in the steam and feeling awkward as she crouched over the pot, trying to listen as Oleg and Mitya discussed what to do next in low tones.

"She's weak," Oleg was saying. "But we should leave this place, get as far away from the cursed stream as possible. And this isn't a good place to stop for the night, either."

"Is there a cabin somewhere on the road?" Mitya asked.

"Not according to Fyokla. We'll either have to camp somewhere for the night, or ride through the dark in order to make it to the sanctuary. And neither option makes me happy."

They both glanced over at Dasha, who pretended to ignore them, hiding her head in the steam. Sweat was streaming down her face and throat and running in rivulets down between her breasts and down her belly, pooling in her navel and soaking her underclothes, but she felt less shaky and hysterical than she had before, and the pain of her moonblood was almost gone.

"Can you ride?" Oleg asked, coming over to her.

"I think so," she told him, lifting her head out of the steam. "I'm feeling better than I was before. I think the herbs are helping. And we don't really have much choice, do we?"

"We could stay here," he told her. "But I don't like being right on the road like this, and I like the idea of going into the woods even less, especially when we're so near the stream. Do you know how far it was from here?"

She shrugged. "Less than half a verst, probably. I don't think I actually walked very far, even though it seemed like I was out there for a long time."

"Too long," he told her, a deep crease appearing between his brows. "Far too long. I almost lost you—again. It seems you have a knack for turning the simplest situations into danger."

"I don't mean to!" Dasha protested. He looked angry, just like he always did when something happened to her, and no matter what he had said about not being angry with *her*, Dasha couldn't help but feel that he was, at least a little, which scared her and made her shrink back from him instinctively.

"I know." He sighed, and she could see him struggle to hide his anger. "I know, but it happens anyway. I suppose I should have expected this. You're too innocent for your own good, Dasha, and innocents like you can't help but stumble into trouble at every turn. And you're— you. You're a target. And not just for scheming princesses and angry common folk. You're a target for spirits as well."

"But wouldn't..." Dasha looked around and then lowered her voice, not wanting the others to hear what she was about to say, embarrassed by the very thought of what she was about to utter. "Wouldn't the, the *gods* protect me from them? Wouldn't spirits be kindly disposed towards me?"

"What do you think, Dasha?" His gaze was steady as he waited for her answer. "What do you *feel*? *Are* they all kindly disposed towards you? Do you want to throw yourself into their waiting arms?"

She shuddered. "No," she said. "When I think of them, I...I have nightmares. Horrible nightmares. And Vika—she was so sad. But she wanted to push me into the water with her, I could tell. But they *should* want to protect me. They all *should* be trying to help me, not hurt me."

"No doubt some of them are," Oleg told her. "But help doesn't always come looking like help. And spirits like Vika—they're nobody's friend. Water-maidens are nobody's friend. They're..." He paused, and looked around, as Dasha had done before. Reassured that the others were all busy eating, caring for the horses, and preparing to set off, he continued, "You know, don't you, that I...I've lived, oh, twice my normal span, at least?"

Dasha nodded hesitantly, excited that he was finally going to tell her something about himself, especially about the part of himself that she was most curious about, namely, his connection to the gods, but also nervous, almost squeamish, at finally hearing it, and hearing details of his life that he'd never shared with her.

"The gods can do that," he told her. "Those of us who've been chosen for a life of service—they can do that for us. To us." He smiled painfully. "It isn't as great a blessing as you'd think it would be. Or maybe none of us are ever happy with what we have. Certainly others have envied my wealth in years, and spurned the other kinds of wealth they've been given instead."

He shook his head. "But the gods can do that," he told her. "Give you more years. Their business is life, and they can give more of it, if it suits them. And take it away, of course. But water-maidens—when they died, they were so angry, so frightened, so heart-broken, so...whatever it was they were, that it gave them—more. More life. Of a sort. Life trapped in that moment of pain. You could say the same for me," he added softly, looking away. "We all have to die for our extra life. But that's no matter," he said more loudly, shaking his head and looking back at her. "What matters is that a spirit like Vika is...not really under the control of anything, not even the gods. Water-maidens aren't servants, like I am. They serve only themselves. And they're always looking for more life, to feed themselves. She could have—she *would* have—pushed you or lured you into the water, and then she would have drowned you, in order to keep herself alive. And you would have died, or maybe you would have become a water-maiden too, and that would have been even worse."

"But she *didn't*," said Dasha. "I took her instead. And I think she's gone now."

"Yes," said Oleg. "And that shouldn't have happened, either."

"But it *did*!"

"Oh, I believe you. I just don't know why you were able to do that. *I* can't, and your mother can't, and I don't know of anyone who *can*. So why you can, how you can—that I don't know. And I'm glad, but it—it worries me, as well."

"It worries me too," Dasha confided.

He smiled at her. "Well, that's something, at least. A lot of young people—or older people—would have something like this go to their head, and we'd never get them to come back from it. If...well, if any of *them*"—he nodded to where Susanna, Svetochka, and Fedya were checking the horses' packs—"were to do something like that, how do you think that would turn out?"

"Susanna would...Susanna would be bursting with pride, and recklessness," Dasha said. "And Svetochka and Fedya would either try to run away from it, or use it for their own ends. I can"—she shivered—"I can *see* it. I just had a vision, and I think it was—I think it was a real one, one that was...almost useful."

"Well, that's something," Oleg told her. "Maybe you'll get these visions under control after all." He smiled at her. "And you're right, by the way. About what they would do. You don't have to have visions to see that. But it wasn't them who found Vika, it was you."

"It was more like Vika found me," Dasha told him.

"And that was not by chance, I'm sure of it. She sought you out amongst all of us, even if she didn't know what she was doing. Which is why you mustn't go off alone again, not for any reason. You'll have to take the guards with you at all times."

"I can't...they can't come with me for *everything*!" Dasha protested, her cheeks flaming.

"Well...I suppose not...but Susanna or Svetochka. Always Susanna, and Svetochka as well, if you can. Don't go off alone for *any* reason, no matter how innocent it seems. After all, you didn't expect to get lost this time, did you?"

"No," Dasha admitted.

"Danger's like that. It catches you when you least expect it. Here, give me that pot. The steam's gone now. How do you feel?"

"Better," Dasha told him. "I think I can ride now, at least for a bit."

"Come on, then," he said. "I'll feel a far sight better once we've put a few versts between us and that stream. The gods alone know how much influence Vika is still having on you, and she may not be the only water-maiden haunting it." He sniffed, looking very wolf-like as he did so. "This is not quite a prayer wood, but it's something like that. People come here to pray, but their prayers are dark and full of rage. More like curses than prayers. I doubt it will be any better closer to the sanctuary—those who come to it are full of despair and rage themselves—but we might be a little safer behind their walls. And we should leave this place before the protection from those herbs wears off. Let's go. Poloska and Seryozha are already ready."

"I have to..." Dasha said, wriggling in embarrassment. "Before we go, I have to...go into the woods again."

"Well, be quick about it, and take Susanna with you," he told her. "And don't stray too far from the road!" he called after them.

This time they went to the South side of the road, rather than the North, and found a fallen tree to crouch behind. As soon as they lost sight of the road, everything went silent, as if the forest was holding its breath, and not even the words of their companions could carry through the thick air. Dasha's neck prickled in unease, as power rose within her, preparing to combat whatever it was that was out there, but when she looked around, she saw nothing.

"We need more water," Susanna said, when they were done, and Dasha had put the bloodsoaked cloths into the oilcloth packet. "We need to wash."

"There's a stream in that direction," Dasha told her, nodding off to where the ground sloped down, away from the road.

"No!" said Susanna. "We will take more water when we cross a stream on the road. If you need more clean cloths, you can use some of mine. Come on, we have to get back."

Susanna chivied her back out of the woods as fast as they could walk, and handed her over to Oleg, who was holding her horses for her. As soon as he had legged her up onto Poloska's back, and vaulted onto Belka himself, he called for them to head out, and they set off at a brisk trot, moving as quickly as they could down the narrow road.

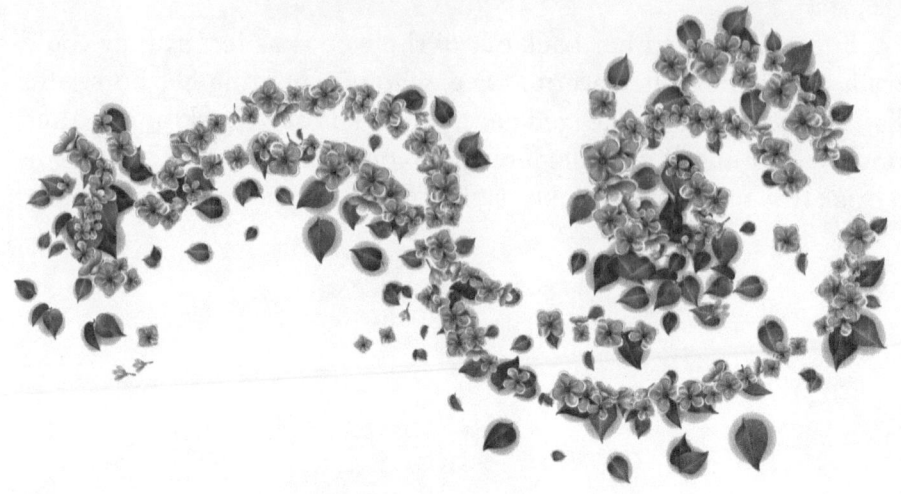

Chapter Twenty-Seven

They rode hard for the rest of the afternoon, twisting and turning through the trees down the winding road. Their brisk pace kept the mosquitoes off them as they moved, but whenever they stopped, the insects would descend with a threatening whine, causing both humans and horses to twist and thrash out with whatever they had at their disposal to try and drive off the maddening creatures.

"Whyever did the gods create mosquitoes?" Dasha moaned, after Poloska had almost unseated her in her desperate attempts to brush off the mosquitoes by brushing against a tree.

"They must have had their reasons," said Oleg, slapping at the mosquitoes swarming around his face. "Or maybe mosquitoes arose on their own, spawned by the spite of the Black God. Or...come on, let's go. The longer we sit, the more we'll get bit. There's no water around here, so we might as well keep going till we find some."

"There's a stream off in that direction..." Dasha began, but Oleg shook his head and told them to keep going. They hadn't encountered any water sources since leaving Fyokla's barn that morning, and the water situation was becoming more and more worrisome. They had given the horses a few mouthfuls at every stop, but they needed more, and the humans did as well. Especially Dasha.

She was sweating so much that Mitya had taken to joking about her melting like a snow-maiden, until Oleg had given him such a look of reproof that he had fallen silent and ridden as far away from Oleg as he could. She could feel all the water in her body draining away in the sweat and in the blood that she was losing, and her mouth felt as if it had been stuffed with sawdust. But she had drunk all her water, which had done her little good, and there was no more to spare for her, not unless the others gave up their shares, which she didn't want, and so she stifled her complaints.

However, Oleg's insistence on avoiding the stream that ran a few paces away from the road was beginning to irritate her. They all needed water, and water was well within their reach, if only they would go to it. After all, nothing *that* terrible had happened to her at the stream, had it? She was still alive, wasn't she? And there was no reason to suspect that there would be any dangers lurking at this other stream—or perhaps it was the same stream, but it was versts and versts away from Vika's haunting spot—while there was every reason to believe that if they didn't get water soon, they would all sicken from thirst.

"We'll stop when we find a stream or a watering spot on the road," he told them. "We won't reach the sanctuary today, not unless we ride all night."

"And if we don't find a watering spot?" Dasha asked.

"Then we'll stop anyway, once night falls. One night without water won't kill us."

Dasha tried to swallow, and felt her lips stick together, and her tongue stick to the roof of her mouth. One night without water might not kill her, but it sounded very unpleasant nonetheless. And she could tell the horses were desperate for water too. Of course, if they did stop by water for the night, the mosquitoes would be unbearable.

What we need is a storm, she thought. *And a swift-flowing stream.* She closed her eyes as they trotted along, trusting in Poloska to carry her. Her skin crawled as she sensed the water floating in the air, and the water flowing through the ground.

"There's going to be a storm at nightfall," she announced, opening her eyes. "And there's a stream crossing the road about, oh, five versts ahead."

Everyone stared at her. "Did you see it?" Oleg asked. "Did you have a vision?"

"Of sorts. I could feel the water. I can feel the water now, both in the air and in the ground."

Oleg frowned and bit his lip, but said nothing. When the wind picked up, blowing away the mosquitoes, he frowned even more, though, and when, about five versts down the road, they came to a ford crossing a wide stream, he frowned yet again.

The horses, however, sensed nothing wrong, and all began sucking it up greedily as soon as they reached it, while the humans jumped down and began filling their waterskins from the clear cold water that was rushing over the pebbly bottom of the ford.

"What are you *doing*!" Oleg's hand landed on Dasha's shoulder, and he jerked her out of the water, where she had been, she realized, kneeling, drinking straight from the stream like the horses, and splashing herself with the water so that she was as wet as if she had been swimming.

"I—I don't know," she admitted. "I didn't know I was doing it till you stopped me."

"We're *leaving*," he announced, his face as dark as the thunder that suddenly pealed out above them.

"We can't!" Dasha protested, and then bit her lip to stifle a groan as a spasm suddenly took her.

"What's the matter?!" demanded Oleg, still holding her by the shoulder.

"It's nothing," she told him, resisting the urge to clutch at her belly. She knew that the second wave of spasms was normally not as bad as the first, but it could still be very bad, and given how terrible the one this afternoon had been, she feared that this one would be very unpleasant as well.

"It's not nothing!" he told her, giving her shoulder a shake. "What is it? Are you taking ill? Are you sickening from the water?"

"No," she told him.

"Don't lie to me!"

"I'm not!" she insisted. "It's not that! It's...it's my moonblood," she told him, dropping her voice to a whisper and looking down at the water, her cheeks flushing painfully bright.

"Oh." To her surprise, when she dared to look back up at him, he was observing her, not with the revulsion she had expected, but the closest thing to compassion she had ever seen him exhibit. "Is it very bad?" he asked.

"That's why I was so sick this afternoon in the forest," she told him, still half-whispering. "It was the worst I've ever experienced, and

I thought I was going to faint away from it! It's not so bad right now, but it still hurts. And I don't want to ride any farther."

"I see," he said, dropping his hand from her shoulder and stepping back, the compassion on his face already being replaced with the expression of slightly irritated problem-solving he tended to wear whenever she presented him with something that didn't fit in with what he wanted to do. "You're sure it's not from...the water?" he asked. "From Vika?"

"It's moonblood," she told him. In truth, it had not escaped her notice that the spasms had come upon her when she had taken Vika, and again when she had drunk water from the stream, but that would only cause him to insist that they leave the stream behind and spend the night perched on some rise, as far away from water as he could arrange, and Dasha had no desire for an entire night of torturous thirst.

And in spite of the pain the water was causing her, she could see no danger in it. What it was trying to do to her, her visions could not say, but they were telling her that whatever it was, it was necessary, while whenever she thought of leaving the stream, all she could see was thirst and misery and missed opportunities.

"I think we'll be safe here," she told him. "That's what my visions say, anyway."

"Yes, but your visions aren't very reliable at all!" he burst out.

"I think they're becoming better," she said. "And what are we going to do? This is a camping place, at least." Which was true. There was a bare patch of ground off the road, with a fire pit in it, and a place nearby where people had set up picket lines for their horses. "This is where people stop," she told him. "They wouldn't do it if it were dangerous. And where could we go that would be safer? There are dangers in the woods, and in the middle of the road, as well."

He sighed and scratched at his beard. "You're right," he said. "Or at least, there's nowhere we can stop that's safe. The Black God take that Fedya!" he added. "If he hadn't been such a thrice-cursed hardhead, we'd be stopping at a nice, normal sanctuary off the main road, instead of losing a week stumbling around here in this uncanny woods."

"Maybe it's for the best," Dasha told him. "Maybe this is where I need to be. Maybe I *needed* to meet Vika. Like I need this pain, or so my mother tells me."

Oleg ground his teeth. "She *would* say that, wouldn't she?" he said. "Well, nothing we can do about it now. The gods are going to punish us as they see fit. And you're right: we might as well stop at a proper camping site if we're going to stop. But"—he held a finger in front of her face—"absolutely *no* wandering off by yourself, understand? You will sit by the fire and not leave its light."

"Except when I need to pee," Dasha told him pertly. The pain had released her for the moment, and she was feeling the giddy euphoria that came with that release.

"Well...yes." He grinned. "But then you'll take Susanna with you, and you won't leave her side, not for any reason. Safety is more important than privacy."

"Of course," Dasha assured him.

"And you won't drink any more water until we boil it," he went on.

She looked down at the cool water, flowing so temptingly around her legs. "Fine," she agreed reluctantly. "But be quick about it! I'm thirsty."

"If you want us to be quick, you'll have to help us. *Out* of the water," he told her. "Go onto dry land, and begin unpacking our things. And"—he gave her a pat on the shoulder, causing water to splash both of them—"you'll need to change into dry clothes, too."

With both Susanna and Svetochka as escorts, Dasha managed to go off and change and wash out all her used bloodcloths. Despite her splashing in the stream earlier, she still felt dirty and sticky, but Oleg resolutely refused to allow anyone to bathe in the stream. The girls were to stay as far away from it as possible, and the guards were only to venture into it enough to draw water for themselves and the horses, before hustling back to dry ground. The girls strung up a clothesline to hang their wet clothes on (although not the bloodcloths: the other girls saw nothing wrong with that, but Dasha hung them more discreetly in the shelter they had constructed out of oilcloth instead) and then settled down to wait for supper to be ready.

Dasha struggled not to squirm in discomfort as she waited: the moonblood pain was, although not as debilitating as it had been earlier, still quite bothersome, and she had to wait for the water to boil before being allowed to make herself an infusion of the herbs Baba

Sofroniya had given her, and then wait some more for them to take effect. At least, she consoled herself, the rising wind meant that they were no longer being troubled by mosquitoes.

The days were already quite long by now, with Midsummer only a few weeks away, and it was still light when the lentil and barley stew Oleg had prepared was ready, although it was a strange, yellowish light, heralding the storm that Dasha knew was coming. Pain had dulled Dasha's appetite, but she forced herself to eat as much as she could, knowing she needed her strength. She also drank and drank, but no matter how much she drank, she couldn't seem to quench her thirst, and she kept sweating, even as the wind rose and the air cooled around them.

"Is it always like this?" Oleg asked her quietly, as she downed more water in thirsty gulps. "Are you always this thirsty during your moon-time?" He made a face. "I should know that," he added, almost too low for her to hear.

She shook her head. "Thirsty, yes, but not like this."

He felt her forehead. "You feel cold, not hot, but you're sweating like you've taken a raging fever."

"I think it's Vika," she told him. "I think she needs the water, or I'm sweating her out, or something like that."

He made a face. "Maybe we should carry on to the sanctuary," he said. "Maybe they'll have a healer there who can help you."

"I don't think a healer can help me," she told him. "And I don't think I'm in any danger, anyway."

He frowned, and wiped away the sweat that was trickling down her face. "You look like you're in danger to me," he said. "And water-maidens are nothing to mess with. I've never heard of anyone doing what you've done, and I have no idea what the consequences will be." He pulled away from her and frowned even more, and she had to resist the urge to point out to him that, once again, he was angry with her for something that wasn't really her fault, and was hurting her because of it.

Dasha closed her eyes. "I don't see danger," she told him. "When I look with my visions, all I see is...me." She scrunched her eyes shut as hard as she could, concentrating on the vision that she could just barely see. She had never tried to chase after a vision like this before. Normally they overwhelmed her, confusing her and filling her with panic, but this one was dancing just on the edge of sight, as if teasing her, trying to get her to come after it.

"I see myself on a shore," she told him. "A vast lake, only it smells funny. The sea, maybe? It must be the sea. The ice is breaking up, and I'm walking out into the water. It must be cold, but I don't seem to feel it. I'm walking out into the water, and then I dive under." She opened her eyes, to meet Oleg's own horror-struck eyes staring back at her.

"It wasn't a bad vision," she told him. "Normally they're full of terrible things, like me falling and hurting myself. Or even worse things. Did you know that I have a recurring vision of having a child, and either you or my mother accidentally killing it?" His eyes widened even further, and he looked like he might be sick.

"I don't think it's a true vision," Dasha told him. She knew she was blabbering, but she couldn't seem to stop herself. "I think it's a warning, telling me of the bad things that *could* happen, of the bad things that happen no matter how careful we try to be. None of us are safe from stupid mischance. I think many of my visions are warnings of what *could* be, warnings to keep me careful and humble. But this vision—it's not like that. I think it's telling me of something that *will* happen. And it's not a bad thing," she hurried to reassure him.

"Diving into the half-frozen sea *is* a bad thing!" he insisted, staring at her with the same revulsion he had shown before, along with fear and horror and anger and every other bad feeling she could think of. "Doesn't it tell you how to stop it?!"

She shook her head. "I told you. I think many of the other visions I've had are warnings of what *could* go wrong. Like when I had a vision of what could go wrong when we were crossing the ford, and then it did. I just can't control them, or understand them. But this isn't like that. This feels different. And I think it's telling me that this is something to strive for, not something to avoid. This is what *needs* to happen."

"Why?!" he demanded.

She shrugged. "I don't know. But I think it does."

"How can you be so calm about it?!"

"I don't know. I've always been afraid of water," she admitted. "But right now I'm not. Maybe that's what Vika's given me. Maybe she's taken away my fear of water. Speaking of water, is there more? I'm thirsty."

"I think you should stop drinking," he told her, his brows knit together so that they almost touched. "I think you've had enough water. Don't have any more tonight."

Dasha tried to argue and protest, but he took away the mug she had been drinking from, and told her no, absolutely not, she should stop drinking and go to bed.

"I'm not going to sleep," she told him. "The storm will hit at night-fall, and that will keep me up."

"Go lie down anyway," he told her, and then added, his voice soft-ening, "you've had a hard day. Lying down will do you good."

Dasha had been prepared to argue some more, to defy his attempts to force her into doing what he wanted her to, but his softening made her soften as well, and she went and crawled into her tent, wrinkling her nose at the strong sheepy scent of the oilcloth, which was soaked with lanolin. She tried not to see visions of where the lanolin had come from, but her mind spent quite some time showing them to her anyway, and she wasn't sure when the visions slipped into dreams.

She was racing through the fog, with creatures chasing after her, reaching out for her. She tripped and fell headlong into the river.

"I'm in the river," she thought. "Let the river take me. I'll drown soon."

Something touched her foot. "Ride on me," said a voice, and she was lying atop the smooth scales of the viper, and she swam sinuously through the water, cutting through the golden moonlight that lit the surface of the river.

"Why did you save me?" Dasha asked the viper.

"Why?" repeated the viper. "Because." And then she dove down into the water, pulling Dasha down with her before she could even think to resist. The water surrounded her, filling her nose and mouth, covering her head... Dasha tried to let go of the viper's back and swim to the surface, back to where the moonlight was lighting a path to the shore, but no matter how much she struggled, she kept sinking and sinking.

Something clutched at her hair. She shook her head desperately, thinking it was a root, thinking it was the viper...no, it was her lover, he was pushing her back under, pushing her back under after he had pushed her in and then hit her on the head when she had tried to climb out. She opened her mouth to scream at him, and water rushed in, flooding her lungs, dragging her down to the bottom of the stream with its weight.

*You don't have to die, the viper said in her ear. **You don't have to let him get away with this.***

NO! screamed Dasha, sucking in more water and driving her body down to the bottom of the stream. She pushed herself off of it with all her strength, as if leaping over a tall log, and found herself flying up over the water, flying through the air, straight at the moon, which wanted to devour her. Just like the viper did, and the water, and the fish in it, and the roots of the trees hanging down from the stream bank. Everything wanted to devour her, tear her apart and turn her into something she wasn't.

"No!" cried Dasha, and jerked awake. Pain was lancing through her belly as if her insides were trying to claw their way to freedom.

She looked around wildly, not recognizing at first where she was. Something reeking of sheep was brushing against her face...she was in the tent. The tent made of lanolin-soaked oilcloth. It was dark. A flash of lightning lit up the tent like a lantern, showing Svetochka and Susanna sleeping beside her. There was a crash of thunder that made the air shake, and set the horses to whickering nervously. Dasha could hear the men cursing as they ran around to check on the horses and secure everything from the wind and rain that burst down on them, filling Dasha's ears until she couldn't hear anything else.

*That was Vika, she thought, curling up in a ball and putting her hands over her ears. That was Vika's death—again! Well, the last part was. The first part was...me. But terrible. Why did I have to see that? Why did I have to see both those things? Why do I have to keep seeing the things chasing me, and why did I have to see Vika's death **again**?*

Because, she answered herself, I have to see them so that others don't. I have to see them so that they don't happen, or don't happen again. I have to see the bad things so that others don't.

Another flash of lightning seared the backs of her eyes even through her closed eyelids, followed immediately by a crack of thunder that made her jump as the air seemed to split around her. She crawled out of the tent and ran towards Poloska, who was pulling back on the picket line, her eyes rolling.

"Get back in the tent!" Alik, who was with Ryzhechka, shouted at her. Another flash of lightning lit him up, showing his hair plastered to his head from the rain pounding down on them. He had run out in nothing but a shirt, which was clinging to his body, the linen transparent in the lightning. Dasha tried not to stare, and then ducked and hid her face in Poloska's neck when the peal of thunder rang out so loud she thought the sound alone must knock down the trees above them.

"Get back in the tent!" Alik repeated, sliding through the water running over the churned-up ground under the picket line to shake her shoulder. "Get back in the tent! It's not safe out here!"

"The stream!" Dasha shouted back at him. "The stream could break its banks!" She could see—or could she feel?—the water rising and rising, overflowing the ford and spilling out onto the campsite, flooding everything in their tents and threatening to carry them away.

The next strike of lightning illuminated Alik's face as he bit his lip. "Stay here," he said. "I'll go tell Oleg Svetoslavovich. But if the horses start to bolt, *get back*. Don't try to stop them, do you understand?"

"I understand," Dasha told him, not mentioning that she had no intention of doing any such thing. The horses, she sensed, were frightened, but not enough to bolt. The lightning was still striking, but the next clap of thunder took longer to reach her ears, and it no longer felt as if the air were splitting and shaking around her. It was the stream that was the real danger. Even through the pounding rain she could hear the water rising, rattling the stones at the bottom of the ford. Only half-aware of what she was doing, she began untying Poloska and Seryozha from the picket line.

"The water!" Susanna came running up to her, soaked to the skin in her nightgown, her head and feet bare. "The water in the stream!"

"I know!" Dasha shouted back. "We need to move the horses!"

Susanna nodded and dashed off towards Chernets, who was whinnying and twisting back and forth in agitation, threatening the other horses. Dasha got Poloska and Seryozha free, and began to lead them away from the picket line, towards the road. The other horses called after them, and her heart twisted. Should she go back for them? The men were occupied with moving their packs to higher ground, ignoring the horses' distress. Dasha's feet slid in the mud as another bolt of lightning struck, making Poloska flinch and shy away.

The water was already spilling out from the ford, covering the campsite.

Dasha blinked. The campsite was wet but not yet underwater. "Come *on*," she said to Poloska and Seryozha. "We have to get to higher ground."

A wall of water came rushing downstream, hitting the ford and exploding outwards, flooding their tents and carrying away half their supplies.

Dasha shook her head and looked back. The men were running back and forth, hauling packs out of the tents and stashing them in tree branches at head height. *Surely* the waters wouldn't reach that high.

The wall of water caught Alik as he ran to snatch up the last of the packs out of the girls' tent...

"NO!" shouted Dasha. "Susanna! Susanna! Take my horses!" She had to shout several times to catch Susanna's attention over the pounding of the rain, and then struggle, slipping and sliding, to convince Poloska and Seryozha to get close enough to Chernets to hand their leadropes over to Susanna. Susanna grabbed her arm, trying to hold her back, when she realized that Dasha was planning to run off, but Dasha wriggled out of her grasp, all her sparring lessons coming back to her and moving her body without her conscious thought.

The pain's gone, she thought as she ran, which caused another bolt of pain to slice through her, but then she was next to Alik, who was stooping down to crawl into her tent, and there was no time to think of the pain.

"No!" she shouted, grabbing him by the sleeve and shaking it. "Come on, Alik, come on! You have to get away from there!"

"Get *back*!" he shouted in reply, pushing her away from him. "Get back to higher ground!"

"No!" she cried, and then screamed "NO!" as she felt the wall of water rushing towards them. Alik's fingers closed around her arm, but she slipped right through them and ran straight at the ford, twisting around Seva and pushing him back towards safety as he tried to grab her, not stopping until she was in the ford, the water already rising past her knees, the stones shifting and rolling under her feet. She could hear faint cries from the others as they attempted to reach her and pull her back, but already the wall of water was coming towards her, drowning out all other sound and repelling all attempts to rescue her.

Let the river take me, she thought as the wall of water hit her with the force of a galloping horse. *I'll drown soon*, she thought as it filled her nose and mouth, forcing her down onto the streambed. *Let the river take me.*

Something lifted her off the streambed and onto the surface of the raging waters. She could *see* herself being forced into the pebbles and mud, held down by the current until her lungs filled with water and the life left her body, and she could *see* herself slipping and sliding back down the bank into the deep pool after her lover had smashed her head in instead of pulling her out, but she could also *see* herself being picked up by the current and carried to the surface, and when her face broke free of the water and she sucked in a great gasping breath, she realized that that last vision had been the true one. She lifted up her arms to try to swim, and she could *see* how her arms were overlapped by other, ghostly arms, and both sets were desperately clawing and churning at the water, trying to lift her up higher.

Vika? she thought. *Can you hear me?*

...a bit...

Vika, you have to let me go.

...why?... ...you took me...

I know. To save you. To let you let go.

...no... ...deserve...vengeance...justice...

Dasha looked up. The rain had abruptly stopped, and the moon was already out, the tiny sliver of the first day of the waxing moon sailing through the sky, but still lighting a golden path on the water in which they floated.

You need peace, she said. *There is no vengeance for you, and you've already taken it a hundred times over. That was so long ago, it doesn't matter what you deserve, and you couldn't get it anyway. But what you **need** is peace, and I can give that to you.*

...why?...

Because you came to me. Because your hunger for justice and vengeance has led to injustice. How many have you killed, to keep you alive for your quest?

...many...

I can't give you justice, and I can't give them justice either, Dasha told her. *You may have started out seeking justice, or something like it, but it's gone beyond that. You've let your pain become the only pain that matters, and it's twisted you into something terrible. I can feel you, Vika, all day you've been riding inside of me and I can **feel** you, and I know that you were once very like me. You wanted things to be better than they were, didn't you? Just like I do.*

*That's why you came to the sanctuary: because you wanted things to be better than they are, you wanted **people** to be more than just mud and blood and stupidity. You wanted them to be something higher, purer, more perfect, than they are, and you wanted to lead the way. And that's what drew you to your lover, isn't it? He felt the same. Or so you thought. Only...he broke, didn't he? When it really mattered, he broke down and betrayed you, he showed you that he was just mud and blood and stupidity, like all the rest of them.*

*...he **murdered** me...* A wail of a pain that even now, generations later, could not be assuaged.

Yes he did. And you murdered him in turn, didn't you? You hunted him down and drained the life out of him, and then you did the same to all the other faithless lovers who crossed your path. And then it wasn't just faithless lovers anymore, was it? You were going to drain me, weren't you, and I've never been anyone's lover, or broken my faith to anyone.

...you've betrayed. I could sense it. You've betrayed, and you will again. I always sense betrayal...

*That may be so. But I've never betrayed **you**, have I? Any more than all your other victims have, other than that first one. And even he...you shouldn't have killed him, Vika. You shouldn't have killed him. It didn't make things any better. You got so caught up in justice, in balancing out the scales, that you forgot about making things better. And so things became worse instead.*

*...I have the **right**...*

*It doesn't matter. You wanted justice, but you wanted only to give it to others, without taking it in return. And then it doesn't matter how justified you are, because this isn't a matter of justice anymore, it's a matter of mercy, and that's what I'm going to give you. All of you. I'm going to **help** you.*

...how?... ...no one else ever could...

Dasha opened her eyes, and looked up at the tiny waxing moon. She looked over at the left bank of the stream, and thought she caught sight of amber slanted eyes, watching her from the trees. And then she looked right, and saw large dark eyes gazing at her expectantly.

I've been carrying you inside me all day, she told Vika. *I've felt your pain. I feel **compassion** for you. And for your victims, as well. But also for you. I can't say I wouldn't have done any differently, if I had been you. And that's why I'll be able to help you. Because you're not something separate from me, something that I want to cut off and throw away in order to pretend that we have nothing in common. If you can't feel for others, you have nothing, and you certainly can't help them. But I **can** feel for you, because we were not just two, but one for a time. You helped me, you brought me to the water, and now I'm going to bring you back to land. We will part ways, but we won't ever part, not really. I'll always have a little piece of you inside of me.*

She took a deep breath and plunged down under the water, diving all the way to the bottom, feeling herself dissolve into its coolness—and then she popped up, thrust back up to the surface by an invisible force. She began to swim towards the near shore. When she looked at her arms, all she could see was the moonlight glinting on them, with no sign of their ghostly doubles.

She brought herself to the bank in a few strokes, and crawled onto land. When she looked back, she thought she saw a patch of mist rise out of the water on the far bank, and then dissipate in the moonlight. Amber eyes blinked at her, and then winked out.

"Come on," Dasha said to the deer who was waiting for her by the streambank. "We have to go back. They must be frantic."

The deer leaned down and lipped at her hair, and then snorted.

"I know," said Dasha. "I'm wet *again*. It's a wonder I haven't caught my death from a chill yet. Come on. Let's go find the others."

The deer led her upstream, weaving in and out amongst the trees, showing her a path in the darkness. The stream had already returned to its banks, the only sign of the storm the water droplets that rained down on them as they brushed through the leaves.

They had not gone very far at all before they heard the sounds of crashing and shouting.

"Yes," Dasha said, when the deer stopped, pricking her ears in the direction of the sounds. "That's them. I think I can find them on my own now."

The doe snorted and shook her head.

"Very well," said Dasha. "But I'll walk in front. You can run away whenever you want to. I'm sure you don't want to be around them."

The doe allowed her to step to the front, but followed close behind, nudging her in the back with her muzzle whenever Dasha hesitated or stumbled.

"Dasha! Dasha!" It was Svetochka who first caught sight of her, and came running up to her, throwing her arms around her, heedless of her soaking clothing. "You're alive! She's alive! Dasha's alive!"

The others came running over, slapping her on the back and whooping with joy.

"Give her some space!" Oleg was the last to arrive, and when he came running up, he was as soaked as Dasha. He must have been out in the middle of the stream, searching for her. He pushed the others back. "Give her some space!" He threw his arms around her, crushing the breath out of her.

"We thought you were dead!" he said into her dripping hair. "We thought you were dead!" He pulled back, wiping his face. Dasha thought that some of the moisture on it was from tears, not just streamwater and rain.

"I'm not even injured," Dasha assured him. "Just a little damp. And the doe brought me back, once I'd gotten out of the water." She looked around, but the doe was gone, and no one else seemed to have noticed her. "I guess they didn't trust me not to get lost." She smiled to show it was a joke, but Oleg didn't seem to find it even remotely funny.

"I won't ask *why* you did it," he said, holding her almost painfully firmly by the shoulder as he walked her back to the campsite. "No doubt you were in the grip of forces beyond your control."

"I just *knew* what had to be done," she told him. "I saw it, and I knew it was a true vision, so I followed it."

"Of course you did," he said. "But couldn't you have told us beforehand?"

"There wasn't time," she said, trying and failing not to sound defensive. It had all been so clear at the time, and it had in fact turned out well, but he was still making her feel as if she'd done something wrong, acted foolishly and thoughtlessly.

"We thought you'd died! Well," he admitted, "we guessed that... *something* was behind your actions, and that you might have a chance at living, but we saw you run out into the water, Dasha, we saw you run out into the water and be carried away by the flood, and we couldn't find you! I—if I weren't gods-touched, if I could die like a mortal man, Dasha, I think I would have died right then!"

"No you wouldn't," Dasha told him. "You'd have run out into the water, just like you did."

He gave her a sideways glance. "Is this something you can *see*?" he asked, his words caustic.

"Yes. I can see it now. You wouldn't have died, you'd have run out to try to save me. And if I had died, you still wouldn't have died with me. You think now that you would, but you'll never give up your life for me."

He ground his teeth. "I..." he began.

"I'm not saying you wouldn't want to. I'm saying that you won't. I can sense it. I'm going to survive...all this," she waved her hands to indicate the road, and the water, and the night sky, "and you're not going to give up your life for me. So don't worry about it."

"I'm glad you're so certain," he said sourly. "Pardon me for saying so, but your visions have never given reason for this kind of certainty before."

"I know. But this isn't even a vision. Visions are possibilities, not certainties. This is a sense of what's almost certainly going to happen."

He stopped and turned to face her, grabbing both her shoulders. "Don't let your certainty in your survival lead you into anything foolish," he told her. "I remember what it was like, when I was seventeen and foolhardy, and even more what I was like when the gods first took me. I was crushed down—and then raised up, filled with more strength, more life, than I could have ever imagined possible, back when I was an ordinary man. I ran through the woods like a wild thing, challenging all who came across me. Which meant elk and wolves and bears." He smiled ruefully. "And I didn't lose, if by 'not losing' you mean 'not dying,' but I didn't win, either. What's happened to you may not be that different. With Vika in you, you may feel like you can take on water, and win. But *no one* can take on water and win. You're not invincible, no matter how you might feel right now."

"I don't think I'm invincible," said Dasha, her voice sounding smaller and more childish, more apologetic, than she would have liked. If he wanted her to be strong and brave, to stand up for herself, why was he always putting her in places where she had to back down and apologize? She shook her head to rid it of the irritation.

"I don't think I'm invincible," she repeated, more confidently. "It's not that. It's not like you're describing about yourself. I just feel like I'm going to survive, that's all. All this time I've been having visions of disaster, seeing myself falling from my horse, drowning, being caught in a burning building, being murdered—but not now. It's like all that's been washed away, as if all those were false visions of possibilities that aren't going to happen, now that they've been washed away by the water I jumped into. I've been running and running from it, afraid of it, and it's been chasing and chasing me, giving me visions of all the bad things that could happen to me if I turn away from it, but now that I've jumped in, those things aren't going to happen."

"So you think now," said Oleg.

"Other bad things could still happen," said Dasha.

"Other bad things could *always* still happen," said Oleg, but his mouth already starting to quirk into a smile.

"I know. But I'm not running and hiding from them anymore, or at least, I didn't run and hide from them tonight, and that's changed things. Made things better."

He sighed. "I hate that you're probably right," he said. "If you were anyone else—if you were someone else's daughter, or even another of my own daughters—I'd say you were surely right. But Dasha, we can't lose *you*. You can't go risking yourself."

"I think sometimes I have to," Dasha told him. "I think that's what I'm here for. I think that's what jumping into the water showed me." *And you of all people shouldn't lecture me on being careful,* she thought but did not say. *You of all people, who agreed to make me to be what I was, shouldn't lecture me on saving my life. Not when you of all people had to know that it was going to be sacrificed. Not when you of all people know what it's like to be used for something greater than yourself, not when you of all people produced me for the sole purpose of being used for something greater than myself.*

He clenched his jaw as if he could guess her unspoken thoughts, and then released it in a long exhale. "Well...you're probably right... but I don't have to like it." He put his arm around her shoulders. "Come on. Let's get you changed into something dry, if you have anything dry left, and see about getting some sleep. We might as well catch a little rest before we put ourselves at the mercy of the castrates." He shuddered. "Which reminds me." He dropped his voice. "Is the pain gone?"

"For the moment," Dasha told him. "It might come back."

"Pain normally does," he said.

The soaking in the stream had, Dasha was distressed to discover when she changed into her last dry outfit, caused her bloodcloths to bleed out onto to her clothes, but at least a lot of the blood had been washed away as she had been tumbled about. She rinsed it out as best she could, surreptitiously, hoping that the others would take it for normal care after the dunking she'd had, and then, aching all over, crawled back into her damp tent and into her damp bedclothes, and closed her eyes. She thought she might not be able to fall asleep, or she might have bad dreams, but she slipped into a deep sleep between one breath and the next.

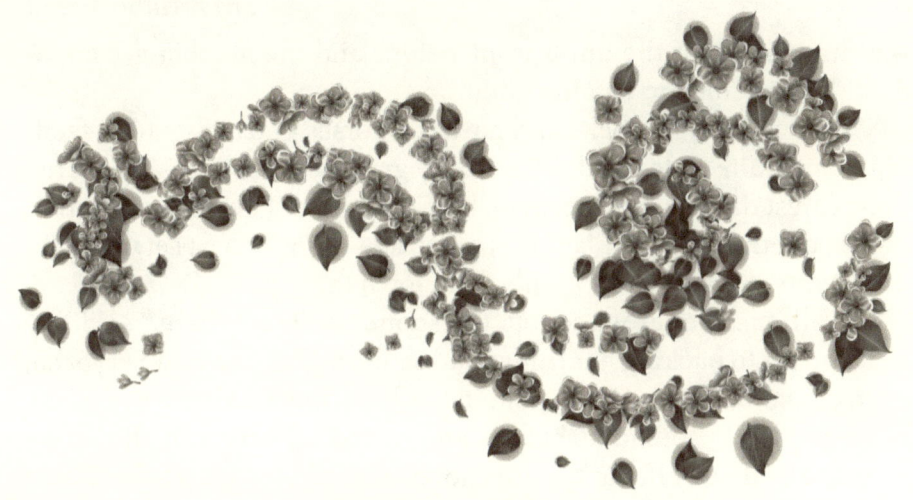

Chapter Twenty-Eight

The next day dawned very early, even under the trees, with a coolness that was more of spring than of summer, no matter the growing length of the days. Their things were still sodden, despite the breeze that was just strong enough to blow away the mosquitoes, but they packed them all up anyway, deciding to take advantage of the clear morning and reach the sanctuary as soon as possible, with the hopes of a warm welcome and the chance to dry their things out there, and perhaps replace their spoiled supplies—some of their food had been gotten soaked in the rain, and would start to mold soon.

"Of course, they may not have much to give us, no matter how much we offer to pay for it," Oleg said, looking with disgust at the wet barley, buckwheat, and oats. "I doubt they're over-rich themselves, and now is a lean time of year for everyone."

"Do we have enough to make it to Lesnograd?" asked Dasha. A vision of them starving in the forest rose before her. *So much for not being troubled by troubling possibilities*, she thought, shaking her shoulders to rid them of the prickles that were running across them. Once she had lain down the second time, she had slept heavily, and awoken feeling much the same as before, except for an unerring sense of which direction lay water. Which could be a handy skill, she had to admit, but it was annoying that the unpleasant visions and the fits that accompanied them seemed to be returning.

"If we tighten our belts and have the horses graze instead of feeding them grain," Oleg told them. "Only grazing takes time, and there's more forest than pasture between here and there. There's a waystation or two, but this isn't the black earth district—things aren't set up for fat merchants to travel comfortably from town to town."

"Well, the sooner we set off, the sooner we'll get there," said Dasha, and set to packing her things and saddling Poloska and Seryozha, trying to ignore the nagging pain in her belly that had returned *again*. It wasn't nearly so bad as before, and by the afternoon it should be over, she told herself, but the afternoon seemed very far off, and it was hard not to hate her body for doing this to her—*again*. As it insisted on doing every month.

Why wasn't she a horse, she lamented to herself as she adjusted Poloska's girth. Horses went into heat in the summer, but that was only for half the year or less, and they didn't suffer the pain of moon-blood. And their labors were much quicker, and thought to be much less painful, than those of human women. She definitely should have been born a horse. Or a deer, she thought, smiling as she remembered the doe from the night before, and the one from earlier on the road as well. That might be even better, because no one rode deer: a deer was unlikely to have a cruel mistress. Of course, deer were hunted and eaten by wolves and bears, and lived out in the woods without so much as a barn for shelter, and had no healers when they were injured or ill, and...probably she didn't really want to be a deer, she told herself, but right now, like so many other nows, she didn't want to be herself either.

I need to stop dwelling on this thought unless there's something I can do about it, she told herself. *And remember all the bad things that happened from pretending to be someone else!* Only—she looked at her arms as they moved to attach her packs to Seryozha—she *wasn't* quite the same person as she had been before, was she? She'd briefly been Vika as well as herself, and while Vika was mostly gone, she'd left a little bit of herself within Dasha, or changed Dasha in some way. Not as much as Dasha would have liked, but—her head swiveled around to look at the stream, which she could feel running through the back of her mind—she wasn't exactly the same girl she'd been before she'd encountered Vika, just the day before.

I hope I'm not becoming a ghost or a water-maiden, she thought, and had to fight off a vision of herself becoming cold and insubstantial, haunting some sorry streambed. *No!* she reminded herself. *That's a warning, not a certainty! That's what you **could** become, if you're not careful, but you **won't** because you've been warned. Now get on your horse and stop thinking about the pain in your belly and how your boots are still wet and they're already rubbing holes in your ankles. It'll all pass soon enough.*

The sun shone down on them through the break in the treetops that was the road, warming their heads and drying off the top of their packs, but the cool breeze continued flowing through the trees, chilling their legs and making them shiver for the first several versts of the journey. The moonblood pain did pass soon enough, just as Dasha had told herself it would, but the rubbing of her wet boots on her ankles only got worse and worse, until she wasn't sure she wouldn't rather have had the moonblood pain back, and she was assailed with visions of the blisters and sores that were surely being created taking septic and poisoning her—no! Because she'd clean the wounds and dress them in order to prevent that from happening. Baba Sofroniya had given her a concoction made of honey from her own bees that she'd said would prevent a wound from turning septic, even better than regular honey would. She would use that, and bandage the sores in clean linen, and then the vision would never come true.

Which is what she did when they stopped to rest, although she was surprised at how small the sores were. It had felt as if all the skin on her ankles had been stripped away, but in fact there were just two small patches, one on the inside of each ankle, each no bigger than a thumbnail.

"I must not be very tough at all," she said ruefully to Alik, who had come over to see what she was doing, and, she felt certain, to make sure she didn't suddenly run off and throw herself into a stream. "I felt like I was being flayed, but there's hardly any skin gone at all." And then she had to suppress a shudder as a vision came to her of what it must be like to actually be flayed. No! That was the kind of thing that the barbarians off to the West did, or maybe in the Hordes to the East, but flaying had never been in fashion in Zem'. Lots of other horrible things, yes, some of which had only ended when her mother had put a stop to them, but not that. Thank the gods, not that.

"Blisters hurt, Tsarinovna," he told her with a smile. "Even the toughest soldiers get brought down by blisters. I've got one right now," he went on, bending down to her and lowering his voice as if about to confide a secret, "that's making me want to cry like a child, my head for beheading."

"Well, sit down and let me treat it," Dasha told him.

"Oh no...I couldn't..." protested Alik, looking uncharacteristically, and rather comically, taken aback by her offer.

"No, I insist," said Dasha, feeling a rush of a new and unknown power as he looked at her uncertainly, and then slowly sat down in front of her and pulled off his right boot.

"It's there," he said, indicating a large burst blister, twice the size of the ones she had been complaining about, on the back of his heel. He kept his eyes on his foot, as if too shy (again, most uncharacteristically) to look at her.

"How long has this been going on?" she asked.

"A day or two, Tsarinovna," he said, still not looking at her.

"It must have hurt like the Black God itself," she said, washing it off with water from her waterskin.

He shrugged, and then bit his lip as she began applying the salve to the wound. She found herself studying the way his teeth pressed into his lip, and saw herself sinking her own teeth into that lip...she jerked her eyes away as if scalded, only to find them landing on the line of his jaw, which was already being covered with a fine dark growth of beard...she saw herself running her nails through that beard, and through the dark hair that was pulled back into a tail that revealed the back of his neck, which also cried out for the touch of her nails, as did the shoulders that strained against the linen of his shirt, and the chest whose fine dark hair she had glimpsed last night, when he had run up to her, soaked to the skin so that his nipples had shown clearly through the white linen...

Stop it! Dasha screamed at herself, her cheeks flaming and her whole body prickling as if about to go into a fit. *What are you **thinking**! He's your **guard**, by all the gods!*

But her errant thoughts reminded her that Boleslav Vlasiyevich was her mother's guard, and that hadn't stopped her mother, had it? Dasha found her eyes land on Alik's face so that she could compare him to Boleslav Vlasiyevich. Dark and slender, like Boleslav Vlasiyevich, but taller, and with eyes that were not only slanted, but, most unusually, dark.

"Are you from the steppe, Alik?" she asked, trying to distract herself and embarrassed to realize that she didn't actually know anything about him.

"I am, Tsarinovna," he told her, still not looking at her. "Or my mother is. My father was from the Hordes. I'm a halfblood. I don't know what my father'd think about this; whether he'd be proud or not of me for guarding the Tsarinovna." He flashed a brief grin at her, finally able to look up. "He loved my mother and the steppe well enough, but I don't think he ever warmed to Krasnograd."

"Well, I'm of the steppe, too," Dasha told him.

"That you are, Tsarinovna, that you are. Well, maybe he'd've forgiven you, then, although I don't think he'd've ever warmed to your eyes. He always said only evil spirits had blue eyes."

"Mine are as much green as blue," Dasha said.

"And so they are, Tsarinovna," said Alik, after peering into them. "Not sure that he'd see much of a difference, to be honest, but at least they're not completely round, like some people's. Maybe he'd be willing to let me guard you, if he knew that. Not that I've been doing such a grand job of guarding you," he added, looking away again.

"I'm still here, aren't I?" Dasha said, wrapping clean linen around the wound on his heel.

"No thanks to me, though. Mostly I've stood by while you've almost gotten drowned."

"I think that needed to happen," Dasha told him.

He snorted. "And next you'll be telling me you need to be wounded in an assassin's attack. Begging your pardon, Tsarinovna," he added. "I meant no disrespect. You're just so...you're just...still like a little girl...like a younger sister, or something."

"I'm not offended," said Dasha, although the remark about her being like a younger sister had nettled her more than it should have, and made her cheeks flame even more. How embarrassing that he saw her as a younger sister, when she'd just been having such...*womanly* thoughts about him. She stood up, and tried not to see the way he looked, sprawled so invitingly on the ground below her. This was *terrible!* Where had these thoughts *come* from?!

Vika, she thought. *Vika had taken a lover, Vika knew these kinds of thoughts, and now I know them.* Which was only sort of true. Dasha had had such thoughts before, but they had always been shrouded in such vagueness that she hardly knew what they were, and overlaid with the squeamishness provoked by the sight of the squeamish princes of Krasnograd, who could hardly bear to look at her, it seemed, or any other girl.

But now, perhaps because of the echoes of Vika's memories, perhaps because it was *time* for her to have such thoughts, whether she willed it or no, when she looked at Alik she saw not just a guard and a companion, but a potential lover as well, and she could imagine the ways in which she might take him.

Those visions led to more vision/realizations, as she saw that she could get a child off of him—not today, obviously, but in two weeks' time she could get a child off of him, if she so desired, make that next step into womanhood and ensure the succession of her mother's line, rather than her aunt's. She could even take him as a husband, as her foremothers had taken commoners before—as her own mother had, when it came to her conception. A whole set of possible married lives, happy and unhappy, played out before her in a fleeting series of visions, before being subsumed by another set of visions, this time of her having his child and abandoning him in favor of a nobleborn husband.

Stop it! she told herself. *He deserves none of this in truth, and not even in vision either!* She jerked her eyes away from him, and over to where Mitya and Seva were sitting together on a fallen tree and joking about something, and she could see, all too clearly, herself taking them as well. She forced her gaze off of them and let it land on Fedya. Who was scratching at the fuzzy beard he hadn't had time to shave that morning, no more than the rest of them had. *No no no*, she thought. *I can't feel that way about **Fedya**! The very thought is repulsive, and no doubt even more so for him!*

He looked over quizzically at her, and she was relieved to feel her blood cool at the entirely un-lover-like expression on his face. He was saying something to Svetochka, and the sight of them together had enough of a chilling effect—the only person Dasha could possibly want to take as a lover less than Fedya was Svetochka; in fact, it was hard to imagine *anyone* wanting to take her as a lover, which was unkind but Dasha couldn't help but think it—that Dasha was able to wrench her mind out of the course it had taken and onto more practical and appropriate matters.

"I think it's time to go," she told Alik.

"As it pleases you, Tsarinovna," he said, jumping to his feet. "And my thanks for the healing." For an instant he gave her a look that made her wonder if he'd been sharing some of the same thoughts as herself, but then he gave her a little bow and went over to the other guards, and soon enough they were off and Dasha was able to turn her mind to other thoughts.

By midafternoon the strip of sky above them had changed from a clear blue to a dark gray, as more clouds rolled in.

"Will it storm?" Oleg asked Dasha, watching her with a curiosity that made her squirm with embarrassment.

"Not this afternoon, I don't think," she told him. "There's not enough water in the air. Maybe later tonight, or tomorrow. But it will be dark and cloudy."

"Well, we should be under shelter soon enough," he said. "The sanctuary can't be too far away."

They had been riding through pines, whose tall trunks let in a little light and allowed them to see out into the forest, but the pines changed back to firs, and the forest darkened and thickened around them, even as the light from the sky faded. The narrow path wound back and forth between the trees, making it twice as long as it needed to be, or so complained Seva as they wove back and forth.

"It's avoiding the stream," Dasha told them. "It's running off there to our left, and the road's avoiding it."

Oleg frowned at that, but said nothing, and after another verst or so of twisting through the trees, they began to pass prayer trees, with ribbons hanging from their branches, and faces carved in their trunks.

"Did you see that?" said Seva suddenly.

"See what?" asked Oleg.

"I thought I saw...something flashed at me, like sunlight, only there's no sun here."

"It was probably nothing," Oleg told him, but he frowned some more, and urged them forward.

Dasha tried not to look at the prayer trees, but her eyes kept going back to them, and she, too, though she caught a glimpse of something flashing at her, or maybe—was it winking? She could hear the stream running off to their left even with her regular hearing now, and had to resist the urge to go to it. The thirst that had plagued her the day before was gone, but the fear of water she had always felt before had been replaced with a pull towards it, and despite the coolness of the air she wanted to go wading and immerse herself in the flowing current.

They came to two tall pine trees, standing on either side of the path like sentinels. The branches had been cut away from the lower part of their trunks, and large freshly carved faces stared out at any travelers who came their way. Ribbons hung from every branch within reach, marking hundreds of silent prayers.

"Is something moving in the branches?" whispered Seva. "Is something *moving* the branches?"

"It's the wind," said Oleg, also speaking quietly.

"There's no wind," Seva objected. And it was true. The cool breeze that had been blowing on them all day had died away, leaving the air feeling breathless and stagnant.

"It's a squirrel!" Dasha exclaimed, catching sight of a flash of red fur. "It's nothing but a squirrel!" Tension she hadn't known she'd been holding released, and the fit that had been building died away. The squirrel poked her head out of the branches, and looked down directly at Dasha.

"We mean you no harm," Dasha called to her. "We only seek to pass by."

The squirrel turned her head this way and that, looking at Dasha out of each eye in turn, and then turned and skittered back up the branch, disappearing into the tree's crown. A breath of wind hit them, making the ribbons on the trees flutter.

"Come on," said Dasha. "It's safe now."

"It wasn't safe before?" muttered Mitya, but quietly. They rode between the sentinel trees and through a thick spruce grove, the wind sighing through the spruce needles and ruffling their hair, and then arrived at a palisade fence with a closed gate. Human skulls had been placed on the points of the palings on either side of the gate.

"What *is* it about skulls?" murmured Mitya, eyeing the skulls with distaste. "Why do these Northerners pile them up at every turn?"

"They're wards," Oleg told them. "They're supposed to warn the people inside if intruders come. And they're like scarecrows, too: they scare intruders off."

"And honest visitors," said Mitya, moving to the back of their group as Oleg rapped on the gate.

"I think the skulls are looking at me," whispered Svetochka, moving closer to Dasha. Dasha glanced up at the skulls, and quickly looked away, trying to convince herself that Svetochka's words weren't true, and that the skulls weren't looking at them. Fedya was looking down at the ground and swallowing, his hands clutching convulsively at his reins.

"You don't have to do this, you know," Dasha said to him, leaning over and speaking into his ear. "We can just stop here for the night and then ride on, taking you with us to Lesnograd. You don't have to do this."

"Yes I do," he said. "I do." He relaxed his hands on the reins and lifted his chin and squared his shoulders. "This is what I must do. I just didn't think"—he gave her a quick sidelong glance—"I'd be so *nervous* about it. I didn't think I'd be so scared of something I know I have to do. I thought once I made the decision, it would be easy to go through with it."

Dasha opened her mouth to tell him once again that he didn't have to go through with this folly, but found herself saying, "Maybe that's part of the test," instead. "Maybe you have to fight through the fear over and over again to show that you're worthy," she told him.

He smiled and straightened his shoulders some more. "Maybe you're right," he said. And then the gate swung open, and they rode through.

Dasha tried not to stare at the brother who'd opened the gate for them, and in truth, he looked much like anyone else in a sanctuary robe. There was no sign of the mutilations he'd undergone—unless he hadn't undergone them yet? But more brothers came up to them once they were inside the compound, and they all looked perfectly normal too.

Or rather, they either kept their eyes fixed on the ground, unable to look their visitors in the face, or they gazed on the newcomers with eyes that burned with a fervent light that raised a faint unease in the pit of Dasha's stomach, but they didn't seem visibly deformed. A couple of them had almost freakishly long faces and round eyes, with cheekbones that weren't visible at all, as if they didn't have a drop of steppe blood in them, and Dasha realized with a jolt that they must be Westerners, from Rutsi or someplace similar. But other than their appearance, they didn't seem any different than anyone else there, and they stood there silently in the background, making no attempt to harm anyone or do anything strange.

Perhaps it's not so bad, Dasha told herself. Fedya seemed to be thinking the same thing as he looked around, taking it all in.

An older man came over to them, smiling the faint smile Dasha associated with sanctuary brothers. "Greetings, travelers," he said with a bow. "Welcome to our sanctuary." When he straightened up and looked at each of them in turn, the fervency of his eyes made Dasha shiver. She would like to be that certain about something—except that she wouldn't. "I am Brother Afanasy. Do you seek shelter for the night?" he asked.

"We do," Oleg told him. "And one of us wishes to join you." He nodded towards Fedya, who gulped but rode forward to stand in front of the others.

"Welcome, brother," said Afanasy, his smile widening. "You have made the first step on the path to wisdom and immortality. And none of the rest of you wish to join us? After all, people come from all over the Known World to take what we have to offer. Our path transcends the petty borders of Zem' and all the lands around it." He glanced from person to person, his eyes, it seemed to Dasha, lingering especially long on her.

"No," said Oleg gruffly. "We're on our own journey. We just picked up Fedya here on the road, and decided to escort him here before he got himself into any more trouble than he already had."

"Your charity is commendable," said Brother Afanasy, and Dasha couldn't tell if he were making fun of them or not. Perhaps a bit of both. "This way, if you please. My brothers and sisters will take your horses, and escort you to your cells. And our new brother will come with me."

The pit of Dasha's stomach clenched at those words, but no vision accompanied her fear, and Fedya dismounted and followed Brother Afanasy readily enough, so she had no choice but to dismount herself and hand Seryozha's reins over to a brother—no, it was a sister, Dasha corrected herself when she looked more closely at the woman's face, it was a sister—who was hovering silently beside her, waiting to take her horses.

"I'll take Poloska myself," Dasha told her. "Seryozha's easy enough to care for, but Poloska can be finicky." This was only partly true. Dasha's real motivation was to avoid going to her "cell"—how unwelcoming that sounded!—for as long as possible, and also to see if she could find out more about the sanctuary from her new companion. Questioning another woman seemed more likely to lead to results than questioning a man.

It took several tries for Dasha to get anything out of the sister other than her name, which was Sister Anastasiya, but she finally managed to extract the information from her that she was the daughter of a minor merchant from Pristanograd, that she had fled to the sanctuary there at the age of eighteen, and she was now thirty-six and had been with the castrates for half her life.

"Or all of my life, really," said Sister Anastasiya, her eyes starting to glow with the same fervor Dasha had seen in the others. "For I count it started when I joined my brothers and sisters here and took the seal. Before that I wasn't really alive. I came to the compound by the sea, where they do all the cutting, so that the wounds may be cleansed with salt, with the immortal, life-giving water of the ocean, and I let them cut away everything I wished to be free of, and, and—it was marvelous, sister, marvelous!"

"Is it so different once you take the seal, then?" Dasha asked, intrigued despite herself. She remembered the feeling of defilement she'd experienced when that man at the waystation had tried to grab her, the awful pain of her moonblood yesterday, and the shameful hunger she had felt when she had gazed down on Alik this morning. The thought of cutting all that out of her, leaving all that behind, suddenly seemed very tempting. One quick cut, and a lifetime of gentle contemplation, rather than struggling with all the ugliness that was life out in the world, all the dirt and filth, of the mind as well as of the body, that was the business of life and living and making more life.

"Oh, sister!" exclaimed Sister Anastasiya, reaching out and taking Dasha's hand. "You can't imagine the peace that comes over you! The sense of *rightness!* The knowledge that you have finally, after so much struggle and doubt, done the right thing!"

How much struggle and doubt could she have undergone? Dasha thought to herself. *She was only eighteen when she came here and took the seal. Only a year older than me.* While it seemed to Dasha that she herself had experienced a great deal of struggle and doubt, when faced with Sister Anastasiya's statement, it suddenly seemed ridiculous. When she thought of what people who had more years than them had gone through in those extra years, things that Dasha doubted she herself could go through—could she really conceive a child with a man she hardly knew at the gods' behest, like her mother? And then carry and give birth to that child, like her mother and so many other women? Overthrow her sister, like her mother? Or lose her mother and her daughter, like Aunty Olga? Or leave her family behind for years, like her sister Vladya? Or die and come back, like her father? Or...sometimes *none* of that seemed possible to Dasha. She looked over Poloska's back at Sister Anastasiya, whose thin face was half-hidden by the hood of her robe. She looked too lined and worn to be only thirty-six, Dasha thought, and the only thing that shone in her was the fervency of her eyes, as if she were burning herself out from the inside with the passion of her belief.

"Did it not...hurt?" Dasha asked hesitantly. "Taking the seal, I mean?" When she thought of *that*, she was astonished that Sister Anastasiya had survived it, just as she was with all the things that others had survived.

Sister Anastasiya tried to smile, but a grimace of pain crossed her face instead. "A bit," she admitted. "I had the breasts removed first, and that hurt the worst. Many sisters don't survive that."

Dasha shuddered. "And...and the other?" she asked. "Pardon me, but they say that you have to, to sew yourself up."

"The area is cleansed," Sister Anastasiya told her. "All the offending flesh is cut away. And then the opening is sewn partially shut. Some have tried to close it entirely, to stop the flow of moonblood, but we have not yet achieved that level of purity and perfection. A small opening must be left for the body to rid itself of the filth of moonblood. The pain..." She made a face involuntarily. "It can make your moontime longer and more painful, as a punishment for your lack of purity."

"I see," said Dasha, all thoughts of joining the sanctuary banished at that horrible news. The thought of cutting off her breasts and damaging the entrance to her womb, horrid as it was, was difficult for her to picture clearly, but with the awfulness of yesterday still fresh in her mind, the thought of voluntarily doing something that would make it worse was too terrible to contemplate. She didn't know whether to offer Sister Anastasiya her sympathies, or rave at her for being a lunatic. She settled for brushing off Poloska as best she could, and giving her the few handfuls of hay that Sister Anastasiya allowed her to take.

"Hay is hard to come by, this deep in the woods," Sister Anastasiya explained to her. "And we all must overcome the weakness and lusts of the body, horses as well as humans."

"I see," said Dasha. She noted that the two horses who belonged to the sanctuary were uncomfortably bony. "You don't...have the horses take the seal as well?" she asked.

Sister Anastasiya frowned. "It was tried with mares," she said. "But to no avail. They are too tied to their filthy, mortal bodies. So now we only keep geldings, and not too many—horses are too much of the earth to have a place here, and we do not have much need of their services, anyway. If travelers come with mares, we only allow them into the sanctuary if they are not in heat. Try as we might, we have not been able to get rid of that abomination."

"Ah," said Dasha, hastily trying to calculate when Poloska could be expected to go into heat. Probably not until next week, she decided with relief. She let Sister Anastasiya lead her out of the stable and over to a low-roofed building that stood a little apart from the main building.

"This is where the cells for visitors are," Sister Anastasiya told her. "You will each have your own little cell, to facilitate contemplation and purity. Our new brother will stay with us, so that Father Afanasy can question him, and help guide his mind."

"Oh," said Dasha. She didn't like the sound of that one bit, but she had already tried to talk Fedya out of this a dozen times, and each attempt had met with failure.

The cell Sister Anastasiya brought her to was just slightly larger than the thin mattress stuffed with pine and fir needles that lay on its floor, and entirely lacking in a stove, fireplace, window, shelves, chests, wardrobe, table, chairs, or any of the other things that Dasha had always thought a bedchamber should contain. There was a single hook on the door for hanging things on; Sister Anastasiya observed with, Dasha thought, a fair amount of censure, that Dasha wouldn't be able to hang all her packs on it, and would have to pile up her things on the floor.

"We do not need all these outer trappings that people living out in the world seem to believe necessary," Sister Anastasiya told her.

"And food," Dasha said, opening one of the packs she had taken off Seryozha. "We carry our food with us, you see. Only some of it got damp in the storm last night, and will need to be used before it spoils. You wouldn't want to trade for it? You could use it for supper tonight, before it goes bad, and give us dry supplies in exchange."

Sister Anastasiya bit her lip, and Dasha could tell that she was interested, even though she thought she shouldn't be.

"Sister Taisya is in charge of the kitchen," she said finally. "Go to her, and see what she says."

Sister Taisya, when Dasha found her and the kitchen after wandering around the compound and getting several strange looks from startled brothers, was slightly less peculiar than the other inhabitants of the sanctuary whom Dasha had met so far. Dasha supposed that having to deal with food forced her to be a little more of this world than the others in the sanctuary. She accepted the damp barley that Dasha had in her pack, and offered to give her dry lentils in exchange.

"Not that we've much," she told Dasha. "It's a hard time of year, before the first harvest comes in, and we only get what people bring us, or what we can buy, and we're not here to earn coin, now are we?"

"I guess not," said Dasha, looking around the simple kitchen. At least it was better than her cell.

"I can see you're used to high living, my heart," said Sister Taisya, patting her on the hand. "Daughter of a noblewoman, are you?"

"Ah...yes," said Dasha. She was about to start in her story of being Susanna's maid and companion, but then stopped herself, remembering how poorly that had turned out the last time she'd used it. "I'm traveling to visit my kin in Lesnograd," she said instead.

"And how's the journey been so far, my dove?" asked Sister Taisya.

"Interesting," Dasha told her. "I've learned many things. For instance, I'd never heard of this sanctuary before."

Sister Taisya laughed. "Most haven't, my dove, most haven't. We keep to ourselves." Her face turned serious. "There's many as wouldn't understand us, and would try to stop us—for our own good, they'd say—or'd attack us for things as don't concern 'em."

"I know," said Dasha.

"And probably you're thinking just like 'em," continued Sister Taisya, a shrewd look on her homely face. She had crooked teeth under a crooked nose, and small deepset gray eyes, and gray hair that she'd pulled back in a plain kerchief, and looked like a strict tutor or someone's dried-up old aunt. Dasha couldn't help but wonder if she'd chosen the sanctuary because she hadn't been able to find a husband. "That's not what I'm thinking," Dasha protested, responding both to Sister Taisya's words, and her own thoughts.

"Sure you are, my heart," said Sister Taisya, with another little pat of her hand. "Because you're young and pretty and noble, and you can't imagine giving all that up and volunteering to undergo pain and privation, can you?"

"Well..." said Dasha.

"Not all of us are pretty and noble, and none of us stay young, my dove," Sister Taisya told her. "And pain isn't the worst thing in life."

"What is worse, then?" asked Dasha. "Whenever I've been in pain, it's seemed pretty bad to me."

Sister Taisya laughed. "And when have *you* ever been in real pain, my dove?" she asked.

"I suppose I haven't, not compared with what others have endured. But that's the point! Even the small amounts of pain I've experienced have been very bad! Much worse than I thought they would be! I don't think taking on *more* pain would make me very happy!"

"And is happiness the most important thing in life, my love?"

"Well...no. But I mean to say, I think more pain would just make me bitter and angry. I don't think anyone would be very well served by my suffering."

"That depends on what you do with the suffering, my love," Sister Taisya told her, now speaking seriously. "That depends on whether you let it make you greater than you are, or smaller."

"I always feel like it's making me smaller," Dasha told her. "Like I'm a mouse caught in the talons of an owl, or something like that."

"And is not a mouse caught in the talons of an owl part of something greater than herself? For she's not just the mouse anymore, she's also becoming part of the owl, lifted up above the forest floor and flying through the air."

"Yes, but...I'm sure she'd rather not become part of the owl. I think she'd rather just stay the mouse."

"That's her mouse-voice talking. But the *world* isn't served by her staying a mouse, and neither is she, not in the long run. Better to be the owl than the mouse, my love, even if that means impaling yourself on her talons. For the pain will not last forever."

"Yes, but while it's happening, it *feels* like forever," Dasha argued.

"And thus gives you its own form of deathlessness!" said Sister Taisya triumphantly. "It gives you the chance to live forever, even if only in your own feelings."

"Yes, but..." Dasha's thoughts were all in a jumble. Everything Sister Taisya said made sense, but it also seemed like the most senseless thing Dasha had ever heard. "Someone has to be the mouse," she found herself saying. "We can't all be owls, nor should we. We have to be mice as well, and it's easy enough to say that it's better to be the owl than the mouse, or that the mouse should suffer and die so that the owl can live, but that's all owl-thinking. We need more mouse-thinking."

"It's the way of the world, my girl," said Sister Taisya. "Nothing any of us can do about it." Which seemed to Dasha like a ridiculous thing to say by someone who had cut off her breasts and sewn up the entrance to her womb, but before she could figure out how to say this to Sister Taisya without being unforgivably rude, Sister Taisya went on blithely, "It's the way of the world, my dear, and we just have to learn how to become the owl."

Owls die too, Dasha thought, as Sister Taisya said, "And the owl is elevating the mouse, blessing her, you know. Pain is a blessing, pain cleanses. Giving pain is a great honor, as much as taking it."

"Mmm," said Dasha, not knowing what to say to this at all. "So where do you get your food, then, if you have so few visitors?" she asked. "Do you have gardens?"

"Some, my dear, some, but the middle of the forest is not the best place to grow gardens. Too many roots and needles, not enough sunlight. We have our little garden, though, that we all work in, and the forest provides, as well. Mushrooms, berries, and game."

"Oh," said Dasha, not liking that mention of game and pretending to ignore it. Hunting seemed like a very strange thing for members of a sanctuary to engage in, unless, she supposed, they were from the Sisterhood of the Wolf. She was certain that no one from her grandmother's sanctuary hunted. But what else could they do, out here in the middle of the woods...it was the way of the world, just as Sister Taisya had said...only she could sense that that was *wrong*, so wrong, although she couldn't form the words to explain why. "Well, I hope you're able to make good use of the barley," she said instead.

"We will, my love, we will. We haven't had barley in two months at least, and I'm sure we'll enjoy it greatly. Now you run along, and we'll call you for supper."

Dasha obeyed, glad to get away from Sister Taisya and her confusing arguments, and went back to her cell, where she tried to wash herself as best she could, which was not very well. They must have a bathhouse here, but it hadn't been offered, and she didn't want to ask. They obviously lived very poorly here, and might not have the firewood to spare—no, living in the middle of the forest, they must have plenty of firewood—or more likely, they frowned on excessive bathing.

Some sanctuaries were like that, Dasha had heard, although she would have thought that a place as concerned with purity as this one would require everyone to steam every day. Maybe they did, but they didn't want their guests to pollute their bathhouse with their uncut bodies. Maybe that was it. Or they just hadn't thought about it. Itchy and sticky as she felt, Dasha decided she didn't want to bring up the bathing issue with them. She hung up her damp clothes as best she could with just the one hook on the door. They must have a place to wash and dry laundry as well, but again, they hadn't offered, and Dasha didn't want to ask. She hid herself as best she could behind the visitors' cells to wash the blood out of her bloodcloths (which were very bloody; the bleeding was heavier this month than usual, and Dasha tried and failed not to worry that something was wrong with her, and that she would run out of clean cloths before the others dried), thinking how wrong and how fitting it was that she should have her moontime right as she was here, as if in defiance of everything they were trying to do, and then snuck back to her cell to hang up the cloths to dry.

Not that they were going to dry very well in the damp air. She would be lucky if everything wasn't completely spoiled with mold by the time they arrived in Lesnograd. Well, if it was, she told herself, surely her family there wouldn't begrudge her some new clothes. Her mother had certainly given Vladya enough things during her time in Krasnograd.

Prickles began building up on the back of her neck as she finished hanging up her things. *No, not a fit!* she thought. The idea of having a fit in front of the people here at the sanctuary struck her as especially embarrassing. Maybe they would take it as a sign she was particularly impure, or try to tell her how she could stop them, and she'd be forced to take their advice, which she was loath to do. She shook her shoulders and rolled her neck, but the prickles kept building, giving her the sensation that something was staring at the back of her head.

Don't be silly, she told herself. *Nothing's looking at you. There isn't anything behind you other than your packs, piled in the corner. There's nothing there but shadows.*

Dasha's breath caught at that thought. She slowly turned around to face the pile of packs in the corner, her eyes the last part of her to make the turn, unwilling as they were to see what was there. But when she finally forced them to look, the only thing they saw was exactly what they should have: a pile of packs, lying in a dark corner.

See, she told herself. *You're just being silly. Now go find Susanna or someone, and sit with them so you won't be alone.* She began to turn back around and head for the door, when she caught sight of something out of the corner of her eye. She whipped back around, but nothing was there. She shook her head and turned to the door.

"I'm down here," said a voice at her feet.

Chapter Twenty-Nine

Dasha's back was pressed against the cell wall, and she was standing on her thin mattress, trying to get as far away from the thing as possible. She thought she might have screamed, but no one was trying to come rescue her, so either they were all too far away, or she had only imagined it. Maybe she was only imagining all of it, or it was all some vision she was trapped in, but it *felt* very real.

"Oh, don't worry," said the thing, arching its back like a cat and then sitting back on its haunches and looking up at her. "I don't bite."

"You're..." Her voice came out as a frightened squeak. She swallowed and tried again. "You're a domovaya," she said.

"Well spotted, young Tsarinovna," said the domovaya cheerfully. She was no taller than Dasha's knees, and looked sort of like a black cat, and sort of like a very tiny woman. Dasha's mother had told her that all the domoviye she had seen had looked old, very old, but this one looked young, not much more than Dasha's age, as much as something like that could be judged with such a creature.

"What are you doing here?" asked Dasha.

"What am I doing here? What do you think I'm doing here, young Tsarinovna. I've come for *you*."

"Why?" asked Dasha, hating the way her voice squeaked and trembled.

"Why? Because your mother agreed to give you to us, before you were even born. That's why."

"She wouldn't have done something like that!" cried Dasha indignantly.

"Why not?" asked the domovaya.

"Because...because she wouldn't have, that's why!"

"Is she opposed to the practice of taking wards, then?" asked the domovaya mildly.

"Well...no. She takes wards all the time. But this is different!"

"Why?" asked the domovaya. "Because you're special, different from all those girls whom your mother took as wards?"

"Well...no. Because...because she didn't *tell* me about it, that's why!"

"Tsk tsk." The domovaya shook her head. "Didn't tell you, did she? Never mentioned anything about you being trained, did she?"

"Well...yes, she did. She said that I might need special training, more than what my tutors could provide me. And she said that there were those who could give it to me, who had offered to give it to me. But I always thought she meant my father, or his companions!"

"You always thought, did you?" said the domovaya, shaking her head slowly. "That's a mistake right there, young Tsarinovna, always thinking. I see we've a lot of training to do with you."

"What kind of training could you possibly offer me?!" demanded Dasha. "You're just, just...you don't do *magic*. You just...guard the home. And most of the time, you don't even do that!" As soon as she said them, she wished she could take the words back, but they had already left her mouth, and there was no retrieving them.

"We don't do magic, do we?" said the domovaya. "And you do, I suppose?"

"Well...that's not what I meant! I meant that we have different kinds of magic!"

"I see. Because you have the magic of women, I suppose, and we have some other kind?"

"Yes! That's what I meant."

"And how good are you at this women's magic, young Tsarinovna?"

"Well...not very good," Dasha admitted. "Not very good at all, to be honest. But what other kind of magic could I have?"

"A very good question, young Tsarinovna. A very good question. And one we would be happy to answer for you."

"I don't think I could have *your* kind of magic," said Dasha, her face twisting into a grimace of distaste as she looked down at the domovaya. It wasn't that she was *ugly*, exactly. In fact, if she could have taken her as a pet, she would have. But she wasn't exactly a human, either, and the thought of Dasha having her kind of magic felt *wrong*, just like the thought of becoming an owl did.

"Probably not, young Tsarinovna," agreed the domovaya. "But you don't have any other kind, either, so you might as well come with us. Which is why I'm here. To take you away."

"Take me away...I can't just run off with you! I can't. I'm on a journey. With my father. I can't just *leave* him. He wouldn't understand."

"I think, young Tsarinovna, that he would understand better than anyone else in the Known World."

"Yes, but...I don't want to! I want to go on my journey, with my father, and visit my kin in Lesnograd!"

"Your kin," repeated the domovaya slowly. "You think they are your kin, then? Your...kind?"

"Yes, of course! What else would they be?"

"A very good question, young Tsarinovna," said the domovaya again. "And I suppose you are right. But they may not be your *only* kin."

"Well, no. I have kin in Krasnograd, of course, and in the steppe."

"Of course you do. And elsewhere, as well. Amongst us, for example."

"Amongst you...I'm not a domovaya!"

"No?" The domovaya laughed. "It seems to me you've been pretending to be everything else, so why not a domovaya as well?"

"You've—have you been watching me?!"

"Since before you had the good fortune to be born, young Tsarinovna," said the domovaya. "Since before you had the good fortune to be born. And you may be right that these people around you are your kin, but you will not always want to acknowledge them as your kind. You will not always look on them and see yourself. Soon, very soon, you may look on them and feel nothing but separation and revulsion, even more than you feel right now as you look upon me. And when that moment comes, call for us, and we will come for you."

Dasha shuddered. "I'll *never* call for you," she declared.

"No? It is the habit of youth to make such declarations, but how often do they keep them? I myself am young, as we count the years, but already I have learned better. Call for us, Tsarinovna, and we will come for you." The domovaya winked at her, and then slipped some-how into the cracks in the wall, and disappeared.

Once she had recovered from the shock, Dasha went running out of her cell in search of her father, knocking on cell doors and disturbing everyone else until she finally found him in the very last cell of the building, closeted with Fedya.

"They let you get away?" Dasha blurted out on seeing Fedya, for-getting her own troubles for a moment. "They don't still have you locked up with them?"

"They're not like that!" protested Fedya, with a force that spoke of secret doubt.

"What's the matter, Dasha?" Oleg asked. "What happened?"

"A domovaya! A domovaya came to me in my cell!"

"And?" asked Oleg.

"She said they wanted to take me away! To train me!"

"Ah." Oleg nodded. "I see."

"You knew!" Dasha accused him. "You knew about this, and you didn't tell me! She said they had made a bargain with my mother be-fore I was even born, and you knew about this and didn't even tell me!"

"I didn't know the details," her father told her. "I didn't know it would be domoviye, but we all knew you would have to go off to the spirits for a while, for training. You knew it too."

"Yes, but...I didn't know it would be *domoviye!*"

"You'd rather someone else?" Oleg asked. "Who would be more fitting?"

"I...I don't know," admitted Dasha. "I just...she scared me. They scare me," she said.

"Why?" asked her father. "Of all the spirits to fear, domoviye are the least likely. They're harmless, well-intentioned little things. And they've done nothing but protect you. Now, and before you were born, too."

"Yes, but...they *scare* me," Dasha repeated. "I don't know why, they just do! I don't want to go with them! I want to stay with you!"

"Are they trying to take you away?" Oleg asked.

"Well...no. Not at the moment. But she said I'd call for them! She said I'd *want* them to take me away, and soon!"

"Well, when that happens, go with them," said her father, with maddening calm. "Until then, stay with us." He turned back to Fedya, who had watched the conversation with bewilderment. "The same goes for you," he told him. "If you want to stay here, in this sanctuary, with these people, then stay. If you want to leave with us, then leave. We'll stay an extra day for you to make up your mind. We need the rest anyway, and so do our horses. But the decision is up to you."

"I have to go now," Fedya said, not looking particularly happy about the freedom Oleg had given him. "They're waiting for me. They want to talk to me some more. I just..." he wrung his hands, "don't know. I thought I was sure, and now once again I'm not."

"So spend another day here, and imagine yourself spending all the days of your life here. It's normal not to be sure at first. But at a certain point you will be sure, and then you'll have to abide by your decision."

Fedya did not appear to find this very comforting, and Dasha could understand why, but he thanked Oleg for his counsel, and left his cell, still wringing his hands.

"He shouldn't stay," Dasha said as soon as he was gone. "They're horrible here."

"Have they mistreated you?" Oleg asked.

"Well...no. But..."

"But you'd rather die than be one of them," Oleg finished for her.

"Well...something like that, yes. And I thought you didn't like them either!"

"I don't," he told her. "But I don't particularly want Fedya hanging on with us for weeks and weeks either, and this seems like as good a place for him as he's likely to find."

"That's not very nice," said Dasha.

"But true," he told her. He sighed. "Dasha, my heart, I'm sorry the domovaya startled you. I'm sorry you feel like your mother and I didn't tell you everything you wanted or needed to know. But it doesn't look like you've come to any *harm* from them, and domoviye are powerful, more powerful than most people know, and they're good. They would never do anything to hurt you. Gray Wolf and all the animal spirits— they wouldn't hurt you either, not on purpose, but they have their own concerns, which are not always those of the world of women. But the domoviye are of the world of women, a bridge between the gods and women. Just like you."

"I'm not a domovaya!"

"No, but you're *like* them. One foot in each realm. Touched by the gods, but part of the world of women too. Maybe they can help you better than anyone else could."

"I just..." Dasha swallowed. "I'm just so scared, and I don't know why!"

"You've spent your entire life, which hasn't been very long, in the world of women." He gave her a steady look. "In Krasnograd, surrounded by civilization and comfort, and also surrounded by your mother and her princesses and all your nannies and maids and tutors. But now you have to leave all that, and become more than you were. It's frightening. I was scared too, when I left my village, even though I was running away from what I thought in my youthful ignorance was the worst place in the world, and I was scared again when I left the boy behind and became a husband and then a father, and I was terrified when I left my first life behind and became what I am now. A servant of the gods. And so was your mother, my head for beheading, although she'd never admit it to me or you."

"I didn't think it would be this hard," Dasha said in a small voice. "I thought it would all be a jolly adventure and I'd come back much braver and wiser at the end, but just riding from place to place is dirty and painful and tiring and dangerous, and I'm afraid of what else awaits me, and I don't feel any braver or wiser than I did—in fact, I feel even more foolish and scared than I did before!"

Oleg laughed. "A sure sign of wisdom," he told her. "Now come. Let's go visit the horses. There's not much here for them, but there's a patch of grass behind the kitchen garden, and Sister Taisya told me we could graze them there."

"I don't want to stay an extra day here," Dasha said, still speaking in that small, little-girl voice. "I don't like this place."

"And neither do I, but I doubt an extra day here will kill us, even if it's not a very welcoming place for people like you and me. And Fedya needs the extra time to be sure of his decision."

"It's not that it's not welcoming," Dasha told him. "It's that it feels like they're trying to draw me in, and a little bit of me wants to go."

"It does, does it? Well, I suppose that's not too much of a surprise. I don't like this place at all, Dasha, but then, I'm...pretty much the opposite of everything they're trying to do here." He looked away, embarrassed, and it took Dasha a moment to realize what he was saying.

Then she blushed too, and wanted to ask him if he really thought she was like him, too, someone who...was supposed to produce a lot of children. Only that was much too awkward a question to ask, so she followed him to the stable in silence, and they talked only of the road to Lesnograd as they grazed the horses.

They were invited to have supper that night with the rest of the sanctuary, in a plain echoing chamber in the main building, decorated only with a long table and splintery, tippy benches. Dasha wondered whether the benches were supposed to be so splintery and tippy as a punishment or a way to make those sitting on them think on higher things than their seats, or if they were just made by someone who wasn't very good at making furniture. None of the people there seemed to be very good at what they did. The robes were plain, made of coarse linen and wool, and sewn, it looked, with a clumsy, unsteady hand, as if the person making them had never sewn anything prior to making these robes.

Which may very well have been true. The barley stew Sister Taisya brought out was plain and undercooked, even though the barley had been soaking all day in Dasha's pack and should have softened up quickly. There were no dried mushrooms or spring onions or any of the things that were normally added to barley stew in Dasha's experience; again, she didn't know if Sister Taisya had done that on purpose, or if she hadn't thought to do it, or they didn't have the supplies. Everyone got a small piece of black bread that was too tough to chew and yet undercooked at the same time. There were also strips of dried meat that, judging by the expressions on the others' faces, was no better than any of the other things they had been served. Susanna tried to press some of the dried meat on Dasha, but with considerably less enthusiasm than she normally did, and when Dasha refused, she only nodded in understanding and went back to stolidly chewing her own portion, looking as if it took every grain of her self-control not to burst out with imprecations against Northern barbarism.

"Have some venison," said Sister Taisya, seeing that Dasha was not partaking. "We brought it out specially for our guests."

"I thank you for your hospitality, but I fear I couldn't manage another bite," Dasha told her, trying and failing to suppress visions of the hunt that had brought back this venison. Was this the flesh of a sister of the doe who had led her back from the stream the other night? Had she known she was being hunted? How long had her dying been? The half-cooked meal turned uneasily in Dasha's stomach, and for a moment she could see *herself* fleeing, arrows in her back.

"Nonsense, you've hardly eaten a thing," said Sister Taisya, getting that look on her face that Dasha knew so well, the look of someone who is determined to force her to do something she didn't want to, for her own good. Her nannies and maids had worn it all the time, and it seemed that putting half the country between her and them was no salvation: the world was, apparently, full of others who were more than willing to take up the office.

"I find I have little appetite tonight," said Dasha. "The strain of travel, you know. The food should go to someone who needs it more."

"If you're traveling you've even more need of it than ever," said Sister Taisya stubbornly, pushing some of the dried venison over towards Dasha. "Take it!"

"I fear I couldn't possibly manage," Dasha said, pushing the platter (rudely carved of pine) away. "Perhaps Fedya would like my portion instead? He tends to have more appetite than I do."

They went through several more rounds of this, which ended in a victory for Dasha, in that she never took any of the venison, but Sister Taisya was red-faced and angry by the end of it, unable to believe that she hadn't managed to force Dasha to eat it against her will, and everyone else at the table seemed to share her mood. Dasha looked over at Fedya, hoping to find him taken aback by this display, but he kept his gaze fixed steadfastly on the table. Dasha was very glad when the meal was finally over, and she could retreat to her cell, which, if not particularly comfortable, at least afforded her some protection from the harrying and bullying of the others.

The doe sniffed at her. "I thought you were dead!" Dasha cried in relief. "I thought they'd killed you!"

"*Part of me,*" *said the doe.* "*Not the part in here, though.*" *She turned and disappeared into the fog between the trees.*

Dasha began running after her. An owl swooped down and hooted at her, nearly getting tangled in her hair. When Dasha straightened up from the crouch she'd thrown herself into to escape the owl, she caught a glimpse on the edge of her vision of amber, slanted eyes.

"*Go* **away***!*" *shouted Dasha.* "*Don't chase her!*"

"*It's the way of things,*" *said Serenkaya.* "*I am a wolf, and so are you.*"

"*I am* **not** *a wolf!*" *screamed Dasha, and started running again, fog covering her face with droplets of water and filling her nose and mouth so that she could hardly breathe. Creatures moved through the woods beside her, shadowing her, their paws making heavy sounds on the ground.*

Dasha pushed herself faster, though her limbs felt heavy and uncooperative, and there was a burning pain in her belly. She raced across two birch poles that spanned a stream—and then stopped dead when the bridge came to an abrupt end, and she reeled on its edge, almost falling into the ravine that opened out beneath it.

"*Hello sister.*" *Something small and soft closed around her calf. Dasha looked down, and saw with horror that a domovaya, not the one who had come to her earlier, but a different, much older one, was gently holding her leg with one small paw.* "*We've been waiting for you,*" *said the domovaya.* "*Come away from this place. You don't want to fall in.*"

"*I am* **not** *your sister!*" *cried Dasha, shaking her leg loose from the domovaya's grip.*

"*True,*" *agreed the domovaya.* "'*Daughter' would be a better word.*"

"*I'm not your daughter either!*" *shouted Dasha, and threw herself off the bridge.*

She landed, not with the bone-jarring thump she had expected, but a cold splash.

"*I'm in the river,*" *she thought, as she bobbed back up to the surface.* "*Let the river take me.*"

She floated along, staring up at the moon and the stars that floated above her in the opposite direction. A mist rose up around her and enveloped her, and she knew that it was Vika, trying to take her, but she floated on past, and the mist soon dissipated, leaving nothing but an unpleasant damp sensation all over her body.

"*I'm soaked through,*" *Dasha thought.* "*I'll drown soon.*"

Something touched her leg, and she found herself riding on the viper's back, its brown and yellow scales glinting in the moonlight, its muscular body moving sinuously under her.

"I'll take you to the shore," said the viper.

"Who are you?" asked Dasha.

The viper twisted her head around to look Dasha in the eyes, and said, smiling as she did so, "I'm you, Dasha."

*"I am **not** a viper!" Dasha screamed.*

"But you rode me to shore anyway," said the viper, and shook, tossing her off of her back and onto the hard ground of the far shore. Dasha tried to crawl away, to get as far away from the river as possible, but her body wasn't working properly, and when she looked down at it, she saw that her hands had turned into wolf paws. Her back twisted back and forth like the spine of a snake, and owl wings beat above her, and no matter how she twisted, she couldn't throw them off.

*"I thought we were one, Dasha," said the doe, stepping out of the fog. "I saved you, and I thought we were one, but you **betrayed** me. You turned yourself into **them**."*

*"I am not **them**!" screamed Dasha, cutting her tongue with her fangs, her belly so knotted it felt like she might be torn apart as her body writhed and changed.*

"Then who are you?" asked the doe. "Whose are you?"

A small hand closed gently around Dasha's leg. "Mine," said the domovaya.

Dasha jerked awake, hitting her head on the cell wall. There was a bloody taste in her mouth, and she realized that she'd bitten her tongue in her sleep. Her stomach was churning, the echoes of moon-blood pain making her belly clench.

It was just a dream, she told herself. *Just a silly dream.* But her words rang hollow, even inside her own head. She pulled herself shakily upright, tripping over the packs piled up in the cell corner and almost falling headlong against the door.

I'll go outside, she thought. *I just need to go outside and clear my head.*

She opened the door and went out into the chill night air, resolutely not looking at the corners of her cell, resolutely not looking at the shadows.

The stars shone brightly overhead, the movement of the trees in the breeze that was rising making them look as if the stars, too, were moving above her.

Nothing can really be so bad if you can still see the stars, Dasha told herself. But she soon found her gaze being drawn down, away from the stars, to a patch of fog that was creeping out from under the tree boughs.

"Vika?" called Dasha softly. There was no reply, but the patch of fog rolled over her, and settled on her before dissipating, leaving droplets of water on her hair. Dasha's belly unclenched, and she was able to go back inside the cell and lie back down. The rest of her sleep was dreamless.

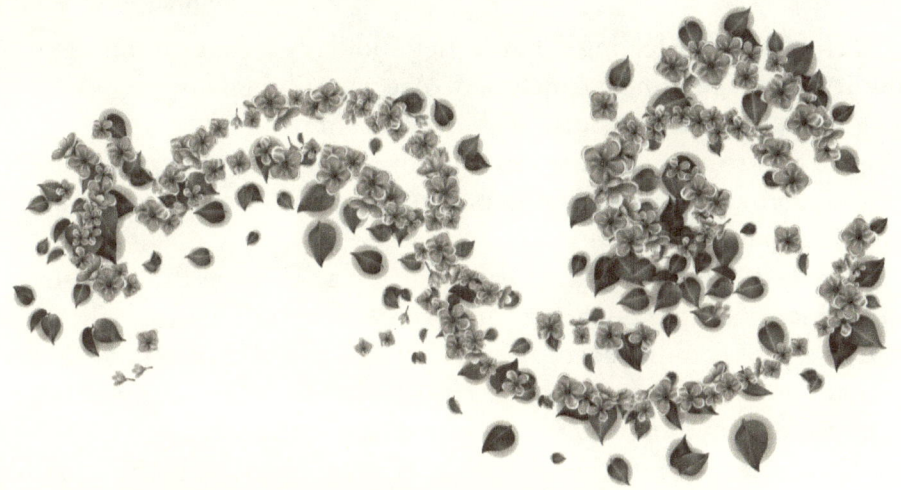

Chapter Thirty

The patch of sky that shone above the treetops when Dasha got up the next morning was a sullen red, that soon changed to an equally sullen gray. The air was breathless, and mosquitoes and flies whined around her face as she went out to feed and walk Poloska and Seryozha.

"Do we have to stay here another day?" Dasha asked Oleg, her voice almost as whiny as that of the mosquitoes, as they stood side by side grazing their horses and slapping at the insects plaguing them.

"Would you leave Fedya here by himself when he still isn't sure what he wants?" Oleg asked in reply. "You were the one who was so keen to help him."

"I don't think he should stay here," Dasha said stubbornly. "I still think we should put our foot down and force him to come with us for his own good."

"And if he never forgave you for your interference?" asked Oleg. "If you were him, how would you feel about it? How would you feel if I dragged you home, or forced you to go somewhere you didn't want to, for your own good?"

"This is different!" said Dasha, her voice ringing hollow in her own ears. Even more annoyingly, her father didn't even deign to reply, but instead just *smiled,* as if she were an amusing child. Dasha could feel her fists clenching, and a hot rage rising up out of the pit of her stomach. How could he think this was funny? This was *serious*!

"How are you feeling?" her father suddenly asked, sounding, to her irritation, genuinely concerned. "Are you still in pain?"

"It's no concern of yours," she told him shortly.

"Of course it is," he told her. "I'm in charge of this journey, and I need to know if you're sick or in pain. And I don't want you to suffer if you don't have to."

"I'm fine," she told him. In truth, she felt as sullen as the sky above her, which made her even more annoyed with herself than she already was, but she couldn't seem to stop herself, and she certainly didn't want to pour her heart out to her father, who was being so annoying.

"Is there anything you need?" he asked delicately.

"No," she said, and then amended that to, "I want to bathe and do laundry. But I don't think they'd let me, and I don't want to ask and have them tell me no. I don't think they like me very much here. That's why I want to leave."

"I could insist," he offered. "I could tell them who you are, and insist."

"No!"

"As you wish," he said. "Will you be able to last one more day?"

"I can if I have to," she said. "I just don't want to."

He smiled again in that infuriating fashion. "I'm afraid that is something that happens to all of us, and much more often than we'd like. But staying another day here might be good for you: this way you can see what it's like to live in a sanctuary. Your grandmother retired to a sanctuary before you were born, and I know your mother often thinks of it as well, so like as not, you'll feel called to join a sanctuary one day, too."

Dasha gritted her teeth. Everything he said was true, which made it even more irritating. "Not this sanctuary!" she protested. "Not this sanctuary, and I already don't ever want to live at *any* sanctuary, after just a single night here."

He laughed. "Fair enough," he said. "But you might change your mind after seeing other sanctuaries, or after spending a few years ruling. The gods know your mother and grandmother found it a trying business, and wanted nothing more than to give it up. I'd be very surprised if the same doesn't happen to you."

"That's just wrong," she said. "People who don't want to rule shouldn't rule. It should be done by people who want to do it."

"Ah, well, that's an argument for another day, with those who know better than me about that kind of thing. But I'd say that rule should be held by those who feel a calling for it. Which isn't the same as wanting power. Your aunt wanted power, wanted to set herself above others, wanted to take without giving back, without suffering, and in the end it broke her. Although I suppose you're right in that she didn't want to rule like an Empress, she wanted to feed her own vanity. Your mother, now, she doesn't want to be constantly telling people what to do, and she never has, but she felt a calling for rule nonetheless, because there was no one who could do it better, and she knew it, modest as she is. And you'll feel the same, unless I'm wrong about you entirely."

"I don't want to be just like them!" Dasha burst out. "It's as if my whole life has already been mapped out for me because of who I am, and I don't get to have any say in the matter at all!"

"You get to have say," said her father. "We all get to have say in how we run our lives. Just not as much as we think we should." He sighed. "But that's a heavy thought and a heavy conversation, best had with someone wiser than me. I'm not much of a thinker, Dasha, as I'm sure you know. All I know is what I've seen, and I've had more time than most to see things and think on them, but I've never been a scholar or a thinker, not like your mother, and I'm still not. I'm still just me, even after all these years, even after all the things I've seen, all the changes that have happened to me, and that's the way things are. You are who you are. There are things you can change about yourself and your life, and things you can't, and if you try too hard to change the things you can't or shouldn't, all you do is break yourself."

"That's not a very happy thought," said Dasha.

"It's the way things are," he repeated. "Now come on, let's take the horses back to the stable, and then go see if we can do some laundry. You're not the only one who needs to wash their clothes."

Dasha followed him back to the stable, and then on their quest to be allowed to do laundry, which, as she had predicted, was more difficult than it should have been, since Brother Feofan, who was in charge of washing, was openly squeamish about letting them use the laundry facilities, but once they convinced him that they would do all the washing themselves, and not let any of their clothes touch any of the sanctuary robes or be seen by anyone—he seemed to think that the mere sight of a sarafan would spoil everything they were attempting to achieve—as they were hanging up to dry, he relented.

"Go tell Susanna and Svetochka to bring their things, and I'll get the guards, and we'll all wash our clothes," Oleg told Dasha.

"I've never done laundry," Dasha confessed, trying to be cheerful

465

about something that she didn't really want to do, but that needed to be done, and that Oleg had just gone to trouble to arrange for her.

"You haven't missed much," he told her. "Laundry is one of the more tedious tasks there is. But it'll be good for you to learn how, and even better for you to know what your maids do for you, every week."

Dasha couldn't argue with that, although the implication that she was lazy, ignorant, and ungrateful did rather rub her the wrong way. It wasn't *her* fault that not only had she never been taught how to do laundry, but that she had been actively prevented from learning. But she could sense that if she said that to her father, he would just say something true but annoying like "Now is the time for you to learn," or something like that. So she wandered off in search of Susanna and Svetochka while her father lit the fire under the big vat and began filling it with water.

She found Susanna and Svetochka sitting in Susanna's cell, mending their clothes, their faces dour. "Tsarinovna!" cried Susanna in delight at Dasha's appearance. "We looked for you! We thought maybe you also wanted to mend your clothes! Or just to sit with us." She made a face. "It is very boring here, is it not? They are not pleasant at all. I do not understand why Fedya wants to live here with them."

"I know," said Dasha. "We're doing laundry. You should bring anything you want to wash."

"All my things!" said Susanna with a laugh. "Everything is so dirty! But I do not think they want us to be naked here, so I will wear this dirty gown, and wash the other things." She put down her mending and began gathering up her clothes. Svetochka ran off to get her things, and Dasha wandered off toward her own cell.

It felt dark and dank when she pushed open the door as much as she could before it was stopped by the thin mattress, and edged her way inside. Dark and dank, but also stifling, and a handful of mosquitoes had found their way inside, and whined around her ears as she sorted through her things and began gathering up her dirty clothes.

"Stop it!" she complained, slapping at the mosquitoes. "Stop it, stop it, stop it! Why do you keep chasing after me! Go chase after someone else!" Suddenly she was near tears. *Everyone* was chasing after her, *everyone* wanted something from her—wanted *blood* from her, wanted her *life* from her, just like these horrid mosquitoes, and she could sense something looming in front of her, something terrible. It was the same feeling she'd had the day her father had arrived with the news of what had happened to Lisochka and Dasha the dog, the same feeling of impending doom, or change, or both.

Stop it, she told herself. *You're just being silly. It's just because you have your moonblood. That always makes you unhappy, and why wouldn't it.* But the bleeding had almost stopped, and normally she felt this way just before it started, not as it was ending. *It's just all these silly dreams*, she told herself. *But that's all they are, silly dreams.* She knew even as she thought them that those words were lies, but she didn't know how to make them true, so she stuffed all her dirty clothes into one of her packs, and trudged off to the laundry house, her bulging pack slung heavily over her shoulder.

The laundry house was already filled with steam when she arrived, rising from the vat in the center of the room. For one horrid moment Dasha had a vision of tripping and falling face-first into that near-boiling water, or—even worse!—pushing her father in, or one of her companions, but she shook her head and the vision passed, if not the heavy feeling it left behind in her breast, and she kept being assailed by flickering visions of scalded hands and faces.

Svetochka, showing a confidence she had never demonstrated before, took charge of the washing, ordering everyone about in firm tones and taking up a position by the vat of hot water, arranging other tubs around her, into which she measured soap with a practiced eye, followed by hot and cold water until she was satisfied with the temperature, and then began adding the clothes, holding up each item and examining it and deciding whether it should go into the tub with warm water or the tub with lukewarm water, before taking up a stick and stirring everything with sure movements.

Dasha and the others were left to hang about and wait until she declared it time to change the water and rinse everything out. This involved a great deal of heavy lugging, and then they had to rinse and wring out the clothes, which was also a heavy, tiresome business, and then hang them up to dry, or, in the case of the linen items, iron them first, which was very tedious. By the time they were done, it was midday, and Dasha, like everyone else, was soaked with steam and sweat.

"We'll just leave these here to hang an' dry," Svetochka announced, looking around at the neat lines of clean clothes with satisfaction. "It'd be better if we could get a bit of a breeze, but they should be dry enough by tomorrow, anyway."

"Looks like you're getting your breeze already," said Alik, as the door to the laundry house rattled. Dasha's stomach clenched. *Something* terrible, the terrible thing she had been waiting for all morning, was on the other side of that door, trying to get in.

"I'll let it in," said Svetochka, walking over to the door as if nothing were wrong.

NO, don't! Dasha screamed, but the scream didn't leave the inside of her head. She watched, frozen as she had been when the waystation mistress had killed the dog, as Svetochka pulled open the door, revealing a couple of the sanctuary's brothers.

"Is the fire still lit?" one of them asked. "Is there still hot water? We just brought back a deer, and we need to butcher it."

Dasha's feet carried her out of the laundry house before the rest of her knew what they were doing, her body shouldering aside Svetochka and the sanctuary brothers as she burst through the door and over to where the body of a doe was lying on the ground, an arrow piercing her chest.

For a moment Dasha couldn't speak, couldn't even breathe. She could not just see the arrow piercing that chest, but *feel* it, feel it tear its way through her lungs to her heart, feel the horrible realization that something terrible, something unfixable, had happened, followed by pain, more pain than she had ever known possible, and then blackness, that was a relief even in its horror. And then that vision was replaced by another one, one of the doe who had come to her when she had crawled out of the stream, and she knew that she was one and the same with this doe, lying here dead in front of her. She whirled around, the rest of her still not knowing what her feet were doing, and raced back into the laundry house.

"You...you..." She was panting, gasping, unable to get the words out. Prickles that were more than just prickles, that were more like flames, were running up and down her spine, and blackness was crowding around her vision, as things flashed and danced in the corners of her eyes.

"You *killed* her!" she screamed. "She was my friend, and you *killed* her!"

Everyone stared at her in horribly mild surprise. "She was just a deer," said Svetochka eventually.

"Not you too! You're my *sister!* You're supposed to understand!"

The others shared a long look between them, one that said they had been expecting something like this for a while, and were now going to deal with it. Her father reached out and placed a gentle hand on her shoulder. Dasha shook her shoulder, hating his touch, trying to get free, but he wouldn't let go.

"Dasha, my love," he said. "I know you find this upsetting. But it's the way of things."

"No it's *not!*" she cried. "It's *your* way!"

"Dasha," he said. "You're upsetting our hosts."

"I don't care! I don't care! I don't care! They *killed* her!"

The sanctuary brothers, after receiving a nod from Oleg, backed slowly out of the laundry house, giving her the looks of irritated patience that people bestowed on half-wits. Dasha wanted to run after them, take their arrows and shove them through their chests so that they would *know* what they had done, she could even see herself doing so, but her father wouldn't let go of her shoulder.

"Dasha," he said, his gentle voice even more annoying than it would have been if he had been angry, "I know you're upset, but…"

"Don't tell me it had to be! Don't tell me it had to be! I *hate* them, I *hate* them, I *hate* them!"

"And me?" he asked. "Do you hate me?" When she said nothing, he pressed on, "Who do you think I am, Dasha? How many times do you think I've done exactly that, bring home game from the hunt? More times than I can count. And I'm your *father*, Dasha, and you are my flesh and blood. It is the way of things, Dasha, and you are part of it, whether you want it or not."

"You're…you're not my father!" she screamed. "I'm nothing like you! I hate you! I'll never be like you!"

"Ah well," said Oleg, giving her a long, calm look. "I hated my own father pretty well when I was your age, too. And I always said I would never be anything like him. The gods alone know how well I've succeeded in that, but I've said the same thing, thought the same thing, and more than once, too. Maybe we all have to."

The calm look on his face, and the calm sound of his voice, made Dasha want to claw his eyes out, and his words made her want to smash those same eyes so hard that they came out of the back of his skull. How could…how could someone who would do something like *that* be so calm? How could someone like *that* say that they were alike? How could…how could someone like *that*, who would do things like *that*, be her own flesh and blood? How could…how could…how could…

"We're *nothing* alike!" she screamed. "Nothing, nothing, nothing! Nothing alike!"

Oleg gave her another long look. "Maybe so," he said after a while. "Maybe so. But I can see my own fire in you, more now than ever before."

"No!" she cried desperately.

"So this is my advice to you," he continued, ignoring her outburst. "I know, because I had to do it too, that you need to go off on your own for a bit. Maybe for more than a bit. Otherwise you'll never not be at the mercy of your own fire, your own burning inside. So I'm going to let you go. But...you have to learn how to control it, Dasha my heart, you have to learn how to let it warm you, drive you, without letting it take over you and burn you to ash."

"I won't!" she cried, although she could have hardly said what it was she was protesting—or was it promising? "I won't, I won't, I won't!"

"Be sure you mean it, Dasha my love," he said. The tiny part of her that wasn't angry enough to kill him saw that he looked tired and sad, but she ignored it. "Be sure that you mean it," he repeated. "And some day you may find that you and I really are the same, more the same than you can possibly imagine, and that you will do the things that I have done, and know that it is right."

If he had only not said those last words...Dasha had almost softened towards him, towards everyone, for a moment, but on hearing those words, Dasha felt once again that the only, the best, the only possible response was to kill herself and everyone else in the room. She looked down at her hands, hoping for flames, but there was nothing there. She looked up and saw her shortsword, that Boleslav Vlasiyevich had given her so trustingly, lying on the table a few paces away, and she could see herself taking it up and slicing through the throats of all her companions, their blood pouring out and assuaging some tiny fraction of her own pain, before the edge of the sword cut keenly into her own tender neck, just as a similar edge had cut through the chest of the doe that was lying there, waiting to be dismembered and eaten, and how she, like the doe, would collapse onto the ground, screaming through the blood that was choking her, before finally finding the only release she could from the evil that was suffocating her.

The vision was so real that for a moment it was all that she could see, and when her sight cleared, she could tell that the others had seen it too, but they were too transfixed with horror to stop her, and too trapped by their fear of changing themselves, of going against what they thought was the way of things, of acting for her sake rather than theirs, of promising to do no more harm, no more killing, to offer her the words that could turn her aside from her path of destruction. It seemed to her that she was actually reaching unopposed for the sword, but whether it was in vision or in truth she could not tell.

"My love." A tiny hand closed over hers.

Dasha blinked, but the tiny hand did not go away. She followed it with her eyes down its arm and to the face of a tiny wizened-up old woman, no bigger than a small child.

"I don't know you," Dasha blurted out. "You weren't here before."

"Better to say that you didn't see me before, my love," said the old woman. She shifted in the light, and suddenly it seemed to Dasha that she was not an old woman, but a bundle of sticks. "I have been watching over *you* since the moment you arrived, and long before that, too."

"How?" asked Dasha stupidly. The old woman shifted again, now looking not like a bundle of sticks, but a creature of the forest of some sort, perhaps a tiny bear.

"You are not the only one gifted with visions, my love," said the old woman. "And if you come with me, I will show you. My sisters and I will teach you many things, just as we promised your mother we would, when you were little more than a hope we all carried in our hearts." She shifted again, and now Dasha saw all three things at once: old woman, bundle of sticks, and creature of the forest.

"You're the domovaya who bargained with my mother," she said. "Aren't you?"

The old woman bowed without letting go of Dasha's hand. "As are my sisters, my love," she said. "And we promised your mother we would watch over you when you were small, and teach you many important things once you came of age."

"I..." Dasha looked around wildly, but it seemed as if the rest of the room and all the others in it were mired in shadow, and could not or would not weigh in on what she was seeing. "I wanted to...I almost..."

"I know, my love," said the domovaya gently. "I know. I always knew it would come to that. I always knew that you would save so many, Dasha my love, my most precious gift, but only if you would let us save you first. You must burn with suffering, you see: it is in your nature. And because you must burn, so may others around you. It is the way of things. But my sisters and I can help you. We can help you take your wondrous gift, the ability to suffer for others, and turn it into glowing coals that will provide warmth and sustenance for all around you."

"And if I don't let you save me?" whispered Dasha.

"Then I fear you and all around you will be overcome by the raging fire, the great tide of blood, that your suffering will release." The house spirit spoke kindly, but her eyes were dark with sorrow.

"And you would suffer too," said Dasha.

The domovaya bowed her head in acknowledgement, for a moment looking for all the world like a grieving bear cub. It was this that decided Dasha: had the house spirit remained wholly human, she didn't think she could have stood to go with her, any more than she could have stood to stay with her own human companions, but she could not turn away from this simple animal grief.

"I will go," said Dasha. "But I must tell the others first."

"Of course," said the house spirit. She released Dasha's hand, which seemed to release the shadows that held the others as well, and the room was returned to its previous brightness and animation.

"I'm going," she announced, before anyone could speak. "The domoviye have called me, and I am going to them."

Mitya, Seva, and Alik all protested loudly, and were only quelled when the shadows came creeping out from the corners and surrounded everyone, and the shadows turned out to be domoviye, who stood in a circle around the room and gazed at the humans with dark and gentle eyes.

"I'm going with them," Dasha repeated. "You don't need to worry about me. It is for the best. It is the only way." Her eyes sought out Oleg, and even though she wanted to smash him, to hurt him more than he had ever been hurt before, she still found herself saying, "This was what was promised by my mother, before I was born. And," she felt herself choking on the words, unable to swallow the rage that was still burning within her, but forced them out anyway, "it's as you said. I have to go with them."

"I know," he said. "But..."

"She will be well cared for, Oleg Svetoslavovich," said the domovaya who had taken Dasha's hand. "You of all people should know that. And when it is time for you to come for her, you will know when and where."

For a moment Oleg bowed his head in acquiescence, but then he lifted it. "I'm not going to let you do to her what you did to me," he said. "I'm not going to—Dasha, you may need to go with them, but don't just take their gifts with your eyes closed! Don't just accept the gifts of the gods on blind faith! I should go with you, guard you the way I haven't been guarding you all along. And maybe I couldn't—I never was much of a father that way. But in this I can do my duty, I can protect you from them the way no one ever protected me. I should go with you!"

Burning

Dasha opened her mouth, whether to accept or deny his request, she couldn't say. But before she could get the words out, the domovaya squeezed Dasha's hand so hard she could feel the bones grinding together, and the others came up and surrounded her, and they stepped into the shadows.

End of Part I
Part II is now available!

Want to know how it all began? Keep up with the latest news and get freebies and insider information? Come say hi at <u>epclarkauthor.net</u> *to sign up for my mailing list and get a FREE copy of the prequel collection* **Winter of the Gods and Other Stories.** *Or you can go to it directly by scanning the QR code below.*

Discussion Questions

1) *The Breathing Sea* is set in a matrilineal, matriarchal world. What are gender relations and gender roles like? Would you call it "female dominated"? How do women treat men in it, and is it a parallel to how men treat women in our own male-dominated society?

2) The question of perception and reality is a recurring theme in *The Breathing Sea*. What examples of that did you notice? What kind of unusual perceptions does Dasha have?

3) Related to that, the question of physical reality versus what people think or want is also a recurring theme. When Dasha says, "You don't wear your body, you are your body," what does that say about the dualist mind-body concept common in Western thinking? How does clothing figure in the text?

4) How does upbringing and influence appear in *The Breathing Sea*? How is this related to the issue of physical versus ideal reality, or the tension between individual desires or subjective perception and objective or shared reality?

5) The issue of gifts comes up repeatedly in *The Breathing Sea*. What are the various gifts that appear? Are gifts a good or a bad thing?

6) Dasha's story is meant on one level to parallel that of the Buddha. How does that play out in the text?

7) The subtitle of this book is *Burning*. How does the concept, theme, or motif of burning appear throughout the text? What kinds of elemental or psychological tension appear in the text?

8) How are figures from Slavic fairy tales worked into the story? How are they reworked or made different from the original, and why?

9) Some of the key works of Russian literature and culture that are alluded to in the story are Dostoevsky's *The Idiot, Crime and Punishment*, and *The Brothers Karamazov*; Chekhov's "In the Ravine"; and Chapter 5 of Pushkin's *Eugene Onegin*. When and how do they appear in the story?

10) How does the epigraph relate to the story?

11) Were there moments that made you uncomfortable or challenged you? What were they, and why? What is the benefit to reading something that challenges you?

12) How does twinning or doubling appear in the text, and why?

13) This is on one level the traditional story of a young woman's sexual awakening and transition into womanhood. How does that appear, both literally and symbolically, in the text? Does this story differ in some way from the traditional or stereotypical story of the (de)flowering of a maiden?

14) How do questions of writing, language, and storytelling appear in the text? Is that related to the issues of identity that are raised in the text, and if so, how?

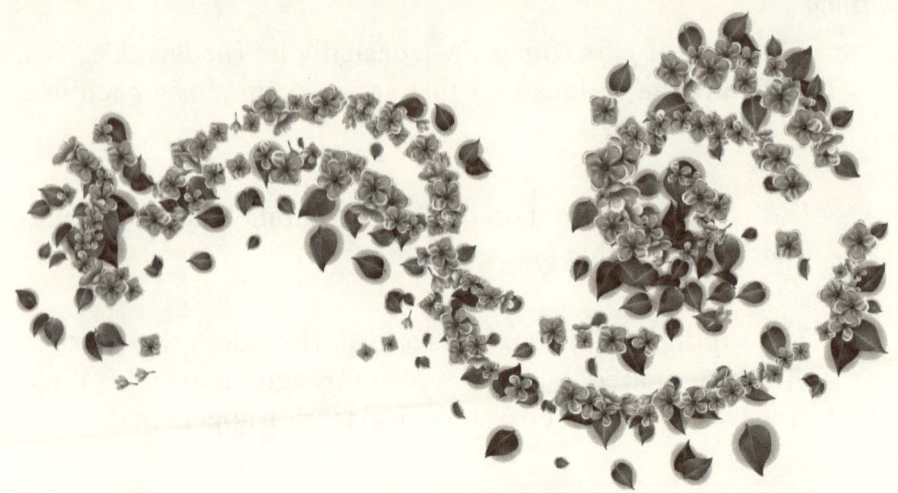

From the Author

What you are holding is the first part of *The Breathing Sea*, the second installment of *The Zemnian Series*, except that since the first installment, *The Midnight Land*, was split into two volumes, this (Part I) is book three in a trilogy that will probably end up being in seven, or maybe eleven, volumes...

Let me explain.

When I originally planned the trilogy, I envisioned it in three volumes, like any sensible, law-abiding person would. Unfortunately, that person is not me. A serious, possibly criminal, case of graphomania overcame me, and when I'd finished the books, I realized that they were too long to be published as single volumes. As in, the spines wouldn't hold in the paperback editions. *The Dreaming Land*, the last part of the original trilogy, was so long it could no longer function as a Word document, and kept crashing whenever I tried to open it. Plus, I'm now eying the possibility of writing even more books in the series.

I guess that's why they call it "epic" fantasy.

So I took a leaf out of Tolkien's publisher's playbook, and divided what had originally been conceived of as single books into multiple volumes, breaking them off at the most fraught moments I could find, à la a TV miniseries or Sam's desperate chase after the retreating orcs in Shelob's lair. The result was the monster you see before you. Each "miniseries" was written as a single book, each with a single main viewpoint character and a whole and complete story arc, but they have been divided for portability and ease of use, like a two-volume set of *War and Peace*. I know the first volumes of each book end on cliffhangers, but don't worry, I won't make you wait: all the volumes of each book will be published simultaneously, or near enough that you won't have to pine for long.

Even though it's the middle book in what was originally conceived as a trilogy, *The Breathing Sea* was composed after both *The Midnight Land* and *The Dreaming Land*, which either means that it is the most mature and developed product of my artistic abilities thus far, or it's a jerry-rigged afterthought, designed to stitch two disconnected works into some kind of a clumsy patchwork. Probably both. I don't know that a work of art can be anything else.

Readers familiar with Eastern European languages, literatures, and cultures will find much that is familiar in these pages, but historical accuracy or anthropological fidelity was never my intention, and there is at least as much here that is entirely the fruit of my own fancy as it is the results of my research. The language and naming customs described in this book are all based on Russian, but with many of the gender conventions reversed; you can find a detailed explanation in the foreword to *The Midnight Land,* which I won't bore us all by reproducing here, but in short, each person is given a first name, such as Darya, and a matronymic created out of the mother's first name, such as Krasnoslavovna. First names also have numerous diminutive versions, such as Dasha or Dashenka for Darya or Masha or Manya for Marya.

As you might have guessed by the use of matronymics rather than patronymics, Zemnian culture is matriarchal and matrilineal. We know from *The Tale of Bygones Years* that there were matriarchal tribes in what is now Russia and/or Ukraine, but in writing these works I was more interested in exploring my own thoughts on relationships between women, and between women and men, as well as sending up a few gender stereotypes, than in recreating any specific pre-modern matriarchal society. So while the setting is medieval, many of the issues I touch upon are deliberately aimed at modern readers.

Although when it comes to human nature, the more things change, the more they seem to stay the same. I have been asked if *The Midnight Land* was based on reality, to which I have to answer "No, definitely not: it's fantasy!" but there are a number of things in *The Breathing Sea* that are based either on my own personal experiences, or the recorded experiences of medieval personages. Firstly, the very title "The Breathing Sea" comes from an old name for the White Sea. The character of Fedya, for example, is based in part on various Orthodox saints, particularly Saint Theodosius of the Caves and **Moses the Hungarian** (check him out at https://oca.org/saints/lives/2014/07/26/102095-venerable-moses-the-hungarian-of-the-kiev-near-caves—the link will take you to a safely anodyne contemporary English version that will give you the gist of the story but lacks much of the original's gleefully misogynistic ball-smashing homoerotic glory). Meanwhile, the castrates' sanctuary is inspired by the Russian sect of the **Skoptsy** (read about them at https://en.wikipedia.org/wiki/Skoptsy, but don't click on that link if you don't want to see pictures of people who have undergone the operation). And the Rutsi were inspired by the word Ruotsi, the modern Finnish name for Sweden, related to the Rhos or **Rus'**, the Vikings who gave us the current name for Russia.

Even more than East Slavic history, though, I drew upon East Slavic fairy tales and literature. Baba Sofroniya and her hut on stilts is an obvious reference to **Baba Yaga**, the witch who lives in the deep woods and sometimes helps the heroine and sometimes threatens to eat her. Leshiye, vodyaniye, water maidens, and giant talking wolves all roam the Russian forests, although my own versions bear only cursory resemblance to the "real" forms. And then there's more modern literature and culture: for example, Dasha's recurring dream is a conflation of Tatyana's dream from Chapter Five of *Eugene Onegin* and a scene from the Soviet animated masterpiece *Hedgehog in the Fog*. References to Dostoyevsky's *Crime and Punishment* and *The Idiot*, Chekhov's "In the Ravine," and no doubt many other works, also abound. How much this will make sense to the non-initiates, I can't say, but if it inspires even a single reader to pick up any of these classics, I will consider my effort well spent.

As for my own personal experiences that went into this, there are many, but I will just mention three, as being the most important. First of all, between when I hand-wrote the first draft of the first couple of chapters, lo these many years ago as I was stuck at home with no power after Superstorm Sandy, and when I wrote the final lines of the final chapter, I was struck by a mysterious chronic illness, which later turned out to be Lyme disease, and discovered firsthand what it was like for your body to take matters into its own hands and, for example, start twitching uncontrollably at inopportune moments.

Secondly, Dasha's experience of being groped by a much older man who keeps comparing her to his daughter is very similar to something that happened to me when I was even younger than she is. I'd like to say that such things are rare, but we all know that they're not, not at all.

And finally, Dasha's struggles to avoid being forced to eat meat by her well-intentioned friends and family members will probably ring painfully, painfully true for anyone who's ever tried to give up meat and animal products. Sadly, while not eating animals is in theory an easy way to make a significant **reduction in suffering** in a world already overfull of it, the vast majority of those who try can't **stick it out,** most likely because of intense social pressure to conform to the mainstream ideology of carnism. As my characters discover repeatedly, attempts to do even a little bit of good on a personal scale can run headlong into serious, sometimes even insurmountable, obstacles (if you're looking for support and suggestions on how to cut back on your consumption and production of suffering, http://www.chooseveg.com/ is a good place to start). However, sometimes merely reading about a fictional character's struggles to overcome the same obstacles we ourselves are facing can be just enough to get us to take one more step, and then another, and another, until you've made it farther than you ever thought you could.

The headings of this paperback edition are in Luminari, a typeface based on elaborately decorated medieval manuscripts. The main body text is in Athelas, a typeface inspired by classical British literature and named after the healing herb in *The Lord of the Rings*. The decorations bring together the elemental motifs of the story: the chapter heading images are a wave made up of flowers, and the scene breaks are poppies, which are flowers that look like flames.

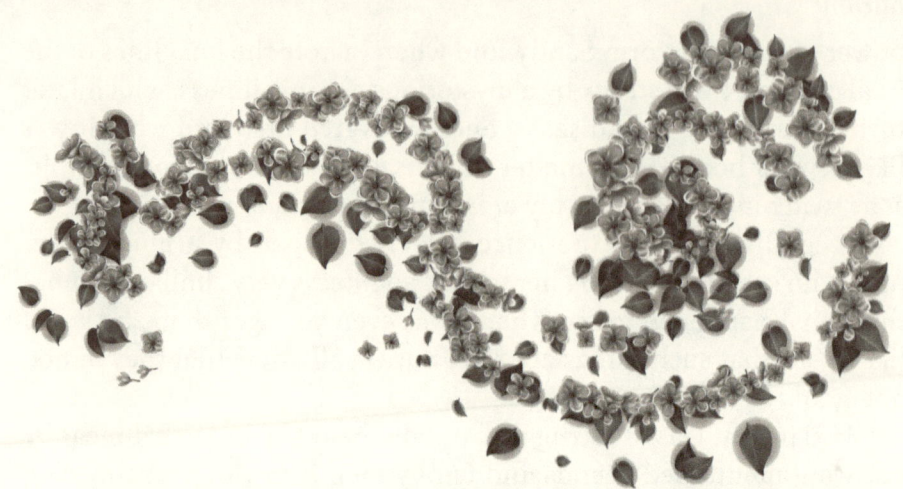

About the Author

When she is not teaching Russian, E.P. Clark is probably playing with her pets or reading a wide variety of literature from around the world. She loves to hear from her readers and can be reached by email at epclark@epclarkauthor.net, or on her website at https://epclarkauthor.net/, Pinterest at https://www.pinter-est.com/EPClarkAuthor/, Facebook at https://www.facebook.com/ep-clarkauthor/, and Twitter at @EPClarkauthor.

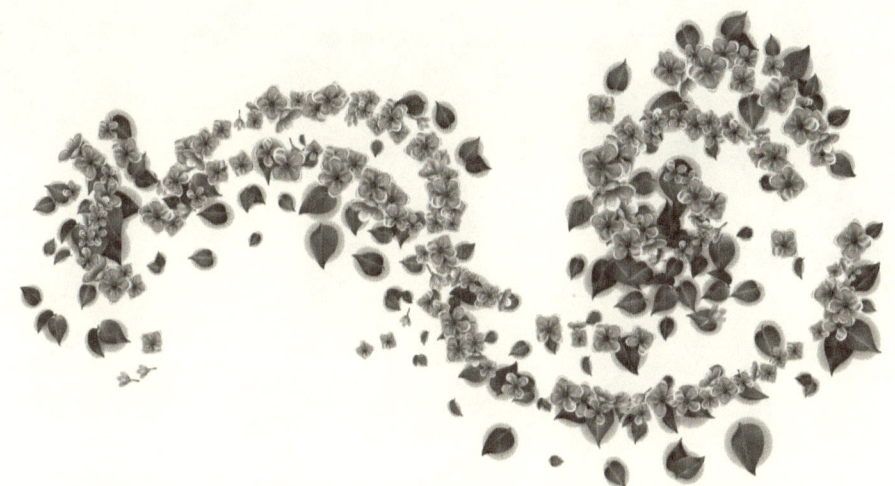

Also by the Author

The Zemnian Series: Slava's Story
The Midnight Land I: The Flight
The Midnight Land II: The Gift

The Zemnian Series: Dasha's Story
The Breathing Sea I: Burning
The Breathing Sea II: Drowning

The Zemnian Series: Valya's Story
The Dreaming Land I: The Challenge
The Dreaming Land II: The Journey
The Dreaming Land III: The Sacrifice

Giaco & Luca
The Shadowy Man: A Renaissance Fantasy Thriller
Half a Dream: A Renaissance Fantasy Thriller
The City of Shadows: A Renaissance Fantasy Thriller
Giaco & Luca Complete Trilogy